Heroes Road

By

Chuck Rogers

D1603400

FIRST PRINT EDITION, OCTOBER 2016

Cover design by Marc Lee

PRINTED IN THE UNITED STATES OF AMERICA

CHAPTER ONE

Coel ap Math hated the steppes.

He clapped his hands to bring feeling back into his fingers. Despite his gloves and the knotted rags tied about them, his hands were numb. He tried to hunch deeper into his cloak but the wind cut right through him. Coel looked about grimly and shivered in his antiquated scale armor. Frozen dirt rang under the hooves of the Second Squadron of the Frontier Cavalry. The sixteen cold, dispirited, and disparate men barely formed two-and-a-half lances of cavalry by normal muster, nor were the nags they rode up to the standard of a Paladin's heavy charger. They were men from many kingdoms, most of them victims of fate or some foolishness that had landed them in the eastern steppes. The horses plodded along wearily under old, patched, felt caparisons. Even with their shaggy winter coats they were every bit as miserable as their riders.

Coel looked over at old Ib. The company sorcerer sat quaking on his horse and clutched his heavy robe and wizard's mantle about him. The sway-backed nag he road was wretched even by the squadron's standards; but Ib was not required to wear armor nor carry a lance, and that left him with the worst of the lot. Pity and contempt moved Coel as the graybeard shook. The wizard shivered with more than cold. It had been two days since Ib had kissed a wineskin, and the lack of it was going ill with him. He sat his horse like a man at sea for the first time. Ib's was an old story. The sorcerer was an old man who had possessed a small measure of power. A young woman with none had taken his teachings and his heart and ran off with both. Ib had filled his loss with wine. Drink had left him destitute and desperate. That desperation had led him to practice unlicensed magics. It had only been a matter of time before the Church had found him out.

Coel glared, red eyed and rueful across the steppes.

The Church always found out.

That had left Ib with the choice of hanging or service on the Frontier. Coel reigned in his scorn for the broken and besotted sorcerer.

The sins Coel carried in his own heart were heavier than any man's in the squadron.

Coel reached behind him and took up his wineskin. "Ib."

The sorcerer looked up from his misery. There were only a few swallows left of the near vinegar they were issued, but the skin sloshed as Coel held it out. "My guts have been running for days and won't stand this swill. You have it, then."

Ib took the skin with a shaky smile of gratitude. They both knew the lie for what it was. "Thank you, Coel. You are a good man."

"It is nothing." Coel clucked his mount forward as Ib sucked at the skin. He didn't want to watch Ib's dissolution even as he was having a hand in it.

The gray cantered forward obediently. Coel's horse was old, but better than most of the squadron's. Coel's size and skill at arms had gotten him first choice of what mounts were available, and the gray beneath him had been bred for war. The old mare's best days were behind her, but Coel couldn't complain. Some of the men might as well have been riding goats for all their mounts were worth. The steed beneath him had been well trained, and Coel could direct her in battle with only his knees. He glanced at the men around him as they rode hunched in their saddles with their heads down. There would be no battle. There had been no battle on the Frontier since time out of mind. There were no bandits to patrol for either. No bandit would be stupid enough to live out here in the steppes. There was nothing to live on. There was nothing in this godforsaken countryside at all. It didn't even have the decency to snow. There was naught but frozen gray hills, frozen gray rocks, and frozen gray dirt.

Coel grit his teeth. There was also the wind. It whistled up under Coel's cloak, and he shivered so that the worn scales of his armor rasped. According to the stars in the night sky it was spring, but the steppes did not know it yet. Far to the west, the forest-covered mountains of his home would be greening. There would be planting festivals and hunts, spring rains would swell the rivers and snow would cap only the highest pinnacles.

The Frontier Cavalry had once been the proud bulwark of the Holy League of Humanity. With the passage of time and lack of an enemy, frontier service had become nothing more than hellish punishment duty. It was now the last place to fall within the Empires, and the lowest duty there was save indentured bondage or rowing in the galleys. Coel grimaced. That wasn't quite true. There was always the Frontier Foot. Those poor bastards spent years posted in the forgotten frontier forts of the League, praying for an enemy that no longer existed to come and put them out of their misery. Coel was thankful for the thousandth time that he was a trained horseman, but it was a small consolation. There was nothing to patrol against this far out. It had been a week since they had seen the one, starving goblin scuttling across the steppe. Lancing it had been more an act of mercy than defense of the realm. Coel stared up at the vault of the iron gray sky and the endless steppe that marched out to meet it on the horizon.

Russia was appallingly large.

He sighed as a horse pulled up beside his. Snorri Yaroslav pushed back the hood of his cloak and smiled. Snorri was an ugly man. His broken nose and the ragged white scar that ran through his left eyebrow did not help matters. The Rus ran a hand over the thick brown stubble on his skull and scratched his cleft chin. He hadn't shaved any part of his head in days. His grin widened enough to spread his drooping mustaches and show his missing left canine tooth. "Cold enough for you, Irish?"

Coel stared straight ahead. The Rus was baiting him. It was an old game, and he was not going to waste his breath explaining for the hundredth time that he was Welsh. To Snorri, anything Celtic was Irish, "no matter what peat bog it might have clambered out of." Snorri, himself, was more Slav than the Swede he fancied himself to be. What hair the Rus had was brown, and he was a good head shorter than most real Swedes that Coel had met. But it was best not to mention that to Snorri. What Snorri was, was broad. The Rus had a broad skull, broad shoulders, broad chest, broad gut, broad thighs, broad everything. He was what Coel's mother would call, and with appreciation, a full-blown man. Snorri was also a former Varangian Guardsman, and the way he swung an axe would do the Norse side of his ancestry honor. The corner of Coel's mouth turned up slightly at the weapon as it sat in the lance rest of Snorri's stirrup. A broad axe was no cavalry weapon. Neither was the huge sax-knife at his waist. Then again, Snorri Yaroslav wasn't much of a cavalryman, either. He had earned his cavalry posting with bribes and his fists.

The Rus' gap-toothed grin widened as he changed tactics. "Give us a song, Coel."

Coel snorted. "My harp is back at the fort, Swede." Snorri smiled happily at the ancestral reference. Snorri's good humor was infectious, and Coel smiled against his will. "Besides, you do not speak Gaelic, and those are the songs I know."

They both knew that was a lie but two could play at this game.

"Who cares?" Snorri rolled his shoulders with vast indifference. "Even in Irish, your caterwauling beats the whistling of this *Hel* cursed wind."

It was a backhanded compliment, but the endless months of patrolling and garrison duty were tortuously boring. Any man with any kind of talent at anything was highly encouraged. Snorri could juggle and beat every man in the garrison at chess. He was also the garrison *Kulachniy boy* fist-fighting champion, and the captain of their wall-on-wall fights, which did something to explain his looks. They both knew Coel would sing. Coel nodded at Snorri with feigned impatience and raised his voice so that the rest of the squadron could hear him. "Very well, Snorri. One song. Just to shut you up, then."

The men nearby rode in a little closer as Coel raised his head out of his cloak and sat up in his saddle. He took off his sallet helmet and shook his red hair out over his shoulders. More of the men clustered near. At the head of the tiny column, the Captain turned around in his saddle to see what was going on. Sir Jean Hainault was a Burgundian. His tonsured black hair was a reminder of his former membership in the Knights of Saint John. Sir Jean had fallen into debt with the Church, and other than practicing banned magics there was no quicker way to get Rome's unwanted attention. Coel was second in command of the squadron because Hainault was a knight. Coel raised a questioning eyebrow at their Captain. The blunt-faced

Burgundian nodded back.

Coel made a show of scratching his week-old beard and searching the sky for a song. Snorri took the bait with indignant relish. "Christ on a crutch, Coel! What do we have to do? Kiss you first? Sing something!"

The men of the column began a chorus of catcalls. "Sing, Coel!" "What are you looking to the sky for, you dizzy bastard!" "Sing, you goddamn bean-pole!" Coel ignored them and waited for Sir Jean's signal. The endless steppe had driven the squadron's morale to rock bottom. Any spark of life had to be fanned. Sir Jean's voice suddenly thundered across the steppe in the trained voice of a Captain of cavalry.

"Give us a song, you prick-teasing Welshman!"

The men roared.

Coel decided his audience was ready.

He had a song in mind. A love song. Love songs were what he was best at. Many a woman in Wales had turned her head when he sang at a feast. No one in this company would know the difference, or care. Not one of them spoke Gaelic. Latin was the binding language of the Holy League. What the men were starved for was emotion, any emotion other than crippling boredom. Coel filled his lungs with the cold air of the steppes and let the loneliness of the desolate place fill him. The shouting quickly died down. Half the squadron either slowed down or sped up to get closer as Coel's voice rose up in his throat and spilled out in a clear tenor.

"*Seoladh, na, nGa--*"

"Goblin!"

The shout rang out from the front of the squadron as the men stood up in their stirrups to see. Coel and his song were forgotten. The little Serbian, Raska, rode point, and it was he who had shouted. His horse was already galloping ahead, and he dipped his lance as he sped away. Sir Jean's voice roared out again as he waved his lance and pennon in the air over his head. "A silver ruble to the man who brings it down!"

The company surged forward like a pack of wolves.

The Church paid a tiny bounty of coppers on the head of each goblin brought back to Moscow. Sir Jean increased it out of his own meager pay to keep the men of his command sharp on the lookout. A silver ruble was not a king's ransom, but a man could eat well on it for a day or stay drunk for a night.

Coel clapped his helmet back on his head and yanked the strap under his chin as he spurred his horse. He scanned ahead and caught sight of the quarry. It stood caught out in the open near a pair of low hills.

A goblin.

It was the size of a child. Spindly arms and bowed, twig legs sprouted from its bulbous torso. Its hairless head was shaped like a gourd, with a pinched face of slit eyes, slit nostrils, and a small mouth filled with teeth like a dog with a bad under bite. The goblin's hands and feet were enormous for its body, and in one of its spatulate hands the creature carried a curved throw-stick bound with strips of hide. The green-skinned creature was barefoot, and wore nothing save a tattered, scavenged deerskin. It froze in place for a moment as the squad of armored horseman bore down on it. The excitement of the hunt swept the squadron forward. The men roared as the little creature stood and hurled its throwing stick.

Snorri hooted at Coel's side as the feeble weapon whirred through the air and bounced in the dirt far short of the mark. "He's a defiant little bastard! I give him that!"

The goblin squealed in terror and bolted for the low hills and the few sheltering trees behind it. Coel sent his horse surging ahead. The tall horse was old, but for a short sprint she was still the fastest mount in the troop. Raska was in the lead. Slavomir, the Pole, was not far behind him. Both men were mounted on steppe ponies, and both had been born to the saddle. They surged down on the fleeing goblin. The goblin milled its arms and keened in terror as it ran looking for some kind of cover in the barren landscape. Coel pulled ahead of the pack. Nando, the Spaniard, was a small man on a small horse, and he blew the war horn right behind Coel, but Raska and Slavomir were going to beat them all to the mark. The Serb and the Pole dipped their iron lance blades for the kill. Coel kept his lance in his left hand with the reins and reached back to pull a javelin from the case behind his saddle. Goblins were not fast runners, but for all their awkward hopping and lurching they were agile as hares. When they were ridden down, the first and even second lance thrusts often missed.

Coel was Welsh, and the son of a Chieftain. He had been throwing javelins out of the saddle in the hunt and in war since he had been old enough to ride. The pittance paid on a goblin's head was almost nothing, but every copper that Coel could add to his tiny hoard was another step towards buying his way out of his horrid Frontier Cavalry commission. Coel grinned fiercely into the wind. Sir Jean's silver pieces shone like hope out of Coel's little mound of tarnished coppers. He had taken the last three goblins the squadron had seen. He intended to take the fourth. Coel spurred his horse to full gallop.

"Yah!"

"Not this time, Celt!" Nando's horse matched Coel's stride for stride, and the wiry little Castilian blew the war horn again. He held his lance high overhand as he spurred forward after Slavomir and Raska. The Spaniard shouted gleefully over his shoulder as he pulled ahead of Coel. "Those dolts will miss, and then, the prize? She is mine!"

Coel grinned with the thrill of the hunt as he leaned low in the saddle and urged his flagging horse on. The goblin reached the edge of the tiny rise and suddenly dropped out of sight. Slavomir and Raska whooped and disappeared as they hurtled after it. Coel and Nando swept after them and found the flat steppe falling away down a steep grade between the low hills. The goblin shrieked as Raska and Slavomir closed and stabbed overhand with their lances. The creature dodged and ran under Raska's rearing horse. Coel raised his javelin for the throw and snarled as Nando sailed between him and the target. Sir Jean and the rest of the squadron came hurtling down the grade in a thunder of hooves.

Hell erupted out of the earth.

Goblins burst shrieking from concealed holes in the hillsides. The howling cacophony startled the Spaniard, and his horse shied. Nando's lance dug a furrow in the dirt as the goblin dodged the blow. The creature's misshapen hand clutched beneath the filthy hide it wore and came out with a barbed dart. Nando drew back his lance for another thrust as the thing beneath him threw. The little Spaniard's eyes flew wide in shock as the dart sank under his chin up to the black crow feathers that fletched it. War horn and lance fell from his hands as he sagged in the saddle and clutched his throat. The howls of the goblins swarming down the hillsides rose as Nando toppled from his horse. The Spaniard's killer capered and shrieked its triumph to the sky.

Coel stood up in his stirrups and threw his javelin with all his might. The goblin's screeching cut short as the javelin punched through its chest and pinned it sitting to the ground. Coel yanked his shield around on its sling. He slipped his arm into the straps and looked about wildly.

The goblins were everywhere.

They surged out of holes in the hillsides on either side of the squadron and flowed forward in swarms. More goblins filled the top of the grade behind them. The soil of the tiny valley ahead seemed to vomit goblins up as if hell had run out of room. Nearly all of them carried wicker shields. They hurled more of the barbed and weighted darts as they came. Others held back and whirled slings. Throw sticks scythed at the horses' legs. Coel jerked up his shield as darts, stones and sticks filled the air.

Coel took his lance in an overhand grip as the rest of the squadron piled past him. Momentum took the squad farther down the grade even as they sawed back on their reins. Slavomir and Raska had wheeled their ponies and were trying to gallop back up the grade, and they nearly smashed into the rest of the squadron as Sir Jean and the men tried to check their downhill plunge. The horses reared as they piled up on the slope and milled as they fought for footing in the loose soil.

Discipline was gone. The men panicked as the goblins fell upon them.

Darts and sling stones hammered into Coel's shield like hail as he raised his lance. A misshapen creature howled forward. Coel drove his spearhead down through its wicker shield, and the goblin shrieked as it was lanced. He struggled to pull his lance free, and two more of the creatures hurled down their shields and seized the shaft. Coel snarled as he yanked on his lance, but the goblins clung to his weapon with grim determination. He released his grip and the stunted creatures fell backward clutching their prize. Coel drew a second javelin and flung it into a goblin's stomach. The gibbering thing fell writhing to the ground. Coel pulled a third javelin as the things closed in.

"Ib!" Sir Jean roared over the pandemonium. "Do something!"

The Danish wizard rose up in his saddle. He reached into his robe and then swept his hand before him in an arc. Golden dust spewed forth from his hand and ignored the wind as it sprayed out before him in a swift wedge of twinkling motes. The glittering cloud engulfed half a dozen charging goblins. Ib's hand shook but his voice was firm.

"Sleep!"

The six goblins stumbled. Their slit eyes rolled and closed. Their weapons fell from their spatulate hands and they collapsed to the earth. Ib thrust his hand into a saddlebag and pulled forth a carved wooden wand and a leather bag. He touched the two together and spoke. "I call--"

Ib twisted in the saddle as a dart took him in the side. His wand and fetish bag fell from his hands as a throw stick scythed into his face.

Coel spurred towards the wizard. "Ib!"

A goblin grabbed Coel's stirrup and stabbed at his leg with a dart. The scales of his armor held. Coel stabbed down with his javelin and the thing fell away with its face a red ruin. He reared his horse, and she put her fore hooves into a wicker shield and sent another goblin tumbling back into its fellows. Coel wheeled his mount. Ib was gone and his horse riderless. "Sir Jean!"

The Burgundian knight had his longsword out and hewed all about himself. The squadron milled in confusion as each man was beset by dozens of leaping, darting adversaries. A goblin seized the Burgundian knight's bridle, and its weight dragged his mount's head down. Coel flung his last javelin, and the creature fell away. Sir Jean nodded grim thanks even as he swung his sword. "Coel! We have to--"

Sir Jean reared back in his saddle as a noose of knotted horsehair fell around his neck and jerked tight. The knight hacked desperately at the rope, but the blade slid off without cutting. The two goblins hauling on the rope were joined by three more. They hauled Sir Jean from his horse to fall in a clattering heap. The victory wailing of the goblins rose higher as the stunted creatures swarmed over the fallen knight. Their knives and hand axes rose and fell.

Coel's sword rang from its sheath as he spurred forward.

The thrill of the perfectly balanced weapon sang up his arm as he charged. Even under the overcast skies the blade gleamed like quicksilver. A goblin ran to block his path and Coel rode over it. The war sword swept down and sheared the wicker shield and the twisted arm that held it. Darts rattled off his armor. They hung by the dozen from the bloody felt barding covering his horse. Coel's steed rolled its eyes as the stinging barbs drove her close to madness. Coel yanked back on the reins as Slavomir's rearing pony nearly spun into him. Goblins hung all over man and horse, stabbing with knives and hacking with hand axes. A goblin clambered onto the Pole's back and tried to stab under Slavomir's helmet. The Pole's pony screamed as it was hamstrung. Man and horse fell together under a wave of goblin knives.

Coel reined his horse up as a goblin ran across his path clutching a severed arm. Two of its fellows chased it and the grisly prize it carried. Goblins were not warriors. They were pack hunters. They dragged their prey down by weight of numbers, and then carved off a piece and bolted away before a larger member of the pack could take it from them.

Panic rose up Coel's spine.

The situation was out of hand. A third of the squadron was down and the rest were being separated into isolated battles. They were being pulled down one by one. Part of the squadron was trying to fight their way back up the grade even as more goblins poured down it. They were being overwhelmed. Coel saw the soft, freshly turned over soil of the grade and the covered pits and trenches opening like graves everywhere. The situation struck him with icy clarity. It was not a natural slope. It had been excavated, just like the goblins' concealed holes.

The tiny valley between the hills was a killing box, purposely built as a trap to kill cavalry.

Momentum was the only asset the Squadron could muster against such overwhelming odds. The only chance they had was to form up and charge down into the teeth of the trap.

Coel wheeled and spurred down the grade. Goblins leaped aside from his charging horse. He reached the bottom of the slope, and for a moment he was free from the press. Coel reared his horse and spun his sword around his head. The mirror-bright blade was undimmed by the blood upon it. The sword flashed like a beacon. His voice roared across the battlefield. "Squadron! Form on me! Form on me!"

Heads turned desperately. Horses wheeled. Snorri burst from the press and spurred towards him. Coel reared his horse and waved his sword like a banner. "Squadron, form on--"

Coel did not see the goblin behind him as it released its sling from only a few yards away. The stone flew up under the wide brim of his sallet helmet and struck him behind the ear like a mallet. Coel's vision tunneled down and the goblins howled louder as he reeled in the saddle. His shield slipped from his grip and hung by its strap around his shoulder. Coel turned his head in dim surprise as his sword slid unbidden from his nerveless fingers. The sword seemed to fall away in slow motion. Coel leaned out and pawed down drunkenly to catch it. The frozen earth reared up at him. Coel met it with bone jarring force.

The victory shriek of the goblin horde rose to fever pitch.

The fall smashed awareness back into Coel. Ice-cold fear took over. He had been unhorsed. He had to get up or the goblins would butcher him alive. Coel raised himself up on his hands and knees. A sling stone slammed into his side. He spied his sword a few feet away. Coel rose to one knee and reached out his hand.

A spitting, clawing weight slammed into Coel's back and drove him back down onto his hands. A filthy, sharp-nailed hand scraped across his face and grabbed his chin. A blade jabbed again and again at Coel's armored back. He grabbed the spindly wrist and twisted. Bones snapped, and the goblin shrieked as Coel yanked the broken limb and hurled the creature off of his back. He crawled forward a few paces and reached out his hand.

He clasped the hilt of his sword as darts skated off of his

armor. Coel rose up. Blood ran down the back of his neck as he slid his arm back into his shield straps. A lasso sailed through the air, and he raised his shield to ward off the loop. The charging goblins drew back and circled about him as he whipped his sword up. The creatures howled and hurled darts as they looked for an opening. Coel saw his horse under siege. Two goblins pulled her head down by the reins while two more jabbed and chopped at her with javelin and hatchet. Blood leaked from beneath the thick green felt of her barding in streaks. A pair of goblins lay dead beneath her hooves with crushed skulls. The old gray spun screaming, eyes rolling and froth bubbling from under the bit.

Goblins gave way before Coel as he charged. One of the goblins tormenting Coel's horse turned as the huge human bore down on it. Coel swatted its hatchet aside with his shield and cleaved the creature's skull. The other goblin's keen of terror cut short as Coel rammed the iron boss of his shield into its face. The goblins hanging on his horse's reins dropped free. One managed to scamper back into the howling pack. The other fell as Coel's sword sheared its spine.

The goblins surged to keep Coel away from his horse. He hurled his shield to smash a pair of goblins off their feet and took his sword in both hands. Coel dropped to one knee and scythed his blade through the spindly legs of one attacker and then rose up and brought the sword down to split the bulbous forehead of another. He reversed his sword and stabbed behind him and a goblin fell back vomiting blood. Goblins leaped forward, stabbing with short spears and swinging hand-axes. Coel spun about in a grim dance. Hour upon hour of grueling practice with weighted blades had burned the patterns into mind and muscle. The patterns of the sword drills manifested themselves spontaneously. Coel had been the best swordsman in his class, but his weapon masters in Paris had never envisioned fencing with a horde of goblins. Coel killed and killed. The frozen dirt beneath him churned into a steaming red mud. Torn bodies lay all about him. The goblins howled and screamed as the glittering sword killed them and the iron clad Celtic giant refused to fall. Above the melee, Coel heard the war horn sounding the call.

The goblins kept Coel ringed, darting in and out in search of an opening. The situation was untenable. Sooner or later he would be dragged down. Coel whirled for his horse. The goblins fell back, and those around his beleaguered mount darted away from his raised blade. Coel leaped. He grabbed the saddle horn with one hand and thrust his foot up into the stirrup. A goblin danced forward, and he slashed it down as it grabbed at his boot. Another goblin hurled a javelin. Coel grit his teeth and took the weapon in the chest as he tried to get on his mount. His armor held and the javelin fell away. Coel heaved his other leg over the saddle, and his foot sought his stirrup as something blurred in front of his face. Coel gagged as a noose settled around his neck and jerked tight. He tottered in his saddle and tried to jam his fingers under the strangling rope. His panicked horse reared and rode out from under him. Coel fell to the ground in a heap.

The pack surged over him.

Screams filled Coel's ears. One of them was his own. Knives and hand axes hacked at him. His issue scale armor was old and had been repaired many times. Some of the iron scales had been replaced with scales of horn or lacquered leather. Coel thrashed as his leg armor failed and cold iron sank into his thigh and stopped on bone. Another blade slid up under a scale and grated across his ribs. He was being butchered alive. Coel screamed and lashed out with his fists. A twisted forearm dragged across his face and he sank his teeth into it. Coel heaved under the mass of howling bodies and curled a leg underneath him. He threw off goblins and lurched to his feet. Coel tottered as goblins grappled at his legs and tried to bring him back down. A goblin hung from his back and slammed its hand axe again and again into his helmet. The call of the war horn sounded like it was right on top of him.

A sledgehammer struck Coel from behind. He fell forward and the goblin on his back fell away in two halves. Coel found himself in a forest of trampling hooves and stabbing lances. Goblins fled in all directions. A hand swung down and hauled him up by his baldric. Snorri's ugly face loomed. His broadaxe dripped blood. "Gods in Valhalla, Coel! We thought you dead for sure! I've never seen anyone fight like that! It was like something out of the sagas! It was--" Snorri roared to the man beside him. "His horse! We ride! Now or not at all!"

Hands heaved Coel up into his saddle. Snorri pressed the reins into Coel's hands. Raska held out Coel's sword. Coel took it as Snorri cut the loop of the lariat around his neck. Raska brought the war horn to his lips and blew the charge. The horses spurred forward. The remnants of the squadron charged straight through the little valley. Ten of the squadron still lived, and a thousand paces ahead the killing box opened out onto the flat steppe again. Scores of goblins stood between them and freedom, but the men were mounted and charging in a wedge. The goblins were too small to stand in formation and stop them. They fell away before man and horse and hurled their weapons. Darts and javelins filled the air. Sling bullets and throw sticks hammered man and animal. Coel clenched his teeth against the blows and watched for lariats. The loops flew through the air. Men desperately swatted them aside with their swords and lances.

A sling stone hit Raska in the face and the Serb toppled out of his saddle to the howls of the horde. The squadron charged on. There could be no stopping. Momentum was their only weapon. The break in the hills drew closer and they flew past the last of the holes the goblins had emerged from. The squadron broke free and spurred for the gap. Snorri roared in victory and the men echoed him.

The ragged cheer cut short as shapes out of madness rode into the gap in the hills.

Such beasts were never seen this far north. Coel had seen them before in the markets bordering Moorish Spain. The creatures were camels. Armored figures rode upon them two per beast. The riders carried crossbows and hooked lances. The faces beneath the hoods were not human. Coel had seen such beings only in paintings. No one had seen such faces in two hundred years, but Coel had spent his life as a warrior hearing about them and how they had nearly conquered all of Christendom.

They were hobgoblins.

Six camels galloped forward. The beings riding them were as large as a large man and wore long felt coats. They dropped from the saddle and took shelter between the long legs of their beasts. Six raised shields and lance. The other half-dozen raised crossbows as the Frontier Cavalry bore down on them.

There was nowhere left to go. A blood-frenzied mob of goblins gave chase behind them. The only way to freedom was forward. Coel raised his sword overhead in both hands and spurred his horse. "Through them! On! On!"

Snorri stood up in his saddle and raised his axe in one hand and a spear in the other. The Rus lost his Latin as he roared his defiance in the pagan tongue of his forefathers. "Odinnnnn!"

The hobgoblin crossbows thrummed. Horses screamed. Two of the squadron fell. The camels snorted and grunted as the horses bore down on them. The hobgoblins were everything Coel had ever heard of them. Their skin was green and their lower canine teeth thrust up past their lips like tusks. The camels honked and milled as the squadron hit them. Snorri cast his spear into one beast's throat and it reared and fell on the hobgoblins beside it. One hobgoblin leaped aside and tried to reload its crossbow. It fell hissing as Snorri's axe cleaved its shoulder. The Rus spurred on and was through. "On! On!"

Two of the men still had their lances, and hobgoblins fell as the cavalry spears rammed home. The hobgoblins had hooked lances of their own; two more men screamed as they were dragged from their saddles. Coel dug his spurs into his mount and bore straight for the gap Snorri had cleared by felling the camel. A hobgoblin dropped its empty crossbow and jerked a curved short sword from its sheath. It aimed at Coel's mount, but Coel had the reach with his war sword. He thrust it forward at arm's length. The hobgoblin fell pierced through the chest. Coel's horse leaped the dead camel like a champion. Triumph surged through Coel's veins. He spurred on, and turned in the saddle to see if the other three men had made it.

The crossbow bolt hit him like a fist. Coel reeled as he stared at the leather-finned base of the wooden quarrel beneath his collarbone.

Snorri cried out. "Coel!"

Coel reached up and tried to pull the finger-thick shaft of wood out of his shoulder. The effort sent his vision spinning. His sword suddenly seemed too heavy to hold, but instinct pounded dimly in Coel's brain. If he lost the blade a second time he would die. Coel clumsily shoved the sword through his war-belt. The effort bent him over the saddle. His skull throbbed from the sling stone he had taken. Coel felt his eyes closing.

"Coel! Hold on!"

Coel was too weary to answer. He leaned on his saddle horn and gazed with far-away interest at the hilt of the goblin long-knife sticking up out of his thigh. He was cold. Coel desperately wanted to close his eyes. Deep down, something told him he would be warm if he did, but the jostling of the galloping horse beneath him kept bouncing his head back up.

"Coel!"

Snorri was yelling. Coel considered that with a fuzzy sort of distraction. Snorri was always yelling, but his voice seemed to be coming from far away and was growing blissfully dimmer. Coel felt himself leaning over his horse's neck.

"Coel! I'm coming! Don't fall!"

Coel closed his eyes and fell out of the saddle.

CHAPTER TWO

Coel awoke stinking and throbbing. He remembered the battle and falling and not much else. Instincts born in war spoke to him and he lay unmoving as his eyes slit open. Coel stared up at a ceiling. It wasn't much wider than the bed he was laying upon, and was an ugly gray where it was not blackened by soot. He tried to rise, and pain screamed through every part of his body. Coel groaned aloud and sagged back onto the bed. It was actually more of a cot than a bed, and it had not been built with a man of his size in mind.

"Hah!" A voice rumbled happily. "You're awake. Good."

Coel looked over. Snorri Yaroslav sat upon a footstool smiling at him. Snorri held a leather jack of beer and saluted Coel with it. Coel peered down at himself. Rank-smelling poultices and bloodied bandages seemed to swath most of his body. His left arm lay bound and slung across his chest. The dressings and the shooting pains wracking him told Coel his wounds had been beyond the power or the willingness of the garrison's resident cleric to heal. The cleric was a surly Norman priest of Saint William of Hastings who bitterly resented having been posted to the northeast outskirts of the Holy League. He was stingy with his healings and hoarded his power like a miser. Unless you were mortally wounded, village midwives were friendlier and far more caring, even if their potions and unlicensed hearth magics were frowned upon by Rome.

Coel was no stranger to pain. He knew he was still badly injured. He turned his head and looked at Snorri. The Rus smiled pleasantly at him. Coel found it very irritating and made his headache worse. "What are you grinning about, then?"

Snorri took another sip of his beer. "We've been drummed out."

Coel blinked.

Snorri nodded. "You've been stripped of your rank. You were second in command, and the highest ranking surviving officer, so the Garrison Commander and the Court of Inquiry say you are responsible for the massacre." The Rus wiped foam from his mustaches with the back of his fist. "They weren't even going to have the cleric heal you. They were just going to saw off your leg and see if you survived."

Coel flung back the blanket. His eyes flew to his leg in terror. It was wrapped in bandages, but the limb still seemed attached to his body. His leg ached and throbbed as if the goblin knife was still in it, but his toes obeyed him. He wiggled them furiously for several seconds before he sagged back into the cot again. Snorri jammed his thumb into his chest proudly. "I didn't let them. I paid for your healing."

Suspicion leaped in Coel's breast. "Where did you get money?"

Snorri shrugged. "I borrowed it from a friend."

Coel bolted upright in bed, his pain forgotten. "You took my money!"

"What?" Snorri looked hurt. "We're not friends?"

The room swam. Coel flopped back on the bed. He closed his eyes and saw his future falling away from him behind his eyelids. He had foregone wine and women and every other possible vice for three years trying to make his miserable hoard grow large enough to get him away from the Frontier. Without his cavalry commission and without money, his only choices would be the Frontier Foot or brigandage on the frontier itself. He had seen the poor wretches who had fallen into both those fates. Coel groaned. "How much remains?"

"Remains?" Snorri spread his arms expansively. "Do you see this room I got for us?"

The room was tiny and filthy. There was the cot, the stool Snorri sat upon, an oil lamp, and an ancient-looking iron brazier that glowed with dull warmth. Coel knew only the pain wracking his flesh kept him from feeling the bed-lice crawling all over him, but time would take care of that. He glared at Snorri coldly. "I see beer in your hand, Slav. Did I buy that, too?"

Snorri met Coel's gaze and his tone lowered unpleasantly. "Listen, Irish, it's warm in here. I stood up for you, and I got booted out of the cavalry because of it. Now you begrudge me my beer. Let me tell you something for nothing, Coel. You could be out in the street. In the snow. Singing for your supper. Without a leg. Would that suit you better?"

Coel clamped his jaw shut. He was the son of a Chieftain of Wales. A third son, but the son of a Chieftain nonetheless. The ancient *Brehon* law of his people was very clear. No Celt could aspire to be a Chieftain or a King if he was not whole in body. Outside the warmth of the room, Coel knew that Moscow would not be showing any signs of spring for weeks. He muttered without meeting the Rus' eyes. "No."

"You see?" Snorri's grin broke back across his face. "I am your friend!"

Coel regarded the Rus sourly. His eyes narrowed as he examined him more closely.

Snorri's head was freshly shaven. His drooping moustaches were combed and oiled. His baggy, striped pantaloons were tightly gathered at the knee and stuffed into boots that had been freshly shined. He wore his best linen shirt and it appeared to be clean. The thick fur fringes at the shoulders and hem of his reindeer fur vest stood up lustrously. Coel realized the Rus had brushed them. Snorri had shaven his forearms so that the blue tattooing of serpents and dragons that coiled from his wrists to his shoulders would stand out clearly. For a half-pagan Rus, Snorri actually looked presentable. Snorri noticed he was being examined and he puffed up with pride and grinned even wider.

Coel's scowl deepened. "What are you all dressed up for? And why the hell do you keep smiling?"

Snorri's smugness grew insufferable. "I found us gainful employment."

"Employment?"

"Yes. Employment." Snorri tilted back the leather jack of beer and finished it. He suddenly raised a distracted eyebrow. "Oh, I am sorry. Did you want some?"

Coel shook his head in irritation. "What do you mean, employment? We've lost our cavalry commissions. We're still in debt to the Holy League. The only jobs waiting for us are in the Frontier Foot or pulling ropes on a river barge."

"Fah!" Snorri made a dismissing wave with one meaty hand. "Marching in lines, bending oars, it's not for me, Coel. Nor you, either. We're too good for that kind of drudgery."

"Just what kind of job did you find, then?"

Snorri's voice hushed conspiratorially. His eyes gleamed. "Bodyguards, Coel! Personal retainers to a wealthy patron!" Snorri waggled his scarred eyebrows up and down disconcertingly as he leaned forward. "Hired swords."

"We're still bonded to the League, Snorri. Neither the Emperor nor the Vatican will look kindly upon us skipping out on our obligations."

"What? You don't think I know that?" The Rus shook his head. "Our employer says if he hires us, he'll pay off our Commissions of Debt. But, he wants to meet you first." Snorri peered up at the tiny window and its dirty pane of yellowed velum. It was starting to get dark. "Speaking of which, we need to make you presentable."

Coel looked up from his sickbed dryly. "I do not feel very presentable."

Snorri looked beseechingly at the sooty ceiling. "I've met fishwives who do less whining than this Irish!" He turned his gaze back on Coel. "Listen, if our employer is willing to pay off our obligation to the League? I think he's more than likely to pay up and have you healed proper, as well. You're no good to him otherwise. All we have to do is get you downstairs and across the street to the tavern."

Coel swallowed a snarl as he propped himself up with his good arm. Pain bolted through his thigh as he sat up and let his foot touch the floor. The weight of his arm hanging in its injured socket nearly brought him to tears. His head throbbed like he might throw up. "Snorri, truly, I do not mean to be an old woman, but I do not know if I can walk."

Snorri nodded sympathetically. "That's all right. All you have to do is totter to the table and look mean. I can carry you down the stairs, and across the street if I have to. God knows how many leagues I carried you across the steppes."

Coel raised his head. He remembered nothing after breaking out of the ambush. "What happened?"

Snorri shrugged. "We formed on you. We charged. We broke free. A few of us, anyway. You were wounded pretty badly. There was a goblin knife in your leg and a quarrel through your shoulder. Your skull had a dent in it. You were wounded all over. I tell you, Coel, the goblins took a good stab at carving you for their meat. Anyway, we cut free. We rode out of those hills and kept riding west for Moscow."

"How many are left?"

"Just you and I," Snorri's face turned grim. "It was those goddamned darts they were hurling. I think they were poisoned. The horses all died within days. Anyone who got so much as a scratch from one took sick. They just bloated up and died. You were hacked up, but not poisoned. You held on. So I carried you."

"Days?" Coel shook his head in confusion. "How long has it been?"

"It took a week to walk out of the steppes after the last horse died. You were raving and soiling yourself in fever the entire time. Only the cold kept your leg from rotting off." Snorri suddenly leered. "Tell me, Coel, who is Maythair? Is she pretty? You kept crying out for her."

Coel felt his face flush and he stared at his toes. He was not about to tell the Rus that *m`athair* was Gaelic for mother.

The Rus tossed his head in dismissal. "Anyway. We made it to a fort. You can imagine the quality of cleric one finds in a Frontier Foot outpost. He wasn't much of a holy man, but the old wine bag did his best for you with the old Laying On of the Hands. It kept the fever from killing you. We got you in a cart and back to Moscow. You were unconscious most of the time." Snorri shrugged his shoulders again. "You slept through your court-martial."

"So, how did you get this employment of yours, then?"

"This employment of ours, and we don't have it just yet. We have to go meet with our prospective employer as soon as we can get you dressed."

Coel frowned. "Snorri, how then?"

Snorri warmed into a story-telling mood. "Well, as you can imagine, when we came back, the Commander had questions. We were under house arrest in the garrison, and then they called for a closed Court of Inquiry. I told our side of it. I think they half bought the part about being ambushed by goblins. One hears stories of travelers falling into goblin holes out on the steppes and being eaten alive. They were willing to believe the squadron was drunk on duty and fell into a goblin hole, or else we didn't post guards around the camp and got ourselves slaughtered in our sleep. I was fool enough to stick to our story. Now, hundreds of armed goblins? The Court of Inquiry was already having trouble believing, but, when I told them about hobgoblins riding giant goats-"

Coel rolled his eyes. "Camels."

"Right. Anyway, when I told them the part about hobgoblins riding giant humpback goats, they knew I was lying. Except of course, I wasn't." The Rus paused in reflection. "Never tell the truth, Coel. It may be easier to remember, but no one will ever believe you. Anyway, I stuck up for you. I told them how you fought like a hero out of the sagas. I told them how the squadron formed on you and we cut free. I didn't even exaggerate. I didn't need to. I got all indignant. I told them I'd swear on a stack of bibles. I demanded a cleric or licensed thaumaturge to give me a Truth-Tell. I demanded a Higher Court of Inquiry. I told them I would take it all the way to Rome."

"And what did they say?"

"They told me to shut my mouth and to keep it shut. They told me that I had failed in my duty. They told me that I was still in bond to the Holy League, the Emperor, and the Church. They told me that if I was so fond of you, I could join the infantry with you, assuming you still had two legs to march with. They told me if I didn't like that, I could always swing from a rope instead, and they told me we had a week to pay off our commissions or they would make the decision for us."

Coel was incredulous. His own Commission of Debt had been deliberately set so high that he would have no hope of paying it no matter how long he served. "How in God's name are we supposed to do that?"

"You know?" Snorri's eyes grew calculating. "I don't think we are. I think they're hoping I'll do something stupid like try to steal the money or desert so they could hang us."

"So, what did you do?"

"I got drunk, of course. Though, first I got us out of the cold and paid to have your leg healed as much as I could." Snorri nodded at Coel's bandaged leg. "Which wasn't much, but you didn't exactly have King Solomon's mines in your war chest. Anyway, like I said, I got drunk, and while I was about it, I was approached for this job of ours. Our employer seemed to have heard our story. He said he tended to believe our side of it." Snorri's frown reversed itself in happy pride. "He said he could use men like us."

Coel thought past the pain in his skull. "I thought you said we were under house arrest at the time, and the Court of Inquiry was closed."

"Oh, indeed, we were, and it was."

"Then how did this, our employer, know our side of the story, then?"

Snorri stroked his moustaches. "Well, now, that's a very good question, and one I've been asking myself, as well."

"And?"

Snorri stood up from his stool. "And I say we go ask him ourselves. He said he would pay for supper regardless. I say we take him up on it. Get dressed. It's nearly time."

"I need to shave."

"You are shaved."

Coel stroked his chin. "So I am." He eased his other leg off of the cot and reached down with his right hand. Coel flinched and snarled as he slowly peeled his sticking bandages from his wounds.

Snorri winced as he watched. "You should do that quick rather than slow. It hurts less. I can do it for you if--"

"I'm fine!"

Coel blasphemed under his breath and managed to get the bandage from around his leg. The wound in his thigh was a ragged, half-closed trench in his flesh. The barest tug would reveal bone. It made Coel green to look at it. He stood up on his good leg, and Snorri re-bind his wounded thigh as tightly as he could stand. Coel shrugged out of the sling and unbound his aching left arm. He tottered to his chest of belongings. There was very little left. There had not been all that much to begin with, and it seemed the garrison had taken back everything they had issued him, including his cloak, his felt coat, his two pairs of riding breeches, and even his boots. All he had left were his own clothes from home, and they were woefully inadequate for March in Moscow. His left shoulder throbbed where the crossbow bolt had holed him. Coel found he couldn't raise his arm over his head. He sighed and turned to Snorri. "Lend a hand."

All Coel had left was his own ragged finery. With Snorri's help, he struggled into his scarlet tunic of linen with gold embroidery around the neck, sleeve, and hem. The color was a match for his hair, and the tunic was hemmed high to show off his calves, as was the Welsh custom. Snorri grinned. "There is a fine breeze outside tonight. You're going to enjoy it."

Coel scowled mightily.

Snorri shrugged. "Well, if you goddamn Irish would wear trousers like civilized people . . ."

"Just help me with my sandals."

Snorri grimaced. "I wasn't lying about that breeze, and you'll be no good to us without toes. Here." The Rus unsheathed his sax knife and quickly cut four long strips from the red woolen blanket on the cot. "Stick out your feet."

Coel leaned against the wall while Snorri wound a pair of the strips around each of his feet and crisscrossed them up to just under his knees and tied them off. Snorri slid Coel's sandals onto his feet and tightened the straps. "There. Not exactly Italian hose, but that's how we do it on the Volga."

Coel shrugged the scarlet and black plaid woolen *bratt* his mother had made for him around his shoulder and clasped the bronze brooch. He stood up to his full height and experimentally put his weight on both legs. Snorri's eyes widened. "Baldur's beard, Coel!

You really do look like something out of the sagas." The Rus blinked. "Oh! Don't forget the sword. You have to wear your sword. That sword will sell us if nothing else will."

Coel's eyes flew about the room in a panic. "Where is my sword?"

"The garrison wanted to confiscate it. They said you'd probably stolen it, and that you certainly didn't deserve to carry it. I hid it. I hid your harp, too. I was going to sell it, but I remembered you said your father had given it to you." The Rus stooped over and pulled the sword out from under the cot. It sat in its sheath with Coel's war belt wrapped around it.

"Just carry it across your shoulder. It will keep your wounded arm in place and make you look like you're ready for anything." Snorri reached under the cot and pulled out another jack of beer and a trencher with some dark bread and pale cheese on it. "Here, eat this."

"I thought you said we were getting our dinner out of the deal."

"Oh, we are," Snorri set the food on the bed. "But Allfather Odin always says a man should eat a little and drink a little before going to a feast. It makes him better company and helps him keep his wits about him."

"You're talking pagan again." Coel bit into the black bread and found he was ravenous.

Snorri watched Coel wolf his food and take his beer by the gulp. "Trust me, we're going to need our wits about us for this."

Coel moved his mouthful of bread and cheese to one side of his mouth. "Why do you say that, then?"

"Well, it's our prospective employer."

Coel's eyes narrowed as he swallowed. He knew Snorri's ways, and he felt the rub coming. "What about him?"

"Well?" Snorri shrugged. "He's a sorcerer."

CHAPTER THREE

The tavern door flew open beneath Snorri's boot. Coel's teeth chattered as took his hand off Snorri's shoulder and tottered in behind him. The front of the tavern was densely packed with people both sitting and standing. Conversation ceased. The patrons turned and stared intently at the strangers. Snorri muttered under his breath. "Well, I'll admit you're a bit of a sight, Coel, but no stranger than some of the truck that comes through here."

Coel looked around and let the warmth and smells of food wash over him. The tavern had not been across the lane as Snorri had said, but four snow-strewn streets away through the timber-lined alleys of Moscow. Coel was surprised by their destination. The Golden Horse was one of the best taverns in Moscow. The ceiling was high, and the yellow, wood-paneled walls were clean. The tavern was brightly lit with many lamps and a fire crackled in the large fireplace. Coel had never drunk at the Golden Horse. He had never been able to afford it. Coel had leaned on Snorri and limped every step of the way from the ratty room they were renting. The exertion had kept him warm, but his leg was killing him. Snorri had been right about the evening breeze up his tunic. Snorri had been right about his toes, as well, and he was thankful for the leggings the Rus had cut for him. The people inside the tavern were mostly fur traders, merchants, and the better-to-do tradesman who supported the lucrative sable and amber trade on which Moscow thrived. They continued to stare at Coel and Snorri with sullen interest. They were both very large men, outlandishly dressed, bearing axe and sword.

The tavern keeper elbowed toward them through the crowd. Snorri muttered into his mustaches again. "Let me do the talking."

The owner was short and Slavic with a round head and massive eyebrows. He looked the two of them up and down and did not appear to like what he saw. "I should have expected this."

"Well, now," Snorri smiled unpleasantly. "And a fine good evening to you, too, barkeep."

"Snorri . . ." Coel put a hand on Snorri's shoulder. They didn't have the job yet, and they didn't need Snorri splitting someone's skull and making their position worse. He hopped between them on his good leg. "We are here to meet someone."

"I could have guessed that," The barkeep jerked his head towards the back of the inn with ill-concealed irritation. "Over there."

Coel and Snorri looked at one another. Snorri shrugged and began to shove his way through the crowd. Coel followed him exerting every effort not to limp. The eyes of the other patrons followed them. They averted their eyes and looked into their cups whenever Coel met their distrustful gazes. Coel bumped into Snorri's broad back and winced as his wounded leg took weight. Snorri had stopped. Coel peered over the Rus' shoulder. The rear of the tavern was deserted. A solitary patron sat by the fireplace eating pickled eggs from a jar and drinking *kvass*. His presence filled in the emptied tables around him. Coel gaped like an idiot.

The pickled egg eating, bread beer drinking patron was a dwarf.

There were some settlements of dwarves in England, but this dwarf was unlike any Coel had ever seen. The dwarves in the Isles had red or brown hair and long beards they tucked into their belts. This one's hair was black, and his thick beard and mustache were neatly trimmed only an inch past his chin with his cheeks shaved clean. The dwarves of England wore somber tunics of green and brown and leather jerkins and tall boots. This one dressed like a mountebank in a black velvet tunic with garish puffs of the purple, gold, and red silk shirt he wore beneath pulled out through the slashings. His huge sleeves were gathered at the elbow and wrist by ribbons and billowed fantastically. It was his features that truly set him apart. Most dwarves could almost pass for powerful, stunted humans. This dwarf's eyes were nearly square, and his pupils were more oval than round. The eyes glittered an almost crystalline gray in the brightly lit tavern. His nose was blunt and squared off. His brow and cheeks were great shelves that seemed to have been roughly chiseled from stone and he had a jaw like a shovel. Everything about him was squared off. Coel noticed with surprise that the fingers of the dwarf's hands were all the same length.

He was the biggest dwarf Coel had ever seen. He was sitting, but looked to be five feet tall with shoulders as wide as an axe-handle. The dwarf shoved a pickled egg between immense white teeth and chewed with great relish. He seemed totally at ease being stared at as he took a long pull from his pewter stein and wiped his beard. The anthracite eyes took notice of Snorri and Coel as they stood staring. The dwarf looked Coel up and down, and his massive horse teeth blazed into a grin. Nearly every human in the tavern jumped at the booming sound of the dwarf's voice.

"God's codpiece! The Norseman has brought Brian Boru with him!"

The silence in the tavern was thunderous. Snorri cleared his throat. "The Boru was the High King of Ireland. Coel here is Welsh."

Coel stared at Snorri in surprise. The dwarf gazed on in amusement.

"Is he, now?" The dwarf peered more closely at Coel. The glittering gray eyes were distinctly inhuman. "And by the way he's standing, I'd say your Welshman friend has a wounded leg or a lance up his arse. Which is it?"

Coel and Snorri gaped. The dwarf snorted at his own humor. Snorri took a cautious step forward. "We have business here."

"Yes, indeed," The dwarf nodded. "You two could be none other than the mighty heroes the Walladid has told me about."

Snorri and Coel blinked uncomprehendingly.

The dwarf sighed. "You are here to see the sorcerer."

"Well," Snorri opened his mouth and then closed it again. "Yes."

The dwarf spread his massive hands. "Well, then! The Walladid and I are associates, and he will make his appearance presently. In the meantime, he asked me if I would be good enough to buy you both your suppers. Please, be seated."

Snorri stepped forward and set his axe in the corner. Coel kept his sword by his side. The dwarf gave the weapon a long and appraising look but kept his thoughts to himself. He suddenly locked eyes with the tavern keeper and snapped his fingers. The little man jumped and moved quickly back through the crowd towards the kitchen. Snorri took a stool. Coel stuck out his injured leg and eased himself onto a bench. An awkward silence fell across the table. The same silence spread out across the tavern as the other patrons studied their cups and pretended not to listen. The dwarf smiled at Coel and Snorri pleasantly but made no effort to communicate further. From where Coel sat, he could see the dwarf wore a silver-studded war-belt and a massive short sword lay across his thighs. The blade was as wide as a large man's hand at the hilt and tapered to a needle point. The dwarf's pantaloons were the same fantastical colors as his shirt and gathered at the knee with ribbons of brocade. His lower legs were sheathed in hose of matching stripes of purple and gold. Black suede slippers with silver buckles encased his block-shaped feet.

The silence dragged on. Coel screwed up his courage and held out his hand to the dwarf. "My name is Coel ap Math, and this is my friend, Snorri Yaroslav. Your name would be . . .? "

The glittering eyes narrowed at Coel's outstretched hand. Coel looked at his hand hanging between them and it felt like it belonged to someone else. He lowered his hand and he fumbled for words. "I meant no offense."

"Yes, Son of Math," The dwarf sighed. "I understand you meant no offense. So I am willing to forgive you. It will be in your best interest to know that Dwarves do not generally go about giving their names to just anybody, though even if I told you my true name, I doubt whether you could pronounce it correctly enough to do me a mischief with it." The dwarf's smile lit up again, and his hand shot out to close like a vise around Coel's wrist in the Roman style. "However, since it seems we are to be working together, you may call me Orsini."

Coel clasped arms with the dwarf and found he could not close his hand around the dwarf's wrist. "Orsini, that is an Italian name, is not it?"

"Indeed, it is," The dwarf nodded amiably as he released Coel's arm. "It means 'Little Bear'." The dwarf smiled ruefully. "I am not sure if I totally approve of it, but the Venetians are given to whimsy, and I believe they meant it with affection. However, and, more to the point, the name has stuck, and there is little to be done about it."

Snorri nodded sagely. "Nick-names are like barnacles. Good or bad? They're nearly impossible to scrape off."

"Wiser words were never spoken." Dwarf and Rus nodded at one another in smug wisdom.

Coel flexed the little Italian he knew. "Well, *Signore* Orsini, I admire your tailor."

The dwarf's face broke into a happy smile. "Why, thank you. It is the very latest fashion with the *Campagni della Calzas*. I have had the good fortune of being elected an honorary member of the *Violetto e Oros*."

Coel bit his lip. "My Italian is limited."

"Ah, well." The dwarf shrugged. "The Purple and Gold is only the most famous Trouser Club in all of Venice, or the most infamous. To be absolutely honest, I suppose it really depends upon whom you ask." The dwarf's eyes narrowed slightly as he leaned forward. "Tell me, by the by, what languages do you speak?"

"Gaelic, English, and Latin primarily," Coel shrugged. "I am fluent in French, and Spanish, a know a few words of the Moorish tongue, and Rus, of course, since I've been posted on the Frontier."

"I see." The dwarf nodded and turned to Snorri. "And you?"

Snorri leaned back and peered at the ceiling in reflection. "Well, now. Latin, of course, can't get along anywhere without it." The Rus began sticking out fingers as he counted. "Rus, naturally enough, and Swedish. Greek from when I served in Constantinople, and some English from the Normans I served with there, as well. I can make myself understood in German well enough, and I know enough of that Laplander yapping of the Finns to do a deal. I picked that up traveling with my father. Some Lett I picked up roving the Baltic with my uncle. I can insult a Turk, which is a good deal more complicated than you might think, and I speak enough of steppe trade speech to get along east of the Volga, I suppose." Snorri looked up as he ran out of fingers. "That's about it, save for some few other words here and there."

The dwarf nodded appreciatively. "Well, now, the Walladid said you were men of interesting possibilities, and it appears he spoke the truth. Ah, and here is your supper."

The tavern keeper staggered forward under the weight of the serving board. Coel had not seen so much food since he had left the hall of his father. There were two roasted chickens stuffed with pine nuts and herbs that dripped with olive oil imported from the south. Two baked heads of cauliflower covered with egg and melted cheese and dotted with browned butter sent savory steam across the table. A tureen of borscht and a bowl of baked sweet onions sprinkled with cinnamon and nutmeg added to the heavenly smell. A stout serving woman followed the tavern keeper with a trencher board. She carried buttered carrots with dill and a stack of potato pancakes smothered in sour cream. Black bread and pot cheese crowded the great platter to nearly overflowing. Coel's eyes widened at the sight of red wine in glass pitchers.

Orsini nodded in satisfaction as he watched the two humans drool openly. "Barkeep, more *kvass*, if you would be so kind."

The serving woman set down her board, and Orsini waved a hand at Coel and Snorri as they stared at the food with wide-eyed wonder. "Let us not stand on ceremony. Please, eat."

Coel attacked the food as if it were his last meal. It was his first real meal since having been rendered half-alive and unconscious. Before that, he had been weeks on patrol, living on thin rations of cracked wheat *kasha* gruel and dried fish. The bill of fare served at the Golden Horse made food seem like a new and glorious experience, and Coel was almost overwhelmed by the smells and aromas. Taste stunned his tongue and a full belly was a forgotten feeling. For a long time there was no sound save the table noises of half-starved men.

Orsini watched Coel and Snorri benevolently as they gorged themselves. Over time, the heaps of food disappeared, leaving the table a sea of emptied dishes. Slowly, Snorri pushed himself away from the table and wiped his mustaches. Coel drained his last cup of wine and sighed contentedly. He found the candlelight shining through the glass ewers endlessly delightful. He sighed again and spoke almost to himself. "Tuscan, if I am not mistaken."

"Indeed, Tuscan. You are a man of taste." The dwarf raised an eyebrow. "Is there anything else you would care for?"

"Well!" Snorri leaned his stool back and propped himself against the wall with his hands clasped over his girth. "Mead is good for settling a man's stomach."

The dwarf nodded. "And you, Coel?"

Coel smothered a belch behind his fist. He hadn't had decent mead since he'd left Wales. "It would be a shame to open a jug for just one cup."

"A wise man. Barkeep! Mead and three mugs please!"

The tavern keeper brought a round clay jar in the shape of a beehive and three wooden cups. Orsini broke the beeswax seal and poured the mead. "To your health, gentlemen!"

Coel and Snorri spoke as one. "And yours!" The three of them clacked cups in comradely fashion and drank. Somehow, Coel found room in his stomach, and the sweet glow of the honey wine spread through him. He found the pain in his leg had distinctly diminished. The dwarf glanced up as he refilled the cups. "Ah, and here is your employer now."

Coel turned to see the crowd in the tavern part again. This time they crowded against one another hard enough so as not to touch the man who passed amongst them. He was clearly from the east, with sun-darkened skin and a slightly aquiline profile. His long tunic, vest, and wide-legged trousers were of plain browns and dark blues, but they were excellently tailored, and Coel recognized the expensive sheen of silk. A heavy, double-edged *kindjal* dagger of the Caucasus Mountains was thrust through his red sash. His beard and mustache were black and short, and Coel could not seem to come to a decision on how old the man was. Slightly wavy hair fell to his shoulders, but it was his eyes that were the most striking. They were as black and penetrating as a hawk's. The man was neither tall nor short, and he was plain featured, but the intensity of his personality seemed to precede him and fill the room with his presence.

The patrons of the Golden Horse refused to even look at him. Several overtly made the sign to ward off the evil eye. The man strode through the crowd as if they did not exist. As he approached the table his face broke into a surprisingly friendly smile. His Latin had a slight, almost-musical lilt to it as he addressed the dwarf.

"So, Orsini. Tell me. What do you think?"

The dwarf waved a hand expansively. "Well, I think you've

found as fine a pair of bravos as one could ask for."

Coel found himself smiling at the compliment. The man sat down at the table and turned to Snorri. "So, Yaroslav, this is the heroic Gael you told me of."

"Yes," Snorri nodded confidently. "He is."

The man nodded in return and extended his hand to Coel. "I am Reza Walladid. I am pleased to make your acquaintance."

Coel clasped the offered hand. "I am Coel ap Math, and the pleasure is mine."

Reza Walladid turned back to Snorri. "And how does the evening find you, my friend?"

Snorri smiled wide enough to expose his missing tooth, but the smile did not reach his eyes. "I'm bloated like a sausage and well towards half drunk, and, were I anyone other than a Norseman, your bargaining strategy would have been excellent. I say enough pleasantries. Let us speak of business."

The dwarf chortled. "Oh, I do like a man of enterprise."

The Easterner smiled. "I, too, appreciate your candor, Yaroslav, and I will be frank, as well. I will not bargain with you. I will leave that to Orsini. He knows the worth of swordsmen far better than I. If you have impressed him, then I am sure you will impress me. We are prepared to be as generous as he thinks you are worth." He turned to the dwarf. "What say you, Orsini?"

The dwarf gave Snorri a measuring glance. "I tend to believe what you have told me about this one. Most Rus these days have given up the broad-axe, and by the way this one clings to his, I'd say he was once one of the Eastern Emperor's axe bearing bodyguard."

"You're right," Snorri nodded. "I was a Varangian."

"So, then, tell me. Why aren't you one now, and what is a man of your apparent quality doing in the Frontier Cavalry, if I might ask?"

"A fair question." Snorri took a sip of mead and leaned forward. "Now, I was in the Varangian Guard, and I served the Emperor in Constantinople for four years, and with distinction, I might add. I fought the Turk, and I rose to the rank of *Manglabites* and wore the gold hilted sword. The problem was a certain woman at court. A goddamned Greek wanted her, and so did I. She enjoyed playing the one against the other. He was one of those tall, dark, handsome types with long curly locks that do so well in palace halls. Wealthy, too, and from a good family."

Reza Walladid looked frankly at Snorri's battered face and shaven head. "And she played you? Against him?"

Snorri shrugged helplessly. "Can I help it if I carry *Gungnir* between my legs?"

The patrons of the Golden Horse jumped again as the dwarf laughed. A ghost of a smile passed over the Persian's face. "The Spear of Odin?"

"Oh, yes," Snorri nodded earnestly. "Anyway, like I said, at first she just liked to hang about my shoulders at feasts to make him jealous. Now, I don't particularly mind having pretty girls hanging about, and I don't much mind if it hurts some goddamn effeminate Greek's feelings either, which, by the way, I believe it did. I guess they had some kind of spat about it, and then her flirting stopped being a game of asking for stories from my roving days or feeding me grapes at dinner parties." Snorri spread his hands. "Now, I'm a loveable fellow, and popular in my own way. But, I'll admit I'm not used to having beautiful and educated Byzantine women of good family scratching at my door in the night, and I'll admit I'm as weak as any man in that regard, perhaps weaker than most. So I let her in, and I let her in the next night, and the next night, too. Soon it was all night and every night, and I'll tell you something for nothing. Such things do not stay a secret for long in the Byzantine court, and, as I said, she was not trying to keep it much of a secret, anyway. She wanted him jealous, and, at that point, I wasn't giving his feelings on the matter any great deal of thought. It was all I could do just to stay awake and stop smiling on duty. Well, anyway, one evening? The goddamn Greek drank a few wineskins' worth of courage and decided he was going to do me a mischief."

Reza looked at Snorri intently. "What happened?"

"Well now, that evening? The lady in queston was at some court function or other, and I was at a tavern, and well into my own wine cups I might add. That Greek came straight at me. There were no flowery speeches or exchanges of insults. He didn't want a fight.

He was in the mood to make murder." Snorri shook his head grimly at the memory and his hand went to his scarred eyebrow. "I'll give him credit, too. For all his silk stockings and scented curls? He was a strapping large lad, and someone had taught him which end of a dagger was which. He had me half-blinded and bleeding like a pig before I knew he was upon me, and, to be truthful, had it stayed at knives, I think he would have put me at the bottom of the Bosphorus."

Orsini leaned forward over his mead. "What did you do?"

"Like I said, he knew knives, and I would bet he was a decent swordsman as well, but I don't think the dandy had ever been in a real tavern brawl before, much less a real Russian wall fight."

"And?"

Snorri shrugged helplessly. "And so I spat in his face. That startled him. Then I kicked him in the codpiece, and that startled him even more. When he dropped his dagger to clutch his aching stones? I took the opportunity to break a bench over his head."

Orsini nodded. "You killed him."

"Oh, no, no, no. Had he died? I'm sure they would have had me publically impaled. Like I said, regardless of the circumstances, he was a Greek of good family, and wealthy. He had connections at court. I was just a glorified guardsman who was sleeping above his station. Nonetheless, the blow did cross his eyes for him, and last I heard he still can't ride a horse without falling off. Still, that was trouble enough. I was arrested, and they were planning on having me castrated to set a good example for the rest of the foreign troops in the Emperor's employ."

"I gather you are still intact?" Orsini inquired.

"Oh, indeed!" Snorri grinned. "The Varangians threatened a riot. Of course, more of the Varangians are goddamned Saxons than honest Swedes or Rus these days. *Hel*, most of them don't even carry axes anymore, and let me tell you, a sourer bunch you've never met!" Snorri's lip curled in disgust. "Sulking about the halls and saluting the Emperor in English. Anyway, like I said, there were still a few hearty Norse souls left in the Guard, and they threatened a riot. Also, Ianthe, the lady in question, was kind enough to use her influence at court on my behalf. Being a Varangian still has some prestige attached to it, even if the Guardsmen are all mostly egg-sucking Saxons now. Anyway, I was quietly given the opportunity of accepting a Debt of Commission with the Holy League on the Russian Frontier. An ugly bargain for sure, but I've never heard of a gelding getting into *Valhalla*, and *Gungnir* and I decided we'd like to go to the grave together. So, I took the Commission. I was sent upriver on the first available prison scow and found myself back in the Russias where I first started my career. I've been riding goats and glue pots out on the steppes for almost three years now and I am no closer to closing out my Commission than when I started. All told, I have been soldiering for seven years in both the north and south, and the dinner before me is all I have to show for it. Oh, and Coel, here."

Snorri tossed back the rest of his mead and leaned back. "And that is my tale of woe."

"Well, now," Orsini nodded slowly. "That is an interesting story."

Reza stroked his short beard. "Indeed," He looked at Snorri frankly. "What other skills have you?"

Snorri shrugged. "Well, I am no centaur like Coel, but I can manage a horse well enough. I am an able sailor. When I was a lad, I went river trading up and down the Volga and the Moscow with my father. When I was older, I went roving upon the Baltic for a few years with my uncle before I went to seek my fortune as a soldier in the Golden City."

The dwarf raised a finger pointedly. "He speaks the steppe tribesmen's trade speech as well."

"Ah," The Easterner seemed to tuck the fact away for later. "Is there anything else about you I should know?"

Snorri folded his arms across his chest and stared at the man long and hard. "Well, since we are all being honest, and you appear to me to be a Persian, I will give you fair warning. I am the greatest chess player I have ever met."

Reza's face grew serious as stone. "You play with the queen empowered?"

Snorri peered up into his eyebrows with infinite patience. "And pawns may move two spaces on the first move. I am familiar with the recent changes in the rules introduced in the East. I assume you are aware of castling?"

Reza Walladid's smile lit up his entire face. "You are all but hired." He turned back to Orsini. "And what do you make of our gigantic Welshman?"

All eyes at the table fell on Coel. Orsini frowned. "Well, he looks likely enough, and if half the bragging this Rus does about him is true, I'd take him on immediately."

The Easterner raised an eyebrow. "But?"

The dwarf's eyes went steely as he stabbed a blunt finger at Coel. "I want to hear the story of that sword he's carrying. You don't see many of its like, much less in the hands of penniless bravos on the Eastern Frontier. There is a story there if it's not stolen, and perhaps even if it is."

Coel looked down at his sword. The plain steel of the cross guard and pommel gleamed at his side. The blade was a good finger's length over three feet long, double edged and terminating in a wicked point. The handle had an extra four finger widths of length so that it could be swung with both hands, but it was so well balanced that a strong man could easily wield it with one. There was nothing ornate about the sword. The hilt was wrapped with plain steel wire. The cruciform guard was a simple bar and the pommel a perfect wheel of steel. The sword was utterly devoid of ornament. There was no maker's mark or signature. Any warrior in the known world would still recognize the blade. The sword had been forged in Grande Triumphe, the Paladin Academy of Paris. Coel spoke low. "The sword is not stolen. It was given to me."

Orsini leaned forward. "Tell us, man of Wales. Who would give you such a blade?"

Coel met the dwarf's stare. "The Swordmaster of Grande Triumphe."

Orsini leaned back and frowned in open disbelief. Reza Walladid leaned forward. "I do not doubt you, my friend, but tell me. Why would the Swordmaster of the Paladin Academy of Paris surrender you such a sword?"

Coel gave a troubled sigh. "I do not know."

Reza Walladid did not blink. His dark eyes widened and held Coel's gaze. "Perhaps you could tell us a little bit about your background. It would be helpful in deciding whether or not to hire you."

Coel's thoughts wandered back to Wales. He thought of his father's hall in the mountains of Snowdon. Being the third son of a Chieftain had brought him rank and privilege, but his future was limited. His eldest brother, Bryn, would inherit the land, and be elected Chieftain as long as the Brehon lawyers of his people found him fit. Of that there was little doubt. Bryn was indeed fit, as well as brave, and wise, and everything their father wanted him to be. His next brother, Evan, the priest, was being groomed for a bishopric at Saint David's.

Coel had been left with nothing but his size, his wits, and his father's name. For a time, that had been enough. Welsh tribal law dictated that there must be six weeks of marauding every summer. Coel joined the warriors for his first raid at the age of thirteen. He had run for miles across the mountains and marshes where no horse could pass, and each year he had bent a bigger bow until his muscles had grown to match his bones. He had raided his neighbors' lands and cattle and ridden out to meet the Norman Marcher Lords patrols in both ambush and open battle. By age seventeen, Coel had firmly established his reputation. He was renowned for his size, his strength, and his luck in battle. But that was the best he could hope for. He would spend his life being his eldest brother's right hand man. However, he had proven himself, and he had made his father proud of him. Proud enough to use his friendship with the Prince of Gwynned to see Coel enrolled in the Paladin Academy in Paris.

Coel's eyes lit up at the old dream.

To be a Paladin. To wear a shining coat of plates and ride a white charger. To have the Mantle of Power descend upon him and become unlike other men. To be the best among men. It was the dream of every young warrior in Europe when he first took up arms. Coel was no different. The dream had filled his earliest memories. It was his father's dream, as well. On Coel's eighteenth birthday, Math had taken his son's shoulders in his hands and told him as much. His first son, Bryn, for the inheritance. His second son, Evan, for God, and his third son, his pride, Coel, to be a hero. Coel had wept openly at his father's words and had eagerly packed his belongings and begun the voyage to Paris.

Paris, and the shining citadel of Grande Triumphe were like nothing in his experience. He was awestruck as he walked the paved streets and craned his neck looking up at the tall stone buildings. When he walked through the marble arches of Grande Triumphe, he joined the ranks of Europe's most promising and well-to-do young men. His reputation had preceded him. The Academy Masters knew of his ability as a warrior and a raider. They turned their efforts to forging Coel into a Soldier of God.

There, the massive destrier of the knight replaced the sturdy Hackney war pony he had ridden for days at a time through the mountains and forests of Wales. Coel learned to ride in formation and charge with the couched lance. A Paladin was the epitome of a mounted warrior, but was also expected to fight on foot, and he learned to wield the poleax and war hammer. Above all else, Coel loved the sword. He spent endless hours on the practice field hewing at posts with weighted blades and fencing with his classmates. It was quickly apparent to all that Coel was the best in his class.

However, skill at arms was but one facet of becoming a Paladin. There were the vows of chastity, humility, and temperance. None of which were in the natural makeup or upraising of a Celtic warrior. Endless study of scripture and ritual, scourging to purge the candidates' minds and bodies, and constant prayer for worthiness filled his hours outside the practice field. Coel considered himself a Christian, but his mother still practiced the old ways, and more of her teachings than he knew had come to color his beliefs. His religious instructors were appalled. Coel was also the son of a chieftain. He had immediately bridled at scourging, and chastity had set with him not at all. On the few occasions Academy pages were let out of the Citadel, he debauched himself like the seasoned veteran he already was. The scourging and penances increased, and they only made him more unruly. Only on the practice field did he continue to be the star pupil, and he channeled his frustration into defeating every opponent set before him. Soon only the Weaponmasters of the Academy themselves could unhorse him or give him a good fight on foot. Sometimes, even they could not defeat him, but even these sweetest victories were hollow.

It was clear to everyone in the Academy that Coel would never be a Paladin.

The Mantle of Power, to heal, to perform miracles, to make an Academy-forged blade blaze forth with divine power, would never descend upon him. Only his skill at arms had kept the Masters of the Academy trying for as long as they did. The Masters urged him to stay. He was a great warrior. He could still serve as a man-at-arms in the Holy Host. If he could not be a Paladin, he could well achieve knighthood and still rise to high rank in the Holy League of Humanity. He would have none of it. He would not carry lances for classmates he had beaten on the practice field, nor watch them ride past him invested with power he would never have.

Coel had packed his few belongings on the eve he would have failed the Ritual of Commencement. He stood alone in the barracks while his classmates paraded to the chapel in white robes to fast and pray before they presented themselves for examination. When Coel had hefted his sack and turned to leave, he had found himself under the scrutiny of Sir Eberhard von Hohenloe, the Swordmaster of the Academy. The Swiss knight was nearly a foot shorter than Coel and gray streaked his blonde hair, but even the heaviest two-handed sword became a thing of lightning in his hands. He stood wearing a Master's white ceremonial robe and mantle for the commencement ceremony less than an hour away. Coel had burned with shame under the Swordmaster's gaze. Sir Eberhard was the head weapons instructor of the Academy, and was the only Academy Master Coel had not failed in his schooling. Now, Coel felt Sir Eberhard was the one he had failed the most.

"So," The Swiss knight stared at him frankly. "You leave."

Coel tasted ashes as he answered. "Yes."

The Swordmaster continued to hold him under his horrible, appraising gaze. "Home?"

Coel burst with three years of frustration. "Home! Home to what, then? Home to my father's shame and my mother's pity? Home to be my older brother's lapdog? Home to the sneers of my brother, the priest? No, I think not!"

"Yet, you will not stay and be a man-at-arms in the Host, nor allow the Grand Master to recommend you to an honorable free company."

Pride and anger steeled Coel to meet the Swordmaster's gaze.

"No."

Von Hohenloe's voice grew steely, as well. "So. A free sword? No master. No company. No allegiance except to gold. Selling your training and Grande Triumphe's reputation to the highest bidder." Sir Eberhard spit forth the words like sour wine. "A hired blade."

Coel had practiced a thousand arguments in his mind to justify his feelings, but he knew it was all a facade for his wounded pride. He was being ungrateful and self pitying. He was throwing away opportunities he barely deserved and would never be offered again. He looked down at his sandals, unable to meet the Swordmaster's eyes. Sir Eberhard had shaken his head wearily and walked to the doorway. Before he left, he had turned to look upon Coel a final time. "You will need a sword, then."

Coel had looked up from the barracks floor in confusion.

The Swiss Knight had thrown back his ceremonial robe and unbuckled the sword around his waist. It was not the Swordmaster's own blade, but one much like it. Double-edged and needle pointed, it could be wielded in one hand or two. It had been forged from the iron of fallen stars into an alloy known nowhere else on earth. It was said such swords never rusted and held an edge like no other. They were the finest swords ever forged, but their real value lay far beyond perfectly balanced steel. A true Paladin, invested with the Mantle of Power, could make such a sword blaze forth into a Holy Weapon.

Coel had sat stunned as the Swordmaster had come forward and held out the sword to him. As Coel looked up from the weapon, the knight had held him unwaveringly with his gaze. "You have not earned that blade, nor is it truly mine to give, and carrying such a sword may well get you into more trouble than it will get you out of," The Swordmaster relented and heaved a sigh. "I cannot explain it, but I feel guided to give it to you. Though I must answer for the act to the other Masters."

Coel's hand had trembled as he reached out, hardly daring to touch the sword's tapered hilt. The barest hint of a smile had twisted Sir Eberhard's lips. "You should not let your mouth hang open like that, Coel. Birds will nest in it."

Coel closed his mouth and took the sword. It was a perfect

weapon, and the feel of the sheathed blade in his hands had filled him with resolve. "I swear to you, I will not shame you, this blade, or the name of Grande Triumphe."

The Swordmaster of Grande Triumphe had scoffed. "Oh, I suspect you will do all three," He had grinned at Coel's shocked look. "But perhaps it will keep you alive long enough to do all three of us some credit, as well. Coel, you are without doubt the best student I have ever had. I may yet have done the right thing."

Coel had left the Academy that night to seek his fortune. Not long after, he had--

The sorcerer's voice spoke in a soft and friendly manner. "Tell me more about your mother."

Coel found himself staring directly into the sorcerer's dark eyes. He realized he had been talking out loud. The Academy blade sang out of its sheath with a ringing of steel as Coel surged to his feet. He ignored the ripping pain in his thigh as he whipped the sword over his head with both hands. "Stay out of my head, wizard! Or by God I will split your skull!"

Patrons of the Golden Horse shouted in alarm. Barmaids screamed. The dwarf's short sword appeared in his hand like a magic trick as he kicked back his bench. "And that will be the last thing you ever do."

"And you, runt!" Snorri's sax knife rasped out of his belt. He snatched up his stool and held it before him in his left hand as a shield.

The dwarf turned. The huge horse teeth gleamed. His gray eyes glittered in delighted outrage. "What did you call me?"

Reza Walladid had not moved from where he sat. His eyes never moved from the sword poised over his head. His voice maintained its calm and friendly demeanor. "Please, Orsini. You of all people should know just how little danger I am in."

The dwarf slid the massive wedge of steel back into its sheath. "You are right, of course," He kept his gaze on Snorri for a moment longer. "I find myself liking you, Rus. Your loyalty is commendable, but a word to the wise. Keep a civil tongue in your head in future."

Snorri didn't drop his sax knife or his stool as he slid an eye over at Coel. "Are you all right?"

Coel stood with his sword poised. His thigh cramped with pain. Sweat broke across his brow. Long ago, Coel's mother had taught him never to look an elf or sprite he didn't know in the eye. He had never met an elf or a sprite, but his mother's advice came to him now, and he made his gaze bore a hole between Reza Walladid's eyebrows. He grunted out of the corner of his mouth. "I am fine."

Snorri shoved his knife back in his belt and set his stool down. He cleared his throat and looked at the dwarf nervously. "Sorry."

Orsini shrugged graciously. "Think nothing of it."

Reza sighed. "Please, put your sword away and sit. You're bleeding again."

Coel lowered the sword but did not sheath it. "Back at the Academy, the priests would perform Truth-Tells upon us. They used their power to dig in our minds and find out our deepest sins for atonement. I did not care for it then. I will not stand for it now."

"What I did was no real sorcery. It was more an exercise of will, and, to be truthful, I am very pleased with your performance. You told me nothing you did not already want to tell, and, when I asked you of what you did not? You were immediately aware. That is good. I have enemies, and you must admit a man carrying a blade like yours raises a number of questions. However, I give you my word. I shall never attempt such a method against you again, and I offer you my apologies."

Coel sheathed his sword and eased himself back onto his bench. Blood trickled down his leg. Reza nodded. "Your story was interrupted, and I would like to hear more of it, but, for now it may wait. As for your other qualifications--"

Snorri interrupted. "Coel can play the harp, and he can sing! He was trained by the Bards of Wales!"

Orsini peered at Snorri and then at Coel. "Really?"

Coel opened his mouth to speak, but Snorri piped in again. "I've heard him. He's good." Snorri raised his finger and nodded smugly. "Oh, and he's the Devil's own with a longbow."

The dwarf ran his eye across Coel's shoulders measuringly. "The English longbow?"

"Oh, no, no, no," Snorri shook his head in disgust. "The Welsh longbow."

Coel stared at Snorri's newfound sense of geography.

"A singing longbowman," Orsini looked to Reza. "Well, now, that is intriguing."

Reza nodded decisively. "As far as I am concerned, these men have far surpassed our expectations. Fortune seems to be with us, and I believe we should strike while the iron is hot. Orsini, if we are in agreement? Make these men an offer."

"We are, and I shall," The dwarf leaned over the table. "Gentlemen, we shall not haggle. Here are our terms. In the first, on the morrow, Coel, we shall go and fetch you a decent healing, at our expense. In the second, both of you shall have your Commissions of Debt to the Holy League paid in full, and all obligations of duty to the Church thereof dissolved. The Walladid and myself, to whom you shall remit the balance, from pay, spoils, plunder, or other negotiable methods of compensation, shall assume these debts. Once your debts to us have been paid, you shall be considered free contractors in our service. In the third, any and all room, board, and medical attention required during your term of service with the Walladid and myself shall be provided for at our expense. In the fourth, all additional armor, weapons, equipment, horses or livestock needed in the course of your duties shall be provided for at the Walladid's and my expense, and, you shall be allowed to keep any and all surviving said weapons, armor, equipment, horses and livestock so issued to you when your duties are finished or terminated by mutual agreement. In the fifth, one hundred pieces of silver shall be paid out to each of you, per month, as wage, or remitted back to fulfill your debt to us. In the sixth, a bounty of twenty-five pieces of gold shall be paid out to you, each, tonight, immediately upon agreement to service. In the seventh, and mind you now, the Walladid and myself shall have first pick over any and all loot, plunder, or spoils taken during your association with us, the remainder to be divided equally between yourselves and any other employees or associates of the Walladid and myself directly involved in the acquisition of said spoils. And, in the eighth, one hundred pieces of gold shall be paid to you, each, as bonus, after each successful year of service. All monies shall be paid out in standard League of Humanity monetary weights or their equivalents. Letters of credit, banking facilities in Venice or any other major city within the League, or other such financial advice and assistance shall be provided for upon request, free of charge."

The dwarf smiled. "Do we have an agreement?"

Silence reigned.

Coel stared at Snorri. Snorri stared at Coel. Coel tried to regain his composure. "Well . . . what kind of duties are we talking about?"

"Oh, well, soldiering, body guarding," The dwarf shrugged. "Being useful at what you are best at."

Coel's mind spun. "Yes, but, where are we going?"

Snorri regained his bargaining face with a struggle. "Oh, yes, where are we going?"

"South," Reza's finger drew a line down the table. "Down the Dnieper to Kiev. If I receive the news I hope for there, we shall continue on to the Black Sea, and then eastward across it, to the Empire of Trebizond. It is possible I will have business there."

"Trebizond?" Coel blinked. The Empire of Trebizond was one of the farthest-flung Christian nations in the East. He had heard little but rumors about the wildness of the tiny empire on the far edge of the Black Sea and the beauty of its women.

"From there?" Reza opened a graceful hand. "That remains to be seen."

"Trebizond! Now there is a place I have never been!" Snorri slapped both of his hands on the table. "I say count me in! What say you, Coel? Let us leave this frozen chamber pot and go someplace warm!"

Coel leaned back. He was leery of the deal. It seemed too good to be true, and he was uneasy about working with non-humans and sorcerers. Dwarves had a reputation for both scrupulous honesty and utter ruthlessness in their business dealings. The Church tolerated their non-humanness because of their wealth and their usefulness, particularly their skills in masonry and metallurgy. But

Orsini was unlike any dwarf Coel had ever seen or heard of, and, as for the Sorcerer, Coel was willing to bet a great deal that this Persian was practicing magics unlicensed by either the Pope or the Patriarch. Coel's leg throbbed at him in unpleasant reminder. Whatever his reservations, there was a simple truth he could not escape. If his leg were not healed properly soon, he would lose it. Even if it healed on its own, it would take weeks of rest. He was penniless and without connections. He had been drummed out of the Frontier Cavalry, and he was still in debt to the Holy League with no way to pay it off.

Snorri nodded at him with child-like eagerness.

Coel shrugged helplessly. "All right, let's go someplace warm, then."

"Hah!" Snorri grinned happily. "Trebizond!"

Orsini raised his hand palm up. "You agree to the terms?"

Snorri nodded distractedly. He seemed too stunned by fortune to haggle. "Oh, indeed."

The dwarf nodded at Coel. "And you?"

Coel took a slow breath and then let it out. With the decision made he felt a dangerous sense of relief. For good or ill, the die was cast. "Yes. We are agreed."

"Excellent." Orsini fetched two jingling pouches from out of his billowing vest. "Twenty-five pieces of gold, each, as bounty, in advance, as agreed."

Coel took the pouch. It was satisfyingly heavy in his hand. He peered at Reza Walladid questioningly while Snorri gleefully emptied his pouch onto the table and counted his newfound riches. "You want no swearing of oaths or signing of contracts?"

"That is not necessary."

"Is that not a little unusual in these matters?"

"I will admit I have been accused of being a devil, my friend, but I assure you, I do not require your names written in blood. You have both shown me that you are men who are honorable by your own standards, and you have both given me your word. That is enough." Reza suddenly laughed and Coel started at the sound. The Sorcerer's voice was almost musical, but his laugh was a short, harsh bark. It was more a sound of personal amusement rather than real mirth. "However, I will tell you something my father told me long ago."

Coel raised an eyebrow. "Oh?"

"Yes. He always said that there is only one man more foolish than he who gives his word to a wizard."

"And who is that?"

"The man who breaks it."

Reza Walladid's barking laugh rang out through the tavern again.

He sounded genuinely amused.

CHAPTER FOUR

Coel leaned on Snorri as they staggered down the snow-strewn street. He felt warm and slightly drunk as they moved away from the light of the Golden Horse. The orderly rows of plank and beam construction quickly gave way to a maze of more rudimentary constructions of logs and undressed stone. Moscow had been the first major city of the West to be sacked during the Goblin War, and its fall had been well documented. Its earthen ramparts and wooden walls had lasted barely a day and a half against the Hobgoblin horde. The city had been razed to the ground, and nearly every man, woman, child, and beast had been killed and eaten. The survivors were tied into long coffles and eaten on the march as the implacable army had marched like ants westward into Europe. In the intervening two hundred years, Moscow had been rebuilt with tall walls of thick stone. It had become the eastern bulwark of the Holy League of Humanity, and it had quickly outgrown the new walls. A tall palisade of heavy timbers now formed a second ring around the city. Haphazard constructions jammed the space between the old and new fortifications. Log halls, huts, and lean-tos had recently begun clustering outside the gates of the palisade and spread out to form a third ring of habitation. The Holy Roman Empire wanted furs and amber, and the southern Empires of the Byzantines and the Venetians wanted timber.

Moscow was booming.

Coel snorted as they moved into the starlit gloom of Moscow's alleys. "The Spear of Odin?"

Snorri spoke with immense seriousness. "The gods have favored me, Coel. It is a blessing and a curse."

Coel changed the subject. "So, what do you think of our employer, then?"

"Reza Walladid? I think he spends his money like water. I think the gods have favored us both this night."

"And what of his warning about breaking our word?"

"What of it? You break your oath to a free company? They

hang you. You run off on your Commission from the Holy League? They excommunicate you and then hang you. We break faith with this Walladid fellow? He turns us into toads. Why should a wizard be any different? *Hel*, he seems a great deal more reasonable than most if you ask me, and he pays a great deal better, as well."

Coel couldn't deny it. It had been many years since he'd worn a full purse jingling at his belt, and the coins were no worn silver rubles or thin copper kopecks, either. They were gold. Thick, Venetian gold ducats, gleaming and sharply minted. Venetian coins set the standard for Europe and were accepted everywhere from Ireland to the Red Sea. Then there was the monthly wage in silver coin and the promise of even more gold to come with successful service. Shares of plunder and spoils had been mentioned, as well. Captains in command of reputable free companies were often paid less.

Snorri read Coel's mind. "What's more, tomorrow we go and get your leg properly healed. And Trebizond!" Snorri's eyes glittered at the thought. "Last I heard? Ianthe had sailed there to attend the court of the Empress."

"The girl who got you thrown out of the Varangians, then?"

Snorri laughed. "Oh, I got myself thrown out of the Varangians, but there was still a stink at the palace. I believe she was sent to attend the Empress in Trebizond while the aroma died down." His tone lowered. "Now, Ianthe is a woman you need to meet, Coel, and if I know Ianthe, which I do, she'll have surrounded herself with the most beautiful and well to-do ladies at court, and, from what I hear, all the women of Trebizond are beautiful. The Empress, herself, is supposed to rival Helen of Troy. They say her mother and her mother before her were beauties, too, and all sorceresses, as well. Every girl-child born to the bloodline. They say they used their beauty and sorcery to take over the place generations ago, and they've held it ever since." Snorri's gaze reached far away into the night. "It's a place I've always wanted to see."

Coel took all this in with surprise. It seemed there was very little that Snorri did not know something about.

"And I'll tell you, Coel. I bet they've never seen a redheaded tree like you before. You'll do well there. The Greeks love novelty." The Rus suddenly snapped back into the present. "But that is tomorrow, and promised to no one. Tonight, we sleep in a warm room with full bellies. Which is more than you or I had any right to hope for this morning. I think we're doing rather well."

Coel looked at the Rus thoughtfully as they limped along. "You have proven a good friend, Snorri."

"Indeed," The Rus puffed up with pride. "I am a fine friend to have."

"Why, then?"

"Why then, what?"

"You risked your life to save mine. You stuck your neck out for my sake and got yourself thrown out of the cavalry for your trouble. We are neither kin or clan, and there are no oaths between us." Coel shrugged his good shoulder. "I am not one to look a gift horse in the mouth, Snorri, but I wonder why you have stuck by me."

"Well, now, that's a fair enough question, and I'll answer it." Snorri's voice dropped low. "Because you're lucky, Coel, and your kind of luck cannot be begged, borrowed, or stolen."

"Lucky? For God's sake, have you looked at my leg, then? Have you noticed I was in the Frontier Cavalry with a Commission of Debt? Have you noticed that our entire squadron has been killed? I am a failed Paladin candidate, I cannot go home, and you call me lucky?"

Snorri nodded thoughtfully. "Oh, indeed. You spend your luck like water, I'll admit, but you always land on your feet. You were born the third son of a Chieftain. You attended the Paladin school. When you failed there, the Swordmaster, himself, offered you a position in The Host. I know you do not like to talk about it, but I have heard rumors about how you earned your Commission of Debt. They usually hang men for that, or burn them at the stake."

Coel's back went rigid as his ugliest memories stirred.

Snorri quickly continued over the subject. "But rather than a rope, they gave you second command of a squadron of cavalry. When all was lost, it was you who cut us out of the goblin horde. And for that matter? It was not me that got us this posh job, but what I said about you that piqued the sorcerer's interest." Snorri's tone grew deadly serious. "Now, my grandfather, the Swede, told me to pick my friends carefully, and I will tell you something for nothing. Most men spend their whole lives wishing for just one of the opportunities you've had, and you? You toss your chances away as if your hat was full of them, which, by the way, I think it is. You are lucky, Coel, and I am practical. It is an unbeatable combination. I am sticking to you like glue, and I say we'll both be kings before we're done."

Coel felt his ears redden. He smiled despite the cold and pain. He found Snorri's view of his life much grander than his own. "Well, then, what do you say we go get a decent room for our last night in Moscow?"

Snorri stared up at the stars with a well-practiced eye. "It's late. Most innkeepers will be barring their doors by now."

Perhaps it was the wine, but Coel could not help grinning. "Aye, but I can pay in gold. And I would not mind another bowl or two of good red wine, either." Coel's grin spread across his face as it truly struck him that he no longer had to scrape for every copper. It also struck him that there were certain things he had been forgoing for quite some time. "For that matter, I would wager there are a couple of women somewhere in Moscow who would not mind meeting men of destiny like ourselves, no matter what the hour. Hell, Snorri, it is the least that I owe you."

"Now you are talking!" Snorri threw back his head and laughed. "We are well-armed men with money! Who's to gainsay us? With an Academy blade and Venetian gold, they will throw open their god damned doors and be grateful!"

A voice spoke out in the dark. It came from the shadows under the eaves before them. It was a low voice, and its Latin was strangely accented. "Venetian gold?"

Snorri stopped abruptly and shrugged his axe from his shoulder. The haft fell into his hand just under the blade. "Oh, indeed, friend. Great, big, bulging bags of it. Why don't you come a little closer, and I'll show you."

A tall, cowled figure stepped out into the narrow lane before them. Coel's nostrils flared as he smelled a strange sweet scent surrounding the stranger. The break between two log houses formed a tiny cross street. More figures filed out from the side alleys. All wore their cloaks draped about their heads and shoulders or else wore rough hoods of sackcloth. The tall figure took a step forward and the sweet smell grew stronger as he spoke to one of the men beside him in Russian. "Are these the ones?"

A stocky man with his cloak pulled low over his face pointed with his sword. "Yes, that's Yaroslav, and the tall one beside him can be none but the Celt."

Coel's eyes narrowed as he heard the crunch of feet in the snow behind him. He silently cursed his game leg and hoped it would hold him up long enough to strike a blow. The stocky figure took a step forward and opened his free hand reasonably. "We've heard you've come into money, Yaroslav. You and your friend drop your weapons. Give us your gold." He pointed his blade at Coel again. "And give us that sword. We let you walk away."

Snorri looked over his shoulder at the three men behind them, and then back at the five assailants ahead. His shoulders sagged in defeat. "Well, *Hel*, its not worth--" The Rus lunged forward and the four foot haft of his axe licked out in an uppercut. The butt of the ash shaft cracked against the stocky man's jaw. The blow lifted the man up in his boots. Snorri caught the butt of his axe with his left hand and the blade swept down. The twelve-inch steel crescent crunched into the stocky man's skull with horrible finality. The man fell to the snow and lay motionless. The two blows had been struck within heartbeats of each other.

"*Khristos*! He's killed Pietor!" Swords rasped from their sheaths as the killers filled their hands. Coel turned to face the men behind them. He put nearly all of his weight on his good leg and let his injured arm hang. He whipped the Academy sword before him with a snap of his wrist. The sheath hissed off of the blade and snaked through the air at the men facing him. The killers flinched back and Coel laughed out loud. The thrill of the perfectly balanced blade sent the old sweet shiver up his arm. The mirror bright steel caught the light of every star shining over the narrow alley.

Coel smiled crazily and jerked his head out at the street behind the three killers.

"Run."

The men drew back a step. The voice of the hooded figure

boomed out like a thunderclap.

"KILL THEM!"

Coel flinched at the inhuman power of the voice. It sounded as if a hundred men had shouted. It was sorcery. The command thundered inside his head like the voice of God, and the two simple words of Russian seemed to bounce around his skull and blaze with an unnatural life of their own. The effect on the killers was galvanizing. They leaped forward like dogs let off the leash. The lead man roared and swung his sword high overhead. Coel raised his own blade and dropped to one knee under the killer's attack. He ignored the wrenching pain in his thigh and scythed his sword out at ankle level. The blade sheared through one shin and bit deeply into the other. The man's roar rose to a scream of agony as he tumbled past Coel and fell howling and hobbled into the snow.

Coel awkwardly thrust himself erect on his good leg. The other two attackers charged forward with sword and club. Another figure appeared behind the killers and joined the charge. Coel hopped a step backward and steel rang as he deflected a sword cut, but his balance was already off. The second killer raised his club in both hands and brought it down at Coel's head. Coel tottered as his foot shifted, and it was all he could do to raise his sword between himself and the bludgeon. The Academy blade rang like a bell in Coel's hand. The force of the blow shivered all the way down his arm. Coel's knee gave way and he sat down in the snow.

His sword had bit deep into the club and stuck. The killer leaned on his truncheon to keep Coel and his blade pinned. Coel tried to yank his weapon free as the swordsman stepped forward for the kill. The hooded swordsman raised his blade high and then screamed in surprised agony. His back arched and he fell to his knees. The newcomer stood behind him with a curved blade gleaming dully in one hand. The clubman managed to yank his weapon free of Coel's blade and whirled to face the new assailant. The newcomer's scimitar whipped across his throat. The bludgeoner fell staining the snow in a spray.

The stranger with the scimitar marched past. Coel levered himself back up onto his good leg and looked for Snorri. The Rus stood with his huge *sax* knife in hand. Two men faced him. A third lay moaning in the snow with Snorri's broadaxe buried in his shoulder. Behind the killers, the tall one stood and watched.

The newcomer walked straight past Snorri and engaged the closest killers. The two of them crossed blades twice, and the killer gasped as his sword hand fell severed from his wrist. The stranger slashed his throat without mercy. The other killer attacked without hesitation. The stranger leaned away from two blows without deigning to cross weapons. On the third thrust, the stranger lopped off the killer's sword hand and then cut him down exactly like the first.

Coel leaned against the rough timbers of the wall and kept his eyes behind them. There was a high-pitched ringing in his ears, and he could still hear the tall one's command echoing like a whisper from around a corner. Coel spread his jaws in a wide yawn and shook his head to clear it of the sorcerous sound. "Snorri, are you all right?"

The Rus walked over to his axe without moving his eyes from the stranger with the curved blade. "I'm fine."

Coel glanced back at the empty alley before them. There was nothing to see but shadow. "Where is the tall one?"

Snorri sheathed his *sax*. "Gone. I swear I did not blink, and yet he is gone." The Rus took his axe haft in both hands and put his foot on the moaning killer's chest. The blade wrenched free with a splintering of bones. The killer screamed. Snorri ignored him and looked at the hooded newcomer measuringly. "Well, friend, that was timely. I admire the way you swing a saber."

"Thank you."

Coel started at the sound of a woman's voice.

Her hooded face lowered to gaze at the two throat-slit men lying in the snow without right hands. Her voice was a smoky alto. Her Latin was perfect. "They fought like foot-soldiers doing the same drill. They both made the same mistakes, and they died the same way. I doubt they had been out of the Frontier Service very long." She shrugged her shoulders. "They were probably deserters."

"Hah!" Snorri leaned on his axe. "Well, you impressed me. You're almost as good as Coel."

Coel felt the woman's hooded gaze measuring him. "The

kneeling cut was most impressive. Sitting down in the snow was less so."

Coel's face reddened in the dark. Snorri laughed out loud. "For a man with one arm and one leg, I think he did just fine." The Rus squatted on his heels and wiped his axe blade on the cloak of the wounded man at his feet. The humor left his voice as he addressed the man with the cloven clavicle. "And you, what's your story?"

The injured man grunted back in words Coel couldn't understand. Snorri tilted his head and then began making pointed inquiries in the same language. Coel narrowed his eyes in the dimness and tried to make out the woman's face. "You work for the Walladid?"

"Yes." The woman knelt and wiped the blade of her scimitar on a dead man's mantle.

"The Sorcerer told you to follow us?"

"Yes." The woman stood. The curved blade stayed unsheathed as she looked up and down the alley. "I was told to wait for you outside the room you are renting, and then to follow you discreetly to the Golden Horse. I went in after you left to see if I was still required to safeguard you. I was told the negotiations were successful and that I was to follow you back to your dwelling. You took a different route back. It took me some moments to find you."

Coel leaned heavily on his sword. The warmth of the wine was gone, and the sweat of his exertion had quickly dried. The night seemed to suck the heat out of his body. He made a determined effort to keep his teeth from chattering. "Well, I am glad you did. I am in your debt, and I agree with Snorri. Even a Bulgar would envy the way you swing a saber." Coel still could not make out her face. He ignored the cold and put on a winning smile. "I am Coel ap Math."

The shadowed face looked back at him for a moment. "I apologize for my remark about you sitting down in the snow. I did not know you were wounded. You are obviously an excellent swordsman." The woman paused again. "My name is Márta."

Snorri bounced up off of his heels and stood. "Well, it seems the lady has guessed correctly." He waved a hand over the dead and wounded men. "These lot are all Frontier Foot. This fellow here is a

Pechneg. Says his name is Bolli. He earned his commission in the Foot poaching the Grand Duke's sable farms. He says this foreigner he'd never met before, the tall fellow with the commanding voice, offered to pay off Bolli and his squad-mates' Commissions of Debt if they would be kind enough to sneak out of their barracks and kill you and me this evening." Snorri turned to the woman. "He says they weren't expecting you, and he's never heard of Reza Walladid."

"I believe him." The woman looked at the men on the ground. "Two still live. Shall we kill them?"

Coel and Snorri looked at one another askance. Snorri cleared his throat. "Well, normally I would say yes, but I can forgive a man condemned to a Commission in the Frontier Foot almost anything. I say leave them. They will be found absent without leave from their barracks and carrying their issue weapons without orders, obviously caught in some kind of crime." Snorri shook his head. "The Church is merciful, though. The Commander of Foot will probably have a chaplain heal the Tartar and add another hundred gold pieces to his debt. The poor bastard will have to kill every stray goblin from here to the ice-pack to pay it off." He glanced grimly at the other man who lay on his side clutching his severed ankle. "As for that one, you don't need both feet to pull an oar on a river barge."

The woman sheathed her scimitar. "We should leave."

Snorri peered at Coel closely. "Are you all right?"

"What?" Coel realized he was swaying. He straightened up with an effort and words came out of his mouth without being bidden. "I am tired."

Snorri grabbed Coel by his good arm and peered up the street. "I say the Boatman's Rest. It's by the West Gate and not far. River captains and wagon leaders frequent it. I sometimes play chess there with the proprietor. They don't allow riffraff, and they are open all hours of the night."

The woman walked up to Coel without a word and draped his bad arm over her shoulders. Coel felt himself being walked up the street towards Moscow's West Gate.

Coel's hand fell on the woman's shoulder. He felt the stiffness of armor under her cloak. Coel, himself, was over six and a half feet in height, and the top of the woman's head came up to his shoulder. She smelled nice. Coel breathed in the faint scent of rose oil in her hair. They moved through the streets and passed through the West Gate without incident. The Boatman's Rest loomed long and low in the dark like a great longship set belly-up in the snow. It had been one of the first inns built outside of the protection of Moscow's new stone walls, and it had been built with defense in mind. Its windows were thin cruciforms that allowed bows and crossbows to be fired outward and allowed very little to get in. Thick shutters were closed against the night, but light came out through the cracks. The ironbound door was very heavy, and it was narrow enough that only one man at a time could go through it.

Snorri banged a fist on the door. "Rollo! Open your God damned door!" He pounded on the door again and threw in several choice remarks in Swedish.

A voice spoke back in Russian. "Who is it?"

"Snorri!"

"Yaroslav?"

"Who else!"

"It's late for a game, Snorri. Go back to your barracks."

The door thundered on its hinges as Snorri put his boot to it. "Open your god damned door you fuzzy bastard! I have a hurt friend! He needs a bed!"

"Can you pay?"

"By Thor . . ." Snorri yanked his purse from his belt and slammed the sack of coins against the door several times. "What does that sound like to you?"

Metal bolts rasped within. The door swung back and a tall lanky man stooped in the entry. His hair and beard were so thick and curly that his face seemed to peer out of a ball of gray lambs' wool. He held a short, thick piece of well-turned wood in his hand. He shook his head at Snorri and tossed the club into a corner behind him. "Well, Yaroslav. Where did you come by such wealth?"

"Hello, Rollo," Snorri shouldered his way in, dragging Coel and Márta behind him. "My friend here is nearly out of blood. He's going to get a good healing tomorrow, but I want him to live to see it."

"Ah," The innkeeper was as tall as Coel and almost half his weight. "I've got a corner vacant. I suppose I can pull out a screen."

Coel let himself be pulled across the hall. It was a spacious but low-beamed establishment. The lanterns had been dowsed, but fires still burned low in the two stone hearths. An axe much like Snorri's hung behind the bar. Men lay on the benches wrapped in their cloaks near the fires. Along the far wall, a number of carved folding screens marked the spaces of those that had brought their families or were willing to pay for a real bed and a little more privacy. Rollo lit a candle in the corner and began pulling a screen around a large bed. The innkeeper's eyes flared in the sudden light, and he rammed a hand against Snorri's chest. "Christ! Bind that bloody leg of his before you throw him down on my best linens!"

"Well, bring some bandages! And some wine while you're at it!" Rollo walked out of the candlelight into the darker red glow of the hearth fires as Snorri and Márta sat Coel on the edge of the bed. Snorri muttered under his breath. "Nappy-headed, beanpole son of a . . ." He suddenly grinned. "How are you, Coel?"

Coel felt a bit fuzzy. "I would enjoy some wine."

"Hah!" Snorri turned to the woman. "That's a good sign. He's going to live."

The woman pushed back the hood of her dun colored cloak. Snorri's grin widened. So did Coel's eyes. Coel gazed at her face. His mother would have described the woman's face as "having character." Coel would have agreed with her. She had a strong chin, and her cheekbones were both wide and high. Her nose was straight and slightly thick across the bridge. She had a generous mouth. Her most distinguishing feature was her eyes. They were very large and brown with luminous flecks of gold in the iris. Her eyebrows were thick, well defined, and expressive. Chestnut brown hair with tinges of gold spilled down to a square cut at the shoulders. A black brocade barrette held her hair back from her face. It struck Coel that her eyes and her hair were the same color.

Snorri liked what he saw and offered his hand. "You and I have not been introduced. My name is Snorri Yaroslav."

The woman nodded, gave a short bow, and then clasped Snorri's hand awkwardly. A smile suddenly broke across her face.

Coel already thought she was pretty. She was beautiful when she smiled. "My name is Márta."

Her brown eyes flared wide as she looked at Coel's face for the first time in the candle light. Her mouth opened slightly and then shut. Coel smothered a frown. "Is something wrong?"

"Oh, no. It is nothing," The woman gave another embarrassed smile. "You remind me of someone."

Coel raised a bleary eyebrow. "Is that a good thing? Or a bad thing?"

Márta blushed deeply and broke into smile that lit up her face. "It is a good thing."

Rollo returned with bandages and a basin of water. He'd tucked a flagon of wine under his arm and held four wooden mugs crooked in his fingers. Snorri took the mugs and the wine and began pouring as Rollo peeled back the bandages from Coel's leg. They were soaked through and came off wet. Rollo sucked in his breath. "Sweet Jesus, that's a deep one. Right down to the bone, and it's been pulled open again more than once."

To Coel the wound was little more than a dull ache. All he wanted in the world was to lie down on the bed but Snorri's hand kept him sitting up. The innkeeper washed out the wound and then rebound it with an expert hand. Snorri handed Coel a cup of wine. Coel swallowed it in a gulp. Warmth spread through his stomach. Snorri refilled the cup. "Another."

Coel poured down the wine without protest. Rollo clapped him on the shoulder. "All right. Rest."

Coel lay back on the bed and felt his head sink into a pillow stuffed with real feathers. He sighed contentedly. The wine was going straight to his head.

Snorri held out a cup to Márta. "Wine?"

"No, thank you. You are safe now. I must return."

Snorri obviously wanted to drink with her, but he nodded affably. "Well, walk safely."

The woman nodded. "Thank you."

Rollo followed her to the door and saw her out. Coel yawned

and looked up at Snorri sleepily. "What do you think of that?"

"Of what?"

"Her. Márta."

Snorri waggled his eyebrows. "I think she has big brown eyes."

Rollo returned. The lanky Swede held a chessboard in both hands. "Well, the wine is open now. We might as well have a game." He looked at Snorri ruefully. "Though I suppose you'll win, you always do."

Snorri nodded. "Tonight, in seven moves."

Rollo blinked. "Bastard."

The two of them squatted on stools at the foot of the bed with the chessboard between them. Coel closed his eyes and his mind wandered a few moments through the fight in the street and the tall killer's shout that still seemed to echo in his head. Those thoughts quickly faded. Coel slept and dreamed of Márta's eyes.

CHAPTER FIVE

"Jesus Christ!" Coel awoke with a shout and tried to leap out of bed as lightning shot down his leg. He struggled and flailed, but strong hands held him down firmly. A deep, melodious voice spoke tersely.

"Do not take the Lord's name in vain, my son."

Coel looked about wildly. Snorri leaned over the foot of the bed and held his ankles. "Steady down, Coel. Let the good Father do his work." A short fat man in black robes and the peaked cap of an Orthodox priest pulled his hands away from Coel's injured leg. Snorri took his right hand from Coel's ankle and shook it out. He blew on his fingers with a laugh. "I felt that one, Father."

The priest stood and nodded slightly as he wiped his brow with the back of his hand. "It was a very deep wound, down to the bone. It had been repeatedly re-opened and was not healing properly. It required some effort to correct." He smiled benignly at Snorri. "You did well. Many men who are untrained let go of the patient during the healing. The pins and needles sensation you are experiencing should subside in a moment."

Coel looked up. Rollo was holding his shoulders. The innkeeper grinned down at him and then whistled at Coel's leg appreciatively. "Will you look at that? That really shines, Father!" Coel looked down at his leg. His wound was gone. There was no scar. There wasn't even a mark. The flesh of his thigh seemed to glow a rosy pink and his whole leg tingled as if ants were crawling up and down it. The big bone of his thigh radiated with pleasing warmth.

The priest nodded to himself. "Sit him up, Rollo, and we shall see about his shoulder."

Coel kept his eye on the priest as Rollo pulled him upright. The priest was stout but he wore his girth well. His every move was dignified and graceful. He folded his hands across his breast and slowly tilted his head and closed eyes. His lips moved in silent prayer. The priest took a deep breath and then slammed his palms together with a sharp clap. His eyes flared open, and he quickly shoved his right hand under the collar of Coel's tunic. The priest's palm pressed against the crossbow wound as his fingers gripped the flesh of Coel's shoulder. Coel yelped, and his body locked as lightning seemed to run across his collarbone and down his arm. Rollo grunted in surprise and his hands spasmed closed on Coel's arms.

The priest took his hand away and hooked the embroidered neck of Coel's tunic with his finger. He pursed his lips judiciously as he peered at Coel's shoulder. Coel could see the stout priest was trying not to breathe hard, and a trickle of sweat ran out from under his cap. The priest looked at Snorri. "Was there anything else?"

"Yes, Father. Coel took a sling bullet to the skull some weeks ago. The cleric at one of the Frontier Forts said his brain was undamaged, but he was the same one who did the healing on his leg."

The priest's eyes lidded disdainfully. "A Roman, I suppose."

"Yes, Father," Snorri searched his mind. "Father Phillip was his name. He was Frankish."

"I see." The priest was clearly unimpressed.

The Roman Catholic Church and the Greek Orthodox Church had joined hands to form the Holy League of Humanity and defeat the Hobgoblin hordes during the Goblin War. In the intervening two hundred years, that spirit of cooperation and brotherhood had swiftly fallen back on its old feuds and jealousies. Of late, the two had actually begun preaching against one another again. Many felt there would soon be war.

The priest stuck his finger behind Coel's ear. Coel winced as it ground probingly against his skull. "Superficial splintering of the skull bone has produced a slight protuberance." He finally deigned to speak to Coel directly. "You still have some tenderness?"

"Yes, well--Gah!" Coel started as his scalp leaped under the priest's finger.

"There." The priest stood back and ran his eye up and down Coel's frame. "How do you feel, my son?"

Coel rolled his arm in its socket. His shoulder felt tingly. His leg felt tingly. His scalp felt tingly. He felt tingly all over. All the colors in the room seemed brighter, and everything he looked at seemed sharper and more clearly defined. Coel felt himself glowing with health. The corners of his mouth turned up in a giddy smile he could not restrain. "I feel . . . well!"

"Excellent."

Snorri cocked his head. "Should he rest?"

"There is no need. His wounds are healed. There is no scarring. His fever is gone. His blood volume has been refilled. His lice are eradicated. He should feel completely rested and refreshed. He is fit for God's work." The priest mopped his brow again. His hand shook, and he looked slightly pale despite his dignified tone.

"Thank you, Father," Snorri grinned. "Will you take some refreshment for your labors? Perhaps some wine?"

"That would be most kind of you. I do feel fatigued." The priest smiled at Rollo. "Some Tokay would be a lovely constitutional."

Rollo blinked. Hungarian Tokay was one of the most expensive wines to be had. Often it could not be had at all this far north. He usually reserved what little he could get for impressing patrons with money and cementing deals. More often than not, he reserved it for himself. The priest smiled on him benevolently. Rollo cleared his throat. "Of course, Father. I will only be a moment."

Rollo's face broke into a scowl as he turned his back on the priest. He turned the look on Snorri as he wandered out behind the screen. The priest and Snorri smiled at one another. Coel flexed his leg and raised his arm over his head. Coel had received the Laying of the Hands before. Some healings burned. Some itched. Many had been less than wholly successful. This priest seemed to carry thunderbolts in his hands. Coel couldn't stop smiling at the feeling of well being pervading him. "Thank you, Father. You are amazing."

The priest spoke a vaguely pleased reprimand. "It is God's works which are amazing, my son. We are all but vessels of his will." He waved a dismissing hand. "I am told you received your injuries in God's service. It was the very least I could do."

Rollo returned with a small cask under his arm. "I'll get some cups, and--"

"Ah, bless you my son." The priest took the cask in both hands and looked at it fondly. The Roman numeral five had been burned into the blonde wood. "Well, I have many I must minister to, both in body and in spirit." He tucked the cask beneath his arm. It seemed the priest was not about to drink such a fine wine in surroundings as rude as the Boatman's Rest. He passed his hand in blessing before Rollo and Snorri's astounded faces. "God keep you both in good health, and God keep you, Coel, for defending the Faith. Good day."

Snorri and Rollo gaped in shock as the priest traipsed out of the inn humming contentedly. Rollo's scowl was so deep that his mouth seemed to disappear into his wooly beard and mustache. He turned on Snorri in moral outrage. "Fat bastard!"

Snorri chewed his lip and frowned. He studiously tried to avoid insulting priests, at least directly. "Yes, well, he might have shared."

Coel jumped up off the bed. He didn't give a good god damn about the wine. He'd never felt better in his life. "Who was that, then?"

Rollo glared. "That was Father Michcalik. Second Orthodox Bishop of Moscow and personal spiritual advisor to the Duke."

Coel looked up in surprise. "What brought him here?"

"Gold probably, and my wine cellar," Rollo scowled. "What brings priests anywhere?"

"No," Coel shook his head. "I mean, he came here, for me?"

Snorri shrugged. "Well, he arrived at the door at first light asking for the wounded warrior of Christ. I know it is a leap of logic, but I figured he meant you." The Rus sighed respectfully. "He surely had the power. Beautiful speaking voice."

"Bugger his speaking voice!" Rollo looked fit to have kittens. "That was my last cask, Snorri! Do you know how hard it is to get five *puttonyos* Tokay? They don't send it up river! You have to go down river, to Kiev, and I don't care how many silver pennies you have in your pouch, you can't afford it!"

"Oh, well." Snorri reached into his pouch and flipped a coin at the innkeeper. "Buy yourself a barrel next time you go to Kiev."

Rollo caught the flashing coin. He lost his Latin and babbled a few words in Swedish as he opened his fist and looked at the thick gleaming metal in his palm.

"Yes, Rollo," Snorri nodded blandly. "It's gold."

"It's Venetian!" Rollo gaped at Snorri. His Russian returned. "A full ducat!"

Snorri clapped him on the shoulder. "You're a good friend, Rollo. You've stood me many a stoop of beer and a bowl of *borcht* when I had no money, and you took your beatings across the chessboard in a manly fashion. Your game is improving as well, and it is good to have someone I can speak Swedish with once in a while. I thank you for the bed and wine, and for helping my friend, Coel."

Rollo looked long at the gold in his hand. "Who did you kill, Snorri?"

"For the money? No one, I assure you. I've just found more profitable employment than the Frontier Cavalry."

Rollo let out a breath. "I've been meaning to ask you about that. I was going to ask you the next time you came by for a game, but last night it was late and I got distracted."

"Well, ask me. I have no secrets from my friends."

"I get all kinds in here, Snorri. Merchants, river captains, soldiers, even priests, though I'll admit this morning was my first bishop. Pouring wine for that kind of traffic? I hear things. All kinds of things, and I'd be a liar if I said I hadn't heard a few rumors about you and your cavalry squadron."

A deep line drew down between Snorri's eyebrows. Despite radiant health and wealth, the smile left Coel's eyes as well.

Rollo locked his gaze with Snorri and his voice dropped low. "Were there really hundreds of them, Snorri? And hobgoblins? Or was that all just a lie?"

"Now, I was told I would be hanged if I spoke such lies again. I gave my oath before the court that I would not, and, last night, I think someone tried to make sure I would never get the chance."

Rollo's eyes were unrelenting. "Were they lies?"

"You have been a good friend, Rollo. So I will tell you something for nothing."

"What's that?"

"I would get out of Moscow if I were you."

Rollo swallowed.

Someone knocked politely on the dividing screen. The three men turned to find Orsini smiling at them. The dwarf was resplendent in his outlandish Italian clothing. He wore an ermine-trimmed cape of black silk with a purple lining, and a wide-brimmed black velvet hat perched on his head at a rakish angle. The hat's purple plume matched the lining of his cape. The dwarf removed his hat with a flourish and spoke in Latin. "Good morning, gentlemen." He looked at Coel and revealed his huge square teeth. "Coel, you are looking well this morning."

The giddy rush of the healing resurged. "I have never felt better!"

"Well then, let us see if I can improve your mood even further," The dwarf reached into his vest and pulled out two flattened scrolls with wax seals. He handed one to Snorri and one to Coel. Coel's stomach tightened as he looked at the red seal. It bore the stamp of the Legate of the Church of Rome in Moscow. Coel steadied himself as he broke the seal and unfolded the parchment. The note was handwritten, in Latin, in heavy script. The note stated simply that the five hundred gold piece Debt of Commission of Coel son of Math was paid in full. He was absolved of all duties in the Frontier Service, and he owed no debt to the Holy League of Humanity. It was signed Waleran Gengelphus, Legate of the Church in Rome in Moscow.

Coel whooped. "Free!"

"Free indeed, by Thor!" Snorri whooped as well. Coel hooked the Rus' right arm with his own. The two of them danced a mad jig beside the bed and waved their writs overhead like banners of victory. The dwarf hooked his thumbs in his war belt and his gem-like eyes glittered approval. Sleepy patrons of the Boatman's

Rest shouted at the crazy men to shut up. Snorri bawled a song in Swedish, and Coel raised his voice to the rafters in Gaelic as they spun each other faster. Freedom was a heady drink, and Coel was suddenly drunk with it. His legs felt like spring steel beneath him as he capered and whirled. He released Snorri and hurled himself about in wild Welsh round. His feet thundered the patterns on the floorboards as bodhrans and pipes only he could hear pounded and howled in his heart. Life surged through Coel's veins as it hadn't in years. His heart wanted to burst from his chest and soar to the sun. Snorri was laughing so hard his face was turning purple. He raised his knees to his chest and pumped his fists as he tried to stomp in time to Coel's wild Celtic dance. The Rus finally collapsed on the bed, clutching his sides with tears streaming down his cheeks. Coel spun to a halt and faced the dwarf. His chest heaved. Sweat poured down him in a river. He grinned like a crazy man.

Orsini matched Coel's insane smile and nodded at him. "Are you ready?"

"Ready?" Coel stabbed a finger at the dwarf. "I will shave the mountains! I will carve the heart from Pharaoh!"

"Hah! A poet, too!" The dwarf jerked his head at the door. "Gather your things. The wagon caravan for Smolensk departs tomorrow at dawn, and we have much business to be about before we leave."

Snorri sat up and wiped his eyes with the back of his fist. "What kind of business?"

The dwarf raised a thick finger and quoted: "*In the fourth, all additional armor, weapons, equipment, horses and livestock needed in the course of your duties shall be provided for at our expense.*" The dwarf waved a cautioning his finger. "The journey to the Black Sea is long and fraught with peril, even in these peaceful and prosperous times. I believe a visit to the Street of Armorers would be appropriate."

Snorri flopped back on the bed and shook his head at the ceiling. "This just gets better and better."

"I suspect it will get rougher and rougher once we leave Moscow's walls. Gather your things," The dwarf cocked a thick black eyebrow. "Have either of you left anything of value at the room you rented?"

Coel jerked up in alarm. "My harp!"

"Very well, then. I have been informed of last night's altercation, but I believe you should be safe enough during the day so long as you stay on the main streets and do not dally at any one place too long. Go to no taverns. Have yourselves something to eat here. Then fetch your personals quickly. Meet me on the Street of Armorers at the noon hour, at the shop of Ugo Dandolo and Sons." The dwarf turned on Rollo. "You, Sir. Good innkeeper."

Rollo tensed. The Swede had been watching the two clearly insane men and the non-human with a wary eye. "Yes?"

The dwarf wriggled his fingers and made a gleaming half-silver appear as if by magic. He flipped it at the innkeeper. "Please provide my associates with some breakfast."

Rollo caught it and blinked at the thick Venetian coin in his hand. People had been throwing Italian money at him all morning. The dwarf turned back to Coel. "The noon hour, if you please. There is much to arrange, particularly if either of you need fitting."

"At noon, *Signore*. We will be there."

"I shall look forward to it, and please, we are associates now. Call me Orsini."

"We will be there, Orsini. You may count upon it."

The dwarf donned his black velvet hat. "Then I will bid you good morning."

Coel watched Orsini leave and then turned on the innkeeper. "What have you got in your cook pot, Rollo?"

Rollo kept an eye on the door. He clearly wondered what other surprises might come wandering in. "There's leftovers from last night's borscht. I could reheat it, I suppose."

Snorri grunted his approval. "Borscht is always better the second day. It gives all the flavors time to get friendly with one another."

Coel agreed. "Aye, and you might bring us a little watered-wine with the change from that silver piece."

"Watered, *Hel*," Snorri snorted. "And bring some bread."

"And butter."

"And pot-cheese."

"You might fry an egg or two if there is anything in the coop."

"And you might fry the bread while you're--"

"Yes I know!" Rollo wandered off muttering. Coel and Snorri looked at one another smugly and waited for their breakfast, each thinking his own thoughts. Coel flexed his fingers. It had been months since he had played his harp, much less wanted to. Now he couldn't wait to get his hands on it.

* * *

Moscow's Street of Armorers was paved with cobblestones and crowded with buildings. It ended in an open court. In the place of prominence was the shop of Ugo Dandolo and Sons. The original building had been a long low hall of stone erected during the rebuilding of Moscow. More recently, a wooden house had been built on top of the stone structure. The bottom of the building had the gray, forbidding aspect of a fortress, but the house on top was painted a merry red with green shingling and whitewashed window frames. The storefront was a low stone arch, and its great oaken double-door were thrown wide. Over the door hung a wooden sign that read 'Dandolo and Sons' in flowing Latin script. Beneath the arch of script hung an oversized triangular tournament shield bearing the Dandolo family coat of arms. The shield was split diagonally with a prancing black dog with a sheaf of arrows in its mouth on a white field, and beneath it the golden Lion of Saint Mark on a field of scarlet. The paint was fresh and bright.

Coel walked with his harp under his arm and enjoyed the morning. There was still snow on the streets, but the day was clear and the sun was shining. The sound of hammering echoed up and down the narrow street, and the smell of charcoal and red-hot iron filled the air.

"This must be it," Snorri observed.

The two of them entered the shop. Weapons of every description festooned the walls. Cuirasses, coats of plates, mail shirts and even full suits of plate armor stood on display on wooden trees. A long stone counter ran along one wall. Orsini stood arguing with the man behind it. The armorer was a short thin man with a laurel of clipped white hair surrounding his pink scalp and a trim white beard and mustache. He was thin-lipped, and his eyebrows were huge and black in startling contrast to his white hair and beard. He wore a blazingly white linen shirt with the sleeves rolled up to his elbows. He looked more like a hatter than an armorer until Coel came closer and saw his forearms. The muscles twisted around his bones like ropes, and thick veins crawled down from his elbows and spider-webbed across his hands. A number of bows lay on the counter top between the armorer and the dwarf. Two were composite bows like those the steppe people used from horseback, and a third was a short and ornately carved flat bow suitable for small game. The armorer and Orsini were speaking to one another in rapid Italian. Orsini shook his head disdainfully, and then the two of them started arguing in German. The armorer spoke with his hands as much as his tongue, and he flung them about like birds as they argued. He finally threw his hands over his head and broke into Latin. "Listen here! These are the bows I have!"

"They will not do," Orsini hooked his thumbs in his warbelt and cocked his head. "I know you are a collector, Ugo, and I know men from all over Europe come here on Debts of Commission and end up pawning you their private arms. Have you nothing in the back?"

The armorer gave Orsini a sour look. "Oh, I have a bow upstairs, and you are correct, Orsini, it is a collector's item. I have collected it, and I have grown rather fond of it. As a weapon, I doubt I could find a buyer for it, even if I wanted to, which I do not. It is twice as tall as you are, and it would take a giant to string it."

Orsini cocked his head the other way at the sound of Coel and Snorri's footsteps. He smiled at the Italian and jerked his thumb at Coel. "Will he suffice?"

The armorer stared up at Coel in shock. "Well. maybe, he--" The Italian looked at the musical instrument under Coel's arm and ran his eye over the scarlet tunic. The armorer reignited his irritation.

"What the hell does a harper know about archery?"

"Why, he is Coel ap Math, a man of Wales. Born and bred in the mountains of Snowdon, and the third son of a Chieftain." Orsini's huge teeth gleamed. "Come now, Ugo. Don't you know an archer when you see one? Just look at those shoulders."

"Hmm." The armorer looked Coel up and down again in wary appraisal. "I still doubt whether he could string it, much less pull it. And I still do not wish to sell it."

Orsini did his coin trick, and gold piece appeared between his thumb and forefinger. "I'll wager you a ducat he can string it." In a blink, he closed his hand and opened it again, and a second ducat sat between his forefinger and his index. "And I'll bet you another he can pull it."

The armorer smiled slyly. "I'll grant you he can string it, he looks likely enough. But, pull it, and, hit the mark mind you, now, that is a wager I will take."

"You have targets in the back?"

"I do."

The gray eyes glittered. "Done! Two ducats to you if he fails, but, should he hit the mark? You shall sell me the bow. Agreed?"

The armorer's eyes went flat as a shark's. "Agreed," He shouted at the ceiling. "Pia! Fetch me down the bow!"

A moment later a woman's voice shouted back in thickly accented Latin. "Which bow you want?"

"The bow! The big one! Over the bed!" He looked at his guests and shrugged. "My wife is Istrian. Latin is not her first language, nor her second. He suddenly grinned and crooked a finger. "But please, I beg of you, follow me."

The three of them followed the armorer back to the forge. Ugo Dandolo was well equipped. He had two massive furnaces ringed by anvils. Tables and benches covered with tools were everywhere. A young man with long black hair wearing a leather apron looked up from examining a sword blade. The armorer waved a hand in introduction. "My second son, Enzo."

Enzo quickly nodded his head at Orsini, Coel, and Snorri and then back at his father. "What is happening, Papa?"

"I am going to deprive this dwarf of his ducats and buy your mother a bolt of silk."

The young Italian's face lit. "A wager?"

"Oh, yes. A wager."

"What is it, if I may ask?"

Ugo cocked his head at Coel. "Orsini of Venice says his friend here can pull the Strongarm's bow."

"The Little Bear!" Enzo gazed at Orsini in awe. Orsini tipped his hat slightly. Enzo bowed deeply. He turned his gaze on Coel with a shrewdness the equal of his father's. "Who is the Little Bear's friend?"

"Coel, son of Math. Of Wales."

"I do not know, Papa," Enzo bit his lip in concern. "Betting against the Little Bear, and a Welshman . . . "

Alarm bells suddenly clamored in Coel's mind. "Strongarm?"

Ugo grinned mercilessly. "Oh, so you have heard the name, have you? I am not surprised. It would not surprise me if you knew his other nickname, as well. Would you care to tell us?"

Coel's shoulders sagged. "The Hammer of the Welsh."

Orsini looked shocked. "Ralf deBarret?"

Snorri frowned. "I'm missing something. Who is Ralf deBarret? And why do they call him the Hammer of Wales? And what is all this strongarm business?"

Orsini looked at Ugo with renewed respect. "Sir Ralf deBarret was a Norman Marcher lord. He held a large fief in southern Wales. He ran it as if it is his own little kingdom, and in a rather red-handed fashion from what I am told. He and his knights were famous for the brutal way they pillaged their Welsh neighbors, and they did it with the King of England's blessing. From what I understand he was nearly invincible in battle."

Snorri frowned. "So who is Strongarm?"

Coel shook his head. "Ralf deBarret is the Strongarm. They called him that because he was seven feet tall and he carried a bow that no man could bend but him. My father had kinfolk in the south that suffered under the Strongarm's shadow. When I was just a lad, my father went to aid his kinsmen. He took some of his best warriors and they raided deBarret's lands," Coel cleared his throat uncomfortably. "They got mauled."

Orsini put his fists on his hips. "Am I to understand, Ugo, that you have one of the Strongarm's bows?"

"I do."

"How, if I might ask?"

Ugo hooked his thumbs into his apron. "The Strongarm got too big for his britches. He began taking territory from other Marcher lords without the King's permission, but he got away with it because he kept the Welsh from raiding into England. He became first among the Marcher Lords. Then he started calling himself the Prince of the Marches. That was his downfall in England. He and the King were not related, and the King took exception to deBarret joining the royal family. When the King marched on him with a thousand men-at-arms, deBarret fled to France to remake his fortune. It went badly. He ended up stealing money from some French pilgrims that was destined for the Church in Rome. That was his undoing in France. The Clerics cast spells of Augury and Divination and sniffed him out in Flanders. They dragged him before a Church Tribunal in chains. He had been knighted on Crusade in Antioch, so they decided not to excommunicate him. He ended up here in the Frontier Cavalry with a Commission of Debt that would give the Doge of Venice pause. That was ten years ago. He died out on the steppe not long after. Some Tartar bandits ambushed his patrol. The Strongarm couldn't pull that great big bow of his from horseback. The Tartars rode right up and filled him full of arrows. It was all very ironic. His surviving men brought his bow back, and I bought it. It's a beauty. I've never seen one to match it in all the Russias." He looked at Coel's face. "From the Welshman's expression, I'd say one wouldn't be likely to see its like anywhere else, either."

Ugo glanced at the door. "And here it is. Gentlemen, my wife, Pia."

A petite, dark-haired woman came into the forge bearing an

unstrung bow in her hands and a bag of arrows. Ugo's smile widened. Orsini's smile lost some of its light. Coel blinked.

"That's . . . " Snorri rubbed his shaved head. "That's a big bow."

It was huge.

Ugo beamed. "Pia, let our guest examine the bow."

The little woman smiled and handed Coel the bow. She gazed lovingly at the harp Coel handed her in return. Coel stood the bow.

It was perfect. No expense had been spared in the massive bow's construction. It was taller than he was and over four fingers thick in the middle. The bow stave had been painted in bright red enamel against the elements and ivory nocks capped both ends of the bow to hold the bowstring. It's vast length curved in a shallow arc to increase performance and then recurved near the nocks to allow an even greater draw. Coel ran his hand up and down the stave admiringly. "Yew?"

Ugo nodded proudly. "From Spain."

Coel stroked the wood. The yew tree was famous for yielding the best bow staves in Europe. Yew from Spain was the best of the best. Coel held the bow up and examined it more minutely. The bow was painted, but he could feel the line of the creamy sapwood that formed the inside of the bow. Sapwood was perfect for resisting tension and it held the bow together when it was pulled. The great outer arc of the bow was of the yew's amber heartwood. The heartwood could take immense compression and was the powerhouse of the bow. Cut and shaped correctly from a single bough of wood, the bow formed a perfect wooden spring. A yew bow stave seemed to have been designed from God on High to store and release force.

Ugo looked at his wife. "Did you bring the strings?"

Pia Dandolo shot him a scathing look. "Of course, I bring strings. What good is bow with no strings?" She slapped a small leather pouch into Ugo's palm. "Strings!" She reached into her blouse and pulled out a black wrist bracer of tooled leather. "Bracer!"

Ugo led them out into the back lot of the shop. The large

courtyard sported a number of striking posts with canvas covers on them. Past a couple of wagons, one end of the courtyard led into a long alley. At the end of the alley stood a heavy berm of packed soil as tall as a man. In front of the target butt three wooden wands stood set in the ground a foot and a half apart. Each wand was two inches in diameter and five feet tall.

"I normally use the targets to test crossbows, but it should suffice for our little archery contest." He handed the little leather to bag to Coel with a smirk. "String it."

"Hey!" Snorri waved his arms indignantly. "How's Coel supposed to shoot with a ten year old bowstring! It'll have dried out or gone soggy long ago!"

Ugo rolled his eyes contemptuously. "Observe." He nodded at Coel to continue.

Coel opened the little bag took out one of three loosely coiled bowstrings. His eyes went wide with shock. "It's silk!"

"Silk indeed," Ugo nodded. "Those strings will never fray like flax or hemp, nor sag when wet. They are the finest in the world."

Coel stared at the string as he rolled it in his hand. He had only heard of such things. The silken cord was the same scarlet shade of red as the bow and still smelled of the beeswax that lined the pouch.

Ugo handed Coel the bracer and then hooked his hands in his leather apron. "Well?"

Orsini hooked his thumbs in his war belt and looked at Coel expectantly. Enzo Dandolo stood behind his father with his arms folded. Snorri was chewing his mustache. Coel was irked to see that Snorri looked worried. Coel strapped the bracer to his left wrist. The bracer would defend his arm against the snap of the bowstring. Pia Dandolo held Coel's harp across her chest and smiled at him encouragingly.

Coel smiled back.

He slipped one end of the string into a nock and wedged the strung end against his instep. He reached up his right hand to grip the other end just below the ivory. Coel pushed at the upright end of the bow and pulled against its center. A grunt of surprise escaped his lips. It was the most powerful bow he had ever tried to string. He relaxed the bow and took a breath.

Ugo was smiling at him.

Coel frowned.

He could stand the bow up, grab one end in both hands and heave down against it with all of his weight, and that was what Ugo was waiting for. It was the method of an amateur, it was bad for the bow, and would be admission to all that Coel had not the strength to properly string it.

Coel's frown deepened. He would be damned before he failed such a beautiful bow.

Back in Wales, his own war bow's draw weight had been over a hundred and thirty pounds, and many a respected archer had marveled at it. The pull of the bow he held had to be close to one hundred and fifty. Coel seated the strung end against his instep and once more took the center and the end in his hands. His shoulders creaked with strain as he heaved against the war bow's weight. The bow slowly bent. His hands shook as he slid the string up the shaft. Coel bared his teeth as he pushed the loop up over the nock with his thumb. The silk hooked into the ivory groove and suddenly all strain was gone.

The bow was taut and alive in Coel's hand.

"Good!" Pia laughed happily. "Good for the tall one!"

"Yes, good for him," Ugo scowled. "Now let us see him pull it."

The armorer took up the arrow bag and pulled forth three shafts. He held the arrows up in the sunlight. All three shafts had wickedly barbed broadhead points that glittered in the sun. "Three arrows. Three chances. Aim for the middle wand. Hit either of the outside wands with any shot, and the wager is forfeit to me. Agreed?"

Orsini nodded confidently. "Agreed."

Ugo looked at his son. "Enzo."

Enzo Dandolo reached into a pocket of his leather apron and

took out a thick piece of chalk. Ugo took the chalk and gauged the distance. He took three steps backward and nodded to himself. "One hundred paces?"

"Aye," Coel nodded. "About."

Ugo drew a line on the cobbles. He stood up and smiled at Coel without an ounce of warmth. "Whenever you are ready, my friend."

Coel stepped to the line. He raised the bow and gave it an experimental tug. The string hardly moved. Coel held the bow out and pulled the string back as far as he could with just the strength of his right arm.

"Good God!" The grunt came out involuntarily. He had been wrong. The bow's draw had to be closer to one hundred and sixty pounds. Coel let the string back and rubbed the fingers of his right hand together. The string had left deep red grooves in his fingertips. He had not pulled a bow in years, and playing the harp had not been enough to keep his calluses longbow thick.

Ugo handed him an arrow and stepped back to the tiny circle of spectators.

Coel took the broadhead and laid it across the bow. He took a deep breath and fixed his eye on the center wand at the end of the alley. Coel slowly raised the bow. In his mind he saw the arrow hitting the wand. He--

"You have a run in your hose, Welshman."

Coel lowered the bow and glared back at Enzo.

Snorri shouted in outrage. "Foul!"

Orsini pointed a condemning finger at Ugo's son. "Now, we will have none of that."

Ugo Dandolo shook his head at his son but his smile stayed fixed. "No, Enzo, we will have none of that. This is an honest wager. Let the man loose his shaft."

Enzo spread his hands. "I am sorry, Papa."

Coel scowled. Enzo Dandolo did not look sorry at all.

Snorri's voice boomed encouragingly. "Come on, Coel!"

"Yes!" Pia Dandolo shouted excitedly. "Loose, Coel! Loose!" It seemed she was tired of the great bow dominating her bedroom wall.

"This is a wager," Orsini rumbled. "Let us give the man some quiet."

The courtyard grew very quiet. A few pigeons cooed from the eaves hanging over the alley. Coel raised the bow again. He eyed the center wand and took a deep breath. Coel suddenly let out a half shout. His left foot stomped forward and his left arm shot out straight as his right arm pulled back. The bowstring expanded out and up to Coel's ear. Ugo Dandolo gasped in surprise. It was no shortened chest pull. Coel had taken the great bow to full draw. Coel's whole frame trembled for a split second while he held the draw and aimed. Coel sighted down the arrow and the bow thrummed as Coel let fly.

The arrow hissed down range and thumped into the butt squarely between the left and center wands.

"Wide!" Ugo's voice was respectful. "Two spans wide of the mark, but I admit I am impressed."

Coel ignored the compliment. He held out his hand without taking his eyes off the center wand.

Ugo laid another arrow in Coel's hand. Coel stared at the center wand and a grin split his face. His fingertips buzzed and stung from the immense, cutting pressure of the bowstring. It hurt, and Coel enjoyed it. Perhaps it was the glow of the healing he had received, but Coel could not remember the last time he had enjoyed anything. He enjoyed the challenge. He enjoyed the fact that rich dwarves and famed armorers were betting gold, and it was his skill that would tell the tale. It was a beautiful Spring morning, and he held in his hands the most beautiful bow he had ever seen, and possibly the strongest ever made. He had taken the great bow's measure and felt its power. Coel thought about his escape from the Frontier Cavalry and his new employment. He thought of returning to Wales with a string of fine horses and sacks of gold. Coel grinned crazily. He pictured the look on his father's face as he handed him the bow of the Strongarm, the Hammer of the Welsh, to hang over his mantle.

The spectators looked askance as Coel threw back his head and laughed.

None of that mattered.

Coel looked up into the cloudless blue sky. The wager did not matter. The wands did not matter. All that mattered in the whole wide world was a smooth draw and the joy of a clean release.

Coel stamped forward a step and drew the arrow to his ear with a shout. He sighted down the barbed head and loosed.

The arrow hissed down the alley. Splinters flew as the arrow scored the center wand on its left edge. The arrow spun as it deflected and shattered against the left wand.

"Hit!" Snorri roared. "By Odin's beard, a hit!"

Ugo Dandolo shook his head in wonder. "A hit indeed."

"Good!" Pia Dandolo hopped up and down and clapped her hands. "Good for the handsome one!"

Coel wedged the end of the bow against his instep and unstrung it. Ugo Dandolo held out the little leather string bag. Orsini stood with his thumbs hooked in his belt staring at Coel appraisingly. A slow smile spread across his face. "I will speak to the Walladid about increasing your wages."

Snorri snapped his fingers in Enzo's face. "Hah!"

Orsini reached up to clap Ugo on the shoulder. "Do not feel too badly, my friend. You will be paid in gold for the bow, and these men need armor and other weapons as well. You are going to make a tidy profit today."

"So be it!" Dandolo smiled warmly. With a wager on the line, the Venetian was a wolf. With the betting over, his gregarious side emerged. "Back to business! Pia, bring bread and wine for our guests, they will be here some hours, and we will all be in need of refreshment. Enzo, heat forge number two." Ugo eyed Coel's frame calculatingly. "If this one wants armor, we will have to do some alterations."

CHAPTER SIX

Coel stood in an exceptionally well-appointed room in the Huntsman's Lodge. The Huntsman was the fanciest inn in Moscow. It had been open for less than a year and did a thriving business catering to wealthy, and more often than not, foreign clientele. It had three floors, four if you counted the wine cellar. Five, if you counted the bridal loft. Coel stood facing the wall and sighed with impatience. "Now?"

"Not yet . . ."

Snorri was acting like a fourteen-year-old bride. Coel shook his head and examined the vividly painted hunting scene on the wall. The panel showed a pack of long limbed wolfhounds holding a great, tusked boar at bay while a hunter on foot charged the bristled beast with a hunting spear.

"All right. You may turn around, now."

"Oh, for God's sake . . ." Coel turned around and looked at his friend.

"Ah? Ah?" Snorri turned in place with his arms spread. "This is how we dressed it up in the Varangian Guard."

Snorri was resplendent. He wore a glittering steel chain mail shirt that ended just above his knees and elbows. Over the mail shirt he wore a sleeveless lamellar cuirass. The small plates of iron were sewn together so that they overlapped like vertical fish scales that rose from his waist to his neck. Thin, vertical slats of steel encircled his legs from knee to foot, and hinged iron vambraces armored his arms from his elbows to the back of his hands. A conical helmet sat on his head. A mail aventail hung from its brim like a hood protecting the back of his head and neck and pinned under his chin to guard his throat.

Coel smiled. It was old-fashioned armor by the standards of Western Europe. But they had been hired as bodyguards, and that was not a job that could be done by men clanking about in full coats of plate armor. Snorri's defenses were layered. He could dress them up or down as the situation warranted. Snorri had upgraded his arms as well. A heavy single-edged sword hung from his shoulder on a leather baldric. Leaning in a corner stood a long-bladed fighting spear, and two lighter spears for throwing. A tear-shaped wooden shield stood in the corner with them. Snorri had not given up his old weapons, either. He'd had Ugo's third son, Pietro, put a new edge on his axe, and he now wore his sax knife behind his back in the same fashion that Orsini wore his Italian *cinquedea* short-sword.

"So," Snorri batted his surprisingly thick eyelashes. "How do I look?"

"You look like a man who is dangerous to know."

"Hah!" Snorri was well pleased. "Well, then, look at this!" Snorri hooked his upper lip with his thumb. Gold gleamed in the gap where his left canine tooth had been missing.

"When did you get that?"

"*Hel*, Dandolo was two hours fitting you for your mail, so, I went to the barber while you were in the forge. It took two-thirds of a gold ducat to fill the gap, and I paid the barber for the operation with the change. I made him throw in a head and arm shaving for free!"

Coel looked over the arms and armor piled on his own bed. Orsini's gold seemed endless, and he'd bought them anything they'd asked for. The great bow lay on the bed with its waxed pouch of spare strings. Strongarm had left four bags of arrows to posterity, and Orsini had bought them all. Two were filled with short shafted, broad head arrows, and two more held longer shafts with narrow, triangular bladed bodkin points for piercing armor. Ugo had contracted the fletcher next door to his shop to have another bag-full ready by morning. Orsini had paid the fletcher and his apprentice double to work through the night.

Next to the bow lay a rolled mail shirt of blackened steel and a sleeveless, red leather jack of studded brigandine armor. Fully armed and armored Coel was a study in red and black. Heavy black greaves of hardened leather would guard his legs from ankle to knee, and he'd bought matching vambraces for his forearms. Coel had not forgotten about his head. An archer could not wear a brimmed helmet. It would interfere with his draw. So he'd gotten Ugo to pound out a steel skullcap with a shallow bill to fit his head.

Coel had absorbed the lesson of Strongarm's fate. He knew he could not bend a bow that powerful from the saddle, either. A case of javelins stood in the corner with an eight-foot light-cavalry lance. Coel had picked up a stout, double-edged dagger with a bronze hilt, as well.

The shop of Dandolo and Sons had not been their only stop. They had also gone to the garment district and bought boots, cloaks, clothing and blankets, and other gear for traveling. Coel's proudest acquisition had been a low, wide-brimmed, black felt hat. The hat had been slashed and tabbed. With the brim turned down, the bonnet hid his iron skullcap from sight. The hat currently sat on Coel's head at a jaunty angle, with the right side of the brim buttoned up and the other turned down over his left eyebrow.

Coel felt like a thousand ducats, and by his own estimation he looked it, too. He could easily forgive Snorri his preening.

Knuckles rapped on the door of their new room. Coel and Snorri reached for sword and axe. Coel called out in Latin. "Who is it?"

Márta answered. "May I come in?"

Snorri tossed his axe back on his bed and flung the door wide. "Of course."

Márta stood in the doorway and smiled tentatively. Snorri smiled back. Coel gaped. She looked very different than she had in the dark, snow-strewn alley, covered by a cloak and wielding a bloodstained scimitar. The swordswoman now wore high-waisted, wide-legged silk pants of shimmering dark blue. Tiny threads of silver ran through the fabric and gave it a lustrous sheen. A tunic of dark green silk tucked into the pants and had been belted with a wide, black brocade sash patterned with tiny pink and white roses. A long silk vest that matched her pants fell to mid-thigh. The lines of the clothes had been exquisitely tailored to drape her frame perfectly. She'd thrust a long, recurved Turkish *yatagan* dagger through her sash.

Coel watched Márta walk into the room. She had perfect posture. Her every motion seemed utterly natural and graceful. Only her facial expression was slightly unsure. She looked back and forth at the two men in the room. "Would the gentlemen care to join us in the dining room?"

"Call me Snorri."

"Call me Coel."

Márta blushed charmingly. "Would Snorri and Coel care to join us?"

"Of course," Snorri raised his armored arms. "But, first, tell me how I look."

Márta smiled. "Very handsome."

Snorri was triumphant.

Coel watched the woman's face. He was irrationally pleased to find that when she smiled widely enough her chin dimpled. Márta looked back at Coel and ran her eyes searchingly across his face for a moment. Coel blinked. "What?"

Márta shook her head and looked away. "It is nothing."

Snorri pulled off his helmet and perched it on the bedpost. He unwound the padded scarf he wore under it, and his freshly shaven head gleamed. "Let me shrug out of all this iron and we will be right down."

"We will await you." Márta turned and closed the door behind her. Both men watched her leave intently. Snorri whirled and stabbed a finger at Coel. "Hah!"

Coel stiffened. "And what are you hah'ing about, then?"

Snorri drooped his wrist at Coel like a dandy. "You like her."

Coel's face reddened against his will. "What makes you say that?"

"Well, I was staring at her the way a man is supposed to stare at woman."

"Oh, and I was not, then?"

"No. You were swimming in her eyes like some moony calf. Drowning, too, I might add."

"What the hell are you--I was not!" Coel's ears burned. His denial sounded infantile even to him.

Snorri rolled his shoulders as if it meant nothing to him. He lowered his eyelashes at Coel demurely. "Help me off with my armor, won't you?"

* * *

The dining hall of the Huntsman's Lodge was done in German style with many long tables. Bows, crossbows, spears, and hunting swords hung all over the walls, as did the heads of boar, red bear and stag. A tall old man in a black robe with a gold plated chain around his neck looked up from a table full of Russian cavalry officers as Coel and Snorri entered. "Gentlemen, your party awaits you in the second dining room."

Coel and Snorri looked at one another. The man smiled tolerantly. "Your party has asked for private dining tonight. The man gestured expansively towards a number of doors along the wall. "Number two, if you please."

"Hah," Snorri nudged Coel with his elbow. "Private dining."

Wealthy merchants from all over Europe sat at the tables, as well as the most prosperous of those in Moscow. In their fine new clothes, Snorri and Coel did not raise any eyebrows as they passed. Snorri knocked on a door marked II in Roman numerals. Márta's voice answered. "Who is it?"

Snorri hooked his thumbs in his belt like Orsini. He seemed to be taking on a number of the dwarf's mannerisms. "Your associates."

Coel shook his head. Snorri was picking up the dwarf's vocabulary as well.

Orsini's voice spoke in return. "Do come in."

The private room was large enough to seat eight comfortably. Márta sat closest to the door, and her scimitar stood in a small floor stand by her side. Reza Walladid sat at the head of the table, and Orsini sat at his right hand. The sorcerer smiled. "Good evening. Please, be seated." He nodded at Coel and gestured at a tall glass carafe in the middle of the table. "Orsini tells me you are something of a connoisseur. We discovered The Huntsman has a Cypriot wine on the menu that Márta is fond of. I believe you will enjoy it."

Coel took a seat at the wizard's left hand. He held up the carafe to the candlelight. The wine within was a very dark amber color, and he could smell its sweetness. Coel poured a cup for himself and for Snorri. He raised the carafe towards the empty cup before Márta. "May I?"

She looked at Reza and then shook her head. "No, I really shouldn't."

Reza extended a graceful hand. "Do have a cup, Márta. If you do not, you will stare at the carafe all night, and I shall feel guilty. Should you swoon to the floor in drunkenness, I suppose Orsini can still defend me."

Márta happily extended her cup to Coel. "Thank you."

Orsini raised his cup. "To a profitable association."

Everyone at the table drank. Coel took a long slow mouthful of the dark Cypriot wine and let the flavor roll around on his tongue. It was very sweet, and the warmth of it expanded as it went down his throat. When he breathed in, the warmth turned fiery. Snorri spluttered and coughed. He was not a sipper. "Now! That is a mead to serve the heroes in *Valhalla*!"

Reza nodded over his cup. "Yes, the Greeks, themselves, liken it to the ambrosia the Gods of Olympus drank. The Mediterranean sun is warm and allows the grapes to naturally achieve a very high sweetness. The grapes are usually ripe by July, but the Cypriots do not pick them until September. Then the grapes are dried another three days on the roofs to consume what little water is left in them before they are trodden."

Coel was enthralled. "They are almost pressing raisins," Coel frowned suddenly. "The yield must be very low."

Reza nodded pointedly. "Yes, indeed, you are correct. The yield is very low, which is why the wines of Cyprus demand such exorbitant premiums. After pressing, the natural fermentation is controlled by burying the wine jars in cool cellars as the ancients used to do. Such a sugar-rich start yields wines twice the strength of the thinner, northern vines, and still leaves much unfermented sugar left over for sweetness. It is this strength, and the high sugar content, that allow the wine to survive years in the cask as well as the jostling of long voyages across land and sea that destroy other wines."

Coel shook his head wonderingly. "You are an alchemist, then?"

Reza smiled tolerantly. "Alchemy is a much misused word, and most men I have met who call themselves alchemists have great flaws in their thinking. However, I will admit to a keen interest in the interaction of phenomena, and what you would call alchemy is a branch of knowledge that my profession requires."

Snorri eyed the Persian slyly. "Does not the Prophet forbid the drinking of wine?"

A slow smile spread across the sorcerer's face. "The Prophet forbids many of the things I do." He looked at Snorri with interest. "Tell me, my friend, is there no religious scruple in your upbringing that you have broken?"

Snorri frowned deeply in thought and rubbed his head before he spoke. "My grandfather, the Swede, he worshipped the old gods. He used to appall the neighbors when he sent burnt offerings up to Odin and Thor on their feast days. When my father reached manhood he had himself baptized in the Greek Church for convenience sake, but he never took it into his heart. He had me baptized when I was born, but that was more to please my mother than anything else. When I served in Constantinople I saw the golden dome of the Saint Sophia, and knelt beneath it under the statues of the Saints as the Patriarch gave his benediction to the Guard," The Rus gazed long into the distance. "But I have seen the great whales breaching in the gray sea, and the pack ice calving into bergs as big as mountains in the frozen north. I nearly wept when I first saw dolphins dance in my ship's bow wake as the sun set on the Black Sea, and a standing stone on a windy moor in Sweden moved me more than any sermon I have heard. An Arab trader once told me that the earth beneath our feet spins about the sun, and the stars in the sky are suns like ours, shining on worlds beyond counting. I think on these things, and . . . "

Snorri's eyes reset upon the room. He met the sorcerer's gaze. "Oh, I have scruples all right. I won't break my oath once I have given it. Nor will I betray a friend. My friends' enemies are mine as well. As for religion?" His gaze hardened. "I accept all I have done and said, and I will say the same come Judgment Day, whether I stand before Christ, Allah, or one eyed Odin, himself."

Orsini slammed down his wine bowl. "Well said!"

Reza stroked his beard in thought. Márta nodded vigorously. She had hung on the Rus' every word. Coel looked at his friend and almost didn't recognize him. Snorri Yaroslav was proving to be a more complex man than Coel had ever imagined. Reza turned his gaze on Coel. "And you, my friend. Our conversation seems to be taking a philosophical turn. What thoughts have you on religion?"

Coel's face tightened against his will. The old anger surged fresh and hot as ever in his veins. Coel took a deep drought of the Cypriot wine and made a conscious effort to unclench his teeth. "I have no love for the Roman Church. The Greeks have given me little reason to love them any better."

The table grew very quiet. Reza nodded. "Yes, as I recall this is a subject of some sensitivity to you. Let us speak of other things." He turned to Snorri. "Tell me more about what you encountered on your last patrol."

Snorri scowled unhappily. "I know I told you some of the tale when we first met, but the morning after, the Court of Inquiry made me swear an oath I would not speak of such things again." The Rus suddenly grinned mischievously. "However, Coel was unconscious at the time, and swore no such oath that I know of. You might try asking him."

Reza nodded at Coel. "Can you tell us something about it?"

Coel refilled his wine cup and thought back to the attack on the steppes. "What Snorri told you was true. There were hundreds of them. Goblins. Everywhere. They led us into a trap, and then swarmed us. They were well armed, too. They had slings, and javelins, and darts of some kind. They filled the air with them. They pulled us out of the saddle with lassos, and then fell upon us with knives and hatchets."

Orsini looked at Coel intently. "And hobgoblins? You saw them as well?"

"They were hobgoblins, all right. Tall as a man or taller, armed with hooked lances and swords. They had crossbows, too, and they were riding camels."

Orsini looked at Reza doubtfully. "Well, they sound like no hobgoblins I have ever known."

Coel agreed. "No, they do not."

Orsini raised a bemused eyebrow at Coel. "Tell me, have you known many hobgoblins?"

Coel matched the dwarf's expression. "Not until recently."

Orsini grunted. "Point taken. I apologize for doubting you. However, you must forgive me if I ask, are you quite sure they were hobgoblins? Could they not have been steppe nomads? Tartars perhaps, or Cumans wearing war-masks or closed helmets?"

"What I know of hobgoblins has all been from books. What I saw on the steppe matched the descriptions I have read."

Orsini raised a knowing finger. "The Book of Saint Yves?"

"Yes." Coel remembered the book well. He had read it dozens of times. The Book of Saint Yves was part of a collection that formed the standardized telling of the great Goblin War, and the only book that was told in the first person. Yves Vancura had been a Nestorian priest in the Russian town of Riazan when it had been stormed by the Hobgoblins at the onset of their invasion. He had been rounded up with the surviving non-combatants and chained to the great food coffle. The hobgoblins had marched out of the steppes of Asia and invaded Europe. They made their food march with them. Yves had survived the trek from Russia all the way to Budapest where the northern Hobgoblin horde had been turned back. The priest had done all he could to comfort his fellow sufferers on the long death march. Father Yves Vancura had taken confessions, given the last rites, and recorded what he saw. Both the Roman and Greek churches had canonized him. Coel quoted the book from memory.

"The Hobgoblins are uniformly tall and strong, strong as a man or stronger. Their skin is green or gray, and great teeth like the tusks of boars protrude from their lower jaws. They gaze upon their prey with huge, canted, cat-like eyes. Their nostrils are but slits in their faces, but their sense of smell is as a keen as a hound. Horses will not bear them. The very scent of hobgoblins drives them to frenzy, and hobgoblins take great relish in eating the fallen steeds of the cavalry. Their marching is remarkable, and would put Caesar and the Legions of Rome to shame. They feast upon the flesh of beasts and men. In times of famine and hardship, they will feast upon the flesh of the lesser race of goblins, and in extremity they will feast upon the weakest among themselves. They do not partake of grains or vegetables, and it was our blessing and our curse on the slave coffle that these foodstuffs were gathered from fallen towns and villages and given unto us to keep our feet marching and our bodies fat enough for their cook fires. They will drink the milk and blood of cattle and goats, and these beasts march beside us. They seem to enjoy eating cheeses looted from fallen towns and villages. Butter pleases them immensely. This was our salvation."

Coel smiled at Yves' ingenuity. The old saint had been one of the men forced to milk the cows for the hobgoblin army as it marched. A bowl of milk and blood was the hobgoblins' favorite morning meal. Frequently the humans who did the morning milking contributed the blood, and then became the meat for the mid-day meal. The humans in the food coffle were allowed to loot the clothes of the eaten, and Saint Yves had found a heavy cavalry boot. Secretly, he managed to milk a cow into the boot. When the milking was done, he and the men with him had passed the boot among them and shaken it for their lives. At daybreak, the first hobgoblin that Yves had offered a dirty boot for his breakfast had nearly split his skull. Yves managed to survive long enough to show the irate hobgoblin the lump of butter floating in the congealed cream. The priest had been dragged before the Great Hobgoblin, Hakak, and through pantomime he had shown that dread creature what he had done. Yves and his men had been made butter makers on the spot. A platoon of men were cut from the food coffle and given to him as boot shakers. Without ever having described them, butter churns appeared to replace the boots when the next village fell to the hobgoblin horde. Saint Yves and his butter men survived. There seemed to be many labors that hobgoblins considered beneath them, and Saint Yves saved countless other men and women from the cook fires by organizing people and finding ways to make themselves useful. The butter churn was his symbol, and he was the patron saint of dairy farmers. All of Europe celebrated his feast day.

"Vancura was a fascinating man," Orsini took more wine. "Can you quote the Hobgoblins' arms as readily?"

Coel recited: "The Hobgoblins are armed with spears and battle axes with great knife-like blades set into the haft at right angles. They protect themselves with wooden shields and crude armors of leather and felt. The poorer tribes carry wicker shields and war clubs studded with nails. War chiefs and their bodyguards may have byrnies of horn scales or split horse hooves. Hobgoblins gladly wear the armors of humans if they can find those that fit them among the fallen, and these are much sought after. In attack, the Hobgoblins drive the lesser breed of goblin before them to disrupt their enemy's formation. When they feel the time is right, the Hobgoblins hurl their spears and then charge to attack with their war axes. Their champions wield war axes in both hands, and few swordsmen in Christendom can stand before them."

Orsini nodded. "Essentially correct."

Coel leaned back in his chair. "That is what struck me so strange. In the military classes at Grande Triumphe, we were told that the hobgoblins were defeated by their lack of cavalry and archers. That, and the Hand of God. These looked like the creatures I had read about, but they did not act like them at all."

Orsini stared deeply into his wine cup. "It is disturbing enough to hear that the race of Hobgoblins walk this Earth of yours again. More disturbing still is your talk of crossbows and camels."

Coel peered at the dwarf. The way he said 'this Earth of yours' struck him as odd.

Snorri reached into his vest and pulled out a piece of cloth. He unrolled it onto the tabletop. Three of the barbed, weighted darts the goblins had been throwing in the canyon clattered to the table. Coel forgot Orsini's words as he saw the weapons again. "Those were what the goblins were hurling. They fell like rain."

"Ah. A *plumbatae*." Orsini picked one up. "The late Romans and early Byzantines used such weapons. They were cheap to manufacture and much easier to train troops on than archery. They have longer range than javelins, and one may carry many more of them. More of a nuisance weapon than anything else, really, though they can be lethal against unarmored opponents." The dwarf peered at the barbed head distastefully. "This one has been poisoned."

"That was Snorri's thought," Coel shook his head as he

remembered his comrades. "Snorri told me everyone in the squadron who was even nicked by them sickened and died, including the horses."

Orsini handed the dart to Reza. The sorcerer sniffed the black iron point and then held the dart head over a candle until a wisp of foul smelling smoke rose from it. He sniffed the air again and his nose wrinkled. "Traces of cobra venom, if I am not mistaken. Mixed with something else I cannot identify."

Coel sat up. "What is a cobra?"

"A serpent you do not wish to meet," Márta shrugged as she sipped her wine. Her cheeks had taken on a rosy glow. "From the East."

"Yes, indeed, Márta, from the Far East." Reza handed the dart back to Orsini and looked at Coel. "Your encounter on the steppe is beginning to have all manner of ramifications."

Snorri finished his wine and poured himself another cup. "I would be interested in hearing more about where we are going."

Reza let the subject change. "Tomorrow morning, we shall take our leave of Moscow and take a wagon caravan west to Smolensk. From there, I shall charter our passage on a river barge, and we shall head south down the Dnieper to Kiev. I have business there. If my business is favorable, we shall be joined by two more of my associates who are waiting to meet us. From Kiev, we shall continue south to the Black Sea. There we shall take ship and sail onward east to the Empire of Trebizond, where I will have further business negotiations. If those are successful? My business may lead us in almost any direction. Your duties shall remain the same, regardless."

Snorri eyed the wizard sharply. "What kind of business are we talking about?"

"My business," The sorcerer smiled. "However, you might think of it as research. I am currently attempting to delve into some rather esoteric mysteries of the past. My studies require extended travels, often to dangerous and uncivilized places. I must often travel quietly, and lightly. I cannot afford to bring an army with me, so I must make up for lack of numbers with quality. Thus, I require the services of reliable and multi-talented men such as yourselves."

"Ah," Snorri waited for the wizard to elaborate. The Walladid didn't.

Coel cleared his throat. "What sort of duties are expected of us, then?"

"Well, as I have said, I often go to dangerous places, and I have enemies. Though perhaps it might be more accurate to describe them as rivals or competitors. Magic alone is often not defense enough. Like armor, one's defenses are best layered. It seems from your encounter last night you have acquired enemies of your own. Márta informs me that the man who led your opponents last night spoke with the Voice of Command, which tells me your enemies have some skills in the art of sorcery. I shall help you against your enemies. You shall help me against mine. I may also require various errands from you from time to time."

Snorri shifted uncomfortably in his seat. "Errands?"

"Oh, only dangerous errands, ones that require your skills, I assure you. Márta is my bodyguard. My wellbeing is her only duty, and I never like to have her far from my side. There are occasions when I need capable men to carry out actions that she would otherwise have to perform." The sorcerer gave Snorri a droll look. "However, you have my promise, I shall not command you to collect my linens or haggle for vegetables in the market."

"That is not what I--" The Rus rolled his eyes. "Oh, *Hel*, for what you're paying me? I would empty chamber pots as long as you said please."

Coel leaned back in his chair and drained his cup. "So, it is to be hired swords, then, and doers of dangerous deeds."

"Orsini told me you had the poet's flair," The wizard smiled warmly. "Those shall be your duties exactly."

There came a short knock upon the door, and the dinner entered. An entire roast pig came in borne upon a silver platter. Everyone at the table set upon the pig with gusto. Coel noted that Snorri had no inclination to ask Reza Walladid about the Prophet and his prohibition upon eating pork.

The Rus was too busy indulging his own appetite.

CHAPTER SEVEN

"Wagons!" The wagon master's shout echoed through the clearing. "Halt!"

Steam rose off the oxen as the wagons creaked to a halt for the noon rest. Coel sat on a buckboard and looked out over the river crossing and the thin forest surrounding it. Spring was coming early to the Russias. The ice had broken on the river, and only watery shards like glass clung to the rocks in the shadowed areas of the bank. The air was cold and the sky was clear and windless. Green shoots were pushing their way up out of the snow. Birds flew from tree to tree singing and jousting for nesting space.

"Rest! One hour!"

Coel leaped off the wagon and stretched his legs. There were twenty wagons in the caravan. All were heavily laden with goods and passengers heading west for Smolensk. The men of the wagon teams quickly began setting up cookfires as the caravan guards dismounted. The guards were lancers from the Frontier Cavalry. Like Coel, they had been conscripted for their crimes with Commissions of Debt. However, these were mostly local men, or men from wealthy Eastern European families. Their connections had gotten them soft duties and the opportunity to obtain work as caravan guards. The work paid in silver, and the risks were minimal. The cavalrymen had eyed Coel and Snorri narrowly in the morning but for the most part had ignored the two of them throughout the day. The troopers had gone well out of their way to pay attention to Márta's every comfort. Their sergeant in particular was a darkly handsome Pole named Sandor. Sandor had spent the entire morning riding beside Márta. Coel sat in the second wagon and found himself displeased with the arrangement.

He took up his long bow and a sheaf of arrows as Snorri unpacked a jar of the strong Cypriot wine. Coel had seen the provisions being laded in their wagon at dawn. It seemed as if Reza Walladid had bought almost half of the Huntsman's Lodge's larder for their journey to Smolensk. Snorri looked up from his labor as

Coel strung the great bow. "Where are you headed?"

"To have a leak, and loose a few arrows."

"Ah," Snorri went back to prying open his wine jar. "Luck with both."

Coel ambled along the riverbank. He quickly lost the camp noises of the caravan and took in the sights and sounds of the forest. He ran his eye over the river as he walked. The sun's light dappled the river with gold as it gurgled over rocks that had only recently been sheathed in winter ice. Coel stopped by a likely looking tree and lifted his tunic. A fool's grin passed over his face as he wrote his name in a patch of snow. Coel took a deep breath and sighed as he relieved himself. He looked around the evergreen forest. During his tenure in the Frontier Cavalry, he had been blind to the beauty of the Russias. Now, it almost overwhelmed him. His grin widened. Beautiful as it was, he was pleased to be leaving it. Coel shook himself and squatted down to wipe his hands with snow. Across the river he spied a tiny hillock. A tree had shattered and fallen from it during the spring thaw. Its fall had torn open a patch of raw earth a yard across. Coel judged it a good hundred paces away. His eyes never left the mark as he pulled an arrow from his belt and nocked it.

He drew the great bow and let fly.

The arrow flew straight and true, and the narrow, armor-piercing bodkin point sank deeply into the soft brown earth. Coel methodically began drawing and firing. His arrows thumped into the target and began to form a rough circle twice the size of a dinner plate around the first shaft he had loosed. It was not a great feat of archery, but he was taking his time befriending his new bow. His shoulders were sore each morning but he was pleased with how smooth his draws were becoming. He and the Strongarm's bow were going to get along well with one another.

"What is that thing you have in your hand?" Coel jumped as a voice spoke behind him. "A barge pole?"

Coel turned. Márta wore the same dun-colored travelling cloak she had been wearing the first time he had seen her in the alley. She carried a bow in her hand and a case of arrows slung at her side. Márta stared at Coel's weapon in disbelief.

Coel laughed. "Just just limbering up." He glanced at the

weapon Márta carried. "What have you there, then?"

"Well, this, I would call a bow." Márta raised the weapon. Her bow was small, little more than three feet across, but it was the classic armament of a horse archer. Coel's bow was primitive in comparison. Cut from a single bough of wood, his bow depended on its length and thickness for its immense power. The short, recurved weapon in Márta's hand was a laminate of many layers of wood, horn, and sinew that gave it power out of all relation to its size. Coel smiled and held the great bow out to her. "Would you care to try?"

Márta rolled her eyes but traded bows with him. Coel's weapon was a head and a half taller than she was. She took the arrow Coel held out and raised the bow. A line of concentration drew down her brow as she began drawing back on the string. An 'umph!' escaped her lips as the string moved back an inch. Her arms trembled as she drew harder. It refused to budge. Márta laughed as she eased off the string. It was the first time Coel had heard her laugh. It was low and throaty, and he found himself liking it immediately. Márta lowered the weapon and grinned as they traded bows again. "The Sultan of Egypt's own Mamluk Guards do not draw bows that heavy."

"Archers in the east loose mostly from horseback, so they must draw with the strength of their arms alone. Welshmen stand to loose their shafts. We lay our whole bodies into the bow."

"Well, your body and your bow seem well matched." Márta suddenly blushed at her own boldness.

Coel grinned at the compliment. He gestured at the bow she held. "Show me what you can do with yours, then."

Márta took an arrow from her case and raised her bow. She peered at the target Coel had chosen and the pattern of arrows he had made in it. She raised a speculative eyebrow. "This is your second day with the bow?"

"Well," Coel looked off to one side. "We are still becoming acquainted."

"Oh, no. It is very good, particularly with an unfamiliar weapon." Márta drew her arrow back and released. Even as it flew, she drew and released a second arrow and then a third. Coel watched in open admiration. In a space of seconds, Márta drew a circle of arrows around the center shaft Coel had released. Her circle was well inside of his and barely wider than a wine bowl.

"Now, that really shines!" Coel grinned. "You must have started young."

Márta blushed again. Coel found it utterly enchanting. "I began my training when I was twelve."

"Did you, then? I too!"

Márta grinned so that her chin dimpled. "When I started my training, the arms masters would not teach you anything else until you acquired proficiency with the bow. Drawing the bow built the base of strength needed for the saber and lance. Of course, they were toy bows when I started, but the draw weights grew heavier as I got older."

Coel looked at her shrewdly. "You were trained at a military convent?"

"I was trained by the Sisters of Limmasol, in Cyprus." She gave Coel a tentative look. "Have you heard of them?"

"I know of the Isle of Cyprus of course, and I have heard of the city of Limmasol. I know the Knights of Saint John have a castle there, but . . . "

"Oh, it is all right. Few westerners have heard of us. Everyone has heard of the Sisters of Antioch in the Holy Land and the Papal Amazon Guard in Rome, but the Sisters of Limmasol are a small order, and Orthodox. They have a high reputation, but they are known mostly in the East."

"I admit I have not heard of them," Coel's stomach sank at a sudden, unhappy thought. "Have you taken vows, then?"

"Oh, no, I was trained by the nuns, but most of the training was secular and done on a contract basis." She brightened suddenly. "But the Abbess told me that she believed there was a place for me if I wished to be ordained. Though I would need to complete my religious education," Márta bit her lip. "It has been somewhat spotty."

Coel smiled wryly. "It seems we have much in common."

"Orsini told me you have trained at the Paladin Academy in

Paris," Her eyes were wide with the thought of it. "That must have been very exciting."

"Oh it was, for a time. But that was years ago," Coel's gaze fell on the river. "A lifetime ago."

Márta searched his face again as she had the night before. She hesitated before she spoke again. "Orsini told me the story of how Snorri was thrown out of the Varangian Guard over a woman and sent to the Frontier." She suddenly dropped her gaze from his. "When you were sent to the Frontier, was it over a woman, too?"

The anger was Coel's oldest companion. On the endless winter patrols in the Russia's, thoughts of the past had smoldered just below the surface of his skin and kept him warm. His hatred had been simmering for a long time. Now, with his new freedom, the anger flared out of him before he even knew what was happening. Coel strode forward and his voice tore out of his throat. "What god damned business is that of yours?"

Márta flinched and took a step back. "I am sorry. I did not mean to--"

"I did not want to talk about it last night!" Coel loomed over her as the floodgate opened within him. "What the hell makes you think I wish to speak of it now?"

Márta's eyes went as wide. She backed up another step and started as she bumped into the tree behind her. Three years of blackest hatred shuddered through Coel's veins. "Did Reza send you to worm answers out of me?"

"No!" Márta gaped. "My Master would never--"

"Master!" Coel reared backward in shock. "You're his slave?"

Márta flinched. Part of Coel wanted to stop, but his voice was chained to his hatred. His lips twisted in spite. Words rose up in his mouth and spilled forth like bile. "So, were you going to bend over to loosen my tongue? Or were you going to drop to your knees and loosen your own, then?"

Coel did not even see Márta's hand move. He saw stars as her palm cracked across his jaw. For a moment he was too stunned to react.

Márta's eyebrows drew down into a vee of fury. "I answer only to the Walladid! Not his paid lackeys! Speak to me like that again and I will kill you!" She spun on her heel and stomped off. She stopped suddenly and jerked her head at the target across the river. "Fetch the arrows!"

Márta stalked away through the trees.

Coel's knuckles went white. The wood of his bow creaked in his hands. Rage twisted in Coel's guts like a serpent, and he spent long moments trying to regain control of himself. Slowly, the serpent turned its belly up, and his rage was replaced with anger and embarrassment at himself.

The question Márta asked had gotten men killed. The answer had ruined lives. It had taken everything from Coel except his life, and even that had been a near thing. It continued to ruin everything around him.

Coel took a deep breath and scowled across the river. He was not about to abandon twelve perfectly good arrows. He gazed hard at the tight pattern her shafts had drawn inside of his own. He had already acted the fool, he was not about to act the infant and leave her arrows behind, either. Coel grit his teeth and began splashing across the river. He regretted his choice of targets immediately and gasped as the melted snow reached the tops of his thighs. He shivered as he reached the other bank and stomped up to the target. Coel pulled his arrows out and cleaned the heads before sheafing them on his belt. He drew Márta's shafts and cleaned them as well. He crossed the frigid river once more and made his back way to the wagons. The wagoneers were breaking camp. Márta was nowhere in sight. Snorri sat against a wagon wheel using a piece of bread to sop the last of the borscht from his bowl. He wiped his mouth on the back of his hand and nodded pleasantly as Coel approached. "So, how was your leak?"

Coel didn't trust himself to speak. Snorri glanced at Coel's sodden leggings. "Looks like you missed."

"You go to hell, then!"

"What?" Snorri spread his arms helplessly. "What?"

Coel glared off into the distance. "Oh, hell, it is not you, Snorri. Reza sent his slave to go digging about in my affairs." He felt his stomach tightening. The thought of it began to fuel his fury again. "I did not care for it."

"Coel?"

Coel turned. "What?"

"We are friends, are we not?"

Coel paused. "Yes?"

"Well?"

"Well, what then?"

"You are an idiot."

Coel blinked.

Snorri sighed. "Listen to me. Reza did not send Márta after you."

Coel blinked again.

Snorri looked at Coel as if he were a small child. "I did."

Coel's mouth dropped open.

Snorri waved his wine jar. "Listen, I know you like her. I have an inkling she likes you, too. I know, I can tell about these things. Anyway, you went wandering off into the woods with your bow. I was minding mine own affairs by the wagon while Márta was unpacking some of her things. I saw she had a bow, too. It occurred to me to mention that you had acquired a fine great bow in Moscow and that the weapon had a history to it. She seemed intrigued, so I took the liberty of suggesting that perhaps the two of you might enjoy loosing a few arrows together while the wagons were stopped. She seemed rather taken with the idea and went off to find you," The Rus shook his head sadly. "Now, when she came storming back hissing like a wet cat? I just figured you had gotten impulsive and tried to get into the seat of those silk pants of hers too quickly." Snorri made a face. "But now I see the only thing you managed to bugger was yourself."

Coel just stared.

Snorri held up his wine jar. "Here, have a drink. You look like you need one. Then I will help you think up an appropriate way to beg Márta for forgiveness," Snorri shrugged modestly. "I've had much practice at these sort of things."

* * *

Smolensk sat on the northern bank of the Dnieper and straddled the long line of trade between the Baltic and Black Sea. The river was its life. Furs and amber came west from Moscow. North from the Baltic Sea came whale oil and wax, amber and hides. Locally, timber, iron, and silver mines swelled the economy and the nations of the south always paid a premium for northern slaves. South from the Black Sea came silks, spices, and all manner of luxury goods. The river piers of Smolensk bustled as busily as any seaport on the Mediterranean.

It was late in the day, and the wagon caravan unloaded near the wharves. Coel watched as bales of goods were laded onto river barges heading north and south and other bales were carted through the city gates. Snorri and Márta stood together and talked on the other side of the wagon. The two were becoming fast friends. Coel knew Snorri had spoken on his behalf during their journey. Márta would have none of it. Coel had returned her arrows to her cleaned and sharpened and received little more than a frosty nod. After that, she had acted as if he did not exist. Coel ignored her back, and Márta had spent the rest of the trek basking in the company of the Polish Cavalry Sergeant, Sandor. Coel's fist clenched. The other night in camp the Pole had quoted love poetry by the old Roman poet Catullus while looking in her eyes. Márta had sat by the fire and glowed at him. Reza never mentioned the squabble. It seemed beneath the sorcerer's notice. Twice, Coel had tried approaching Orsini about it. But each time the dwarf had turned his glittering eyes on him Coel had gotten embarrassed and ended up changing the subject to wine or siege tactics. He had spent most of the week by himself angrily practicing his archery. Coel knew Snorri was right.

He was an idiot.

Snorri ambled over with his axe in hand and his sealskin sea bag over his shoulder. "Hello, Coel."

"So, what is happening?"

"What? Oh," Snorri sighed. "She still thinks that you're an ape."

Coel scowled. "No, I mean what is happening now? I saw you speaking with Reza a few minutes ago."

"Oh, well. He is going to charter us a berth on a river barge. He says he has no duties for us presently, and you and I are free to wander about the city as we like." Snorri grinned. "I say we go find an inn and get drunk."

Orsini appeared out of nowhere. "An excellent idea. I know of an inn close by. It is somewhat rustic and caters mostly to soldiers and river sailors, but they serve an excellent wheat beer in the German style."

Snorri elbowed Coel knowingly. "Wheat beer, in the German style." Coel shook his head. Snorri basked in the dwarf's presence and hung on his every word. If the Rus began wearing puffed and slashed pantaloons, Coel felt he might hit him. The Rus grinned. "What say you, Coel?"

Coel glanced back over at the wagon. Márta stood in the bed holding a bag of her belongings. Sandor stood beside the wagon and took her bag as she handed it down. Márta smiled warmly. Sandor twirled his glossy black mustaches gallantly as he smiled back. Their hands brushed for a second too long as they passed the bag. Márta's chin dimpled. Coel ached to smash the Pole's face in. He turned to Snorri instead. "I think getting drunk is an excellent idea."

Orsini was pleased. "Well, then, gentlemen! Let us be about it!"

The two men followed the dwarf through the bustling press of wagons, oxen and people. Orsini moved unerringly along the wharves. People gaped and quickly moved to give way as he passed. Coel and Snorri walked in the dwarf's wake. Orsini pointed a thick finger. "There, as I remembered it. The River Inn."

The River Inn was long and low and hewn from rough logs. The inn faced the wharf. Its wide, double-doors were flung open to the afternoon. Smoke rose from its roof hole. Music and the sound of laughter came out along with the smell of roasting meat. Coel followed Orsini's lead. The River Inn was doing a brisk business. Many of the tables were filled with teamsters and soldiers from the wagon caravans and sailors and bargemen from the river. Two saddles of moose turned on a spit over the central fire, while a cook poked at it. A lean, gray-haired harper sat near the fire. His voice belied his wrinkles as he sang a song in Russian and plucked at a three-string *gudok*. Orsini took a table along the wall and sat with his back to the heavy logs. Snorri sat beside him. There was no room for a third along the wall, so Coel unbuckled his sword and took a stool at the side.

Tavern girls moved between the tables. The innkeeper had chosen them with care to separate men from their rubles. They were tall and strong enough to carry a serving board laden with heavy beer steins. They were also pleasingly well formed and kept the top two buttons of their white linen blouses perilously unbuttoned. They smiled at anyone with money. One of them approached Orsini's table warily. The tall blonde girl could not remove her gaze from the outrageously dressed dwarf. She spoke halting Latin. "Yes?"

Orsini smiled good-naturedly and spoke in Russian. "And who might you be?"

The girl drew back slightly. "I am Sasha."

"Ah." A silver ruble appeared in Orsini's palm. He flipped it onto the back of his hand and began walking it back and forth across the tops of his fingers. "Would you be so kind as to tell me, Sasha, do you still buy your beer from Brewer Kutner?"

Sasha stared, mesmerized, as the silver piece walked back and forth across Orsini's hand with a seeming life of its own. "The German? Yes. We have several barrels."

"Ah. Well and good. May we please have three mugs of the wheat? My friends Snorri and Coel here have never tried it. Oh, and some lemons, if I may be so bold."

Sasha giggled at the dwarf's good manners. Orsini's eyes suddenly glittered. "I will tell you what, Sasha. We shall flip a coin. Heads, you shall buy our first round, tails, you shall keep the change."

"What?" Sasha started. "I--"

"Good. Done." The silver coin rolled onto Orsini's thumb and rang off of his nail with a ping. The ruble ascended towards the rafters. Sasha's breath hissed inward. Orsini opened his hand and held it over the table. The coin seemed to pause for a moment at the apex of its flight and then tumbled back down. Orsini's hand never moved. The ruble simply fell into his palm. He peered down at the coin. Orsini shrugged mightily and gave Sasha a helpless grin. "Well, it appears I have lost again."

He flipped the coin back to his thumb and sent it high and slow over the table. Sasha caught it between her hands with a happy clap. The barmaid beamed and left without a word. Orsini leaned back against the wall. "The service here is excellent."

Coel's foul mood faded and he smiled against his will. "I have the feeling you often lose to pretty barmaids."

"My friend, what man has not lost something to pretty barmaids?"

"Hah!" Snorri gazed upon the dwarf in awe. "By God, you have a sense of style!"

"Thank you," Orsini's brow furrowed as men entered the inn. "Well, now. It appears to be Márta 's new acquaintance."

Coel sat up straighter. It was indeed Sandor. He was accompanied by two of his men. The Pole looked over at the table and shot Coel an insufferable smile. Coel started to rise. Orsini's hand clamped implacably on Coel's wrist. "Look, Coel, here is our beer."

Coel studiously turned his attention to Sasha. She had returned carrying a large serving tray laden with a wooden ewer, three pewter steins and a small bowl of sliced lemons. Sasha set down the tray. Coel raised appalled eyebrows as she squeezed a lemon wedge into each mug. Orsini caught the look. "Patience, Coel. One must try new things."

Snorri nodded sagely. "Yes, patience, Coel."

Coel examined the beer with interest as Sasha poured. He was used to the brown ales of his homeland and the paler brews of the Russias. The beer that flowed out of the ewer was a cloudy gold. Sasha dropped the lemon wedges into the steins with a splash of foam. Orsini turned to Coel with a wink. "It fights the scurvy, if nothing else."

Coel snorted. Snorri raised his stein. "To a good journey."

"Yes, a good journey," Orsini raised his mug.

Coel raised his own. "Good journey." They clacked their mugs together. Coel blew off the foam and took a brave pull of the fruit adulterated brew. His eyebrows shot up as he swallowed it. Coel raised his mug in salute. He couldn't remember when beer had tasted so good. "It is perfect."

Orsini laughed. "Well, now, perfect is a mighty high praise." He raised a finger. "And, I will tell you, the nut brown ales of your own Welshlands have given me pause. I have had some fine portage ales from Sweden, and I had a beer brewed by Trappist monks in Flanders once that renewed my faith in humans, however . . . " The dwarf took another swallow and sighed contentedly. "To my taste, nothing smacks more of springtime than a good German wheat."

Snorri looked at Orsini. He looked at Coel. He looked deeply into his beer. "This is . . . " The Rus searched for words. He looked about the room. He looked at Sasha. He looked back at his beer and then his drinking companions again. He looked as if he might burst with good will. "This is great!"

It seemed as if there was no place on earth the Rus would rather be than where he was now and doing what he was doing.

"Well, good beer, good companions, beautiful women?" Orsini raised his mug again. "What more needs to be said? To Sasha!"

They toasted again and savored their beer. Sasha made a pleased noise as Snorri snaked his arm around her waist and pulled her onto his knee. "Tell me, Sasha, what would you do if I carried you away with me?"

"My brothers would hunt you down and kill you." She gave Snorri a heavy-lidded smile. "But in the meantime, I would spend every piece of silver you have, and you would still be smiling when they put you in the ground."

"Hah!"

Sasha draped an arm around Snorri's shoulder and looked at Coel. "Tell me, who is your friend with the strange accent?"

"Why, that is Coel, son of Math, son of a Chieftain, and a son of Wales." Snorri waved his stein expansively. "He's my best friend."

This was news to Coel but he found himself immensely pleased by the statement.

"Wales?" Sasha's nose wrinkled delightfully. "I have never heard of it."

Snorri lowered his voice mysteriously. "Coel is a Celt, Sasha. A barbarian from the Western Isles, on the edge of the Irish Sea."

"Ireland!" Sasha's eyes grew wide. "The Island of the Elves!"

Orsini nodded knowingly. "And he is a harper, as well. Perhaps he will give us a song later."

Sasha clapped her hands. She looked Coel up and down. "I have never seen a man with such green eyes before." Her eyes went heavy lidded once more. "He is big, too."

"Oh, indeed. Tall as a tree." Snorri smiled wide enough to expose his gold tooth. "But I am bigger. Trust me."

Sasha frowned. "No, but he is-Oh!" She clapped her hand to her mouth and blushed. "You are terrible." She looked at Snorri with renewed interest. "Tell me, you are not here under a . . . " She looked away for a moment, and her smile dimmed slightly. "Commission of Debt?"

"Oh, no." Snorri jingled the pouch at his belt. "We are free men."

Sasha's smile grew bright again. "Where do you go?"

Snorri took another pull of his beer. "The Black Sea, and beyond."

"The Black Sea? What will you do there?"

Snorri looked to Orsini. "Yes, what do you think we shall we do there?"

Orsini shrugged nonchalantly. "The world is wide, our swords are sharp, and our pouches full. We shall go wherever adventure takes us."

Sasha looked around wonderingly at the sumptuously dressed

dwarf, the Celtic giant from the fabled Western Isles, and the local boy who dressed like a Norseman and whose pouch jingled with gold. Together, they were unlike any table she had ever served. She suddenly noticed her platter. "Oh! You need food!" She looked over at the cook fire. "The meat isn't done yet, but I can bring you some apples and cheese."

Snorri's arm stayed around Sasha's waist. "Coel can get it."

Sasha smiled warmly at Coel. She seemed pleased to stay right where she was. Coel laughed. "I can get it. Watch my sword." He jerked his head at Orsini. "And keep Snorri away from my mug."

Orsini smiled blandly. "And what makes you think it is the Rus you must worry about?"

"Well, then, I guess I shall have to buy another round as well." Coel took another swallow as he kicked back his stool and strode across the inn. The fresh sawdust on the floor competed with the smell of roasting meat. Coel stopped by the cook fire to breathe in the aroma of roasting moose basted in oil and herbs. The cook nodded at him and smiled. "Soon, friend. Soon."

Coel turned to the minstrel sitting by the fire and listened. The greybeard's *gudok* was smaller than Coel's harp and didn't have the same quality of tone, but the old man's voice was good. Too good to be singing by the riverside. Coel thought he must have offended someone in town to be working an inn near the piers. Coel tossed a silver ruble amongst the coppers in the cap at the man's feet.

The minstrel was startled by the gleam of silver, but he quickly regained his composure. "You are generous."

Coel nodded. "Aye, but you have talent, and I know what it is to sing for one's supper."

The old man looked Coel up and down warily. He had stomached too many fools who had bought the right to sing a song with a big tip and then driven away the paying customers as they howled to their ancestors in bad voices made worse by drink. The man sighed. He could forgive much for a silver ruble. "You play, then? Or just sing?"

"A little of both."

"You have a strange accent. Have you any training?"

"Some."

The old man's eyes narrowed. "Where did you receive it?"

"In Gwynned."

The man shook his head. "I have never heard of it."

"It is in Wales."

"Wales?" The man leaned forward slightly. "You have had Bardic training, then?"

Coel nodded. "Some."

The old man stared into the distance. "It has been more summers than you have seen since I have heard a song in the Celtic tongue." He looked at the silver piece in his cap. "Well, you have more than bought the right to sing a song, if you like."

Coel smiled. "I bought a song from you, my friend, and I will have one of your best if you do not mind."

The minstrel rubbed his chin. "Well, my best is not what it once was, but for a silver ruble I will do what I can for you."

Coel glanced back at his companions. Snorri raised his empty mug and held it upside down over the table in silent accusation. Coel waved at him and turned back to the minstrel. "Listen, I am with friends and we have yet to eat, but I have a harp of my own in my bag. Perhaps we might play something together later. I--" Coel bit his lip at his temerity. The old man's seat by the fire was his livelihood, and as a harper himself, Coel realized his silver did not give him the right to intrude upon it. Coel looked at his feet sheepishly. "That is, I mean, if you're of a mind to."

The minstrel raised a calculating eyebrow. "You sound like a tenor."

Coel looked up with a shy grin. "I am that."

A slow smile spread across the old harper's face. "Well, then, perhaps after you've eaten, you and I shall see about relieving this crowd of their rubles."

Coel grinned. "Save a spot by the hearth for me."

The old man grinned back. "You may depend upon it."

Coel turned happily to the bar. It had been a long time since he had played to a crowd, and he looked forward to it. The barkeep was an immensely fat man with a thick blonde beard. He smiled at Coel and nodded back at the minstrel. "Paulus is good, isn't he?"

"He is very good. I would like to send him a cup of your best, if it is not too much trouble, then."

"He would like that. I give him his beer for free, but he has a taste for wine when he can get it."

Coel nodded his head back at his table as he put coins on the bar. "Oh, and another ewer of the wheat for my friends, and some apples and cheese while we wait upon the roast, please."

The innkeeper pulled another wooden ewer from a shelf behind him. "Done."

Coel turned and listened as Paulus' voice rose by the fire and slowly began to fill the air. Before, the minstrel had been singing more to himself and plucking the strings of his instrument as a background for the conversation at the inn. Now, his voice rose in steadily growing power and he had taken out his bow and expertly sawed the strings. The man's talent demanded attention. Much of the conversation in the inn died down as people stopped to lend an ear. Coel listened intently. He would have thought the Russian language a harsh one for song, but the old man made it sound beautiful. Coel glanced around at the crowd. He did not recognize the tune, but it was obvious the crowd did. Many were moving their lips as Paulus' voice rose to fill the corners of the inn. Coel smiled. There would be more silver in the minstrel's cap before nightfall.

A voice spoke loud enough for the entire bar to hear. "So, that is the coward you told me of in Moscow?"

The song died. Heads turned towards the bar. Coel looked to his right and found Sandor and another man standing together staring at him. They sneered in open contempt. The man standing next to Sandor was stout and had a ragged scar on his chin. He wore the livery of a Cavalry Commission of Smolensk. His small eyes narrowed at Coel. "Indeed, he is the one. Coel, son of Math. He lost his entire squadron on the steppes. He was drunk on duty and got them all killed."

Sandor stroked his mustaches. "Yes, I have heard the story.

To think I spent an entire week on the wagons with the villain and did not know it."

"Surely you could tell just by the smell of him."

Coel's fists clenched.

"Indeed," Sandor made a face. "He was always sniffing about a lady I made the acquaintance of during the trek. He gave her great offense the very first day out, and then acted the sullen churl thereafter. I was going to teach him some manners, but the lady begged me to ignore him."

Coel felt his blood go hot. He kept enough of his composure to see the trap. Sandor was leaning arrogantly on the bar, but his hand rested casually on the hilt of his dagger. Coel's sword rested well out of reach across the tavern. The two men Sandor had come in with stood at the bar a few paces away regarding Coel with steely eyes. Four other men wearing the colors of Smolensk sat at a table a few strides away watching the stout man for the signal. The stout man made a pretense of indignant anger. "Sir Jean Hainault was a good man. He was knighted on crusade in Antioch. He deserved better than to die on the steppes due to his second in command's incompetence and cowardice."

Coel's knuckles went white.

Sandor arched an eyebrow. "I am surprised they did not hang the knave."

"So was I, but it seems some rich Persian bought his Commission of Debt." The stout one curled his lip in distaste. "One can only imagine the kinds of 'services' he is performing for the Persian in gratitude."

Sandor shrugged himself off of the bar. Coel stood a head taller, but somehow the Pole still managed to look down upon him. His lip curled. "Yes, I had heard he had a reputation for immoral character. As a matter of fact, I heard something of how he earned his Commission of Debt. It seems there was a woman. If you can believe this, she was a--"

Coel rammed his forehead down into the bridge of Sandor's aristocratic nose. Cartilage cracked and the Cavalry Sergeant's head snapped back. Coel kicked Sandor's feet out from under him as he staggered. He grabbed the Pole by the hair with both hands and bounced his face off the bar.

Sandor fell unconscious to the floor with his looks in bloody ruin. Coel smiled unpleasantly at the cavalrymen. "Which one of you eunuchs is next?"

The stout man stepped forward putting his hand on his dagger. Coel put his hand on the man's throat. The man choked as Coel's fingers squeezed, and he gave a strangled shriek as Coel's other hand slammed up into his crotch. Coel heaved upward and hurled the cavalryman bodily over the bar. Barmaids screamed, and clay pots and bowls shattered as the fat man fell. The two troopers at the bar attacked in a rush. The four Smolensk troopers leaped up from their table.

Snorri's voice boomed across the inn. "Coel!"

Coel kicked one trooper in the groin and then stood him back up with a knee to the face. The other trooper leaped upon Coel and they grappled. A Smolensk man hit Coel from the side and the two attackers bore Coel backwards against the bar. Snorri leaped into the fray and two of the local troopers turned to meet him. Coel struggled with the men holding him. A fist crashed into his mouth. Coel heaved as the men kept him pinned. A voice hissed behind him. "Hold the bastard!"

Coel managed to tear partially free as a dagger rammed into his back. Coel grunted. The armored jack he wore under his tunic held. Coel whipped his head about. The fat man had tried to stab him from across the bar. Blood streamed from his forehead where his face had met with the crockery. The dagger flashed and plunged into Coel's side. The blow drove the air out of Coel's lungs, but the blade failed to penetrate. The fat man snarled. "Armored, are you?"

Coel heaved forward and pulled the two troopers holding him along. The fat man vaulted his bulk over the bar. "I said hold him!"

The stout man lowered the dagger and went to thrust it up under Coel's tunic.

A huge hand swallowed the stout man's wrist. Orsini held the wrist for a moment and smiled as the fat Smolensk man struggled. The dwarf suddenly clenched his fist. The fat man screamed as his bones cracked and his blade fell to the floor. The men holding Coel suddenly noticed the dwarf amongst them. Orsini reached out and seized one of the troopers by the elbow. The trooper howled as Orsini squeezed. The dwarf yanked and the trooper flew from his feet and went tumbling back into the tables.

Coel spun into the trooper still holding him. He rammed his forearm under the man's chin and drove him backward across the inn. Patrons scattered from a table as Coel shoved the man backward across the top of it. Coel seized a stein of beer and crushed the pewter around the man's forehead. The trooper went limp. Coel snatched up a stool and looked for a new opponent.

Snorri stood with his axe held reversed in his hand. The two troopers he had beaten with the haft lay moaning on the floor. Orsini dusted one of his still-immaculate puffed sleeves with his fingertips. He glanced at the innkeeper. "Such an embarrassing misunderstanding. Beer has been spilled and crockery broken." He produced a gold ducat. The coin gleamed as it sailed through the air and landed on the bar.

The innkeeper looked at the gold piece and then looked at the non-human with apprehension. "I think I would like you to leave."

"Yes, I believe that would be best. No one would want any further misunderstandings," Orsini looked to Snorri and Coel. "Come, gentlemen. Let us retire."

Coel dropped the stool and went to fetch his bag and his sword. Snorri followed. Orsini stood watch as the two of them went out the door. The dwarf swiftly joined them. "Let us be away before the city watch comes."

Coel looked back over his shoulder. No one came out of the River Inn after them. "Where is Reza?"

Orsini marched at a quick pace towards the south gates of the city. "He will have arranged our berth on a river barge to Kiev by now, and, I believe, gotten our accommodations within the city, as well. We had best go there and lay low for the evening."

The sun began to set as they entered the city proper of Smolensk. Orsini quickly moved to the back streets and began winding his way through the alleys unerringly. They moved along a back row of large houses. Orsini stopped at a small, heavy wooden door and rapped his knuckles on it with three rapid taps and then a fourth. In the narrow alley the houses stacked almost one against another, but from the back the houses looked very expensive. The lengthening shadows in the alley made Coel nervous. "Where are we?"

"At the house of an associate of the Walladid's. We should be safe enough here for the night."

Moments passed and someone unbarred the door from within. Light spilled into the alley. Márta stood in the doorway with her scimitar in one hand and a lantern in the other. Snorri grinned. "Hello, Márta!"

Márta smiled. "Well, hello!" She looked at Orsini. "I thought you would return much later."

"Things happened."

The three of them filed through the small door and into the house. Márta barred the door behind them as they walked down a narrow, paneled hall to another heavy door. They entered and found themselves in a very comfortable and brightly lit parlor. Four heavy couches formed a square around a small table in the middle of the room. Thick Persian rugs hung on the walls and a crystal candelabrum spilled light from the ceiling. A brazier stood in each corner full of glowing coals. Orsini doffed his felt hat and ermine cape and draped himself upon a sofa. He glanced at Snorri. "Would you be so kind as to see if there is any wine in the cupboard? The Walladid's associate must have left something in the larder for guests."

Snorri set down his axe and went to the cupboard. He opened the ornate double doors and pulled forth a small oak cask. He squinted at the writing on the side. Orsini put his feet up upon an ottoman. "What manner of refreshment is it?"

"I think it's Frankish."

Coel peered over. "It is claret."

"Hmm," Orsini frowned. "A thinner potation than I would have preferred."

Coel took the cask and examined it. "It is a Bergerac, from Bordeaux. I have had its like when I was in Paris. If it is less than a year old, it should still be good."

Orsini waved a careless hand. "I defer to your judgment. By all means, let us give the French an opportunity to impress us."

Snorri drew his sax and went to work on the stopper. Márta looked at Coel's face with clinical detachment. "Your lip is bleeding."

Coel raised a finger to his swollen lip. He had barely felt the trooper's blow at the time. Now it throbbed.

Márta rolled her eyes contemptuously. "What did you do, walk into a door?"

"My face is fine," Spite leaped out of Coel's mouth unbidden. "You should see Sandor's."

Márta went rigid. "What did you do?"

Orsini sighed tiredly. "Oh, can the two of you not make some kind of effort to get along?"

Márta whirled on the dwarf. "What did he do to him?"

"Well, Sandor is somewhat, less handsome, than he used to be."

Márta's hand went to the hilt of her scimitar.

Orsini rose up between them. "Wait!"

Márta loomed over the dwarf. "Wait nothing! I told this savage I would kill him if he gave me offense again!" Her eyes locked with Coel's over Orsini's head. "Draw your sword!"

Coel stepped backward before Márta's fury. His hand went to his hilt defensively.

"Draw!" Márta's scimitar hissed free of its sheath. "Or I'll cut you down where you stand!"

Snorri stepped back out of Márta's view and cocked the wine cask back for a throw. Márta never took her eyes off Coel. "Oh, don't think I don't see you, Rus."

Snorri sent Orsini an imploring look.

Orsini raised his hands. "Márta! Please! I beg of you! Listen to me!"

Márta dragged her eyes back to the dwarf. "What!"

"Márta," Orsini's tone grew very calm. "I understand your ire, but Coel was provoked. Sandor and some of his friends made a very real attempt to kill him tonight." The dwarf reached into his vest and pulled out a short, wide dagger. "I picked this up during the excitement. Sandor's accomplice at the inn tried three times to shove it into Coel." Orsini held the blade over a candle. After a second, acrid black smoke rose up from the blade and an ugly smell filled the room.

Coel's eyes flared. Snorri slammed down the wine cask. "The same stench as the goblin darts, by Thor!"

"Indeed, and our friend, Sandor, had a hand upon his own hilt even before the fight began, though Coel never gave him the chance to draw it." Orsini looked apologetically at Márta. "Now, my dear, I admit your charms are such that men might well fight over them, but would they use poisoned blades? For that matter, one must ask, what was a Smolensk cavalry trooper doing with a poisoned dagger in the first place, if he did not have a premeditated mischief in mind?"

Márta's lip trembled. She bit it to keep it still.

Orsini sighed. "I am sorry, Márta, but I believe Sandor knew of the friction between you and Coel. I believe the attentions he showed you during the journey from Moscow were intended to inflame it. If Sandor had murdered Coel on the wagon trail, there would have been trouble. Clerics might be called in, and Truth-Tells administered. However, were Coel were killed in a tavern brawl, over a woman? There would be little notice. No one in authority would care. The poison was to make his death a certainty, and I feel a similar certainty that a poison blade lurked for our friend, Snorri, as well."

Márta looked as if she might be sick.

Orsini spread his hands helplessly. "I am sorry, Márta. I know you had developed a certain fondness for the man."

Márta sheathed her scimitar. Her eyes were bright with tears she refused to spill. She spun and walked away without a word.

Orsini dropped his hands to his sides as the door closed behind her. Coel sat heavily on one of the sofas. A long, uncomfortable silence followed. Coel noticed a small, leather bound book lying on the table and picked it up. The book had the slightly battered look of literature that has been well cared for but has traveled far and been read many times. Coel's eyebrow rose slightly as he read the title. The book bore the title "The Love Songs of Sappho" painted in gold leaf. A piece of parchment fell from the book into his lap. It was a note written in a flowing hand. The ink was still wet, and some of it had smeared from being hastily folded.

> *~Sandor,*
>
> *To me it seems,*
>
> *I have the fortune of the gods,*
>
> *to sit beside you, and close,*
>
> *to listen to you sweetly speaking*
>
> *and laughing temptingly,*
>
> *my heart flutters in my breast.*
>
> *I say nothing, my tongue broken,*
>
> *a delicate light plays under my skin.*
>
> *An indelicate fire burns in my blood.*
>
> *My eyes see nothing, my ears roar,*
>
> *cold sweat rushes down me.*
>
> *trembling seizes me,*
>
> *I am greener than grass,*
>
> *with but a spark*
>
> *I would burst into flame.*

~Márta

Coel had read the poem before. Márta had personalized Sappho's words. A pang of jealousy stabbed him. Márta had changed the words for Sandor. Coel put the parchment back in the book on top of the page Márta had been copying from. He set the book on the table and found Orsini staring at him. Orsini waved at Snorri tiredly. "Perhaps you should pour the wine, my friend. I will take some to Márta presently."

CHAPTER EIGHT

Coel could see his breath as the sun rose over the Dnieper. Below Coel's feet, the river ran dark, deep, and swift past the piers as once frozen waters raced south to the warm reaches of the Black Sea. Coel smiled. He had risen before dawn and run to the Street of Merchants for all he was worth to return from his errand and meet the barge before it embarked. He was pleased to find himself early. He had spent the last half-hour watching the sky lighten over the spires of Smolensk. The few scattered clouds had slowly turned pink and then orange and then gold. The clouds were whitening now, and the morning breeze had risen. Coel held a small parcel wrapped in used parchment in his hands. Before dawn, he had banged on the poor merchant's door with all his strength to bring shopkeeper down from his rest. It had taken the sight of silver to make the disgruntled man open his door, but it had been worth it. He slid his purchase back into his bag. Coel pulled a small round loaf of dark Russian bread from his bag and bit into it as he resumed watching the morning manifest itself. A pair of large, lanky, red-coated hounds lay near the gangplank. They raised their heads as footsteps vibrated the wooden boards.

Snorri threw down his sea bag. "A fine morning. The river is running swift and steady. We will make good time to Kiev."

Coel handed the bread to his friend. Snorri tore into the loaf happily and spoke around the wad of bread in his mouth. "We could use something besides river water to wash this down with."

Coel bent to his pack. He produced a small wine bag. "It is the last of the night's claret. It would have turned to vinegar soon, and I thought it a shame to let it sour in the cupboard."

"You are my true friend."

The two of them finished the bread and wine while the barge crew began loading goods. A fat farmer stood with his hands on his hips while two crewmen ushered his prize pig squealing down the gangplank with barge poles. The farmer followed, and behind them came a trader and two of his men bearing bales of fur. The barge captain was a small wiry man with a potbelly named Tsapko. He stood on the dock with his legs spread wide and oversaw everything with a critical eye. The barge was wide, long and low. A small leather tent stood lashed along the barge's midline, and its sides were rolled up to allow the stowage of the paying passengers' gear.

Reza, Márta and Orsini came walking down the pier. A pair of hired men accompanied them with pack mules carrying the party's considerable baggage. Reza and Orsini spoke quietly together as they walked. Márta walked a step behind Reza. Her eyes were red. As she approached, she would not meet Coel's gaze. Reza waved in greeting. "Good morning, my friends. How does the day find you?"

"Well!" Snorri handed the wineskin back to Coel. "I am eager to see Kiev again, particularly with money on my belt!"

"Yes, it has been some time since I have seen the spires of Kiev, as well." The sorcerer looked upon Coel. "And how are you this morning? Orsini has informed me of last night's incident. You are uninjured?"

"I must thank you again for my new armor. The jack saved my life last night."

"Think nothing of it. An investment in your safety is an investment in mine." Márta gazed out over the river as they spoke of the brawl at the River Inn. Reza's eye fell on her for a moment and he waved a dismissing hand at Coel. "We shall speak more of it later. Let us board."

Snorri ran a practiced eye about the deck and threw his sea bag down against a large bale of furs. He draped his wool cloak across them with a flourish and sprawled out in Roman splendor. His berth for the voyage down the Dnieper was established. Coel grinned and wished he'd been quicker.

The captain glanced about and counted heads. Reza's bearers clambered back up the gangplank counting coins. Tsapko nodded to himself. "That's it! Cast off!" He clapped his hands. "Otto! Odo!"

The two hounds rose lazily and stretched before leaping from the pier onto the barge. Crewmen cast off the mooring ropes and dipped their poles into the river. They bent their weight against the poles and the vessel's nose swung south with the current. The river ran swift and smooth and they moved downstream with deceptive speed. The spires of Smolensk swiftly receded. Coel turned away from the low rail. Reza sat on a campstool with a bench set before him. He called to Snorri. "Yaroslav, you mentioned some interest in the game of chess, as I recall?"

Snorri sat up with a smile. "So, you are prepared for your drubbing?"

Reza arched an eyebrow. Snorri's smile stayed fixed. "You are an educated man, and a sorcerer. I will not pre-surrender you any major pieces nor grant you any extra moves until I know the caliber of your play."

The Persian gazed upon the Rus with bemused outrage. "I shall endeavor to make the game interesting for you."

"Good." Snorri sat down while Reza brought out a wooden case from his baggage. He unlatched the case and unfolded it. The inside halves formed a chessboard. Snorri gazed upon it admiringly. "Cunningly wrought."

"I believe you shall enjoy this even more. Pull out the brass knob before you."

Snorri pulled the little brass knob as Reza did the same. A pair of thin drawers emerged. Snorri's brows shot up. "Coel! Come look at this!"

Coel peered over the Rus' shoulder. Each drawer was divided into sixteen tiny, felt lined compartments. Each compartment snugly cradled a chess piece. The white pieces were intricately carved ivory. The king was the Holy Roman Emperor. The queen was carved in the likeness of the Empress Ariadne of Byzantium who had reigned during the Goblin War. The black pieces were not black, but green jade carved in the likenesses of hobgoblins. They were the most beautiful chess pieces Coel had ever seen. "May I?"

Reza nodded. "Of course."

Coel picked up the green pieces and examined their detail. The king was the squat figure of Hakak, the legendary Great Hobgoblin. Hakak and his hordes had been the terror of Europe and the instrument of God's anger for the sins of man. Hakak's wide cat-like eyes glared out from under heavy brow bones. His tusks jutted up before lips curled in a cruel sneer. His left hand extended a knife-axe urging his hordes ever westward across Europe. Coel handed the king back and looked at the queen.

It was the first representation of a female hobgoblin he had ever seen.

She was broad shouldered and long-limbed, and bald except for a long comb of hair like a horse's mane that ran down the middle of her head and continued to the small of her back. Her ears were pointed, and her nose much more pronounced than the nictitating slits of the males and made her look much more human. Her chin was pointed like a witch rather than being lantern jawed like a male, and rather than upward jutting male tusks, the points of a pair of canine fangs were barely visible beneath her upper lip. She was naked to the waist and six small, human looking breasts jutted from her chest. Beneath her ribs her stomach was muscled like those of a Greek statue. The figure reclined on a couch with a whip across her knees. Her face wore the same domineering sneer as the Great Hobgoblin.

Coel glanced at Reza curiously. "Is it accurate?"

"Oh, I assure you it is. This set was carved by the dwarven mason, Bruno of Flanders."

Coel looked respectfully at the tiny piece again. Bruno of Flanders had carved the world-renowned Triumphal Arches that guarded both sides of the bridges connecting the twin cities of Buda and Pest over the river Danube. Coel handed the piece back. Snorri and the sorcerer began setting the board. Lines of ivory spearmen faced crouching goblin pawns with heavy daggers and wicker shields. The Pope and the Patriarch stood as bishops across from a pair of Hobgoblin shamen standing on mounds of human skulls. Knights carved in old Norman style sat astride their horses and couched their lances at armored Hobgoblin champions who wielded knife-axes in both hands. A pair of square towers faced Hobgoblin tents. Snorri smiled lovingly at the board and looked up at Reza. "I will grant you the first move."

Reza looked insulted. "You may have it."

Snorri grinned and twisted the board so that the ivory pieces stood before him. "If you insist."

Snorri casually took up his king's knight and jumped it out to the king's bishop three. Reza's eyebrow remained arched as he moved his king's pawn forward a space. Snorri immediately jumped his queen's knight out to the queen's bishop three. Reza sat up straighter. Coel stared. Snorri's moves were bold to the point of recklessness. Reza's hand hovered over his queen's knight's pawn. His hand closed without moving the piece. He looked up at Snorri and the Rus looked back. The two men held one another's gaze for long moments. A slow smile spread across Reza's face. Snorri's smile grew to match the wizard's own. The two men hunkered down over the tiny table.

Márta sighed under her breath and turned away. "They will be at this for days."

Coel suspected she might be right. He had seen that look on Snorri's face before. A quicksand-slow battle of wills had begun. Coel had played Snorri three times in the barracks during their service in the Frontier Cavalry. Snorri had swiftly annihilated him each time. Once the first move had been made, it was life and death to the Rus, and it seemed he had met a man of the same mind in Reza Walladid. Coel looked at Márta. She stood watching the trees pass by along the river.

"Do you play chess?" He asked.

Coel took a step back. Márta's brown eyes were capable of remarkable coldness. "No. I know the rules, but it is not a favorite of mine."

Coel cleared his throat. "May I speak to you for a moment?"

Márta's expression did not change. Coel swallowed his pride. "Please."

Márta's eyes narrowed slightly. She turned and walked to the rail without speaking. Coel followed. Her expression turned openly hostile. "What do you want?"

Coel threw caution to the wind. He squared his shoulders and loomed to his full height. "There is something I want you to know."

Márta looked up at him with impatience. "What?"

"I am a horse's ass."

Márta stared at him for a long moment. "I know that."

"Well, I just wanted you to know that I know it too, then."

Márta did not smile, but her expression softened. Coel tried to put his thoughts into words "I said many unforgivable things to you. I have a wound. A deep one, and personal. One that has never truly healed." Coel felt his chest tightening. "I was not the only one who was hurt. My family was dragged into it, we were torn apart by it, and someone who I loved was . . . " Coel felt his eyes stinging and he realized his fists were clenched. Márta watched him intently. He cleared his throat again and shook his head. His voice steadied. "What I mean to say is, my words were not meant for you. I mean, they were, but they would have been meant for anyone who asked the same question of me. You were there, and asked innocently. I know that now, and--"

"Very well. I forgive you."

Coel blinked. "You do?"

"Yes."

"I—wait!" Coel ran to his belongings. He ran back with the parcel he had bought before dawn. "I wronged you, and I apologize," He held out the gift. "This is for you."

Márta took the package hesitantly. "What is it?"

"Open it, then."

Márta looked at Coel suspiciously as she untied the twine and pulled away the scraps of parchment that wrapped it. "It is a book."

Coel nodded eagerly.

It was a small book, bound in glossy black leather. Its pages were heavy parchment with gilt edges. Coel could still smell the freshness of the binding from where he stood. Márta turned the book over, and her eyebrows shot up. On the front cover was the single word ~MÁRTA painted in gold leaf. Márta slowly opened the book and the spine cracked with newness. The inner cover bore a simple inscription in gold leaf that simply read ~FROM COEL. Márta turned a few of the pages. The entire book was blank.

Coel's ears burned as he made clumsy, explanatory gestures with his hands. "I thought you might write your thoughts down in it, like a journal, or perhaps write poetry, or . . . something."

"It is beautiful." Márta closed the book, and her fingertips softly caressed the leather cover. "Where did you get it?"

"This morning, before dawn, I went to a bookbinder and asked him to bind pages that had not been transcribed or illuminated yet. Then I asked him to put your name upon it." Coel began making apologetic gestures. "It was glued and pressed rather than sewn, and in haste, so it is not--"

"It is beautiful, and a very thoughtful gift. I shall treasure it," Márta's smile lit up her entire face. "I will go put it someplace safe."

Coel watched her disappear beneath the tent shelter. He felt positively giddy.

"That was well done."

Coel turned and found Orsini standing at his elbow. "It was the least I could do." Coel frowned. "You know of what happened between us, then?"

"Who does not? Besides, she tells me everything." The dwarf gave Coel a prosaic look. "You would best be aware that there is little she hides from the Walladid, either."

"Ah," Coel had dreaded that.

The dwarf reflected for a moment. "I will tell you something, Coel, and I believe you are gentleman enough to understand what I say and not take advantage of it. Márta has little experience of men. She was trained by a military order of nuns from the age of twelve. Since the age of eighteen, she has been the Walladid's personal bodyguard. The position of women in much of the East is restrictive, even more so than in Europe. Márta's position as an armed and unmarried woman left her status rather outside the cultural mainstream, and while she is well traveled, she has spent most of her life as an adult in the company of the Walladid and his associates. In the East, strange men who sought her out were trying to get to the Walladid. It would be no jest to say that until recently she has killed more men than she has had conversations with. Since she has come west with the Walladid, many things have been different for her. He is not known here, and she is having many new experiences. I believe her upbringing left her somewhat susceptible to the charms of a man like Sandor." The dwarf grimaced distastefully at the name. "No one likes to be used, and Márta had thought herself too professional to let something like this happen to her. However, it seems she developed an infatuation for the cad, and I believe the whole experience has hit her rather hard."

Coel looked at his feet. "My behavior could not have helped matters much."

"It most assuredly did not. However, you have been man enough to admit it, and your atonement has done you credit. Both your apology and your gift showed a great deal more empathy and taste than I generally attribute to humans."

Coel eyed the dwarf. "You overheard, then."

"Well, it was not my intention to pry. As I said, Márta would have told me of it anyway, and, while I am no long-eared elf, my sense of hearing is somewhat keener than that of most people of the taller persuasion."

Coel tucked that away in his mind. An unhappy thought rose up to replace it. "Orsini?"

"Yes?"

Coel bit his lip. "Is she really his slave, then?"

"Slavers took her at the age of six. The Walladid purchased her in Alexandria when she was eight. As I told you, she began her education and training at arms with the nuns in Cyprus when she was twelve. If you wish to know anything more of her personal history, out of propriety, I must ask that you bring your queries to her yourself. However, I may add, slavery is looked upon very differently in the East than the West. In Europe, almost all slaves are either their masters' whores if female, or chained to plows or oars like animals if they are male. In the East it is very different. Slaves are much better treated, and their status can often be much higher. In a number of circumstances, slavery is even quite honorable. Márta, you may note, wears a scimitar rather than chains. She is free to come and go as she pleases, and has been trained in the arts of war. Consider if you will the Mamluk soldiers of Egypt. They are world renowned, and currently hold your Christian Crusaders to a standstill in the Holy Land. Yet, to a man, they were first recruited as slaves. In the East, slaves have become scholars, statesmen, holy men and kings. Perhaps you have heard of such things. For example, in your own Christian Bible, Joseph was a slave, and yet Pharaoh set him over all the land of Egypt."

Coel's frown remained. "Yes. I have heard such things."

"But the fact remains she is a European woman, a pretty one, and the slave of a Persian sorcerer. This bothers you."

The dwarf read him like a book. "I would be a liar if I said it did not."

"Well, in your defense, I must say if I, myself, found a dwarven woman enslaved to a human, unthinkable as that might be, blood would be spilled."

Coel's eyes narrowed intuitively. "Dwarves do not practice slavery, do they?"

"Oh, good heavens, no," Orsini looked at Coel askance. "Not amongst ourselves, nor against any other race." The dwarf grunted to himself at a private joke. "However, since you have been so brave as to admit your own faults, I will tell you, that as a society, we do have our own peculiarities."

Coel waited for him to elaborate. The dwarf didn't. A thoughtful silence fell between them. They turned and looked to the chessboard. Snorri's eyes were unreadable. Reza had yet to make his second move. Orsini and Coel watched the two commanders face one another across the tiny battlefield. The dwarf eyed the board. "They seem well matched."

Coel nodded as Reza moved a pawn decisively. "Snorri is the best I have ever seen, but he has never played a Persian or a sorcerer, much less someone who is both." Coel shook his head. "Still, I would be hard pressed to pick the victor."

"Indeed, I would not care to wager on it." The dwarf yawned. "Well, perhaps I shall have a nap." The dwarf turned and began walking to the front of the barge where he had stowed his gear. He stopped and glanced over his shoulder. "Coel."

Coel looked up from the game. "Yes?"

"As you have already guessed, she likes poetry."

* * *

The barge halted before sunset and they moored to pilings set in a stretch of gray stony shoreline. Rocks had been cleared in a rough oval, leaving a public camp area of level sand with several blackened stone fire rings surrounded by split logs for seating. Beyond the sand the rocks resumed for a few dozen paces. Beyond them, the shore gave way to thick pine forest. The barge crew quickly began setting up tents and starting cook fires. The two hounds charged into the trees on their own business. The fat farmer sat with his pig lying in the sand next to him. Both appeared ready for their dinner. Coel glanced up at the sun as it started to set over the trees. There would be little time for archery practice. He smiled to himself as he rubbed the fingertips of his right hand against his thumb. They were still sore. A day's rest wasn't going to kill him.

Coel left his bow in its waxed canvas wrapping and drew his wool *bratt* over his shoulders. A breeze had risen. The night was going to be cold. Coel moved to the fire as the sun sank and the moon began to rise yellow and full over the trees. Reza had purchased a trio of chickens in Smolensk and given them to the care of the captain's mate, Oleg. The young man had them plucked and spitted. Fat dripped into the fire and spread the smell of roasting fowl over the encampment. The hounds returned and circled the fire ring with their tails wagging. A lidded iron skillet sat in the coals and pan bread baked. The universal Russian mush of salted herring and millet gruel began bubbling in a pot.

Reza and Orsini sat off to one side and spoke in low tones. Coel took a seat beside Márta. "Have you written anything in your book, then?"

"Oh, no," Márta laughed. "I am too embarrassed. I have opened it a dozen times, but when I look at all that blank paper my mind becomes blank as well."

Coel's own early education had been with the Celtic *Brehons,* and all of their teaching had been passed down by word of mouth for a thousand years. Coel had been required to memorize everything by rote. When he grew older, his father got him a tutor to prevent him from becoming too much like his mother. Coel remembered his teachings in letters and Latin. The first time he had sat with a pen in hand and a blank piece of parchment before him he had been terrified. "Perhaps you should just spill your inkpot all over the first page and get it over with."

Márta laughed aloud.

Snorri plopped down and gazed rapturously upon the spitted chickens. He sighed happily and turned to Coel. "Too dark for archery?"

Coel looked up into the falling night. "I suppose I could loose a few at the moon."

Márta grinned upward. "Well, that bow of yours just might make it!"

"No," Snorri glanced up pursing his lips. "It is bad luck to anger the Man in the Moon."

The sky was quickly going from purple to black. The rising yellow moon owned the sky. Coel's memories returned to his childhood in Wales. "The moon is a woman."

"You're wrong," Snorri was adamant. "There is a man inside it."

"No, she is a woman," Coel mused. "The Bride of the Sun. Every child in Wales knows that. The Romans knew. They called her Luna, and the Greeks before them named her Selene. Artemis, the huntress, hunted with her bow beneath the stars, and her shafts were made of moonbeams. Her brother, Apollo, his shafts were made of the sun."

Márta beamed at Coel.

"There is a man. In the moon." Snorri pointed his finger up into the sky and stared at Coel as if he were simple. "Do not tell me that you cannot see him."

One of the barge sailors looked up from the pot of salted herring and millet he was stirring. "I knew a Polish whore once who told me the moon was made of cheese."

Snorri regarded the man sourly.

The sailor swiftly dropped his gaze and went back to stirring the gruel. Snorri shook his head. "The moon is a man," He jerked his head. "Tell them, Márta."

Márta gazed upward thoughtfully. "The moon is a woman. My nanny told me once in a story, when I was very young." Márta nodded to herself as a long forgotten memory came to her. "It was the story of the Prince with the Terrible Temper."

Snorri scowled. Márta hesitated. Coel grinned and gave Márta his undivided attention. "Tell us, what about this Prince with the Terrible Temper, then?"

"Oh, well, once, long ago, there was a little prince who was playing foxes and hounds with his friends in the forest. He was not looking where he was running, and he knocked down an old woman who was gathering firewood. Her sheaf of kindling broke and spilled all about. The little prince stuck his tongue out at her and then laughed and ran away. But the old woman was really a witch and she cursed him. She said the magic words 'Dirom-Durom-Darom! May the first wish you say aloud become!' When the naughty prince returned home, he began teasing his sisters. They chased him and threw their pincushions at him. He got angry and shouted 'I wish you all would disappear!'" Márta waved her hands. "Poof! His wish came true. His sisters were gone. When his mother found out, she cried and cried and the little prince's heart broke. So he told his mother he would find his sisters. He had the castle blacksmith make him a pair of iron boots and forge the finest sword in the world. As he turned to leave, the little prince swore a great oath by the gate that he would never stop looking for his vanished sisters until the iron shoes wore out and the fine sword had rusted down to nothing. The prince traveled to the ends of the earth and sailed across every sea, and still he could not find his sisters. He finally traveled so far west that he came to the House of the Sun. The Sun said he had not seen the little prince's sisters, but he only worked during the day. So the Sun gave the prince a lock of his golden hair as a token, and sent the prince to the house of his sister, the Moon, who might have seen the prince's sisters by night. So the little prince went off to the House of the Moon, and she . . . "

Márta's voice trailed off as she looked at Snorri. The Rus' lower lip jutted out in defiance. Márta shrugged awkwardly. "So, you see, the moon was the sun's sister. Which makes her a woman." She bit her lip uncertainly. "Oh, and the Wind was their uncle, but, that was later."

"Fah!" Snorri stomped off towards the barge.

Márta looked at Coel incredulously. "Is he really pouting?"

"Snorri is a man of many moods."

Márta looked up at the moon again. "I have heard rumors you own a harp."

"I do, then."

"I have never heard you play it."

"I have been pouting."

Her chin dimpled. "Are you finished?"

Coel searched the sky as if considering the question. Márta laughed. Coel nodded. "Yes, I believe I am. For the moment."

"For the moment?"

"Yes. For the moment."

"Oh, well, do you think you might favor us with a song while you are in a one of your rare good moods?"

Coel grinned at her. "And what is in it for me, then?"

Márta paused. For a moment, Coel thought he might have taken his flirting too far. She suddenly smiled. "You may have Cypriot wine with your supper. I have a personal cask I bought from the Huntsman's Lodge."

"Oh, well, then!" Coel rose up off of his stool. "I shall return presently." Coel walked across the camp with a spring in his step. He left the sand of the encampment, and his feet crunched in the smooth round river stones of the beach. He could dimly make out Snorri's bulk outside the light of the fires. The Rus stood by one of the wooden mooring posts. Coel laughed as he approached his friend. "Still sulking, then?"

"No. It is a bright night, but staring into the fire ruins your eyes for it."

Snorri's tone was strange. Coel looked back the way he had come. "What are you looking for?"

"I am not sure. Perhaps nothing."

"You are making no sense," Coel scanned the encampment

again. He heard a whimpering noise behind him by the mooring post. "What's going on?"

"Look and see for yourself."

Coel squinted. He could see shapes around the Rus' boots. Snorri spoke quietly. "Otto. Odo."

The two hounds whimpered and cringed at Snorri's feet. Coel grimaced. He looked back to the camp. "What is wrong with them?"

"I don't know. As I was walking to the barge, they were whining about the feet of the captain. He kicked them and told them to stop begging for food. Then they saw me and came over whimpering and shuddering like squids."

Coel's eyes adjusted to the dark. The dogs were scraping the rocks with their bellies and shaking. "They are not begging for food."

"No, they are not."

"They are scared to death."

"Yes."

"This is the Russias. It could be wolves, or boar. Possibly a bear."

"No, were it wolves they would be slavering for a fight. Every dog in the Russias hates wolves. If it were boar, they would be off chasing it. Bear might frighten them, perhaps."

The Rus did not sound convinced. Coel saw the gleam of Snorri's axe. Snorri held it low against his side. Coel peered out past the glow of firelight and into the dark of the forest beyond. He sniffed the air. In Wales, hunting placed a close second to raiding in every warrior's heart. Coel had hunted stags in the mountains of Snowdon and bear and boar in the lowland moors of the valley of Dee. He knew dogs well, and the Russian hounds' behavior made his fingers itch. "If it were men, bandits or the like, they would be barking."

"I agree. But these mutts are writhing about my legs like snakes and wetting themselves with their own fear." Snorri kept his eyes on the trees as he spoke. "These are the barge master's dogs. I think they have been up and down the Dnieper many times. I think it would take something very unusual to unman them like this."

"I am going to go aboard and string my bow."

"That is a good idea." Snorri ran his gaze across the tree line. "Throw me a spear and I will go speak of this with Walladid."

Coel quietly walked into the river. His belly already felt cold, and the frigid water around his ankles did nothing to help matters. He grabbed the edge of the barge and vaulted aboard. He quickly walked to Snorri's space. He took up the Rus's heavy fighting spear and one of the lighter throwing ones and went back to the rail. He tossed first one and then the other towards the shore. Snorri caught a spear in each hand and walked back towards camp. Coel ran to his own berth and quickly strung his bow. He looked at his arrows and chose a sheaf of the barbed and wickedly sharp broadheads. He laid an arrow across his bow and quietly slid over the side.

Coel froze in the shallows.

There were eyes in the trees.

He blinked and they were gone. Coel almost did not trust his eyes, but he knew he had seen them. They'd been the glowing red lenses of an animal's eyes reflecting firelight. Coel gazed hard at the trees and estimated with an archer's eye. The eyes had been high off the ground, at least as high as the height of a bear. Coel stood with the cold water swirling around his shins. Very softly he ground his heels into the stones of the riverbed until he felt he was standing firm. He raised the bow. Snorri was just walking over to where Reza and Orsini sat. The sorcerer and the dwarf looked up as the Rus approached with a spear in either hand. Coel looked beyond them. He knew if he stayed in the frigid water much longer his limbs would start shaking and--

There.

The red eyes hovered a moment in the blackness between the trees. Coel drew the great bow and took half a heartbeat to aim a foot below the glowing eyes. He let out half his breath and let fly.

Márta snapped around as the arrow whistled over her head. Coel's voice boomed. "Ware! In the trees!"

A great roar of rage tore forth from within the forest. The roar rose to a howl and from a howl to a vibrating shriek. The sound shook Coel to his bones, but he nocked another arrow and drew as his target erupted out of the trees.

A thing bounded towards the fire rings.

Coel had been right about its size. It was as tall as a bear, but its proportions were horribly wrong. It bounded forward on four legs like a coursing hound, and it moved with grace and speed beyond any bear's. White fangs slathered, and its shriek continued to echo over the forest. Coel let fly again and his arrow sank into the thing's shoulder. The white flight feathers of his first arrow stuck out of its neck. Snorri hurled his casting spear with a shout to his Grandfather's gods. The long diamond-shaped spearhead took the creature full in the chest. The thing came on.

Coel splashed ashore and cast down his bow. His hand went to his sword. Márta leapt up with her scimitar hissing from its sheath. Snorri charged forward with his fighting spear held in both hands. One of the sailors stood frozen in terror before the cook fire. The thing leaped upon him. Long white claws flashed. The man's scream cut short as he came apart like a ruptured doll beneath the thing's talons. The cook fire hissed and steamed as blood sprayed into it. The man's body followed it a moment later in a geyser of sparks.

Snorri roared in defiance.

The creature fixed its red eyes on the charging Rus and leaped. Snorri skidded in the sand and leaned back as he jammed the butt of his spear against his heel. The heavy, eight-foot shaft bent against the creature's weight as the iron spearhead sank in bloodlessly. The thing pushed forward as if against a heavy wind. It crawled up the spear shaft, impaling itself to get at the Rus. Márta lunged forward with her scimitar raised. The curved blade flashed down and slashed the thing's flank.

Blood spurted, and the thing's howling turned to a snarl of real pain. Its head whipped about and Márta ducked her head under rending talons. Her blade licked up and slashed the creature's forelimb to the bone. More blood spurted. Snorri's spear shaft bent back upon itself and snapped. The thing surged forward. Snorri screamed in rage and terror as he stumbled backward and fell. The thing raised its talons to rend the Rus even as Márta slashed it again. The creature suddenly staggered to one side as it was deflected from its prey. Another howl of pain escaped its maw before it could savage Snorri with its claws.

Orsini stood with a spear in his hand, and the head was imbedded high in the thing's ribs. The thing tried to run up the spear shaft as it had done with Snorri, but the dwarf's spearhead had winged lugs at its socket that held the creature at bay. Orsini's shaft did not bow or break. The dwarf's face set in a grimace of effort as he braced himself. The creature drove forward, slavering and howling. Orsini's heels dug furrows in the sand as he was slowly pushed backward. The dwarf's voice thundered across the beach.

"Reza! Do something!"

Reza Walladid thrust his palms out at the creature with a great shout. Whatever word he shouted was in no tongue Coel had ever heard and the very sound of it almost halted him in his tracks. The thing paused for the briefest of moments. It looked at the sorcerer and its black lips skinned back hideously. It returned to attacking Orsini. Márta slashed it again and danced back to avoid its backhanded swipe.

The sorcerer hissed in frustration. "*Bismallah!*"

Coel reached the fire rings. His eyes flared as Reza bent forward and thrust his hand into the campfire. The wizard brought forth a burning log and shouted. "Get back!"

Márta leaped away. Snorri rolled. Orsini turned his head. "Do it!" Another word of power hissed through Reza's clenched teeth and the burning log flared in his hand. The sorcerer suddenly held a six-foot spear of flame. The bolt of fire trailed sparks like a comet as Reza hurled it at the beast.

The thing screamed as fire engulfed its head.

Coel leaped over Snorri and lunged beneath the creature's screaming halo of fire. He thrust at the abomination's chest. The Academy blade punched through flesh and sank into sternum. Blood sprayed. The creature screamed in agony. It flung out a forelimb and smashed Coel off his feet. He landed heavily in the sand but retained his sword as he rolled and came up once more.

The thing's head emerged as the fire around it faded. Its fur had burned away to the shoulders, and blistered red flesh bubbled around its snout and jaws. Coel's arrows flared like torches where they stood up out of the thing's neck. Coel fell in shoulder to shoulder with Márta. Orsini wrenched his spear free and held it poised for a second thrust. Snorri's *sax* knife was in his hand as he jumped up. The thing whipped its smoldering head from side to side at its opponents. It let out a terrible scream and bounded away for the forest.

The pig farmer screamed in answer.

He had fled towards the forest's edge with his pig when the creature attacked, and now he stood between the beast and the trees. The farmer froze in fear. Coel shouted his challenge as he charged. "Here! Here!" The beast ignored him and fell upon the pig farmer. Claws scythed through the fat man's middle and he made a horrible noise as he fell spooling out his insides. His pig squealed and ran for the forest. The thing was upon the pig in two leaps. Its drooling jaws crunched down into the prize pig's spine and lifted it up off of the ground. The beast bounded on as if it were unencumbered by the two-hundred-pound pig. Orsini cast his spear and the lugged head sank deep into a tree trunk in the creature's wake. The thing disappeared into the darkness beneath the trees.

Coel ran to the pig farmer but he was beyond helping. The man's innards lay scattered across the stones and his eyes glazed over sightlessly in the moonlight. Coel stood over the dead man. He shook as he stared into the forest.

Snorri's feet crunched in the stones behind him. "Are you wounded?"

Coel's hand went to his chest. His gray travel tunic was torn open, and the red upper layer of his brigandine was rent in four long furrows. Several of the small iron plates dangled by threads. Coel took a deep breath. His ribs ached with the effort. His armor had saved his flesh, but he knew that in the morning he would feel like an ox had stepped him on. "How is the sailor?"

"Somewhat worse off than the pig farmer."

More feet crunched in the stones. Orsini pulled his spear from the tree. The shaft was seven feet long, thick as a barge pole and spiral bound with iron. The spearhead itself was a massive leaf of blue steel with a lugged cross guard at its bottom. Blood smeared the razor-honed edge. Coel looked at his own blade. There was blood on it as well. He turned to Snorri. "Help me."

The two of them put the pig farmer back together as best they could and laid him down in the sand. Reza sat cradling his right arm. His hand was badly burned. Márta poured some kind of clear oil on it from a tiny clay jar. The barge captain and his young mate Oleg pulled their fellow bargeman out of the fire and laid his smoldering body by the pig farmer. The young man wept. The air over the camp stank of charred flesh.

Coel glared at Reza. "And what would you call that, then?"

Reza looked up from his blistered hand. "A beast."

"It stank of sorcery."

"You are observant."

"You are the sorcerer, Walladid. Should you not you have sensed it?"

"Yes," Reza nodded more to himself than Coel as Márta bandaged his hand. "I should indeed have been aware of its presence."

Snorri pointed to the trees. "I put two spears into the thing's chest! Not one of them drew blood! What kind of a beast can take wounds like that and leap about like a hare?"

"Come now, Yaroslav," Reza chided. "You were born in the Russias, and there is Viking blood in your veins. Are you really going to tell me you do not know?"

"*Ulfhednar*," Snorri spat in the sand. "Wolf-shirt."

"A werewolf?" Coel looked at Reza long and hard. "I have never seen one, but that thing was bigger than a bear."

"Oh, I believe you are right. I got quite a good look at it. I do not believe it was some unfortunate man whose veins boil with the blood of the wolf with each cycle of the moon. I suspect there was nothing human in the beast at all."

"So what was it, then?"

"A demonic spirit of some kind. Someone summoned it, and then bound the captured spirit by moonlight in the flesh of the beasts of the forest. There was bear and wolf in it, perhaps boar, as well, all twisted into shape by a malevolence that hungers for blood." Reza shook his head absently. "Cold steel will do it no harm."

Snorri turned to Orsini. "Your spear tickled it."

"Silver." Orsini held the great boar spear's blade near the fire. Blood clumped the red silk fringe of the blood-guard. The spearhead was blue Dwarven steel, but intricate silver inlay glinted along its length in the firelight. "Silver for the shape shifters. The blade, itself, did it no real harm, but it did not care for having silver within its body."

Reza nodded. "Indeed. Great energy is required for the shifting of one flesh into the shape of another. That energy must bind the flesh into its new form and hold it. The energy permeates the flesh to its lowest foundations. It is this same energy binding the flesh into its new form that prevents most forms of mortal damage. The properties of silver, however, disrupt this transaction between flesh and energy. Where an iron weapon would enter without harm or bounce off, a weapon of silver will disrupt the binding energy in the flesh it encounters and then wound according to its nature."

Coel kept his eyes on the forest edge. "So when the sun rises? This thing will die, then? Or fall apart?"

"That is doubtful. A wolf-shirt, as Yaroslav names it, is a man upon whom the interaction of the moon's emanations and the disease of lycanthropy bring about his transformation. With the fall of the moon and the coming of dawn, the creature becomes man again. I do not believe the creature we encountered tonight is such an unfortunate victim of fate. I believe it is a weapon, purpose built, of summoned spirit and the sacrificed flesh of the forest. The moon's emanations increase its powers, as they do for all shape shifters, but the energy that binds this beast to new form is the demonic spirit within. I suspect the creature will continue to exist by both night and day, and with or without the moon. I strongly suspect we have not encountered it by accident."

Coel suspected as much. "It was sent."

"Indeed."

"By whom?"

"And who for?" Snorri asked.

"Both pertinent questions," The sorcerer acknowledged.

"I have a more immediate question," Snorri picked up his shattered spear haft and tapped it against his palm. "Will it come again?"

"Without a doubt," Reza stood up from his stool. "Destruction is its purpose. The beast will not stop hunting until it has killed its designated prey or it has been destroyed."

Snorri's expression was unreadable.

Coel looked at the rent bodies and the spreading stains in the sand surrounding them. "Then I say we hunt it down and kill it first."

Reza nodded. "An excellent strategy."

"Have you any suggestions, then?"

"Kill the creature's flesh, and the demonic spirit will leave it, or possibly even perish with it. Drive the spirit forth from the flesh, and there shall be nothing to hold it together."

Snorri tossed his splintered spear shaft into the fire. "I do not much like the idea of hunting that thing in the dark."

"That would be folly," Reza agreed.

Coel looked out into the trees again. He knew he would not sleep while that thing was out in the dark, but he did not relish the idea of hunting it by night any more than Snorri. "So it will be weaker during the day, then?"

"For tomorrow, perhaps. It will eat the pig to regain its strength and then wait for the rays of tomorrow's moon to bathe its injuries and rebind its disrupted flesh. Then it will hunt us again."

Tsapko spoke for the first time. "I've lost a paying customer, and one of my best men is dead. Why don't we just untie and get out of here?"

Reza shrugged. "It will follow."

Coel shook his head at Tsapko. "That thing will catch up with your barge, even if you run at night." He held the captain's gaze. "I say it is better to be the hunter than the hunted. I say we kill it. Before it kills us."

Tsapko's anger masked his fear. "Well, I say maybe it is not hunting me or my crew at all! I say maybe the evil thing is just hunting you, and this is none of my business!"

The unspoken threat lay between the two of them. Coel nodded thoughtfully. "There may well be truth in that." Coel whipped the point of his sword beneath the barge captain's chin. Tsapko goggled and went up on his toes. His crew shouted in alarm. Tsapko stepped backward, but Coel's blade stayed pressed against the flesh of his throat. The barge captain retreated two more steps and found himself against the fire ring. The blade stayed under his chin implacably. Coel's voice was cold fury. "But by God, if you even think of stranding us here? I will bleed you and hang you by your heels for bait."

"Sweet *Khristos*!" Tsapko arms flapped to keep from falling in the fire. He was nearly bent backward by Coel's blade. "I wouldn't! I swear it!"

"Good," Coel whipped the bloody blade away. "We hunt at dawn." He caught Reza's gaze and held it. "I am just going to assume that you are going to do something more effective than throw firewood tomorrow."

Coel was surprised to see Reza smile grimly. The sorcerer seemed to be reappraising him. "I admit my first spell failed. It was the kind of spell any sorcerer would use in such a situation, and the beast was warded against it. The fire trick was a spur of the moment affair, peasant magic really, and poorly done at that." Reza held up his burned hand. "But it was the quickest thing I could muster. However, I have something more elaborate in mind for the beast tomorrow. I believe you will be impressed."

Coel turned to Snorri and handed him the Academy blade. "Get a rag. Wipe down every weapon that drew blood. Let the dogs sniff it. Let them lick it. Let them fight over it if they want. Maybe if they taste the thing's blood, they might grow some guts and be of some use tomorrow."

Snorri nodded. "Done."

Reza waved a hand at Márta. "Assist Yaroslav."

Márta took Orsini's spear without a word and followed

Snorri towards the river.

Coel turned to Orsini. "Have you any ideas?"

"I do. I will need ten of your arrows and ten of Márta's, as well." He turned to Tsapko. "I assume you have an anvil on the barge?"

"Of course." The captain rubbed his scorched calves. "I have anvil, and a hammer."

Reza looked at the captain. "I shall require a file as well." The wizard turned to Coel. "Between us, Orsini and I will require all the silver available, including the current pay I have given you and Yaroslav. It will be refunded to you in Kiev. I have assets there."

"Take it." Coel glanced at the camp. "We spend the night on the barge." Coel locked eyes with the captain. "Tsapko and I will take the first watch."

CHAPTER NINE

Coel watched the dawn rise over the Dnieper. The day would be clear and cold. Thin snow clung to winter beneath the shelter of the trees and would give them the beast's tracks. The wind blew softly in Coel's face from the forest. Good for the dogs and bad for the beast. The conditions were almost ideal for hunting. That assumed there were any ideal conditions for men to hunt demons. Coel's hand went to his chest. His ribs ached as he stroked the armored jack. Márta had re-sown the separated plates for him during her watch. Coel had surprised himself. After the first watch, he had fallen asleep immediately and slept like the dead despite Orsini's hammering and Reza's filing. Coel sat on the edge of the barge facing the forest. Beneath the jack, he wore his chain mail shirt. The hardened leather greaves and vambraces girded his legs and arms. He wore his steel cap under his hat and he had it strapped securely under his chin. His sword rested unsheathed across his knees. Where iron arrows and steel spears had failed in the night, the Academy blade had drawn the beast's blood. Coel considered that. His eyes never left the edge of the forest.

Footsteps clinked behind him. Snorri clambered up past Coel onto the bulwark of the barge. The Rus wore his full armor. He took a straddle stance and reached under his mail to unlace his trousers. Snorri stood silhouetted against the dawn with his armor gleaming like a golden halo around him as he relieved himself into the Dnieper. The Rus let out a deep sigh of contentment. He grinned back over his shoulder at Coel from under his mail hood and helmet.

"Well, good morning your Excellency!"

"I will settle for Grand Marshal of the Host if you are handing out titles."

Snorri shook himself and tied his trousers. He stepped off the bulwark and landed lightly on the deck. The Rus leaned out and washed his hands in the river. "Well, last night you were barking orders like you were Pharaoh, himself."

Coel looked at his friend seriously. "You object, then?"

"Oh, no. *Hel* no," Snorri's grin turned sheepish as he waved his hands dry. "I'm glad somebody did. Just between you, me and the river? The only thing I managed last night was to make water on myself."

"You looked brave enough to me, Snorri. Hell, you charged the god damned thing."

"Yes, I did, and I'll tell you something. I made as good a cast as I ever have. I put a spear right where that thing's heart should have been, and it did not bat an eye. Then I shoved another spear in right next to the first, and it came crawling down the shaft after me. When the spear shattered?" Snorri's shoulders twitched. He looked Coel in the eye. "I was under its claws, Coel. I thought I was dead. I screamed like a woman."

"We were all screaming," A sudden smile split Coel's face. "Except for Márta, speaking of women."

"Yes," Snorri nodded thoughtfully.

"Speaking of taking command . . . "

Snorri perked an eyebrow. "Oh?"

"I do not think I took it so much as Reza let me have it."

Snorri gazed out upon the forest in thought. "I have the same feeling. I think he wanted to see what you and I might do having faced a thing like that. I think he liked your style."

"How did you do with the dogs?"

"Well, now! Snorri perked up. "Márta and I wiped down the weapons like you said."

"And?"

"Behold!" The two hounds lay curled up by the tiller. Snorri hissed softly. "Otto! Odo!" The hounds lifted their snouts and yawned wide as they looked up at him. The Rus reached under his cloak and took out a small ring of rope he had tied in the night. Rusty red smears stained it. He waved it at the dogs and they came forward wagging their tails and sniffing. As they smelled the rope their tails dropped, and they began growling low in their throats. Snorri tossed the loop, and the hounds snapped at it. Within seconds, they were snarling and scrabbling around the deck in a furious tug of war. "That was an excellent idea, Coel."

Coel watched the dogs. "My father had a dog once, as fine a hound as you could want, save that the damn dog would wet itself at the smell of a bear. Father used the same trick on it, and that hound became the terror of the mountain."

The snarling of the dogs brought the rest of barge awake. Sailors looked up from their bedrolls. Reza came out of the tent shelter. He glanced at the growling hounds and nodded at Coel. "I see you have performed some magic of your own."

"They are brave enough here on the barge. We will see how they do on the hunt, then."

Reza held up a sheaf of arrows. "These are for you. Orsini fashioned them in the night."

Coel took the arrows. The dwarf had taken ten of his shafts and replaced the arrowheads with points of his own devising. They were four sided and diamond shaped. The edges were wickedly sharp. "Pure silver?"

"Indeed."

"Awfully soft, then."

"Yes, but they need only strike once, and the force of your bow should drive them deep, even if the heads deform upon impact."

Coel considered this.

Snorri pointed. "Well, look at that!"

Coel watched as Márta emerged from the tent shelter. The woman was sheathed from head to toe in glittering chain mail. A large bronze disk with a shining sun etched in it was set into the chest of her armor. She wore a scarlet vest of quilted silk over her mail that reached just above her knees. Her yatagan was thrust through a matching silk sash. A round shield of cane bound with silk rode over her shoulder by its strap. Under her arm, she carried a silvery, spiked helmet turbaned with gold. Márta smiled out from her gleaming mail hood. She had kholed her eyes for the occasion and the effect was striking. "Good morning!"

Coel smiled back. "You seem in good spirits."

Márta's chin dimpled. "I have never been hunting before!"

Snorri looked past her. "Would you look at that!"

Orsini came around the tent. The dwarf was fully sheathed in blue steel plate. Coel had seen Paladins in full horse armor wearing less steel. The dwarf wore the full panoply of a man-at-arms. Coel noted the plate armor made almost no noise as the dwarf stepped forward. Orsini waved his steel-gauntleted hand with a flourish. He wore the heavy infantry armor with the careless ease that another man might wear a linen nightshirt. The dwarf held a massive, two-handed war hammer. The back-spike was the same dark blue steel of his spear and short sword. Its single, square peen gleamed like a massive silver molar. Orsini caught Coel's stare. "I hammered a few silver pieces around the striking head. I'm thinking of giving the beast a few licks on the skull and seeing what happens." He nodded at Snorri. "Why don't you take my spear? You need something that will make an impression upon the creature, and I fear your axe, fearsome as it is, may prove inadequate."

Snorri was visibly relieved. It was obvious he had spent much of the night pondering just what, if anything, he might do next time the beast came for him. The Rus went to the tent to fetch Orsini's silver inlayed spear. Coel looked at the curved blade hanging at Márta's side. "Reza, I understand what you said about silver last night, but how did Márta's blade wound the beast?"

"Because Márta's blade was forged by magic."

Coel looked warily at the weapon on the swordswoman's hip.

Reza smiled. "I had that blade fashioned in Damascus by the Sultan's master smith, and it was I who called forth fires hotter than any forge and enchanted the blade with every strike of the hammer. The watered steel blade was folded a thousand times during its forging. Incantations were embedded deep within every fold. The blade never needs sharpening, for it refolds itself to its razor sharpness with every blow, indeed, its edge refolds itself even during a blow. Rust will never eat it. Márta's blood and mine were used in its tempering. It was forged so only Márta could wield it, and forged to defend me from my enemies, and the kinds of resources they can call upon," Reza shrugged. "As you have seen."

Márta slapped the ivory hilt proudly. "There is none finer!"

Coel looked at his own hilt. "My blade is not magic, but it drew blood." He drew the Academy blade and the sweet shiver went up his arm. Everyone on the barge stared as he held it up to the dawn. It drank in the golden light and seemed to glow from within. "I will tell you, most of the legends about these blades are lies. They hold an edge unlike any other sword, but they do need sharpening now and again, and it is a lie to say they do not rust. They simply do not rust easily. They are the finest swords in the world, but they are still steel."

Orsini raised an armored finger. "Now, that is true in the strictest sense. They are steel, but of an alloy known nowhere else in the word. A Paladin Sword is forged from fallen stars by the smiths of the Great Arsenal of Grande Triumphe in Paris and blessed by its Bishop. It is an alloy of unparalleled purity. The balance and symmetry of a Paladin blade is a kind of magic in itself. Anyone who has held such a blade knows they hold something very special. Twice, for but a moment, I have had the honor of holding a Paladin blade, and I will tell you, even the finest smiths in the dwarven halls envy their forging. Short of their souls, there is little any smith in the world would not give to know the secrets of their making."

Coel ran his eye down the perfection of the blade. Over the years it had become a part of him. In battle it was an extension of his will. "Yes, but it is still steel."

"No, it is more," Reza ran his eye over the upraised blade. "The blade, the guard, the pommel, the hilt and the wire wrapping it are all of exactly the same alloy, all made from a single forging. There is no adornment. No engraving. No leather wraps the grip or precious metal blemishes its hilt. Everything that makes up that blade is made at the same time, of exactly the same material. No two are exactly alike, and yet, all share the one same attribute. What a Paladin blade is, more than anything, is an expression of purity."

"I do not follow you."

"Come now, Coel, you were a candidate. What is it that a Paladin strives for more than anything else?"

It was everything he lacked. "Purity."

"Yes, purity, and what happens to a Paladin, who has purified his mind, body and spirit on his Day of Commencement?"

Bitterness came to Coel. It was something he had spent his youth striving for, and failed. "The Mantle of Power descends upon him. He becomes an instrument of God's will. He can perform miracles, and a Paladin Blade in his hands becomes a thing of power."

"So, if a Paladin blade is not of itself magical in nature, what does that make it?"

Inspiration struck. "A lens."

"Yes," Reza regarded Coel with approval. "Very good, Coel. A lens for the Mantle of Power. A holy weapon in the hands of a holy warrior."

"But, it was I, I mean, me," Coel stuttered as he suddenly felt embarrassed and stupid. "Who wounded the werebeast with the blade."

"Yes."

Snorri cocked his head. "Does this mean Coel is a Paladin?"

"No." Reza shook his in bemusement at the idea. "Coel is not. However, the beast we fought was not a pure creature. Sorcery holds it together. In similar fashion, demons must transform themselves when they enter our plane of existence. This is why they are often described as monsters and grotesques. The sorcery involved in such kinds of change often make such creatures invulnerable to normal weapons, but the purity of a sword like Coel's can unbind such energies, and cleave them. Like a shining diamond that can scratch anything, even glass."

Orsini gazed respectfully at the blade. "You were given a gift beyond price, Coel."

"Aye," Coel was mesmerized by the sorcerer's words, and he wondered for the thousandth time what might have motivated the Swordmaster of Grande Triumphe to do such a thing.

Orsini spoke low. "Let us attend to the present, task. I believe we have some dissension in the ranks."

Tsapko and his five remaining crewmen had risen. They stood off to one side with the fur trader and his two henchmen. They all leaned on spears. Coel measured their mood. They were armed, but not to go hunting.

Coel lowered his sword but did not sheath it. "Well?"

"Listen, you!" Tsapko snarled. "I've taken your coin, and I'll take you to Kiev. That's our contract, and I'll honor it. But I'm not going into the trees after that thing out there. Nor are any of my men. We will stay here and wait for you. My man, Dobrynya, and the pig farmer need burying."

The young mate turned on Tsapko imploringly. "But Uncle!"

"Shut up, Oleg! Your mother would kill me if I let you go out there," Tsapko shook his head again at Coel. "You want to go out there and get yourself slaughtered? That's fine by me. Kill it? I'll be the first to buy you your beer in Kiev. But we're not going out there. We stay tied up here until noon. If you aren't back by then I'm sailing, and that's final."

The sailors and furriers nodded and glared their approval. Coel's weighed his options. A brawl with the captain and his crew would solve nothing, and he could spare none of the party to stay and watch them. Coel glanced at Reza. The sorcerer was watching him. Coel knew he was being tested again. He turned to the young sailor who had spoken up. He was large, but he could not have seen more than seventeen summers. "Oleg, is it?"

"Yes, sir!"

"Are you coming, then?"

"Yes!" The young man brandished his spear fiercely. "I will!"

"He will not!" Tsapko shouted.

Coel took a menacing step forward. "I was not talking to you."

The captain took a step back, but two of his sailors stepped forward to stand at his side. No one pointed his spear yet, but their knuckles were turning white upon the hafts. Tsapko grew some backbone. "I'm Oleg's captain, and I'm his uncle. He stays here. That's final."

Oleg stepped from the line and faced Tsapko. "You are my step-uncle, yes, but I am of age! Dobrynya was my friend! I am to marry his sister, and his body lies burned in the sand!" Oleg's voice shook with passion. "You are my captain, but I will not go to my wedding a coward in my bride's eyes! I have the right of revenge! Do you deny it?"

Tsapko spluttered and swore.

Oleg's deadly seriousness belied his youth. "I am going, uncle. I will bring you back the demon's head, and you can sell it in Kiev for a profit." He walked across the deck and faced Coel determinedly. "What would you have me do?"

Coel thought. Other than acting as insurance against Tsapko stranding them, he did not think there was much the lad could do save get himself killed.

Orsini scratched his beard. "Walladid, have you any of your silver filings left over?"

Reza looked at him curiously. "Perhaps a handful, why?"

"It may serve." He turned back to Oleg. "Listen, lad. Take the Walladid's silver, and get some grease. Take your spear, and two more, and grease their heads. Then sprinkle the silver upon them as thickly as possible, so it sticks. Take Snorri's shield. He will need both hands to manage my spear. When we flush the beast forth, you stay back as we attack it. Pick your throws when you see an opening. Understand?"

Oleg nodded firmly at the dwarf and looked back at Coel. "I understand."

"All right, then," Coel looked up into the dawn. "Everyone gather whatever else you need. We leave as soon as the sun clears the trees."

* * *

Coel moved through the woods with his bow in his hand and a silver-headed arrow nocked. The warmth of the sun did not find its way beneath the pines but Coel was already sweating in his armor. He glanced at the ground before him. The beast's trail was not hard to follow. Its great claws left deep prints in the earth and snow. The stolen pig had bled everywhere leaving dark stains. Coel looked to either side.

Márta moved to his left with her bow in her hand and a silver-headed arrow laid across it. She had pinned the mail aventail of her helmet up between her eyes like a veil of steel. Orsini moved to Coel's right. The dwarf had donned a close-fitting blue-steel helmet. His visor was up and he held an immense crossbow. Its bow was of steel. Coel couldn't begin to imagine what its draw weight must be. He had nearly spilled his morning broth on himself when the dwarf had spanned and cocked the crossbow by hand. A silver-headed bolt sat in the guide. Snorri, Reza, and Oleg marched shoulder-to-shoulder a dozen paces behind the main skirmish line. Snorri held the dwarf's lugged spear in one hand and short ropes leashing the dogs in the other. Oleg carried Snorri's shield and his three silver powdered spears glittered like faerie dust in the rays of light filtering through the tree boughs. Reza strode between them holding a bulging leather sack. The sorcerer had a long, thin package tucked under his arm.

The hounds gave choked whines and growls as they strained against their leashes. Coel looked ahead through the trees. The land was flat, but the trees were growing thicker and closer together. They crossed a shallow stream that still had sheets of ice clinging to its banks. Coel froze as he sighted a small clearing ahead overgrown with shrubs. Coel moved closer and held up his fist as he knelt beside a tree.

The rest of the party halted behind him.

Coel peered intently. The clearing ahead was not natural. It was a hundred paces across and formed a circle. There was a mound in the middle of it. The mound was tall as a man and covered with grass. Shrubs had taken over the clearing long ago and choked out any new tree growth. Two thick posts rotted with age and sheathed with moss stood like guardians before the mound. Coel could not tell what kind of carving was on them. He stared harder. The shrubbery was very thick in front of the mound. Much of it had been torn up and piled there only recently. Coel motioned Snorri forward. Snorri came and crouched down beside him. Coel spoke in a hushed tone. "What do you make of that, then?"

"Looks to me like someone important was buried here. The pagan Slavs in these parts used to bury their chieftains and heroes in hollow mounds, just like the Swedes of old."

"I think someone is keeping house in that mound, and it is not some old Slav's bundle of bones."

"Well," Snorri regarded the mound warily. "I think you're right."

Coel motioned the rest of the party forward. "The trail leads right up to that mound, and something has pulled a lot of brush up in front of it. I think the beast has ripped open the grave and taken it for a lair."

Márta drew her scimitar and pointed it at the mound. "The beast lays within," Snorri elbowed Coel. Coel was already staring. He had seen Damascus steel before. Smiths in the East folded the steel while it was forged, producing wavy patterns like water through the finished blade. The intricate patterns in the steel of Márta's scimitar dully shimmered and crawled with a life of their own as she pointed. "The blade remembers it."

Reza took up his sack of silver filings. "Very well. Keep an eye on the entrance. Loose your arrows at anything that comes out." He nodded at Márta. "Come with me."

Reza began pacing the periphery of the clearing. He poured a tiny stream of silver dust as he walked. Márta followed closely. Coel kept his eye and his arrow pointed at the mound. Orsini knelt beside him. They watched Reza slowly walk around the clearing. The sorcerer's lips moved silently as he drew his circle of silver. Coel whispered. "What is he doing, then?"

Orsini rumbled low in his throat. "I believe the Walladid is locking the beast within the clearing."

"Then what?"

Orsini regarded Coel dryly. "Then we slay it."

Time moved with unbearable slowness. Eventually, Reza came back to his starting point. He was sweating slightly. He unwrapped his package and withdrew a pair of long wooden tubes. He fitted them together and then poured the remaining silver dust down into the open end. Coel looked at Reza. "Now what?"

"Now we drive it forth. Oleg, come."

Oleg knelt and looked at the mound. "What do you want me to do?"

"I wish you to take this tube and go to the mound. Unplug the end. Stick the tube through the brush and into the entrance. Blow into it as hard as you can."

Oleg's eyes widened as he considered the implications. "And then?"

"Then, I would recommend you get out of the way as fast as you can."

Oleg looked at the wizard for a long moment. "All right."

"Very good," Reza addressed the rest of the party. "Step within the circle of silver. Make yourselves ready. The enchantment will not last long. If we do not kill the beast quickly, it will escape to grow stronger and hunt us on its own terms."

Coel stepped within the circle. He drew three more arrows and thrust them into the earth before him. Márta held her own bow at the ready. Orsini knelt with his crossbow cocked. Snorri stood with the great dwarven spear in his hand and held the straining hounds.

Oleg approached the mound. The young man flinched at the sound of every leaf and twig beneath his shoes but he did not stop or hesitate.

"Brave lad," Snorri muttered.

"Aye," Coel raised his bow.

Oleg moved to one side of the mound and gingerly set down his shield and glittering spears. The young Rus held the tube in both hands and glanced back. His face was pale but he looked resolute. Reza nodded at him. Oleg stooped and thrust the tube through the shrubs piled before the mound. Reza began murmuring under his breath and raised his hands before him. Oleg took a great breath and blew.

A bellow of rage thundered from within the mound.

Oleg flung himself aside.

Reza shouted something and clapped his hands.

Blinding silver light erupted from the mound. The piled shrubbery burst apart as the beast bounded out of the mound screaming. Coel drew his bow. The thing was horrible in the sunlight. Its great head was a hideous burned mask of wolf and boar and bear with dripping fangs and tusks. It had the shoulders and arms of a bear, and the bristled ridge of a boar ran down its spine to giant wolves' haunches. Márta's bow thrummed. Coel released his own shaft. The thing jerked and howled as the silver arrows hit it. Márta loosed again, and Coel sent a second shaft deep into the creature's chest. Orsini's crossbow snapped, and the creature slewed in mid-bound as the heavy bolt slammed into its shoulder. The monstrosity veered and headed for the trees. Reza clapped his hands again and the clearing lit up as a circle of roaring silver fire shot up ten feet tall around its perimeter. The creature howled and dug furrows in the dirt and snow as it reared up short before the wall of shimmering flame.

"Now!" Reza ordered.

Orsini dropped his crossbow and slapped down his visor. Márta let go her bow and drew her blade. Coel loosed a third arrow. The shaft sank into the creature's side. His bow fell to the snow as the war sword sang from its sheath.

Snorri released the hounds and charged forward calling on Odin. He wanted revenge for having been unmanned the night before. Otto and Odo coursed ahead barking and snarling. Coel leaped after them with his sword in both hands.

Oleg struck the first blow. The beast's back was to him, and he hurled a glittering spear at its spine. The creature reared back on its hind legs and howled as the spearhead smeared with silver paste plunged deep into its body. The hounds leaped upon it. Snorri drove in and rammed the dwarf's spear into the monster's chest. Metal tore as the creature's claws ripped scales from the Rus' armor and Snorri was thrown aside by the blow. Coel leaped in and drove his sword in low and deep into the creature's vitals. The thing shrieked in agony. One of the hounds hung from the creature's arm by the teeth. The beast lifted the dog high and snapped its jaws forward. The hound came apart as the thing whipped its head from side to side and savaged it like a dog with a shoe. Half a hound struck Coel in the face. Coel sat down heavily in the snow with his eyes full of blood.

Márta leaped in. Her scimitar swept up underneath the creature's armpit. Blood sprayed, and the limb fell useless to the creature's side. Coel vaulted back to his feet. Márta's second cut slashed the thing's chin and narrowly missed its throat. The creature dropped to its haunches and lunged forward.

Coel cried out. "Márta!"

The creature lashed out. Márta yelped.

Her legs bent brutally as she was scythed off her feet.

Coel's stomach tightened as she fell. "Márta!"

Oleg's second spear sank into the thing's leg. The surviving hound held tenaciously to the other. The creature reared up and sent its howl into the sky. Coel lunged. The war sword tore into the creature's bowels again. The thing bent over in agony and Orsini charged in with his hammer on high. The silver coated hammerhead crunched into the creature's skull. It reared up screaming. Claws shrieked on metal and Orsini's visor ripped off of its hinges. The dwarf took the blow and swung the great hammer again. Fangs shattered as the massive hammer peen took the creature in the teeth.

Coel swung his sword into the thing's neck and the blade sank to the spine. The beast went down on three legs. Coel yanked his sword free and raised it overhead. The creature struggled to rise. Oleg drove his third spear into the creature's side and forced it back down. The perfectly balanced Academy sword was a butcher blade in Coel's hand. It rose and fell again and again across the thing's neck like he was chopping wood. The sword suddenly clove through. Coel stumbled as the blade met no resistance.

The beast's body shuddered and collapsed. Its head rolled into the shrubs.

Coel rose. "Márta!"

Snorri knelt beside her and eased her helmet off. He looked up at Coel grimly. "See if you can straighten out her legs."

Márta's shining mail armor had kept her legs attached to her body, but both limbs lay twisted and badly broken.

Márta moaned weakly. "I want Reza."

"I am here," The sorcerer knelt beside her. He looked to

Coel. "There are priests in Kiev for whom this healing will present little difficulty. But we must splint her legs until we can get her there."

"Aye," Coel took a deep breath. "Hold her."

Márta moaned again. The initial shock was fleeting. The agony of shattered bones and torn sinews asserted itself. Her jaws clenched. "Master!"

"I am here." The sorcerer took Márta's chin in his hand. "You fought magnificently, Márta. Your first hunt, and the great beast lays dead. You are my champion. My champion of champions."

Reza held her face. "Look into my eyes," The sorcerer's eyes widened. He held Márta's gaze. "I am going to count backwards from five. At five, you will relax. At four, the pain will be gone. At three, you will close your eyes. At two, you will smile for me. At one, you will go to sleep. Do you understand?"

Márta's golden brown eyes went glassy. "Yes."

"Good. Five . . . four . . . three . . . two . . . one." Márta sagged in Snorri's arms. Her eyes closed. Her lips turned up in a smile as if she were having a pleasant dream. Reza nodded. "Straighten her legs. Oleg, fetch the tube I gave you. We will use it to make splints."

Reza scowled in irritation. "Oleg!"

Oleg threw up.

Coel looked up from Márta's legs. Oleg stood doubled over with his hand over his mouth. Before him, the decapitated body of the beast undulated. Flesh writhed and fell from the bones in great steaming chunks. The bones themselves bent and twisted like dying snakes. Entrails spilled into the snow and the stench of putrefaction became overpowering. Blood and fluid seeped and dissipated as if it were fleeing from the great beast's body. The flesh peeled back as the great skeleton twisted and bent. Coel started as the bones burst apart with a great crack. All motion ceased. Three sets of bones lay entwined like lovers. The skeletons were yellowed as if they had been in the earth for a long time. The flesh, fur, and fluids sank back to the soil from which they had risen. To one side, the skulls of a bear, a boar, and a wolf lay impossibly jammed together.

"Oleg," Reza spoke calmly. "Please fetch the tube I gave you."

Oleg staggered off to his task. Coel eased off Márta's chainmail leggings with Reza's help. He cut away her silk trousers high on the thigh. Coel sucked in a breath as the silk came away. Márta's left knee was shattered. The joint was terribly swollen and her lower leg stuck outward in an unnatural knock-kneed position. Her right leg had been snapped below the knee, and the lower bone stuck out through the skin.

Coel took off his hat and iron skullcap. He took one of Márta's legs by the ankle. "All right, Snorri, hold her."

The knee joint popped and ground horribly as he gently pulled the twisted limb back into a semblance of normality and laid it straight. Coel tensed at each muffled sound the shattered joint made as it shifted. He looked up as Márta made a noise. Her head lay pillowed on Snorri's armored thigh. Her lips parted in a winsome smile. A little wheeze came from her mouth as she breathed softly. Coel shook his head wonderingly. Márta was snoring. She was also drooling on Snorri's mail. Coel moved to the other limb. He took her ankle in both hands and pulled down until the bone slid back under the skin. He gingerly twisted until he felt the bone ends fit together. Coel bound the break with a strip of silken pants leg.

Orsini stood to one side and leaned on his hammer. There was blood on his face where his visor had been ripped away. "That was well done. Where did you learn to set bones?"

Coel spoke absently as he worked. "My mother." At ten his mother had watched as he had set the broken wing of a dove. At twelve she had praised him when he has splinted the foreleg of one of his father's foals. Coel frowned at Márta's purpling legs. The breaks were very bad. There were bits of bone free in both injuries and bleeding inside the flesh. Without a true healing, she would be a cripple. The skin was broken along with the bones in her right leg. If infection set in, she would lose the limb. Reza seemed to read his mind. "It is not perfect, but neither is our situation. It will suffice until we reach Kiev. Do the splinting quickly. She will wake up soon."

Coel barked. "Oleg!"

Oleg came back looking green, but he held the tube. Coel pulled the two sections apart, broke them in half and splinted Márta's limbs. He wiped the sweat from his brow and nodded to himself as he finished tying them off. It would serve. "Oleg, get two of your spears. Snorri, give me your cloak, then."

Coel took the cloak and spread it on the ground. Oleg handed him two of his spears, and Coel laid them on the cloak. He folded a third of the cloak over each spear so that the ends met in the middle. Oleg grinned at the field litter. "Her weight will hold it together!"

"Aye."

Oleg looked at Coel with great respect. "You have done this before."

Coel took a hold of Márta's legs to support them. More than once he had been forced to use what little medicine he knew on battlefields where there were no healings from barbers or leeches, much less holy men of power for the defeated. Coel had made more field litters for wounded and dying comrades then he cared to think about. He nodded at Snorri and Oleg. "All right, then. Ease her onto it."

They gingerly moved Márta onto the litter and covered her with cloaks to keep her warm. Coel nodded at Snorri as he took hold of the litter by Márta's head. "All right, lift."

Orsini and Oleg collected the weapons and spent arrows. The dwarf held up the jammed animal skulls of the beast to Oleg. "Well, lad. It is not quite the trophy it was when it was alive, but there are curio shops in Kiev that would still pay you a fair price for it."

Oleg shuddered as he picked up Márta's bow. "Leave the cursed thing. I do not want it." The young man collected Coel's bow and followed the litter. Orsini tossed the twisted mass of skulls into the shrubs and located his helmet's missing visor. Otto the hound sniffed mournfully at his brother's torn remains. Snorri glanced back over his shoulder. "Otto!"

The dog gave his dead littermate a final whine and followed.

It was a long walk back to the river and Coel was thankful the land was flat. Reza walked alongside the litter. He held Márta's hand and spoke very softly in a language Coel did not recognize. Márta murmured back but her eyes remained closed. She did not stir or cry out when the litter jostled.

The sun rose in the sky. Coel figured it was close to the hour of ten. Orsini and Oleg both put a hand on either side of the litter to steady it as the party trudged along. Oleg still looked green. Coel nodded at him. "You fought well, Oleg. Your uncle will be proud, and you will have a tale worth telling your grandchildren."

Oleg reddened and looked at his boots. "It was not so much. Blowing silver dust and hurling spears."

"Do not sell yourself short," Snorri glanced back at the young man proudly. "You drove the beast forth, and your every spear found the mark."

Orsini nodded. "It took all of us to kill it, my good lad, and without you it might have gone much worse."

Reza looked up from Márta. "And no one forced you to go, either, Oleg. You volunteered. I shall see that you are rewarded appropriately when we reach Kiev."

The young man grinned shyly. "It was quite a battle, wasn't it?"

The litter lurched as Snorri stopped. The Rus' voice was as ugly as Coel had ever heard it.

"I will kill him."

Coel looked past the Rus' broad shoulders. The river lay just ahead through the trees. The camp lay abandoned. The fires were out. The party's belongings were nowhere to be seen.

The barge was gone.

"He stranded me!" Oleg was horrified. "Mine own uncle! He stranded me!"

"He has stranded all of us," Orsini's voice was very calm. "He has left us to die."

Coel kept a lid on his fury as he looked at Reza. The Persian's face was unreadable. Coel took a breath. Thoughts of revenge could wait. He had spent much time hunting and fighting in the wilderness of Wales. He knew what was necessary to survive.

"Oleg! Go to the fire-rings, quickly! Find some embers and start a fire burning!"

Oleg ran to the fire ring and began sifting through the ashes. As they got Márta's litter into the camp area, the young man was already sheltering a red spark with both hands and blowing on it for all he was worth. He tore a strip of linen from his tunic and wrapped the ember as he blew. Smoke came out of his hands, and a moment later a tiny flame flared. He set the fire down in the ashes and began feeding it bits of unburned kindling.

Coel and Snorri lay Márta down in the sand. Coel considered what supplies they had. There was precious little. "Snorri, unlimber your axe and start cutting boughs, long ones, with lots of needles to make a shelter. Orsini, gather firewood, as much as you can find that is dry."

Orsini went to the river's edge and began gathering driftwood. Snorri stood motionlessly staring downriver. Coel did not envy Tsapko. The barge captain had made himself a deadly enemy. The hound, Otto, whimpered at the Rus' feet.

"Snorri?"

Snorri whirled. His face was white with rage as he stabbed his finger at Coel. "I'm keeping the bastard's dog! The goddamned mutt deserves better than a coward for a master!"

Coel took a step backward. "He is yours. Take him."

Snorri's voice lowered but it still shook with anger. "Come on, Otto!" Snorri took up his axe and stomped off towards the trees. Otto the dog bounded after him. Coel knelt among the pile of weapons and meager supplies they had carried with them into the forest. Between them, they had two skins of wine, a loaf and a half of bread, a half-eaten dried sausage and small waxed round of cheese.

Reza rose from Márta's side. "Thin rations."

"It will have to do. We can make a mid-day meal of it. Snorri knows the river. Once we have a shelter up, perhaps we can see about catching some fish." Coel eyed the misshapen lumps of Márta's legs under the cloaks. "We cannot march her out of here."

"I agree. We should stay where we are. It is unfortunate that

Tsapko saw fit to steal our belongings. It limits what I can do to improve our situation. But I believe we can survive a day or two until help arrives."

"If help arrives."

Reza stood. "I believe I can do something about that."

Coel watched as the wizard walked into the woods alone.

CHAPTER TEN

Coel sat near the fire beside Márta. The night had been miserable. The day promised to be no better. Snorri had caught no fish, and the snares Coel set were empty. A handful of bread and a bite of cheese had been their last two meals and they were gone. Except for a few mouthfuls of wine, they were out of provisions. The party lay arrayed around the fire, wrapped in their cloaks and covered with pine boughs. Reza sat cross-legged with his shawl around his head and shoulders. Coel could not tell if he was asleep or not, but he had sat in the same position all night. Snorri and his new dog lay spooned together like puppies. Coel envied his friend the hound. Coel, himself, sat beside the tiny lean-to he had made for Márta and shivered. Márta lay in her cloak, and Coel had covered her with own as well. He had only the clothes on his back and the leather-covered brigandine armor for warmth. Coel wished vainly for the woolen brat his mother had woven for him. His lips skinned back from his teeth. That was one more ill favor he owed Tsapko. Coel threw another chunk of wood on the fire. Orsini had cut enough wood to build a house. The dwarf's strength seemed limitless. Coel huddled closer to the crackling flame. The fire's warmth was the only luxury to be found.

Márta spoke quietly as the fire flared. "What time is it?"

Coel looked up at the wan light creeping through the clouds. "The hour of five, perhaps a little after."

"I cannot sleep anymore."

"Good."

"Good?" Márta frowned at him out of the cloak hooded around her head. "What do you mean, good?"

Coel shrugged. "You snore."

"I do not."

"Of course you do."

Márta's eyes flashed indignantly. "I do not snore!"

"You drool, too," Coel poked the fire with a stick. "I've seen it."

Márta's eyes narrowed, but her lips smiled. "I hate you."

"Aye, I get that a lot," Coel looked down at her limbs. "How are your legs?"

Márta paused. "They are all right."

"You are a liar."

Márta would not meet his eyes. "They are swollen. They throb. It could be worse. I just wish that I could turn over. My back is in knots."

Coel held out the wineskin to her. It was almost limp. "There's still a little wine left. Finish it."

"We should save it."

"No, drink it."

"Are you trying to get me drunk?"

"I have been on the Frontier a long time, Márta. Now I have a warm fire and a woman with two broken legs and nowhere to run." Coel leered. "This is my big chance."

Márta smiled wanly. "You have the bedside manner of an ape."

"I made you smile." Coel held out the wineskin again.

"Just do not make me laugh." Márta winced as she raised her arms to take the wineskin. She took a pull from it. "What will we do?"

"Reza says help is coming, but it will take a few days. A boat or barge may well come down river from Smolensk before then." Coel stood up and stretched. "In the meantime, how would you like venison for breakfast?"

Márta sagged back into her bedding. "I have not eaten of deer in a long time."

"Then I shall go and fetch it for you." He glanced at a mound of pine boughs by the fire. "Orsini, are you awake?"

"I am." The pile of boughs cascaded away as the dwarf rolled to his feet. Coel envied him. Beneath his plate armor, Orsini had worn a heavily padded arming doublet and quilted cotton trousers. The soft under-armor helped absorb the shock of heavy blows. It looked quite warm. The dwarf's eyes twinkled in the firelight. "Venison, is it?"

"We'll settle for hedgehogs if we can find them. But spring is here. The new shoots are pushing up through the snow. The stags will be out gamboling. With the demon dead, perhaps some will come frolicking our way to claim its territory."

"I shall fetch my crossbow."

Coel unwrapped his great bow and strung it. He chose six iron broadhead arrows from his bag and sheafed them in his belt. Orsini returned with his massive crossbow crooked in his arm. The dwarf carried a quiver of bolts and his short sword. "Are we ready?"

"Aye, let us be about it."

Márta looked up at the two of them and lifted the wineskin. She smiled up from her sickbed. "For luck."

Orsini grinned out of his beard and took the wineskin. "To a hot breakfast." The dwarf shot a quick stream of wine into his mouth and handed the skin to Coel.

Coel raised it in turn. "To a hot breakfast." The sweet Cypriot wine warmed his belly. Coel knelt and gave the wineskin back to Márta.

She sighed as she finished it. "A hot breakfast."

Orsini bent down and put his foot into the massive crossbow's stirrup. Coel took up a spear and shook his head in wonder as once more the dwarf grabbed the heavy cable and cocked the steel bow by hand. Orsini slid a bolt into the guide and grinned. "Shall we?"

* * *

Patchy fog shrouded the forest at waist height and curled about the trunks of the pines. The two of them had walked slowly for the last half-hour. They had not spoken. They were totally absorbed with the sights and sounds of the forest about them. Coel halted and watched a huge eagle-owl return from the night's hunting. It swooped on silent wings into the bowl of a hollow tree. Orsini's voice rumbled low. "Owls are good luck."

Coel had never heard that, but he would take luck wherever he could find it at the moment. Birds began chirping in the treetops. The owl's return to its nest signaled that the last of the night hunters had gone to their beds. The human and the dwarf were the first hunters of the day.

Coel spoke in a hushed tone as he scanned the forest ahead. "May I ask you a question?"

"You may ask."

Coel bit his lip. He was not sure of how to go about asking what he wanted to know. "What did you mean, in Moscow, when you said that it was bad enough that hobgoblins were walking my world again, then?"

Orsini regarded Coel dryly. "I meant it is too bad that they appear to be walking the world again. You disagree with the statement? You harbor some fondness for hobgoblins? To be frank, I find this somewhat surprising after some of your more recent adventures."

Coel gave the dwarf a hard smile. "That is not what I mean, and you know it. It is how you said it that I am curious about. You spoke as if this were my world, and not yours."

"Ah," Orsini nodded sagely.

Coel waited for Orsini to elaborate. The dwarf did not. Coel cleared his throat. "Well?"

For a moment, Coel thought the dwarf would not answer. He feared he had insulted him or pushed too far. Orsini raised his gaze up into the treetops and studied them intently for long moments. Coel nearly jumped when he spoke. Orsini's voice was so pleasant it was forced. "Would you like to know something?"

"Ummm," Coel found himself clearing his throat. "Yes, very much."

Orsini took a step forward and looked up into Coel's eyes. Coel resisted the urge to take a step back. "Did you know," The dwarf seemed to dwell on each word before he spoke it. "That large numbers of my people, entire clans, in fact, have sworn great oaths over the years, to your Popes in Rome, and, to a lesser extent, to the Patriarchs in Byzantium, that in exchange for their tolerance," Orsini made a face as if he smelled manure. "My race will not go about disseminating our, how do they put it?" The dwarf's eyes bored into Coel's. "Heathen, non-human beliefs amongst Christendom's faithful?"

Coel retreated a step. He had only seen this expression on Orsini's face once before. It had been in the Golden Horse. In Moscow. When Snorri had called the dwarf a runt. Coel shook his head rapidly. "No. No, I did not know that."

Orsini nodded. His voice lowered an octave. "Oh, indeed, it is true. Of course, no clan may speak for another. As a matter of fact, no dwarf may speak for another, unless the individuals or clans in question have personally sworn fealty to one another. This is something you humans cannot seem to grasp. You seem to think we dwarves are some great nest of ants who come boiling up out of the earth all marching to the same drum." Orsini snorted. "As if you humans were so organized. Which, my friend, you are not. Yet, nevertheless, were I to have this conversation with you which you seem so keen upon, and this would not be a conversation about my personal beliefs, or the beliefs of my people, mind you, but a conversation about only mine own personal experiences, there could be all manner of repercussions. If it got out, it could well cause untold grief for myself and members of my clan, and you, my tall friend, if you went farting off at the mouth about what I told you, might find yourself in a situation where cordwood was being stacked about your ankles and the word 'heretic' was being bandied about."

Orsini's smile was not particularly pleasant. "Do you take my meaning? Are you still the curious human?"

Coel met the dwarf's gaze with difficulty. The glittering gray eyes held power comparable to the stare of the sorcerer. Coel steeled himself. He had questions. Questions that had plagued him the moment he'd seen a horde of goblins howling for his blood on the steppes. Since that day, he had been too busy staying alive, too close to death, or just too distracted to ask them. He had been too busy to ask them of himself, much less anyone who could give him an answer. Here, in this lonely wood, alone with Orsini, it was too much of an opportunity to pass up. Coel swallowed hard but met

Orsini's gaze. "I read something once."

The dwarf eyed Coel blandly. "Do tell."

"Let the truth be told though the heavens fall."

Orsini blinked. A big-toothed smile crept across his square face. A slow laugh rumbled out of his throat. The dwarf shook his head in bemusement. "Well, now, who am I to deny Coel, son of Math, seeker of truth?" Orsini rested his crossbow across his shoulder and put his fist on his hip. "Very well. What, exactly, do you wish to know?"

Coel's mind went blank. He stared down at Orsini stupidly. The dwarf glanced back up with infinite patience. The words lamely fell out of Coel's mouth. "How old are you?"

Orsini raised an annoyed eyebrow. "I was born three hundred and seventy-two years, nine months and seven days ago, and, unless you are planning me a birthday party, I really do not see how it is any of your business."

"I mean," Coel struggled for an intelligent question. "Where were you born?"

"Ah. Geography." Orsini pondered a moment. "I was born in the mountains where my clan once made its home. In your language, there, it would be called the Wild Place. In this place, here, your people call that range the Carpathians."

Coel frowned. "This place?"

"Correct."

"As opposed to another place, then?"

"Indeed."

"What other place?"

"A place much like this one."

"A place much like this one?"

"Yes. But very different."

"Ah," Coel nodded not understanding any of it. He stopped nodding and shook his head. "I am afraid I do not understand any of this."

"Hmm." Orsini nodded sympathetically. "Let us try another tack. You are Celtic, are you not?"

"Aye," Coel drew back expecting insult. "I am."

"You know of the *Lebor Gabala*?"

"The Irish Book of Invasions. Yes, I've read it."

"Good. As a historical document it is virtually worthless. However, like all mythos, there is enough truth there for the clever to tell the tale. Tell me, who were the *Tuatha De Danann*?"

"The Children of Danu, the Old Gods. They ruled Ireland."

"Gods indeed," Orsini rolled his eyes in disgust. "If they were gods, what became of them?"

Coel quoted the old legends. "The Sons of Mil, the Gaels, came across the sea from Spain and conquered Ireland."

"Indeed, and what happened to the *Tuatha De*, these 'gods' of yours?"

It was a tale every child in the Celtic reaches knew. "They went to the Hollow Hills."

"Yes, and where exactly is that?"

"Well, I do not know."

"Answer me this. If I were to go to Ireland, with a spade, and start digging in some muddy hillside, am I likely to uncover the Children of Danu?"

"I doubt it."

"As do I. However, if I were to go Ireland, or Wales, or Cornwall, or any number of places in Europe, for that matter, and went to a circle of standing stones, during certain conjunctions of the stars, whom might I meet?"

Coel knew the answer but he was hesitant under the dwarf's gaze. "Elves?"

"Yes. Very good. Elves."

"The elves are gods?"

Orsini snorted. "No, but long ago, your people, the Celts, were foolish enough to worship them as such. Gullibility has always been one of humanity's more endearing traits. Of course, so are greed and aggression. These were the downfall of the *Tuatha De Danann* in Ireland. That, and the fact that you humans breed like rabbits. The elves just could not compete."

"Oh."

"Now, assuming that we are correct in our hypothesis that one does not pull elves out of hillsides like turnips, where might these famed Hollow Hills be?"

Coel considered everything the dwarf had told him. "Someplace else?"

Orsini nodded.

"A place much like this one?"

Orsini raised an encouraging eyebrow.

"But very different?"

Orsini milled his hands expectantly. "And?"

Coel stood straighter as the thought really hit him. "Another world?"

Orsini sighed with grudging satisfaction. "I shall continue to hold forth some hope for you."

Coel's brow furrowed. "But the elves now rule Ireland again."

"Well, actually, they only really rule the Isle of Man, but I will grant you they have great influence in much of Ireland, currently."

"But they live under the sun there, the same as the Irish do. They do not live under hills, or the Hollow Hills, or someplace else."

"No. They do not."

"So," Coel considered. "The elves returned from the Hollow Hills."

"Yes."

"Just like the hobgoblins have now returned."

"Yes."

"From another world."

"Indeed."

"Into this one."

"Precisely."

Coel let out a long breath. "My world."

"You have an agile mind, Coel. Your brain seems able to jump hurdles that trip many humans into the mud of organized religion."

Coel blinked. "Are you a Christian?"

Orsini stared steadily back. "Are you?"

"I . . ." Coel balked. "I was just asking."

"So was I."

Coel felt his stomach tightening. "I was baptized at Saint David's."

"You have not answered my question."

Coel frowned deeply. His hands began twisting around his bow. It was a question that had been troubling him for a long time. "I believe in the Ten Commandments."

"Ah. Do you keep them?"

Coel flinched. "I have been inspired by the words of Christ."

"Mmm."

Coel's jaw set decisively. "You have risked telling me your heresies, so I shall return you the favor and tell you mine. If a priest with the Power laid his hand upon my head and performed the Truth-Tell, they would hang me for what I hold in my heart."

For a moment silence fell between them. Orsini nodded soberly. "I appreciate your candor, and your trust in me in revealing it. I will tell you that I, too, have read your Ten Commandments. They are much like the Great Codex of my race. Actually, I will admit that yours is the much cleaner document. Dwarves are often too lawyerly for their own good, and I, for one, personally, do not believe that all the sub-clauses and codicils that the clan councils argue interminably were present when the Great Spirits first wrote the Words Of Fire over the Mountain." Orsini stroked his beard thoughtfully. "I will tell you, also, that I have read the words ascribed to your carpenter from Bethlehem, and his was a spirituality to which any race might proudly aspire."

Coel relaxed. Orsini was so utterly reasonable that Coel's rage against the Church could not seem to kindle itself. The dwarf smiled up at him. "I am glad that you and I have had this conversation."

Coel found himself smiling back. "I am, too."

Orsini looked about. "Well. It seems the fog is lifting. Unless we intend to talk a deer to death, perhaps we should go about hunting one."

* * *

It was well past noon when Coel and Orsini marched triumphantly into camp with their burden. They carried the stag between them on the spear. It was a good-sized animal. The stag had just begun putting on fat again from eating the new shoots of spring. They lay the deer down and Coel set about skinning and dressing it. Coel looked up from his work. "Oleg, build another fire in the second pit."

Oleg took a brand and went to work. Coel glanced at Snorri. "How was the fishing?"

Snorri rolled his eyes.

"How was the gathering?"

Snorri extended an embarrassed hand at his shield. Upon it lay a pile of scraggly-looking wild onions, small head of wild garlic, a sheaf of edible rushes, a handful of herbs, and a few fistfuls of nettle shoots. Snorri might have been shamed by his inability to contribute meat, but he was an excellent forager. Coel saw their supper coming together. "Perfect. Lend me your knife, then."

Coel sweated as he worked the carcass with the *sax*. After a time he took a few strips of hide and tied the skinned and dressed stag around a spear shaft. He looked at Oleg. "See about roasting this." Coel began scraping the inside of the hide. He nodded at

Snorri. "Take some spears. Make a tripod."

"Ah. Good thinking."

Coel finished with the hide and gave it to Orsini. Orsini joined Snorri, and the two of them tied the ends of the hide to the tripod of spears to make a skin pot over the fire. They began filling it with helmets of river water. Coel sliced the stag's liver, kidneys and tail fat and chopped the onions, garlic and nettles. He split the rushes to get at the pith inside and bruised the herbs with the butt of Snorri's *sax*. Snorri's shield was turning into a fairly impressive trencher of food. Coel went to the fire and scraped the shieldful of fixings into the bubbling water. He looked over at the venison. "They should be done at about the same time. Oleg, take the first turn over the fires. Keep the soup simmering, but don't let the skin burn through."

Oleg nodded and began whittling a stick for stirring.

Orsini reappraised Coel yet again. "And he can cook."

Coel went to the river and sat on his heels as he washed his hands and cleaned Snorri's knife. Snorri squatted down beside him. The Rus looked back over his shoulder to where Márta lay in her little lean-to of pine boughs. She slept fitfully once more under Reza's mesmerism. "Soup for the sick?"

Coel handed Snorri his knife. "It is the most I can do for her until help arrives."

"You've done more than most could do. You continue to surprise me, Coel."

Coel felt his cheeks redden at the compliment. "Reza says help will arrive in three days from Kiev."

Snorri ran a calculating eye over the river. "That is an interesting prediction."

"You do not think it's possible, then?"

"Kiev is well over a hundred leagues away. They would be rowing up river, and against the spring current. I would say it is completely impossible," Snorri shrugged. "But, then again, I am not a wizard."

The smell of roasting venison began to waft over the rocky beach. "Speaking of sorcerers, how is your chess game going?"

Snorri scanned the dark waters before him. "Reza Walladid is the greatest opponent I have ever faced."

Coel watched Snorri's face. Until this moment, Snorri had spoken of every chess opponent he'd ever played with varying degrees of smug condescension. "Can you beat him, then?"

"The only man who ever beat me at chess was my grandfather, the Swede, and he was the man who taught me. I beat him when I was twelve. He is long dead, and no man has beaten me since," Snorri smiled like a shark. "I am not about to lose now to some Persian in silk pants who thinks he invented the game."

Coel could not suppress a smile. "You are sure, then?"

Snorri's eyes went back to the river. "Oh, Reza is clever. Far too clever for his own good. It will be his downfall." Coel stared at his friend. Snorri sounded like some prophet returned from the mountain pronouncing Reza's doom. "I am going to beat him. Bet your harp on it. The only way Reza can win is if he cheats or uses sorcery, and then I will have to kill him." He gave Coel a crazy grin. "I will expect you to help me."

"Right," Coel nodded slowly. He was not entirely sure if Snorri was joking. "If Reza cheats at chess, we kill him."

"You are a good friend."

CHAPTER ELEVEN

"Here," Coel knelt down in front of the lean-to and set his steel skullcap down in Márta's lap. Steam rose up from the last of the marrowbone broth within it. "Eat."

Márta's voice was a hoarse croak. "I am not hungry right now. Why don't you have it?"

Coel gave her a mock scowl. "Eat it anyway."

"All right."

Márta lay propped up with Snorri's shield for a backboard. She was wrapped and hooded in cloaks. She held the helmet of soup with shaky hands and took a tiny sip from it. She set the bowl down on her lap and sagged back on the shield as if taking the swallow of soup had utterly exhausted her.

Coel bit his lip. Márta was not well at all. Her face was gaunt and she had dark circles under her eyes. It was a cold morning but sweat sheened her brow. The swelling in her legs had gotten worse. The massive purple bruises had turned black under her skin. The torn skin where the bone had broken through had turned an angry red despite Coel's cleaning the wound daily. The rest of her leg was streaked with pink and felt hot to the touch. Her fever was climbing. Márta resolutely refused to show her pain, but she moaned and cried out in her sleep. Her lack of appetite boded nothing good. Coel's nose wrinkled involuntarily. It was their fourth morning at the river camp. None of the party smelled like roses, but Márta reeked with the stench of illness. The wound had festered. Rot had set in.

She smelled like death.

Márta spoke very quietly. "Do not cut off my leg."

Coel paled. The thought had kept him awake all night. He knew that when worst came the duty would fall on him. Coel struggled to arrange a smile on his face as his mind raced for something to say. Márta interrupted him before he could utter some inane assurance.

"If help does not come."

Coel's voice went steely. "Help will come."

Márta's eyes closed and she took a deep breath. "If help does not come. I do not want you to cut off my leg."

"Márta--"

"I want you to kill me."

"I will not," Coel shook his head vehemently. "I cannot."

"I know you can," Her shoulders twitched with a sudden chill. "I do not wish to live as a cripple. Without a leg, I cannot wield a sword. If I am maimed, no man will marry me. I will not be a beggar, or sit in a corner of one of Reza's houses gathering pity and dust." Her gaze fixed on Coel again. "If it comes to it? Do this for me."

Coel could not meet her gaze.

Márta's voice was a hoarse whisper. "You know, I had a friend when I was being trained at the convent in Cyprus. A great big horse of a girl. Her name was Blandine. She was French. She was my best friend. We did everything together. We promised each other that if we were ever in the same battle and one of us was badly wounded, we would not leave the other to be ravished by the enemy. We pricked our fingers and promised in blood," Márta sighed. "We were very young and foolish, but the promise does not seem so silly now."

"Must it be me?"

Márta's eyes closed again. "Oleg is young and about to be married. I would not have a woman's blood on his conscience before his wedding, even if he could do it. Snorri could do it, if it was you, or another man. But I do not think he could push his sword through my breast. I do not think killing a woman is in his nature. Even in mercy."

Coel looked everywhere except Márta's face. He looked at the edge of the forest where the dwarf was cutting boughs.

"I already asked Orsini last night." Márta whispered. "I do not think he can do it, either."

Coel met Márta's gaze. "What about Reza? He is your

master, is he not?"

"He is, but . . . " Márta seemed at a loss for words. She looked at Coel searchingly. Her hand trembled as she pulled a silver chain up from under her tunic. A small silver pendant hung from it. "My friend, Blandine. She gave me this. Look."

Coel took the pendant. It was a triptych. The icon was made of silver, and its edges framed in gold. Coel unfolded the double doors of the miniature and opened them. Inside was a tiny enamel painting. The painting depicted the head and shoulders of a man with long red hair wearing a red mantle. He stood with a sword across his breast and a shield across his shoulder. A halo illuminated his head from behind. Coel's eyes widened.

It was as if he gazed upon a decent portrait of himself.

Márta swallowed painfully. "It is Saint George. At the convent, the library had a beautiful illuminated volume of how he saved the princess from the dragon. During my first years at the convent I was always looking at it. Blandine said I was in love with Saint George and waiting for him to ride up and save me from the nunnery. She had the triptych made for me in Nicosia, and gave it to me when we graduated from our training. I have carried it ever since, for luck."

"It is beautiful."

Márta gave him a tremulous smile. "That is why I looked at you so strangely in Moscow. It looks like you." She closed her eyes again. "If it comes to it. I want you to have it."

Coel took a deep breath. His fist clenched around the triptych. He let the breath out and lay the icon back on Márta's breast. "I give you my word. I will kill you before I cut off your leg."

Márta's eyes opened. "Coel . . ."

Coel cut her off. "I also give you my word that I will swim to Kiev and return with the Archbishop on my back before it comes to that."

Márta's eyebrows rose slightly. "I have heard that the Archbishop of Kiev is the fattest man in the all Russias."

Coel rose. "Then I will sit on his stomach and paddle him

upstream."

Life flickered in Márta's eyes as she smiled. "I believe that is blashphemy."

Coel perched his fists on his hips implacably. "And, I promise that if you do not eat your soup, I will sit on your chest and pour it down your throat."

"I will eat my soup."

Coel stood unmoving.

Márta sighed. "Are you going to stand there and watch me?"

Coel folded his arms across his chest. "Yes."

* * *

Coel examined an arrow as he prepared to go hunting. Márta moaned in fever. Her lungs gurgled with each breath. For the last two days Coel and Orsini had gone out hunting and come back with nothing. The snares continued to come up empty, as well. Coel could think of nothing else he could do.

Márta was dying.

Coel looked up at a clatter by the shore. Snorri had thrown down the fishing pole he had fashioned. It had been about as much use as Coel's snares. Snorri stood on the boulder he had been sitting on. He cupped his hands over his eyes as he scanned downriver. His voice suddenly boomed.

"Ship!"

Coel jumped up with a fistful of arrows and his bow in hand. The party was in bad shape and piracy was not unknown on the Dnieper. Snorri was of the same mind. He kept one hand over his eyes as he took up spear. Coel ran across the rocky beach. "Barge?"

"Longship! A small one! Eight oars to a side by my count! A river trader!"

Coel jumped up on the boulder with Snorri. He nocked an arrow but held his bow low. He glanced back. Orsini and Oleg stood by Reza. The sorcerer closed his eyes for a moment and his brow furrowed in concentration. "Put down your weapons. Help has arrived."

The ship came rowing smoothly against the current. Coel became aware of a deep bass voice calling out the strokes. A figure clad in black stood at the prow. As the boat approached, Coel saw the figure was as short as Orsini, but infinitely more pleasing in shape than the dwarf. The oars dipped onward in the same rapid rhythm against the current. The little ship came straight at the encampment. She suddenly back-oared. A sailor threw out a mooring rope as the ship slowed into the shallows. Snorri caught it and tied off on a piling. The woman in the prow looked Coel up and down in frank appraisal.

Coel returned her gaze measure for measure.

Looking upon the woman was not difficult. She was like no woman in Coel's experience. She was just less than five feet tall, but her limbs were exceptionally well turned. Her shape and the way she stood reminded Coel of a female acrobat he had once seen in the circus in Paris.

Coel had never seen a woman wearing woolen hose before.

The fine black wool clung scandalously to her hips and thighs. Men normally wore codpieces or doublets over their hose. Staring up at her where she loomed in the prow, Coel blushed at how little the tight garment left to his imagination. She had thrown a short cape of gray wool over one shoulder and pinned it at her waist with a gold brooch. The face staring down at him was heart shaped and her large eyes were perfectly framed by her cheekbones. Her face swooped down to a pointed chin. The effect made her look like a kitten. Under a sable hat, her black hair was cut short so that it fell around her ears. Her flawless olive complexion provided a striking contrast to her eyes. Coel started as he looked into them. One of her eyes was blue. The other was green.

She stood wide-legged at the prow. Her hands were concealed in a sable muff that matched her hat. Her lips were generous, and unpainted. The lips parted in a slow smile as she looked down at Coel. She spoke in the most melodious Latin Coel had ever heard. "You are big."

"Thank you."

"You are welcome."

"My name is Coel."

She raised her chin slightly. "You are Irish?"

Coel put his fists on his hips and grinned proudly. "No, Welsh."

"Ah," Her chin lowered again. "My name is Zuleikha. My friends call me Zuli. I would be pleased if you would do the same."

"Zuli," Coel savored the exotic name as he stepped into the shallows. "May I assist you to shore, then?"

"How kind of you." Coel started as the woman stepped off the prow. He grunted as her weight fell into his arms. She was heavier than she looked. Her hands stayed in her muff as she slid her arms in a circle around Coel's neck. Zuleikha smelled like jasmine. Coel carried her to shore. Reza stood waiting. The woman kissed Coel's cheek as she slid out of his arms. "Thank you."

Coel watched her as she approached the sorcerer. "Reza."

"Zuleikha. You look well."

The woman took her hands from her muff and spread her arms dramatically. "Do I look suitably barbaric?"

"Indeed. You must be careful lest some Rus carries you off to be his snow princess."

The woman tossed her head. "Now, I will tell you, I was prepared to hate the Russias until I found these pants." She took a pinch of the tight material between her fingers and pulled it from her leg. She let it snap back to hug her thigh again. "I have worn nothing else since I found them, and I nearly died when I found this hat. I may move to the mountains just so I can wear it all the time. I--Orsini!"

The woman ran forward and flung herself into the dwarf's arms. Orsini lifted her up to hug her and then set her back down. "Zuli, my dear. How are you?"

The woman took a step back, and the two of them clasped wrists. "I was informed you had run into some difficulties."

"Yes." Orsini scowled a bit. "Through unfortunate circumstances we have found ourselves stranded here for the last four days."

Zuleikha ran a revolted eye around the encampment. "How awful." Her gaze stopped as she looked at the little lean-to by the fire. A smirk passed over her lips. "Oh. I see you have little Márta with you."

Orsini cleared his throat. "Yes."

Zuli's nose wrinkled. "She does not look well."

"No. Her legs are broken. Infection has set in."

"Oh. Well. I am sorry to hear that."

Coel's eyes narrowed. Zuli did not sound sorry at all. Her tone was not lost on Orsini, either. The dwarf changed the subject. "Tell, me. Did you meet the priest?"

She shrugged carelessly and glanced at the longship. "I brought him with me. That is how I came here so quickly."

"Ah. Come, Coel. There is work to be done." Orsini went to the mooring rope and pulled himself up to the prow hand over hand. Coel jumped to grab the gunwale and heaved himself up. He stopped and stared at what he saw. Sixteen men sagged moaning across their oars at the rowing benches. They shuddered as their muscles clenched and cramped uncontrollably. They acted like men who had been pushed beyond all endurance. It struck him that none of the twitching, tortured looking men wore the chains of slaves or criminals sentenced to the oars.

A man sat behind the rowers and leaned back against a bale of goods. He wore a long black mantle of a cut that was out of fashion in most of Europe. His straw colored hair was cut tightly around his head. There were a few streaks of gray in it, but he did not look much older than Coel, himself. The man's skin was very fair. He might have been handsome had it not been for the expression on his face. Even in repose the man looked tense as a drawn crossbow. His eyes were closed, and he held his fingers to his brow as if he were exhausted or had a splitting headache.

Orsini cleared his throat. "Father?"

The man opened pale blue eyes that were rimmed with red.

The eyes focused on Orsini. They were not pleased at what they saw. The man's mouth twisted. He spoke his Latin in a clipped, Germanic accent. "You are a dwarf."

"You are correct."

The man heaved a heavy sigh. He ran his gaze over the men shuddering over their oars. He raised a hand over them almost like a benediction. The priest spoke a single word. "Sleep."

All twenty men collapsed like puppets with their strings cut. They fell unconscious between the benches in heaps. The priest rose wearily. He was tall, taller than Snorri but still shorter than Coel and lean. "The rowers will sleep until dark. Then they will require large quantities of food." He turned his eyes on Coel. "There is an injured woman?"

Coel took Orsini's cue. "Aye, Father. On the beach. In the lean-to."

"Very well." Coel had to step out of the way as the priest drew a course down the deck straight at him. Coel noticed the ancient Christian Chi Roh symbol hanging around the man's neck. It was the symbol of the Christians who had been persecuted in the Roman Empire. Coel scrutinized the pendant more closely. The ancient symbol had been modified. Five swords met to form the crossed arms of the symbol. The priest grabbed the mooring line and swung deftly off of the boat. Coel glanced at Orsini. "Not the most pleasant sort, is he, then?"

"No. Indeed, not." The dwarf's face was full of foreboding. "He is not what I was led to expect."

Orsini glanced at a wine cask and a bag of rations. "Come. Let us take these ashore. I believe we could all do with some food, and these men will be ravenous when they wake." Coel took the ration bag and looked back at the comatose rowers. They still jerked and twitched in their unnatural sleep. Coel's own shoulders twitched with unease at the sight of them. He shook himself and hopped from the prow and followed the priest ashore. The German stopped before the sorcerer. "Reza."

"Father Marius."

The priest turned his gaze back at the boat as Orsini slid

down the mooring rope. "Must you drag non-humans into this?"

Reza's head cocked slightly. "You wish to express some objection about my associates?"

The priest looked at Reza long and hard. "No." He looked over at the lean-to. "She is the one in need of healing?"

"Yes. Her legs are broken. She has taken on fever and her left leg will require amputation without swift assistance." Reza looked at the ship meaningfully. "Do you need to recover from your exertions first?"

"That will not be necessary."

Coel followed the priest closely. Márta was still unconscious. The man knelt and uncovered her twisted and bloated legs. They barely resembled human limbs anymore. Snorri and Oleg crowded around. The priest ignored them all. He raised the Chi Roh and pressed it to his lips. He dropped the pendant to his chest and raised his hands to the sky. He held them there for long moments.

Coel and Snorri looked at one another.

They jumped as the priest's eyes flared open.

"By the will of God!"

The priest slammed his hands down across the breaks in Márta's legs.

Márta screamed. Her head flew back and her spine locked in an arch. Her limbs spasmed and flailed. Coel put his hand to his sword hilt, but the priest had already released her legs. Márta lay trembling. Coel looked down at her legs in shock. Other than goose bumps, both limbs were whole and unmarked. Márta sat up with a stunned look on her face. The bruised look about her eyes and the pallor of fever were gone. Her cheeks were flushed with health.

Zuli smirked down at Márta. "Someone has not been shaving their legs."

Márta looked down at her exposed thighs and yanked the cloak back over them. Zuli turned her back on Márta and began speaking with Reza and Marius. Coel put a hand on Márta's shoulder. "Are you all right?"

Márta rubbed her legs and bounced her knees up and down

experimentally under the cloak. She looked up at Coel in awe. "That priest has great power."

Coel nodded. The man's power rivaled the Bishop of Moscow. "I almost beheaded him when you screamed," Coel looked over at Zuli. "Who is that woman?"

Márta's face fell in an instant. "That is Zuleikha."

"Yes, but who is she?"

"An associate of Reza's," Márta's voice dropped to an angry mutter. "He must require her services for something."

Coel admired the way Zuli's woolen hose clung to her behind. Oleg and Snorri were doing the same. "What services would those be?"

Márta shot a look of pure malice at the woman's back. "Whoring and thieving."

Coel quickly changed the subject. "Who is the priest?"

"I do not know," She looked up at Coel sheepishly. "May I borrow your cloak for a little while longer?"

"Of course. I will let you arrange yourself."

Coel rose and listened as Zuli spoke with Reza. The sorcerer's face was grim. So was Orsini's. Zuli shrugged carelessly as she spoke. "So, as to this unscrupulous river-captain of yours, Tsapko? He is in Kiev. He has rented a booth in the marketplace. He has many interesting things for sale. Exotic clothes, weapons, strange instruments of various descriptions, a harp."

Coel snarled. "My harp!"

"Yes, it's very nice."

Reza turned to Coel. "You have met Zuleikha already. This is Father Marius von Balke, of Westphalia. He will be accompanying us on our journey. Marius, this is Coel ap Math, of Wales."

Marius nodded curtly. Coel kept his smile fixed to his face and nodded back. "Father."

Reza gestured at the rest of the party. "This is Oleg, son of Igor. We count ourselves fortunate that his step-uncle stranded him among us."

Oleg dropped to one knee and piously kissed the hem of Marius' mantle. "Greetings, Father. What you did with Márta's legs was a miracle. I have never seen such a healing."

Oleg's sincerity seemed to force politeness out of the priest. He waved a blessing over Oleg's head and gestured to him to rise. "God keep you, Oleg Igorson."

"And this is Coel's friend, Snorri Yaroslav."

Snorri stood with his legs wide apart as he looked the priest up and down. He'd folded his arms across his chest with his axe crooked in one elbow. He smiled pleasantly. "Greetings, Father," He raised a scarred eyebrow at the pendant the priest wore on his chest. "So, you're Brethren of the Blade?"

"Yes," The priest's pale eyes fixed in cold defiance. "I am an ordained Brother of the Blade."

Snorri's smile widened so that his gold tooth gleamed. "Well, now, and I'd thought the Pope had suppressed you goddamned butchering bastards years ago."

Stunned silence fell across the beach.

Marius' face flushed. He slowly shrugged back his black mantle. His hands tensed at his sides. Beneath the mantle he wore a mail shirt of blued steel. Thrust through his war belt hung a brutal mace and chain.

Snorri grinned from ear to ear. "Why don't you try it you German son of a bitch."

The priest's weapon slid from its perch with practiced ease. Marius shook out the chain, and the spiked steel ball began making small, lazy figure eights near his calf. Snorri unfolded his arms, and his axe fell into his right hand. Reza stepped in front of Marius. Coel put a hand on Snorri's shoulder.

Snorri stood unmoving. His smile was ugly to behold. "Oh, I know your kind, priest. I was in the Baltic when your brotherhood was doing its Christian duty. My uncle's ship plied the Dvina River. I saw what you did in your crusade against the Livonians. Salvation on the end of a sword," Snorri spat on the ground. "Christ wept."

Marius trembled with rage. "No worse than what your kind has done, Rus! Your pagan outrages against the Roman Christian cities of the north are well documented!"

"That was raiding! That was hundreds of years ago!" Snorri pulled against Coel's hand. The Rus pointed his axe accusingly. "You and your bastard brethren burned every village! I saw it with my own eyes! You split the head of every man, woman and child!"

Marius' lips thinned. He shrugged indifferently. "They were pagans."

Snorri went white. Coel seized him with both hands. Márta grabbed Snorri's other arm. Orsini stepped in front of the priest with Reza. Oleg looked back and forth between the Rus and the German priest fearfully. Zuli looked back and forth between them and her eyes shone with excitement.

Snorri's arm tensed under Coel's hand. "Well I'm a pagan, too, you red-handed son of a whore. Why don't you try saving my soul with that skull-crusher of yours?"

The anger went out of the priest's face like a light. He regarded Snorri from some unfathomable depth. With a twitch of his wrist he doubled up his mace and chain and slid it back into his belt. "I have more pressing concerns than the state of your soul, Rus, or that of your skull."

Father Marius turned towards the ship. Snorri's mouth opened and shut as the priest walked away from the fight. Reza whirled on Snorri. His dark eyes flashed. Snorri's own anger faltered as Reza turned on him. The sorcerer's voice was as cold as the grave. "Listen to me, Snorri Yaroslav, and listen well. I require Father Marius' services. More than I require yours. I will not tolerate the two of you fighting. It interferes with my objectives. If you cannot control yourself, I shall leave you in Kiev, and we shall consider our association mutually dissolved. If you ever pick a fight with the priest again while he is in my employ, you will be picking a fight with me. Do you understand?"

Snorri gaped.

Reza eyes held Snorri's relentlessly. "You will give me an answer."

"I . . . " Snorri's face twisted with conflicting emotions. He kicked the stones at his feet angrily. "Oh, very well! If you need him, I will tolerate him!"

"That is all that I require," Reza stalked after the priest. Orsini followed him.

Coel released Snorri's arm. Márta held onto him and pulled him towards the fire. "There is wine from the ship. Let me pour you a cup. You and Coel have been waiting upon me hand and foot while my legs were broken."

Snorri shook with anger. He took a deep breath and forced a smile at Márta. "I suppose it's that or go jump in the river. I think I would rather drink with you." He followed Márta and the two of them sat down by the fire. Snorri set aside his axe and the two of them went to work on the wine cask.

Coel jumped as a finger lazily traced down his bare forearm and sent goose bumps racing along his skin. Zuli stood at his elbow and smiled up at him. "You know, I really thought they might kill each other."

Coel nodded. So had he. "Snorri is a very passionate man."

Zuli looked at the Rus's broad back speculatively and then at Coel. Her blue-green gaze was disconcerting. Coel looked back at the boat. "What is wrong with the rowers?"

"They have been rowing for three days without stopping."

"Truly?"

Zuli seemed bored by the subject. "They have not laid down their oars since we left Kiev. They signed on for silver, but I do not believe they truly knew what they were in for."

"Marius made them?"

Zuli rolled her eyes derisively. "They say when the spirit is willing, the body has the strength of ten. Marius raised his hands and filled their bodies with the will of God. Or perhaps the will of Marius," She shrugged uncaringly. "The priest is a very passionate man, as well. I think he truly believes they are one and the same."

Coel was increasingly aware of the smell of jasmine. He found himself grinning. "And what are you passionate about?"

"What are you passionate about?" She countered.

Coel put his fists on his hips and grinned. "I asked you first."

"I do not care," Zuli gave Coel a very glad eye. "Tell me."

The words came to him with ease. "Music. Dancing," He shrugged. "Kissing."

Zuli's chin lifted with interest. "Kissing?"

"Well, back in Wales, I was popular with women. I was tall, and the son of a Chieftain. It was not hard. But, to be honest, I never, really, quite understood kissing, until . . . " Coel let the point dangle as he examined the toe of his boot casually.

Zuli cocked her head. "Until?"

Coel looked up and grinned mischievously. "Until I spent a few years in France," He ran his eyes down her body. "It was there that I first learned what a tongue is for."

Zuleikha's smile lit up the rocky shore. Her hand slipped into Coel's. "Would you like to go for a walk in the woods?"

Coel grinned in happy shock. "I would be delighted."

Zuli gave Coel's hand a squeeze and tilted her head at the ship. "There are blankets in the boat."

"I shall fetch them." He turned with a spring in his step and grinning like a fool.

Coel froze in his tracks. Márta was staring at him. Her eyes were huge. Her knuckles were white around the cloak Coel had given her. Coel's stomach twisted as she looked away into the fire. Snorri looked between the two of them and chewed his mustaches uncomfortably.

"So," Zuli spoke. Coel cringed at the sudden scorn in her voice. "That is the way it is." Her voice dropped to an open sneer. "You are wasting your time, Coel. You will never get anywhere with that little priss."

Coel did not turn around. He clenched his fists at the sound of Zuli's laughter and walked resolutely over the stony beach. Snorri jumped to his feet as Coel approached. "I will go check the ship's rigging!" The Rus nearly ran across the rocks.

Coel knelt by Márta's side. "Márta . . ."

Márta would not look at him. She stared bitterly into the fire. "So, the two of you were going to go into the woods like dogs?"

Coel's face twisted with sudden anger. "Well, hell, I didn't, did I?"

Márta's eyes were wet but they stared hard into Coel's without blinking. "And if I had not been here? Had I been on the boat? Or still lay unconscious? You are saying you would not have done it?"

Coel surged to his feet. The old anger burst into flame in his breast. Frustration fueled it. He spoke through clenched teeth. "I am no saint, Márta, mooning about with unrequited love. I promised to stick a sword in you if it came to it, not to never look at another woman again." Bitterness filled his stomach like bile. His lips skinned back from his teeth and ugliness leaped from Coel's mouth before he could stop it.

"If Zuli speaks the truth, a sword is probably the only thing I would ever stick you with, anyway."

Márta's jaw dropped. Coel withered. Márta leaped to her feet. She ran barefoot across the rocks clutching his cloak about her hips. Coel's fists clenched helplessly as he watched her run crying to the ship. The heat of his anger poured out of him like water from a bucket with a burst bottom. He dropped to his haunches and put his head in his hands.

He had done it again.

He stared miserably into the fire and wondered how his heart had ever become so twisted. He cursed himself for a hypocrite. He knew all too well why his heart was twisted. He thought about his mother, and how as a boy she had taken him into the mountain forests and taught him the old ways. He thought of his father, and the tutors he had hired to teach him letters and Latin and make a nobleman out of him. He thought of his music teacher and the *Brehons* who had taught him Celtic law. He thought of his instructors at the Paladin Academy in Paris. Coel shook his head bitterly. He had failed all of them.

He thought of the one great love of his life, and the fate that had befallen her because of him.

A self-pitying fatalism crept into his breast. It was best if Márta hated him. He would only fail her as well.

Sand crunched behind him. Coel refused to look up. Out of the corner of his eye, he could see the squared off, black leather toes of Orsini's boots. Coel's shoulders sank miserably. "I suppose you heard every word."

"Oh, indeed. I think you handled that remarkably badly."

Coel looked up. Orsini was not smiling. "I find myself liking you, Coel, and I believe there are things you carry in your heart that you are struggling with. I realize these things will continue to color your behavior in certain situations until you deal with them. To a point, I am willing to forgive you." The dwarf paused meaningfully. "However, I will tell you, in all frankness, Márta is a lady, and a friend of mine. Should you ever speak to her like that again, you and I shall come to blows. Do we understand one another?"

Coel did not doubt it, but he had no answer. He could not meet the dwarf's eyes. He was pathetic. The dwarf's stern gaze just made him shrivel more. Orsini's steely eyes softened in the face of Coel's abject misery. The dwarf sighed. "Oh, buck up. It could be much worse."

"I do not see how, then."

"In another day you might have had to kill her."

Coel was silent for a moment. "I know it is not you I should be apologizing to, but I am sorry."

"I know you are. That is why I have not smashed your skull in."

Coel stared back into the embers. He rather wished Orsini would. A war hammer to the back of the head would solve most of his problems. "I do not think a blank book or any other apology will buy me out of this new mess I've made of things."

"No. Not immediately," Orsini gave Coel a long look. "I know what you carry is your business, and yours alone. However, were I you, I would tell Márta about it, whatever it is. She is a good listener, and I believe it is the one kind of apology she might accept." Orsini grimaced. "I will tell you something, Coel, as a friend.

Whatever is twisting about in your guts, it is eating you from the inside. Do not try to hold on to it, however much of an old friend it seems to be. You cannot hold on to anger forever. Anger leaves men, like youth, while they are not paying attention. As youth turns to age, anger shrivels to bitterness. I would unburden at least some of it if I were you, lest it hollow you out and leave you a lesser man."

Coel stood and faced Orsini. He offered the dwarf his hand. "I swear, on our association, I will never insult Márta again, and I will think upon what you have said."

"Very well," Orsini took Coel's wrist and clasped it. "Let us put this behind us."

"Besides," Coel managed half a smile. "Snorri worships you as a god. What would become of him if you and I were to come to blows?"

Orsini snorted. "I had not thought of that. It would undoubtedly send our beloved Rus into a moral decline."

Coel looked up suddenly. "What was Snorri about with the priest? I have never seen him like that."

Orsini's look of foreboding returned. "German and Rus have never had any love for one another. The Brethren of the Blade were a German Crusader Order, and they were fanatics. Snorri said he plied the Baltic some years ago with his uncle. It was among the pagan Livonians, Letts, and Samlanders there that the Brethren brought their crusade."

"I thought Snorri said the Pope had suppressed them."

"Indeed. Even the Pope in Rome could not countenance the Brethren's outrages in the name of God."

"Then what is he doing wearing the Order's badge and livery openly?"

"They were suppressed, and dispersed by the Pope in Rome, Coel. We are in the Russias. These are Orthodox lands we are standing upon."

"Oh," Coel stood feeling stupid. "I had not thought of that."

"You undoubtedly had other things on your mind."

Coel straightened. "I should probably go say something to

Zuli."

"You will have to wait your turn."

Coel followed Orsini's gaze. Zuli was near the shore with Oleg. She was holding Oleg's hand. Oleg carried a blanket over his shoulder and wore a stunned smile on his face. Zuli tugged the young man's hand, and the two of them walked towards the edge of the woods.

Orsini let out a very weary sigh. "The Heavens knows I am fond of her, but that one is trouble."

CHAPTER TWELVE

Coel watched Kiev approach from the prow. Snorri clapped him on the shoulder. "It's not the Golden City, but Kiev is something to see, is it not?"

"It rivals Paris," Coel marveled.

Kiev was the pride of the Russias. It, too, was one of the New Cities, and had been rebuilt to greater glory after the final defeat of the hobgoblins. Kiev made Smolensk look like a poor relation. It made a backwater out of Moscow. Kiev was the true nexus of the north and south. It was a city-state in its own right. Almost all other Russian cities were its satellites. It was here the Tsar of the Russias made his home. Coel took in the dozens of golden spires. They soared into the sky and their onion-shaped golden domes gleamed in the noon sun. It was warmer here, too. Spring in Kiev and spring in Moscow were two different affairs, entirely. Here, the endless open pine forests of the north fought for light with oaks and elms and flowering bushes. After years in the north, Coel marveled at the sight of green leaves on the trees instead of endless boughs covered with pine needles.

The trip in the longboat had been swift. The rowers had been given a day of rest. They had eaten like starving wolves and slept like dead men. The ship had set out down the Dnieper the next morning. The swift spring current was with them, and the rowers set a steady pace without the impetus of Father Marius' power. They had shot like an arrow down river towards Kiev.

The wharves of the city were bustling. Barges and longships crowded the docks. Sloops and pleasure boats sat amongst them. Nobles from the south came for the spring hunting of bear and boar in the forest, and with the spring thaw many people from the outlying towns and villages came to pray and receive blessings in the great cathedral.

The long ship pulled along the wharves looking for a berth. The piers were swollen with men, livestock and trade goods.

Pennons flew from a forest of masts. Coel had never seen so many boats in his life.

"There!" Snorri's hand gripped Coel's shoulder fiercely. "There's the bastard!"

Coel scanned the wharves. "Who?"

"Tsapko," Snorri's smile was ugly to behold. "That's who. That's his barge. There."

Coel sighted down Snorri's accusing finger. It did look like Tsapko's barge. Then, to his eye, so did every other barge on the wharf. "Are you sure, then?"

"Oh, yes." Snorri barked over his shoulder. "Walladid!"

The sorcerer, Marius and Orsini were steeped in deep conversation about something. Márta sat at Reza's right hand. She had not spoken to Coel since the river camp. Reza looked up at Snorri expectantly. "You wish to make a move?"

Coel shook his head. The fact that Tsapko had made off with Reza's chessboard had not stopped the sorcerer and the Rus. The night before they left the river camp, Snorri had looked over his stew bowl at Reza and said "Rook to King's Bishop's five."

Reza had grinned delightedly.

Both men clearly remembered the position of every piece. The lack of a board had barely slowed down their game as they each reviewed the chessboard in their minds. The two of them had sporadically called out their moves to one another on the trip down the river to Kiev. It was a level of play beyond Coel's understanding. From a sorcerer, one might expect such things. Snorri Yaroslav never ceased being a source of new amazements.

Snorri jerked his head at the wharf. "Tell me, do you see anything familiar?"

The sorcerer stood. His black eyes scanned the docks and and stopped on the barge. "Indeed, Yaroslav. I do."

Snorri nodded vehemently. "I say we burn it!"

"An attractive idea, but I suspect that would bring a great deal of attention." Reza turned. "Oleg!"

Oleg looked up with a startled expression. The young man sat against the stern. He played with Zuli's hair while she leaned against him. Coel envied the young man. Zuli's hair was so black it had a blue sheen to it. It was barely longer than one of Coel's fingers, barely long enough to lie down rather than stand up. Oleg seemed to find her hair endlessly fascinating as he combed his fingers through it. Zuli lay back against the young man's chest and smiled with her eyes closed. The sun shone on her face. Coel suspected if he came close enough he would hear Zuli purring. Coel felt the pang of lost opportunity.

Oleg leaped to his feet and followed Reza to the prow. Zuli's eyes followed his backside with lazy pleasure. Oleg stood before the wizard with great seriousness. "Yes, Sir?"

"Tell me, Oleg. Do you recognize that barge?"

"Yes, Sir," The young man swallowed hard. "It is mine uncle's."

"The owner of that barge has made himself my enemy. However, you have served me loyally and with courage. You must come to a decision."

"He is my step-uncle, and he stranded me," The young man's jaw set. "I must face him."

Reza nodded. "Very well."

Snorri tapped his axe in his palm. "So, we split Tsapko's head. Then we burn his barge."

"No. Tsapko made his bargain with me, and he broke it. It is to me he shall answer." Reza watched Oleg hurry back over to Zuli's side. He turned his gaze to Snorri and Coel. "Leave the barge alone. I strongly suspect Oleg may soon inherit it. With that, and the silver I intend to give him, he can go into business for himself." The sorcerer smiled. "It is a fitting enough wedding gift for the young man."

"You are generous," Snorri smiled prosaically as Zuli settled back into Oleg's arms. "But, he may not be so eager to go back to his bride."

"Oleg is young and strong. For Zuli that is enough, for the moment. However, I predict she will soon tire of him once we are within the walls of Kiev."

Snorri's face hardened again as he looked at the barge. Coel felt his own ire rising. He owed Tsapko. They all did. He turned to Reza. "So, you will deal with the barge captain alone, then?"

"Oh, no. Márta will be by my side, and Oleg must confront him. The two of you shall be there, as well. We shall all be there. I believe you will find it very educational."

* * *

Zuli swept into the room. Coel looked up from his mug of broth. It was flavored with enough expensive black pepper to give it real heat. The heel of hard, dark bread he dunked in it hung forgotten in his hand. Had Coel had not seen Zuli leave two hours earlier he would not have recognized her. She had changed from her clinging black wool garments and sable accessories. A shapeless, bleached linen dress concealed her figure. She had tied a red kerchief around her head and a brown-fringed shawl covered her shoulders. Battered shoes made of birch bast covered her feet and she did not wear any stockings. She carried a great round wicker basket with linens in it. Her transformation was startling. Even Zuli's complexion was changed. The olive hue of her skin was now pale and her cheeks were rosy and her lips red.

Zuli looked like a little Russian peasant girl barely past the age of twelve.

"Well," She pulled off the kerchief and tossed it on the bed as she shook free her hair. "Tsapko knows you are here."

Reza reclined upon a divan with his feet on a cushioned stool. The house they inhabited was well off the beaten path, but well furnished. Reza seemed to have associates who owed him favors everywhere. The sorcerer nodded. "I suspected he would have spies out on the docks. What has he done about it?"

"He has used some of your gold to hire himself a small army of bully boys off the waterfront, and several swordsmen of low morals but decent reputations to lead them."

"Indeed," Reza did not sound concerned.

"He has also hired a wizard."

"Has he now?"

"I have never heard of him. His name is Borislav. They say he is a conjurer. People in the marketplace are afraid of him."

Reza steepled his fingers. "Is he licensed by the Church?"

Zuli nodded. Reza's lips twisted in contempt. "Where are they now?"

"They are at a tavern on the wharves, called the Pig and Pipes. They are waiting for you."

"Did you acquire the things I asked of you?"

"Oh yes, and some other things, too," Zuli grinned impishly and reached into her gigantic basket. "Here is your chess set."

Reza took the board and opened the drawers to count the pieces. "Excellent."

Zuli smiled at Coel coyly. "This could only be yours." She pulled Coel's scarlet and black plaid *bratt* out with a flourish and flung it at him.

Coel grinned stupidly as he caught the garment and rubbed the soft wool between his fingers. "Thank you."

"You are welcome." Zuli shrugged carelessly. "Oh, and here, Márta. I got you some pants." Zuli pulled out a wad of gray material and tossed it to Márta. They were the same kind of clinging wool hose as Zuli's. Even to Coel's eye they appeared to be several cuts too small for Márta's frame.

Márta held up the leggings and examined them. She looked absolutely scandalized. "I am not wearing these."

Zuli tossed her head. "Fine. Go face Tsapko's bravos with Coel's cloak wadded around your hips for all I care."

Márta flung the garment in the corner. Her fists clenched as she glared at Zuli. Reza seemed unamused. "Zuleikha."

Zuli cocked her head innocently. "Yes?"

The sorcerer's tone of voice was dangerously neutral. "Márta is my bodyguard. If she is to fight for me, she must be suitably attired. I should think you would understand this. I asked you to acquire her some trousers or suitable tunic. You told me you understood when I asked this of you."

It was the first time Coel had seen Zuli lose control of a situation. Her smile faltered. She forced it back onto her face with effort. "It was only a jest."

"You have failed me."

Zuli's eyes flared open in naked fear. "I will fetch them immediately."

She snatched the kerchief and shawl from the bed and ran from the room. Oleg looked as if he wanted to say something, but thought wiser of it. Snorri sat on the edge of the bed running a honing steel over the single edge of his heavy sword. He ran his eye down the blade. "Walladid."

"Yes?"

"You do not seem worried about Tsapko's precautions."

"No, I am not."

"Now, I'll split the heads of his paid bully-boys without a qualm," Snorri ceased his sword maintenance. "But Zuli says he has hired a sorcerer."

"So it seems."

Coel did not like the sound of facing rival sorcerers, either. He had seen men brought down by magical means in battles when he had been a mercenary. Far too often cold steel and a strong right arm were not enough against sorcery. Faith failed far to often as well, unless you were a priest or a paladin upon whom the Mantle of Power had descended. Coel was neither, and he had seen too many good men die by the black arts, both sanctioned and unsanctioned by the Church. "Do you know this Borislav, then? Zuli says he is feared in the marketplace."

"I know no more about him than you," Reza cocked his head in question. "As I recall, Coel, you told me your father hired you tutors in Latin and other classical subjects. Tell me, did you study the Greeks?"

"Aye, I did."

"Socrates?"

Coel answered cautiously. "Aye."

Reza wore the same expression he'd had on the Dnieper after the beast's first attack. Coel tensed inwardly. He was being tested again. Reza opened one hand in a graceful gesture. "Well, then, Coel. Using deductive reasoning, tell us, what do you make of this Borislav?"

All eyes turned.

Coel's broth sat growing cold in his hand. He felt himself start to sweat.

Coel remembered summer days in Wales shut up in a small, stuffy room with his tutor, dying to play hurly with the other boys, or hunting, riding, playing his harp, or, better yet, to be walking through the mountain forest as his mother told him its secrets. Anything other than sitting in the hot little room while his tutor stared down at him with the dreaded switch tapping in his palm. Coel also remembered his iron resolve. One overriding imperative had kept his nose to the grindstone. He would do anything to please his father. Anything to take his father's smile away from his older brother Bryn and make it shine down upon his own brow. Anything, including learning the useless lessons of his dandified Norman tutors.

Coel remembered Socrates, and his god damned deductive reasoning as well.

Coel pondered.

All he knew of Borislav was what Zuli had told them. However, Reza was right. It was more than enough. Coel sipped his broth and smiled.

"Borislav is the kind of warlock who can be hired by a barge captain. Borislav is available to a man like Tsapko, to do his dirty work, even though the Church licenses his magic. His tricks are enough to earn him silver to pay his license, but I would venture to guess that he is not powerful enough for the Church to see him as a threat and suppress him, nor has he shown enough potential for the Church Magicians to conscript him into their ranks. They allow him his mercenary behavior in the markets because he is a source of revenue. Perhaps he does some of their dirty work for them among the commoners as well. Fishwives and laborers in the marketplace fear him, but I suspect few else. My deduction is that he is more of an illusionist than a true conjurer." Coel tossed back his broth decisively. "Smoke and mirrors are his trade."

Reza clapped his hands. "Excellent!"

Coel beamed under the sorcerer's approval. Snorri ceased his sharpening. "You know, Coel? It never ceases to amaze me that a man with a mind as keen as yours could be so terrible at chess."

Coel regarded Snorri sourly. Both of them turned as Márta spoke.

"I agree with Coel."

Coel stared at Márta in surprise. There was no smile of approval on Márta's face. She was simply stating her opinion. She'd had no smile for him since the river encampment. The two times Coel had tried to talk to her she had walked away from him without a word. They had gone back to the awkwardness of ignoring each other. "Nevertheless, even if Borislav is as weak as we believe, Tsapko is wily. It would not surprise me if the Captain tried to put an arrow into you while you are dealing with this market-stall magician he has hired. I think we should be prepared."

"Of course," Reza nodded. "As always, I leave these matters in your hands. Tsapko is mine. That is all I shall say on the matter."

Márta turned her eyes on Coel. "I stay by Reza's side. Bring your bow. If any of Tsapko's men have missile weapons, kill them."

"Aye," It seemed like sound strategy to Coel. "As you say."

Márta tilted her head in thought. "Kiev is a civilized city. Even on the docks, we cannot run about in full armor without attracting attention from the city watch." She looked at Oleg. "I do not think you can walk about with your glittering spears, either. Have you anything else?"

Oleg shrugged unhappily. "I have my knife."

"You have a sword," Snorri held out his blade and smiled. "Consider it a wedding present."

Oleg took the heavy, single edged blade wonderingly. Snorri

grinned at the awe on the young man's face. Oleg held up the sword and savored the feel of it in his hand. Oleg's expression clouded as he lowered the blade. "I thank you, Yaroslav."

"Call me Snorri, my friends do."

Oleg ears turned red, but he sighed unhappily. "Thank you, Snorri, but I think you should keep it. I have never even held a sword before, much less swung one. I would not know what to do with it."

Snorri chewed his mustaches in thought. "You've used your knife in your barge work, have you not?"

Oleg looked at Snorri in confusion. "Of course."

"Oh, well, then. A sword is just a great big knife. Pretend you're back on the barge. Your opponent is a piece of thick rope. Pretend you have to cut the rope, or you're going to lose the mast. You have to cut through it with one swing."

The young man nodded thoughtfully.

Snorri nodded back. "Do it."

Oleg blinked.

Snorri roared. "Do it!"

Oleg stomped forward and whipped the blade around at shoulder height. The keen edge hissed through the air. Coel nodded. Oleg had naturally good wrist action. He also recovered and held the blade in front of himself again without being told. Snorri nodded his satisfaction. "Good. If it comes to it, strike just like that, and strike first. If you miss? Just jump in close and ram the sword home like a spear. It is amazing how many fools forget about the point."

Oleg tested the point of the blade with his thumb as he considered Snorri's wisdom. The young man had been receiving education in all manner of things lately. Coel drew his woolen *bratt* around his shoulders and appreciated the wool's familiar weight. The *bratt* smelled fresh and still held the sun's warmth from being displayed in the market place.

Zuli came back into the room and threw a pair of white linen trousers at Márta. Reza rose from his chair. "We shall go visit Tsapko in half an hour. All of you all should wear as much armor as you can conceal under your clothing. Zuli, go to the docks and tell me if anything changes. Marius, come with me."

The sorcerer and the priest went into the adjoining room and closed the door behind them. Coel looked over at Márta. She regarded him coolly. Orsini, Oleg and Snorri caught the look between them and turned to one another and began speaking loudly about nothing in particular. Coel met Márta's gaze and inclined his head toward the open window.

Márta shook her head.

Coel silently clasped his hands together in prayer and raised his eyebrows imploringly.

Márta's brow furrowed. Her eyes glanced off to the side as if she were doing something against her better judgment. Coel walked to the window. The linen curtains blew in the afternoon breeze. The house they inhabited was tall and narrow. Two floors below, a paved street drew a straight line deeper into the city. Looking out over the city, there was a good view of the houses and shops that clung to Kiev's inner wall. Márta appeared at Coel's elbow. Her brown eyes stared up into Coel's. Coel swallowed. He had been afraid of an angry "What?" but it was worse to have her just standing there staring at him like he was a bug.

Coel sighed. "You and I must speak."

Márta's lips thinned. "Now is not a good time."

"Aye, I know," Coel searched for words. "And I know that I have wronged you."

"I know you know, but you have said that to me before. I grow weary of your apologies. I am sick to death of your insults. I will not stand for it anymore."

Coel's tongue deserted him. He could think of nothing to say. There was no reason why she should put up with his wretched behavior. He would break the bones of a man who spoke to a woman of his acquaintance the way he had spoken to Márta.

"Coel, I see that you are sorry. I have seen you moping about after what you have said to me, and I know you suffer over it," Márta shook her head in exasperation. "Sometimes you are the most beautiful man I have ever met, and then, the next, you are such sheep dip!"

Orsini, Oleg and Snorri looked up. Coel and Márta glared at them. They hurriedly looked down again and began speaking of sailing. Márta bit her lip. "I leaned upon you when I was wounded, I know that. I had thought I might die, and the healing left me a bit unbalanced, and then Zuli showed up, and she always makes me angry." Márta's eyes grew shiny with held back tears. "But I never, ever, did anything to deserve what you said to me," Her eyes looked into his searchingly. "How could you be so evil?"

Coel flinched. He looked at Orsini's massive back. He knew the dwarf could hear every word. The dwarf's words came to Coel. He had to speak to someone. No matter how hard he held on, his anger was sifting through his fingers like sand. The only thing he could close his fists around were the empty ashes of bitterness. Orsini was right. He was becoming less and less of a man.

Coel swallowed his pride. "As you say, this is not the time. However, if both of us survive this afternoon, I owe you an explanation. Will you have dinner with me, alone, tonight?"

"No." Márta leaned back warily. "I cannot. My first duty is to see to Reza and his safety, at all times. You know that."

Coel's shoulders sank. He looked over at the huddled group by the bed, and he squared his shoulders again. "If I pay Snorri and Orsini, in gold, to stay by Reza's side and guard his life, and Reza himself is willing, would you come?"

Márta looked out the window.

Coel spread his hands helplessly. "If I am going to walk the earth like a bucket of sheep dip with legs, it would be best if you knew why."

Márta did not answer.

Coel threw caution to the wind. "We can eat anywhere you want. You choose."

Márta deigned to look at him. "There is an eating house I have heard of here in Kiev, called the Golden Horn. It has a very high reputation. You could not afford it."

Coel loomed to his full height. "Reza has promised to make good the money Tsapko stole from us, and I still have twenty pieces of unspent gold from my last pay."

Márta looked like she might spit out the window. She was not happy with herself or him. "Very well. If both of us live, and if Reza gives his permission, I will allow you to buy me dinner. I will listen to what you have to say. However, I still do not forgive you, nor am I making any promise to do so."

Coel nodded eagerly. "That is fairer than I deserve."

"We had best prepare for Tsapko and his friends. I must armor myself," Márta went into the other room.

The tightness in Coel's stomach gave way to a giddy glow. Márta was talking to him again. Márta would have dinner with him. Coel's chest swelled as he savored her words. Sometimes, he was the most beautiful man she had ever met. Coel grinned like an idiot. He might just take on Tsapko and his gang of cutthroats single-handed.

* * *

The crowds on the docks of Kiev thinned in the late afternoon. Coel wore his brigandine beneath his *bratt* and his steel skullcap underneath his hat. The longbow was taller than he was, but he kept most of its length close to his side and his arrows thrust out of sight through his belt. With their weapons under their cloaks, the party looked purposeful if not particularly war-like. The six of them strode down the docks to the place Zuli had indicated. Zuli was nowhere to be seen.

Coel eyed the passers by and people lounging on the dock. No one took much notice of the party. Orsini drew a few stares, but he was a dwarf. Kiev was the jewel of the Russias and the Queen of the Dnieper. Non-humans were not unknown here and were more of a curiosity than an event. Márta drew more looks, but those were mostly appreciative leers from workers on the docks. Reza spoke. "Keep an eye out. We are approaching our destination."

Coel slid an arrow out of his belt and held it along his arm. Snorri, Oleg, and Orsini's arms all shifted beneath their cloaks as they gripped their weapons.

"There!" Oleg spoke low and urgently. "There is Meklin!"

Coel glanced off towards the river. Coel had not known the man's name, but he recognized one of Tsapko's crewmen. The man leaned against a stack of planks and chewed a piece of straw. He turned his head and nodded once at someone further down the docks. A man Coel did not recognize acknowledged the nod and walked around the corner of an inn. Coel fingered the bodkin headed arrow under his *bratt*. "How do you want to play this?"

Márta eyed their surroundings. "I say we follow him around the corner. It is probably where they have set their trap, and probably where Tsapko will be found."

"I agree," Reza said. "Let us finish this quickly. I have other matters to attend to here in Kiev."

The party approached the inn.

The Pig and Pipes was more a tavern than an inn, and a shabby-looking one at that. Its roof needed re-thatching, and by the piles of offal lying nearby, it seemed to cater mostly to the local fishermen. It was afternoon, and the fishmongers were pulling down their stalls. The best of the morning catch had been sold, and what remained was quickly being salted and packed into barrels. The remnants were thrown onto the docks. The cats picked disdainfully through the piles of tails and guts, choosing the choicest morsels. They were the fattest bunch of strays Coel had ever seen. They were well tolerated on docks. In winter they more than earned their keep culling the rats from the grain stores in the warehouses. Coel watched them eat leisurely. There seemed to be plenty for all. The spring thaw was good to everyone in Kiev.

Coel pulled a second arrow from his belt and held it with the first along the length of his arm. They were drawing close to the inn. In the confines of an alley, there would be time to loose one, possibly two shafts at most, though he had brought eight with him. With luck, there would be no loosing of shafts at all, but Coel was not willing to bet on that. Tsapko had taken all of their equipment and gear, as well as the gold and silver the party had taken with them out of Smolensk. Tsapko seemed the kind of man who that once he got his fingers on something, it would have to be pried forth from his clenched fist.

Coel kept his eye on the door to the inn. It stood open and

typical tavern sounds came out of it. They walked past and moved to the corner. An alley wide enough for a pair of wagons to pass opened before them.

The party halted.

A dozen men lounged about in the street behind the inn. All of them were large. About half were dressed in the rough woolen tunics and trousers of men who worked the docks. Some carried axe handles and knives. One carried a long gaff with a wickedly curved iron hook mounted to its head. Several leaned on axes. Four of the men were better dressed. Sword scabbards hung down from beneath their cloaks.

Reza stepped forward. "Where is Tsapko?"

One of the swordsmen banged on the back door of the tavern. Tsapko walked out with a huge swordsman by his side. The man was as tall as Coel and as stoutly built as Snorri. Tsapko himself wore his long knife and carried a hatchet thrust through the front of his belt. The river captain smiled thinly. "I had thought you dead, Walladid."

Snorri thrust out his axe from beneath his cloak and brandished it accusingly at the barge captain. "You are a rodent, Tsapko, and I'm going to cut off your goddamned head!"

It struck Coel that Snorri was holding his axe in his left hand. His right remained hidden under his cloak.

Oleg threw back his cloak and put a hand on the sword Snorri had given him. "Damn you, Uncle! You stranded us! You left us to die!"

Reza held up a restraining hand. He kept his gaze on Tsapko. The wizard's voice was calm. "You have money and goods that belong to myself and my associates. Return them, and you will live."

"Oh?" Tsapko's thin smile turned sneering. "And you will forgive and forget our misunderstanding?"

"I said you shall survive. You will still suffer for stranding us and breaking your contract with me, but I give you my word I will not kill you."

Tsapko scoffed. "I think my compensation has been fair. You put my barge in danger. You endangered the lives of me and my crew. One of my crewmen is dead because of you. One of my customers died, and his family lost a very valuable animal."

"That is true," Reza conceded. "And that is why I am willing to show you a certain measure of mercy."

Tsapko was unimpressed. "You know, I have grown fond of the Welshman's harp, and--" The barge captain suddenly noticed that Coel was wearing his *bratt* once more. Tsapko's eyes turned mean, and his glance slid to the inn. "And there is a bar girl inside who looks well in your whore's silk pants."

Márta rolled her eyes.

Coel ignored Tsapko's remarks and kept his gaze ranging across the assailants arrayed before him. The swordsmen in the alley kept their arms hidden beneath their cloaks. Coel did not care for it. Bravos liked to brandish their swords and show off their finery, not cover themselves like monks. Something was wrong.

Tsapko shook his head disparagingly. "I saw your sorcery on the river, Walladid. You threw a log. I know hearth witches living in the forest who can do better than that."

Reza nodded amiably. "I hope you have hired one to defend you."

Tsapko's grin soured. He turned to his gigantic swordsman. The big man banged on the back door. Tsapko looked upon Reza in mock pity. The back door of the inn opened, and two more men came out into the street. One was another gigantic swordsman who was the twin of the first. Coel frowned at the second man. He was tall, and wore a long blue velvet tunic and matching wide-legged trousers. A thick belt with heavy silver medallions circled his waist. A silver circlet held back his long black hair. He was a big man with piercing eyes and a jutting, cleft jaw. He looked every inch a sorcerer. He regarded Reza measuringly and then turned a disappointed eye on Tsapko.

"This is the Persian you told me about?"

Tsapko's lip curled. "The very one."

Reza looked the man up and down curiously. "You are Borislav."

Borislav rose to his full height. "I see you have heard of me."

"No, I had not heard of you until today. However, I am informed by my servants that you are feared in the market stalls." Reza opened his hands dismissingly. "Of course, I do not frequent such places. So it is not surprising that you are unknown to me."

Borislav's face clouded. "I have heard about your magic upon the river, Persian. Using fire to make fire, and burning yourself in doing it." The Russian sorcerer snorted. "A real wielder of power can call upon fire without its presence."

Coel's fist tightened on his bow. Borislav held up his right hand. Fire blazed in his palm. He tossed the crackling flames to his left hand and then back. When he did, he suddenly held a glowing ball of orange fire in both hands. Borislav smiled his condescension as he passed flame from hand to hand. "Like so."

"Now, what you say is true," Reza admitted. "A true wielder of power should be able to produce fire without its presence. Perhaps a demonstration would be in order."

Borislav ceased his juggling. The flames crackled in his hands as he looked at Reza askance.

Reza's smile widened and he held up his own hands. "You see, Borislav, what you hold in your hands is an illusion."

Borislav blinked.

Reza's black eyes went flat as he clenched his fists. "Real fire burns."

Borislav screamed. Coel started as the balls of fire Borislav held flared blue and engulfed his hands. The Russian wizard howled and flailed as the smell of scorched flesh filled the alley.

"Kill them!" Tsapko screamed. "Kill them all!"

Coel ignored Borislav and drew his bow. Tsapko had his hand-axe out of his belt and raised it for a throw. Coel loosed his shaft. Tsapko gasped as the arrow skewered his shoulder. The hand-axe clattered to the cobbles. Coel nocked his second arrow as Tsapko fell to his knees. Weapons leaped from their sheaths all around.

Borislav screamed hideously as his hands burned down to bone. Reza's brow furrowed, and the blue flames flared higher. He suddenly threw his hands up into the air. Borislav's whole body went up like a torch. He flailed and staggered like a marionette of flame. The heat he threw off filled the alley. The stench of scorched flesh was nauseating. Borislav's silver circlet melted and ran down his burning face. The wizard threw back his blackened head and let out a howl of blind agony.

It was more than Coel could stand. He sighted down his shaft and loosed. Borislav's head jerked back, and he fell dead and burning to the cobbles with an arrow through his eye-socket.

The hired swords threw back their cloaks and revealed the mail shirts they had been hiding as they drew blades. Coel nocked his third arrow.

The bravos had been hiding more than mail. Two of them held small hand-wound crossbows. Coel had seen their like in Scotland. The Border Reivers called such weapons a 'latch'. They were too light for hunting game and not powerful enough to penetrate armor in war. It was weapon made only for murder. Coel loosed his arrow as one of the swordsmen took aim at Reza. The Welsh longbow had originally been made with bear and boar in mind. The bow Coel himself carried had been designed for war. He had chosen bodkin points rather than broadheads for this encounter. The bodkin points were long, narrow, three-edged pyramids of armor-piercing steel. Sparks shrieked on the swordsman's stomach as mail links burst. The shaft sank into the man's middle up to the fletching.

Coel pulled another arrow from his belt.

Another hired swordsman aimed his latch at Reza.

Snorri let out a shout and hurled something in his right hand. The hired sword staggered and clutched his throat. Crow feather fletching stuck out from his neck. Snorri had kept three of the goblin darts from the ambush on the steppes. It appeared the Rus had been practicing with them. He pulled another dart from his belt.

Coel hurled down his bow and drew his sword. One of the huge twins was pulling Tsapko to his feet. Coel roared at him. "You!"

The big man dropped Tsapko back to the ground. The bravo drew his sword and filled his left hand with a dagger. The giant brandished both weapons and roared back in bad Latin. "Come, skinny! Come on!"

Coel came on.

He eyed the knife in the giant's left hand. It was a style of fighting he had seen in Spain and he thought he could counter it, but there were too many opponents, and Coel had no time to fence. He would have to rely on his armor. Coel lunged in and swung his blade as hard as he could with both hands at the big man's sword. The two swords rang together. The big man grunted with the shock but held onto his weapon. He thrust his dagger up at Coel's belly in return. Coel grit his teeth as the dagger jabbed against the pit of his stomach. The blow hurt, but his armor held. He leaped forward and rammed the steel pommel of the Academy blade into the bridge of the big man's nose. Blood burst from the man's nostrils, and tears squirted from his eyes as cartilage crunched. Coel struck him a second blow to the septum and the giant staggered as facial bones cracked. Coel gave him no time to recover. The war-sword whirled around and chopped into the big man's temple. The giant's eyes rolled upward and he fell without a sound.

Tsapko clutched the arrow in his shoulder as he rose to one knee. His left hand fumbled for his knife. Coel strode forward and kicked the barge captain in the teeth. Tsapko collapsed to the cobbles again. Coel sought another opponent. Márta had cut down two men already. Her scimitar was a gleaming blur in her hands and two more men with axes retreated before her. Snorri traded blows with a dock man armed with an axe handle. The river brute was clearly outclassed. Snorri hooked the club out of the man's hands and whirled in a short, vicious circle. The broad-axe sank into the hired fighter's side. The man groaned and folded in half around the embedded blade. He fell as Snorri kicked him to free his axe.

Snorri brandished his axe high and roared his defiance. Oleg stood with his chest heaving. His chin was cut and his left arm was bloody where the gaff had torn him. The sword he wielded was red, as well. A dockhand lay dead at his feet. The remaining dock bullies threw down their weapons and fled.

The giant's twin stood his ground and weaved back and forth in front of Orsini. The dwarf held his short sword in one hand and a small, blue-steel buckler in the other. The giant had filled his hands with sword and dagger like his twin. He edged around the dwarf warily. Orsini gestured him forward with his short sword. "At your soonest convenience, if you please."

The giant snarled. He thrust his dagger out and raised his sword high over his head. Orsini leaned away from the feint with the dagger. The sword whistled down upon the dwarf from on high as the giant swung with all his might. Coel's eyes widened. It was a butcher's blow, and Orsini made no move to maneuver. The blade hissed down like an axe. At the last moment the dwarf punched his steel buckler up.

Steel rang on steel. The big man gasped in pain and his sword shivered in his hand. His fingers spasmed as the shock went up his arm. His sword fell hopelessly bent from his hand. The giant yelped as Orsini whipped his buckler about. The dwarven steel shield broke bones as it slapped the dagger from the big man's other hand. The giant staggered back before the dwarf.

Orsini nodded mercifully. "You may run."

The big man shoved his battered hands into his armpits and ran for his life down the alley.

Coel knelt on Tsapko's chest and relieved him of his knife. The alley ahead was empty save for the wounded and the dead. Borislav lay smoking on the paving stones, his body folded upon itself like a charred and blackened cricket. Coel looked back over his shoulder. Reza and Marius had not moved. Reza favored Coel with a smile. "Good, you have kept the Captain alive. Be so kind as to let me speak with him."

Coel stood away. Snorri pulled his goblin dart from the throat of a dead bravo. Coel nodded at his friend. "A neat trick."

"It was," Snorri wiped off the dart head on the dead man's beard. "I am getting rather good with these things."

They both turned at the sound of Reza's voice. "Tsapko!" The Persian slowly raised his hand. "I bid you, rise, and face me!"

The barge captain lurched to his feet like he had been yanked up by a rope. He clutched the arrow in his shoulder. Blood ran down his chin. His face was ashen horror as he stared at Reza. The sorcerer's face was implacable as he held the man with his eyes. "Snorri Yaroslav has named you, Tsapko son of Maxim! You are a rodent! As a rodent on the docks you have lived and as a rodent on the docks you shall die, for breaking your word to me!"

Tsapko froze, shivering in place as Reza's hand closed into a single pointing finger. A great line of concentration drew down between Reza's eyebrows as he turned his hand over and opened it. Tsapko trembled violently where he stood. Reza's mouth twitched open. His teeth bared with effort. He raised his hand slowly. Tsapko whimpered in fear and rose up on his toes as if Reza's hand lifted him. Reza's hand stopped. His lips moved. Coel could not hear what he said, but his skin began crawling and his shoulders twitched.

Reza's hand shook as his lips moved faster. Something unseen seemed to emanate from the sorcerer. Coel felt the hairs on the back of his neck stand up. His teeth seemed to buzz in his mouth. He looked to Snorri. The Rus' fists were white around his axe. Tsapko stood on his toes shuddering violently. He bled from his nose, ears and eyes. Reza's whole body shook with effort. The air filled with a strange whining noise like the keening of locusts. The noise grew until it hurt Coel's ears.

Reza let out a great shout. His hand snapped down in front of him as he made a fist.

The barge captain let out an inhuman scream.

Snorri shouted in consternation. Coel jumped back in horror. Oleg threw up.

The barge captain's body collapsed upon itself. His limbs snapped and broke as they curled inward and sucked into his clothes. His skull fell inward and pulled into his neck, and the arrow in his shoulder broke into halves and fell away. Tsapko disappeared. His clothes fell in a limp pile.

A small rustle of wind filled the space where Tsapko had been.

Reza wiped his brow and smiled to himself. He strode forward to the pile of clothes and knelt beside them. He tossed aside Tsapko's trousers and tunic and picked up a boot. He shook it and tossed it aside. He picked up the other boot and upended it.

A rat fell to the stones and twitched.

Coel stared dumbstruck.

Oleg doubled over heaving.

The rat bled from its right fore shoulder. It appeared to be nothing more than a rat, but as Coel stared at it, there was something undeniably Tsapko-like about it. Coel had no doubt in his mind whatsoever. The bleeding, twitching rodent lying upon the cobbles was the barge captain.

Snorri made the sign against the evil eye with a shaky hand. He spoke low. "Coel?"

"Aye."

"Did you see that?"

Coel nodded slowly. "I saw it."

Reza picked the rat up by its tail. It jerked and twisted feebly. He walked over to Márta. The swordswoman stood over one of the surviving bravos. The tip of her scimitar pressed painfully into his Adams-apple. She had cut him badly under his arm in the fight, and blood ran down his side and pooled beneath him. He stared up at Márta piteously. Reza loomed over him. Márta pulled her blade back slightly as the bravo screamed in fear.

Reza scowled. His eyes widened even as his eyebrows drew down. He stared deeply into the man's eyes. "Control yourself."

The man trembled in terror, but he held his tongue under the sorcerer's gaze.

"You saw what I did to Borislav?"

The man's voice came out in a strangled gasp. "Yes!"

"You saw what I did to Tsapko?"

The man turned white.

"Do you want something similar to happen to you?"

The man cringed against the stones and shook his head desperately.

Reza knelt and dangled the bleeding rat in front of the man's eyes. The bravo flinched as drops of blood spattered in his face. "Go to the market. Tell all you meet what happened here. I want my property returned. Let it be known to all that what belongs to me is cursed. Neither the Pope in Rome nor the White Christ himself will be able to help those who choose to keep that which is mine. Do you understand?"

The man nodded violently. Reza nodded his satisfaction. "Marius."

The priest came forward and knelt by the bravo's side. The man shrieked as Marius slapped his hand against the wound under his arm and clenched it shut. Marius made no intonations to the heavens. He simply grimaced and shook the wound under his palm.

The bravo howled and flailed his limbs. He suddenly sagged like a boned fish.

Marius wiped his hand on the front of the man's shirt and stood.

Reza gestured down the alley with the rat. "Be gone."

The man stared about for a moment in fear and confusion, then leaped to his feet and bolted down the alley. His wound no longer seemed to bother him. Both his arms pumped furiously as he ran for his life.

Reza held the bleeding rat out to Márta. It twisted on the end of its tail and made pathetic squeaking noises. "Márta. Go give this to the cats on the wharf."

Coel and Snorri watched in shock as Márta sheathed her blade and took Tsapko by his tail. She held him out at arm's length distastefully and walked out of the alley for the fishmonger's stalls.

"Coel."

Coel jumped as Reza spoke to him. The sorcerer smiled amiably. "You have my permission to dine with Márta tonight."

CHAPTER THIRTEEN

Coel stared at the bed. Every possession he'd brought from Moscow and Smolensk lay upon it. The party's belongings had been appearing in piles on the doorstep all day. Reza's curse was being taken with deadly seriousness.

Even the chest of money had been returned.

Snorri sat on his bed counting coins. Oleg sat next to him and held the sack of silver Reza had given him with disbelief. It was a large sack, and it bulged. He pulled out handful and watched the heavy silver pieces sift through his fingers and clink back into the bag. Within the last week the young river hand had killed a demon, been seduced by a beautiful woman, won his first sword fight, inherited a barge and earned a knight's ransom. He was a seventeen-year-old peasant lad born on the river, and he'd had more adventures than most men lived in a lifetime.

Coel took up his harp and ran his fingers over the bronze strings. The instrument was a little out of tune, but other than that it had survived their separation. He cocked his head as he plucked the first string and turned its peg. Oleg cinched his sack of silver closed and looked to Snorri.

"Yaroslav?"

"I said you might call me Snorri. Indeed, now that we are brothers in arms? I would prefer it."

Oleg blushed. "Snorri?"

Snorri kept counting coins. "What?"

"You saw what Reza did to my step-uncle."

"Yes."

"And to Borislav."

Snorri set down his sack. "If you are asking if was I unsettled by it, Oleg, I have no cause to lie. I will have nightmares about it for the rest of my days."

"You have been to the Golden City. You were a Varangian and guarded the Emperor. Have you ever seen such thing?"

Snorri ran his hand over his freshly shaven head. "Well, with my own eyes I saw the old Patriarch, Milos the II, heal a leper; and it was long before my service in the Guard, but I was told he called lightning from a clear sky to strike down the pagan Uzbeks when they tried to overrun Armenia years ago. But he is the Patriarch of the Orthodox Church and rival to the Pope in Rome. One would expect such a man to wield true power. What Reza did in the alley?" Snorri trailed off shaking his head.

Oleg turned to Coel. "Have you ever seen such things?"

"I am no Paladin, Oleg, but it is part of a Paladin's duty to face the sorcery of those who have given themselves to the Black Arts. I saw men brought down by sorcery when I fought in Spain against the Moors. In Wales, there are woods witches who can blight crops, bring disease, and cause children to be stillborn. I knew a Druid who could call birds to his hand and claimed he communed with the trees. Many believed him. My mother had the Sight. She could--" Coel stopped and shook his head. "One hears stories of wizards who can turn men into toads, but for all I have ever seen, stories are all they are. Stories for frightening children and tall tales by the fire. As for turning a man into a rat? That is magic of the highest order, and banned magic. Banned by the Pope and the Patriarch, and, I would bet all the silver in this room that it is banned by Moor, Saracen, and Turk alike."

Oleg was clearly disturbed. "And Márta, she just took Tsapko and threw him to the cats. She did not even blink. I tried not to look as we left the alley, but I saw. A cat had him under its paws, it was . . . " Oleg's shoulders jerked with revulsion.

Coel, too, had been giving the matter a great deal of thought. Márta had disposed of Tsapko with as much emotion as emptying a chamber pot. It gave him pause.

"Speaking of Márta," Snorri perked a scarred eyebrow. "Don't you have a dinner appointment?"

"Aye." Coel's initial giddiness of the morning had drained away. As the hour approached for his dinner with Márta, he felt an increasing sense of dread. He threw off his white linen shirt. He had no idea what he would say to her. Orsini had told him to tell her the truth about his past, but whenever he thought of the past his feelings grew tangled and the only thing that straightened them out again was rage. Coel kicked out of his wool trousers. He reached into his belongings and pulled out his scarlet tunic. He frowned determinedly as he donned it. It was a fine spring night. He would forgo trousers or hose and let the citizens of Kiev think whatever they wanted. It was his best, and the familiar cut and feel of the tunic was a comfort. He needed all the assurance he could get. He pulled on his sandals and tied back his hair with a black ribbon as he stood. Coel took a deep breath. "How do I look?"

Snorri rolled his eyes. "Like some pagan Irish."

Oleg ceased his pondering and stared at Coel in surprise. "You are not wearing pants!"

"No," Coel's eyebrows drew down. "I am not."

"You're not wearing any under breeches?" Oleg blinked incredulously. "Or linens, or hose?"

Coel's back stiffened. "No."

"Nothing at all?"

"No!"

"Oh," Oleg quickly looked away. "I see."

The young Rus was appalled.

Coel scowled as he buckled on his sword belt and hooked his pouch to it. He threw his *bratt* over his shoulders. He turned on the two Russians sitting on the bed and glared at them defiantly. "I am going to go have dinner with Márta now."

Oleg's gaze fixed unhappily on Coel's naked knees. "So, you are going to the Golden Horn?"

"Yes! I'm going to the Golden Horn! With Márta! Dressed like this!"

"Oh," Oleg's face reddened with embarrassment for the both of them. "I see."

Coel spun on his heel.

Snorri spoke in a loud whisper as Coel strode to the door.

"Coel is a barbarian, Oleg. A Celt. Just be thankful he did not strip naked and paint himself blue."

Coel's spine went rigid, but he forced himself to open the door. He stepped through it with grim determination.

Oleg was incredulous. "Are the Welsh really painted savages?"

"Oh, for God's sake, then!" Coel whirled. "It was the Picts that painted themselves blue! That was in the time of the Romans! Centuries ago!"

Snorri nodded. "Yes, the Pictish Welsh."

Coel exploded. "The Picts were *Scotti*! They lived in the North! Welshmen are *Cymru*! We live in the West! What the hell is wrong with you?"

"Oh, well, I am often mistaken. Thank you for explaining things," Snorri nodded at Oleg sagely. "So, you see, Oleg. Picts paint themselves blue, and Welshman do not wear pants."

Coel spoke through clenched teeth. "I am going to go have dinner with Márta now."

Snorri nodded absently as he went back to counting his coins. "Oh, well, have a good time, then."

Coel's knuckles creaked. He ached to punch Snorri in the mouth.

Oleg nodded at Coel earnestly. "Oh, yes, please, have a good time."

The door shuddered on its hinges as Coel slammed it behind him.

* * *

Coel sat tongue-tied and stared across the table at Márta.

She was beautiful.

Candlelight made all women pretty. It made Márta absolutely radiant.

The Golden Horn was not an inn, but an eating-house. There

was no straw or rushes on the floor, nor any benches that doubled as beds. It catered exclusively to those who wanted the finest food and wine and did not care how much it cost them. The floor was polished hardwood, and the walls hung with rich tapestries portraying Roman splendor. Legions of candles filled every nook along the walls and clustered in the centers of the tables. A great, gold-painted horn of plenty hung over the door. At its mouth were wooden apples, bunches of grapes, and sheaves of wheat so cunningly painted they looked real.

Márta and Coel had an intimate table for two near one of the fireplaces. The table alone had cost Coel several silver pieces. The owner of the establishment was a long-bearded Rus named Kropotkin. He had almost turned them away at the door. The restaurateur seemed to have his doubts about women who wore pants and men who didn't. One flash of the gold in Coel's pouch quickly filled Kropotkin with the spirit of hospitality. Coel had never seen a man bow and scrape with such hand-wringing obsequiousness in his life.

The Golden Horn boasted of its husband and wife Magyar cooks. Coel's mouth watered at the smells that came from the kitchen. Márta and Coel sat munching Hungarian fry-bread and drank white wine from Lake Balaton. Coel was not much for dry whites, but it was perfectly thirst quenching when paired with the bread fried in butter and garlic. Coel watched Márta eat. She had manners, but she was not dainty about it. Márta was a woman who enjoyed her food. She licked her fingers after she finished. "My nanny used to make bread like this."

Coel leaped at the opportunity to talk about something besides what they had come to talk about. "Your nanny was a Magyar, then?"

"I am a Magyar," Márta finished her wine and poured herself another cup. "I was born in Hungary."

Coel cocked his head. "Really?"

The brown eyes locked with his. She seemed prepared to take offense at anything he said. "You doubt me?"

"No," Coel shook his head quickly. "It is just, there are not many Magyars left. One does not often meet them."

Márta nodded. "That is true. Most of the great families were wiped out long ago. Most of those that remained became vassals of the Austrians or shared the same fate as I did."

Coel sipped his wine. The story of Hungary's fall was one of great heroism and tragedy. It was at the twin cities of Buda and Pest that the northern hobgoblin horde was finally turned back, and the hobgoblins had devastated the entire eastern half of Hungary in their passing. Pest had burned to the ground as the battle had raged back and forth across the Danube. Buda held on for months while the rest of Europe raised Crusader armies and bickered amongst themselves. When the hobgoblin horde was finally broken and driven back, the Hungarian kingdom was broken as well. The flower of Magyar manhood had died in the defense. For two hundred years what was left had been a battleground between rival powers. The Germans claimed much of it, and Venice, the Byzantines, and the Poles carved up the rest of it. All of them raided deeply for slaves.

"When were you taken, if I may ask?"

"I was six, I believe," Márta stared deeply into her wine bowl. "It is strange what one remembers and what one does not."

"Where did you live?"

"In the mountains. I am not sure exactly where. We lived in a small castle. My father had been off fighting somewhere with his retainers. One night, slavers were within the walls. I think they must have paid someone to open the gates. They killed the few guards. My older brother, Arpad, was fourteen. He took up a sword. They killed him, too. I remember . . . " Márta's eyes grew very far away. "My mother took me by the hand, and we fled to the top of the keep. She wanted us to leap from it rather than be taken. She hugged me very tightly and told me not to be afraid. But I did not want to jump. I looked over the edge, and I kicked and screamed and broke free. The slavers smashed down the door, and I ran into their arms. My mother spit at them and cursed their unborn children. Then she hurled herself over the parapet to the stones below."

"I am sorry."

Márta's gazed into her bowl as if she could see her past in it. "I have almost no memories of my parents. My father was always away and had no time for a daughter who was too young to be married off. My mother was busy running our lands and holding court with the other Magyar clans who still lived free in the mountains. I hardly saw her. I was raised by my nanny." Márta's eyes focused on the room again. "It was my Nana that I cried for when they took me. I cried for her for weeks."

"Who were the slavers?"

"Byzantines. I remember being carried away. Then sailing in a ship. I was six, so I was made to do scullery work. Whenever I was beaten they yelled at me in Greek. Then I was sold again. There was another sea voyage. I did more scullery work in some woman's house. She spoke Arabic. She had a daughter my age, and we played together sometimes. A plague broke out, and most of the people of that household died. Then a man bought me." Márta shuddered. "He was horrible. He would always say to me, 'When you are older, just a little bit older.' I did not know what he meant then, but he gave me nightmares. His wife hated me, and so did his daughters. It was a very unhappy time. Fortunately, he went into debt and had to sell me." Márta brightened. "Reza bought me when I was eight. That was in Cairo."

Coel refilled her wine bowl. "What was that like, then?"

"Oh!" Márta smiled happily. "You cannot imagine what it was like to be an eight-year-old girl in the house of a sorcerer! He hired tutors to teach me reading and writing in Arabic and Latin. He was always traveling, and he often took me with him. He let me help him in his research. I carried things and stirred things and saw him perform all kinds of magics. It was a marvelous adventure, and I never scrubbed a floor unless I was the one who had dirtied it."

"How did you become a bodyguard, then?"

"Oh, well," Márta smiled bashfully. "I turned twelve."

Coel smiled back. "You started noticing boys."

"Oh, no," Márta blushed. "I was totally in love with Reza. He was my world. I could not have been more his slave if he had put a collar around my neck and chained me to the foot of his bed. If he had asked me to fling myself in boiling oil, I would have done it with a dreamy smile upon my face." Márta shook her head ruefully. "It must have grown too much for him. One day, he asked me if I would like to learn to ride horses and have friends my own age and live on an island. I was torn, but having friends and riding horses was more than the soul of a twelve-year-old girl could withstand. I let him convince me. So we took a ship to Cyprus, and I was commended to the care of the Sisters of Limmasol."

"That must have been hard."

One corner of Márta's mouth turned up. "Well, when Reza went to leave me I cried my eyes out. But there was this big French girl there who was sobbing as her parents got back in their carriage. That was Blandine. I told you about her. Reza told me she was sad and that I should go make friends with her. So I did, and that day I had a new best friend, and the next morning the sisters assigned me my own horse to take care of. Then everything was lessons and training and work around the convent. Reza wrote me and sent me gifts, and he would visit me at least once or twice a year. Reza took me from the convent when I was eighteen, and I have followed him as his bodyguard ever since."

"Why would the Sisters of Limmasol train a Persian sorcerer's slave girl?"

Márta took another sip of wine. "Well, I suppose it was an opportunity to give a European captive a Christian education, and Reza told them, and myself, that when he freed me I could rejoin the sisters and take vows, or else he would arrange a good marriage for me. I suspect he also donated a large sum of gold to the convent's coffers as well."

Coel smiled. "I suppose he did."

A shadow fell across the table. Kropotkin stood at Coel's elbow and gestured at the menu slate on the wall. "Has the gentleman decided?"

Coel looked at Márta. "What would you like?"

Márta smiled up at Kropotkin. "May we have a few more moments please?"

"Of course." Kropotkin backed away nodding ingratiatingly.

The smile died on Márta's face as she looked at Coel. "There was something you wanted to tell me?"

Coel felt his stomach tighten. With effort he relaxed it.

"Aye."

Márta's brown eyes stared into his without emotion.

Coel took a deep breath. "You asked me once if I had been sent to the Frontier over a woman," Coel let his breath out. "I was."

Márta's head cocked with interest. "And?"

Coel's hands tightened around his wine bowl. "She died."

"What happened?" Márta drew back at the expression on Coel's face. "If I may ask."

"It is what we are here for," Coel steeled himself. "I left the Paladin Academy, as you know. I sold my sword arm to anyone with gold. I fought a little in France and Burgundy. I drank a great deal. I gambled. I spent my money like water. The sword I carried always found me a job, but it brought problems. Many priests did not like the fact that I carried a Paladin's blade. I made enemies. After some attempts were made to separate me from my sword, I decided to leave France. I thought of joining the Crusade in the Holy Lands, but there would be even more priests there, and true Paladins. So I went to Spain to fight the Moors. The Christian lords in Spain were not giving away lands and titles like those you could get in the Holy Lands, so few Crusaders went there. But they paid gold to anyone who had skill at arms, and they asked few questions."

"I ended up in Aragon, serving with a border noble named Don Obregon. His family had been fighting the Moors for generations. Most of that fighting had been raiding, and he wanted good archers. There were some English warlords who had brought their retinues to seek their fortune in Spain. I convinced Don Obregon to hire one that had a contingent of Welsh bowmen. It cost the Don dearly, but he got a hundred good longbowmen for his gold, and we gave the local Moors a hard time of it."

Márta leaned forward. "What happened?"

"We raided deeper and deeper into Moorish land. One morning, we were ambushed in a tight place by cavalry. I took a spear in the stomach, but our healer had been killed. My men stuffed the wound with rags and carried me back into Christian lands. The wound was more than Don Obregon's own priest had the power to deal with. Don Obregon was only minor nobility, but his unceasing war against the Moors had attracted the favor of the warlord Lucas of Aragon. Lord Lucas in turn had attracted the favor of the Pope by creating several Spanish Crusader Orders. The Pope had sent a number of the Divine Daughters of Mercy to Lord Lucas to aid those Crusaders who were struck down in service to God."

"I have heard of the Divine Daughters. The nuns of that order are said to have extraordinary powers of healing."

"The Pope himself is their patron. They go where he sends them, often as a reward to those who have pleased the Pontiff. The Pope was pleased with Lord Lucas. Lord Lucas was pleased with Don Obregon. Don Obregon was fond of me. The Lord was fighting nearby, and the Don sent a messenger to him saying one of his best warriors was on the brink of death, one that killed a Moor with every arrow he loosed and carried a sword from Grande Triumphe. A litter arrived for me, and I was taken to the Lord's castle in Zaragoza. The trip nearly killed me. Stomach wounds are very bad. The only thing that can be said in their favor is that you can linger on in agony for days before you die. Still, as you know, healings work better the fresher the wound is. I was wounded in the vitals. It had taken days to get me to the capital. The wound had festered, and I was running hot with fever. A piece of the spearhead was still in my belly. It was thought I would surely die. I was given onto the ministrations of one of the Daughters of Divine Mercy."

Coel felt his eyes growing hot. "Her name was Marisol."

Márta was rapt. "Was she beautiful?"

"I thought so." Coel thought of the dark eyes that had haunted his dreams for years. Coel smiled in the candlelight. "She was thin, and small. But she had beautiful hands. My fever broke the moment she first laid them upon by brow. When she took off her habit, her hair fell down past her waist like a waterfall. I have never seen hair so dark and thick. She said it was her one vanity." Coel's voice trailed off for a moment. "Yes. She was beautiful."

"She healed you?"

"She did. She reached her fingers into my belly and drew the rusting spear-shard out of me. Then she set about putting my torn guts back in place and healing their wounds." Coel relived the memory. "It was no lightning healing like you received from Marius.

It was done over days, a little bit done with each touch of her fingers or the caress of her hand."

Márta sat entranced. "What was she like?"

"She was from Vigo, a coastal town in the Rias region of Galicia. It is the far northwest of Spain. They still speak a strange form of Celtic there, and their women folk are famed for their talent in witchcraft. Marisol was the seventh daughter of a seventh daughter. The weight of all those dowries was crushing her father's finances, so he sent his youngest off to the convent. When she took the vows of a nun, her power to heal began to manifest itself. She grew famous, and she was summoned to Rome. The Pope himself ordained her as a Daughter of Divine Mercy. She said that God was her only love until she met me."

"She fell in love with you?"

"We fell in love with each other. I never set out to seduce one of the Pope's handmaids, and I believe she was happy in her service to God until it happened."

Coel stared into the candle flames. "She would sing to those she was healing. She had a beautiful voice, and she played the dulcimer. When I was well enough, I asked for my harp and we played and sang. We spent more and more time together, and then, one night, she came to me." Coel looked into the candles. Once more he saw Marisol in the Spanish moonlight. He saw again how her habit had puddled around her ankles as she had stepped out of it. He saw her unbound hair falling about her as she came to him.

"She told me she loved me. She said she would forsake her vows and follow me wherever I went. I told her I would take her wherever she wanted to go."

Márta's eyes were huge. "What happened?"

"We were found out, of course. When Marisol abandoned her vows, her powers faltered. I was not the only person she was tending at the castle. She feigned illness, but a Chaperon always escorts the Daughters. Hers was a sharp-eyed Italian priest named Tomba. We should have waited until I was completely healed or taken a horse and fled that night."

Coel's stomach tightened. "I awoke one morning being

beaten with clubs. I was clapped in irons at Tomba's order. I could hear Marisol screaming from the nuns' quarters. I was dragged before Lord Lucas and the Archbishop in Zaragoza. I was accused of seducing a Daughter of Divine Mercy. It was deemed impossible that a holy woman of her power who had given her life to God and the Pope could love a lowly Welsh savage like myself. It was assumed that I had used witchcraft. A Court of Inquisition was called. They were going to burn me at the stake."

Márta swallowed. "But they did not."

"No. Marisol swore that I had done nothing. She swore it was she that had come to me. She demanded that the Chaperon and the Inquisitors use their powers to look into our hearts. They were going to ignore her. They were very angry. They were going to use the old methods and torture a confession out of me, but a letter of recommendation of my character came from Grand Triumphe in Paris. I think perhaps my old weapons master was behind it, but it was signed by the Grandmaster of the Academy. It gave the Inquisitor enough pause that they decided to use Truth-Tell magic rather than the rack." Coel shuddered at the memory. "It was bad enough. Both the Inquisitor and Tomba took turns reaching into my skull."

Márta nodded her head fervently. "But they found the truth, did they not?"

Coel nodded bitterly. "They found more than the truth. They were searching for witchcraft and unlicensed magic use."

"But, what could they find?"

Coel found his hands were shaking around his wine bowl. "They found out my mother was a pagan."

Márta blinked. "Your mother is pagan?"

"She practiced the old ways of the Celts. She was a Druidess."

"I was taught the Romans had destroyed the Druids."

"No, they were suppressed, but not destroyed. Even with the coming of the Christians, the old ways are still practiced. Even today, in Wales, in Devon and Cornwall, in the wild places, the old ways endure."

Márta nodded. "And in Ireland."

"Yes, and in Ireland. There the elves still hold sway. They protect people who practice the old ways."

Márta looked at Coel intently. "What happened to your family?"

"I think the Church was afraid they would anger the Masters at Grande Triumphe if they put me to death, and they did not want the embarrassment of burning one of their own Daughters of Divine Mercy. But they wanted us punished. They wanted examples made. They went after my family. It was an open secret in the mountains of Snowdon that my father was married to a pagan. My mother had given up her status as a Druidess to marry my father, but she refused to be baptized; and unlike a nun who has sworn herself to God, she did not forsake her powers when she married him and left her circle."

Anger began to simmer inside Coel's breast. "But my brother Evan was a priest. He had ambitions. From our youngest days, I have known his mind. He wanted to be the Archbishop at Saint David's Cathedral. My mother was a source of embarrassment to him and his plans. It broke her heart that Evan despised her. He was serving at Saint David's when the Inquisitors came. He came back to my father's hall and denounced mother before the Grand Inquisitor. He said she practiced witchcraft and consorted with the Devil. He said he had tried many times to convert her." Coel nearly spat. "That was true enough. He waved his Bible in her face and told her she was going to burn in Hell whenever he saw her. With Church troops and Inquisitors within the halls, there was little my father or my oldest brother, Bryn, could do. They were going to burn my mother as a heretic."

Márta gaped. "They burned your mother?"

"No. She fled. No one ever saw her again. It destroyed my father. He had risked his chieftainship to marry a pagan. He loved my mother more than his own life. After she fled, he climbed into his wine cup and stayed there." Coel's eyes began to burn with hate at the memory of his brother. "The Inquisitors praised Evan for his loyalty to God and the Church. They made the little maggot a Monsignor. It would not surprise me if he were a Bishop by now. With my father worshipping Bacchus, my brother, Bryn, was elected Chieftain. But the Church was not through with my family. To save the clan, Bryn had to publicly swear his loyalty to the Church and the Pope in Rome. He had to burn out anyone who practiced the old ways on our lands. Even then, it took every last copper the clan had to get the Inquisitors off of our mountain. Our family was broken and penniless. Penniless was what they wanted. For consorting with a nun, I was given a Commission of Debt my family would never be able pay. They wanted me somewhere where Marisol and I could never be together. I was chained in the bilge of a trading lug with a load of commissioned criminals and shipped off to the Baltic. When we reached the Russias, I joined a chain of prisoners and we were marched to Moscow. It was midwinter. Many died on that journey. Most have died since. Some tried to flee their debt and were tracked down and hanged. I served three years in the Frontier Cavalry. I lived."

Márta's eyes were huge. "What happened to Marisol?"

Coel threw back his wine in a single gulp. "They excommunicated her."

"Could she not have joined you somehow?"

Coel gripped his wine bowl for dear life. His world seemed to spin as the tale came out of him. "No. We were both told if we were ever found together we would be burned. The Church has ways of tracking people they wish to find. I have seen skilled woodsmen flee into the Frontier to escape their Debts of Commission, only to be dragged back in chains by the Church's trackers. There was no way she could ever reach the Russias without them knowing. Much less any way of us being together."

Márta's lower lip trembled. "You said that she is dead?"

She jumped as the wine bowl snapped apart in Coel's hands. "She committed suicide."

Márta's face broke and tears spilled from her eyes. "Oh, Coel."

Coel lost control of his voice. The candles blurred into yellow smears before his eyes. "She . . . " Coel choked. "She did it the old Roman way. She drew a bath. There was no knife in her chambers, so she broke her mirror. She took a shard of glass, and she . . . "

Coel's shoulders shook. He tried to crush the sobs in his chest, and he shook his head as they rose to close his throat. Hot tears spilled down his cheeks. Coel wept against his will. For long moments, the agony of remembering wracked him. He felt Márta's hand on his wrist, but tears smeared his sight as the memories filled him. It was all he could do to keep from rising up and screaming at the rafters.

Slowly Coel's fists unclenched. Tears still coursed down his face, but he regained control of his voice. "They found her the morning I was to be sent off. They dragged me up from the dungeon in chains to show me what I had wrought. They held my head by the hair so I could see Marisol floating naked and pale in a bath full of water turned scarlet with her blood. They made me look at the torn flesh of her wrists. They showed me the bloody shard of glass on the floor. They held me there and rubbed my nose in it like a dog that had messed in the hall. They told me this was the price of my lust and the inheritance of my pagan blood. They told me suicide was a sin and her soul would burn in hell because of my lechery. They gave me a good, long, look. Then they wrapped her body in a sheet and buried her somewhere out in the hills, unshriven and without a marker."

Agony wracked Coel's insides. Hatred rose to meet his pain. "Marisol had written me a letter before she killed herself. The Chaperon, Tomba, held it up to my face so that I could recognize her writing. Then he snatched it away before I could read any of it. The bastard held it to a candle and made me watch while it burned."

Coel looked up. Márta was weeping openly. Coel's shoulders sagged. "That is my tale of woe. Sometimes it makes me act like sheep-dip."

Márta wiped at her face. She took Coel's hand and squeezed it. "Thank you for sharing your story with me. I promise I will not tell it to anyone."

Coel squeezed Márta's hand back. His insides unknotted. Even his bones and muscles felt looser. He took a deep breath and let it fill his lungs before he let it out. Orsini had been right. Telling his story to Márta had lifted a great burden from him. Life was loss. Loss could be borne. It was shame and bitterness that killed.

"You can tell anyone you like. I am tired of carrying secrets."

* * *

Coel staggered back into the room he shared with Snorri. Both lamps were still lit. The Rus lay on his bed wearing nothing but a long linen nightshirt. He'd laced his hands together behind his head, and he was humming tunelessly to himself and wiggling his toes. He grinned as Coel entered. "How did it go?"

Coel smothered a belch behind his fist. "You are waiting up for me, then?"

"Of course. I wanted to see if Márta had lopped anything off of you."

Coel grinned tipsily. "She saw fit not to."

Snorri raised his scarred eyebrow. "So it went well?"

Coel belched again. "Well, indeed."

"She forgave you?"

"She forgave me."

"So?"

"So, what, then?"

Snorri propped himself up on his elbows. "So how was your supper?"

"You remember the dinner Orsini bought us in Moscow?"

Snorri smiled at the memory. "Indeed, I do."

"Pig slop."

"Really?" Snorri sat up. "What did you have for your firsts?"

"Smelts, fried in beer batter and drizzled with vinegar, oh, and toasted black bread with eggplant caviar."

Snorri stared intently. "And what did you have for soup?"

"Suckling pig broth with mutton kidney pirogues."

Snorri's jaw dropped. "And for the fish?"

"Trout." Coel rubbed his distended stomach with pleasure at

the memory. "Stuffed with the meat of crayfish."

Snorri's brow creased with jealousy as he waited. "Well?"

"Well, what?"

"Well, what did you have for your meat?"

"Oh, well," Coel sat down heavily upon his bed. "Márta and I could not decide between roasted pullets five days fed on juniper berries or boiled lamb with cumin sauce."

"So which did you choose?"

Coel shrugged. "Both."

"Both?" Snorri bore the betrayed look of a man who had missed a feast. "And for the sweet?"

Coel flopped back on his bed and laced his hands over his stomach. "Toasted pear bread, covered with whortleberries and cream."

Snorri's jaw muscles flexed. "I suppose you had wine."

"Oh, aye."

The Rus waited several moments impatiently. "Well?"

"Well, what?"

"Well, what wine did you have?"

"Oh, well, we had a Hungarian white from Lake Balaton, and a Hungarian red from Eger. The cooks at the Golden Horn are Magyars, and both wines came highly recommended. Then we had a red from Tyre, and then more of that wine from Cyprus Márta is so fond of," Coel sighed. "I find myself growing fond of it, as well."

"Hmm," Snorri grunted. "So how did Márta look?"

Coel stared up at the ceiling. "She wore a long tunic of red silk without sleeves. It reached to her ankles, and she wore black velvet slippers without hose. Beneath the tunic she wore black brocade and wide-legged pants of--"

"I asked you how she looked! Not what she was wearing!" Snorri shook his head angrily. "You are the worst storyteller I know! It is like pulling teeth with you!"

"She looked good enough to eat, Snorri," Coel turned his

head and smiled. "Bones and all."

"Oh, well." Snorri quieted as he painted the picture in his own mind. "I am glad all went well."

Coel sat up as his anger flared. "No thanks to you!"

"What?" Snorri looked startled. "What did I do?"

Coel's voice grew mocking. *"Just be glad he did not strip himself naked and paint himself blue!* What the hell were you doing? Picking a fight with me moments before I am going to meet Márta!"

"Hel!" Snorri threw his hands up in the air. "I had to do something!"

"What the hell does that mean!"

"Oh, for God's sake! You should have seen yourself! If I hadn't done something to get your blood moving, you would have gone to dinner as gray as a corpse. And then you would have said something stupid and insulting again, and then Márta really would have lopped something off of you!"

Coel worked this over in his mind for an angry moment. He clearly remembered his previous dread. "Did I really look that bad, then?"

"You looked like you were going to your father's funeral," Snorri shook his head reprovingly. "It was no way to go dine with a lady."

"Oh."

"I am your true friend, Coel. I look out for your interests."

Coel grumbled as he blew out his lamp. "I suppose I should thank you, then."

"I suppose you are welcome, then."

"How did you spend your evening?"

"Orsini and I played bodyguard to Reza."

"What did you eat?"

Snorri regarded him sourly. "Borscht, and I had enjoyed it until you came back."

"What did you do?"

"Reza went and met a well dressed Greek in a tavern near in a fancy part of town. He, the Greek, and Orsini went into a corner, and I was set to keep an eye on the rest of the patrons. I do not know what they discussed, but both Orsini and Reza seemed pleased with themselves when we left the place. I think they got whatever it was they wanted. We returned to the house, and Reza and I played chess. Orsini drank beer and poured over some thick book of accounts. Then I was dismissed."

"How goes your chess game?"

"Ah, well!" Snorri brightened. "If Reza runs true to form, I will fork him in seventeen moves. He will lose his bishop or his knight. He will have to choose between them, and either way, it will be his undoing. I will have him."

"He has not cheated?"

"Not yet."

"Then we need not kill him, then?"

Snorri smiled mischievously and blew out his lamp. "Not yet."

The room plunged into darkness. Coel flopped back upon his bed and refolded his hands over his stomach. It gurgled at him. He had eaten the finest meal of his life tonight. He had made Snorri jealous. Márta was talking to him again. He was in a warm room, and he was pleasingly drunk. He stared into the dim red glow of the brazier. Moscow and the Frontier Cavalry seemed very far away. He smiled as he thought of the fight Snorri had picked with him before dinner.

It occurred to him with great clarity that Snorri was his best friend in the world.

"Snorri."

Snorri's voice spoke sleepily. "Yes."

"Am I really such a bad storyteller, then?"

"Stick to singing."

Coel was silent for several moments. "I have never told you

the story of how I ended up upon the Frontier, have I?"

The room grew very quiet. Snorri's voice was wide-awake when he spoke. "No, and it always seemed a very poor idea to press you about it."

"Snorri?"

"Yes?"

"You are my best friend. There should be no secrets between us."

"You do me a great honor."

"I will tell you the story if you wish to hear it."

"I will listen if you wish to speak of it."

Coel found he had no anger or trepidation as he began his tale. His throat did not tighten, nor his stomach knot up. He felt very relaxed. There was no agony in recalling the events again so soon, and no healing sorrow in retelling it. It was his history, and a story he thought his best friend should know. Coel gazed into the shimmering red heat within the grate of the iron brazier. "When I left Paris, my sword was for hire. That much you all ready know, but, in the end, I went to Spain. I went to fight the Moors . . . "

CHAPTER FOURTEEN

It had rained late in the night but the morning was bright and clear. Coel took the clean air into his lungs as he stepped from the house. Porters stood ready with a mule-drawn cart. Otto, the dog, lay on the doorstep and watched the mules with a drowsy eye. Coel put his baggage in a cart and knelt to give Otto a scratch behind his ears. Otto thumped his tail. He liked Coel. Orsini stepped outside with a steaming wine bowl in his hand. "Good morning to you, Coel. Mulled wine?"

"Good morning to you, then, Orsini, and thank you." Coel took the bowl and let the hot wine and the taste of cinnamon and cloves fill his mouth. He took another swig and handed it back. "We take ship today?"

"Indeed. While you were plying Márta with choice viands and conversation, our business dealings were very successful. We sail south to the Black Sea at noon."

"And then to Trebizond?"

Orsini smiled. "Indeed."

"Trebizond!" Snorri came out of the house and threw his sea bag into the cart. He raised his arms to the sky. "Trebizond!"

Orsini handed him the bowl. "To Trebizond!"

"Ah!" Snorri tossed back what remained in a gulp and wiped his mustaches with the back of his fist. "The Empire of Trebizond!" Snorri looked down at his new dog. "Hullo, Otto!"

Otto thumped his tail.

He liked Snorri.

Reza came out of the house with Márta at his side. Coel smiled at Márta. She smiled back. Coel's stomach felt fluttery. Otto wagged his tail. He liked Márta. The sorcerer looked about as his associates beamed at one another. "You all seem very cheerful."

Snorri stretched his out arms to encompass the world. "Well, it's a mulled wine and Trebizond on the horizon sort of morning!"

The morning's good humor was infectious.

Marius walked out of the house and stowed his baggage. Otto stopped wagging his tail. Coel frowned. A well full of mulled wine wouldn't drown the sour look on the priest's face. Zuli stepped out and yawned. She looked rumpled, sleepy, and satisfied. Her hair was wet. Coel found it hard not to stare at her. She noticed Coel's look and favored him with a lazy smile. She turned the smile onto one of the porters. "Fetch my baggage, would you?"

The porter leaped to do her bidding.

Snorri looked about. "Where is Oleg?"

Zuli shrugged carelessly. "He was with me last night, but when I awoke this morning he was gone," For the slightest moment, her blue-green gaze grew peeved. She tossed her head. "It matters not. I am not particularly fond of good-byes."

The porters loaded the rest of the baggage and clucked at the mules. Snorri whistled at Otto and the red hound rose and stretched. Márta's scimitar suddenly hissed from its sheath. "Ware!" Blades came out all around. An armored figure approached. He wore a simple conical steel helmet with a nasal and a chain mail shirt that gleamed with fresh oiling. He was a big man and a heavy sword hung at his hip from a baldric. In his left hand, he bore a round shield and a pair of throwing spears; and in his right, he carried a stout spear for fighting. A dark green cloak of wool hung from his shoulders. Brown boots shiny with newness shod his feet.

Otto barked happily.

Márta peered at the eyes on either side of stranger's helmet nasal and lowered her weapon. "Oleg?"

Zuli started. "Oleg?"

"By Thor, it is Oleg!" Snorri grinned. "Look at you! You come to say your goodbyes in full panoply!"

Oleg leaned on his spear the way he had seen Snorri do. "I have come to join you. If you will have me."

Zuli rolled her eyes and turned to Reza.

Reza frowned. "I do not think that would be wise."

Orsini looked at the armed and armored young man curiously. "What of your bride to be?"

"I have sent Svetlana's father a sack of silver, and Svetlana a ring of gold, backed with a sack of silver to match her father's. She will wait willingly enough."

Coel raised an eyebrow. "What about your new barge?"

"I am wearing some of it. More of it went to my father-in-law and my betrothed as I told you. Still more went to the family of my friend, Dobrynya. He has an old mother, and two sisters who will need dowries; and now that Tsapko is dead, my step-aunt is a widow. So I sent her silver as well." Oleg took the fighting spear in the crook of his arm and patted his pouch. A few lonely coins clinked together. "I am in need of employment."

Reza's frown stayed fixed. "I do not mean to insult you, Oleg, but you are young, and you are inexperienced."

Orsini measured the young man. "Well, he has settled his affairs with great maturity."

Snorri nodded. "Yes, and he walked up to a were-demon's den when you asked it of him."

"These things are so, and I applaud his actions. However, he has seen only seventeen summers, and he has never been off the Dnieper."

Oleg faced Reza resolutely. "Yes, I am young. I am inexperienced. That is why I want to go with you. I have been to Kiev many times since I began plying the river with my step-uncle, and only yesterday, in your service, did I ever spend a night within its gates!" Oleg trembled with sudden passion. "When Snorri was my age, he was roving the Baltic! When Coel was my age, he was already a veteran and training at the Paladin Academy in Paris!" Oleg jutted his chin in challenge at the sorcerer. "What age were you when you left your father's village, Sorcerer?"

The party feared for Oleg's life.

"I was born second son to Shams Walladid, First in the Great House of Walladid, in the City of Shiraz." One corner of Reza's mouth turned up grudgingly as he looked at the impassioned seventeen-year-old. "However, to answer your question my young friend, I was apprenticed to my craft and travelled to Isfahan to serve my first master when I was fourteen."

Oleg opened his arms beseechingly. "I want to go with you! I will serve for food and lodging alone if that is what you will pay! I will fetch! I will carry! I am not afraid of hard work! I will work as a dog for you, and come your enemies? I am no swordsman but I will fight like a Fury! I have proven that!"

Reza stared at Oleg unblinkingly. Oleg met his gaze without flinching. Reza's voice grew stern. "If you follow me for Zuleikha, know that when she tires of you, which I assure you she will, she will break your heart. Know also that I value her services far more than any you could ever hope to perform for me." He pointed his finger in warning. "Know this as well, Oleg son of Igor. Come the time you become the jealous lover and a burden to me, I shall deal with you in the harshest manner."

Oleg drew himself up. The young man gazed long upon Zuli and spoke with dignity beyond his years. "Zuleikha is the most beautiful woman in the world. But it is to you, Reza Walladid, that I would swear my oath, and I swear, this moment, should you tell me that your path leads to the great ice of the north, and Zuleikha's leads to the pleasure palaces of fabled Cathay, then it is you that I shall follow into the frigid waste."

Snorri jammed his thumb against his chest. "I shall vouch for him!"

"Yes, but will you bear responsibility for him?"

"Responsibility and more! Should he fail you? You may take from my pay whatever you feel the injury requires, and, should you order it? I, myself, shall beat him forth from your company with the handle of my axe and send him home at mine own expense!"

Reza looked to Márta. "What are your thoughts?"

"He showed his loyalty upon the barge, his bravery against the beast and his honesty in settling his affairs. It is hard enough finding just one of those virtues in a retainer, much less all three." Márta suddenly smiled upon the young Rus. "What he does not know of swordsmanship? Coel and I can teach him."

Oleg's eyes leaped eagerly to the Paladin blade at Coel's hip.

Reza looked at Coel. "Will you teach him?"

Oleg looked at Coel pleadingly. Coel found himself helpless before the young man's earnestness. He shrugged and made a show of carelessness. "If you will have him? Márta and I will see what kind of a swordsman we can make of him."

Oleg looked as if he might burst into flames.

Reza's eyes rested upon Zuli. "Will you have him among us?"

"Let him come, let him go. What is a beardless boy to me?"

Oleg looked stricken, but his jaw set. Reza nodded to himself. "Very well. Orsini, I leave the matter to you. If you would hire him, offer our young friend terms."

"Come inside with me, Oleg. Let us not haggle in the streets like fishmongers, and put your armor and all but your sword in the carts," The dwarf's eyes ran merrily over the fully armed and armored young man. "We are not laying siege to Kiev today, and you are likely to attract the city guard."

Oleg grinned proudly. He even grinned at Zuli, and he was brave enough to keep it when she did not smile back. Oleg seemed a youth of his convictions. Oleg bowed deferentially to Marius as he followed Orsini back into the house. It struck Coel that Reza had not sought Marius' opinion, nor had the priest offered it. He looked sidelong at the priest. Father Marius seemed ill pleased with the course of things. The priest always seemed ill pleased. Father Marius' presence left Coel distinctly disturbed.

Orsini turned to Reza as Oleg eagerly began stripping off his armor and piling it on top of the cart. "We shall meet you on the docks within the hour. Oleg and I must settle upon terms and then drink to seal the bargain."

"Very well. We sail upon the *Olga*, the ship of Abt. It is berthed at the southern end of the docks." Reza looked to the porters. "Let us go."

The porters clucked at the mules. Snorri looked up suddenly at the name. "Abt?"

Reza nodded absently. "Yes."

"Iron Abt?"

"So some call him."

Snorri blinked. "Ooh!"

* * *

Coel looked upon Iron Abt.

He was not sure what all the fuss was about. Abt was short. Abt was fat. Abt was barely taller than Orsini and shaped like a barrel. His head was shaved and he wore a short, white turban. Wind and sun had burned his skin a ruddy red and his eyes seemed fixed in a permanent, crow-footed squint. Someone had bitten off a good deal of his left ear. His right ear was intact, and a massive gold earring hung from it. He wore voluminous pink pantaloons stuffed into scarlet boots that curled up at the toes. He wore a white linen shirt like any other Rus, save his was cleaner than most. His black brocade vest and golden sash smacked of voyages to eastern shores. A short, wide-bladed hunting sword hung at his hip and he'd thrust a hand-axe thrust through the front of his sash.

Coel stood on the gangplank and stared down at the diminutive ship captain. The Captain squinted back up at Coel and jerked his head at Reza. "Who's the tree?"

"Coel ap Math. He is an associate of mine."

"Coel ap Math?" Abt snorted. "What the hell is a Celt doing in Kiev?"

"It is a tale of some length."

The captain looked Coel up and down. The lines in the corners of his eyes deepened sharply. "Yes, the Frontier Commissions are full of such stories."

Coel winced at Abt's shrewdness and stepped onto the ship. It was a longship in the northern style, only much larger than the one Zuli and Marius had brought with them up river from Kiev. Abt's longship had 20 oars to a side, and his crew were no dockworkers looking for extra silver. They were sailors and fighting men. Many of them had silk pants and fine boots and wore earrings and bands of gold or silver on their limbs. Most looked to be Russians like Abt; but others looked Greek. A few even looked suspiciously like Turks. They lounged about like freemen. All carried swords or daggers. Painted shields lined the sides of the ship and racks of javelins lay mounted fore and aft. The prow of the *Olga* was a carved, violent serpent's head. Awnings for the passengers were lashed fore and aft and a leather tent shelter had been erected in front of the mast. Coel noted that the ship was scrupulously clean.

"Women?" Abt asked.

Coel turned.

Abt stood in front of the gangplank with his hands on his hips. Márta stood before him. Oleg stood at Reza's side at parade ground attention. He was taking his office as personal retainer with deadly seriousness. Reza bowed slightly to the captain. "She is my slave."

Coel winced.

"Ah." Abt looked past Márta to Zuli. Zuli wore her tight-knit black woolens and stood with her hands in her sable muff. She lowered her thick eyelashes at Abt demurely. Abt snorted in amused admiration. "And what of her? Another slave?"

"An associate. You have objections to women passengers, Captain?"

"Some say it's bad luck," The captain revealed a mouthful of gold teeth. "As for me? I like women, and your party comprises my only passengers. I think there will be few complaints."

Crewmen laughed.

Márta stepped down and ignored the roving eyes of Abt's sailors. She looked about and joined Coel. "It is a very clean ship."

"Snorri seems to hold this Abt in high regard."

Snorri joined them with Otto at his heels. "I do."

"You know him?" Márta asked.

"I know of him. Abt roves from the Baltic to the Black Sea." Snorri shook his head wonderingly. "They say in his youth he sailed all the way to Vinland."

Márta and Coel looked at Snorri blankly.

"Vinland. The land beyond Greenland."

Márta and Coel looked at one another. They could not be sure if Snorri was making a joke.

"The land on the other side of the Atlantic! My grandfather sailed there!" Snorri rolled his eyes at such ignorance.

Márta looked about the boat and changed the subject diplomatically. "He seems ready enough for pirates, anyway."

Coel took in the racks of javelins and long, hooked pikes mounted along the rails. "He looks as if he is not averse to an act of piracy or two, himself."

"Oh, Abt is honest enough. He does some trade for the Varangians in Constantinople. When I was in the Guard, they said if you wanted to send gold or silver home to your family, then Iron Abt was your man. He charges a stiff fee, but your gold and your goods are safe enough. Once he swears his oath, you have to take his ship and his life before you take his cargo. If Reza has paid him to take us to Trebizond, then to Trebizond he shall take us. As for being a pirate?" Snorri looked back at the little man mysteriously. "I have heard it said he did not earn the name Iron Abt by shipping linens."

Márta gazed at the ship captain curiously. "How did he earn the name?"

Snorri lowered his voice. "I have heard it said that years ago, Abt and his men came upon a Saracen ship in the Aegean Sea. It was a pirate ship, and riding low in the water with plunder. Abt chased it down and stormed it. The ship was as full of cutthroats as it was treasure. There was a great battle. During the fight, the Saracen captain took his great curved shamsheer and laid a stroke on Abt to cleave his head in half. They say the great blade shattered on Abt's head, and Abt ran the Saracen through. Even with his skull half riven, they say Abt fought on with his crew and took the Saracen ship."

"What happened?" Márta asked.

Snorri's voice dropped lower still. "They say the Saracen's blade all but sank through the bone of Abt's skull, and there is a horrible scar down the middle of his head. They say that is why he has taken to wearing turbans, and he has been known as Iron Abt ever since."

Coel and Márta peered wonderingly at the back of Captain Abt's head.

Abt scanned the docks and turned to Reza. "That is all of your party?"

"Indeed, we are ready when you are."

Every person on the boat jumped as Abt's voice boomed out of all proportion to his size. It was a voice that could be heard in the midst of a hurricane. "All right! You heard the Lord! Make ready! This ship is a sty!" He strode forward and kicked the stool out from under a man who sat playing dice. "I said move!"

The sailors rose grumbling, as sailors were wont. Coel noted that they did not grumble too much, nor were there any sullen glares. Abt ran a tight ship, and his men wore wealth won by his mastery of the sea. A crew would take much from a good captain.

Abt turned back to Reza. "We dip oars on the hour, and we sail down river to the Crimea. Then straight on to Trebizond, as agreed."

Reza nodded. "Excellent."

Abt walked over and addressed the party. "His lordship and his bodyguard will have one half of the tent, and I take the other. The rest of you lot may make your own arrangements beneath the awnings. The voyage to Trebizond is not over long, but neither are we stopping except to take on water, so make yourselves as comfortable as you can."

Márta went over to speak with Reza. As she did, Zuli approached Snorri from the side. She rose up on her tiptoes and tugged at his sleeve. The Rus bent down, and Zuli whispered in his ear. Snorri's eyes flew wide at whatever she had said, and he shot a furtive look over at Oleg. Oleg was still busy standing by Reza's side and looking every inch a hired sword. Snorri frowned, but his eyes roved back irresistibly over Zuli's body. He looked over at Oleg uncomfortably again and coughed into his fist. Snorri quickly walked away and struck up a conversation with Abt.

Zuli watched Snorri walk away with predatory amusement.

The woman seemed to have a sense of when she was being watched, and she raised her gaze from the seat of Snorri's trousers and regarded Coel. Her chin lifted slightly. Zuli's body language spoke volumes. If she had paid Captain Abt in silver to bellow, 'You had your chance, Coel!' her meaning could not have been clearer.

Coel reddened against his will.

Zuli's lazy smile spread across her face, and she turned her gaze on the bare-chested sailors who were busy about the ship. Orsini's words rang clearly in Coel's head.

Zuli was trouble.

CHAPTER FIFTEEN

Coel sighed. Now that it was finally quiet he couldn't sleep. The noise had begun at midnight and not stopped until the stars had begun to dim. When Zuli had been with Oleg on the river, she had gasped and sighed for all to hear in ways that inflamed a man's mind. This night she had crept into Snorri's bedroll. Coel had never heard such caterwauling. She moaned and howled and cried out in at least three languages that Coel was unfamiliar with. It had driven poor Oleg from the prow and sent him to the stern with his blankets trailing forlornly behind him. Marius had quickly followed muttering about the wages of sin loud enough for the whole ship to hear. If Snorri and Zuli heard his imprecations, they did not heed them. It seemed to renew their fervor. There was no place on the ship it could not be heard. Coel had tried to ignore it. The sounds of their ardor were distracting enough, but being next to them, he could hear the very sound of their flesh meeting. He had finally moved amidships and flung down his bedroll among the benches. He had not slept. He doubted anyone else on the boat had, either.

Coel flung off his blankets and rolled to his feet. He wore only a pair of knee breeches he had bought in Kiev. A good breeze filled the sail and ruffled his hair. Coel breathed it in deep and draped his bratt over his shoulders as he walked over to the water barrel. He nodded at Abt's right hand man, Vasiliy. Abt's second in command was a lanky fellow with the bowed legs of a horseman and the deep chest of a man who had pulled oars for many years. Long gray hair fell to his shoulders. He wore a sheepskin vest and a long red cap against the cold. Vasiliy was slaking his thirst as well. He handed Coel the copper dipper.

Vasiliy smirked at the awning below the dragon prow as Coel drank. "Did you hear all that?"

Coel rolled his eyes and handed the dipper back. "Who did not?"

"Well," Vasiliy sipped in reflection. "They may not have heard it in Norway, but then I am old, and my ears are not what they once were."

Coel laughed despite himself. The Rus sailor looked at the awning again in speculation. "I wonder how much he paid her?"

"She went to him of her own accord."

"Really?" Vasiliy stared at Coel disbelievingly. "With a face like his?" He looked with renewed interest at the darkness under the awning. Coel turned his eyes upon the Black Sea. It was purple in the pre-dawn and seemed vast beyond measure.

"Here," Vasiliy prodded Coel's shoulder. "Break your fast."

"My thanks." Coel took the piece of brown bread Vasiliy offered. It was slathered with butter and covered with a thick slab of white cheese and strips of smoked eel. Coel bit into it and gazed out over the whitecaps. They had rounded the Crimean Peninsula in the night. To the north, the Sea of Azov lay behind its narrow straits. To the west lay the Golden city of Constantinople and the Mediterranean beyond. Coel gazed east out over the bow. The ship's wake rippled out to the sides like an arrowhead in the dark waters. It was an arrow pointing straight to the ancient Empire of Trebizond. It looked to Coel like the arrow of his destiny. It was an arrow that had always pointed east.

Vasiliy smiled at the faraway look in Coel's eyes. "Your first time upon the waters?"

Coel wadded his bite of food into one cheek and shook his head. "No."

Vasiliy nodded. "I thought not, but your first upon the Euxine Sea, I would wager."

Coel smiled around his food at the poets' name for the Black Sea. "I have sailed upon the Irish, the North and the Baltic."

"Now, I have never been upon the Irish Sea, or seen the Elvish Isle of Man," Vasiliy leaned forward with interest. "Nor have I seen the North Sea. I have seen a bit of the Baltic, but only at its mouth upon the Russias. How did you find them?"

Coel thought back to his first time on a ship at the age of twelve. "The Irish Sea is more beautiful than you can imagine," The memory of the dappled waters filled his eyes. Coel smiled ruefully as he thought of his later voyage. "The other two I found poor indeed, though, in their defense, I spent them chained naked in the bilge."

Vasiliy looked at Coel in sympathy. "A Commission of Debt?"

Coel felt no shame in admitting it. "Aye."

"Well, now, there is a knot few men ever untangle." Vasiliy looked at Coel with renewed respect. "You seem well away from it, and much the richer, besides."

"I was lucky."

"Then I am glad to have you aboard. Wind and luck sailors must take on wherever way they can. "

Coel smiled. Vasiliy seemed a good man. The Rus looked over Coel's shoulder. "I think I shall go spell Tomar on the steering oar."

Coel turned and swallowed his bite of food. Zuli padded barefoot across the deck. Coel marveled at the smallness of her feet. She was wearing Snorri's linen shirt and nothing else, and hugged herself against the chill. She limped slightly as she walked. Zuli grinned up at Coel. "If I had to ride a horse today, I think I would die!"

Coel stared.

He started as Zuli sucked in a quick breath and plunged her head into the water barrel. She flung her head back up with a happy gasp and shook her hair all about. Water sprayed everywhere. Zuli seemed to glow in the dawn's light. Coel watched as the water dripped from her lips and chin and ran down the front of Snorri's white linen shirt. The fabric turned translucent and clung to the curves of her flesh. Coel had an immediate desire to bend her across the water barrel. With an effort he wrenched his gaze back up to her face.

Zuli's smile thinned. "What are you scowling at?"

"You."

Zuli tilted her head and spoke with mock pity. "Now, do not tell me Coel son of Math is jealous?"

"I was thinking more of Oleg."

"Oh," Zuli shrugged. "Him."

Coel's fist went to his hip. He gestured with his bread and eel at the awning in the stern. "What do you call that, then? Using one man to break off with another?"

Zuli lost all facade of amusement. "I would call it a lucky thing indeed, if the man was Snorri Yaroslav."

Coel's upper lip curled. He found himself despising her.

Zuli's eyes went cold. She smiled without any friendliness. "You should not act so proud, Coel. If you were one half the man Snorri is, you would not wear your tunic cut so high."

Coel blinked. Zuli raised her palms up before her measuringly and lifted her eyebrows in challenge. "Not every woman gets to ride the Spear of Odin."

Zuli held her hands more than a foot apart.

Coel found he had no immediate response.

"Listen to me, Coel son of Math. I cannot have Oleg following me around like a lost dog. It will interfere with my work, and his duty to Reza. I broke with Oleg last night so that he and everyone else on this ship would know of it. It is best for him. It is best for me. You do not have to understand it, nor approve," Zuli's voice dripped scorn. "You just stick to pining after Márta and courting your right hand."

Zuli spun about and stamped back to the awning. Coel looked down and found he had made a fist around his food. Eel, butter and cheese extruded between his fingers. Coel flung his crushed breakfast out to sea. He watched it splash into the purple water. He was angry, but save for the top of the mast there was no place on a longship to go and be alone. He stomped back to the steering oar. Tomar quickly looked away and began examining the braid of his scalp lock. Vasiliy smiled. Coel ignored the two Russians and watched the *Olga's* wake. Vasiliy spoke in a genial tone. "It looks like you lost the argument."

Coel refused to acknowledge the sailor.

Tomar nodded. "It looks like you lost your breakfast, as well."

Coel glared. It seemed like all Russians shared the same infuriating sense of humor.

Vasiliy shrugged in a none-too-convincing act of contrition. "Not that it is any of our business."

"Why, I will . . ." Coel looked away angrily. He found his gaze turning to the stern. Oleg lay in a corner. He was curled upon himself like an infant with his blanket pulled over his head. He looked pathetic.

"Oleg."

The lump shifted but did not respond.

"Oleg!"

Oleg spoke in a miserable monotone. "Leave me alone."

"It is time for your first fencing lesson."

The lump was resolute in its sulking.

Coel noticed a bucket by the steering oar. He spoke quietly to Vasiliy. "What's in the bucket, then?"

Vasiliy grinned. "Sea water."

Coel pulled a javelin from the rack by the oar and picked up the bucket. He strode over and tilted most of it over the young Rus.

Oleg shouted with outrage and burst up from his sodden blankets. He looked down and seemed surprised to find that the sword Snorri had given him was drawn. Coel held his javelin by its socket and pointed the butt end at the single edged sword in Oleg's hand. He poked Oleg in the chest none to gently. "Let us see what you can do with that iron, then, boy."

Oleg flinched.

"That's a live blade the lad has there!" Vasiliy warned.

Coel shrugged his contempt and prodded Oleg again. Oleg flinched. "If the young fool can lay a lick upon me, I will give him a gold piece."

Oleg glowered.

Orsini appeared in a red silk robe with wide quilted gold lapels and matching slippers. He hooked his thumbs into his golden sash and observed the situation. Marius sat up. A number of sailors looked up from between the benches where they slept. Oleg stood in his soggy nightshirt and looked about himself uncertainly as a crowd began to gather.

Coel smiled. "Now look who is not wearing pants."

Oleg looked down at himself instinctively.

Coel snapped his wrist and the remaining water in the bucket splashed into Oleg's face. "Never take your eyes of off your opponent."

Oleg spluttered in shock.

Coel shrugged. "I am waiting."

Oleg's face twisted with rage. He let out a great shout and charged. He attacked with the cut Snorri had shown him in Kiev. Coel had expected that, and he stepped back from the blow. The heavy steel blade hissed through the air. Several of the sailors exclaimed at the earnestness of the attempt. Oleg had found an outlet for his jealous anger at Zuli and Snorri. The young man followed through with the thrust that had served him in the alley fight. Coel was awaiting that, too, and he beat down Oleg's blade with the bucket. He hooked shins with Oleg as they passed and sent him sprawling to the deck.

The sailors roared their mirth.

Oleg looked up with murder in his eyes. Coel tossed aside the bucket and tapped the butt of the javelin against his palm. Abt came forth from the tent to see what the ruckus was about. Reza and Márta joined him. Oleg rose shaking with fury. Coel shook his head. "You forget, Oleg. I was in the room when Snorri instructed you, and I saw how you fought in the alley as well. Now, see if you have the wit to improvise."

Oleg punched forward with his point. It pleased Coel to see Oleg pull it back suddenly. It was the young man's first feint. Coel smiled as Oleg committed to his second thrust and plunged in. The lunge was swift and sure, but he had given away his intent with the bunching of his shoulders. Coel whirled his *bratt* from around his shoulders and flung it in Oleg's face. Oleg squawked and flailed like a plaid ghost. Coel stepped away from Oleg's wild swing and cracked his javelin across Oleg's wrist. Oleg's sword clattered to the deck.

Orsini spoke quietly behind Coel. "Perhaps you are enjoying this a bit too much."

"Aye," Coel nodded without taking his eyes from Oleg. "Perhaps."

Oleg yanked the *bratt* from his head and cast it aside. He clutched his bruised wrist and glared at Coel. The young man's eyes smoldered as he moved to his fallen blade.

"Oleg!"

Oleg turned. Márta held a javelin in her hands. She beckoned Oleg over. The Rus approached her reluctantly. His eyes never left Coel. Márta spoke in his ear for long moments. Some of the anger drained out of the young man's face. She took him by the shoulder and pointed at Coel, then whispered in his ear again rapidly. Oleg took the javelin from her with a smile. Márta smiled at Coel and then swatted Oleg's behind. "Get him, Oleg!"

Oleg stepped forward and bent to the bucket Coel had tossed aside.

Orsini's voice boomed. "Ware, Coel! The lad means to have that gold piece you promised!" The dwarf produced a Venetian ducat and held it high in the morning light for all to see. "Oleg! Lay a welt upon the Welshman, and I shall match his gold!"

Abt's crew roared their approval.

"Make it three!" A gold piece shown in Abt's hand.

Coel raised his javelin in a high guard as the sailor's chanted. "Oleg! Oleg! Oleg!"

Oleg leaped in. He raised the bucket high before him and then suddenly dropped to one knee. His javelin shaft scythed around at Coel's ankles. Coel's knees went to his chest as he leaped over the blow. It was the same strike Márta had complimented Coel upon in Moscow. Coel grunted in surprise and leaped again as Oleg reversed the blow and brought his shaft about backhanded. Coel lashed out and was surprised again as Oleg managed to bring the bucket up to block the blow.

Coel leaped back. Márta waggled her eyebrows at him.

The sailors roared. "Oleg!"

Oleg leaped up and lashed at Coel furiously. The wooden shafts clacked and clacked again. Coel parried the blows as Oleg thrashed away. Coel let the young man vent a moment and then launched into his own attack. Oleg's defensive skills were nearly non-existent. Coel swiftly beat down Oleg's guard and leaped to his left flank. He swept his javelin shaft in and snapped it to a halt an inch away from Oleg's neck. The young man froze in acknowledgement. With steel blades he would have been beheaded.

"Now!" Coel commanded. "Again! As Snorri showed you!"

Oleg leaped in with his cut and then the thrust.

Coel parried them. "Now! As Márta taught you!"

Oleg dropped to cut Coel's ankles out from beneath him.

Coel leaped the blow. "Defend and thrust!" He swept his shaft down and again Oleg took it upon the bucket, but this time he thrust back at Coel's middle.

"Aye!" Coel knocked the blow aside. Again!"

Coel made Oleg practice the same few cuts again and again. The javelin shafts clacked and rapped against each other. Steam rose from the two men as they fenced back and forth across the deck. The entire ship cheered them on. Oleg's blows began to slow and grow wilder. He did not know how to relax yet, and he forced every blow through his arms rather than using his body. He was quickly exhausted. Past this point, all he would learn would be bad habits. Coel stepped back. "Enough!"

A cheer roared across the ship. Oleg took great gasping breaths and grinned as the Russian sailors descended upon him and pounded his shoulders. Márta brought him a wineskin and swatted him on the shoulder. She beamed with pride at the way her pupil had performed. Coel smiled himself. The young Rus was a natural. Oleg approached Coel with his hand outstretched. Coel took it. Oleg looked back toward the awning. Both Snorri and Zuli had risen and watched from the rowing benches near the prow.

Oleg addressed Coel with great seriousness. "Márta told me why you started the lesson the way you did, and I thank you for it. I was sulking like a child, and I would have made everyone miserable for days. Reza probably would have ended up turning me into something unfortunate. A good beating was what I needed, and I thank you for the lesson in swordsmanship." Oleg suddenly gushed. "You are the greatest swordsman I have ever seen!"

Coel looked meaningfully to Snorri and Zuli where they stood upon the benches. "You can live with that, then?"

Oleg sighed as he bent to pick his sword up from the deck. "Well, Márta also told me that Zuli is a slut. She said she is likely to bed every sailor on the boat before the trip is over." He took up his sheath and slid the heavy blade home. "She told me I had best get used to it."

"You can live with that, too?"

"Well, she was slut enough to sleep with me, and I was but second-hand upon a river barge." Oleg grinned good-naturedly. "We had never even been properly introduced."

Coel clapped the young Rus on the shoulder. "Oleg, you will do."

"I will," Oleg's jaw set. "And I mean to have that gold piece of yours, as well as Orsini's and Captain Abt's."

"Well then, in the afternoon? We shall practice again the cuts we did this morning, slowly this time, with live blades, for form. Then, tomorrow morning, you will have your chance at winning your pieces of gold." Coel grinned. "But tomorrow? Tomorrow you must win them from Márta."

Oleg's head snapped around at the swordswoman eagerly.

Orsini joined the conversation. "All that wand waving was most impressive. However, perhaps I will take it upon myself to inquire if Captain Abt has some tools, and then see about shaving down a spare plank or two into decent practice weapons."

Oleg gazed upon the dwarf rapturously. Coel knew that practice at arms would be all that filled the young man's mind for the rest of the voyage. Orsini recognized the look and smiled. "I shall need to borrow your swords to get the weights and balances correct."

Oleg shoved out his sword without hesitation.

Orsini rolled his eyes. "Perhaps I will simulate Oleg's first."

* * *

The sorcerer sat cross-legged on the foredeck of the wargalley *Al Qarsh*. He wore the bright turquoise robes of his sect. His turban was blinding white and a matched the long woolen shawl draped across his shoulders. He had not moved since dawn. His eyes were closed. He looked as if he were asleep. Only the single line of concentration between his eyebrows gave sign to the immense strain he was under. Despite his comatose appearance, his senses were terribly aware as they reached out across the Black Sea. It was a nerve-wracking business.

Reza Walladid had not used his power since Kiev. It made tracking him very dangerous.

A small part of the sorcerer's attention cursed the name of Reza Walladid for the thousandth time.

Without using their power, neither Reza nor the infidel priest in his employ left any of the Lines of Power disturbed for the sorcerer's inner eye to detect. The sorcerer could not sit passively and wait. He was being forced to actively send his senses across the waters to find them. He had to be very careful. To actively lock the inner eye upon Reza across the ethers would incur Reza's immediate attention. The opening of such a direct line would be two-way, as well. The sorcerer feared what the outcome of such a meeting would be. There were but a handful of living wizards of the First Rank, and Reza Walladid was one of them. The sorcerer knew that if he locked wills with the Walladid across the ethers he might very well lose. The cost of losing such a battle would be catastrophic. It could leave his inner eye blinded forever and his power broken. That was if he was lucky. Losing such a battle to the Walladid could also leave him insane, enslaved, mindless or dead.

The priest was the key.

His healings were powerful, startlingly so. They were like great flashes in the dark to one who knew how to see. The priest had not used his power since Kiev, and yet, he had been the key to tracking the Walladid's party once they had set out upon the Black Sea.

There was something very wrong with the priest.

It was not as if his presence bent the lines of force. Indeed, it was the opposite. It was almost as if there were an absence in the ethers where the priest should be. It was constant, and made a tenuous shadow that could be followed, albeit with great difficulty. It was like looking for a shadow in darkness, a darker patch within a black tapestry. The line between the sorcerer's brows deepened. It made the sorcerer very nervous. It could be a trick of the Walladid, a tremulous thread that must be clumsily groped for in the dark. It was a thread that might instantly thicken into a rope that hanged him.

It was a nerve-wracking business.

There were also the glimmerings of a sword. The sorcerer's senses had not seen it drawn for several days, but, when it left its sheath, it left reflections upon the ethers for those with the sight. The sorcerer had seen such flashes before, at the head of Crusader armies in Acre and Tyre. They had been Holy Swords in the hands of the Christian Paladins. The Mamluk armies of Egypt had similar holy champions. An unoccupied part of the sorcerer's mind frowned at the thought. Those flashes had been much brighter than the glimmers he had seen in Reza's company. The dimness of the glimmering bothered him. The glamour of a Holy Sword in the hands of a true Paladin should be much brighter. He again considered the idea that what he sensed might be some kind of decoy or diversion. Or a trap. Nothing could be put past the Walladid.

He did not know the Walladid's destination, only that the Persian was on board the ship of Iron Abt. That presented another set of problems. It would be fatal to underestimate Captain Abt and his crew. The sorcerer's best guess was that the quarry was somewhere south and east of the shores of the Crimea, and they had a full day's start upon the waters.

The sorcerer opened his eyes as someone approached him.

His gaze fell upon the captain of *Al Qarsh*. Ramah was a very large man. The winding of his white turban and his saddle-leather colored skin marked him as *Mahgribi*, a North African. Ramah was from Tunis. He had served the Mamluk Sultan of Egypt as a marine and had risen to captaincy. The Blue-Robe sect had assisted in Ramah's rise. Ramah was troubled by their task. He did not like the idea of facing sorcery. Ramah did, however, like the idea of absolving his considerable debt to the Blue-Robe sect. He was also enamored of the idea of killing the infamous Iron Abt. Abt kept most of his acts of piracy confined to the southern side of the Mediterranean to curry the favor of the Christian churches. The *Olga* was big for a longship but could not compare to a galley. Abt could not bring down a shipping fleet or assault entire coastal towns. He was little more than a thorn in the paw of the Lion that was the Caliphate. It was the sheer audacity of Abt's attacks that were galling.

At Ramah's side stood Tawfiq, a Mamluk *Amir* of One Hundred. Tawfiq was as long and lean as a lance, and he held the flanged iron mace that symbolized his command crooked in his elbow. Tawfiq led a thousand warriors in the Sultan of Egypt's service, and his rank allowed him his own personal retinue of one hundred men. Twenty of his best soldiers were on board the ship.

Ramah fell to one knee politely. "Great one."

"Yes?"

"The *Amir* and I have spoken."

"Indeed?"

"I have spoken with Juba, as well."

The sorcerer frowned. He glanced down upon the main deck and the man who lounged there. Juba sat against the foremast and held his face up to the rays of the late afternoon sun. His long brown hair fell to his shoulders. His beard was short and both beard and hair had blond streaks from the kiss of the sun. His tattered robe of doeskin only fell to his elbows and knees, and an equally mangy shawl of brown-and-white-striped wool covered his shoulders. The sun had browned the skin of his arms, legs, and face, but his blue eyes and the flashes of pale skin beneath his raiment betrayed his Berber origins. He wore a string of turquoise prayer beads around his neck. The Berber left the sorcerer disturbed almost as much as the prospect of Reza Walladid. Juba looked more like a shipwrecked Christian than a powerful sorcerer. For that matter, Juba looked disturbingly like some of the images the sorcerer had seen of the

Christian savior when he had come forth from the desert. Juba was barely thirty years of age, and by reputation he wielded power out of all proportion to his years and training. His training was another concern. He was a mystic, and had gathered his power among the ascetics in the great North African desert. He was not accredited through any recognized or sanctioned school or sect. As a mystic, his very nature was highly suspect. There was also his power. It was said he could influence the weather. Even the Christian infidels forbade magic that affected the weather. Who should receive rain and which way the wind blew was the provenance of God.

The sorcerer scowled down upon the Berber. Juba had brought four musicians of equally poverty-stricken appearance with him. They all laughed and joked amongst themselves entirely too much for the orthodox sorcerer's liking. He turned his disfavor back upon Ramah. "And what words of wisdom have passed between yourself and this heretic friend of yours?"

Tawfiq stood at attention, but his eyes slid off to one side uncomfortably. Ramah squirmed under the sorcerer's gaze. He was from an ancient family in Tunisia. His family had maintained connections with the Berber clans of the desert since the Arab conquest of North Africa. The thought of battling sorcery made Ramah nervous. When the Blue-Robe sect had summoned him for this mission, he had called upon his family connections.

Juba and his musicians had appeared on the dock unannounced the dawn he was to set sail from Tunis.

Ramah bowed his head respectfully. "Juba says he is fairly sure that Reza does not possess that which you seek. He says he is fairly sure that the thing which both you and Reza seek is in the city of Trebizond."

The sorcerer stiffened. He, too, had considered the tiny empire on the Black Sea among the most logical of several destinations. But these words coming from the mouth of the mystic were unsettling.

"Tell me, ship's captain. How does Juba know of such things? How does he know the Walladid does not yet possess his heart's desire? How does he know what it is that Walladid and I both seek? How is it that he knows what we seek resides within the walls of Trebizond?"

"Juba did not say that he knew," Ramah could not meet the sorcerer's gaze. "Juba has said only that he is fairly sure."

"And to what does Juba attribute this three-quarters measure of surety?"

Ramah's eyes traveled unhappily to every aspect of the ship except the sorcerer seated before him. His voice dropped low. "Juba says the wind told him."

The sorcerer controlled his temper with difficulty. "Bring Juba before me."

Ramah bowed low and backed away as he rose. He turned towards the mast. Juba looked up without being hailed. The mystic jumped to his feet and strode barefoot across the deck. He bounded in unseemly fashion up the stairs. He smiled and nodded with familiarity to Ramah. Ramah nodded and stepped back to stand beside Tawfiq, clearly relieved to have escaped the sorcerer's undivided attention. The sorcerer looked up as Juba stood before him. Juba nodded his head with the barest amount of courtesy, but his smile was so genuine and friendly it was galling. "Greetings, Great One." The sorcerer had never seen so many white teeth in his life.

He locked his gaze with Juba. "I am told you think our destination is Trebizond."

"I am fairly certain of it."

"The wind has told you this?"

"I have heard it upon the wind," Juba corrected.

The sorcerer's jaws clenched. The verbal gymnastics of mystics set his teeth on edge. "So, am I to understand that you can command the wind?"

"Oh no, Great One," Juba's eyes widened in shock. "Where the wind will blow is the provenance of God."

"So, it is God who will give us the winds we seek?"

"Perhaps," Juba smiled guilelessly. "If I ask him."

The sorcerer smothered his outrage at such impudent heresy. He turned to Ramah. "Your vessel is faster than that of Abt, is it not?"

Ramah nodded. "Indeed, it is. We are a war-galley, with two sails to his one. But a stern chase is a long chase, and Abt has over two day's start, and, if Juba is correct, Abt has been headed straight for Trebizond from the beginning. We, on the other hand," Ramah paused as he sought a way not to be insulting. "Have meandered, somewhat, as we have sought him out."

The sorcerer ignored the comment. "Can you overtake him before he reaches the shores of Trebizond?"

"I can try, Great One." Ramah did not seem confident.

The sorcerer scowled. The Empire of Trebizond was a place of great intrigue, but an empire only in name. It was so far flung to the east and so surrounded by enemies that it tried to remain as neutral as possible. Muslim trade was welcomed there, and embassies of many nations had quarters within the city. The Blue-Robe sect, itself, had a holding there. However, one could only guess at what kind of allies the Walladid could call upon in such a strange land. It would be best to take him upon the open sea where he would have only his own power to defend him. That, alone, was a formidable enough prospect. The sorcerer turned his gaze once more upon the Berber. "Can you help us overtake him before he can reach sanctuary within Trebizond's walls?"

"If God wills it."

The sorcerer came to a decision. Reza Walladid had to be stopped by whatever means necessary. If it required blasphemy, so be it. This duty had been squarely laid upon him. The sorcerer sighed inwardly. Indeed, he had asked for the honor specifically. The sorcerer put all of his will into putting a tolerant smile upon his face. "Then, Juba, do what you can, with my blessing."

Juba smiled so that the sun brownd lines around his eyes wrinkled. "I am your slave in this, Great One," He turned and clapped his hands. "Let it be as God wills!"

Juba's musicians took up their instruments. Two were drummers. One played a deep, wide drum, and the other had a pair of smaller drums of unequal size. One musician played the goatskin pipes. The fourth held a strange, many stringed instrument. The musicians sat cross-legged and put their instruments between their knees. The deep drum tapped. The thump repeated very slowly, and it was counter-pointed by a double tap on the double drums.

Juba cast off his robe of doeskin. Clad only in his breechclout and beads he leaped high in the air with a great shout. The deck shivered as he landed before the mast and leaped high again. He landed and then stood on one leg with his arms outstretched and his leg cocked before him. The deep drum throbbed again, and Juba put his foot down. The drum throb came, and his hands shifted with infinite grace. Slowly, Juba began to contort himself in a strange, slow moving dance. His every movement was in time with the drums. Indeed, the sorcerer was hard pressed to say whether Juba led the music or the music led him. The sorcerer watched with grudging fascination. Juba moved as if he had no bones in his body. His muscles writhed like snakes under his flesh as he danced and curled about himself in a circle before the mast. The musician with the strange stringed instrument began slowly plucking his strings. It was almost too soft to hear, but the sorcerer could feel the rhythm of it in the roots of his hair.

The rhythm increased in tempo. Juba increased his speed to match it. His motions became longer and wider, as well. He no longer seemed to coil in upon himself, but his motions opened out to the tips of his fingers. Juba's eyes were closed. He wore a beatific smile upon his face. His dance seemed one of pure joy.

The sorcerer rose to his feet and looked about himself. There had been a slight cool breeze blowing while he had sent his senses across the water. He still felt it now, but, behind the dancing Berber, the twin sails of the war-galley were filling. The sorcerer's eyes widened. There could be no doubt of it. The wind was increasing, and it was warm. Swiftly, it grew in strength. Its warmth ruffled his clothing. He could almost taste the dust and smell the sand upon it. The wind grew hotter as it grew stronger.

"*Bismillah*!" Tawfiq took a step back. He had put one hand to his turban as the hot wind plucked at it. He pointed his mace of office at the whirling Berber. "He calls the wind of the desert across the waters! He calls the *simoom*!"

The wind rose higher.

The sorcerer spread his feet to steady himself. The wind became a searing gale that blasted across the deck. He brought his hands before him as if in prayer as the music spun ever faster. The line of concentration drew down between his brows again. His hands turned over and he gently closed his fists before his belly. His eyes closed.

His Inner Eye opened.

The sorcerer gasped.

He could see the light of the Berber's life whirling before him. It flashed and shifted, then expanded and contracted. Even more, it was the lines of force that fascinated the sorcerer. They were not bent about the Berber mystic as if he were harnessing them to his will. The lines of power curved and shifted about Juba more in reaction to the rhythmic expansion and contraction of his personal power. It was a far different sort of sorcery than the Blue-Robes practiced. It reminded the sorcerer of snake charmers he had seen in the market place. The sorcerer was not a poetic man, but an image suddenly struck him very clearly. The mystic was not trying to command the wind.

Juba was inviting the wind to dance with him.

The sorcerer opened his eyes as the pipes let out a droning howl and the desert wind answered it. The *Qarsh's* sails snapped tight. The music whirled and throbbed as Juba's dance grew ever wilder and the burning wind whistled and shrieked through the rigging. The pipes skirled higher to be heard over the wind and then joined its howl to become one. The masts groaned. The ship rocked as the wind continued to mount. The sorcerer squinted against the heat of the wind.

The *simoom* roared across the Black Sea. War galleys were calm water and coastal ships. They could not face heavy weather. The desert storm threatened to tear the ship apart. The sorcerer raised a worried hand to Ramah.

Every man on the ship started as Juba let out a roar as loud as the wind and leaped into the air. The deck shuddered again as he landed. The air was calm. Men who had stood tensed against the wind staggered as they suddenly resisted against nothing. The pleasantest of warm breezes blew across the ship. Juba stood with sweat pouring from him. He tilted his head back and laughed up into the rigging. "Thank you!"

The sorcerer followed his gaze.

The twin sails filled with wind. It could barely be felt on the deck, and there was no sign of it upon the water, but the ship itself knifed forward through the sea under full sail. Juba's chest heaved. He steadied himself with a hand against the mast and laughed again. He waved at Ramah. "Steer your ship where you will, my friend! But be swift! Winds are fickle things and grow bored easily!"

The sorcerer looked down from the taut sails and turned his gaze upon Ramah. "Can you catch the Walladid?"

Ramah was gazing about in awe. The white caps upon the water were small, out of all relation to the speed of his surging ship. The wind in the sails was his and his alone.

"Can you catch the Walladid?"

Ramah snapped out of his wonderment. He looked up into his sails and then upon the ocean again, but this time with the practiced eye of a ship captain. "Indeed, Great One." He looked up into his rigging again. The *simoom* no longer blew. What he had filling his sails was a wind nearly perfect for a ship rigged as his was. "If the Walladid sails straight for Trebizond, we shall sight him before high sun tomorrow."

CHAPTER SIXTEEN

Oleg stood reeling and panting on the deck. His shield and practice sword drooped in his hands. Sweat dripped from his face. At dawn Márta had taught Oleg a single cut and parry. Then she had driven on the young Rus from every angle and taken the two moves through every possible permutation.

She had also taken a pot of red lip paint from her box of cosmetics and smeared the smooth edges of their wooden weapons. Had the blades been real, Oleg would be missing his head and all four of his limbs. He had red marks on every inch of him save his face. There were so many red streaks on his white linen shirt it looked like he had been beaten with a whip. When the paint streaks were washed away, there would be red welts beneath them and blue bruises to replace them on the morrow. Every time Márta landed a blow she stopped Oleg and showed him his mistake, and then made him perform the movement ten times correctly so that he would not forget. Coel smiled in professional admiration.

Márta was merciless.

Coel watched Oleg gasp with exhaustion. He stood by his summation of the previous morning.

The young Rus was a natural.

Márta nodded her approval. "Enough."

Oleg dropped his shield and flopped gasping upon the deck. He stared dazedly up into the rigging and the blue sky beyond. Crewmen clapped enthusiastically. One of the sailors brought him a dipper of water. Otto padded over and licked Oleg's sweaty face. Oleg pushed wearily at the happy dog but he was too weak to defend himself. Oleg surrendered as Otto slobbered all over him.

Márta's chin dimpled in amusement. She had little more than a light sheen of sweat on her upper lip. Coel gazed upon the swordswoman with great respect.

Márta was an extremely dangerous individual.

Her style was a joy to behold. She had a deceptive, lazy, kind of speed. She rarely parried. She did not engage in any one-two, block and strike combinations. Only rarely did she even attack off of a deflection. Márta had taken the science of evasion and elevated it into art. She did not engage unless she wished to. More often than not, she reacted to an attack by slipping the blow as she came in with a direct counter attack of her own.

It was amazing technique, and almost unstoppable if one had the reflexes and the talent for it. Márta had both. Towards the end of the lesson, Márta had let Oleg engage her in free sparring. The young Rus had instinctively tried to cross swords with her and use his considerable size and strength advantage against her. The more Márta had slipped and evaded, the wilder Oleg's attempts to make any kind of contact became. Then her counterattacks began to fall upon him like rain. Coel could see experienced swordsmen falling into the same trap. He smiled ruefully. He could see himself doing it if his blood was running hot. Coel regarded Márta long and hard as she walked over to the water barrel. In armor, he was fairly sure he could take her. However, if the two of them were to fight stark naked, with only their blades to rely upon . . .

Of that he was not so sure.

Márta's eyes locked with his over the dipper. The wooden saber hung loosely in her hand. Her cheeks had a rosy glow as she sipped. The challenge on her face was clear for anyone to see. Márta put the dipper down and wiped her mouth with the back of her wrist. She smiled sunnily at Coel and spoke loud enough for the entire deck to hear. "Coel? Is that a practice sword I see in your hand?"

Every sailor's head snapped around.

Coel looked down at the wooden replica of his Academy blade he held. "Aye, it is."

Vasiliy shouted gleefully. "A gold piece on the girl!"

Snorri's voice roared out. "Make that two!"

Coel turned a betrayed look on his friend. The Rus' stuttered with guilt. "Two! Two, on my friend, Coel!"

Coel scowled.

"Make it three!"

Coel glared. "Do not do me any favors."

The damage was done. Márta smiled from ear to ear. Snorri took both chess and gambling with deadly seriousness. It was clear to everyone on the ship that Snorri believed Márta was the superior swordsman.

Coel shook his head disgustedly as a furor of wagering erupted from stem to stern of the *Olga*. Every unoccupied sailor began to gather. Bets flew back and forth. Márta seemed to be favored two to one. Coel turned to Orsini. The dwarf had watched his wooden weapons with satisfaction as Márta and Oleg had fenced.

"You are familiar with Márta's style?"

"Indeed, I am," Orsini nodded sagely. "Well familiar."

"Do you have any advice, then?"

The dwarf pondered the question for a moment. "Yes, I believe I do." He crooked his finger at Coel.

Coel leaned in eagerly. "What is it?"

"In a moment, Márta will turn to Reza and ask him to wish her luck. In that moment, take up your longbow, and put as many arrows as you can between her shoulder blades."

Coel slowly straightened.

Orsini gave him a jolly smile. "Then, were I you, I would leap overboard, and swim back to Wales as fast as you can, before Márta has the chance to become genuinely angry with you."

Coel considered breaking his practice sword over Orsini's head.

The dwarf held up his hands placatingly even as he grinned at his own humor. "I am sorry, Coel. You wish my advice; I shall give it to you. It is my belief, given the circumstances, that Márta will defeat you. Were I you, I would take my beating like a man, and look for the lesson in it. A fencing match with Márta is very educational. It will make you a better swordsman, if you can keep that pride of yours out of the way."

Coel found his pride was all ready well in the way.

Snorri's betrayal was bad enough without getting

condescension from some goddamn dwarf. Orsini ignored Coel's fuming and surveyed the throng of wagering sailors. The dwarf cupped his hands before his mouth. "I offer ten to one odds on Márta! Ten to one!"

Heads snapped around at the offer. More shouting began.

Coel lowered his voice. "I will take that bet."

Orsini smiled up at him pleasantly. "Oh, and how much will you wager?"

Coel considered what remained of his war chest and what was promised in future. "Ten Venetians ducats of gold."

"Coel, are you sure you wish to do this?"

Coel gave the dwarf a hard smile. "Can you cover the bet, then? I will allow you to re-adjust the odds if you wish."

"A wager is a wager, my friend," Orsini's eyes glittered. "I will abide by it if you will. Indeed, should you defeat Márta, it will be my pleasure to eat my hat."

"That will not be necessary. But you may wish to go count your gold while you still have it."

Orsini smiled indulgently. "Good luck, Coel."

"Thank you."

Coel strode forward. Boos from the sailors greeted him. Coel threw off his white linen tunic with a flourish. Whistles and wolf calls rang out as he kicked off his sandals and stood in nothing but knee breeches. Márta raised bemused eyebrows. Coel smiled back.

"Shields?"

Márta spoke for all to hear as she raised her wooden saber. "This is all the shield I shall need. However, I will allow you one if you wish."

The sailors shouted their mirth.

"Take it while you can, Coel!" Vasiliy called.

"Ask for armor, too!" Tomar shouted. "And a horse! You seem to lose your battles with women!"

Crewmen roared.

Coel glared.

Márta whooped and tossed her saber high. The wooden weapon revolved up to the top spar of the mast and then came pin wheeling down. Márta caught it by the hilt to the resounding cheers of the sailors. She regarded Coel with supreme confidence. "To the first touch? Or two out of three?"

"Two out of three." Coel knew he needed all the opportunity he could get to figure out her style and still have a chance to win.

"Who shall act as judges?"

Coel glanced about. "Reza is your master. His opinion may be biased."

Reza rolled his eyes but said nothing.

Márta frowned. "Snorri and Orsini have already laid wagers."

"Then I nominate Captain Abt."

The sailors cheered the choice. Abt bowed deeply. "I will endeavor to be fair."

Márta pointed her weapon at Oleg. "And I nominate Oleg. We have each given him equal beatings. He should not favor either one of us too much."

The sailors approved of this, as well.

Coel accepted. "The Rules of Tournament require at least three judges for foot combats. Who else would you have?"

Márta looked about the ship for a suitable choice. Almost all of the sailors had laid bets already.

Coel smiled. "Zuli loves us both the same."

Márta's eyebrows bunched.

Zuli left Snorri's side. The sailors quieted as they watched her enter the circle. She and Snorri had managed to be somewhat quieter during the night, but she had taken to wearing Snorri's shirts on the deck during the day, and leaving them barely buttoned. She looked around the throng with the heavy-lidded eyes. "I am afraid I must remove myself from the judging."

A chorus of disappointment greeted her words.

Zuli smiled with pleasure as she walked up to Coel. "However, should you defeat Márta?" She looked over her shoulder at the swordswoman as she put the tip of her finger between Coel's collarbones. She looked back up at Coel and let her finger lazily trace down the hard muscles of his chest and stomach. Coel's flesh clenched slightly beneath her fingertip as he smelled the scent of jasmine. Her finger stopped at the drawstrings of his breeches and gave them a tug. She raised her voice for all to hear. "I shall make it worth your while."

The sailors roared.

Márta was appalled.

Snorri looked none too pleased, either.

Coel threw back his head and laughed. He pointed his sword at Márta and shook his head. "You are a dead woman."

Márta pointed her saber back. "We still need a third judge."

Father Marius' voice cut through the clamor of rude suggestions by the sailors. "I am a knight, and I have sat in judgment in both tournament and in trial by combat. I shall judge the match if you wish it."

Coel gazed upon the priest. Marius stood wearing a shorter and lighter version of his belted black mantle and black hose beneath it. For a moment, Coel was taken aback. He had never seen Marius smile before. It gave the usually grave priest an almost boyish look. It reminded Coel that Marius could hardly be older than himself. It was his usual haunted demeanor that made the priest seem ancient.

Márta nodded. "I accept."

Coel took a chance and raised his wooden sword in salute.

The priest actually grinned as he saluted back.

Marius walked across the deck to one of the javelin racks and drew three of the missiles. He tossed one each to Abt and Oleg. The crew quieted expectantly. Marius addressed Márta and Coel formally. "Abt is Captain and his ship the field of combat. On his word, the contest will commence. You have both agreed to two out of three touches. I shall judge what is a worthy blow. If either of you dispute me, Captain Abt and Oleg shall cast their votes, and two out of the three shall decide. When I cry halt and throw down the baton, you shall both withdraw. If you do not, Oleg, the Captain and I shall come between you. Do you both agree?"

Márta nodded. "I agree."

"Aye."

"Very well, approach."

Coel and Márta stepped forward and regarded one another. Márta held her practice saber loosely by her side. Coel found himself grinning. Márta shared his sense of enthusiasm and grinned back. Coel could not help but think of Orsini's words. Whichever way it went, the bout was bound to be very educational.

Abt's voice boomed out. "Fight!"

Márta's saber rose up in front of her body in a whipping cut and then down in a slash. It happened so fast Coel barely had time to lurch backward and raise his blade to block it. The wooden weapons clacked sharply as they met. Márta's blade lashed at Coel's crotch. Coel jerked back and shoved his sword in the way.

The two blades scraped against one another hilt to hilt. Without warning, Márta was beneath his blade and shoving it high into the air. She suddenly whipped her blade out from under his. Coel nearly fell backwards as she aimed a draw cut at his neck.

Coel risked being brained and ducked beneath the blow. He hurled himself forward and rolled over his shoulder across the wooden deck. As he came up to one knee Coel swung his sword in a wild blow behind him to ward Márta off. The momentum of his roll and the desperation of his backward blow left Coel spinning off balance. He tottered in a twisted, half crouch and sat down gracelessly upon the deck.

The sailors roared. Catcalls rang out around the ship. His blow had done nothing but cut the empty air. Márta stood half a dozen paces away. She had not bothered to pursue him during his desperate plunge. She leaned on her saber with her free hand insultingly cocked on her hip. "You have a bad habit of sitting down during swordfights."

Coel glowered.

Reza spoke from behind Coel as another round of jeers rang out. "You surprise me, Coel. I thought she would have had you by the second stroke. I am impressed."

Coel glared back at the sorcerer. "Thank you."

He rose to his feet and looked around the throng. Snorri would not meet his eyes. The Rus was already missing his money. Orsini watched him with an infuriating smile. Coel struggled to rein in his temper. The hell with Snorri, and, if he won the match? He would hold the dwarf to eating his hat. Coel grimaced at the thought. If he lost, he would be walking about with his own hat in his hand until he saw his next year's wages.

Márta yawned.

Sailors hooted.

Coel looked about himself again and arranged a defeated look on his face. The catcalls grew louder as Márta's supporters sensed victory.

"He's lost!"

"He knows it!"

"Give it up, Coel!"

"Try fighting the dog!"

Coel let his shoulders sag in defeat as he forced his body to relax. As he did so, he slowly filled his lungs with air. The shouts of the sailors mounted.

Coel let the point of his sword lower. He turned guilty eyes on Snorri. Everyone on board knew they were friends. All had heard Snorri bet gold against him and then lamely reverse himself. For a moment, all eyes turned on Snorri. The Rus spread his hands unhappily and rolled his eyes at his lost wages. In that moment Coel lunged.

As he lunged, Coel screamed.

Coel's father, Math, had first put a sword in Coel's hand and taught him the wordless war-scream of the Celts. Coel's mother had taken him aside and taught him to make it into something more. His Bardic tutors had taught him music and shown him how to sing from his diaphragm. Coel's mother had taught him to go even deeper and bring his war-scream up from the very pit of his belly, to make the breath of his body erupt from the center of his being. The ancient heroes of the Celts were said to be able to freeze the blood of their opponents with their war cries. His mother had shown him how to make his voice as much a weapon as the sword in his hand. The first time Coel had used the technique during a raid in the Border Marches of Wales it had saved his life. The first time he had used it on the practice fields of Grande Triumph had been his last. Paladins were the Soldiers of God. It was His glory they called upon in battle. They did not shriek like demons from hell. Coel had been severely punished. It had been more than a decade since Coel had let the war-scream free.

Coel's power rose up from his belly and ripped from his throat in an inhuman howl. Márta's eyes flew wide with shock. Her sword arm tensed and went rigid. For a split second, the shouts of the sailors were silenced as if their throats had been cut.

The rounded point of Coel's wooden weapon plunged towards Márta's midriff.

Márta blinked. Then she moved with liquid speed. There was no attempt to retreat or dodge. She lunged in to meet him. Her saber slid along his sword just enough to deflect it from its path. Márta slid by as well. Coel's scream cut short as he spun about furiously. Again, he brought his blade about in a defensive arc behind him. Márta was already beneath the blow. Coel staggered as her wooden saber slammed into calf with a meaty thud.

Cheers thundered over the moans of Coel's outnumbered supporters. Snorri clapped his hands to his head in financial anguish.

"Point!" Marius' javelin clattered to the deck as he threw it down between the two combatants.

Oleg pointed his javelin like a baton of office. "A hit! I saw it! A hit!"

"Aye, a hit, and a good one." Captain Abt pointed the butt of his javelin at Coel condemningly. "He would have lost his leg with live blades."

Coel didn't bother denying it. As he took a hesitant step, his limp was clear for all to see.

Marius retrieved his javelin and raised it over Márta. "One."

Everyone had seen the hit, but a rousing round of cheers greeted the pronouncement. Snorri waved his hands beseechingly. "For god's sake, Coel! Steady down!"

Reza spoke again. "Very good, Coel. You almost had her."

Coel clenched his teeth as he put weight on his leg. He listened to Snorri's words rather than Reza's praise. He needed to steady down if he was to have any chance at all. Coel took a deep breath and regarded Márta with a clinical eye. She was faster than he was. He had far more strength and actual linear speed, but her reactions were a half step ahead of his own. It was a bitter draught, but Coel swallowed it as he looked her up and down. Her blow to his lower leg had done him no good, either. Now, he would be a step slower still.

There had to be a way to beat her.

Márta had recovered from the shock of the war-scream. She was watching him intently. Coel knew no trick would ever work on Márta twice. She nodded at him. "Whenever you are ready."

Captain Abt held up his baton and waited on Coel.

Coel considered. Márta had been trained as a horse archer in Cyprus, and he could only guess at what kind of fencing schools she had attended in the East. An idea kindled in his mind. The East was the key. To a man, the warriors of the East had long ago gone to curved blades. Tulwar, scimitar, saber, or shasqua, it made no difference. The dimensions varied from region to region, but the curved blade of the horse archer was king in the East. It left their warriors with a whirling, cutting style. When they fought opponents in heavy armor, they used maces and axes to crack it. Their Christian opponents, both Crusaders and Byzantines, to a man, used longsword and shield.

In the East, two-handed swordplay was almost unknown.

Coel limped several steps forward. Márta's saber rose up into a low guard. She smiled at him again.

Coel smiled, too. Orsini had wrought well. The wooden sword in his hand was nearly a duplicate of his Academy blade. Right down to the extra four finger widths of length in the hilt. Coel suddenly tossed his blade into his left hand. Márta raised an eyebrow at the possibility of a left-handed attack. After a moment, Coel tossed the sword back into his right hand.

Márta shook her head at him. "You're stalling."

The catcalls began again.

Coel ignored Márta and the throng of shouting sailors as he tossed the sword between his hands again and pursed his lips as if unable to choose. He shrugged and slowly took the sword in both hands. He wrapped the fingers of his left hand around the bottom of the hilt and let the pommel fill his left palm. He raised the sword over his head in the high guard he had been taught in the Academy.

"I am at your convenience."

A wary look flashed across Márta's face.

Zuli shouted out with malicious glee. "Get her, Coel!"

Abt's voice boomed. "Fight!"

Márta stepped forward to attack. Coel snapped his sword down and held the point between them. Márta's brow furrowed as she watched the tip of his sword. She feinted from side to side, and Coel followed her with his point. The wooden blades clacked as Márta flung an experimental cut at him. Coel relaxed and took the blow. His blade dipped away and with a snap of his wrists jumped back into place before she could attack again. Coel took a step forward. Márta stepped back with a frown as his point hovered nearer.

Coel moved around to his left. Márta circled warily. Coel stepped forward suddenly and brought his point closer. Márta leaped back, and Coel moved further to his left. Márta's eyes widened as she realized her back was now to the mast.

Coel began cutting off the deck.

The ship of Abt was no spacious merchant galley. The *Olga* was a longship. She was long and thin through the beams with a single deck. Deck space was limited and Márta needed room for the sweep of her weapon. Coel pressed his attack. He stepped in her way when she tried to get around him and always presented her with his point. He kept close to her, always attacking with short thrusts and slicing attacks that only used the top third of his blade. Coel gave Márta nothing to counter-attack off of. A good thrust could be made while backing up, but Márta's scimitar was primarily a cutting weapon, and she could not put her body into swinging her blade while she retreated. Márta's parries and slashes lost power and speed as she was forced to use the strength of her arms alone.

The throng parted as Coel drove in on Márta point first. She back-pedaled and slapped his point away. Coel's sword dipped and snapped back up to press towards her breastbone. Márta slapped Coel's point with all the strength she could muster and risked a great leap backward. Coel leaped after her with a thrust at her belly. He nearly paid for it as her edge whistled towards his wrists with blinding speed. Coel parried and thrust again to drive her backward.

His plan had worked.

Márta found herself dancing off-balance amongst the rowing benches.

Coel risked a great overhead swipe. Márta thrust up her saber desperately and took the blow full on her blade. Coel felt his wooden sword shudder in his hands. Márta gritted her teeth. Coel knew the force of the blow had shivered all the way down her arm. He chopped again with all his strength as Márta tried to negotiate the benches backwards. She hopped and dodged with amazing dexterity, but she could not look where she was going and defend against his sledgehammer attacks at the same time.

Márta tried to hop over a bench backwards while she slashed at Coel's elbow. She let out a gasp and windmilled her arms frantically as her heel caught the bench's lip. Coel thrust. Márta parried as she tumbled and fell between the benches. Coel leaped in and stopped his follow up just short.

Márta glared up as Coel as his point lifted her chin.

"Point!" The butt of Marius' javelin pushed Coel's blade away from Márta. Zuli and Snorri whooped. Coel's minority of supporters cheered lustily over the boos of the men betting on Márta. Márta stood up and rubbed her behind where it had met the deck. Her jaw set as she looked at Coel. He nearly took a step back. Márta was a study in ice-cold intensity.

Marius pointed his javelin at Coel and then Márta. "One

apiece! The next touch shall tell!"

The din of the sailor's shouts rose to a deafening level. Abt raised his javelin over the combatants. "Are you ready?"

Coel looked over at Márta. "Aye." He slowly began filling his lungs again. He knew she would not let herself be maneuvered onto uneven ground again. Coel came to a decision. He would give her the war-scream and attack two-handed. He would hold nothing back. He raised his sword overhead in the high guard.

Abt looked to Márta. "You are ready?"

Márta's saber drifted back behind her. Her left hand drifted back as well. Both of her palms turned upward. She lifted her chin defiantly. Her guard was utterly open. She was inviting Coel to attack. She nodded almost imperceptibly at Abt's question.

Abt slashed the air with his javelin. "Fight!"

"Sail!"

Marius threw down his javelin between Coel and Márta. "Hold!"

"Sail!" The call came again from the steering oar. "Sail astern!"

All eyes turned to Tomar. The steersman stood at his oar with his finger pointed northwestward over the stern.

Abt rushed to the steering oar shouting orders. "Everyone to your oars! Vasiliy! Up the mast! You have the sharpest eyes!" Sailors scrambled to their benches as Vasiliy clambered up the mast like a monkey. Men crowded around Tomar at the steering oar.

Coel glanced at Márta. For a moment he was tempted to tell her she had been lucky. He held out his hand instead. "You are magnificent."

Márta took his hand. "You were lucky."

"Aye, more than you know," Coel admitted. "I was running out of surprises for you."

Márta beamed. "You certainly did surprise me. Your skill with a sword is quite remarkable. I thank you for the match. You have given me a great deal to think about."

Coel looked along the edge of his weapon. There were some nicks and dents from the furious fighting, but both of their weapons had held up. Orsini was a genius with his hands. Coel looked up from his blade slyly. "Of course, this is not over between us."

"How is your calf, Coel?"

"It hurts. How is your rear-end? It seems that sitting down during swordfights is catching."

"You are right, Coel." Márta's chin dimpled. "This is not over between us."

It struck Coel that Márta smelled nice when she was sweaty. Her cheeks were flushed. Coel could not seem to take his eyes from the faint dusting of freckles across the bridge of her nose. Márta's eyes narrowed. Her smile widened as she spoke. "You may let go of my hand now."

Coel blushed and let go of her hand.

"Vasiliy!" Abt's voice boomed across the deck of the longship. "What do you make of her?"

Vasiliy called down from the crossbar that constituted the Olga's crow's nest. "Twin sails! Lateen rigged! A war galley, and a Saracen! Under full sail and under oars! She is coming straight for us!"

Abt looked to Reza. "Friends of yours?"

"I would say it is more likely that they are former associates."

"I do not like the way you said former."

"I suspect my capture or demise may be their main intent."

"And everyone with you, I suppose."

"That is a fairly safe assumption."

"Can you find out for sure?"

"To look through the ethers would be to invite attack or entrapment. Yet, there may be a way." The sorcerer mounted the stern deck. "Move aside."

Sailors quickly scooted out of the wizard's way. Reza stood looking out at the white smear of sail on the horizon behind them.

His fists clenched at his sides, and he began speaking under his breath. The hair on the back of Coel neck prickled as it had when Reza had unleashed his power in Kiev. Reza raised his fists and extended his forefingers. He drew a great circle at arm's length in the air before him. His left hand drew back into a fist at his hip, and his right hand opened and flattened. He seemed to wipe the air before him like a man cleaning a mirror.

Coel started.

The air before the sorcerer shimmered and shifted.

Coel stepped back. Sailors shouted in alarm.

The beak of a war galley's ram seemed to hover over the ship's rail. Reza pulled his hand back, and the ram receded and more of the war galley's bow came into view. Behind the bow, oars threshed the waters into white foam.

"Now that is a trick!" Abt peered intently at the ram and bow of the oncoming vessel. "Can you get us a look at her decks?"

Reza moved his hands. The bow deck of the galley came into view. A spare looking old man in turquoise silks and a white turban glanced up in surprise from where he stood on the enemy deck.

Reza smiled through his immense concentration. "Why, it is the Long-Eye, himself."

Abt snarled and pointed at the image angrily. "He's Blue-Robe sect! What ill-fate have you called down upon me, sorcerer!"

"I have called down upon you?" Reza's smile stayed fixed. "And who is the dark skinned one beside him, can you tell me?"

Abt peered as another man came into view. "Aye, I know him. That is Ramah. A Mamluk Marine Captain of some reputation. And I know that ship. It is *Al Qarsh.*

"What does *Al Qarash* mean?" Coel asked.

"The Shark," Abt answered.

Coel gazed upon the image in the air with trepidation. The name seemed appropriate.

"And tell us," Reza asked. "What price has the Mamluk Sultan put upon your head, Abt?"

"A thousand gold dinars, on delivery of my head and my ship to the harbors of Alexandria."

Reza lifted his chin at a third man who carried a mace and wore costly armor. "And that man is Tawfiq, an Amir of One Hundred. It seems we have enemies in common, Captain."

Coel took in the image of the man in the blue robe. "Who is this Long-Eye, then?"

"His name is Kamose al Ah-Ay. He is an Egyptian, from the city of Memphis."

"A sorcerer, then?"

"A very powerful one."

Abt spat upon his deck. "The Blue-Robe sect is one of the most powerful wizard's guilds in the East. Everyone knows that."

Coel had not known that. "What do we do?"

Reza did not take his eyes from the shimmering image before him. "Were I you, Coel, I would go and string my bow, and then exchange the wooden sword you carry for one of steel."

CHAPTER SEVENTEEN

Kamose al Ah-Ay looked up at the circle of distortion hovering before the ship. Even through his anger, he was awed. Reza had fashioned a lens out of the very air to gaze upon his enemies across the waters. From where Kamose stood, the images in the distortion were smeared, confused and tiny. Kamose held no doubts that Reza could see them all perfectly from his vantage. Nor could Kamose think of any opening the spell left him to strike back with. He had never seen such a thing. The Persian's skill was truly remarkable.

"Remarkable," Juba spoke wonderingly. "I have never seen such a thing."

Kamose scowled. "Tawfiq!"

The Amir of One Hundred stepped forward. Kamose never let his eyes drift from the distortion. "Your men are ready?"

"Yes, Great One." Behind Tawfiq, twenty men crowded the war galley's foredeck. Most of the men were Circassians from the Georgias or nomadic Kurds. An Egyptian Senior Amir of Recruitment had bought each man as a slave in his adolescence. Likely subjects were sent to *tabaqah* schools in Cairo and rigorously trained for years in literature, religion and the arts of war. They had then been freed as highly paid professional soldiers in the service of the Sultan of Egypt and his Amirs. Most had been pagan nomads in their youth, and the opportunity for wealth and advancement in Mamluk service was highly prized. The men with Tawfiq were hardened veterans and intensely loyal to the Amir and the Mamluk State of Egypt that had trained them. It was men just such as these that had taken Jerusalem back from the Crusader Armies of Europe and now fought them tooth and nail for Antioch and Tyre.

Tawfiq's men were well armed even by Mamluk standards. Each man wore a long, hooded shirt of mail that fell to his knees and a cuirass of lamellar plates over it. Vambraces and greaves of heavy iron sheathed their limbs, and the spiked points of steel helmets rose up out of their turbans. They were armed with long straight swords and heavy circular shields sheathed in shining brass. Each man was a trained archer as well and carried a short composite bow and a case of arrows. The gleaming Mamluks would sink like stones if they fell into the sea, but with luck, they would overwhelm Abt's more lightly armed crew.

"We should overtake them within one half of an hour, Great One," Ramah eyed the shifting apparition over his bow unhappily. "What would you have us do?"

Kamose had been considering his strategy very carefully. "The Walladid has vast objectives to the East. He will feel the need to conserve his power at all costs. He will be loath to use his strength on any grand scale unless absolutely necessary. He will prefer to use the men he has hired and Abt's crew to defend him as long as possible. We shall grant him this. Ramah, I wish you to come along side the *Olga* and board her. Let it be a battle of iron and steel instead of sorcery."

"You wish us to take the Olga by storm?"

"If you can, good Captain."

Ramah had been doing some calculations of his own. The *Olga* had at least fifty men in her crew, each of them a veteran of many sea fights. Abt also had Reza Walladid and his strange assortment of associates. On the war galley, Ramah had twenty of Tawfiq's handpicked Mamluks and another forty of his own *Maghribi* marines. All of the war galley's thirty-man crew were fighting men, as well. He had ninety-six men at the oars, but they were slaves and of no consequence. Numbers and the nature of the two ships were both on Ramah's side. His decks were higher, and his ship was faster. He should be able to take the *Olga* in a straight sea fight without great difficulty. However, Iron Abt was the captain of the *Olga*. His reputation was well earned, and he had Reza Walladid aboard his ship. Proof of the Persian's power hung in the air before him. "Great One, what of the Walladid?"

"What of him?"

"You wish him taken alive?"

Kamose had been turning that thought over in his mind

throughout the night.

"That would be preferable. If it appears we are winning, Reza will use his power to defend himself. But before that happens, we will have him within arm's reach. I have it within my power to bind him if I can get close enough," The sorcerer let out a long breath. The Walladid was a devil. Getting close enough to use the Spell of Binding would be both uncertain and fraught with peril. It would be best not to tie Ramah's hands in a pitched battle. "However, if it is necessary, I will settle for his body at the bottom of the sea."

Ramah turned to Tawfiq with relief. "Amir, have your men string their bows." He looked up into the rigging where Juba's wind filled the sails and turned his gaze upon the mystic. Juba smiled at him. "Shall the wind go its way?"

Ramah nodded. "Yes. We can overtake Abt under oars, now, and I do not want them setting our sails ablaze and filling our decks with fire."

"As you will, my brother," Juba pressed his hands together as if in prayer. He took a deep breath and held it. His body relaxed, and he slowly let it out. The mystic's lungs and the ship's sails seemed to be joined. As Juba exhaled, the rigging sagged, and the twin sails deflated. The desert wind no long filled them. They flapped in the ocean breeze.

Ramah shouted to his first mate. "Harun! Take in the sails! Step the masts!"

Harun barked, and men began furling the sails and prepared to pivot the masts and lower them to the deck. Ramah moved aft and peered down through a hatch into the gloom of the hold. The drummer gazed up as Ramah's shadow fell over him. Sweat gleamed from his shaven head and dripped down his massive chest and fat belly. His round leather mallets rose and fell on the wood drum between his knees without missing a beat. The drum thudded in one-quarter time. The drummer squinted up into the square of blue sky above him. "Yes, my Captain?"

The die had been cast and a sea-fight it would be. "Ramming speed."

The drummer bellowed and his mallets thudded on the drumhead as fast as heartbeats. "Ramming speed!"

* * *

"Pull! Pull for your lives!"

The sailors of the *Olga* heaved on the oars with all of their might.

Abt stood at the stern. The look on his face was grim. Coel strung his longbow. The Saracens had stepped their masts and now pursued them under oars. Abt was under full sail, and his men bent their oars for all they were worth. It would not be enough. He had but one sail and forty oars to drive his ship. The war galley was close enough so that Coel could make out the beak of its ram, the triple banks of oars rising and falling and the surge of the ship each time they swept. The *Al Qarsh* looked like some great bird of prey swooping down on them. It was steadily closing.

Coel wore his brigandine vest, knee breeches, and little else. He had forsaken his chain mail and limb defenses, and he had laced his jack loosely. Snorri had been in sea fights and had said he had no intention of going down into the deep. He wore only his scale vest, and Coel had followed suit. Marius, Márta, Orsini, and Oleg had other ideas. Each one of them gleamed in full armor.

Coel had never been in a sea fight. He looked up at the sail and then at Abt. "What do we do?"

"We run."

"And?"

"Ramah will catch us."

"And?"

"And then we fight him."

"Then why do we run, then?"

"It is traditional," Abt turned and looked upon Coel blandly. "Have you some other suggestion?"

Coel could not think of one. "What will they do when they reach us?"

"Ramah has stepped his masts. However, I do not think he intends to ram us. That is in our favor. I think he intends to come alongside and board us. That gives us a chance to make a fight of it. However, his decks are higher than ours. That gives him a substantial advantage. His Mamluk archers will loose down upon us and rake our deck. My crew will be throwing javelins up at his armored men. That means we will get the short end of the exchange. He will use grappling irons to hook our ships together, and it will go hand to hand. Tawfiq's armored Mamluks will lead the attack, followed by Ramah's marines and then his crew. They will try to overwhelm us with numbers. It is very likely they will succeed."

"Is there anything we can do?"

"Well how do I know!" Abt looked over at Reza. "Hey! Sorcerer! Why don't you summon a sea serpent to rend their ship and drag them down?"

Reza shrugged without taking his eyes off of the window he had drawn in the sky. "That is not exactly the line of sorcery I specialize in."

"Well, why don't you turn them all into turnips, or something!"

"I shall take your overestimation of my abilities as a compliment. However, I will see what can be accomplished." Reza spread his hands and began intoning strange words low in his throat.

Abt shook his head and muttered. "He will see what can be accomplished . . . "

Coel frowned. "Why do we not--"

"Why do you not take that tree trunk of yours and see if you can do some good with it!" Abt glared back out across the water. "It ought to outrange their bows for a few moments. Perhaps you could see your way to thinning their ranks a bit."

"I think that is an excellent idea," Orsini stepped forward. He was sheathed in blue steel plate from head to foot and had repaired his visor. It still startled Coel at how little noise the dwarf's armor made when he moved. Orsini held his massive crossbow cradled in his arms. "Come, Coel, let us see who between the two of us is the better shot at sea."

Coel drew a long flight arrow from his quiver. "Aye, then." He laid the arrow across his bow. Orsini grinned and put his foot in the great crossbow's stirrup. Even Abt stared as the dwarf wrapped his gauntlets around the string and cocked the steel crossbow with the strength of his arms alone.

Coel looked over at Reza. The sorcerer stood staring through his magic window. "Tell me, where are they most crowded together on the foredeck, then?"

* * *

"*Bismillah!*"

Kamose looked up as Tawfiq staggered back a step and nearly fell. Two Mamluks grabbed the Amir's arms and steadied him. A ridiculously long arrow shaft stood up out of the Amir's spiked helmet. The point had just managed to pierce the gilded dome of steel. That it was there at all was remarkable beyond words. The Amir shook off his men angrily and yanked the shaft out of his helmet. The wood snapped, and the point stayed embedded in the steel.

"Impossible!"

Kamose started as something smacked at his feet. The squat length of a crossbow quarrel stood embedded in the deck. He turned at the sound of a scream. One of Ramah's sailors fell overboard with an arrow shaft sticking up from between his collarbones.

Mamluks suddenly crowded around Kamose and lifted their shields over the sorcerer in a protective awning of brass and wood. The sorcerer snarled. "Loose back at them!"

A number of the Mamluk's threw down their shields and drew bows and arrows. They raised them uncertainly. Tawfiq's snarl matched the sorcerer's. "They are still out of range! They are--wait! Look!" Tawfiq pointed with his mace. Reza's window was rapidly receding back across the water. Kamose squinted as he lost it and then caught sight of it again. It was visible as a golden smear in the air that distorted their view of the *Olga*.

Ramah pointed. "Great One!"

Something was wrong. The smear in front of the *Olga* was growing. It spread until the entire ship seemed to shimmer. Kamose squinted as the smear shifted into a greenish hue and then violet. The colors shifted and shifted again. The view of the *Olga* twisted within the rainbow fluctuations. The colors grew brighter and fused and whirled. The *Olga's* image skewed sickeningly as the colors twisted. Kamose felt his vision reel and his stomach turn as the light grew ever brighter and began pulsing.

A Mamluk threw down his bow and ground his palms over his eyes. "My eyes cross to look at it!"

Kamose looked away and still the shifting pattern of lights twisted and shimmered like sherbet colored ghosts across his vision. Tawfiq strode forward with his face twisted into a terrible grimace. His raised his bow and aimed it at the miasma of sickening light that covered the *Olga*. His eyes watered and his arm trembled at full draw as he tried to keep his eye on his mark. Kamose watched the Amir loose his arrow. The shaft went far wide and short. Tawfiq staggered and dropped his bow. The Amir of One Hundred fell to his knees and vomited upon the deck. His men averted their eyes as they dragged their commander back beneath the canopy of shields.

Ramah and Kamose crouched behind the armored screen. One of Ramah's sailors leaned out over the rail to gaze upon the apparition and heaved his mid-day meal into the sea. Ramah shook his head. "Great One, how can we fight what we cannot even look upon?"

Kamose calculated. The cleverness of the Walladid knew no bounds. But it would not be enough to save him. The obscuration was impressive. The shimmering light was an amplification of the spell he had used to make his window across the waters. It was a matter of light diffraction. The prismatic shifting and the warping of image was a trick even a soap bubble could perform on a tiny scale. It was an extremely clever innovation, but it took no great energy to do. It was an illusionist's trick. It betrayed the Walladid's intent. The Persian was conserving his power at all costs. He would let them get too close. He would wait until the last possible moment to expend any real power. It would be a fatal error. "The Walladid has woven his spell like a bubble around his ship. When we board the

Olga, we shall be inside it, and then we shall take them by storm."

"How can we steer close enough? If he can maintain the spell, he can evade us until dark. Then we will lose him again, and before that happens, every man amongst us shall be spewing his guts upon the deck!"

"No," Kamose formed his plan. "The Mamluks will keep their shield wall up to protect me on the foredeck. Let no man look forward. I will direct you to the *Olga*. You will direct your crew."

Ramah sounded dubious. "Truly?"

"Have your rowers maintain full speed." Kamose turned to four of the Mamluks. "Hold your shields high to protect me from arrows, and look not upon the *Olga*."

The Mamluks obeyed. Kamose's stomach clenched as he turned his gaze upon the *Olga*. The shimmering light and slewing image made his feet feel unsteady beneath him. Kamose knelt and closed his eyes, letting the after-images die behind his eyelids. Kamose opened his Inner Eye. Across the water, the light of the Persian's power and the energy of his spell enclosing the *Olga* were clear within the lines of force. Using the Inner Eye was dangerous, but Reza would not be able to strike mentally through the ethers while he maintained his own spell about the *Olga*. Kamose spoke to Ramah.

"Bring your ship seven degrees to starboard."

* * *

"They still gain upon us!" Tomar's cry was news to no one. The war galley was very close. Her triple banks of oars tore through the water. The war galley shot towards them like an arrow. Coel loosed an arrow in return. He was still amazed that no arrows answered back. There was a shimmering, golden haze about the Olga, but other than that, Coel could not tell exactly what Reza had done. Abt stood beside Reza and watched the war galley near. "They can still see well enough to steer by."

"No, they cannot. It is Kamose. They do not call him Long-Eye for no reason. He guides the galley with the Inner Eye.

However, the closer they get, the worse it will be for any who look upon the Olga. You and your crew will still strike the first blow. You must make the most of the opportunity."

Márta's bow thrummed and thrummed again. Coel arced an arrow high to land amidships of the galley. Orsini lowered his crossbow and peered over at Coel. " Márta and I will continue to loose. Perhaps you and Snorri should don the rest of your armors."

"What are you thinking?" Coel did not relish the idea of swimming in steel.

"They will throw grapnels and tie the ships together. Then they will board us. I believe we must take the battle to them."

"Onto their ship?"

"Yes."

"We are going to board them, first, then?"

"Precisely."

"Ah." Orsini had clearly gone insane. Coel turned and walked over to his bundle of belongings. He found Snorri gazing intently at the looming war galley. "Don the rest of your armor."

"Why?"

"We are going to board the Saracen ship."

"That is the stupidest thing I have ever heard."

Coel shrugged out of his jack and began drawing on his chain mail. "It is Orsini's idea."

"Oh, well, then," The steel scales of Snorri's armored vest clicked and scraped as he pulled it off. He yanked his long mail shirt from his sea bag. Coel tugged his jack back over his own mail and pulled on his greaves and vambraces. He strapped his skullcap under his chin and took up his bow again. Coel and Snorri jingled slightly as they went to the stern. Orsini conferred with Apt.

The Captain stared down at the armor-clad dwarf. "You are insane."

"Ramah will never expect it."

Abt snorted. "Well, now, that is true enough." He looked

upon his crew as they heaved at the oars. If the chase went on much longer, they would be too tired to make a fight of it. "Very well. Upon your signal, we shall hurl a volley of javelins. Then you will attack."

"Excellent. Have your men make preparations."

Abt began barking orders. Sailors began throwing ropes up over the yardarm. Coel and Snorri stood in their full armor. Orsini nodded his satisfaction. "Ah. Good."

"So, the three of us are going to climb up the galley's side while the Mamluks chop us to bits," Snorri frowned mightily. "Are you sure you cannot think of a better plan?"

"Such a plan would be extremely foolish if that were my intention, however, I do, indeed, have a better one."

Coel cast a nervous eye at the approaching war galley. "Just what are your intentions?"

Orsini's eyes glittered. "When the ships clash, Abt's men will shower the galley's deck with javelins. Then, we three shall swing from the yardarm on ropes and fall upon the Mamluks with both feet. We are going to chop a hole in their ranks. Abt has a couple of barrels of whale oil he intended to sell in Trebizond. His men will heave them up onto the war galley, and we will break them open onto their decks. Then we shall set the Saracen ship afire, leap back onto our ship, and cut their grappling lines. That should be enough to dissuade them until nightfall. Reza says if we use no magic in the night, we can lose the Long-Eye."

Coel was dumbstruck.

Snorri stared at the dwarf. "You are insane."

"I will go first if it will make you feel better."

Snorri looked at Coel. Orsini had become Snorri's unofficial mentor in all things. The Rus appeared to be having a crisis of faith. Márta put a gleaming mailed hand on Snorri's shoulder. "Marius, Oleg, and I shall throw up a boarding ladder and come in right behind you. We do not need to take their ship, simply set it afire and give Abt's crew time to cut the grappling lines."

Abt snarled from the stern. "Make up your minds! They are

almost upon us!"

Coel glanced over at the streaking galley. Its deck was a curtain of shields. No one upon the *Qarsh* would look upon the *Olga*. Coel stared up the *Olga's* mast in dread.

He had never liked heights.

Márta gave Coel's shoulder a squeeze. "I have faith in Orsini. It can work."

Coel shook his head in disbelief. "God . . . damn it . . ."

Zuli spoke at Coel's elbow. "Do not worry, Coel." She stood in her clinging black wool again. A braided leather sling hung loosely in her hand, and a small bulging pouch was tucked into her belt. She opened her palm and lightly tossed a lead sling missile the size of a partridge egg into the air and caught it. "I shall be your guardian angel."

Orsini nodded at her and thrust his war hammer through his belt. "Quickly, then! Up into the crows nest!"

Zuli nodded and caught a halyard. She pulled herself up like a spider to the short crossbeam at top of the mast. She nodded at Vasiliy, and the Rus shinnied back down to the deck and took up a javelin. "The ropes are ready!"

"All right, then! Up onto the yardarm!" The dwarf took the rope and pulled himself up with the strength of his arms alone. He rapidly reached the top of the sail and scissored his legs around the yardarm. Orsini took up the rope that Abt's men had stretched from the other side.

Snorri gaped. "He really means to do this."

Coel bit back a mounting sense of panic. "God . . . damn it . . ."

"Quickly lads!" Orsini shouted from above. "Now or never!"

"God . . . damn it . . ." Coel threw down his bow and took the rope in both hands. He leaped up and began pulling himself aloft. Snorri held the rope taut for him as he climbed. The yardarm tilted under Coel and Orsini's weight. Coel smelled the canvas of the sail as it snapped and cracked before him. He kept his eye on the wooden beam above him as he climbed.

Zuli called out from above. "Hurry! They come!"

Coel reached up and seized the yardarm rigging. Orsini grabbed him by the shoulder and pulled him up. The dwarf grinned maniacally from his perch and handed Coel a rope. The yardarm tilted sickeningly as Snorri began to climb. Sailors down on the deck took up a hawser and pulled the yardarm back in trim. The wood of the beam bent under the weight of the three armored men. Coel's gorge rose as he looked down upon the swaying deck and the sea beyond. Everything was tinted gold within the globe of Reza's spell. The war galley closed. It was much larger than the Olga and shaped like a spearhead. Coel took in the forest of shields and swords lining its rails. There were too many of them. Far too many. The yardarm lurched as Snorri reached it. Coel's stomach lurched in response. Coel's teeth chattered in the cold and the wind drew tears from his eyes. He could hear the drums of the approaching war galley and the hissing sweep of its oars. Coel's knuckles whitened on the rigging. He could not recall ever having been so scared.

"God damn you, Coel! Lend a hand!"

Snorri hung by his armpits as he tried to heave an armored leg over the yardarm. Coel reached out from his own precarious perch. He seized the collar of the Rus' scale vest and pulled. The yardarm bent even more as Snorri managed to lever himself on top of it.

"All right!" Orsini began tossing the ends of the lines up to Zuli in the crosstree. He grinned at Coel and Snorri. "If the mast does not snap when the ships clash--"

Coel's voice cracked in horror. "What!"

Orsini ignored him. "Then Abt's men will give us a shower of javelins to keep the Egyptians' heads down! Then we shall swing across and have at them! Myself, first! Then you, Coel! Then Snorri!"

"Have you ever done this before?" Coel shouted.

"No! But forty years ago, I was on a Venetian galley that was attacked by Genoese freebooters. They used this very same tactic against us!"

"What happened?"

"We shot them out of the air with our crossbows!"

"What!"

Abt's voice boomed to his crew. "Port side! Ship oars!"

The war galley was upon them.

The crew on the portside of the *Olga* heaved their oars up into the air and yanked them desperately onto the deck. The ram of the war galley sheared along the Olga's side in an attempt to break her oars. Timbers shrieked as the two ships scraped across each other. Several sailors were too slow, and their oars snapped between the two vessels. The *Olga* vibrated down to her keel. The mast shuddered and swayed like a tree in a high wind that had far too much weight up top. Coel yelped as he nearly fell. Iron hooks hurtled through the air and thudded to the deck of the *Olga*. Men on the Saracen war galley heaved on the lines, and the hooks dragged across the *Olga* and sank into her rail. Timbers groaned as the two ships locked together in battle.

Abt roared. "Now!"

His crew to the starboard rose from their benches with javelins in hand. They flung them with all their might up at the row of shields along the galley's rail. A few javelins stuck, but the angle was bad. Most of the missiles skated off and fell back onto the Olga.

"We go!" Orsini clapped down his visor. He popped up onto the yardarm for a split second and then leaped out into the air. Coel gaped as the dwarf arced down like a steel pendulum above the deck of the Olga and then ascended towards the rail of the galley.

Snorri roared in Coel's ear. "Go!"

Coel got a foot under him and teetered on the yardarm. "God . . . damn it . . ."

Snorri's palm slammed into Coel's back and knocked him off the beam. "Go!"

Coel screamed in terror as he swung out into space. Ahead of him, Orsini smashed into the Mamluk shield wall like the ball and chain of a siege engine. Three of the Egyptian soldiers fell back. Orsini landed on the deck with a clank and yanked his war hammer from his belt.

Coel clung for dear life as he swooped down towards the deck. His scream went up a notch as he nearly smashed into the war galley's rail. He jerked his knees into his chest and his rear-end cleared the rail by inches. A shield rose up before him. A bearded face under a conical helmet blinked in surprise. Coel kicked with all his might and planted both of his feet into the shield. The Mamluk flew backward into his fellows. Coel clattered to the deck of the enemy ship in a heap.

An armored boot instantly stomped down on Coel's chest and pinned him to the deck. A sword rose to cleave him. Coel's hand went to his dagger. The sword sheared downward. Sparks flashed from the forehead of the Mamluk's helmet. His head rocked back with a great dent in the front of his gleaming helm. A sling bullet fell onto Coel's chest. Coel rammed his dagger up under the Mamluk's chain mail skirt and buried it in the Egyptian's thigh. The man fell back screaming into the press. Coel jumped to his feet.

Orsini waded through the ranks of the armored Egyptians. Sparks shrieked from his blue steel armor as blows rained down upon his head and shoulders. His war hammer buckled shields and smashed limbs. Coel drew his sword. Snorri was suddenly at his side. The Rus's broadaxe rose and fell. Oleg stepped in beside him and lay to with his sword.

Coel's sword flashed. A Mamluk fell. Whatever sorcery Reza had wrought, it had unmanned the Egyptians. Their blows were weak and hesitant, and they seemed pale and disoriented as they swung their weapons. They tried to keep their eyes down while they fought and faltered when they looked ahead. Coel found the golden haze no longer surrounded him, but strange colors reflected from the Mamluk's shining armor before him.

"We are outside of the Walladid's spell!" Orsini's muffled roar came out of his visor. "Look not behind you! Press forward! Forward!"

Marius came shoulder to shoulder with Coel. His mace and chain arced overhead and a Mamluk helmet stove in. The German priest rammed an African marine off of his feet with a buffet of his shield. Márta's veil of mail hid her face. Her scimitar licked out and clove limbs. Orsini formed the point of the wedge as they drove through the Saracen ranks. The Mamluks and Marines fell back before them. Abt's men leaped up to fill in the gap at the rail. Abt's voice rose above the din of battle.

"We have the barrels aboard!"

Orsini smashed down a Mamluk with his hammer and suddenly there was no one ahead of him. Coel shouted over his shoulder to the ship captain. "Roll them forward!"

Coel ran past Orsini without looking back. Saracen crewmen with hand axes and curved shortswords rushed to meet him. Coel faced them with his sword in both hands.

One of the crewmen fell instantly as he was hit in the throat with a sling stone. Coel grinned ferociously. Zuli was an angel watching over him. Coel skewered the second crewman and dodged a blow from the third. Coel cut the man down and found himself at the mast-step. The lowered mast and rolls of furled sail and coiled rope lay at his feet. Coel turned and carefully kept his gaze down and pointed behind him. "Here! Roll the barrels!"

Marius stood with a barrel lying on its side before him. His mace and chain whirled and the iron ball smashed the barrel top. Marius grunted and shoved the heavy barrel with his boot. The barrel rolled lazily across the deck towards Coel, spewing whale oil as it went. The barrel spun as it came, and Coel kicked it into the mast. It turned perfectly, and its contents flooded all over the furled sails. A Mamluk leaped out of the press at Coel. The man's gilded helmet rang like a bell as Zuli's sling bullet struck him. Coel cut the Egyptian down as his shield sagged in his hand.

The plan was working. Coel turned with a victorious wave of his sword and shouted. "The next barrel! Quickly--"

Coel reeled as he looked back. His stomach flip-flopped as the pulsing wall of colors twisted across his vision. Coel squeezed his eyes shut and turned away from the nauseating sight. He rubbed his fist against his eyes and fought the urge to throw up. He shook his head against the after-images that crawled under his eyelids. Someone on the ship shouted at him. "You!"

Coel opened his eyes and turned to face his opponent.

Jesus Christ stood pointing an accusing finger at him. He wore nothing but a breechclout of doeskin and a necklace of blue beads. The Savior stood barefoot upon the deck, and his blue eyes blazed with an intensity that locked Coel in his place.

Jesus' voice thundered across the deck in very bad Latin. "You fight on the wrong side, brother!"

Coel gaped.

"Coel!" Marius' bellowed. "The barrel! The barrel!"

Coel turned and found the second barrel rolling straight at him. He leaped over it as it spun across the deck. Coel landed in the flood of oil behind it, and his feet shot out from under him in two different directions. His nose and chin took the full brunt of the fall. Coel tasted blood and the musty stench of whale oil filled his nose. He shoved himself up with his hands and they slid out from under him in the slippery spill. People shouted his name as he flopped about. He stabbed his sword into the deck and managed to get his knees under him.

"We've cut the lines!" Abt's voice thundered over the clash of arms. "Heave the lamp!"

"Wait!" Snorri's voice shouted louder. "Coel is down!"

Márta screamed. "Tomar! Do not! No! No--" Her scream rose in panic. "Move, Coel! Move!"

Coel looked up. An object arced over the heads of the combatants. Coel strained his eyes as the pulsing lights blurred his vision again. The object was a ship's lantern. It was lit.

Coel heaved himself up blindly and fell on his back as his heels skidded out from under him. Something hit the deck nearby. Coel heard the sound of glass breaking.

"She burns!" Abt's voice thundered again. "Cast off lads! Heave away!"

Oars thudded into the side of the *Qarsh* as the men of the *Olga* pushed away.

Márta screamed again. "Coel!"

Coel crawled blindly towards the mast. He was covered with oil. If he could get over the mast, he would be safe from the fire. If he just--

Blue flame flowed beneath him. Coel thrashed as heat seared his legs. Excruciating pain closed around his hand and flowed up his arm. He could hear the whoosh of air as he ignited. Coel screamed.

He was burning.

Coel thrashed and flailed as he went up like a torch. Agony beyond endurance engulfed him. Coel screamed and screamed again. The flesh of his arms and legs scorched and burned. The screams tore out of his throat as his hair alit and the flesh of his neck seared. Coel's screams suddenly cut off in a strangled gag. Something yanked his chinstrap into his throat and pulled his head back. His war belt cinched and he was hoisted into the air. Coel windmilled his burning limbs as he was borne aloft. His mind went white in unendurable anguish. His screams came out in horrible gurgles as he burned and strangled. All the world was burning flame and twisting lights. Coel's throat was suddenly free. His ears and face were burning. His agony tore out in fresh screams as he fell weightless into the horrible colors.

Cold smashed into Coel like a fist to the jaw.

Coel's body clenched in shock. His lungs filled with seawater, cutting off his screams. Coel sank. Something flashed in the dark water, and a part of Coel's mind cleared. His sword was still in his hand. His fingers had clenched around it in the rictus of fiery agony, and he still held it now it as he descended. His burned limbs obeyed him as he pushed the blade under his war belt and cut it free. Pressure built in Coel's ears as he went down. He shoved the sword under his jack and felt the flesh of his chin part as the point edged up out of the neck of the armored vest. Coel sawed back and forth, and the leather lining rent. His pulse thundered in his temples as he worked the sword with failing strength. The threads holding the diamond-shaped armor plates parted. With a jerk, he cut out of the vest. Coel's charred fingers fumbled at his chain mail shirt.

The water grew darker and darker. His legs kicked less and less. His arms grew heavy. Coel plucked listlessly at his mail with his free hand and stopped. His flooded lungs no longer strained. His hand had only enough strength to hold his sword, and that seemed enough. His limbs no longer burned. He gently clutched his sword across his chest and let the sea take him. He felt very peaceful. His eyes closed. He was free of the fire. Free of pain. Free from the want of air. He was free of all--

Coel jerked listlessly as something seized him by the neck.

Bubbles blew against his face. Distantly, he heard the bizarre, hollow sound of someone screaming at him underwater.

"Kick! Kick!"

Coel kicked his legs feebly. It was too much effort, and he stopped. The arm around his neck tightened. The sea around him began to grow brighter. Coel did not care.

He cradled his sword and closed his eyes again.

* * *

Kamose al Ah-Ay watched the *Olga* sail away into the distance. The twisting prism of lights was gone. Some of her oars had been broken, but most of them were back in the water steadily pulling. In his anger, the sorcerer wished to hurl a magic at the fleeing ship, but his sense of survival prevailed. The Walladid had hardly exerted himself during the battle, and he would be waiting for such an attack. Kamose looked back upon the deck of his own ship. The slaughter had been appalling. Nauseous, half-blind men simply could not hold their own in hand-to-hand combat, no matter how well armed and armored they were. Half of the Mamluks were dead or injured, and as many of Ramah's marines and crewmen had fallen as well. He looked down at Ramah. The ship's captain stared at his masts. The deck was blackened and still smoldered, but the damage to the ship, itself, was minimal. Ramah's frown was reserved for his sails. The sailors had thrown sea water upon them, and that had only spread the oil fire further along their lengths. Great scorched stripes blackened the canvas. They were not incinerated, but Kamose suspected from the look on Ramah's face that the sails would tear apart in the first decent wind.

Ramah shook his head helplessly.

"You!" Tawfiq's voice was a roar of outrage.

The Amir of One Hundred trembled with fury as he pointed his mace at Juba. His eyes were reddened with smoke and fury. "Yes, you!"

The entire ship had seen the mystic stride through the flames and hoist the burning unbeliever into the ocean. Kamose, himself, had watched stupefied as Juba had done this. Nor had it escaped Kamose's notice that the nearly naked Berber had emerged from the fire seemingly unscathed. He had stamped his feet and swatted out the patches of burning oil on his body like a man brushing away flies.

Juba turned his blue eyes upon the Amir and faced him calmly. Tawfiq stalked forward. He thrust out his mace. He came inches from stabbing its top spike into the mystic's chest. Juba did not blink.

Tawfiq was almost wordless with rage. "You!"

"Yes?"

Tawfiq gnashed his teeth. "You threw the infidel into the sea!"

"Yes."

The Amir was torn between outrage and incomprehension. "You threw him! The infidel! Into the sea!"

"Yes."

Tawfiq raised his mace. Kamose thought he would surely strike the Berber, but the Amir lowered the weapon again. "Why?"

"He was on fire."

Kamose stepped down from the foredeck and raised his hand. He feared the Amir might have a seizure. Tawfiq's voice rose to a scream. "He set fire to our ship!"

Juba regarded the Amir with great patience. "Shadrach was thrown into the fiery furnace, and God preserved him."

Kamose mouth opened as the mystic spoke from the Old Testament. Juba raised his hands before the Amir of One Hundred in supplication. "The red-haired one carried a Holy Sword, Amir. The son of Ah-Ay knows this. Ask him. He has known this for some time. I say the infidel's heart is good. He is somehow either ignorant or deluded by the Walladid." Juba sighed. "For that matter, Amir, I would not let an idol worshipper, nor even a disciple of fire perish in flames. I would not let a man's soul leave his body in such torment. There is no worse death for a living man. I gave him the peace of the waters. If you judge this a betrayal, then I pray you, strike me down."

Juba lowered his head for the blow.

Tawfiq's hand slowly opened. His mace of office thudded to the deck. He shook his head as he regarded the mystic. "Allah loves the merciful, and perhaps you are a better man than I. But I would dance my joy to God to see the infidel burning and twisting upon the deck again."

Juba's brow furrowed. "He killed many of your men. Your anger is understandable. I will pray for you both."

"Pray for new sails." Tawfiq spat upon the deck and turned about on his heel. His adjutant scooped up his mace. Juba frowned and went aft. Kamose and Ramah looked upon one another. Kamose prepared himself for what he already knew. "Well, ship's captain?"

Ramah sighed. "We are but a day and half from the Crimean Peninsula, but our rowers are spent and our sails are damaged. It will take us several days to make port. Under oars alone, we are weeks from Trebizond. Cherson, on the peninsula, is the nearest major city with any kind of shipyard. It is claimed by the Rus, but it is the Genoese who run its port. The Genoese are known to ask few questions, and do business with anyone who has gold."

Kamose smothered his anger. They had been defeated, and the Walladid had barely lifted a finger to do it. The sorcerer admitted his defeat. "Bring the ship about, and bring us to Cherson as quickly as you can without killing the rowers. See to your men."

"As you command, Great One."

Kamose turned and climbed back up to the foredeck. He sat down cross-legged and closed his eyes. He calmed his breathing and found his center.

Reza Walladid would not find safety in Trebizond. Kamose had a card he could play there, though it galled him to do it.

The Walladid had enemies in the east he had never dreamed of.

CHAPTER EIGHTEEN

Coel screamed as fire consumed him. His flesh seared. Flames burned him down to his bones. He howled in agony as liquid fire climbed up and blazed between his legs. His nose and mouth filled with burning oil. His tongue charred and contracted as his teeth blackened. Coel screamed in damnation as fire filled his lungs and they burst and shriveled in his chest.

Coel awoke screaming.

"Steady down, Coel!" Hands grabbed his shoulders. "For God sakes!"

Coel jerked and twitched and looked about himself in panic. He was aboard the *Olga*. He was under a blanket. Snorri held him down. Márta and Marius knelt at his side. The priest rose. "He is awake now. The disorientation will pass. He will be fine."

Marius walked away towards the prow. A crowd gathered there.

Coel snatched his hands out from under the blanket and examined them. His fingers were not twisted and blackened. He was unscathed. He threw the blanket aside to look at himself and snatched it back as Márta gasped at his nakedness. Coel's face turned bright red. Márta blushed.

He was, indeed, whole.

Coel collapsed back. "So, Marius has healed me?"

Snorri handed Coel a wineskin. Coel's hand shook as he took it. "Yes, and it was a near thing. You were very badly burned, and you had drowned. He said it was not a resurrection he performed, but you had almost gone beyond his powers. He said it was best if you slept through the healing. He put his hands upon your chest, and you vomited up half the ocean and began breathing again. Then he put his hand upon your brow, and your eyes closed. Then he healed your burns while you slept. Anyway, the effort seemed to nearly do him in. He fainted when he was finished."

"He seems fine."

Márta nodded. "That was three days ago."

Snorri's lips pursed. "What do you remember?"

Coel shuddered. "I remember burning. I remember drowning," Coel blinked. "I think I saw Jesus."

Snorri grunted. "It would not surprise me if you had. You dance closer to death than any man I know."

"No, I mean on the war galley. I think he saved me."

Snorri coughed uncomfortably. "We all have a friend in Jesus, Coel, but it was Zuli who saved you."

Coel cocked his head. "Zuli?"

Snorri nodded in admiration. "It was the damnedest thing I ever saw. Zuli, as you know, was up in the crow's nest. You came flying out of the flames and fell burning into the deep. She grabbed a line from the rigging and dove in after you from the mast. Well, you'd gone down in your armor. I was sure we had lost you. Then Zuli was down so long I thought we had lost you both to the Old Place. I was going to haul up the rope, but Reza told me to wait. The rope suddenly went tight, and then Orsini and I hauled the both of you out of the drink. You weren't breathing, and you should have seen yourself, Coel." Snorri's shoulders twitched. "You looked like a ruined roast. I was sure you were dead." Snorri regarded Coel with great seriousness. "I have said it before, Coel. Your kind of luck cannot be begged, borrowed, or stolen."

Coel looked about the ship. He could see no obvious signs of damage. "We drove them off?"

Márta nodded. "Orsini's plan was marvelous madness. Had you not been so stupid as to look back into Reza's spell, it would all have gone off perfectly."

Coel flinched. "Was anyone else hurt?"

"Oleg took a sword cut to his chin." Márta raised an indulgent eyebrow. "He is very proud of it."

Orsini called from the prow. "Snorri!"

"Yes! Coel is awake!"

"Then come and look!"

"Take a moment or two to collect yourself, Coel," Snorri said. "And then come forward. You should see this."

Márta looked at Coel. Coel looked back. Márta blushed and looked away as Snorri walked off.

"What?"

Márta shook her head and blushed more. "It is nothing."

Coel frowned. "What, then?"

Márta would not meet his eyes. "Your hair is red."

"Aye," Coel nodded. "And?"

Márta's eyes traveled unwillingly to the blanket that covered his loins. "Well, I mean, it is red everywhere."

Coel stiffened. "So?"

Márta flushed to the roots of her hair. "No, I mean, there is nothing wrong with it, it is just, well, I have never seen such a thing." Márta began stumbling over her words. "I mean have never actually seen one, at all. I mean a . . . thing. I mean, a man's thing. I have seen a horse's thing, but your thing is not that big."

Coel simply stared.

Márta stammered out of control. "Not that it should be, though Zuli says that Snorri has thing as big a horse. Not that I have ever seen Snorri's thing, of course, nor that your thing is small. That is not what I am saying. Other than the color, it seems fine to me, I mean, the color is fine, actually—I would like to talk about something else!"

Coel gathered what little dignity he could muster. "Why have I been awakened?"

Márta took a deep breath. "Trebizond."

Coel sat up. "We have arrived?"

Abt suddenly loomed over the two of them. "You should come look. It is quite a sight."

Coel made a robe of his blanket and went to the prow. The coastal water of the Black Sea was a deep blue. The walled city lay less than a league away. Orsini waxed eloquent, and his audience hung upon his every word. Coel followed the dwarf's finger as it traced the land before them.

" . . . As you can see, it is as if the gods themselves made this land a castle before the Greeks ever arrived."

Coel looked at the massive, crenellated sea wall that faced the wharves. Towers and domes rose behind it. Orsini pointed off to the east and west. "Look to the gorges along the coast. Just beyond the city to the south is a deep valley that forks as it stretches to the sea. The city of Trebizond, itself, as you can see, lies within this triangle of land. The gorges on either side of the city and the Black Sea before it create the greatest defensive moat that man has ever seen. Two great bridges of stone span the ravines on either side. Double portcullises of iron guard the bridges where they meet the city walls. Now, look to the sea wall."

Coel looked at the great stone wall that faced the sea.

"On either side you will note a castle, nominally belonging to the Venetians and the Genoese, respectively, though both are mostly manned by native Greeks. Beyond the great sea wall lies another wall, which is actually a string of castles that house the Trebizuntine ruling families. Between the two walls is the commercial district, where traders from throughout the known world ply their trades. Beyond the inner wall lies the ancient city proper and the Imperial Palace of the Angelis."

Tomar frowned. "You keep calling them Greeks. Do they not call themselves Romans as the Byzantines do?"

"An excellent question. Hellenic Greek colonists first founded Trebizond, long before the Italians ever built Rome. It was many generations later, and just a scant handful of years before the coming of the hobgoblins, that the Normans took Constantinople during the Fourth Crusade. One of the great Byzantines, Alexius Comnenus, fled the Norman occupation and sailed with 10,000 men east across the Black Sea. The Greek-speaking population of Trebizond initially welcomed him, and he and his 10,000 soldiers never left. Subsequent generations of Comnenids drove the border of Trebizond south all the way to the mountains and nine days' ride both east and west. The Comnenids held Trebizond for half a dozen generations."

Coel gazed up at the towers and domes rising over the walls. "What happened to them?"

"The women of the Angeli happened to them." Orsini waved his hand at the city. "The women of Trebizond have always been famed for their beauty. The Angeli women were famous for their beauty before the first colonists among them left Greece for the farthest shore of the Black Sea. The Angelis were one of the oldest unbroken lines of ruling families before Alexius came with his 10,000. It was not long before the male Comnenids began marrying women of the Angeli family. The Angeli women also had a reputation for witchcraft, a reputation that has grown stronger with each generation. Some say the Angelis were never completely Christianized and still worship the Greek Pantheon. Hecate, the goddess of magic, in particular, is rumored to be their patron deity.

Four or five generations ago, rumor has it, the Angeli women tired of being concubines and brood mares for the Comnenid males. Peter Comnenid, the then-Emperor, died of a particularly horrible wasting disease, as did his son, his brothers, and the greater part of the Comnenid male line. When the Comnenid's now mostly unemployed royal bodyguard found this suspicious, many of them found themselves similarly afflicted. This plague seemed to have the habit of selectively ravaging the enemies of the Angeli family. Hypatia, the deceased Emperor Peter's wife, proclaimed herself The Angeli, Hypatia I, Autocrat of the East, Queen of the Transmarine Provinces, and, most importantly, Empress of Trebizond. Unsurprisingly, her assumption was unopposed. The first-born daughters of the line have been Empress ever since, and they have fallen back upon the old Greek ways. Hypatia V currently rules, if I am not mistaken."

Abt nodded. "They say she is a sorceress of the First Rank, and her beauty unmatched in the east, and perhaps the world."

Zuli spoke softly. "It is true."

Coel looked over. Zuli looked upon the walls of Trebizond with far away eyes.

Abt shouted out in command. "All right, look alive! Bring her in!"

Sailors scurried to their benches. The sail dropped and oars dipped into the waters of the Tideless Sea. Trebizond's shore swept ever closer. Ships of every description filled the harbor. Vasiliy clapped a hand upon Coel's shoulder excitedly and pointed. "Look there, Coel! Do you see that?"

Sailors began exclaiming in surprise. All eyes on the *Olga* turned and stared in fascination. Snorri rubbed his head. "I have only heard of such things. I never thought to see one."

It was huge. The ship had four masts. Square sails filled with strange rods hung furled in the spars. Red windsock banners in the shape of dragons billowed for dozens of feet from the top of the masts. Armored men in bright silks stood on station around the rails leaning on fantastical polearms with curved and wavy blades. The great ship looked like a wooden fortress anchored upon the water.

"It is a junk!" Abt nearly lost his composure. "An ocean-going junk from fabled Cathay!"

Coel could not believe it. Cathay was the source of silk. When the Hand of God had descended upon the hobgoblins in the steppes of Asia, the Silk Road had been closed forever. Traders from Cathay came only rarely and had to travel the pirate-infested southern coasts of India and Araby and sail the Red Sea, and there the voyage ended. What a ship from Cathay was doing at the eastern edge of the Black Sea and how it had gotten there was beyond imagining.

Abt squinted. An open berth at the docks lay directly ahead of the *Olga* as she swept into port. "That seems awfully damn convenient."

Reza appeared at the captain's side. "It is possible we are expected."

Men moved on the dock. A pennon ran up a pole. The pennon had the image of a black raven upon a blue field. Abt grunted. "Indeed, we are. When I am roving, I fly the raven standard over the *Olga*. That device is close enough that my mother might have sewn it." Abt raised his voice. "Take us in, Tomar! Dead ahead!"

Snorri looked at Coel. "Coel, put on some pants. Or a tunic, or something."

Coel went to his sea-bag and pulled on his best red tunic and slipped on his sandals. Snorri gazed back at him as he buckled on his sword. "And do something about your hair."

Coel suddenly felt the wind on the back of his neck. His hands flew to his head. His thick red hair had once fallen in waves to his shoulders. Now the nape of his neck was naked to the breeze. He ran his fingers through his hair in panic to find it was only a few scant inches long. Coel's hand went to his sword. He flung his gaze about furiously for the culprit. "Who has done this to me!"

"You did," Snorri shrugged. "When you set yourself on fire. Actually, Tomar did. He did not see you floundering about in the oil when he threw the lantern. The fire burned off everything below your helmet. Zuli trimmed what remained for you."

Coel whirled on Zuli in mounting horror. "What have you done?"

Zuli smiled demurely. "You look very barbaric. All the Greek girls will go mad."

Coel seized his mirror from his sea bag. In the bronze surface his hair stuck up out of his head in unruly, red shocks. Coel turned on Marius in terror. "Do something!"

The German priest stared at Coel incredulously. "You wish me to heal your hair?"

"I will pay you! In gold! Name your price!"

Marius' pale blue eyes looked upon Coel scathingly. "Despair is the deadliest sin, and Vanity is the road that leads directly to it." The German turned a cold shoulder to Coel and his gaze back upon the approaching city-state.

Coel ran his fingers through his decimated locks in despair. "My hair . . ."

"Look sharp!" Abt put a hand on his sword. "We have company!"

Coel looked up as the great gate of the sea wall opened.

The *Olga* slid smoothly across the blue waters towards the wharf. As she closed, cavalry galloped out of the gate and clattered across the docks. The horsemen gleamed in gold washed mail and rode black Arabian horses with purple plumes and harness. Their lances waved above them in a thicket of shining steel, and each lance sported the purple pennon denoting royalty. Coel scanned their ranks. There appeared to be about a hundred of them.

Márta shouted happily. "Look!"

Coel looked to where she pointed. At the head of the column rode a lancer with a red pennon, and its device was a bow and scimitar at the foot of a double armed cross.

Márta was beside herself. "It is the arms of the Sisters of Limmasol!"

Coel forgot his hair for a moment. "Where you were trained?"

"Indeed," Reza peered at the horsemen as they formed into ranks before the berth. "This is most unexpected."

Coel looked at the rows of lancers in their gleaming golden armor. Each carried a bow and quiver attached to their saddles and curved scimitars hung from their war belts. Veils of golden mail armor hung from their helmets and covered all but their eyes. The eyes beneath were kohled black. It suddenly became very clear to Coel that all one hundred cavalrymen were women.

"Back oars!" The *Olga* slowed and came to a stop in her berth. Vasiliy threw a mooring rope to the dockhand. The rider with the red pennon rode forward. Coel noted she wore a war horn gilded in silver on a strap around her shoulder. She unhooked the mail aventail that veiled her face. Márta seized Coel's hand in excitement. Coel examined the woman on the horse.

She had a large nose, a large chin, a large mouth, and large brown eyes. Gazing up at her, Coel could see everything about the woman was large. She appeared to be in her twenties but held herself with great dignity. She turned her gaze upon Abt and spoke in a throaty voice.

"You are Abt Svytaslav, captain of the *Olga*."

"Indeed, I am Abt."

The woman held up a gilded baton of office. "I am Blandine de Gossard, Captain of the Empress's Royal Amazon Guard. You will debark your passengers and then row your ship three hundred yards from the dock and drop anchor. A rowboat will be dispatched to your ship once it is anchored. No more than six of your men at any one time may come ashore until further notice. Your crew must stay within the inner and outer walls and not enter the city proper. All ashore must be back aboard ship before nightfall."

Abt exploded. "This is outrageous! I have weighed anchor on these shores thrice before! Each time I have obeyed your laws and brought valuable trade. What have I done to warrant such a welcome?"

The Captain of the Royal Amazon Guard lowered her eyelids slightly. "You wish to question the orders of the Empress?"

Abt looked at the one hundred lances that faced him and then looked back over his shoulder. Coel followed his look. A pair of war galleys had backed oars and pulled out into the harbor. Their rams now faced the Olga from a distance of several hundred yards. Abt gazed up sourly at the Amazon Captain. "No, I do not question the orders of the Empress. I simply reflect upon happier hospitality I have received in the past."

"The orders of the Empress are subject to her whim. However, they will be obeyed without question." She turned her gaze to Reza. "You are Reza Walladid of Shiraz, the son of Shams."

"I am he."

Márta could no longer contain herself. "Blandine!"

The woman sat up in her saddle as Márta pushed forward. "Márta!"

The two women stared at one another in happy shock. Blandine suddenly seemed to remember her office. Her face became serious. "So, you are still with the Persian?"

Márta's face drew down at the question. Her face grew serious as well, and her chin lifted slightly. "I am his bodyguard. My life is sworn to his. Anyone who would strike him must first strike through me."

Blandine grimaced. She turned her attention back to Reza. "You and those with you shall accompany me to the Imperial Palace immediately. You are to be privileged with an audience with her majesty the Empress of Trebizond."

"We will be honored to bask in the presence of The Angeli."

The Captain of the Guard jerked her head to the lancers behind her and eight horses were brought forward. "Surrender your weapons."

Coel's hand went to his hilt. Márta had done the same. Reza lifted a hand. "You may surrender your weapons. I assure you they will be returned."

It took all of Coel's self control to unbuckle his sword belt and lay his weapon on the deck. Márta laid her scimitar and *yataghan* upon the deck, as well. The rest of the party's weapons joined them.

The Amazon Captain nodded in satisfaction. "Your possessions will be taken to your chambers."

* * *

Coel rode beside Snorri as the cavalry column flew through the city of Trebizond. The streets were narrow and paved with wide flat stones of exceptional smoothness. Like all great cities that had reached the limits of their walls, Trebizond had grown up when it could no longer grow out. The houses were all several stories high, and many actually touched one another forming bridges over the streets. They swept through the district between the walls and entered the city proper. The course twisted and curved but led unerringly south. The Amazon Captain gave Reza a steady stream of instructions as they rode.

"You are being privileged with a private audience. The Angeli and her consort, Sir Roger of Syracuse, Strategos of the Empire, will meet you. You will not be expected to perform the triple prostration. You and those with you shall kneel in the presence of The Angeli and then rise only when you are bidden. You shall speak only when bidden. Any attempt at sorcery in The Angeli's presence will be met with your utter destruction and the destruction of those with you."

"We look forward to the honor of observing all required forms of protocol in the presence of the Empress."

Snorri muttered close to Coel's ear. "I don't like this. I don't like this at all." The Rus shot his eyes around the column of woman warriors that surrounded them as they rode. "Treating Apt like a common pirate, taking our weapons, and look about you. There is hardly anyone on the streets. Nothing good is happening in this city."

Coel noticed the shuttered windows and closed doors. "Something is afoot, then. I will grant you that."

Snorri's voice grew belligerent. "And where is my god damned dog! If they have messed about with Otto--"

"Quiet in the ranks!"

Snorri bristled but clamped his mouth shut.

The narrow streets opened onto a wide promenade. The Imperial Palace lay before them. The iron gates swung open. Before them were a dozen men in full mail who made way for the column. They held long, tear-drop-shaped shields and heavy lugged spears. Snorri hissed. "Normans, or I'll be--"

"Silence!" The golden armored woman drove the butt of her lance into Snorri's side.

Coel thought for sure the Rus would snap. Snorri's jaw muscles flexed as he ground his teeth and kept silent. The column rode past the gates into a wide courtyard and dismounted. The Amazons swiftly gave their horses and lances to the horse boys. They drew their curved swords in a single rasp of steel and surrounded the party again. The Amazon Captain jerked her head. "Blindfold them."

Coel tensed as a black silk hood descended over his head.

A hand grabbed his elbow. A woman spoke. "March."

Coel found himself being marched through the inner gate.

The interior of the palace was cool, and Coel could feel the wide-open spaces of the hallway and the vaulted ceiling. He sensed people around them silently watching. They turned and then turned again. Coel felt the passages becoming smaller. They walked down a flight of stairs and then up another one. They began a long winding descent. Coel could smell dampness in the air. They came to level area, and everyone crowded closer. The space was becoming distinctly more confined. Coel began feeling a distinct sense of dread. The only place they could be going was the dungeon.

"Halt!"

Coel halted. Long moments passed. There was nothing to hear but the sound of many people breathing in a confined space. The wait grew interminable. He heard a door unbarred. The hand on his elbow led him into a room. "Kneel."

Coel stiffened, but there was little to be done. Coel dropped to one knee with as much dignity as he could. The woman who led him sucked in her breath at the impropriety, but it seemed she was unwilling to do anything about it. It occurred to Coel that whomever they were to meet was already in the room.

A woman spoke. "Remove their hoods."

Coel blinked in the light. He was in an octagonal chamber filled with glowing candles. A massive chandelier hung from the ceiling. Rich tapestries in the Hellenic red/black style covered the eight walls.

Coel gazed upon the most beautiful woman he had ever seen.

She sat upon a throne a dozen paces away from him. Black hair fell from her brow in great glossy ringlets. Her violet eyes bored a hole into Coel's. The purple depths seemed so vast and dark that they became all that he saw. A part of Coel's mind sparked as he remembered Reza's gaze when they first met in Moscow. He remembered his mother's words about locking gazes with sprites and elves he didn't know. Coel wrenched his eyes up between the woman's arched eyebrows and fixed them there with every ounce of will he had. The woman blinked, and her eyes narrowed at him momentarily. Her purple gaze left him to rove over the rest of the party.

Coel's shoulders sagged. Even with her gaze elsewhere, it was impossible to take his eyes off of her. She was perfect. There was no other way to describe her. She wore a simple Greek chiton of deep purple. Her bare arms and calves were perfectly turned. Her olive skin was flawless. Coel's eyes roved over her voluptuous body and then back to her face. She was so beautiful it made something inside his chest ache. Coel tore his gaze away and managed to look over at Snorri. The Rus stared unblinkingly at the woman on the throne with his mouth hanging open. Oleg stared in similar stupefaction. Even the priest Marius knelt stunned by the vision of the woman on the throne. Reza and Orsini looked at the woman intently but seemed to have their wits about them. Márta's expression was awestruck if not adoring. Zuli stared at the woman and her eyes shown with a strange intensity.

Coel noticed for the first time that a man sat on a throne at the woman's right hand. He was large with long brown hair and drooping brown mustaches. He had pale skin and a strong, oval face. He wore a sumptuous robe of black and gold and a massive sword with a golden hilt hung from his studded war belt. Incongruously, a heavy, and well-weathered wooden club rested across his knees like a royal scepter. Coel had seen such things before. The club was a *baculus*, and was an ancient symbol of authority in the northwest of France. The man's blue-gray eyes fixed on Coel. Even without the title of Sir Roger of Syracuse or the club across his knees, the *Strategos* of the Empire of Trebizond looked every inch a Norman knight.

Coel found his eyes drifting inexorably back to the woman on the throne. He clenched his teeth and dragged them back to the man. The Norman snorted silently and smiled his approval. Coel found that he was sweating with effort, but he grinned back. Inside, to his very core, Coel ached to look upon the woman on the throne again. His hands trembled at his sides with the want of it. Coel searched for resolve. He found it at his hip. His flesh itched at the uncomfortable lightness where the weight of his weapon should have hung. He turned his gaze back upon the Empress on her throne and summoned his anger.

The woman had taken his sword.

Coel rammed his elbow into Snorri's side. The Rus jerked, but his gaze did not waver from the woman's face. The Amazon Captain spoke. "The Angeli will speak with you now."

The Empress of Trebizond looked upon the German priest with obvious distaste. Even in disgust, the woman's voice shivered down Coel's spine and settled in his loins. "You are Father Marius. I am aware of what you are and what you represent." She lifted her hand slightly from the carved arm of her throne. "Escort him to his chambers, and let him wait upon his master."

Marius rose dazedly and a gold mailed Amazon led him from

the chamber. The Empress looked upon the two stupefied Rus. "There is one in my court who has spoken for you, Snorri Yaroslav. You have the freedom of our city. I do not know this Oleg son of Igor, but it is clear he is of little consequence. Take them to their chambers, and see that they are comfortable."

She looked upon Márta as the two bewitched Russians were escorted from the room. "The Captain of my guard has told me of you. Since you are the Walladid's bodyguard and his property, I shall allow you to stay in our presence."

The Angeli gazed upon the dwarf and inclined her head in the slightest of nods. "Orsini of Venice, you have never graced our Empire with a visit before, but your reputation precedes you. Your presence does us honor, however strange the circumstances and your travelling companions may be. I am sure our consort, the *Strategos*, has much he would discuss with you."

Orsini doffed his hat and bent low at the waist. "I am at the Angeli's service in all things."

Zuli and the Empress met one another's eyes. They regarded one another for long moments. The Empress's smile became strangely tentative. "You are exactly as I remember you, Zuleikha."

"You are as beautiful as your mother."

The Empress of Trebizond blushed. Coel's heart leaped at the sight of it. Something passed between the two women.

The woman's purple gaze finally fell again upon Coel.

"You, I do not know. You bear the sword of a Paladin of the Academy of Paris, but you appear to be nothing more than a barbarian savage." Her violet eyes widened. Coel felt his defenses crumble as her gaze bored into him. He found himself in a purple whirlpool and he spun helplessly towards the twin black abysses in the pupils of her eyes. Her voice seemed to speak from inside his head. "Who are you?"

Coel clutched at his anger like a drowning man. He would not have anyone peering into his mind ever again. Not priests, Persian sorcerers, or witch queens gone renegade from Byzantium. He fanned his fury with thoughts of Marisol, his sword and his best friend being led from the room like an addled sheep. The anger surged up out of Coel and spilled from his mouth in a choked outrage. "Where is my sword? And what have you done with Snorri's god damned dog!"

The words sounded lame even to him.

Their effect was thunderous.

The Empress drew back in open shock. Her consort rose from his throne. The gnarled wooden club rose in his hand. An Amazon's curved sword whipped under Coel's jaw and lifted his chin up. Another sliced down in front of his face and rested on his throat. The point of a spear pressed into the small of his back. Coel grinned at the Empress of Trebizond with savage exultation. Her spell was broken. She was inhumanly beautiful, but he found he could look her in the eye.

Reza spoke quickly. "I beg the indulgence of the Angeli. My retainer's name is Coel ap Math. He is, indeed, a barbarian. A Celt, from the uncivilized land of Wales in the Far Western Isles. His belligerence is unforgivable, but it has served its purpose in preserving my life on a number of occasions. I beg you to spare him."

The Amazon Captain snarled at the sorcerer. "You will speak only when you are bidden!"

The Angeli gazed down upon Coel for a long moment. She lifted her perfect chin slightly. "You are very strong," She ran her eyes across Coel's shoulders with interest. "Can you swim?"

The question caught Coel off guard. "All my life."

"Good." The woman turned her attention to Reza. "Time is short, and we have many affairs of state to attend to. I will be brief." The Empress lifted a finger. From behind one of the tapestries an Amazon brought forth a carved ebony box. Coel could not make out what was inscribed upon it. What he could see was that the hinges and the lock were large out of all proportion to the size of the box, itself. They were made of blackened iron rather than gold or brass, and they encircled the box to bind it closed.

The Empress frowned at the box steadily. "You and I have never met, Walladid, but I believe we know one another. I will not bandy words with you. I am prepared to give you what you want. It was not necessary for you to bring Zuli here to steal it from me."

Zuli bit her lip.

The Empress kept her eye on Reza. "Take it. I do not want it. Let it and whatever doom it brings you be far from my shores."

Coel looked upon his employer. It was the first time he had seen Reza display any real emotion. The sorcerer gazed upon the box and his black eyes burned with a hunger beyond imagining. Coel looked at the hunger in Reza's eyes and knew there was nothing the sorcerer would not do to acquire the box before him and possess whatever lay inside it.

The Empress read Reza's look as well. "Of course, I will require something in return."

Reza tore his gaze from the box and regained his chess-playing face. "What is the Angeli's wish?"

"I shall require the services of Zuleikha, and those of your retainer, the barbarian, Coel. I shall forgive his insult and spare him his life. I shall also return his sword and pay him handsomely should he succeed."

Reza gazed upon the box once more. "Coel shall do whatever is required."

Coel strove to rise but the blades upon his body held him in place. He bared his teeth. "The hell I will."

Reza rose to his feet. His eyes flashed, and the finger he stabbed at Coel trembled with sudden fury. It was the first time he had ever seen the Persian lose his composure. "You will do as you are told!"

Orsini spoke calmingly. "*Hired swords, and doers of dangerous deeds.* Your own words, Coel, exactly, when you accepted the Walladid's terms. Until this moment, you have done little more than defend yourself. Admirably, I may mention, and to the benefit of us all, but the circumstances were unavoidable. Now, the time has come for you to earn your pay." The anthracite eyes suddenly glittered. "However, you are within your rights to terminate your contract with us. We are neither kith nor kin, nor are you slave or bondsman. You owe neither the Walladid nor myself any feudal obligations. You are a contractor. You may dissolve our association, return all unspent funds from this month's wages, and present us with an alternative plan as to how you shall refund us the five hundred gold pieces we remitted to the Church for your Commission of Debt. You may then throw yourself upon the hospitality of the Empire of Trebizond if you wish. Of course, if you choose to desert us, I suspect Snorri shall join you out of loyalty, and Oleg, in a likewise mien, to him. I cannot in good conscience guarantee what would become of any of you."

Coel stared at Orsini long and hard. The dwarf met his gaze. Coel was between a rock and a hard place, and they both knew it. It was swiftly becoming clear to Coel that Snorri was the only person he could truly trust, and the Rus had been led from the room like a bull with a ring through its nose. Coel looked over at Zuli, and in his mind he heard the words of his father. There always remained one refuge for a true warrior. That refuge was honor. Were it not for Zuli, his burned body would be at the bottom of the Black Sea. She had risked her life for his. "Are you willing to do this thing, whatever it may be?"

"I am prepared to do whatever the Walladid requires of me."

Coel felt the noose snap tight around his neck. He looked back at the Empress. "What is your wish?"

"It is Zuleikha who shall do most of the work. You seem to have proven your worth to the Walladid, and you have proven your strength to me. You shall simply assist as is needed."

Coel nodded impatiently. "Yes, so just what is it you would have me do, then?"

The spear point jabbed harder against his back. The blades pressed into his chin and throat. The Empress smiled, but her eyelids lowered in irritation. "You are so blissfully unscarred by any sense of your station that it is amusing."

Coel's blood began to simmer. "I am Coel ap Math, my father is Chieftain upon the Mountain, I--"

The Empress waved a dismissing hand. "I am the Empress of Trebizond. As was my mother and her mother before her. Emissaries from the Emperor of the Byzantines, the Patriarch, the Pope, the Mamluk Sultan of Egypt, and the Seljuk Sultan of the Turks all pay homage at my court. What is it, exactly, that you think you are? The second or third son of a minor barbarian noble from some cattle-pasture kingdom of foggy Albion? Look at you. You come into our presence a hired lackey, yet you are filled with foolish pride. Pride is all you and your kind have. You clothe yourselves with it. It fills your bellies and keeps you warm at night. Your kind are nothing but savages and beggars dreaming of the past. The Celts are finished. Caesar, himself, subjugated your race a thousand years ago, and my consort's kinsmen make slaves of the last of you as we speak. You are a weak and pathetic man, Coel son of Math, born of a weak, spent, and pathetic people," The Angeli shook her head in derision. "You are nothing."

Coel was surprised to find himself icy calm. There was a time when he would have hurled himself upon the Amazon's blades to avenge such insults. Now, he gazed mildly at the Empress. "Then you must be very desperate to require the services of a man such as me."

For the second time, shock registered on the Empress's face.

The flesh of Coel's chin parted under an Amazon blade. Another pressed his Adam's apple so that he could not swallow. The armored women looked to their empress for the order to slay him.

"Coel?" Márta spoke from between clenched teeth. "You are going to get us all killed."

"No," The Empress' voice was very calm. "I shall not kill him. The barbarian is, indeed, correct. We are desperate." She opened her hand. "I bid you rise and make yourselves comfortable. I told my Captain this would be an informal audience. Let it be so."

The tapestries parted, and servants slid pillowed stools across the tiled floors. Coel took a seat and dabbed at his chin with the back of his hand. The guardswoman gave Coel a nervous smile and handed him a square of red silk from her belt. Coel smiled back as he took it and pressed it to his bleeding jaw. He looked from the Amazon to the Empress. "May I speak?"

The Empress tensed but inclined her head.

"How is it, then, that I may be of service to the Angeli?"

The tension in the small chamber eased significantly. The Empress regarded her chandelier for a long moment. Her tone lost its sense of majesty and became conversational. "Would you care to hear something of our history? It would amuse me to speak of it."

"Very much."

"A millennium ago, our forefathers came from Greece as colonists to this unexplored place. They built our city between the gorges, and they thrived. When the Romans came, we became a part of their province of Asia Minor. When the western half of the Roman Empire fell to the barbarians, the Emperor Constantine had already moved the capital from Rome to the city of Constantinople. Over time, the remaining eastern half of the Roman Empire became more Greek in culture than Italian, and came to be known as the Empire of the Byzantines."

Coel nodded. "I studied history at the Paladin Academy in Paris."

"Ah, then you are educated, after all. Did you know that my city was once the capital of what was known as the Byzantine province of Chaldia? We were a small and far away province, but wealthy. At one time, we were so wealthy that our citizens did not even pay taxes. Tell me, Coel, can you guess from where such a river of wealth flowed?"

Coel knew. "The Silk Road."

A bitter smile crept across the face of the Empress. "Yes, indeed, the Silk Road. The Silk Road led from far Cathay across almost impassable mountains and deserts and finally came to our shores. We were the point from which unimaginable wealth flowed out into the Black Sea, up to the mouth of the Dnieper River into the north, and west to Constantinople and the Mediterranean beyond. From every bolt of silk, every cask of costly spice, from every chest of jade we took our tariff. Now, can you tell me what happened in the Year of our Lord 1071?"

Coel answered immediately. "Manzikert."

"Yes, the Battle of Manzikert, and what occurred there?"

"The Byzantine Emperor Romanus IV led an army of over 400,000 men against the army of the Seljuk Turk Sultan, Alp Arsalan."

"And what became of the largest army ever to take the field?"

Coel shook his head. He had pored over every account of the battle he could find in the Academy's library. "They were annihilated. The Emperor Romanus was wounded and captured."

"And what was the result of this military catastrophe?"

"The Byzantines lost nearly all of the Anatolian peninsula."

"Indeed, and, yet, Trebizond survived. The mountains to the south and our fortress city made us too costly to conquer. We remained semi-autonomous. We remained the Black Sea conduit of the Silk Road. We survived. Now, tell me, do you know the history of the Goblin War, particularly what unfolded in the south?"

Coel frowned. "I know they ravaged Anatolia and that they reached the walls of Constantinople before they were turned back." Coel shrugged. "Most accounts I have read dealt with the northern invasion through the Russias and the siege of Budapest."

"It occurred much as you said. The southern hobgoblin horde left Persia in ruin and swept into Anatolia. They marched through the mountains and ravaged the lands of Turks. They marched up to the very gates of the Golden City, itself, but, once again, Trebizond remained free. Once more, our mountains defended us, and the hobgoblins were no sailors and could not assault us by sea. When the hosts of the Holy League of Humanity finally drove the shattered hobgoblin armies back, they consolidated for a last stand in the plains of Kazakhstan. Do you know what transpired in that final confrontation?"

It was an event called upon at least once during every sermon in every Christian Church. "Saint Tomas sent the Holy Host back and stood alone before the hobgoblin horde. Father Sander beseeched the Heavens, and the Hand of God descended upon the Hobgoblins."

"Yes. Tomas Sander and the Hand of God. The hobgoblin horde was struck down by holy fire. So utter was their annihilation that the scar of their destruction became the Great Waste. Can you guess what God's victory did to my city?"

"It closed the Silk Road."

"Yes, the Silk Road was closed forever. The Hand of God left an impassable desert of scorched horror from the southern foot of the Ural Mountains to the north of Persia. A vast plain where all living things sicken and die, and those that survive become vile and cursed by the gods. A fitting burial place for the bones of Satan's army, but it was a victory from which Trebizond never recovered. Our river of wealth ran dry."

The Empress stared into a bank of candles and mused to herself. "Oh, we are a comfortable little kingdom. Our land is well watered by the snows of the Caucasus Mountains that protect us to the south. Our soil is fertile with rolling fields of grain and our hills well laden with vines." The attention of the Empress fell back upon Coel. "I accused you of being borne of a weak and spent people. I might well have accused myself of the same. Trebizond is now an empire only in name. Our only overseas possession was Cherson, on the Crimean Peninsula, but the Genoese took that from us with the help of the Rus over fifty years ago. We had no fleet that could match the ships of Genoa and no army we could afford to send to take it back from the Rus."

Hypatia Angeli's face flushed with sudden anger. "We are surrounded by our enemies. Our land is green, while the lands about us are dust and rock. The Turks, the Georgians, the Armenians, and now even the Rus, all would like to see us under their yoke. The Byzantines, themselves, would like to bring us back under the shadow of their shriveled little empire. We make treaties. We play one side against the other. We hire mercenaries, and, when we must, we fight desperate little wars. My sisters, my cousins, my aunts, we stretch our powers to their limits, and still, more and more, we are forced to debase ourselves to remain free. I married my sister, Lydia, to Vahram, the King of Cilician Armenia, for the promise of a thousand horsemen. My youngest daughter, Chloe, lies in the arms of the Seljuk Vizier, Orhan the Cruel, to keep his mind on things other than conquering our city.

"And now a junk from far Cathay lays anchored in your harbor."

"Yes, after nearly two centuries, envoys from the Far East come to our shores." The Angeli looked beyond Coel. The clear brow furrowed. Her perfect fingers touched her chin in thought. Her every movement was enthralling. It occurred to Coel very clearly that if every wall in Trebizond fell away she would be staring directly at the Cathayan ship where it lay moored. "How did they do it? Could

316 | CHUCK ROGERS

they have truly sailed around the Africas? Is such a thing possible? Did they put their great ship on rollers like the ancient Pharoahs and portage across the Eastern Desert to the Nile? And done this without the Mamluk Sultan of Egypt, much less the Blue Robes knowing of it? I cannot divine it, and nor will their envoys tell me." Her gaze fell once more upon Coel. "Would you like to know what they do say?"

"Very much"

The Angeli's voice dropped low. "They say a way has been found through the waste. They say they the Silk Road shall be opened once more. Can you guess what this would mean to my kingdom?"

Orsini's voice rumbled low at the thought. "Wealth beyond the dreams of avarice."

The eyes of the Angeli shone. "Wealth to build a new fleet. Wealth with which to hire as many soldiers as need be. Wealth to rebuild the garrisons and strengthen the frontier. Real power with which to bargain with our neighbors, rather than whoring the flesh of the Angeli line for a few more scant seconds of sovereignty. It would mean wealth, it would mean power, and it would mean freedom. It would mean the rebirth of our empire." The Empress took a deep breath. "And yet, I have looked into my power; and when I close my eyes, I see fire and blood from horizon to horizon. I smell sorcery on this junk that sits in our waters. It is a sorcery whose smell I do not recognize, and it is veiled in ways through which I cannot see without revealing my hand."

A cold, sinking feeling began to creep into the pit of Coel's stomach. "What is it you want of me?"

The Empress leaned back on her throne. "I wish someone to go aboard that junk and find out what it is that disturbs me."

Coel cleared his throat. "To sneak aboard, then."

"Precisely. Zuli shall do it, and, since you have proven yourself so resourceful, you shall accompany her."

Coel's sense of dread mounted. "Why us?"

Orsini gave Coel sympathetic look. "I believe it is a matter of plausible deniability."

The Angeli nodded. "Indeed. This is a crucial moment. I

cannot afford to offend the Chinese. My city is the natural outlet for the Silk Road onto the Black Sea, but that does not mean the men of Cathay could not travel farther west to the Turkish port of Samson. For that matter, the King of Georgia would carve a port city out of his rocky coast with his bare hands to acquire the Silk Road's trade. Yet, I must know what it is aboard that ship which pricks my skin. That is why I need your services. Zuli's reputation as a thief is known from Cairo to Karachi. Stealing aboard the first Cathayan junk to drop anchor in this century is exactly the sort of thing she would do, and you?" The Empress eyed Coel's hair in amusement. "You will appear to be nothing more than her thatch-headed barbarian accomplice."

"Tell me, then." Coel liked the sound of things less and less. "If we are captured, what is to keep these envoys of Cathay from taking fire and tongs to our flesh, or sorcery to our minds and finding out all about us?"

The Angeli shrugged. "It is within my power to arrange it so that you will die conveniently before you reveal too much."

"I . . ."

"Zuli has already said that she will do what is required. All that remains for you to do is lurk and assist her as needs be."

"Well . . ."

The Empress waved a casual hand. "As to your initial questions of me, your sword is in my safekeeping. It would only encumber you on your swim, and, should you be captured, it would be so strange a thing to find in the hands of a hulking, barbarian thief that it would raise too many questions in the minds of the Cathayans. I shall return your sword to you on the completion of your task. Should you be killed, I give you my word I shall return the blade to the Academy in Paris with the tale of your demise."

"But--"

"Ah, yes, your friend Snorri's dog. Otto is currently in a stall in the royal stables. I assure you he is warm, watered, and well fed."

Coel restrained his anger. He did not relish being played like a harp. He did not like the naked feeling of not having his sword. He did not like being coerced into the deal with veiled threats to his friends. He did not like the idea of boarding the ship of an official envoy of Cathay. He liked the idea that there were sorcerers aboard even less. He found he did not like the idea of swimming in the sea so soon after having drowned at all. Coel closed his eyes. It did not matter what he liked or disliked. She had him by his stones and they both knew it.

Coel refrained from spitting on the tiles. "I owe Zuli my life. I will help her if she is willing."

The Angeli's face softened as she looked upon Zuli. "Will you do this thing, Zuleikha? Not because the Walladid orders you, but willingly, for me?"

Zuli spoke very softly. "I will do this thing, for you."

The Empress visibly relaxed. A great weight seemed to have dropped from her. She smiled upon Coel with genuine warmth. Coel could not prevent his heart from leaping in his chest. She was disturbingly beautiful. "You have our gratitude." She inclined her head at Blandine. "Take the box to the Walladid's chamber, and give him whatever he requires." She looked back at Zuli and Coel. "Tomorrow night, there shall be no moon, and with luck, the clouds that gather in the east will be upon us and shroud the stars. Before dawn, you shall swim out to the junk Until then? You have our every hospitality." The Empress lifted a graceful hand. "I bid you, indulge yourselves."

CHAPTER NINETEEN

Coel blinked as his blindfold was removed. Two of the Amazon Guards stood at his side. Their weapons were sheathed. The tall redheaded one nodded at the brass-gilded door before him. "This is your chamber. You shall share it with your friends, the Rus. There is a bell hanging by the door. You have but to ring it if there is anything at all you desire."

Coel struggled to keep a civil tongue in his head. "Thank you."

The two women marched off down the hall, glittering and clinking in their gold-washed mail armor. Coel gingerly pulled the bloodied square of silk from his chin as he entered his chamber. He was greatly relieved to find the room was above ground. The room was spacious and lit by numerous oil lamps set in the walls. Intricately tiled frescoes of the ocean floor populated by mermen with tridents and sea nymphs reclining in seashells tiled the walls. Persian rugs covered the floor beneath his feet. The ocean breeze stirred the curtains in the narrow window-slit. Snorri sat on a couch looking at nothing. Oleg gazed out the window dreamily.

Coel scowled at his welcome. "Well, hello to you, too, then."

The two of them stared at Coel as if he was very far away. Coel's scowl deepened. "What the hell is wrong with you?"

"Coel?" Snorri blinked sleepily. "Your chin is bleeding. Did you cut yourself shaving?"

"No! I did not cut myself shaving!" Coel's temper simmered as he strode into the room. "One of the Amazon Guards did this to me, while the Empress lectured me on the history of the Roman Empire and the unfortunate nature of my pedigree!"

"No," Oleg shook his head slowly. "Hypatia would never do that."

Coel stared at Oleg incredulously. "I was not aware that you and the Empress were on a first-name basis."

Oleg's head tilted like a dog that has heard a sound it does not understand. "What?"

Coel's open hand cracked against Oleg's cheek like a whip. The young Rus staggered and clutched the side of his face. Snorri blinked and rose. Coel's voice dropped to snarl.

"Wake up, God damn you! She has bewitched you both! While you were led away like moonstruck fools, Zuli and I were blackmailed into committing suicide tomorrow night! Reza and Orsini are willing to throw the three of us to the wolves for an antique breadbox! Look at you! You are like a couple of bullocks who have just come out from under the shears, and that Greek bitch still holds both of your shriveled sacks in the palm of her--"

Coel saw stars as Snorri hit him. His jaw almost unhinged from his head. The room tilted crazily as he staggered and fell to one knee. Coel caught himself with his hands and shook his head to clear it. He saw red as he surged up at the Rus.

"By God, I will--"

Coel's nose broke under Snorri's knuckles. Tears squirted and smeared his vision. Blood filled his mouth. His knees buckled, and he fell forward heavily onto his hands. Coel spat blood and stared at Snorri's boots. The bare-knuckle boxing champion of the Moscow garrison stood over Coel with his ham-like fists clenched. Snorri's voice dropped very low. "We don't have to take that from the likes of you."

"No," Coel's swelling lips skinned back from his teeth. "No you do not."

Snorri raised his fist to strike Coel down.

Coel lunged headfirst and speared Snorri in the belly. The Rus' breath whooshed out of his lungs. Coel rammed Snorri with his shoulder and drove the Rus all the way across the room. Snorri crashed backward into the wall by the window. Coel seized the stunned Rus by his war belt. He turned and heaved with all his might. Snorri flew over Coel's hip in a pinwheel of limbs.

Tiles shattered as the big Rus crashed against the window nook and fell heavily to the floor. Broken tiles and mortar dust showered down on Snorri where his impact had obliterated a frolicking merman. Coel caught movement in the corner of his eye and whirled. Oleg reared back as Coel rounded on him. The young man stood with a clay water jug cocked back in his hand. Coel bared his bloody teeth at the young Rus. Oleg's eyes flared wide. He looked back at the jug he held in his hand and then at Coel in a horror.

"No! Wait! I--"

Coel punched Oleg in the mouth. He was irrationally pleased to see the young Rus fall and the crockery in his hand shatter on the stone floor. Coel turned back on Snorri with the idea of kicking his gold tooth down his throat.

"Leave him alone!"

Coel snapped around at the sound of a woman's voice.

Three women in costly silk gowns stood in the doorway. A short blonde ran into the room and hurled herself between Snorri and Coel. She dropped down and cradled Snorri's head in her lap. Her blond curls fell all about Snorri's face as she brushed bits of tile and mortar off of him. She looked up and shook back the veil of her hair. Her blue eyes glared murder at Coel. "Heathen savage!"

Snorri looked up into the woman's face. "Hello, Ianthe. You look beautiful."

The woman rubbed Snorri's head. She peered into his eyes one at time and checked his pupils. "Are you all right? Do you want me to have him impaled?"

"Oh, no. Coel is my best friend. He was helping me."

The woman wrinkled her nose at Coel in distaste. "This bloodstained barbarian is your friend?"

"Well I was the one who stained him," Snorri grinned up from her lap. "Oh, and the Empress was another."

Ianthe's expression changed. Everything was suddenly crystal clear to her. "Ah, yes. Your audience with the Empress."

Snorri's eyes grew vague again. "Hypatia . . . "

Ianthe slapped Snorri on side of his shaven head. "Be strong."

Snorri blinked back into clarity. Coel scooped up the square of silk the Amazon guard had given him. It was becoming rather rumpled and crusty. He pressed it to his face anyway. His nose and chin were bleeding freely. Ianthe's blue eyes looked Coel up and down with interest. "I had heard your behavior at the audience was absolutely insufferable."

Coel raised a swollen eyebrow. The woman did not seem at all displeased with the notion.

"You are Ianthe?"

"Yes, I am," Ianthe shook back her blonde curls and smiled. "And these are my friends, Tabitha, the Empress' handmaid of Thessaly, and Ghiday, of the court of Ethiopia."

Coel looked at the two women. Tabitha looked like a dark-haired statue of Athena. Ghiday's tightly coiled copper hair fell in thick horsetails over the cinnamon-colored skin of her shoulders. Both women were absolutely beautiful. They looked Coel up and down like horse traders examining some strange breed they had never seen before.

Coel nodded and lowered the bloody silk. "I am pleased to meet you both. I am Coel, son of Math."

Ghiday's smile lit up the room. "You have green eyes."

Coel grinned through his mangled face. "I have just had to beat these two Rus because the Angeli bewitched them. If you smile upon me again, it is I who shall need beating."

Ghiday's hands flew to her mouth as she flushed with pleasure. Coel turned his attention back to Ianthe. "You are the woman Snorri was thrown out of the Varangian Guard over."

"Why, yes, I am." Ianthe seemed pleased. "Has Snorri mentioned me?"

It was increasingly painful, but Coel managed a smile. "Often, and fondly."

Ianthe beamed. "Perhaps I have misjudged you. It is hard to make determinations about a man whose face has been so rearranged." She gazed down at Snorri warmly. "The *Strategos* has honored the three of you with an invitation to dine with him tonight.

Will you go?"

"Who?"

Coel shook his head.

Ianthe's disgust was evident. "Sir Roger of Syracuse, the Consort of the Angeli and *Strategos* of the Empire. You were introduced. You probably were not paying attention. The Empress has that effect. Sir Roger would like the three of you to join him informally in his chambers tonight, along with Orsini of Venice. The *Strategos* dislikes petty intrigues and does not often dine at court. However, he dearly loves to hear news of Europe from travelers."

Snorri gazed up from Ianthe's lap. "Tell the *Strategos* Oleg and Coel will be delighted."

"But what of you?"

Snorri put his hands behind his head and grinned up from her lap. "I will only go if you kiss me."

Ianthe bent over Snorri and her blond hair shrouded the both of them for long moments. She was blushing as she arose. "You have a new tooth!"

Snorri smiled so that the gold glittered in his mouth. "Do you like it?"

"Very much," Ianthe gathered her skirt about her as she rose. "You are expected within the hour of nine. I will inform the *Strategos* that you have accepted his invitation." Ianthe inclined her head at Tabitha and Ghiday, and they left the room in a flurry of whispers.

Snorri sat up and grinned. "Hah!"

Coel frowned as blood soaked through his borrowed handkerchief. "What?"

Snorri snapped his fingers at him. "Dinner with the *Strategos*!"

He suddenly looked over at Oleg. The young Rus sat on the floor holding his bleeding mouth in pain. Snorri looked at him for a moment in sympathy and then back at Coel.

"So, what is this about you and Zuli committing suicide

tomorrow night?"

* * *

Snorri tsked into his wine cup. "Well, now, that was damn fool thing to agree to."

Coel's knife froze. He held his skewered cube of grilled lamb in mid-dip over the honey pot and glared out of his swollen face. "Well, why don't you try your luck making deals with the Empress, then? I am sure you would drive a harder bargain than I!"

Sir Roger spoke in Coel's defense. "Your friend had little choice in the matter, Yaroslav," He tossed back the remainder of his goblet. "Few of us do."

Snorri looked into his wine with a troubled brow. "Was I truly that bad?"

Coel spent a moment enjoying the juice of the seared meat and the honey mixing in his mouth and then washed it down with a draught of red Trebizuntine wine. The wine made him forget his face. "You would have willingly scraped the royal barge of barnacles with your tongue, and then asked for seconds."

Snorri flushed. Oleg looked down at the tiles. Orsini smiled over the rim of his cup at the *Strategos*. "I told you Coel was a poet."

Sir Roger snorted in amusement.

Snorri muttered as he speared a piece of pear with his eating knife. "My pride is wounded enough. You do not have to rub salt into it."

Sir Roger sighed. "Neither you nor your young friend should feel ashamed, Yaroslav. Hypatia has broken better men than you and I with the arch of an eyebrow." He looked over at Coel. "Indeed, I will give you full credit, Celt. You are the only man to ever look into the eyes of the Angeli and demand the whereabouts of a dog. Even eunuchs and sodomites are completely in her thrall. Had it been a public audience before the court, I suspect she would have had you killed. It would have been a terrible blow to her power and prestige. You shook her. I can tell. She will remember you for a very long time." The Strategos peered into the candle flames again. "I wish I could shake her like that."

"But you are *Strategos* of the Empire!" Oleg protested.

"Indeed, son of Igor. I am *Strategos*. I command all the might of Trebizond, save for the one hundred of the Royal Amazon Guard. For whatever that failing might is worth."

Snorri glanced about at the tapestries that covered the walls and the gold and silver they ate off of. They all reclined on Roman-style couches circling a low table laden with choice foods and wines from half a dozen lands. Snorri gestured about at the opulence with his wine cup. "Forgive my impertinence, *Strategos*; but from where I sit, you seem not so badly off."

Sir Roger raised a distracted eyebrow as one of the servants went to the door unbidden. The door opened, and a staggeringly beautiful woman entered the chamber accompanied by a pair of the Empress's Amazons. She looked like an older version of the Empress. A few silver strands gleamed out of the long black waves of her hair, and her chin was slightly square compared to the perfection of the Empress Hypatia. She was tall, as well, and wore a white chiton with purple at the neck and hem that denoted royalty. She carried herself like a queen. Just looking at her kindled desire in depths of Coel's belly.

Sir Roger muttered ruefully. "May I present the Empress's first cousin, Eulia. Her talents lie in healing, rather than fortunetelling, bewitchment, and affliction."

The woman ignored Sir Roger and turned purple eyes upon Coel. "It is my cousin, the Angeli's wish that your face be made whole again."

"I would appreciate that."

Eulia took his face in her hands. Coel breathed in the scent of her hair and struggled to slide his eyes over at the *Strategos* as he spoke. "To answer your question, Yaroslav, indeed, my situation could be worse. My men and I have all that a warrior could ever wish for. Gold, richly appointed chambers, our choice of the finest steeds and equipage. I can have any woman in the Empire I choose, including the Empress, herself, whenever the mood strikes me. Indeed, I have had Eulia come to my chamber a number of times."

Coel winced as Eulia's hands tightened on the bridge of his nose.

Snorri peered at the Norman shrewdly. "And yet?"

Sir Roger took a deep draught of his wine and waved his empty chalice at Eulia. "And yet, whenever I start to have an interesting conversation with anyone other than a god damned Greek, one of the Empress's relatives appears without fail to spy upon me."

Coel looked hard at the *Strategos* as Eulia's hands pushed at his face. He realized that Sir Roger was drunker than he appeared. The *Strategos* refilled his cup. His voice became bitter.

"I will tell you something. I have sired four children by the Empress. Hypatia has seen to it that all of them are girls, and damn me if I know how the witch did it. I have had four other children by ladies of the court and another six with women outside the city. Not a single man-child was born among them. Fourteen daughters, and none will bear my name, nor will any woman in this bewitched land ever bear me a son who will." Sir Roger sagged back and took another long pull from his goblet. "Hypatia wants no male heirs to disrupt the Angeli dynasty, and the witch has done her work well."

Coel jerked as Eulia shoved his nose back in line. He blinked as a burning itch flowed through the break. His eyes immediately felt less puffy. Snorri shook his head at the *Strategos*. "Then why not leave?"

Eulia smiled serenely at Sir Roger. "Yes, *Strategos*, why do you not leave?"

"Because Hypatia is a witch of the First Rank, as well as the queen of whores!" Sir Roger glared from under his brows. "She came to Syracuse and unmanned me. I followed her half way across the world like a dog drooling after a piece of meat. I have tried to leave a dozen times, and every time I do the witch looks into my eyes and I am lost. If I were a man, I would pluck out my eyes. It would be a fair trade to have my balls back." The Strategos looked upon Coel long and hard. "I would pay you anything you asked if you would tell me how you defied her this day."

Coel had no idea what he could say to him. All he could offer the warlord was the truth. "She took my sword. It made me angry."

Sir Roger snorted and gazed deeply into his wine. "She took my sword long ago, and I gave it to her gladly."

Orsini spoke in a diplomatic tone. "Surely, there is something more worth staying for?"

Sir Roger peered at Orsini for a long moment. His eyes looked into the distance. "Perhaps."

Eulia gazed upon the *Strategos* with interest even as her thumb stroked the wound on Coel's chin away. Coel looked at the Norman lord's face and the answer was clear to him.

"The people."

Sir Roger stared at Coel in amazement. "Indeed. The people." He shook his head at Coel. "I will tell you something. In Syracuse? The people hated my family. They hated all Normans. I swear the Sicilian wretches preferred being ruled by the Saracens. Revolt was always fermenting, and daggers always awaited us in the dark. Here?" Sir Roger stared back into memory. "When I first came, the people bowed and scraped, and I took their words of love and loyalty for what I thought they were worth, which was nothing. I had been elevated above all others in the land save the Empress. They had no choice. Then, a year later, I fought my first battle on these shores.

That was fifteen years ago. Six Janissary *Ortas* had managed to breach the fastness of the mountains and were looting the villages in the foothills. It was the first such incursion in many years. It was more than just a raid. These were the Sultan's *Serdengeçti*, what the Turks call 'head riskers,' their elite. I believe they were testing the new *Strategos*. I rode out with my knights and men at arms. Hypatia's magic had given me ample warning of their whereabouts, and her power allowed me to meet them at a place of my choosing, but those Turks did not lie down for us. We fought them tooth and nail, and we crushed them. We hung their bodies by their heels in the mountain passes as a warning."

The *Strategos* gazed back in memory. "I shall never forget the day my men and I rode back into the city victorious. A hundred horns announced us as the great gates opened, and the fifes and drums played as we rode down the street in column. The entire population had all turned out in their finery. Flowers rained upon us from the rooftops, and the people hailed us as heroes. Children ran beside us waving pennons with my coat of arms upon them. Maids threw ribbons from windows and balconies. We were feasted in every house and hall. Three times I have ridden out to fight the Turk, and each time I have ridden through the streets in triumph. Even in peace, the people hail me as Defender. The heads of the oldest Greek families offer me their hospitality with open hands, and the lowest rag picker in the streets will come out of the shadows to press his hand to my boot and bless me when I pass."

"Adulation," Orsini nodded thoughtfully. "It is a coin that glitters brighter than gold."

Eulia rose from the couch. Her gaze grew impassioned as she regarded Sir Roger. "You are the Defender. You were not chosen out of a hat from amongst the available warlords of Europe. When Hypatia came of age to take the throne, she knew she must take a consort. A consort to defend the Empire. She looked deep into her power. She saw fire and blood on all the horizons, and she saw you, Roger of Syracuse, on your white horse, your sword on high, the banner of Trebizond flying behind you as you rode through the flames. You are the undefeated sword and shield of Trebizond. Our hero. How can the people not love you? Hypatia, herself, loves you. As much as she can love any man."

Sir Roger reddened at Eulia's earnestness and gave Snorri a lopsided smile. "And you ask me why I do not leave."

Eulia went to Oleg's couch and put her palm across his bruised mouth. Coel stroked his healed face and watched as Sir Roger drank more wine. Coel decided it was time to take a chance.

"*Strategos.*"

Sir Roger nodded benignly. "Yes?"

"May I ask a question?"

"You have agreed to risk your life for us tomorrow night," Sir Roger shrugged. "Ask. I will answer."

Coel found no diplomatic way to frame his question, so he simply spoke his mind. "What is in the box the Angeli gave Reza, and why is it worth my life?"

Sir Roger sat up straight. Eulia tensed visibly. Coel was surprised when Orsini spoke. The dwarf's voice was not unfriendly, but neither was it yielding. "That is the Walladid's business, Coel, and mine. It will remain so until we choose otherwise."

Coel matched Orsini's tone. "I appreciate that, but tomorrow night it is I who will be swimming out to sea, not you, nor was I speaking to you when I asked."

Orsini's brows drew down. "You have been paid, and paid handsomely, Coel. Paid to be brave and fight well, both of which you have done admirably up to this point. You and I have shared confidences, so I will give you some advice. You have not been paid to snoop. That is Zuli's area of expertise. I suggest you leave such activities to her."

Sir Roger raised his hand. "I will tell you honestly, Coel. I do not know what Hypatia has given the wizard. The business of sorcery is something I prefer to stay well clear of." The *Strategos* rose from his couch. "However, I will show you something. Come."

Coel rose and ignored Orsini as he followed the *Strategos* to a large window shuttered against the night wind. Sir Roger threw back the bolts and pulled the double shutters wide. "Do you see?"

Coel looked out across the Imperial Palace. A white marble tower stood apart from the rest of the main keep. It was narrow, round and windowless except for a single shuttered slit at the top. The shutter on the window was brass, and it gleamed in the night as strange lights flickered around its frame. Above the window a crenellated balcony surrounded a narrow cone-like spire of brass. Coel watched as yellow and blue will o' the wisp lights crawled down the spike of the spire. Some seemed to dance among the crenellations to fade away or disappear in a flash. Others split or stretched out, appearing to fill the cracks between the stones. The wind blew strongly in Coel's face and smelled of rain. Coel's skin crawled as he seemed to hear the whisper of voices on the wind.

Sir Roger pointed his finger at the tower. "That is where the Angeli women make their magics. On more nights than I can count, I have heard whispers and shrieks upon the wind and seen the light of sorcery crawling in the dark. I think she gave me this chamber precisely so that I would always be witness to her power. I will tell you what little I can, Coel, since you risk your life tomorrow. I do not know what is in the box. But I do know that the box and whatever lies inside it are in the top of that tower, and I know also that Reza and the priest, Marius, are up in that tower this night. It is they who are making magics, not the Angeli. The sorcerer's swordswoman, Márta, stands guards within the lower door."

Coel knew suspected this, but he did not like hearing it.

Snorri spoke beside him. "Reza is a sorcerer, Coel. We knew that when we took the job. His sorceries have saved our lives. Now is not the time to be squeamish."

Orsini spoke in agreement. "I advise you to listen to your friend, and bend your mind to the task which lies ahead of you."

It was sound advice, and Coel knew it. Reza had saved their lives. But the mission before him was so vague in nature and so desperately dangerous he no longer knew what to think, and looking out the window at the tower left his stomach feeling cold and jittery despite the food and wine.

Something was wrong.

Coel kept his thoughts to himself as he returned to his couch. "I apologize for my impertinence, Orsini. You know that you have my deepest respect, but a man cannot help but be curious."

"It is perfectly understandable," The dwarf nodded and poured more wine. He seemed glad to put the subject behind them.

Sir Roger seemed glad, as well. "The Angeli has said you are to indulge in our hospitality tonight. What is your desire? Dancing girls? Jugglers? Perhaps magics of a lighter nature? The court has recently retained an Armenian illusionist who can conjure images of a most remarkable nature." Sir Roger gave a slight leer after the last suggestion.

Snorri drained his cup and set it upon the table. "Actually, I have an acquaintance I would like to rekindle, and I thought I might take Coel and Oleg along with me."

The *Strategos* nodded. "Ianthe, and her friends, Ghiday and Tabitha."

Snorri grinned. "The same."

"Very well. For me? A quite evening in. Perhaps Orsini of

Venice would be kind enough to help me finish the wine and tell me the latest news of Europe."

Orsini nodded and filled both their cups. "Nothing would please me more, *Strategos*."

Snorri rose and snapped to attention. He slapped his chest with his right hand and then shot his hand palm out. "By your leave, *Strategos*."

Coel was impressed. It was a very snappy Roman-style salute, worthy of the parade ground. It seemed Snorri's years in the Varangian Guard in Constantinople had not been spent entirely in taverns. Sir Roger was impressed, as well. He rose from his couch to return it.

Oleg bowed clumsily. Coel bent a knee as he had learned in Paris. Sir Roger raised a hand towards the two Amazons standing by the door. "See to it that they have whatever they need."

The Amazons opened the doors and followed the three of them out. Snorri was quiet as they were escorted back to their chamber. At the door, the tall redheaded Amazon smiled in a friendly fashion. "Is there anything you require?"

Coel nodded. "Yes, may I have pen and paper, and a pot of ink?"

"It shall be brought to you." The woman blushed slightly and pointed at Coel's belt. "May I have my kerchief back?"

Coel looked at the bloodstained square of silk he had thrust into his belt. He plucked it out guiltily. "I am afraid I have ruined it."

"Well, my mother gave it to me. I would still like to keep it."

Coel handed it over and watched the two Amazons march away. Snorri grabbed his shoulder and jerked him inside. He slammed the door shut and his voice dropped to an angry mutter. "What the hell are you doing prying into Reza's affairs!"

"I am the one swimming out to sea tomorrow night! I want to know what this is all about!"

Snorri rolled his eyes. His voice dropped to whisper. "I am trying to see what I can do about that, and I don't need you raising suspicion by asking stupid questions!"

Coel's voice dropped to a hiss. "What the hell does that mean?"

"Never mind! The less you know the better!"

Coel glared. No one seemed to think he could be trusted with anything except taking insane risks. Snorri clapped him on the shoulder. "Forget about it. Come! Ianthe and her friends await us." He leered suddenly. "At the palace baths!"

The image of Ghiday, handmaid of Ethiopia lying in a scented bath waiting for him filled Coel's mind with startling clarity. Snorri grinned as he read Coel's expression. "Worry about tomorrow, tomorrow, Coel. Tonight, you have other concerns.

Oleg gaped. "They are awaiting you?"

"Yes."

"In the bath?"

Snorri nodded happily. "Indeed."

Oleg looked uncertainly between Snorri and Coel. "All three of them?"

"Indeed, yes." Snorri read the young Rus' expression. "Three of them, three of us. It will all work out very nicely." Snorri leaned forward. "Tabitha likes strong young men."

Oleg's jaw dropped.

A small voice nagged in Coel's mind. "What about Zuli?"

"What about her?"

Coel found himself flushing. "Well, you and she . . . "

Snorri waved his hand. "We are not married, you know. She knows about Ianthe and me."

"Aren't you afraid she might find another man for the evening?"

"No," Snorri grinned. "Tonight, she is with the Empress."

"What is she doing with the Empress?"

Snorri rolled his eyes. "What do you think she is doing with the Empress?"

Coel suddenly understood what Snorri was implying, and the image of it blurred his mind.

"Listen to me, Coel. The Greeks are a very ancient and interesting people. They take their sins of the flesh very seriously. Did you not notice the look that passed between them during the audience?"

Coel had, but the picture Snorri painted still shocked him.

Snorri sighed. "You know, Coel, you have traveled half the length of civilization from west to east, and still you have the morals of a bumpkin from Wales."

Coel blushed against his will. The Rus folded his arms across his chest. He pulled back his chin as he regarded Coel. "Oh, it is quite a thing to think of, I admit." Snorri suddenly jutted his chin mockingly. "But you are not thinking of Zuli and the Empress, tempting as that is, nor are you thinking of Ghiday lounging naked in a bath scented with oil." Snorri's finger stabbed Coel in the chest in gleeful accusation. "You're thinking about Márta, aren't you?"

Coel flushed to the roots of his hair.

"Paper and a pot of ink, what are you going to do? Spend the night by yourself, writing love poetry?"

Coel could not make up his mind whether to kill Snorri or crawl under the bed and hide. A knock at the door saved Coel the choice. Oleg opened the door to find a steward in dark blue livery holding a silver tray laden with a sheaf of clean parchment, an inkpot, two quills, a sharpening knife, and a small bowl of sand.

Coel took the tray. "Thank you."

Snorri nudged Oleg with his elbow. "Come, Oleg. It is for the best if Coel stays in his chamber, anyway. It will keep him out of trouble, and he needs to conserve his strength. He has a big day ahead of him. Let us you and I go join the girls at the bath."

Oleg glanced between Coel and then Snorri. "But . . ."

Snorri grew impatient. "But what, Oleg?"

"What of Ghiday?" The young Rus seemed genuinely concerned for her feelings.

"Ah!" Snorri brightened. "Normally I would take care of that, but this night I must give Ianthe my full attentions. Coel's loss is your gain. I would make the most of it were I you."

"But then what of Tabitha?"

"Yes, she will require attention, too."

Oleg was shocked.

So was Coel.

"Me?" Oleg blinked. "Both?"

"Oleg, do you understand what I told Coel about Zuli and the Empress?"

Oleg stammered. "I . . . yes."

"So ask Tabitha and Ghiday to play Empress and the Thief for you. Pay attention to the details, you might learn a few things that will serve you the rest of your life."

Oleg was shocked.

So was Coel.

The slowest, stupidest, happiest grin slowly spread across Oleg's face from ear to ear.

Snorri nodded. "Good lad."

Coel watched the two Rus walk out the door. He started as Snorri's head suddenly reappeared around the corner. "Mooncalf!"

Coel nearly hurled the tray at him. The steward looked back at Coel nervously. "Is there anything else?"

Coel let go the scowl from his face. "Have you any wine from Cyprus?"

The steward nodded. "Kommandaria, from the city of Limmasol."

"Bring me a cup, if you will." Coel looked at the writing instruments before him and decided the two Rus could go straight to hell. He grinned suddenly and silently wished them both luck. Snorri was right. Coel's thoughts were about Márta. His Muse was speaking in his ear, and Coel could see the lines begin to form in his mind. "Make that a jar."

CHAPTER TWENTY

Coel blinked up into the rain. The night was black as pitch. The rain fell straight out of a windless sky in a heavy, ceaseless shower upon the rocky shore. Across the harbor, the great lamps of the junk shone like beacons in their shades of waxed red paper. Coel stood upon a tiny strip of beach just west of the docks and listened to the sounds of the night. The Black Sea was very calm. She was often called the Tideless Sea, and the rain falling on the water made more noise than the ripples that lapped feebly at the rocks. It would be a long, miserable swim to the junk, but the sea itself would present no problems. Coel drew off his soaked tunic. Even with Zuli, Márta, and six Amazon Guards at arm's length, there was no need for modesty. It was the darkest, wettest night in the world.

Snorri's hand gripped Coel's shoulder. The Rus pulled him aside and spoke in Coel's ear. "Listen to me. You do not have to do this."

"Now is a fine time to tell me that, then."

"Now is the perfect time. There are only six of the Empress's Amazons watching us. Márta will not draw steel against us, and neither will Zuli. I have Oleg hiding in the rocks less than a stone's throw away. He has a spear and shield for you. Say the word, and we cut our way out of here."

"And go where?"

"Listen, Abt is with us. He has sold his goods at a profit and taken on new cargo. His crew is back aboard the *Olga*. Nothing holds him here. He remembers the way you fought when his ship was attacked. He likes you. He does not like the reception he has received in Trebizond. I sent a message to him through Ianthe. Abt says if we can get to his ship without being caught, he will take us aboard and weigh anchor this very night. Abt can lose anyone who pursues us with ease on a night like this. I say we run. Now."

"I cannot."

"Hypatia has your sword, is that it? It is the most beautiful blade in the world, Coel, but it is not worth dying for. Let the witch have it."

"That is not it, and you know it."

Snorri was silent for a moment. "Well, Márta is as fine a woman as a man could want, I grant you, but corpses do not steal kisses. You will have even less of a chance with her if you're dead."

"I gave my word."

"Damn your word! You gave your word to a Persian sorcerer and a Greek witch who do not give a good god damn whether you live or die! It is a fool's errand! If they had told you that the fabled Pearl of the Ocean was on that ship and that you were to steal it, that would be one thing. It would be suicide, but at least it would make some kind of sense. But you are sneaking aboard and poking about without even knowing what you are looking for! You will die! For nothing!"

"I gave my word to Zuli. She risked her life for me. I cannot let her swim out to that ship alone."

Snorri seethed in silence.

"You would do the same, Snorri. Admit it."

"By Odin, I do not like this! I do not like it at all!"

"Neither do I."

"Then listen. I was afraid of this. I have a fallback arrangement with Abt."

Coel sighed. It seemed everyone in Trebizond had spent the day plotting except for him. "What kind of arrangement?"

"Once you have swum out with Zuli, Oleg and I will go to the wharf and steal a rowboat. We will row out a few bowshots west of the junk. If things get out of hand, go over the side. Swim for your life. We will fetch you and take you to the *Olga*."

"What of Zuli?"

"We take her, too, if she will come. If the two of you would come to your senses, I would take the both of you now."

"You have already asked her, then?"

Snorri muttered unhappily. "She is determined to do this thing."

The two of them jumped as Zuli spoke beside them. "It is time to make ready."

Coel could barely make out the pale gleam of her flesh in the darkness. She grasped his hand and slapped something into it. Coel found he held a jar. "What is it?"

"Rendered grease, mixed with indigo dye."

Coel turned the jar over in his hand dubiously, even though he could not see it. "What is it for?"

"It will make the swim easier and keep out the cold. It also makes you very hard to hold onto if guardsmen seize you. The grease is rendered so that it will not smell. The paint will make us harder to see."

"Why indigo, then?"

"The night is not actually black, but a lack of light. At night, dark blue fools the eye better."

Coel pondered this. He nearly jumped again as Zuli spoke in her normal voice. With all the hushed whispering and the tension that filled the air, it sounded like shouting.

"Márta, come here."

Márta's boots crunched as she blindly picked her way across the rocks and sand. "What is it?"

"Grease Coel."

"I will not."

Zuli's voice dropped to a throaty purr in the darkness. "You may grease me, instead, if you like. I would not mind so much."

Márta 's voice sounded very tightly controlled. "I will grease Coel."

Zuli took the jar from Coel's hand. She spoke to Márta. "Here," Her voice dropped back to its purr as she addressed Snorri. "Will you assist me?"

Snorri's spirits improved measurably with the idea. "Oh,

indeed."

"Come, then, let us give them some privacy." Zuli spoke over her shoulder as they moved away. "Everywhere except the palms of his hands, Márta, and the bottoms of his feet."

Márta was a rigid shape in the dark.

Coel shivered in the rain and awkward silence. "I did not know this was part of the preparations."

"I know that."

"You need not--"

"Kneel down."

Coel dropped to one knee. Márta's hand groped out for a moment and found his head. The jar grated as she pulled off its lid. "Here."

Their fingers fumbled together a moment, and Coel took the jar in both hands. Márta made a perturbed noise as she dipped her fingers into the grease.

"Eew!"

She ran her fingers through Coel's hair. The thick grease pasted his hair down around his head like a helmet. "Close your eyes."

Márta smoothed the grease across his face and neck and ran her thumbs around his ears. Coel felt the calluses on her hand from holding swords and pulling bows. Her hands lingered on his chin for a moment and then tapped his collarbones. "Turn around."

Coel stood, and Márta painted wide swathes of the grease down his back with her palms. "I do not like what they are making you do."

"Neither do I."

Márta 's voice dropped low. "Coel."

"Aye?"

"I want you to know that if you try to escape, I will not try to stop you."

Coel felt a tiny star shining on him out of the rain and

blackness. "That means a great deal to me, Márta. More than you know."

"But if you do, I warn you. Reza will kill you. Horribly. Even if you get away from the shores of Trebizond, even if you make it all the way back to your mountain in Wales, Reza will have his revenge. Even if it takes him decades. You saw what he did to Tsapko, and think carefully, it is not just Reza you would be crossing, but the Empress as well." Márta's voice trailed off for a moment. "Coel, when the Amazon cut you, what became of the kerchief she gave you?"

"She retrieved it after my face was healed. Why?"

"They have your sword, Coel, and now they have your blood. I know something of these things. They have enough to make terrible magics against you."

Coel's worst suspicions were confirmed. "I had thought as much. When the Empress told me she could see to it that I died if I was captured, the thought of escape left my mind. I made up my mind to die with honor." Coel looked out across the water at the blood red light of the ship's lamps. "Now, it is in my mind to succeed. I will board that ship of Cathay. I will return to tell the tale. I will hold my sword in my hand again."

"I like hearing you talk like that."

"Snorri says I am lucky. I am starting to believe I am."

Márta seized Coel's shoulders and spun him about. "Never say you are lucky! Let others say it about you, but never claim it yourself! No god loves it! It is the worst kind of hubris and the death of heroes! Say you are brave, say you are bold, but never say you are lucky!" Márta shook him with greasy hands. "Do not tempt fate! Not on a night like this!"

Márta's passion startled him. Coel squared his shoulders and gravely addressed the sky. "I am a luckless man, foolish and dull. I will probably be eaten by sharks before I ever reach the junk, and deservedly so."

Márta began smoothing grease down his chest. "Better."

Coel grinned in the dark. "But my luck turned the day I met you."

Márta paused. Coel could not see her face in the dark, but he knew she was blushing. "You are lucky there are no sharks to speak of in the Black Sea."

They were silent for a moment. Coel vainly tried to make out her face. "Márta?"

Márta rubbed the grease down Coel's arm. "What?"

"What is inside Reza's box?"

Márta's hands stopped on his biceps. "I swear to you, Coel, I do not know."

"Would you tell me if you did?"

"If I had been foresworn to keep it secret, I would tell you as much, but I do not know its contents. There are many things Reza does not tell me. That does not matter. I know my place, and what is in the box is my master's business, not mine, until he chooses to make it so."

Coel bridled at her use of the word master, but let it pass. "I appreciate your honesty."

"I want there to be no lies between us," Márta knelt and began greasing Coel's leg. Her voice grew tentative "Blandine told me about the Ethiopian woman at court, Ghiday."

"Aye," Coel tensed despite himself. "And?"

"And, I want you to know I do not mind if you and she are, I mean--"

"I thought you wanted there to be no lies between us, then."

Márta was quiet as she finished his other leg.

"I did not go to Ghiday last night. I spent the night alone in my chamber."

A suspicious silence ensued.

"I made something for you instead. It is in my harp case. If I do not come back, I want you to have it."

Márta's breath hissed inward to protest, but he cut her off. "But I think I will come back and give it to you personally."

Coel jumped as Márta quickly ran her greased hands over his

flanks. "There, now you are ready."

Coel turned back around.

Zuli's voice spoke out of the darkness. "You missed a spot."

"I did not miss any--" Márta suddenly choked off her words.

Zuli took Coel's hand and put something in it. "Here. We cannot have that thing of yours flopping about shining like a flagpole."

Coel did not feel much like a flagpole in the rain and cold. He found a length of fabric in his palm. "What do I do with this, then?"

"You wear it."

"How?"

The fabric was snatched from his hand. "Stick you arms out."

Coel went up on his toes with a wince as Zuli pulled the fabric up between his legs. She pulled it up snugly between his flanks and then wrapped it around his waist twice. She pulled it down and around again and then knotted it at his hips. "There."

Coel plucked at the scant swaddling. "For modesty?"

"No, to hold your knife."

"I lost my dagger fighting the Saracens on board the *Olga*."

An object slapped impatiently into his hand. "Here."

Coel ran his hands over the leather of a sheath. It was a very large knife. Coel felt the knurling of the horn handle. "This is Snorri's *sax*."

"Yes, and he wants it back. Now, thrust it through the waist of your breechclout unless you intend to swim with it in your teeth."

Coel secured the knife at his waist.

"Here," Márta spoke in the dark. "Take this as well."

They fumbled for each other's hands. He found he held Márta's hand axe.

"If you have to cut a rope on board the ship, it will be faster than the knife, and better if you have to kill a guard. Many a man has still raised a ruckus with his throat cut. No man makes a noise with a hatchet in his head."

It still shocked Coel to hear Márta speak such things. He took the axe and thrust the handle under the cloth at the small of his back. "Thank you."

Zuli spoke quietly. "Let us go."

Márta grabbed Coel's arm and pulled him close. "Coel."

"Yes?"

Márta's face came close. Her lips pressed into his cheek and slid a little on the grease as she stood on tiptoe. She steadied herself with her hands on his shoulders and pressed her lips against his flesh more firmly. "For luck."

Zuli's voice was a hiss in the black. "Now, Coel!"

Márta's hands squeezed Coel's shoulders and fell away. Coel turned and walked to the water. His right cheek tingled from her lips. His shoulders still felt the grip of her hands. The rain beaded and ran off his greased flesh. He heard the slight splashing ahead as Zuli stepped into the sea. The water closed in over Coel's feet. It was not as cold as he had feared. He followed the sound of Zuli's splashes. Coel's stomach tightened as the cool water reached the top of his thighs. There was a deeper splash ahead. Zuli was swimming. Coel leaned forward and kicked out. His feet left the bottom and his arms stroked. The breakers coming in were barely a few inches high and presented no resistance as he swam.

Zuli sounded pleased. "You know the breast stroke."

"The what?"

"You can swim with your head above water, yet without paddling about like a dog."

"I can swim on my back, as well, and under the water."

"Indeed? And how long have you been swimming?"

"Since my father threw me into the tarn on my fifth birthday."

The two of them smoothly stroked through the sea together. Coel strained his eyes, but he could not see Zuli even as a dark outline. Only the sound of her voice and the tiny noise of her passage let him know she existed at all. The junk ahead of them was an island of red light in the black.

Zuli spoke quietly. "We climb the anchor rope."

"So I imagined."

"I shall go first, then signal you to follow me. Do not speak. Make no noise. Do not do anything. Simply follow me when I signal you to do so."

"Aye." Coel could think of no objections to the plan. He had no idea what to do once they boarded the ship. He was more than happy to let Zuli lead.

There were no more words between them. Coel concentrated on swimming. He fell a few strokes behind Zuli and matched himself to the wake of her kicks. The grease kept out the cold, and made his strokes very smooth. As they neared the junk, the reflections of the red lamps on the water shivered as the rain struck them. The lights appeared close, but it took an eternity to get near the ship. Coel kept his eyes on the junk. It was massive and had multiple decks. The great hanging lamps gave everything a roseate glow.

Zuli swam astern of the junk and carefully kept out of the glow of the lamps. As they rounded the ship the great anchor rope silhouetted itself against the light of the lamps. Zuli kicked towards it. Coel followed. They made no sound as they reached the rope and clung to it. The steering oar was a vast blade of wood a few yards away, and the stern deck hung out over the water like a balcony. Zuli's hand suddenly clamped onto Coel's shoulder. Coel instinctively sank in the water up to his eyes.

A figure appeared at the stern. The man was tall. He wore red lacquered armor over his chest and shoulders that looked like the carapace of a beetle. The man wore a wide straw hat that shadowed his face and held a spear as tall as he was. Its glittering blade was long and curved sinuously like a tongue of steel flame. The man leaned out over the rail and peered down into the water.

Coel's hands tensed on the anchor rope. It seemed like the man was staring directly at him. Coel's heart hammered in his chest as he took in the man's exotic features. The man leaned on his spear and frowned out over the water. After a long moment, he leaned back and looked up into the sky. The guard pushed his hat back and stuck out his tongue. He stood for a moment and let the rain fall on his tongue and then smiled at himself self-consciously.

A thin smile of relief passed across Coel's lips. Pulling the night watch was as boring for the men of Cathay as it was in West. Coel relaxed as the man pulled his hat back over his head and resumed his sentry walk along the rails.

A tiny wake crested around Coel's neck as Zuli pulled herself up on the rope. From Coel's view, her diminutive form was a black silhouette against the red lanterns. She cupped her hands against the thick rope and vized the bottoms of her feet against it as she pushed her way up one span of limbs at a time. The water dripping from her body was soundless in the rain.

Coel watched as she scaled the rope and disappeared over the side of the ship. Long moments passed. A dark arm slid over the side and beckoned him in the glow of the stern lamp. Coel gripped the anchor rope and started climbing.

The rope was wet, but the twisted hemp was thick and ridged. Coel jammed the inside edges of his feet against it and pushed himself up out of the water. He cupped his hands against the rope and pulled himself up as Zuli had. Zuli's orders not to grease his palms or the bottoms of his feet suddenly made a great deal of sense. Coel heaved himself up the rope and stretched out to grab the rail. His feet left the rope. Coel hung by his hands for a moment and scanned the deck.

No one was about. Coel's biceps tensed with the strain of holding himself aloft as he looked back and forth. The little aisle formed by the starboard side of the junk was abandoned. Zuli was nowhere to be seen. Coel's muscles locked as he heard a tiny noise.

Several coils of ship's rope the size of barrels lay stacked on the deck. A dark hand beckoned to him from the pool of shadow between the coils.

Coel hooked a heel over the rail and rolled to the deck. He scooted over to the coils of rope in a crouch. Zuli knelt against the cabin wall. She brought her hand up before his face and pointed up at the top of the cabin they leaned against. Coel nodded and made a stirrup out of his hands. Zuli stepped into it. Coel heaved. Zuli vaulted up and disappeared onto the roof.

Coel waited long seconds. Zuli's head appeared. The whites of her eyes and her teeth gleamed out at him. Coel grasped the eave of the cabin and pulled himself up. The two of them stood atop the junk. The four great masts stood like trees with their sails furled. A smaller cabin rose before them. Zuli crept towards one of its shuttered windows in the dim glow cast from the lamps beneath them. She pressed her head against the shutter and stood motionless for a long time. She beckoned Coel forward with a finger.

She pressed her lips against his ear as he crouched beside her. "Give me the knife."

The blade seemed bright as a beacon as Coel drew it. Zuli took it and slid it between the shutter doors to work the latch. She moved with agonizing slowness for long moments. "Open it."

Coel opened the shutter. Zuli lowered the latch silently and wriggled through the window. Her arm slipped out and beckoned Coel to join her. He awkwardly managed to snake his frame through. Heavy curtains brushed against him. Zuli drew them shut behind him.

The glow of the lamps outside barely broke the blackness of the room. Zuli spoke in Coel's ear. "I heard what you said."

Coel tensed. "About what?"

"About coming tonight. For me."

"I--"

Zuli's pressed her lips fiercely against Coel's. Her tongue slipped into his mouth for a startling moment before she pulled away. Her finger pressed his lips closed before he could speak.

"Thank you."

Coel spoke low while his lips tingled. "What do we do now?"

"Ships are the same the world over. The lower down you go, the less interesting things are. The bottom is the bilge. Above that, the cargo holds. Above that, the sailors' berths. Above that, the officers' and the Captain's quarters."

"So, the cargo hold, then?"

"No. The most valuable cargo would be stored in the Captain's cabin. Passengers of importance would share his cabin or displace his officers. Everything interesting is at the top."

Coel looked about himself in the gloom. "So where are we now, then?"

"I don't know. This cabin is new construction. There are windows on all four sides. The windows have curtains as well as shutters. The curtains are heavy, yet perforated. This cabin was made for observation, and made so that the observers could not be seen."

"So whatever it is we are looking for should be right below us?"

"It should be, but then who knows what the men of Cathay are thinking when they build ships?"

Coel did not find this comforting. He drew Márta's hand axe. "Let us go below, then."

"Wait."

"What is it?"

"There is a hatch in the floor. I am rubbing some of the grease from my arm onto the hinges."

It occurred to Coel with great clarity that Zuli could see in the dark.

Light flooded into the tiny cabin from a crack in the floor. Zuli lifted the hatch. "Here."

Coel held it while Zuli silently slid down a ladder without using the steps. She waved and Coel lowered the hatch and followed. They found themselves in a cabin lit by a pair of lanterns. There were four cots with sea chests beneath them. Suits of foreign armor hung from pegs on the walls. Zuli examined a table covered with charts. Coel stared at Zuli's naked, indigo-dyed body in the lamplight. Zuli ignored his gaze and swiftly searched every inch of the cabin. "This would have been the captain's cabin. Four now inhabit it."

Zuli took a lantern down from its hook and flicked its hood up and down with her thumb. She closed it and went to the door and listened. She cracked the door and peered out. "Come."

They slid out of the cabin and found themselves in a narrow corridor. Coel could hear voices. Zuli crept to a door and put her ear against it. She cocked her head and her eyes narrowed. Coel listened. It was like no language he had ever heard. A voice rose and spoke in a language unlike the first. Two tongues were being spoken.

The voices suddenly stopped. Zuli's eyes popped wide in her painted face. Coel listened harder. There was a low noise. Like a hiss, but different. He realized it was a sniff. It came again and was joined by a second.

Coel jumped as an ear-splitting roar erupted behind the panel.

Zuli tore past him. "Run!"

Coel ran down the corridor. Shouts joined the roaring behind the door. Calls of alarm rang throughout the ship as Zuli and Coel reached the door at the end of the corridor. Feet thudded on the decks outside. Zuli snarled as the barred door failed to open. Coel whirled about as the door down the hall flew open and a man leaped out.

Coel froze.

It was not a man. Tusks thrust up from a shovel-like lower jaw. The nictitating slits of its nose flew open and shut. Great, slanted, cat-like yellow eyes flared wide as it looked at Zuli and Coel. Only a short apron of gray wool covered its hairless green flesh. The hobgoblin held an axe with a huge dagger blade set at a right angle to the halft. It thrust its knife-axe at Zuli accusingly. Its roar thundered in the corridor.

Coel hurled his hand axe. The hobgoblin reared back as the weapon flew end over end. The wooden handle slammed between the creature's eyes and it reeled backward.

Coel grabbed Zuli's hand. "Move!"

The two of them ran back down the corridor. Zuli yanked Coel's arm as they passed a ladder. "Down!"

Coel leaped down the hole in the deck and nearly broke his ankle as he landed. Zuli landed on top of him and bounced to her feet. "Move!"

"Where?"

Zuli pressed Snorri's knife into his hand. "There were shutters in the hull! Pick a door!"

A door flew open. A half-dressed Cathayan burst forth with a heavy curved sword in his hand. Zuli lunged right at him. Coel charged after her. The Cathayan raised his sword and Zuli dove at his ankles. Coel lunged in and blocked the sword blow with his knife. The Cathayan tumbled to the deck. Coel stomped on his belly and Zuli slammed her lantern against the side of the Cathayan's head. She leaped up and ran past. She snarled as she looked in the room. "No shutter!"

An armored man slid down the ladder behind them followed by another. Coel ran past Zuli to the door at the end of the corridor and kicked it open. It was unlit, but the light from the corridor revealed a large cabin full of boxes and barrels and the hope of a shuttered window along the hull. "Here!"

Zuli skidded into the room. Coel shut the door and shot the bolt. The decks pounded with running feet. There was shouting above and below them. Zuli opened her lantern. Light spilled forth as she ran to the shutter. "It has been nailed shut!"

The door hammered on its hinges. Coel grunted as he shoved a heavy barrel against the door. A spear point suddenly punched through the wood. Coel ran to the shutter. It was an inch thick and had been sealed with iron nails for the voyage. Coel seized a small cask and raised it above his head. He let out a shout and smashed it against the shutter. The cask burst its sides and Coel spat as grit showered him and the smell of brimstone filled his nostrils. Black powder stuck to the grease paint that covered him. Coel hurled the shattered cask away and sought about for something heavier. More spear points pierced the door. They bored and twisted and shafts of light began to bleed in from the besieged portal.

Zuli knelt and took some of the spilled powder and sniffed at it. Coel found another cask and hefted it. He stepped back and ran at the shutter. He rammed the cask into it with all of his strength. The shutter burst apart. Pieces of it hung by the nails while the rest fell into the sea.

Zuli shone the lamp all around the cabin at the casks and

crates. Large bundles were racked in rows that reached the ceiling. She looked again at the powder beneath her feet. Coel spat again at the acrid stench in his nose and the bitter taste in his mouth.

"Go!" Zuli hissed. "Now!"

"But--"

"Go!"

Coel clambered up into the window and looked back. Zuli raised the lantern high as if she were going to throw it. "Zuli!"

Zuli rammed her shoulder into Coel's posterior and sent him sailing into space. Coel slapped his hands together and turned his fall into a dive. He punched into the sea and water closed over him. As he turned to the surface, the water above thumped as something struck it. Zuli's hand seized his hair and pulled him back downward.

Thunder rolled through the water. The water above lit up in lurid orange and Coel's eardrums seemed to meet in the middle of his skull. The muffled thunder boomed and boomed again, and the orange light flashed and flared above them. Zuli released his hair and swam ahead. Coel's lungs strained, but he stayed under the water and followed her. The sea above splashed as objects began to hit the surface.

Zuli kicked up and Coel followed. Her head broke the surface for a second, and she dove down again. The thunder grew louder as Coel came up. He barely drew half a breath when the sky fell on him. A great weight pushed him down and he flailed in a tangle of limbs. A huge clap of thunder rolled through the sea, and the surface lit up in brilliant orange again. Coel found himself face to face with a hobgoblin.

Coel screamed under the water as he pulled his knees up to his chest. He shoved his feet against the creature and propelled himself away. As he flailed backwards, the hobgoblin slowly sank. Its head hung at an angle. It was stunned or dead. Coel was sure it was the one he had met in the corridor.

Coel kicked up to the surface and took a strangled gasp of air. The junk was afire from stem to stern. Flames crawled up its shattered masts. Meteors of fire screamed and hissed up into the night and burst like exploding stars. Coel shook his head and dove again. He kicked down and wrapped an arm around the hobgoblin's neck and found it broken. Coel strained to pull it to the surface. His head broke the water for a moment. "Zuli!"

The hobgoblin was heavy beyond endurance. Coel kicked and stroked with his free arm and yelled as he went underwater again. "Zu--"

The weight suddenly lessened. Zuli was by his side and held the hobgoblin's arm. She pointed out into the darkness with her free hand. "Swim!"

They kicked out with their burden between them. Their progress was painfully slow, but there was no pursuit. Fire and thunder lit up the night sky. The junk was dying in a chained orgasm of explosions. Zuli shouted out. "Snorri!"

"Snorri!" Coel roared at the top of his lungs. "Oleg!"

"Coel!" A voice called out of the black. "Zuli!"

"Snorri!"

A rowboat pulled out of the darkness. As it neared, Coel saw Márta at the prow with an arrow laid across her bow. "Coel!"

The boat slid up. Snorri and Oleg shipped their oars. Zuli caught the gunwale and gasped in exhaustion.

Snorri froze in alarm as he looked at their burden. "Baldur's beard!"

Coel gasped. The muscles in his arm burned with fatigue. "Pull it in!"

The load lifted, and Coel clutched the side of the boat. Oleg pulled Zuli aboard. Coel pulled himself up feebly. Snorri grabbed his arm and heaved him in. Coel flopped down into the bottom of the boat beside Zuli and the dead hobgoblin. Oleg dragged the corpse to the back of the boat. Zuli spooned into Coel and shivered. Snorri threw a blanket over the both of them. The night sky glowed orange and was lit by occasional flashes and shooting stars that rose up into the clouds. Coel gasped and hugged Zuli as his heart gradually slowed.

Zuli clutched Coel as she lay against him. Snorri and Oleg bent their oars. Márta stood over the dead hobgoblin and held the tiller as they rowed into the sheltering darkness. Snorri grunted as he pulled his oars. "That's a hobgoblin you have there, Coel."

"Aye," Coel shivered. "It is, that."

"And just what was a hobgoblin doing aboard a Cathayan junk in the Black Sea?"

Coel clenched his teeth to keep them from chattering. "Giving orders."

CHAPTER TWENTY-ONE

Coel, Snorri, and Oleg strode down the marble hall. Coel relished the familiar weight of his sword on his hip. The Angeli had returned his sword as she had said she would. She had also said she would reward him, and her generosity flowed from an open hand. Coel wore a scarlet tunic that was a perfect match of the one his mother had sewn for him, except this one draped his frame in the luxury of pure silk, rather than wool, and the thick embroidery at the neck and hems were spun of real gold. Coel had two more like it in his room, another of scarlet and one of dark green. Another tunic cut in the Greek style had been given unto him as well. It was bleached a blinding white and hemmed with gold, but a thick stripe of purple ran down the right shoulder to the thigh to show the imperial favor of the Angeli. She had given him full access to the royal armory, and Coel had replaced the armor he had lost as well as upgraded it. A sack of a hundred gold pieces lay on his bed, along with a letter of credit worth 500 more signed by the Angeli, herself, and the chamberlain of the Venetian bank of Trebizond. The Angeli's entire demeanor had changed towards him. Coel's breath caught at the memory of it.

She had given him back his sword with her own hand. Her perfect fingers had touched his. For the briefest of moments her violet eyes had looked into his in such open speculation that Coel's will had nearly left him. He had broken her spell once. Only having his sword in his hand kept him from being unmanned this second time. Coel gripped the hilt of his sword reflexively. He knew, in the depths of his soul, that if he took the unspoken reward promised in that purple gaze, he would remain in Trebizond forever as the Angeli's most willing slave.

Coel gripped his sword hilt tighter. Just the thought of Hypatia left his limbs loosened and an aching loneliness inside of him. Her face would haunt his dreams for the rest of his life.

"So," Snorri interrupted his thoughts. "Have you given Márta her poem, yet?"

Coel's ears reddened. "I have not."

"Well, you should. It's quite good, actually."

Coel's head whipped around. Snorri ignored him. The Rus peered up into the arched ceiling and quoted from memory:

"Márta, Fairest of Helens! To capture the light of your radiant gaze,
in array would I launch my thousand ships,
to hear the whisper of your voice in the night,
words framed by the sweetest of lips,

Coel was horrified. Snorri recited on.

Márta, in golden dreams, golden, you haunt my fevered rest,
dreaming, the curve of your thigh, the supple tilt of breast,
to lay enshrouded in the mane of your chestnut hair,
to feel it fall about my face, it's touch a zephyr's caress

Márta, Iron, sheathed in silk, a tawny-limbed delight,
you--"

"God damn you!"

Snorri looked at Coel in admiration. "I liked the 'Fairest of Helens' part. Very romantic."

"You went through my things! You read my poetry!"

"And how do you know about the supple tilt of her breasts, anyway? Is there something you haven't told us? Or are you just guessing?"

"You go to hell, then!"

"Well, I liked it very much," Oleg looked at Coel with great seriousness. "But I am not sure about the word chestnut for her hair."

Coel spluttered.

"Well," Snorri stroked his chin and pondered. "Márta has beautiful hair, but brown is a difficult color to make sound romantic. Chestnut may actually be the best--"

"Bastards!" Coel whirled on them.

Snorri kept an eye on Coel's fists. "You're not going to start punching people again, are you?"

Oleg took a wary step back. Coel began walking again determinedly. The Russians fell into step on either side of him. Snorri began waving his hands. "What if you had drowned? What if some Cathayan had cut your head off? What if a hobgoblin had carved you for his meat? Someone had to get the poem to her if you wound up dead. I should think you'd be pleased."

"You were snooping!" Coel's eyes flicked angrily to Oleg. "And I expected better of you!"

"I was in the room. Snorri read the poem aloud. Should I have covered my ears?" Oleg shrugged. "It is really very good. I think Márta will like it."

They turned the corner, and thoughts of Hypatia and nosey Russians left Coel's mind. Márta stood before the door to Reza's chamber talking with Blandine. Márta gave them a cheerful wave and opened the door. Blandine favored Coel with a smile. Reza, Orsini and Zuli sat upon sofas drinking tea from a golden service. Marius sat off to one side. The priest looked utterly exhausted. Reza had dark circles under his eyes and looked pale, but his eyes shone. Márta and Blandine entered and closed the door behind them. The Persian could not seem to stop smiling. He waved a hand at the sofas and couches around the room. "Please, sit, my friends."

Coel took a chair by the window and glanced at Márta. The poem sat burning a hole in his chest where he had tucked it under his tunic.

Reza nodded and smiled as they all were seated. Blandine remained standing. Reza did not ask her to leave. "Well, we have come to something of a cross-roads."

Snorri took a cup of tea. He sniffed at it and dumped in a fistful of beet sugar. "I trust you have met with success, whatever it is you are doing."

"Indeed," Reza's smile was startling. "I have met with a great deal of success. More than I had dared to hope for. The three of you have also met with great success. You have proven yourselves beyond all expectations."

Coel took a cup of tea. It had a light golden color and smelled of jasmine petals. The scent made Coel look over at Zuli. She sat against the arm of the couch with her knees pulled up to her chin. She gave Coel a heavy-lidded stare over the rim of her teacup. She smiled as she read the thoughts that came unbidden to his mind.

Reza put down his cup and addressed his hired swords. "The question is, do the three of you wish to continue on with us?"

Coel sipped his tea. "To where?"

Reza shrugged. It was a gesture totally out of character for the wizard. He seemed giddy as a lad who had left his village for the first time. "I do not know."

Snorri dumped more sugar into his tea. "What direction?"

"East, or south. I am not sure yet."

"Can you tell us anything, then?" Coel asked.

"I can tell you this. As I have said before, I seek knowledge of the past." Reza shook his head in wonder. "It is strange, the course of things. I went all the way to the frozen Russias searching for clues of what I seek, and they have lead me back south, almost back to where I started."

"What is it you seek from the past?"

"I seek sorcery, Coel. Have you not guessed?"

It was an ambiguous answer, but Reza still made him feel stupid for having asked. "You have no idea at all where we might be going, then?"

"I know not, but I suspect to one of the large cities of the east. Baghdad, perhaps. Perhaps Kandahar, or Calicut."

"Calicut!" Snorri slammed down his cup. "That is in the Indies!"

"Yes, the Indies. Does the idea not make your feet itch, Yaroslav?"

Reza read the Rus all too well. Snorri sat wearing the same look he'd had in Kiev when he had been told their destination was Trebizond. "Calicut, the land of spices." He shook his head in wonder and sipped at his tea again. "They have elephants there."

"Yes, but as I said, I am not sure of it. My destiny may lie all the way to Cathay. It may lay anywhere." The sorcerer fixed his eyes on Snorri. "I am prepared to follow it all the way to Vinland if I must."

Snorri strangled on his tea. Reza smiled. "The world is round, as you have long suspected, Yaroslav. Perhaps it shall fall upon you and I to prove it. If I must sail beyond the Indies, I must commission a ship of my own. I can think of no better a vessel than a Norse longship for the voyage. I will need a captain whom I can trust and an able opponent across the chessboard with whom to pass the hours."

Snorri was no longer in the room. "To circle the world . . . "

Reza raised his hands. "I cannot promise that. All I can promise is that my journey continues, and to where I am not exactly sure. What I can promise you for certain is an increase in wages if you follow me."

Coel set down his teacup. "What about the hobgoblins?"

The room grew very quiet.

Coel pressed. "Travel to the East has always been dangerous, long before the hobgoblins, and long before the Hand of God descended upon them and created the Great Waste. Now there are hobgoblins in the Russian steppes and hobgoblins in Cathayan junks upon the Black Sea. Are you sure going east is wise?"

"That is a very good question, Coel. We have, indeed, seen disturbing things. I do not know what they mean. We all know some goblins scattered and survived the Hand of God. You, yourself, hunted them on the steppes during your tenure in the Frontier Cavalry. I have long suspected some hobgoblins must have survived as well. Perhaps they seek to carve themselves out a land of their own in the steppes. I do not know. It is something I have never bent my will to learn of. I have more pressing matters to attend to."

Reza leaned forward. "But, I will give you my honest

opinion, Coel. I believe the hobgoblins, whatever their number or intentions, are the least of your concerns. The fact is there are those who want you dead. The Church in Rome is your enemy. You escaped your Commission of Debt, but the offense you have given them will never be forgiven. Your garrison commanders in Moscow set you up to be hanged for your unpaid debt or to be killed trying to escape it. Attempts were made on your life both in Moscow and Smolensk. Further, the sorcerers of the Blue-Robe sect would see you dead, as well. Though, I will admit that is because of your association with me. You have powerful enemies. Both you and Yaroslav. All of them lie to the West."

Coel peered unhappily into the leaves in his teacup. "True enough."

"I value you very highly, Coel. You and Yaroslav have far exceeded all expectations, and Oleg proves his worth every day. I believe you are safer with me going east than anywhere else on earth."

"Coel?" Snorri gripped Coel's shoulder fiercely. "Where else would you go? France? Spain? Back to Wales? You have been to all those places already! What is there that you have not seen in the West? But the East! The Far East! I have yet to see the court of the Caliph of Baghdad or the pleasure palaces of the Rajahs of the Indies! Why not Cathay, itself! Why not the Land of Silk!" Snorri's fingers tightened. His eyes burned with religious fervor. "And why not keep going, Coel? Why not keep going east until you and I both stand upon the shores of Wales?"

For the first time in his life, Coel pictured the world as round. His mind reeled as he tried to grasp the idea of going east until he saw Wales again. "From Trebizond, to Cardiff?"

"From Wales to Wales, for you, Coel. Who's to stop us?"

"Take me!" Oleg lunged to his feet. "I will go!"

Reza raised a cautioning hand. "I cannot promise you that you will circumnavigate the world in my service--"

Snorri's smile verged on the insane. "We will take it one step at a time."

Reza's eyes matched Snorri's in their intensity. "But I

promise you, you will go places no Rus or Welshman have ever gone before."

Snorri turned shining eyes on Coel. All eyes in the room followed suit. "What say you, friend? Shall we go where the Walladid leads?" He leaned in and voice dropped low so that only Coel could hear it. "I ask you this as a personal favor, Coel. I need time to finish my chess game. Beating this Persian is harder than I thought."

Coel looked about the room. Everyone looked at him expectantly. Even the Amazon Captain, Blandine, seemed excited. Coel reined in his own excitement and picked up his teacup casually. "I suppose we will need horses, then?"

* * *

Blandine spread her hands expansively. "The Angeli gives you leave to pick whichever mounts you wish."

The horse market of Trebizond was a great, tented square of open walled barns and a labyrinth of stalls. The smell of hay, horses, and dung would have been overpowering were it not for the offshore breeze. Reza and Orsini were in audience with the Empress. Reza had sent Márta to acquire horses. Coel, Snorri, Zuli and Oleg had gone with her. God only new where Marius was. Márta and Blandine ran off together like schoolgirls. Zuli wandered off thoughtfully by herself as she looked at the horses. Coel ambled through the stalls. He had never seen so many breeds quartered in the same place. Great destriers and warhorses that Sir Roger's Norman soldiers must have brought with them munched oats as he passed. Steppe ponies, Turkmenes and Bactrian warhorses from Persia all stood in their stalls as men from a dozen nations haggled with one another. Coel knew something of horses. He was looking for a mount with the size and strength to carry him but one with stamina as well. Their destination could be anywhere. He needed a horse that could reach it.

Coel stopped, stunned. In the stall before him stood a beautiful horse. It was absolutely snow white. It was an archetypal example of an Arabian. It was the most beautiful horse in the world.

"Mine!" Snorri leaped in front of Coel before he could speak. A horse trader wearing a huge pink turban and flowing garments bowed before Snorri. With perfunctory politeness out of the way, the trader looked the Rus up and down with the same professional eye he would have judged a horse. The trader seemed dubious. "And how much is the master prepared to pay?"

Snorri's smile showed the horse merchant his gold tooth. He gestured at the gold-mailed Amazon Captain two stalls down. "Whatever the agent of the Angeli sees fit."

The merchant bowed deeply. "I am the servant of the Angeli's servants."

Coel glared. Snorri ignored him and stepped forward to run his hand on the white stallion's muzzle. The merchant turned to Oleg. "And you, Master, how may I be of service?" Oleg wandered off with the Arab. Coel burned with jealousy as he watched Snorri and his new horse fall in love with one another. A hand came to rest on his shoulder. Coel turned and found Márta pointing down the stalls.

"You want her."

Coel followed Márta's finger.

A smile broke across Coel's face. The mare was magnificent. She was big for her breed, but her lines were unmistakable. She was thick necked, full loined and deep through the heart. She lifted a Roman nose to sniff the air, and her tail was set low in her sloping rump. The cleanness of her legs was a joy, and her coloring was flawless. She was a deep roan red with a white diamond star crowning her brow and white stockings on her forelegs. Coel had ridden such horses on Crusade in Spain. They had a short charge, but they could run at a steady pace forever. The mare was a Barb. The Moors had boiled out of North Africa and conquered nearly all of Spain on such horses.

Márta's hand stayed on his shoulder as they walked up to the stall and admired the horse. "You and she wear the same color tunic." Márta grinned as she reached up and rumpled the unruly shocks of Coel's shorn hair. "And you have matching manes as well. Look at the way she stands. She is as proud as you are."

"She is beautiful."

Coel lifted a hand to her muzzle. The mare shifted and shied away. Coel clucked his tongue, but the horse skittered sideways. Coel drew back his hand as the horse reared.

Márta tsked. "Really, Coel, you must be gentle."

Coel sniffed the air. There was a sweet scent that did not belong in a stable. It was a scent he had smelled before. It raised the hairs on the back of his neck. The mare rolled her eyes and pawed the air with her hooves. Coel whirled and drew his sword. A stable boy in the next stall threw down his spade and ran screaming at the top of his lungs.

"*Hashasheen!*"

A man came out of the stall. The sweet stink filled the air around him. Black robes covered him except for his bare hands and feet. A black burnoose concealed his face except for his eyes. The eyes fixed on Coel with a malevolent glare. The whites of those eyes were bloodshot webs of reddened veins. The man reached beneath his robes. A short curved sword came out of its sheath with a wet sucking noise. Black vileness dripped from the blade. Another voice screamed in wild panic.

"*Hashasheen!*"

The horse market erupted into chaos. Horses reared and peopled ran screaming in all directions. Márta's scimitar hissed from her sheath. "Assassin!"

Another man draped in black seemed to step out of nowhere behind the first.

Márta lunged forward. The Assassin slashed and streamers of black ichor flew from the dripping blade. She sidestepped the blow and her scimitar flashed. The poisoned blade and the hand that held it fell to the straw. The killer did not blink. Blood spurted as the stump of his forearm flew up and clouted Márta beneath her chin. Márta's head snapped back and she staggered and fell into an empty stall.

"Márta!" Coel lunged. The killer reached under his robe and drew a second blade with his left hand. Coel's point pierced the killer's stomach. Coel leaned back desperately as the killer slashed back at him.

Blandine's voice rose above the chaos of screaming people and rearing horses. "Wounds will not stop them! Strike for the head or the heart!"

The Assassin slashed again. Coel leaned away from the attack and used the reach of his longer blade. The keen edge of the Academy blade whirled into the Assassin's neck and stopped on bone. The poisoned blade fell as the killer raised a hand to his half severed throat. He took a step forward and dropped to the straw.

"Coel!" Snorri shouted. "Watch out!"

The second Assassin pulled a length of metal from beneath his flowing black robes. The javelin was three feet long and made of iron. Its fluted, diamond shaped head dripped with poison. The killer held two more missiles sheafed in his left hand. Coel flung himself wildly into the empty stall with Márta as the heavy javelin flew past and sank deep into a hitching post behind him. The killer filled the stall's gate and raised another javelin of iron. Coel rose up in front of Márta and raised his sword to try and block the cast.

"Odinnn!"

The killer looked around at Snorri's war cry. Snorri held the stable boy's manure spade in both hands. The shovel blade bent around the Assassin's skull with terrible force. The killer fell twitching with his brains scrambled in his head. Snorri tossed away the mangled spade and pulled his *sax* knife. Another killer came for him with a curved sword.

Zuli leaped down from the rafters. She had her leather sling wound around both hands, and the braided leather whipped under the Assassin's chin as her knee struck between his shoulder blades. She cinched the sling and yanked back with all her strength.

The Assassin's body bent backward like a bow. Snorri seized the killer's flailing sword arm and rammed his *sax* knife up under his sternum. He buried the blade up to the hilt and twisted. The killer's bloodshot eyes rolled up into his head as Snorri yanked his knife free from his heart. Coel pulled Márta to her feet. Snorri searched the stalls with his eyes. "Where is Oleg?"

Blandine screamed.

Oleg charged down the aisle. Coel vaulted the stall ahead of him.

The Amazon Captain had fallen. Her scimitar lay in the straw and she clutched her slashed right hand in agony. An Assassin stood over her with a sword in one hand and an iron javelin in the other.

Coel roared. "You!"

The killer looked up as Coel charged him. The dripping head of the iron javelin rose. The Assassin took a step forward and put his body into the cast. Coel jerked aside as the javelin flew past him. Rivulets of poison spattered Coel's cheek and tingled his flesh. He came on and swung his sword down with all of his might. The killer raised his sword to parry and the two swords rang with the impact. Coel ignored the shuddering ache that ran down his arms and rammed his shoulder into the Assassin's chest. The killer stumbled back and Coel drove on. The Assassin crashed back into a beam as Coel drove into him with all of his weight. The poisoned blade flew from the killer's hand. Coel dropped his own sword and seized the Assassin's burnoosed head in both hands. He bounced the Assassin's skull back against the beam. The killer weakened in his grasp. Coel twisted the stunned Assassin's head to the side. Coel smashed his forehead into the Assassin's temple with the breaking of bones.

Coel's vision darkened with the impact, and pinpoints of purple light flashed. The killer went limp in Coel's hands. Coel flung him to the dirt as his vision cleared.

"Coel!"

Coel scooped his sword out of the straw.

Márta knelt beside Blandine. The Amazon lay on her side and twisted in pain. The Assassin's blade had slashed the top of her sword hand. Blood and black ichor spurted from the wound. Her fingers swelled like sausages, and her veins distended up out of her flesh. Márta had cinched her hair ribbon around Blandine's wrist and the blackened veins pulsed against it. Darkness crept beneath the ribbon.

"Cinch it tighter!"

Márta pulled on the silk. Blandine screamed. Her skin broke under the binding. The blackness beneath her flesh pulsed under the tourniquet and crawled beneath the flesh of her arm. Coel shook his pounding head. He dropped his sword and picked up Márta's scimitar. The curved sword was made for slicing.

"Hold her."

Márta blanched. "Coel!"

"Hold her!"

Blandine made a terrible noise. She squeezed her eyes shut and jerked her head away.

The watered steel of the enchanted blade sheared through the Amazon's arm as if it was a twist of straw. "Bind it! Quickly!"

"Coel!" Zuli was screaming at him. "Coel!"

"Márta, bind the wound, I'll--Sweet Jesus . . . "

Oleg lay writhing in the dirt between the stalls. The iron javelin meant for Coel stood up out of his stomach. Snorri and Zuli knelt by his side and held him down. The young Rus moaned and thrashed. Whatever poison had crawled up the Amazon's arm was deep in Oleg's guts on the end of the spear.

Coel knelt and jerked his head at Snorri. "Find Marius!"

"He's in the Citadel, he--"

"Find Eulia!"

Snorri was close to panic. "I don't--"

"Anyone!" Coel shoved him to the straw. "Go!"

Snorri leaped up and skidded to a stop by Blandine. He pulled the Amazon Captain's war horn off of its strap and ran on.

Coel gripped the haft of the iron javelin impaling Oleg. Oleg screamed.

"Hold his shoulders!"

Zuli leaned all of her weight on the thrashing Rus. Coel pulled up with smooth strength. Oleg howled as the javelin came free. Coel's face twisted as he looked at the weapon. Vileness dripped from the grooves in the diamond shaped spearhead. Coel cast it aside.

Oleg's back arched in agony. "God!"

A war horn pealed out. It rang across the rooftops and echoed from the walls of Trebizond. The horn of the Empress's Amazon Guard called and called again the summons to battle.

Coel pressed his hand against Oleg's wound and held it firm. The blood beneath it tingled and itched against his palm. "Help is coming, Oleg! Hold on!"

"Coel!" Oleg flailed and clawed. "Jesus, God! Coel!"

Zuli held Oleg's head as he twisted and screamed. "Marius is coming, Oleg! He can heal you!"

Oleg screamed and screamed again. Black blood welled up beneath Coel's hand. Oleg was bleeding all over. Blood poured from his mouth and nose and leaked out of his eyes. His screams turned to drowning gurgles. His torn guts heaved, and blood splashed down his face and neck. Oleg's throat cleared with the upheaval and a fresh scream tore out of his lungs. He thrashed uncontrollably. Oleg's every vein stood out of his body pulsing with the terrible darkness that filled them. His skin burned with fever. Oleg screamed like the damned in hell.

Zuli was white as a sheet. Her hands were soaked with blood to the elbows. She looked at Coel with helpless horror. "Do something!"

There was but one thing. A thing of mercy his mother had taught him long ago. Coel seized the thrashing young Rus by the throat. His thumbs found Oleg's pulse hammering in his carotid arteries. Coel pressed in hard and cut them off.

Oleg gurgled, and his jaw worked. His eyes went glassy. He relaxed under Zuli's hands. His jaw went slack even as blood poured out of his mouth. Oleg sagged unconscious.

Zuli cradled his head. Oleg was bleeding a river. Coel could not believe a man could have so much blood in his body. Zuli looked at Coel desperately. "How long will he--"

"I do not know! I may have killed him!"

Oleg jerked. A deep, wet noise like tearing cloth came from deep within Oleg's body. His entire body sagged. The young Rus no longer moved. The blackened blood continued to flow out of him as if it no longer wished his dead body for a home.

The floor of the stables began to tremble beneath Coel's knees. The horses in the stalls reared and screamed in panic. The rippling thunder of hooves rang on cobblestones out in the city streets. Armored Amazons charged into the stables with their scimitars drawn. Zuli rose and waved her arms frantically.

The leading Amazons skidded to a halt. Others fanned out and swept the stables. Coel recognized the redheaded Amazon as she pulled back the mail guarding her face. She leaped down from her horse and ran to her Captain's side. Blandine was ghostly pale. Márta held the tourniquet around the stump below her elbow.

"Bring the Abbess forward!"

An ancient woman in a nun's habit dismounted from amongst the golden armored Amazons. Her eyes flicked to the maimed Captain, but she knelt beside Oleg. Her hands went to the rosary around her neck. Her eyes filled with sadness as she looked upon the young Rus. Zuli screamed at her.

"Do something!"

The nun shook her head slowly as she made the sign of the cross over Oleg's body. "Only our Savior can raise the dead."

* * *

The skies over the citadel of Trebizond were lead. Rain drizzled down miserably upon the assembled mourners. The black iron gate of the Royal Mausoleum swung open soundlessly on freshly oiled hinges. Father Marius had given the liturgy over Oleg's body. The beauty and passion of the German priest's service startled Coel. He had wept openly as Marius spoke. The Empress and the *Strategos* wore black robes. The ashes of mourning they had combed through their hair ran in streaks down their faces. They mixed with their tears. An honor guard of Amazons stood at attention. Their freshly polished, golden mail gleamed dully in the rain. Blandine stood in full regalia as their Captain for the final time. The stump of her sword arm lay across her chest in a sling. She returned Coel's gaze, but there was little warmth in it. Coel had saved her life, but he had also maimed her. No healer could grow her a new arm. Oleg's funeral would be her last military function before she stood down. Ianthe, Tabitha, and Ghiday rent their clothes, tore their hair and howled in the old Greek fashion of mourning. They had quieted as the Mausoleum was opened. Snorri stood off to one side. His head hung low. His axe was in his hands. Otto shivered at his feet. Snorri had not spoken since sounding the horn.

Coel could not see Orsini's face beneath his hat. Zuli was nowhere to be found.

Oleg's body lay in his full armor. His hands clasped his sword hilt across his breast. Coel could not tell what had been done, but Oleg's face showed no signs of the death that had taken him. Beneath the rim of his helmet, his eyes were closed and his expression serene. The young man looked like a sleeping warrior, waiting the clarion call to arise for battle once more. The Angeli had said she would send money to Oleg's family. She had insisted that he be buried in the Royal Mausoleum rather than the graveyard outside the city. She had spoken over his body before the mourners and praised his bravery. He had died fighting a menace to the Empire. Oleg would lie in state beside empresses, kings, and heroes.

Coel felt fresh tears well up in his eyes. Márta's hand slid into his. She wore a black shawl and head scarf over her armor. The party had hardly spoken to one another since the attack. They had seemed almost charmed during their travels. Whatever lucky star had shone upon them was gone. Oleg was dead. The charm was broken. Coel found thoughts coming to his lips unbidden.

"The javelin was meant for me," He murmured.

Márta spoke very softly. "Yes."

"I did not even think of Oleg behind me when I dodged it."

"Yes. It could have been you with a javelin in your belly instead of Oleg. Or me. Nothing is certain in battle." Márta's face was wet with tears as she looked up at him. Her hand squeezed his. "I am very glad you are alive."

Coel's eyes went back to Oleg's body as bearers raised it upon a great ceremonial shield of brass. Oleg lay dead. Murdered in the foulest method Coel had ever seen. Even as tears spilled down his cheeks, other thoughts began to kindle and burn in his breast. Coel began to think of vengeance. "The ones who attacked us. "

"The Assassins of Alamut."

"Who are they?"

"They are a fanatic sect, feared throughout the East. They kill for their religion, and they kill for gold. It is said they live in fortresses high in the Elburz Mountains."

"Where is that?"

"In northernmost Persia. On the southern coast of the Caspian Sea."

"They stank of something."

"Hashish. It is a drug for which they are named. It is said they smoke the drug and put themselves into trances before they kill. It makes them almost impossible to stop."

"Then it was not sorcery."

"No, I do not think so. But it is said the Assassins number terrible wizards amongst them who practice banned magics. It is said they have strayed so far from Islam that they have become worshippers of demons. It is said they consider the Great Waste a holy place, and each Assassin initiate must make a pilgrimage into it. Their leader is called the Old Man of the Mountain. It is said he is no longer human. It is said he is immortal."

Coel looked up. "There was a man in Moscow. Amongst those who tried to kill us. He wore robes of black, and he had the same stink about him."

"I heard someone use the Voice of Command, but I smelled nothing."

"He was there. Then he was gone. It was the same stench. I am sure of it," Coel averred. "Ask Snorri. He must have smelled it."

Reza spoke for the first time during the ceremony. His voice was low and steely. "I wish very much that you had told me of this, Coel."

Coel could think of nothing to say. He watched Oleg's body as it was borne beneath the marble arch and disappeared into the gloom of the Mausoleum. Reza spoke. "I have had an audience with the Angeli. Never before have the Assassins dared to do their business within her realm. She does not wish their kind of trouble within her borders, nor war with the Old Man of the Mountain. After the ceremony, we have the rest of the day to gather our horses and take what supplies we need. She grants us one night of sanctuary within the citadel. We must be out of her city by dawn."

CHAPTER TWENTY-TWO

The sun came out from behind the clouds as they ascended the Caucasus Mountains. The party plodded silently through misting rain as the rolling fields and vineyards of Trebizond's outlying districts passed by. Coel and Márta rode together and took comfort in each other's company. Reza and Orsini rode together murmuring. Snorri spoke in little more than uncaring grunts. Zuli spoke to no one at all. She rode apart during the day and crept away at night. The hood of her dark blue cloak covered her face against the rain. She had made no move to push it back since the sun had broken out.

Coel looked over at his friend. Snorri rode with his head hanging. Otto no longer knew what was wrong. He had forgotten Oleg. The red hound only knew his master was miserable. He mirrored Snorri's misery and padded along the wet lane with his tail drooping. Coel clucked at his horse and rode over.

"Snorri."

"What."

Coel found he had nothing intelligent to say. "Are you all right?"

"That is a stupid question."

"You are my friend."

Snorri looked up at the breaking clouds. "He was a good lad."

"He was."

"He should not have died like that!" Snorri's voice trembled with anger. "He was only seventeen! He came a thousand leagues to die in a stable, his guts torn open and filled with poison! He never even struck a blow!" Snorri spat. "He died lying in dung."

"He died going forward, Snorri. That means something where I am from."

Snorri was silent for a moment. He cast his eyes down

bitterly. "I sponsored him in Reza's service. I should have been beside him."

"And I should have taken the javelin, and Marius should have been with us to heal him, and Blandine should have been wearing gauntlets. Hell, all of us should have worn full armor to shop for horses within the inner walls of Trebizond." Coel shook his head. "You are worrying this like a bone, Snorri. I was, too. Márta showed me that."

Snorri looked away.

Coel smiled wearily. "You will break your teeth if you keep worrying it. You're my best friend, and it breaks mine to see you like this."

Snorri took a deep breath. Some of the tension seemed to leave him as he let it out. "You know, Coel?"

"What, then?"

"You never sang that song of yours out upon the steppes."

"No, I did not."

"Nor at the River Inn in Smolensk."

"No. I keep getting interrupted."

"Why don't you give us a song now? God knows we need something."

Coel turned a wary eye at the sky. "With my luck I may be struck by lightning."

"Sing anyway."

Coel reached back for the halter rope of his pack pony and drew her forward. He unbundled the blanket around his harp case. It lay rolled next to the iron javelin that had killed Oleg. Coel did not know why he had kept it, but he had wrapped its poisoned head in waxed leather and thrust it through his bundled belongings. He pulled out the instrument. He ran his fingers over the strings and listened carefully. He spent several moments quietly tuning the harp until he was satisfied. All of the party turned at the sound except for Zuli. Her face stayed shadowed within the hood of her cloak.

Coel gazed up into the Caucasus Mountains before him. The

northern slopes were green and lushly forested. He had been told the southern side was arid, but looking up at the snowy peaks above the tree line, with sunset breaking out of gray clouds of rain and painting them a fiery pink, he could almost fool himself he was in Wales, and that just across the mountains lay the Valley of Dee. The song he had felt on the steppes came to his heart once more. Coel decided to sing it in Latin. He was not sure what it would do to the rhythm, but to him the words felt more important than the music on this day. The song spilled forth from him as if he had spent the last month in practice.

> *But now my love as you are leaving*
>
> *it remains our love was not in destiny*
>
> *I place three kisses upon each finger*
>
> *to you my love farewell five hundred times . . .*

Coel no longer saw the mountains. He was no longer aware of his audience. Oleg's death had inspired the mood, but the song had taken on its own life in Coel's breast, and it had woven itself into the shape of Marisol's face. Coel wept as he broke into the second verse. His fingers stopped on the harp strings. His voice trembled once at the chorus and then filled out with even greater power as he sang *a cappella*. Coel's tenor soared. It was a singing song, and an ancient one. It had no need for accompaniment. From a time out of mind, the song had come east to Wales from across the Irish Sea. Coel held the final note and sustained it high and clear, and then it tore and swooped low to a fading drone of inconsolable loss. The song ended. Coel could not recall at what point the words had reverted back to Gaelic on his lips.

The silence was deafening.

Coel looked about himself. Everyone was staring at him awestruck.

Coel's head turned at a choked sound. Zuli sat her horse a little way apart from the rest of them. Her cloak still covered her and her hood concealed her face, but her shoulders shook.

Zuli was weeping.

She spurred her pony and plunged down the road away from the party.

Snorri shook his head in self-reproach. "I've been wallowing in guilt when I should have been thinking of her. I think she cared for Oleg more than any of us thought." He clucked at his Arabian. "I will see to her." He rode off with Otto at his hooves. Coel began to re-wrap his harp.

Márta rode up beside him. "You sing beautifully."

"Thank you."

"I have heard many singers in the East sing with great passion, but rarely with such power."

"Well, every man of Wales fancies himself a singer. If you have no timbre to your voice, the Welsh will not listen."

"Even the horses were listening."

"Well, between warhorses and Welshmen there is not much to choose, though, by temperament, some would liken us more to mules."

Márta laughed and admired his Barb. "Your horse likes you."

Coel leaned forward in the saddle and rubbed the Barb's withers. "I like her." He gazed at Márta's mare. She was tall, with a deep golden coloring and a jet black mane. "What breed is yours?"

"Kazilik. The Armenians breed them. They are not an easy ride, but in the hands of a skilled horseman there is little they cannot do. My first horse in the convent at Limmasol was a Kazilik." Márta ran a hand lovingly through her horse's ebon mane. "Kaziliks and I have had an understanding ever since."

"I am sorry about your friend, Blandine. I could think of nothing else to do."

Márta's face clouded. "I know. It is sad. When her term of service was up, she had wanted the Empress to arrange a good marriage for her rather than return to the convent and take vows. Now that she is maimed, the convent is all that remains for her."

"You have never told me the story of the Sisters of Limmasol."

Márta perked up in the saddle. "Oh, it is a fascinating story. Would you like to hear it?"

"Very much."

"Well, two hundred years ago, even as the hobgoblins were coming out of the steppes, a convent was formed on the island of Cyprus. We were a charitable Greek Orthodox order, but circumstances led to the Sisters acting more like Hospitalers and tending to wounded and needy Crusaders who were returning from the Holy Land. Well, as you know, during the hobgoblin invasion, the Great Horde split on the Russian Steppes. Half went north, and the other south. The Southern Horde was stopped at Constantinople, and they laid siege to it. Christian countries on the Mediterranean sent hundreds of ships laden with soldiers to help lift the siege. When the hobgoblin siege was broken, most of them retreated in good order before the armies of the Holy League of Humanity. Still, many of the hobgoblins were cut off on the western side of the city. Small bands of them fled in all directions, pillaging as they went.

A few dozen hobgoblins managed to flee to the west coast of Anatolia and seize a ship. They were no sailors, but they drifted about without being found and somehow ended up making landfall in Cyprus. They were starving, and when they swarmed ashore the first thing they came upon was the nunnery. It had been a lookout fort of the Byzantines before it was a convent. It was isolated, but it had decent walls. Many of the wounded and sick from the siege of Constantinople had been taken out by ship and sent to the hospitals and churches in Cyprus. Most of the wounded soldiers being tended at the nunnery at the time were horse archers and light cavalry from Istria and Dalmatia. When the hobgoblins besieged the convent, the sisters took up the weapons of the sick and wounded soldiers and manned the walls. They held off the hobgoblins for three days before people in the city found out what was happening and sent the militia. The Mother Superior, Gillian, was killed on the wall during the final night of the siege, and the Patriarch, himself, declared her a holy martyr and canonized her. The Sisters of Limmasol have been a military order ever since."

"That is a noble--"

The screech of a hawk interrupted Coel. He squinted back into the blazing pink clouds and saw a black shape hurtling towards them out of the dying sun. The party reined in. Márta's bow was in her hand and she nocked an arrow as the hawk streaked low over the party and then climbed high again to circle.

A piercing whistle matched the hawk's shriek. Reza held up his wrist. Márta lowered her bow. The hawk plummeted down at the wizard and then snapped out its wings to perch upon the sorcerer's riding glove. Jesses of purple silk hung from the raptor's legs. One carried a thin, tin tube of parchment. Reza withdrew the paper and held out the hawk to Márta. It hopped to its new perch as Reza unrolled the tiny scroll. Orsini rode to Reza's side and the two of them conferred quietly.

Snorri rode back down the road and reined in beside Márta and Coel. He shook his head dejectedly. "She will not talk to me." He looked over at Reza. "What's going on?"

"A hawk came from the north and landed on Reza's hand."

Reza spoke aloud. "The hawk is a messenger from the Empress. She says, because of Zuli and Coel's service to her, she has bent her powers on our behalf. She says the Assassins await us in Baghdad."

"Well, that's a black piece of news," Snorri said.

"There is more. She says they also await us to the south in Aleppo."

Coel saw what was coming. "And to the north?"

"In Tiflis."

Coel tried to lay out cities he had only dimly heard of in his mind. "They are casting a net. They do not know which way we are going."

Snorri grunted. "Neither do we."

Orsini's eyes glittered for the first time in days. "That is to our advantage. It makes us unpredictable."

Snorri was somewhat mollified. "So, we go back?"

Reza shook his head. "No, the Angeli also says a Saracen galley has weighed anchor in her harbor," Reza smiled thinly. "The Long-Eye still follows us."

Snorri rolled his eyes. "Well, why doesn't she do us a favor and kill this Egyptian friend of yours?"

"As the Angeli, herself, has said, Yaroslav, her empire is

surrounded by enemies and she walks a political razor. She cannot afford to antagonize the Blue-Robe sect. For that matter, I suspect she wants nothing to do with the Assassins of Alamut. This warning was the most she could risk. She will not help us again."

Coel ran his eye over the mountains before them. "What course were you thinking of before?"

"I had thought that Baghdad would be a good place to get our bearings. If our path led to the Far East, then it would have been an easy trek to Basra and then take ship to the Indies through the Gulf of Persia. That course is now denied us."

Snorri nodded. "So?"

"So, tonight, I shall bend my will to finding our path. This is not the time or place I would have chosen, but so it must be. There is an inn a few leagues up in the mountains where I had thought we might rest for the night. I have changed my mind. We do not stay at inns or stop in villages anymore save to replenish our supplies."

Coel looked up into the mountains. The thick forest that covered them no longer seemed friendly. He saw an Assassin behind every bend in the path before them.

Reza seemed to read his thoughts. "From here on, we make camp outdoors and keep well off the road."

* * *

The campfire had been small and nearly smokeless. With the coming of dark, it had been allowed to burn down to embers. They had picked their way nearly half a mile from the road and put a thick stand of trees between themselves and anyone who might come along it. Coel had taken his bow and taken first watch on an outcropping of rock that looked up and down the road. It was now well past midnight, and Coel was back in his bedroll. He stared up into the night sky. He found Orion's belt shining through a ragged hole in the clouds. The wind slowly pulled the clouds apart, and the great hunter shone through the misty shreds. Scorpio chased him from the spring sky. Coel tracked down from Orion and found Sirius, Orion's faithful dog, glittering at his feet. Coel's mouth quirked. Out in the darkness beyond camp, Snorri leaned on his spear on the cold lookout perch with Otto. Snorri and the lanky hound had become inseparable.

Coel stretched out his arms. The great bow lay strung on a blanket next to him. He'd folded half the blanket over the bow to keep dew from dampening the string. The silk string would never go slack but water would make it heavier. A half dozen arrows stood ready with their heads thrust into the soft grass. Coel's sword lay with him in his bedroll. It was a cold companion, but it was the only one he'd had for years.

Coel turned his head. He could barely make out the dark shape of Reza's canvas tent. Reza and Marius had gone off into the trees and spent hours doing God only knew what. When Snorri had come to spell him on watch, he had told Coel that when Reza and Marius had returned, Reza had the strange box in his hands. Coel wondered for the hundredth time what might lie within it. He--

Coel froze. A faint sweet scent came to him. He parted his lips slightly and he breathed as shallowly as he could through his mouth so there would be no noise. Coel strained his senses out into the darkness. There was no movement except for a slight breeze through the grass. Coel relaxed. The smell was faint, but it was not the sweet stench of the Assassin's hashish. It was something subtler.

It was the scent of jasmine.

Coel spoke very quietly. "How long have you been watching me?"

"How did you know I was here?" Zuli's voice purred with soft certainty behind Coel's head. "You could not have heard me."

"No," Coel smiled in the dark. "But your scent set my belly to fluttering."

"You say nice things."

Coel looked up and found Zuli standing over him. Her cloak ruffled and fell to the grass. Her naked flesh was ghostly in the scattered starlight. Before Coel could speak she slid into his blankets. Zuli made a small noise and pushed his sword out of the bedroll. "Why are you wearing a tunic?" Her hands grasped the hem and began sliding the garment up. Coel's arms rose up with a will of their own as she pulled the tunic over his head and cast it on top of their feet. She slid back down into the blankets. Zuli threw her leg across his thighs. Her arm slid across his chest as she spooned her body against him. She rested her head upon his chest. Coel could feel her breath upon his throat as she spoke. "Warmer than your sword?"

Coel's throat caught. He could barely swallow. His stomach tightened as she trailed her fingernails down his belly. He stifled a groan as they closed around what they sought.

"How long has it been since you have been with a woman, Coel?"

Coel's first instinct was to lie. He found himself smiling ruefully in the dark instead as he ran his hand through Zuli's hair. It was remarkably soft and thick. "More than three years."

"Good God!" Zuli raised her head. Her hand stopped. "Couldn't you have tumbled a tavern wench? Or some little peasant girl who thought you were handsome?"

"Whores cost money. I was scraping every copper to try and free myself. As for peasant girls, they bolted their doors and made the sign against the evil eye when we passed. We were men under Commissions of Debt, being punished by the Holy Church. We were pariahs." Coel's tone lowered. "There were some men who took what they wanted. That kind of scum always hanged."

"How about a sheep?" Zuli suggested.

"Now, I knew a man who did that."

"Really."

"Oh, yes. He was a complete loon. I think his family trumped up some charge just to send him to the frontier and be rid of him. He was very generous, though. Invited the rest of the squadron to come into the forest and join him."

"And what did you do?"

"Well, we beat him senseless, then."

"You did not."

"We most certainly did. We were Frontier Cavalry on Commissions of Debt, billeted in a drafty barracks outside of

Moscow, living on millet gruel and small beer. We were starving. So, this dizzy bastard goes and steals a sheep, fair enough, but then, rather than roasting it? He goes off and commits sins against God and nature with it. Of course, we beat him. Then we tracked down his beloved, barbecued her and ate her."

Zuli laughed. "You are horrible."

"The steppes are vast. They do strange things to a man."

Zuli made a derisive noise. Coel tried to make out Zuli's face. Starlight reflected in her eyes as she spoke.

"I read your poem."

Coel sighed in defeat. "Everyone has."

"Everyone except Márta."

The words stung. "What are you doing here, Zuleikha?"

"Do you want me to leave?"

"If you are here because Snorri is on watch and you are bored, then yes, leave. My sword is cold, but at least it does not make fun of me."

Zuli was silent.

Coel shook his head. "First you chose Oleg, then Snorri--"

"I chose you first, if you will recall."

Coel recalled all too well how Zuli had dropped into his arms on the Dnieper. "Aye."

"You cannot have her, Coel. She is Reza's slave. She cannot go to you without his permission, which he will never give. If she comes to you without it, he will punish her, and while you are it remember Tsapko, and what Reza might do to you.

"She will not stay in his service forever."

"Four more years, Coel, and she may indeed decide to remain in his service. Or she can return to Limmasol and take the vows to be nun of the order. She could return to Trebizond and easily rise to Captain of the Angeli's Amazon Guard. Neither of which allows for a husband. For that matter, if she wishes a man, Reza can arrange a marriage for her with great men, men of wealth, even princes, from half a dozen countries in the East," Zuli sighed. "For that matter, she would probably marry Reza if he asked her. He was like a father to her, and he was her first love when she came of age. He is the only man she has ever truly loved. She would die for him, and you could spend the rest of your life waiting for her."

Zuli's words cut like knives. Coel turned his head away.

Zuli whispered in Coel's ear. "But you can have me, if you like."

"So, you love me, then?"

"No, but I want you, tonight." Her hand crept down his torso again. "I fancied you when I first saw you on the river, and then?" Her voice broke. "Then Oleg died. Then your song made me weep. It has been so long since I have felt anything. Now, things are stirring inside me. Things I cannot control." She seized his hand and dragged it down her body. "Can you feel it, Coel? Can you feel how things stir inside me?"

Coel felt it. His hand moved with a life of its own. Her hand closed around him and pulled him on top of her. Coel's voice was a strangled rasp in his throat. "What about--"

Zuli breathed in his ear. "No one will hear."

"You made noises like you were being killed with Snorri."

Coel's whole body went rigid as she fitted herself to him. Her finger pressed against his lips and stifled his groan.

"I can be very quiet when I want to be."

* * *

Coel stared up at the stars. The dimmer lights had faded, and the black of night had just begun to turn purple. The morning was chill against his face and mist dewed the top of the blankets. Zuli lay against him. She whispered in his ear in a language he had never heard. Her hand moved upon him. They had not slept. He would have thought it impossible that he could be aroused yet again, but he felt himself stirring under her hand. She made a pleased sound low in her throat and kissed his neck.

Morning was the time of guilt. Coel felt a twinge as he gazed up into the fading stars. "What about Snorri?"

Zuli's cheek pressed against his as she looked up into the sky. "Yes. It will be light soon. I must go back to my own blankets."

"No, I mean, he is my friend, and you were with him."

"I was."

A thin needle of jealous curiosity stabbed Coel at the sound of satisfaction in her voice. It got the better of him. "Is it true?"

"Is what true?"

"About Snorri."

Zuli's lips smiled against his cheek as she kissed him. "The man puts Arabians to shame."

"Oh," The jealous twinge tightened. "I had not heard that Arabs had that reputation."

"I meant Arabian horses."

Coel stiffened.

Zuli giggled. "I swear, Coel, the man is deformed!" She stuck her tongue in his ear and rolled on top of him. She smiled down as Coel's hands roved over her acrobat body. His fingers traced her mouth. Her smile widened and her lips and tongue began to caress his fingers. Coel's breath caught as she slowly sank her lips around his thumb and engulfed it.

Coel gave no more thoughts to Snorri. His hands went to her hips. Zuli thrust her face against his and kissed him. Coel grunted with surprise as she pushed away and rolled to her cloak. "It is nearly light. I must go."

Coel was appalled. "And leave me? Like this, then?"

Zuli's nose suddenly pressed against his. Her eyebrows waggled against his. "Yes, like that, then. I want you to think of me today while you ride, Coel. I want you to think about tonight. You bragged on the river about the things you had learned about tongues in France. Tonight I shall make you prove them."

She pulled her cloak about her and disappeared soundlessly into the gloaming. Coel flopped back into his blankets and looked skyward again. He could not believe he could be frustrated after the last six hours, but once more his flesh ached and yearned. The rest of him was utterly exhausted. Coel hoped whatever the dawn brought would be uneventful.

He had the feeling he was going to be absolutely useless the rest of the day.

CHAPTER TWENTY-THREE

"What are you grinning about?"

Coel looked up from his food. "What are you looking so sour about?"

Snorri watched Zuli's back as she rode beside Orsini. "Oh, it is nothing." Snorri muttered. "Perhaps it is her time."

Coel nearly choked. Snorri sniffed. "What is that you are eating?"

"Herrings, preserved in red vinegar. I found a cask of them in the provisions and rolled some flat bread around them." Coel held it out. "Here."

"Ah." Snorri brightened at the prospect of food. He bit off half of the roll and chewed reflectively. "It would go better with beer."

Coel looked up at the brown, scrubby peaks that surrounded them. "Do you know where are we headed?"

"Well now. This morning, Reza took Marius, Orsini, and that box and the three of them wandered off behind some rocks. They were gone for an hour. Let me tell you, they came back with strange looks on their faces. Then Orsini pulled out a map." The Rus sighed with wonder. "I tell you, Coel, you have never seen such a chart. Marvelous! Anyway, the city of Erzurum lies to the south of us. Orsini says it is fairly large and mostly Turkish. From there on the land gets flatter and more populated. The great river valleys are full of towns and villages until you get past Baghdad. From there you either go on to the Persian Gulf or reach the deserts of Arabia. We are heading east, into Kurdistan instead."

"I have never heard of it."

"It was little more than a name to me."

"When did all this happen?"

Snorri rolled his eyes. "While you were asleep. I was going

to wake you, but Orsini stayed me. You were smiling in your sleep. I've never seen you look so peaceful. You must have been having a good dream."

Coel examined his saddle horn.

Orsini's head craned around. Coel had forgotten how well the dwarf could hear. The dwarf reined in as Zuli moved on. The dwarf and the thief both rode Bactrian ponies. The Bactrians' brown coats were dappled with white snowflakes of white and they were less shaggy and more horse-like in their lines than the other steppe breeds. The dwarf smiled at Coel and Snorri as they approached and fell into line with him.

"Indeed, our path seems to lead due east now. In some ways, this is fortunate. To sneak past the major cities of the south would be dangerous work. Kurdistan is a wild place and vast. There are few cities there except for a few Turkish outposts. The Kurds are a warrior people, and nomads. It is a dangerous place. Every clan feuds with every other, and the mountains are infested with bandits. However, they can be bribed easily enough, and despite that they have a sense of honor well worth remarking upon. Besides that? They have no love for the Assassins. In fact--

Otto barked in alarm.

The Barb reared and Coel sawed back on the reins to bring her back down. Snorri let out an oath and pulled his axe from behind his saddle. Márta's bow was out with an arrow nocked. The spiked head of Marius' mace and chain uncoiled with a rattling of iron links.

Otto's barking dropped to a snarl in his throat. His hackles rose as he lowered his head. Saliva dripped from his teeth.

The Assassin had appeared out of nowhere. The black robed figure was huge, as broad as Snorri and a head taller than Coel. Flowing black cloth covered his gigantic frame save for his bare hands and feet, and a slit in the veil of his burnoose that showed sun-darkened skin and red-rimmed eyes. The Assassin stood in the middle of the road a stone's throw away. His voice boomed out in thick Latin. Coel knew the voice. He had first heard it in a dark alley in Moscow.

"Son of Shams!"

Coel flicked his gaze to Reza. The sorcerer nodded at the Assassin politely. "I am Reza Walladid, of the House of Walladid, the second son of Shams of Shiraz."

The Assassin bowed so low it was insulting. "I bring you a message."

"What is the wish of the Old Man of the Mountain?"

"It is Ibrahim, First of the Blue Robe Sect, whose wish we humbly serve. The Old Man has taken Ibrahim's gold. It is his wish that the will of Ibrahim be carried out, as has been contracted."

"What is the wish of Ibrahim, First of the Blue Robes?"

"He wishes only the pleasure of your company. His hospitality awaits you in Cairo."

"And should, by unhappy circumstance, my business not take me to Cairo?"

"Ah, well," The Assassin spread his hands in a helpless gesture. "We are told your presence in Cairo is required, willingly or unwillingly. Indeed, should circumstances force it, we are told your head shall be sufficient company to please mighty Ibrahim. Your head, and the contents of the box given unto you by the Angeli."

"Ah." Reza leaned an elbow upon his saddle horn. "And should I attend the court of Ibrahim in Cairo, what shall be the accommodations of my companions?"

"Gold has been taken. The deaths of Coel ap Math and Snorri Yaroslav have been bought and paid for." The red eyes fixed on Coel and Snorri. "Think well upon the death of Oleg son of Igor, for his fate was a blessing compared to what I, myself, shall do onto the two of you."

"Bastard! By Thor, I'll--!" Only Orsini's hand stopped Snorri from charging. Coel felt rage kindling within him.

The Assassin's eyes smiled above his burnoose. "Now, we have taken no specific contract for the death of Orsini of Venice, however, we believe the dwarf's head will fetch its own weight in gold when presented to the Doge in Genoa."

Orsini sighed at the Assassin. "Now you insult the both of us. Go to Genoa, to the Hall of Captains, and have your agents seek the

Brothers Trentadue and their allies. My head weighs sixteen pounds if it weighs an ounce, and they will double its weight in gold easily."

The Assassin bowed in deference.

The reddened gaze fell upon Márta. Coel's anger leaped from his stomach to his chest as the Assassin spoke. "Your safety is assured, Walladid, until you reach Cairo and are within the House of the Blue Robes. You will have no need for a bodyguard." The Assassin looked Márta up and down appreciatively. "Pale skinned virgins are rare upon the mountain and not to be wasted. The priests shall find a purpose for her, I am assured."

Coel's knuckles went white. The killer turned his eyes upon Zuli. "And you, little sister, for your betrayal? Your flesh shall serve the every pleasure of every Assassin upon the mountain. When we tire of you, we shall give you unto the insane ones. When even they have grown bored with your broken mind and flesh, then you shall be sent out into the Waste where you shall serve the pleasure of those who dwell there."

The red eyes narrowed. "As for you, Marius Von Balke, we have no use for a creature such as you, you may . . . "

Coel muttered under his breath next to Reza. "The Assassin used sorcery to appear the way he did?"

Reza lips did not move. "Yes."

"Can you prevent him from disappearing?"

"I can."

Coel gave in to the red rage boiling within him.

The Assassin turned his gaze back to Reza. "What is your answer, Son of Shams? Shall I tell my--"

"Yah!"

Coel spurred the Barb forward. The Assassin's eyes narrowed above the edge of his burnoose. He took up the corners of his flowing cloak and crossed his hands before him.

Reza barked out a word. The Assassin's red eyes widened. He looked about himself in confusion. Something had gone wrong.

He had failed to disappear.

Coel pulled a javelin from the case behind his saddle. It was a Moorish style weapon, with a wide dagger-like head and short shaft he had taken from the armory of Trebizond. Infantry javelins were long and thin with small heads for distance throwing. Cavalry javelins were short with heavy heads to take advantage of the horse's momentum.

Coel spurred the Barb to full charge. The Assassin threw back his shoulders and his chest expanded. Coel knew he was filling his lungs, and Coel's own filled in preparation. He had heard the sorcery in the Assassin's voice in Moscow and seen how it had enslaved the deserters he had used as henchmen.

The war scream of the Celts ripped up from Coel's belly and exploded from his throat as he raised the javelin high. The Assassin started at the sound. Coel flung the javelin with all his might.

The Assassin staggered. His sorcery stuck in his throat as the javelin sank into his chest. Coel bore down on the killer. The Assassin reached his hand beneath his robes. Coel spurred on. The Barb had been trained for war and did not balk. The huge Assassin flew from his feet as the mare slammed him down with her shoulder.

Coel wheeled the Barb and reached back to his javelin case. The heavy iron javelin he had taken from the stables of Trebizond slid free. Coel leaped from his horse. The Assassin lay on his back. His poisoned sword lay in the dust out of his reach. His hand went to the broken shaft of the javelin in his chest even as his eyes rolled dazedly. Coel ripped off the leather he had wrapped the poisoned javelin head with. He took the three-foot length of iron in both hands and spiked it through the Assassin's heart so hard it thrust into the earth beneath. The killer's arms and legs jumped once with the blow and sagged still.

Coel stood over the massive Assassin's body. His chest heaved and his limbs still shook with fighting rage.

"Coel!" Snorri pulled his horse to a halt beside him. "Are you hurt?"

"Give me your axe."

"What?"

"Give me your axe."

Snorri handed down the weapon without a word. Coel took it in both hands. Márta cried out in alarm. "Coel!"

The axe rose. Orsini's voice joined Márta's in protest. Coel ignored them. He swung the axe down with all of his strength. Marius shouted with outrage. "What kind of pagan outrage is this?"

Coel reached down. Blood flowed over his hands as he stood and finished his grisly business.

Reza rode up. His black eyes were unreadable. "I understand your anger, Coel, but--"

"They killed Oleg."

"The man was a messenger."

"The man told me he was going to kill me," Coel pointed the bloody axe. The iron shaft of the poisoned javelin stood up out of the Assassin's heart. The Assassin's head stood spitted upon it. "That is my answer."

Reza stared at Coel inscrutably.

Coel thrust the broadaxe back into Snorri's startled hands. Márta was aghast. Orsini was grim. Marius' face filled with open disgust.

Zuli did not seem upset at all.

Coel could not stop shaking. He took his horse's reins. "Let the Assassins come. Let it be war between us."

* * *

Coel looked up into the night. The clouds had given up trying to cross the Caucasus. The stars of spring shown down in full array upon the mountain peaks. The air was cold, but his blankets were thick and he found he enjoyed sleeping without a tunic. He heard no sound other than the wind, but his arm reached out automatically as his blankets lifted and Zuli slid in beside him. He could feel her watching him in the dark.

"Are you all right?"

"I am all right."

"Do you wish to speak of it?"

Coel took her hand and traced the smallness of her fingers with his thumb. "I do not wish not to speak of it. Why?"

"You took his head."

"I did."

"Everyone is appalled," No one had spoken to Coel for the rest of the day. Coel had eaten his supper by himself and then taken the first watch.

"You did not seem appalled."

Zuli's hand closed and squeezed his thumb. "No. I am not appalled. I am glad you killed him, but it startled me."

"It startled me, too," Coel looked intently into the thousand stars above him. He had not felt that kind of blood fury in many years. "He made me angry."

"What he said of Oleg?"

"Oleg was my student, a fighting companion and a friend. Then there was what he implied about sacrificing Márta." Zuli stiffened for the briefest of moments. Coel turned his head and smiled at Zuli. "But I believe it was when he spoke of you that I decided I would take his head."

Zuli squeezed his thumb again. "I spoke with Snorri. He told me the Celts have always been headhunters."

"Mostly it is only the Irish who take heads, now. In Wales, it is rare to do so, and then you do not take it as a trophy. If you take a man's head, you mount it on a stake, preferably on his own land, as close to his clan's hall as you dare, where his relatives are sure to find it. You do it to declare a blood feud."

"You have declared a blood feud against the Assassins?"

"Yes, no one shall use your flesh for their every pleasure except me."

Zuli pressed her lips to his throat. Coel rolled onto his side and took her face in both hands. "I must ask you something."

He felt her smile die beneath his hands. "What?"

"Why did he call you 'little sister'?"

Zuli went rigid. "Do you want me to leave?"

"I want you to tell me the truth."

Zuli's voice went dead. "I served them."

"You served them?"

"Yes."

"The Assassins?"

"Yes."

Coel's stomach knotted. "Why?"

"There was no place left to go."

"I do not understand."

"I am a woman, Coel, and alone. I never met my father. My mother died when I was child. I had no brothers to protect me and no clan to call upon. I grew up an orphan on the docks of Alexandria. I was small. My eyes are two different colors. I do not know what that means in the West, but in the East, it thought to be a sign of the devil."

"It is the same."

"They called me witch-girl and hurled stones at me in the streets. Stealing was the only way I could live. When I grew older, I fell in with street performers. I tumbled and danced and did tricks. Amongst them, being exotic was an asset. Street performers have always had a reputation as thieves. It is well deserved. I learned my trade from experts. Even so, stealing and tumbling are uncertain work. You often go hungry. Many die in the streets. I learned whoring was much more certain employment, even during famines and plague.

"After a time, it was obvious I was barren. No child would ever come of what I did. I went crazy. I would sleep with anyone. Men fought over me in the street troupes. I grew bolder in my thieving and my whoring. I often combined them. I grew wild and reckless. I began to get into trouble. My name became known. I had to keep moving. As my reputation spread, the thieves and street people in the cities refused to take me in. Soon, I had a price on my head, and I would soon have been on the slave block or dead. I made one final attempt to find my family." Zuli's voice grated with bitter memories.

"And?"

"And then I fell in with the Assassins. They took me in."

"You became an Assassin?"

"No, first I had to prove myself. The Assassins you have seen, the robed killers who do not care if they die, they are recruited from the mountain villages. They are ignorant, illiterate, and their lives are very hard. The mountains the Assassins live in are much the same, but they have a valley hidden high and deep in the Elburz. It is a Garden of Eden. It is green with trees and grass, blossoms, and flowing streams. The dwellings there are pleasure domes of silk and incense. The recruits are drugged and taken there. They are given many intoxicants; they are put into trances. Their every appetite is seen to. There are rituals of pleasure you could not conceive of. After weeks of unspeakable delights, they awaken again to the rock and desert of their homes. They are convinced that they have visited paradise, and that if they die in the service of the Old Man of the Mountain, the Land of Delights is where they shall return. I was one of the pleasures there."

Zuli's voice grew challenging. "There is no perversion you can think of I did not commit, and I did them all, willingly. After a time, the Assassins made use of my other talents. I went back into the world. I stole for them. I seduced for them. I murdered for them, Coel, and I did not care. I did not care whether I lived or died. I did not care about anything, or so I thought."

"Yet you left them."

"Yes, I left them, but not because I did not like what I was doing."

"Why, then?"

"I excelled amongst them. I was granted an audience with the Old Man of the Mountain." Zuli shuddered. "The Old Man told me he was pleased with me. I was to be rewarded. I was to be initiated into the Inner Circle. I was to make the pilgrimage into the Great

Waste."

"I thought nothing could live there."

"Nothing can, unless it becomes part of the Waste. I had seen some of those who have come back from the Waste changed. I have seen those who have become One With the Waste." Zuli shuddered uncontrollably. "I have gazed upon the face of the Old Man, himself, and I found I cared enough about myself not to become as them."

"You fled, then."

"Deep into Persia. I stuck to the wild places and avoided the cities. I came upon a tent in the forest. A man had made camp in some ruins. He seemed wealthy. He was alone, without guards, and I was desperate for food and money. I tried to steal from him. He caught me."

"Reza."

"Yes. He decided he had use for my talents. He gave me a choice. I took it. He hid me from the Assassins. He put me to work acquiring things for him that he could not acquire through normal means. He has sheltered me. I owe him my life." Her voice grew hard again, daring Coel to despise her. "What do you think of me now?"

"I think you are beautiful."

"You do not--"

"I failed my father. I destroyed my family and my clan. The woman I loved committed suicide. I have killed more men than I can count. I am not fit to judge anyone," Coel's lips brushed hers as he spoke. "But I was burning, drowning, sinking to the bottom of the Black Sea. It was you who dove from the mast and pulled me from the deep. I owe you my life. If the Assassins wish to take you back, then they must kill me to do it."

Zuli made a choking noise. Coel tasted salt as her tears ran down to her lips. Her finger pressed against his mouth before he could speak any more. The eastern wind blew cold across them. The sky above was bright with hard unblinking stars. In the shadows of the mountain the world around them was pitch black. Their past was full of sins unpaid. The future dark with the promise of poisoned blades and retribution. Only the moment had meaning, and Coel and

Zuli felt it slipping through their hands like sand.

They made love with a new and terrible urgency.

CHAPTER TWENTY-FOUR

"Fools! Who was it that taught you how to load a horse?"

The Amir snarled at the fearful Greek stable boys as they laded the caravan. Kamose al Ah-Ay looked over his war party. Reinforcements had awaited them in the city of Cherson on the Crimea. Kamose had purchased Ramah new sails and they had used every inch of them to make Trebizond. Kamose's welcome in the tiny empire had been cold and formal. The Empress had done nothing to hinder them but neither had she made any effort to be helpful. The Angeli granted Kamose the audience he requested and freely admitted the Walladid had been within her walls. Beyond that, she would reveal nothing other than that they had left her city. Kamose' powers confirmed the Walladid had been within Trebizond. The reverberations of the sorceries the Walladid and Father Marius had performed still echoed in the ethers. Kamose could only assume they had been successful.

He had confirmed that the Assassins had failed. He also knew the Empress Hypatia was all but certain of his involvement. The Assassins had not operated within the tiny Empire of Trebizond in over a century. Even the Old Man of the Mountain paid wary respect to the power of the Angeli women. It made Kamose ill that he had stooped so low as to employ such creatures. Even though they had failed, it made him ill at ease that Assassins had been bold enough to take a contract within the walls of Trebizond.

Something within the balance of power had shifted, and Kamose could not guess what.

Ramah bowed low. "I take my leave of you, Great One. I wish you well."

"I thank you, Captain. You were most skillful. Despite my defeat, your worthiness has been noted, and shall be mentioned in the Sultan's court."

"Many thanks."

"Juba!" Tawfiq pointed his mace angrily. "Why are you not

ready?"

Juba bowed respectfully. "Because I am not going with you."

Kamose sat up in his saddle. "What do you mean, you are not going with us?"

Juba looked from side to side as if he wondered which word he had mispronounced. "I mean that I am not going with you."

"I require your skills, Juba."

"To do what?"

"To kill Reza Walladid."

"No," Juba shook his head. "I will not kill anyone."

"Very well, since you are squeamish about killing infidels, you need not bloody your hands. You will only be required to help me find him and capture him."

"So that you may then kill him."

Kamose ground his teeth.

"I will not be a part of this thing, Great One."

"Fool! You are already a part of this thing!" Tawfiq was livid. "Why did you come this far if you are not a part of this thing?"

Juba spoke with immense patience. "I came because the threads of Captain Ramah's family and mine have been woven together since time out of mind. Before I was called out into the desert, Ramah and I played together as children in the shade of his father's patio. How could I refuse the summons when his family requested aid? I knew the nature of your quest, Son of Ah-Ay, long before Ramah told me of it. I came to ensure my friend's survival. That I have done. Ramah has served you well. In serving him, so have I."

"Served us well?" Tawfiq rode in a close circle around Juba. "Filling the sails with wind? Fah! To serve us well, you should have called down lightning to sunder the ship of Abt! Or summoned the maelstrom to pull them down into the depths!"

"I will not kill for you, Amir. I will not kill for anyone."

Kamose's frustration spilled over. "Whip him, and put him in chains."

Tawfiq's Mamluks stared at Kamose in shock. They looked at Juba fearfully and shot looks of consternation amongst themselves.

Kamose's smile was tight. "Fear not. He will not kill you. He has said so himself."

Ramah clasped his hands pleadingly. "Please, Great One! I beg of you!"

"Do you wish to join him, Ship's Captain?"

Juba closed his eyes wearily. "Please. Do not do this."

The Amir held his mace of office reversed in his hand. The shaft of the mace was a tube of iron. The Amir leaned out from his saddle. The leather wrapped grip of the mace swung down and cracked into the back of Juba's skull. The Berber fell face first to the cobblestones.

Sandor sat his horse next to the sorcerer and stroked his mustaches in a bored fashion. The cavalry captain had come with the reinforcements from Cherson along with a small contingent of Rus. His jet-black stallion shook its head and pawed the cobblestones as if would kick the fallen mystic. Sandor casually snapped his studded leather quirt across its withers and the horse lowered its head. Sandor spoke in fairly decent Turkish. "Who is this beggar?"

Kamose looked the Pole over. The man was so handsome he was almost evil looking. It was easy to assume he was just a useless dandy from the court of the Polish Queen, Justyna. Kamose studied Sandor's mount. The Pole had chosen a Chahri from Khorosan. It was said the breed was vicious by nature and dangerous to approach. They were known to wheel and trample their riders if they were foolish enough to fall from the saddle. To their credit, Chahri were known for incredible toughness and not feeling wounds, and they could be trained to fight for their rider with hooves and teeth. The Pole's choice in warhorses and the ease with which he controlled his mount spoke of abilities that belied his fancy riding breeches and bloused shirt.

"Someone who has displeased me."

"Will you kill him?"

Kamose thought about that. Killing a mystic might have

unforetold consequences. He nodded at one of the Mamluks standing about. "Roll him over."

The soldier prodded Juba onto his back with his lance butt. The mystic's blue eyes rolled back in their sockets. Blood began to stain the cobblestones beneath his head. Kamose pointed at his chest. "Beneath his robes should be a pouch. Do not open it. Take it and burn it, and take from him his necklace of blue stones. Take them and crush them."

The Mamluks divested Juba of his fetishes and set about destroying them. Kamose dismounted and knelt beside the Berber and closed his eyes. He sought his own center and opened the Third Eye.

Kamose's Inner Eye sought the light of the mystic's life. He was impressed, even envious at what his Inner-Eye saw. All but one of the Thrones of Power within Juba's body had been awakened. Juba's light lay resting in the Throne of Power above the heart. Tawfiq's blow had smashed Juba unconscious. Juba's light had retreated back to the Throne of Power the mystic used most. It lay there quiescent.

Kamose summoned his own power. He pulled it into the pit of his stomach and concentrated it. His breathing became a long, slow bellows as he fanned his power and kindled it into flame. With a great cry Kamose raised his had. His eyes flew wide and his hand swung down like a falling rock. He let out an explosive breath as his palm slammed down over the Berber's heart.

Juba went into convulsions.

His limbs jerked and flailed and his head bounced against the stones. Kamose took heavy breaths and wiped his brow as the Berber's body subsided into gentler twitches and jerks. The Egyptian closed his eyes and peered into the mystic's power once more. The light of his life was still strong, but his power was broken. His power had been clear white light, now it was a smeared yellow and flickered with bruised blues. The Throne of Power above the heart had been crushed. The lines of power in the human body paralleled the lines of power in the universe. Juba's broken power bled from his heart. The mystic shuddered as his power leaked down lines it was not meant to go and disrupted the patterns of his subtle body.

Psychically, Juba was crippled.

Sandor peered down from his horse. "Now what shall you do with him?"

Tawfiq leaned out and spat upon the Berber where he lay. He pointed his mace at one of his men "Take this lover of infidels and give him a hundred strokes of the whip. Then take him to the market," Tawfiq thrust his mace back into his belt. "Take him to the pens of the slavers."

* * *

The Caucasus marched on in an endless order of mountains and valleys. On the high paths, clumps of wildflowers sprang from cracks in the brown rocks. The dead looking shrubs suddenly leafed and bloomed. The snows were melting, and little rivulets and waterfalls fell from the cliffs and made pools among the boulders. The river valleys below were lakes of green grass and trees. Reza kept them on the high paths through the peaks. Their route twisted and turned, but the line it drew invariably headed east. They pushed hard and only descended to isolated villages to trade for supplies when they had to. Reza frequently consulted his box. He no longer seemed to need Marius' help to do it. He no longer hid himself, either, but rode a little bit away and stared into the box, murmuring from horseback. They saw no more of the Assassins. Coel suspected Reza had more to do with that than the declaration of blood feud he had left behind. During the day, Zuli spoke little more to him than she ever had. Yet, every night she crept into his bedroll. Coel felt greatly relieved. His one fear was that Zuli would use their stolen nights together to hurt Márta. Coel suspected Orsini knew of their trysts, but the dwarf kept his suspicions to himself.

Snorri grew increasingly grumpy.

Their second week in the mountains left them facing peaks that looked exactly like the ones they had passed. Coel looked out despairingly. "Do they never end?"

"They end," Snorri spoke at his side. "These are the Lesser Caucasus. The Greater lay to the north, in the lands of the Georgians and the Circassians. I have spoken with Orsini. We have been heading east for two weeks, and have passed Lake Sevan in the land of the Armenians. We should come to the great plain of the Kur River soon." Snorri grinned smugly at his ever-expanding geography. "We should spy the Caspian Sea within days."

Coel looked out across the peaks. The Caspian had been little more than a name to him until he had come to the Russias. The idea of a landlocked sea boggled his mind. "How far have I come?"

"From Wales?" Snorri searched his scarred eyebrows as he calculated. "Judging by Orsini's map, I would say well over two thousand miles, perhaps more."

Coel tried to wrap his mind around that.

Snorri sighed. "So."

Coel looked up. "So?"

"She's been with you."

Coel started.

"Don't bother to lie. You cringed like a kicked dog, and your face reddens like borscht." Snorri shook his head in slow disgust. "God help you if you ever really have to lie about something, Coel. You're pathetic."

"How did you know?"

"Well, *Hel*, Coel. She had to be sleeping with someone. She wasn't going to Marius' bedroll, that I knew, nor Reza's, and she's not been sleeping with Orsini."

The image gave Coel pause.

"I asked him. Man to dwarf. He says he does not tumble humans. It goes against his principles." Snorri face turned sour. "That leaves you or Márta. Frankly, I was betting on you. The look on your face says I was right."

Coel drew himself up in the saddle. He found himself unwilling to shoulder any more guilt. "You are my friend, Snorri, and I am sorry, to a point. But I did not write her love poetry or seduce her behind your back. She came to me of her own accord. You know her, and you know I speak the truth."

Snorri looked away.

"Now, you and I can go off behind a boulder and beat each other senseless if you wish, but you and I both know that Zuli will sleep with whomever she chooses. Whenever she chooses."

"You and I are friends, Coel," The Rus flung up his hands. "But *Hel*! Do you have to have both of them?"

"Snorri, I would settle for the one."

"You haven't given Márta the poem yet, have you?"

"No."

"Perhaps you should."

Coel's fingers reached up to press the folded poem inside his tunic. His shoulders sank. "I cannot have her Snorri. There is no reason to give it to her."

"Well, I'll give you a reason, by Thor!" Snorri sidled his horse over and thrust out his jaw. "Because tomorrow you may be dead! Tomorrow she may be dead! The Assassins hunt us, Coel! Tomorrow it may be you, me, her, and the rest of us with our heads stuck on spears!" Snorri shook with sudden passion. "Every woman should have a poem written about her! Even if we have to turn the whole goddamn world upside down to do it! By God, if you don't give her that poem, then, then . . . " He shook his scarred fist in Coel's face. "I'll beat you to a pulp!"

Snorri reined his horse around in a tight circle. He glared once more before he spurred away. "Fool!"

Coel watched in shock as Snorri rode ahead to rejoin the party. He spoke to empty air. "I will . . . give her the poem."

* * *

Coel found he could not work himself up to give Márta the poem. Not that night. Nor the next. They descended out of the Caucasus and into the great plain of the Kur River. The blue expanse of the Caspian Sea glimmered in the distance. They made camp in a copse of trees as they approached the landlocked sea. Reza gathered them together around the tiny fire they'd lit at dusk to cook their food.

Reza poked the fire with a stick. "We must make a choice.

The Assassins of Alamut have spread forth their hand. Their fingers are everywhere. They shall try to close their fist around us. The Long-Eye still follows our trail, and our path leads us ever east. We must decide which route shall serve us best." Reza gestured with his hand. "Orsini."

The dwarf thrust a twig in the tiny fire and used it to light an oil lamp. He pulled out a scroll from a bundle and spread it out on the blanket he sat on. He lifted the lantern high. "Gather about."

Coel marveled. He had never seen such a map in his life. Orsini took his twig and pointed at an elongated blue kidney shape. "This is the Caspian Sea. We are here, but a few miles west of it." He pointed at a small peninsula just east of where they were. "Here is Baki, the biggest city of the Azerbaijan. We must assume the Assassins wait for us there. If we go south along the coast, the next great city is Rasht, which is part of Persia."

Snorri peered over Orsini's shoulder. "The Assassins are there, too?"

Reza nodded. "The city of Rasht is infested with them and their agents. The Assassins do much of their trading there."

Coel pointed at the Caspian's southern coast. "What lies there?"

Reza smiled. "The southern coast of the Caspian is girded by the Elburz mountains. That is the very home of the Assassins of Alamut. There are no cities there. Only the strongholds of the Assassins, themselves."

Orsini drew a line east across the landlocked sea. "Directly across from Baki is a bay. There are a number of fishing villages there. The inhabitants are a mix of Persians, Turkmens, and Rus. They trade and pay tribute to the city of Baki. Barges and fishing boats sail between them."

Snorri nodded. "It would cover a quick two hundred miles to take ship across the sea, but the Assassins will expect it. They will be waiting on the other side as well."

Orsini tapped the map. "Indeed."

Coel stared at the map intently. "You say the Assassins own the southern coast?"

Reza nodded. "They do."

"There are no cities? No villages?"

"No. The Assassins wiped them out centuries ago. The Assassins do most of their trading through Rasht, and through agents in Tehran on the southern side of the mountains. What people there are exist high up in the mountain valleys. They are settlements of slaves who tend the Assassins herds and crops."

"Then I say we slip by them using their coast. If everyone fears the Assassins, then no one will be there, nor will the Assassins themselves be looking for anyone."

Orsini frowned. "That will mean a six hundred mile march along the coast. Three hundred of it through the Assassins' own homeland."

"My father always said the best place to hide from a Norman was under his nose."

"Hah!" Snorri nudged Coel with his elbow approvingly.

Reza stroked his beard. "Orsini is correct. I admit the Assassins will not expect it, but we would be travelling the entire length of their northern border with the sea. Sooner or later, someone would spot us. It is simply a matter of odds."

"No, no, no," Snorri shook his head. "You see, Coel's problem is that he is full of good ideas, but he needs someone like me to think them through for him."

Reza lifted an eyebrow. "You have an idea, Yaroslav?"

"I do. Coel is right; but rather than marching, we will use boats and hug the southern coast."

"Boats?" Márta grimaced. "There are seven of us, with sixteen horses, laden with gear. A ship or barge large enough to carry such a load could only be bought or stolen in the port city of Baki. We would be discovered."

"I did not say ship or barge, nor did I say Baki. I said boats. I say we go south a ways and find a fishing village. We buy fishing boats, the biggest we can find. It will probably take two of them. With luck, it will be several days before our purchase is reported. Even then, they will be expecting us to head east straight across the

Caspian as fast as we can. That is the direction they will pursue us, and on the eastern shore is where they will wait to welcome us. Instead we go south. We hug the coast. We put ashore at dawn and dusk only to run the horses and take on water. We sail at night. By day, we drop sail out of sight of land."

"Transporting horses?" Marius spoke gravely. "On fishing boats? While sailing at night?"

"I did not say it would be easy. But the Caspian is landlocked and calm. I can manage the sail on one boat and teach you to handle the tiller. Orsini must have learned something of sailing from the Venetians, and Coel has been upon the waters many times. They will handle the other boat. It can work. We can make it work."

Reza mulled the idea over. "And where would we disembark?"

"That would be up to you. You seem to know the mountain ranges. How well do you know the Elburz?"

"Not well. I have never penetrated the holdings of the Assassins."

"What lies beyond them?"

"Directly east, the Kopet Mountains, and beyond them the Karakum desert. The Kopets form the barrier against the southern edge of the Great Waste. South lay the plains of Persia and Khorasan beyond."

Coel looked at the map. Questions he had wondered all his life occurred to him. "Just how big is the Great Waste, then?"

Orsini took a piece of ash and crushed it between his thumb and forefinger. He dragged his thumb across the map. The dark gray smear went from the Kopet Mountains up to the southern feet of the Urals. The Waste was bigger than the Caspian Sea. "That big."

Reza's finger pointed within the swathe. "When the Hand of God descended upon the Hobgoblin Horde, his wrath engulfed the Aral Sea. The lands of Khwarazim, Transaxiona and Kazakhstan were laid to waste. Ancient cities that are only legend now, Merv, Bukhara, Tashkent, and Samarkand, all were destroyed. The hobgoblin advance had already decimated their civilizations. The Great Waste annihilated what remained of them and left the survivors in the Russian steppes and those in Asia forever separated. It closed the Silk Road and cut the world in half."

For a moment there was no sound but the crackling of the small fire.

Orsini licked his thumb and wiped it across the map. Coel marveled as the ash rubbed away clean without staining. Coel's eyes tracked to the islands of the west and his home. He thought it odd that on the map they were white. In fact nearly all of Northern Europe down to the Alps was white. White covered nearly half of the map.

"What does the white mean?"

Orsini shrugged. "Ice."

Coel was taken aback. "All of these places are not covered by ice."

"It is an old map," Orsini shrugged the question away. "The question remains, where do we make landfall, and how do we make our way through the eastern edge of mountains of the Assassins? It is the only weak point in an otherwise sound plan."

Coel and Snorri looked at one another. The dwarf had deliberately changed the subject. Coel was tempted to press him.

Zuli spoke very quietly.

"I know the secret paths of the Assassins. Some of them, anyway."

Once more the camp grew quiet.

Reza stood. "Very well. It is a dangerous plan, but the best option available to us. Coel, take the first watch." The sorcerer turned on Snorri. "Shall we resume our game?"

"Ah!" Snorri grinned delightedly. "I shall fetch the board."

Coel watched in tongue-tied fascination as Márta ate pan bread with bacon and honey and washed it down with goat's milk they had bought from some herders. Marius was a surprisingly good cook. Coel had learned the Brethren of the Blade were celibate and before being violently disbanded had kept no women servants in their keeps. The brothers took turns serving one another. Eating well was one of their few vices and they were adept at cooking on campaign.

Marius's camp fare was plain but hearty, and--Coel started as Snorri's boot collided with his rump. Snorri jerked his head meaningfully at Márta as he walked past carrying the chessboard over to Reza.

Coel waited in schoolboy trepidation until Márta had finished eating. She licked her fingers clean and then went to see to her horses. Coel rose with a fluttery sense of dread and followed her. He reached into his tunic and pulled forth the poem.

"Márta?"

Márta stopped running her brush over her horse. "What is it?"

"I have something for you."

A strange look came into her eyes. "What?"

"I told you, in Trebizond, before I swam out onto the boat, that I had made something, for you."

"Yes, I remember."

Coel held out the folded parchment. "Here."

Márta unfolded it and held it so that the firelight would fall upon it. Coel watched her face as she read. He watched Márta's eyes move across the page and he read the lines in his mind as she read them.

. . . Márta, iron sheathed in silk, a tawny limbed delight

lissome of neck and sculpted waist

would that you might turn your head

lips open, parted to my embrace

Márta, bright soul, shining through the lamps of your eyes

bright life, glowing beneath . . .

The parchment shook in Márta's hands. She looked up from it and her eyes were wet as they met his. "It is beautiful."

Coel felt like his heart might burst out of his chest.

His heart tightened like a fist as the poem crumpled in Márta's hand. The parchment crackled as she wadded it into a ball. Coel's heart fell out of his chest as Márta dropped the wadded poem to the dirt.

"Give it to your whore."

CHAPTER TWENTY-FIVE

"Well, what do you think?" Orsini asked.

Coel looked at the southern coast of the Caspian. In the distance the sharp peaks of the Kopet Mountains loomed dark blue in predawn. The boat sat with its sail lowered three hundred yards from shore but Coel still whispered. "I do not know, Orsini. It looks quiet enough. What do you think?"

"Snorri!" Orsini hissed across the water to the other boat. Snorri had casually taken command once they had embarked upon the sea. The Rus leaned out over the prow of his own boat.

"Otto!"

The hound leaped from the prow without hesitation and began paddling towards shore. The dog quickly disappeared into the gloom. Snorri waited with the patience of a tree. They had bypassed the city of Baki and gone down the western coast till they had found a likely fishing village. They'd been told the two biggest boats were the village's livelihood and not for sale. The headman's tone changed when Reza had shown him gold minted in Byzantium. They'd sailed out of sight of land during the day, and only put ashore briefly at dawn and dusk.

The horses were not pleased. The two boats stank of horse manure despite all the shoveling they had done, and twice the horses had grown upset and nearly stove in the deck and capsized the boats with their rearing and stamping. Coel was proud that his Barb had engaged in none of this, but the boats were overcrowded, they lay perilously low in the water, and they stank. They'd gone the last day and night without making landfall. Once they'd spied the Elburz Mountains, no one had wanted to put ashore. Now it was a matter of necessity. Coel glanced over at the other boat.

Márta would not sail in the same boat with him.

Coel hissed at Snorri. "Well?"

Snorri's voice called out once. "Otto!"

A happy bark answered. Surf splashed as the hound ran back into the water. "He doesn't smell any Assassins. I think it is safe, as long as we light no lanterns and have no fire."

Coel and Orsini began hauling up the sail. The canvas ruffled and Orsini adjusted it to catch the morning breeze. The two fishing boats began to slowly move towards the beach.

"How far to the eastern shore do you make it?"

"A day, two at the most." Orsini eyed the fading stars. "We are more than halfway across."

The two of them jumped over the side and guided the boat into the shallows. The keel ground into the sand. The horses began stamping and nudging forward to get off. Disembarking their steeds was easy. Getting them back aboard was becoming increasingly difficult.

Coel clucked at his Barb. The little boat rocked in the sand as the Spanish horse leaped obediently into the water. The other horses quickly followed her, and the surf churned into a froth of foam and stamping hooves.

Márta's bow was in her hand as she looked about the beach. "Snorri and I will exercise the horses. Father Marius, a quick meal please. Zuli, keep watch. Coel, clean out the boats. We need to be back out to sea before the sun rises."

Coel stiffened. He knew Márta was baiting him, and he knew it for the trap it was. Someone had to clean the boats. He would no more have his Barb stand in dung than she, but ordering him to shovel manure and scrub the deck in front of the whole party was a calculated affront, and if he refused, it would mean someone else would have to do it. Coel simmered. Orsini's laugh cut the tension. "Come, Coel. I would consider it an honor to scrub dung with you."

"The honor is mine." Coel gave Márta's back a hard look as she and Snorri roped the horses in two lines and led them out onto the beach for a run. Coel leapt aboard the boat and seized a spade. Orsini pulled himself aboard and filled a bucket with seawater. "You took that well."

Coel began scraping the square of deck where the horses stood. "I am just glad my father is not here to see me reduced to shoveling shite at a woman's order."

"Correct me if I am wrong, but my guess would be your father did everything your mother ever told him to, directly or indirectly."

Coel smiled. His father Math was Chieftain upon the Mountain. His mother would never embarrass her husband in front of others, but Math and everyone else on the mountain knew he'd married a woman wiser than he was. Her will had always been gentle law in their hall. "Oh, aye, she played him like a harp, I will admit, but she never made him contend with turd in public."

Orsini slopped seawater and sand onto the decking. "Did you truly believe Márta would not find out?"

"She spoke with you, then?"

"Of course she spoke with me."

"What did she say, then?"

"She thought the poem was beautiful."

"Oh?" Coel perked up an ear.

"She thinks you are a baboon."

Coel scraped the wet sand across the deck to scour it and flipped it back into the Caspian. "Ah."

Orsini seemed hard-pressed to suppress his mirth as he filled the bucket and sluiced. "Coel?"

"What, then?"

"Do you know what a baboon is?"

Coel's ears burned. "I do not."

"Ah."

For several seconds there was nothing but the sound of sloshing and scraping as they cleaned the boat. Coel dug the spade into the deck harder than he needed to. "So?"

"So, what?"

"So, what is a baboon, then!"

"Oh, well, a baboon is a very large and mean tempered sort of monkey from the Africas."

Coel's spade rasped across the deck. "Ah."

"They walk upon their knuckles and have swollen red behinds they wave in the air. It is said they are cannibals. They fling their feces at one another and bark like dogs. They often--"

Coel stabbed the spade into the deck. "You are worse than Snorri!"

Orsini lay down his bucket. "Very well."

"Very well what!"

"I am sorry I have teased you on a matter upon which I know you are sensitive. To atone, I shall allow you to ask me a question."

"What do you mean ask you a question?"

"Coel son of Math is usually bursting with questions. I mean what I said. Here, in private, you may ask me a question. Within reason I will answer it."

Coel glanced back at the beach. He could hear the horses' hooves churning the sand as Márta exercised them. Marius knelt over a large wooden bowl and moistened parched grain with a little oil and vinegar. "What is in Reza's box?"

"That is Reza's business, and mine. I would not recommend you asking that again, and you are wasting this opportunity."

Coel recoiled from the menace in Orsini's voice. "All right, then. On your map, Wales is covered in ice. Why?"

"Because where I come from Wales is covered in ice."

Coel pondered that.

"Ask Snorri. He has seen glaciers. They are great sheets of ice. They cover everything. They move with the speed of stone, but they move, inexorably. Where I am from, the cold has come. The ice is upon the land, and has been for generations."

"You said before that you are from what I would call the Carpathians."

"That is essentially correct."

"All covered in ice?"

"Yes." Orsini's voice grew far away. "The ice came, filling

the valleys and covering the mountains. Only the tallest peaks stuck up from the ice like islands in a frozen sea. We built castles upon those barren spires, and even tried to dig cities in the ice. They were beautiful, like cities of glass, but they were lifeless. The windswept rock was no place to raise our cattle. The valleys where we grew our wheat were buried beneath hundreds of fathoms of ice. Slow and sure our greenhouses failed. My ancestors watched the ice come and fought it. It was my generation who finally abandoned the land."

"You came here."

"Yes."

"How?"

"Tell me of *Samhain*, Coel."

Coel looked about himself warily. The Church had changed the name of the ancient festival to All Hallow's Eve to commemorate the Christian Saints, but in the mountains of Wales it was still celebrated in the old way, and in defiance of the Church in Rome. "What about it?"

"What is it that happens on *Samhain*?"

"It is the time when the veil between the land of the living and the dead is thinnest, when spirits walk the night."

"There is, indeed, a veil between the living and the dead, Coel, as there are veils between the worlds. In some places, the veils are thinner than others. Conjunctions of the stars can make these veils thinner still. At the right time, and with enough power, one can make doorways between worlds, between the living and the dead. Between Heaven and Hell, themselves."

"You came through such a door?"

"Indeed, I, and many of my people. It is something we are still indebted to the elves for," Orsini's voice rumbled low. "They never let us forget it."

Coel looked over Orsini's massive form and square hewn features. "You are unlike any dwarf I have ever seen."

"Ah, well." The dwarf's grin flashed. "I am of the mountain breed. We are hardier souls than the hill dwarves you may have seen in your islands."

"Why come here?"

Orsini snorted. "Because it is warm, Coel, and much the same as what we left."

"The hobgoblins came from your world, too?"

"No. Only the Great Spirits know where hobgoblins come from. But I suspect it is a world far less akin to yours and mine. Their shamans are crude compared to Elvish or even human sorcerers, but they have a grasp of the veils that exceeds all others. They are like locusts, migrating according to their own cycles. And only the Great Spirits know what motivates them, other than meat and war."

"So, they have returned, then?"

"Well, now, they may never have left. We know some goblins survived the Hand of God when your Saint Tomas Sander invoked divine intervention for the Holy League of Humanity. Some hobgoblins may have survived as well. Asia is vast."

"I saw them in the Russian steppes. Then they were on the Cathayan junk, in the Black Sea."

"Yes, that is troubling."

The horses came back in a thunder of hooves and flying sand. Coel and Orsini moved on to the other boat. Coel was silent as he scrubbed, and pondered what Orsini had told him. Everyone looked at Snorri and his Arabian stallion. The horse was magnificent, and Snorri sat upon him like a king. The Rus looked at the boats and then around the ring of faces. No one wanted to get back aboard the boats again. "What do you think, Reza?"

The wizard stared back over towards the mountains. "I have looked and listened with the inner senses. If we are observed, it is by far more skillful sorcerers than I."

Snorri stared up into the sky. "It will be an hour until dawn. I propose we take a rest here on the shore. I bought a pair of poles from the villagers. I will take Coel and see what we can do about catching some fish. Parched grain is losing its luster." He looked down the shore towards a heap of man-sized boulders that walked out a good way into the gentle breakers. "There, that's where the rockfish shall hide. I'll bring the poles. Coel, bring your bow, just in case." He jerked his head Otto. "Come!"

Coel took up his bow and a sheaf of arrows. Snorri took up a pair of poles half again as tall as he was and a roll of twine. Snorri clambered over the rocks and leaped down into the sand on the other side. He grinned and pointed the poles. "You see?"

Coel nodded. The jumble of rocks extended out into the water. Several smaller jumbles stuck up like small islands in the surf beyond. Snorri drew up his battle plan against the Caspian. "Between the rocks, that's where the big ones will be doing their dawn feeding, and look!"

Snorri unrolled a cloth. Coel gaped. Inside lay two rolls of smoked eel. "Nothing in the Caspian has ever smelled the like. They'll go mad."

Coel salivated at the smoked eel. "You have been holding out on me, then?"

"Yes, and you've been poking Zuli, haven't you?"

Coel cleared his throat. He took a pole and began tying his hook. Snorri tore him a strip of smoked eel and the two of them baited their hooks. They tied small rounds of wood to their lines for floats and made twine baskets for pebbles to make sinkers. Coel walked to foam on the beach and held his slack line loosely. He snapped his pole and sent his line across the submerged rocks.

Snorri tsked. "You cast like a woman."

"Had ever seen my mother fish you would not say such stupid things."

"It did not rub off." Snorri cast. Coel had to admit the Rus had a beautiful style. His line hissed through the air like a snake, and his sinker plopped down directly between two rocks that barely crested the water. Snorri grinned smugly. Coel jammed the end of his pole deep into the sand and spread out his *bratt* to sit upon. Snorri joined him with a satisfied grunt. Otto sat between them and sniffed longingly as Snorri offered Coel a strip of eel.

"My thanks." Coel bit off half and gave the other piece to Otto.

Snorri took a deep breath. "It's a fine morning."

Coel took the salt air deep into his lungs and watched the rippling tide turn to foam by his feet. "It is that."

Otto thumped his tail in agreement.

"It is a beautiful morning."

Coel and Snorri turned at the sound of Zuli's voice. The little thief stood with her hands on her hips. Coel was dumbstruck. Snorri opened his mouth and closed it.

Zuli was naked.

She shrugged impishly. "I just cannot get the smell of manure out of my nose. I need a bath." Both men started as Zuli charged them. They ducked as she hurdled over their heads. Coel and Snorri watched in awe as Zuli charged into the surf. Her feet threw up water as she pumped her arms in a full sprint. Otto chased after her barking joyously. Zuli suddenly hurled herself forward into a handspring. Her naked form popped into the air and twisted diagonally in the pearly light. She tucked into a ball and let out a happy shriek as she smashed into the water with a tremendous splash.

Her head and shoulders emerged. Zuli shook her head furiously and grinned at them. "You could use a bath as well."

Snorri shot a look at Coel and then matched Zuli's grin. "Which one of us?"

Zuli stood up. Water ran down her olive complected flesh and followed the contours of her body. Her blue-green gaze did not blink. "Why not both of you?"

Snorri and Coel looked at one another in momentary panic. Snorri leaped to his feet. "Coel!"

Coel leaped up. His pole wrenched over as the line tugged. He seized the pole in both hands, and it immediately bowed deeply. He jammed the end against the buckle of his war belt and dug in his heels as he hauled in.

It was a big fish.

"Don't jerk it!" Snorri waved his arms. "You'll lose it!"

"It's a big one!" Coel shook his head in excitement as the pole bent in his hands. "By God, it's a big one!"

Zuli clapped her hands excitedly. "Get it, Coel!"

Otto leaped and barked in the surf.

The ash pole bent in a severe arc. Coel took a step forward to relieve the tension. He pulled up again against the strain.

"You're jerking! You'll lose it!" Snorri jumped up and down in a frenzy. "Don't jerk it!"

"Well, lend a hand, goddamn you!"

Snorri charged into the water as Coel fought. When Snorri was in waist deep he grabbed the line. "All right! Hold her steady! Zuli! Lend a hand!"

Zuli splashed forward. Snorri pulled in slowly and then took up slack before releasing some line. "Here! Hold the slack!" Zuli took the slack as Snorri pulled in and released again. Coel felt like he could have landed the fish himself, but he had to admit that Snorri played the line like a bard tuning a lyre. Snorri grinned back over his shoulder as he began reeling in the fish in earnest fist over fist. "Odin's eye, Coel! You've caught--"

Zuli screamed.

Snorri's head whipped back around.

Snorri screamed.

A thing lurched up out of the water. Snorri staggered backwards as the thing came at him. Its body was as thick as a man's leg and what came out the water was as long as Coel was tall. Its black skinned form lunged like a cobra. White spines stuck up along its back. Its head was a great knob of exposed bone with sunken milk-white eyes and snapping, jagged jaws. The lobe of a stunted second head stuck out just in front of its gills and hissed and snapped blindly.

Coel threw down his pole.

Snorri screamed as the thing honked like a goose and fell upon him. It snapped inches away from his face and Snorri continued to scream as it twisted about in his grip.

Zuli plunged beneath the water. She came up with creature's thrashing tail in both hands. Snorri let out another high-pitched scream and hurled the thing's head away from him. His scream cut short into a gargle as he toppled backwards into the water and went under.

The thing whipped about and turned on Zuli. Zuli flung the tail away and leaped through the shallows in great splashing bounds. The thing knifed after her with sickening speed.

Coel charged. "Zuli!"

Zuli turned about and rolled backwards into the surf as the thing fell upon her slashing with its maw of saw teeth. Black slime oozed between Zuli's fingers as the creature twisted in her grasp. Otto lunged and seized the creature by its paddle-like tail. Coel's sword rang from its sheath.

Otto dug his paws into the sand and tugged furiously. The creature suddenly coiled half of its length and the hound's paws left the sand. The tail snapped out and Otto flew a dozen feet through the air.

Coel skidded in the sand. The thing writhed all over Zuli as it fought to bite her. Coel feared to strike it with his blade. He let out a snarl and swung his boot up against its gills with all of his might. A great honk came from the creature and its body twisted around Coel's leg. The distorted lesser head sank its teeth through Coel's boot and bit deep into his instep.

"Gah!" Coel yelled in agony and toppled over into the sand.

The thing released his foot and undulated up between his legs. Coel yelled again and snapped his knees together. The thing thrashed back and forth with its head pinned between his thighs. Coel screamed as the stunted head's teeth sank into his inner thigh. His legs parted and the creature's weight slammed down on his chest. The dominant head struck like a snake. Coel caught it by the gills. He struggled to hold the thing up and away from him. Its body oozed black slime and it slipped and slid between his hands. Razor sharp gill rakers sawed into his fingers. The snapping jaws dipped down towards Coel's face.

"Coel!"

Zuli stood over Coel. Blood and black slime covered her naked body. She held a rock the size of a bread loaf overhead in both hands. Coel shoved up with all of his strength. The thing's twin snapping skulls rose and Zuli swung the rock down. The thing's head bounced down against Coel's chest under the blow. It's long body whipped around. The oar-like tail slammed into Zuli's stomach and smashed her to the sand.

The head reared up out of Coel's grasp and coiled to strike.

An arrow thudded into its gills. The thing let out a shrieking honk and thrashed wildly as a second and third arrow sank into its side. Coel rolled aside as the thing twisted and flailed. Its tail struck him between the shoulder blades and swatted him down like a wet piece of iron. Coel tasted sand as he was driven down face first.

Orsini's voice boomed. "Coel stay down!"

Coel had no choice. The oozing wet weight suddenly fell across his back. It twisted and shuddered and then suddenly lay still.

Coel pressed himself up painfully and spat sand. The thing slid off of him wetly as he rose to one knee. Half a dozen arrows sprouted from its gills. The squat bolt of a crossbow had smashed in its primary skull. The second head let out a dying hiss like a kettle taken off the fire. Márta and Orsini stood upon the pile of rocks with their weapons in their hands. Reza and Marius stood behind them. Márta looked coldly at Zuli where she lay curled naked in the sand.

Snorri reeled up onto his knees in the surf and fell to his hands, retching like he had swallowed half the Caspian.

"We must make sail as soon as possible." Márta turned on her heel and disappeared behind the pile of rocks.

Coel picked up his *bratt* and covered Zuli. Reza looked upon the thing lying in the sand. Coel retrieved his sword and wiped it off. "What was it?"

Reza squatted on his heels and mused over the dead horror. "An eel, once? Perhaps a sturgeon."

Coel was revolted. "You are saying someone has sent a demon made of mud feeders after us?"

"No," Zuli rose to her knees and clutched Coel's *bratt* about her. "That is a thing born of the Waste."

"So what is it doing here, then?"

Reza examined the skull-like heads and sunken milky eyes

with interest. "That is a good question. From what I know, spending time in the Waste can change a living creature, but this thing was obviously born there. Most things that are born this changed die. A thing born with extra limbs or a twin growing out of its side usually cannot survive. This one's differences did not seem to hinder it. There are tributaries of the Caspian that empty from out of the waste. This thing may have swam its way down from its poisoned spawning ground and found better hunting here in the clean sea." Reza nodded to himself and rose up. "Márta is right. We must make sail at once. It is nearly sun-up. Coel, once we are under sail have Marius look at your wounds."

Coel steadied Zuli while she painfully washed and pulled on her clothes. He looked down at the vileness that had attacked them. "You told me you had seen Assassins who had been changed by the waste."

"I have."

Coel gazed at the twisted heads and the body that oozed black slime. "Is it like that, then?"

"You told me you have sworn an oath against the Assassins of Alamut."

"I have."

"Will you swear another?"

"I will."

Zuli looked down upon the thing in the sand. "Don't let the Assassins take me, Coel. You they will only kill. Me?" Her eyes never left the abomination lying before her. "Don't let them give me to those who live in the Waste."

"You will die in my arms before you die in theirs," Coel took Zuli's face in his hands. "I swear it."

CHAPTER TWENTY-SIX

"No such people have come into the city, Great One, much less purchased a ship. I would know of such a thing, I assure you."

Kamose gazed out over the Caspian. The dock master of Baki bowed and scraped before him. Kamose had no doubt the man spoke the truth. The question was where could the Walladid be. He had either somehow gone on undetected from Baki, or doubled back upon the trail.

"They have gone south."

Kamose turned in the saddle and looked at Sandor. The Pole smiled with a smugness that tempted Kamose to have the man lashed. "South? The land to the south is flat with few places to hide. South would take them to the city of Rasht, which the Assassins of Alamut own in all but name. What makes you think they would take such a reckless course?"

Sandor gave a languorous shrug. "Because that is what I would do."

Tawfiq and Kamose stared.

"You, yourself, Great One, know the cleverness of the Walladid better than I. However, anyone who has served in Moscow has heard of Snorri Yaroslav. The man is infamous. Further, contacts I have in the Church inform me that Coel ap Math was trained at the Paladin Academy in Paris. Barring all of these things, Orsini of Venice rides with them, and I must at least assume the four of them together must be as clever as myself."

Kamose waited a moment to see if Allah would strike the man down for his hubris. If God did not, it was likely that Tawfiq would.

The *Amir* had taken an instant disliking to the man. He stared incredulously at the Pole. "South?"

"Yes, *Amir*, that is what I said."

"South? Into the very shadow of Alamut?"

"Of course not, that would be foolish. They have most likely made some kind of attempt to cross the Caspian."

"Cross the Caspian?" Tawfiq's face twisted. "They must have at least at twelve horses. They would need Rus long ships, or a barge. They could purchase or steal such things only here in Baki. We know they have not."

Sandor looked down his aristocratic nose. "They could use fishing boats. Of those, there are plenty throughout the region."

"Fishing boats? Impossible!"

"You could do it, *Amir*, could you not? If you had to?" The Pole sighed in dismissal. "Ah, well, perhaps you could not, but I could. With skilled sailors, and skilled horse handlers, it could be done."

Tawfiq gripped the handle of his mace. Kamose raised a restraining hand. "What is it that you propose?"

"Just this. The Walladid must now be well across the Caspian. If we take longships under sail and oar, we can make time. But the Walladid will make the eastern coast before we can catch him."

"If things are as you suggest, I am afraid I must agree."

"Then we must delay him, or kill him, if we can. The farther east he goes, the more difficult it will be to catch him."

Kamose stroked his beard. The Walladid's mission in Trebizond had been successful, of that he was sure, despite the reticence of the witch queen Hypatia to give him information. The first step towards the blasphemy the Persian craved was accomplished. The question was what direction would his search take him to complete it. Kamose suspected even the Walladid did not yet know. That was perhaps the Persian's greatest defense. It was impossible to predict the path of a man who did not know it himself. "What is it you suggest?"

"You are the Long-Eye. Use your power. Find Walladid. Alert the Old Man of the Mountain. Have the Assassins strike before Walladid can get deep into Persia."

Kamose's lips thinned. It was an act he contemplated daily, and not without fear. "That would entail a direct confrontation across the ethers with the Walladid, with my mind open to his. I cannot be entirely sure I would win such a confrontation, and if I lost, the Walladid would have a free run towards wherever his objective led him."

"I have brought a sorcerer with me."

"So I see." Kamose glanced back at the Belgian wizard Sandor had brought with him. The man looked every inch a fool in his peaked hat and scholar's robe. Kamose viewed any user of magic who had ended up in Frontier Service for the Christians with extreme dubiousness. "The Walladid would crush the mind of this Renatus of yours in seconds if he were so stupid as to seek him out across the ethers."

"Exactly," Sandor's voice dropped low. "Have Renatus actively seek out the Walladid. While the Persian crushes him, he will be distracted. Could you not then, safely, use your power to observe and locate him, and then tell his whereabouts to the Old Man of the Mountain?"

Kamose blinked at Sandor's unscrupulousness. "You mean to sacrifice the Belgian to the Walladid's power?"

"If you wish to hunt bears?" Sandor waved a careless hand. "You must surely lose some hounds."

Kamose looked over at Tawfiq. "*Amir*?"

The *Amir* looked upon Sandor with grudging respect. "It is not the worst idea I have ever heard."

* * *

"You were useless!"

Snorri wouldn't meet Coel's eyes. "I swallowed seawater!"

"The dog was of more use than you!"

"I don't like serpents!"

"It was an eel!"

"What do you think an eel is?"

"A fish, fool!"

"By Thor!" Snorri wheeled on Coel with his fists clenched. "If it's a fight you want you'll have it!"

Zuli's voice hissed in the gloom. The sun had fallen and the narrow valley was an envelope of shadow. "Shut up! Both of you!"

"And you!" Snorri's head whipped about. "Changeling child of Loki! Save that you'd probably like it? I would take my warbelt and—Gah!"

Snorri fell to one knee in agony. Coel let out a matching noise and dropped beside him. Orsini held both their elbows. His thumbs ground with paralyzing force into the soft inner joint. "Cease this ridiculous behavior at once or I shall hang you by your heels and beat you like rugs!" He shoved the both of them to the ground. "We are not yet clear of these cursed mountains, and the two of you squabble like fishwives!"

Coel clutched his elbow. He'd refused to speak to Snorri since disembarking. The party silently followed Zuli's lead as they ascended. They lead their horses by foot on the high paths. They were in the heartland of the Assassins. Night had fallen, but Zuli lead them unerringly up through the eastern edge of the Elburz. She said the Assassins had no fear of being invaded, and the night was their time of ritual. If they lit no fires and used no magic, they might just pass through the Elburz and make it safely into the Kopets.

Coel glared first at Orsini and then the Rus. The dwarf ignored both of them as he took up the halters of his ponies. Snorri sat up rubbing his arm and muttered low. "You know, I was trying to say I'm sorry."

Coel massaged his arm. He had been a champion wrestler back in Wales. Orsini had brought him to his knees with a thumb and forefinger. The day he locked collar and elbow with the dwarf he suspected he would be broken like kindling. Coel rose muttering. "These things happen."

Snorri lifted his chin defiantly. "I am not a coward."

"I know," Coel held out his hand. "I would not have a

coward for a best friend."

Snorri made a pleased noise and took Coel's hand. Coel hauled the Rus to his feet. The matter of the beach was no longer between them.

Reza dropped the reins of his horse and made a noise of pain. Márta leaped to his side and steadied him. Reza waved her away. His face bunched with terrible concentration. "Come, Ah-Ay, grapple with me if you dare." He seemed to be speaking to no one. "No, wait, not the Long-Eye. Who, then?"

Coel's hand was upon his sword. "What is happening?"

Márta watched her master intently. "Reza is attacked."

"What?"

"He contends with someone across the ethers," Márta made a disdainful noise. "He will crush them."

Reza's hands slapped together before his chest as if he was praying. His eyes clenched shut but a smile slashed across his face. "Fool."

* * *

Renatus shuddered and jerked in the dirt. His eyes rolled as blood leaked out of his nostrils. Only a small part of Kamose's attention noticed this as he closed his eyes and searched across the lines of force for the disturbance of Reza Walladid. He sought out the flare of the Walladid's power as the Persian crushed the personality of the unfortunate Renatus with his own.

Kamose's eyes flicked open as Renatus spoke. Blood stained the Belgian's lips and he spoke with great strain. "Reza was wounded in Trebizond!"

The Long-Eye's eyes flared wide.

Renatus' voice grated. "The light of his life is weak! I have withstood his assault, but I cannot hold him for long! You must strike! Strike now or I will lose him!"

Kamose's eyes slammed shut and the sword cut deep line of

concentration drew down his brow. He pooled his strength in the pit of his belly and summoned his will. With Reza injured, his concentration would be weak. His power would be divided as he tried to tear himself from Renatus' psychic grasp and face Kamose's own onslaught at the same time. Kamose decided to end the game here. The danger was great, but it was the greatest chance he would ever have. He would leave his body and fly along the lines of force. He would crush the Walladid with one massive blow of his entire being. He would--

Kamose's eyes flew open.

Reza Walladid was a chess player. The greatest Kamose had ever met. Kamose had learned this to his shame across the board, but the hard lessons had shown him something of Reza's style. Kamose divorced himself from his desperation to capture or destroy the Walladid. His every instinct clamored that this was a feint. Kamose could smell it, and even if his instincts were wrong, he would not make the cardinal mistake of diverging from an already sound plan. Kamose calmed himself. His Inner Eye opened. He passively scanned the lines of force. He looked for the signature of the Walladid's power without exposing his own. Reza's power was like a lightning bolt in the ethers that stretched across the short arc of the world between them landing with annihilating force in the brain of Renatus. Kamose looked across the bright arc as it crossed the fluid water force of the Caspian and erupted out of the solid aura of the Elburz Mountains. He had found the Walladid.

Kamose was shocked again at Reza's boldness.

Renatus spoke with a voice that was not his own. "Your level of play has improved, son of Ah-Ay."

Kamose's eyes flew open. Renatus jerked erect like a puppet whose strings had been yanked. The Belgian's dagger hissed from its sheath. The point plunged murderously towards Kamose's heart.

"Great one!" Tawfiq's mace lashed out. The bones of Renatus forearm snapped and the dagger flew out of his hand. Tawfiq brought the mace around in a backhanded blow that shattered the Belgian's jaw. Sandor lunged and the point of his saber thrust through the Belgian's chest. Tawfiq's mace swung down and Renatus' skull sundered under the steel flanges.

The Belgian flopped dead to the ground.

"Great one! Are you all right?"

Kamose shook slightly from his brush with death. "I am well, *Amir*. Almost, I was taken in by the Walladid's ruse," He looked at Sandor with renewed respect. "But the Pole's plan was perfect. I have found the Walladid."

Sandor shrugged nonchalantly and wiped his saber on Renatus' robe.

Kamose closed his eyes again. The Inner-Eye opened. Kamose actively sent his mind across the ethers. Another mind awaited shockingly close to the Walladid. The mind was open to Kamose's communication. The Egyptian twitched with revulsion as the other mind embraced his own. Kamose pictured the lines of force as he had seen them and their relation to the Walladid. In his mind he painted it like a tapestry across the arc of the world between them. The alien mind tracked the Walladid's arc and did its own calculations. Kamose opened his eyes and broke contact with the vileness he had been in communication with. Every rumor he had ever heard in his long life was true.

A man who went into the Great Waste ceased to be a man.

Tawfiq knelt by his side. "Great one?"

"It is done. Sandor was correct. The Walladid and his servants have crossed the Caspian. They are in the Elburz Mountains. They walk within the very shadow of Alamut," Kamose stared off into the east. "And so I have informed the Old Man of the Mountain."

* * *

"Ride for your lives!" Reza swung up into the saddle. "Zuli! Lead us! As fast as you can!"

Zuli vaulted onto her pony and spurred forward. Coel jumped into the saddle. "What is happening?"

"We are discovered!" Márta's horse reared and she sawed on

the reins to pull it back down. "We must ride!"

Coel followed Márta's golden horse as it galloped after Reza and Zuli. The Barb easily matched the furious pace and held it. Snorri's Arabian thundered behind him. The horses galloped along the narrow mountain pass at break-neck speed through the falling dark. Zuli's Bactrian pony set the pace, and they raced around boulders and skirted the black depths that fell away from the cliffs. Coel held the reins loose. The Barb instinctively followed the tail of Márta's Kazilik. The horses blindly followed Zuli's lead as she led the party in a suicidal plunge through the mountain pass.

"Look!" Orsini's voice boomed over the clatter of hooves. "To the west!"

A winking orange light lit the mountain peaks far to the west. A moment later, another flickered into life much closer. A third blazed closer still some twenty miles away. Coel's heart went into his throat. Signal fires lit across the Elburz. A mile ahead another fire lit up the peaks.

"That is their last lookout!" Zuli's voice was a shout on the wind. "If we can win past it, we will have a good run at the Kopet Mountains!"

"Damn you, woman! You've killed us!" Snorri's roar was both fear and outrage. The glare of the signal pyre lit the embrasure of a watchtower just ahead of them.

Reza's voice carried above the sound of the charge. "Look to your weapons! Ride!"

Sparks of light separated from the signal fire as the defenders lit torches. The droning wail of goat horns moaned like judgment through the peaks.

Coel slowed his Barb to come along his packhorse. He nearly lost his shield as he yanked it free in the dark. His lance slid into his hand. "Snorri! We take the front!"

The Rus' spurred his Arabian and they quickly passed Orsini and a string of the spare horses. They flew by Reza and Marius. Márta had fallen back and rode before her master. Zuli's pony pounded ahead of them.

"Zuli! Fall back behind Marius! Help Orsini with the

horses!"

"Straight ahead Coel!" Zuli cried. "Straight for the next thousand yards!" Zuli dropped back between them and suddenly Coel and Snorri led the headlong charge shoulder to shoulder. Coel could barely see the stony path beneath his horse's hooves. He desperately wished he were wearing his helmet. Coel hunched low as something smacked into his shield.

"Ware, Coel!" Snorri snarled. "They're loosing at us!"

Coel looked about the starlit crags wildly as another missile struck his shield. "I cannot see them!"

"By Odin the bastards see us!"

The mountain path abruptly lit with incandescent brilliance. Three men in black robes of Assassins stood out in high relief blocking the path before them. Coel threw a glance backward and saw Father Marius standing in his stirrups. He held the silver pendant of his Chi-Roh symbol high. Yellow light poured out of it like a sun. Coel squinted against the glare as he turned round and lowered his lance. More Assassins ran headlong down the rocky slope. Their robes were in disarray, and they carried whatever weapons they'd at hand at the sound of the horn. Coel spurred the Barb to full charge at the men in the path before them.

Márta's arrows found targets. Coel jerked as a crossbow bolt punched through the wooden slats of his shield and flew past over his shoulder. Coel wielded his lance over arm and thrust it into an Assassin's chest. The shaft bent, and Coel yanked the lance free as he rode past. Even lanced, the Assassin's sword scraped Coel's shield. Snorri flung a spear that snapped back an Assassin's head. They rode down a third killer beneath their horses' hooves.

They were clear.

Coel flung his shield across his back and hunched low in the saddle. He spent long moments fearing poisoned arrows as they plunged on. Marius' light winked out as suddenly as it had blazed forth. Coel's dazzled eyes saw nothing but blackness and after-images.

Zuli's voice was a shriek on the wind. "Coel! Snorri! Slow down! Ride straight!" Coel kept the Barb pointed ahead with his knees and pulled gently on the reins. The panicking Barb slowed. He could sense another horse pulling between himself and Snorri. Zuli's voice was clear beside him. "Give me the reins. Both of you."

Coel felt the reins lifted from his hand. Zuli's pony bumped against his leg as the three animals rode shoulder to shoulder. Zuli pressed a rope into his hands. "I've strung the rest of the horses! Snorri, follow Coel! Coel, let your horse follow my lead! I will take us down into a valley where the riding will be smoother! The Assassins are killers, not horse warriors! The fortress we passed was their easternmost outpost in the mountains! If we ride through the night they cannot catch us!"

Coel sat up in the saddle. His eyes adjusted to the night again, but it was little comfort. Zuli was but a lump in the darkness beside him, and he could not see the ground beneath his horse's hooves as it flew by. He did not relish the idea of spending the night riding blind, but once before Zuli had taken a rope and pulled him out of the darkness of the Black Sea. He would let her pull him from the valley of death.

CHAPTER TWENTY-SEVEN

The Old Man of the Mountain sat upon a divan. The shackled bodies of those who had failed lay before him. Some were still alive. The flayed and vivisected creatures moaned and gurgled as they slowly died beneath the curved scalpels of the torturers.

The Old Man's guest forced his mouth awkwardly around Persian words. "Why do you not kill them?"

The Old Man glanced up from the writhing of the condemned. "They have failed me."

The guest made another overt and vain attempt to peer into the darkness within the Old Man's hooded and veiled burnoose. He failed and returned his attention to the men on the floor. "Yes," The guest watched the dying men without expression and repeated his question. "Why do you not kill them?"

"I wish them to suffer."

The guest stared at him blankly.

"Their suffering pleases me."

The Old Man's guest gave this new thought weighty consideration. He ceased his pondering and sniffed the air as servants set a tray on a low table before him. The guest took an eating knife and stabbed a cube of rare lamb that had been simmered in its own blood. He chewed on the meat and then stabbed another cube.

"The meat is to your satisfaction?" The Old Man asked.

The guest swallowed and deliberated again. "It pleases me. It pleases me how this meat has been prepared."

"I am pleased." The Old Man turned his attention back to the dying. The men had failed to stop Walladid and his associates. The Old Man considered this. Reza Walladid was a sorcerer of the First Rank and a renegade of the Blue Robe sect. The Walladid had devoted his life to the study and practice of banned magics. Orsini of

Venice had been famous for two hundred years, both for his valor in the Great War against the hobgoblins and for the subtle financial empire he had built in its aftermath. His gold had paved the way for the Walladid, and he was a powerful ally. The Sisters of Limmasol in Cyprus had trained Reza's guard slave, Márta. Since the age of eighteen she had foiled numerous attempts on Reza's life, and won eleven registered duels. The Old Man's thoughts turned to an even more interesting subject.

Zuleikha.

The Old Man gazed upon the dying men before him. Their death was a mercy compared to what awaited little Zuleikha. Her employment with Reza was a bonus. Father Marius Von Balke, on the other hand, was an enigma. From what the Old Man's spies could glean, the Roman Church had censured Marius and disbanded his order for their behavior in the Baltic. He was rumored to have power beyond his years or his training. Why such a Christian fanatic would serve the Walladid was a mystery.

Coel ap Math and Snorri Yaroslav troubled the Old Man even more. A failed Paladin candidate and a half-pagan Rus had resisted every attempt upon their lives. The Celt carried a Paladin blade, given to him for reasons unknown by the Swordmaster of Grande Triumphe. Snorri Yaroslav was a former Captain of the Varangian Guard of the Byzantine Emperor. They had both been underestimated. Furthermore, the two of them had fallen in with the Walladid, which had both confused and consolidated two separate business ventures. This was so unexpected that even the Old Man's Vizier had not been able to see it in the Incense of Trance. Such a collection of characters smacked of Fate. The Old Man of the Mountain did not like Fate. It was one of the few things he could not intimidate or control.

The Old Man of the Mountain looked at his guest. He would not tell him that the mewling, dissected things on the dais were being punished for failing to kill Coel ap Math and Snorri Yaroslav. There was no need at all to mention Reza Walladid. That was separate business. For a moment, the Old Man wished he could bring Reza to the Mountain and break him to his will. A sorcerer of such power would be an invaluable addition to the brotherhood, but such thoughts were idle. He was the Old Man of the Mountain and the Lord of Alamut. He had taken gold. He would not stop until Reza

Walladid was presented, dead or alive, in the hall of the Blue-Robe sect in Cairo. He would not stop until Coel ap Math and Snorri Yaroslav died screaming.

The Old Man raised a long finger that remained covered by the black sleeve of the robe. The garment concealed his every feature. "Gassim."

A powerfully built Assassin rose from where he knelt at the Old Man's right hand. "Yes, Lord?"

"I wish you to go down into the catacombs." Gassim's eyes widened for the briefest of moments. The Old Man continued. "I wish you to waken those who have been Blessed by the Waste."

Gassim bowed low and moved quickly from the hall. The Old Man looked over at his guest. He continued to eat lamb and watch the death throes of the condemned expressionlessly. The Old Man suspected his guest thought it was a waste of good meat.

* * *

The horses were tired. The sun shone high overhead, but no one wanted to stop with Assassins somewhere behind them.

Orsini fell out of the saddle.

"Orsini!" Márta reined in and dropped to Orsini's side. "Yaroslav! Go back along the trail! Keep watch!"

Snorri spurred his Arabian without a word, and he and Otto went charging back the way they had come.

Coel slid from the saddle and knelt beside the dwarf. Orsini's face was fish belly white. Sweat ran down his face and streaked the dust that covered them all. The broken shaft of an arrow stuck out from low in the dwarf's side. Blood stained the sumptuous shirt he wore beneath his travel cloak.

"You are hit! For God's sake, why did you not say something?"

"There seemed little time to stop and perform surgery in the night, and I must confess I have been unconscious most of the morning."

Márta leaped up and went to her horse. A pair of arrows stuck out of her cane shield. She yanked one out and held it up. Black vileness they all recognized clotted the wicked barbs of the broadhead point.

"Orsini! You have been poisoned!"

"Most assuredly."

"You will die!"

"I will not."

Coel stared in horror at the arrow. "Marius! Heal him! Quickly!"

Marius stared steadily down at the dwarf. "I will not."

"Marius!" Reza's voice cracked like a whip.

The priest flinched and froze in place. "I will not perform a Laying of the Hands upon a non-human. It would be an affront before God."

Reza's voice went flat. "You will obey."

"I will not have that man laying his hands upon me," Snorri stated. "It would be an affront to my honor and my own religious scruples. I shall not allow it."

"You will die!" Marta begged. "Just like Oleg!"

Orsini drew a deep breath. "I do not wish to demean the young man's memory, but Oleg was human. I am a Dwarf."

The entire party looked at the dwarf as if he were insane. Orsini sighed. "The Greeks believed the Titan, Prometheus, formed man from clay. Your own Old Testament says God formed your like from the dust of the earth. The legends of my people say the Great Spirits carved the dwarvish race from stone. Not to be insulting, but dwarves are killed by sterner standards than those to which you humans are accustomed. Remove the arrow. The poison shall not slay me. I will live."

"We cannot pull it out or push it through. I will have to cut it out," Coel eyed the barbed arrowhead Márta held. "It will hurt like hell."

"It hurts like hell now. Remove it."

Coel drew his dagger. "Someone make a fire."

* * *

Kamose looked out towards the Kopet Mountains and was pleased. The Assassins had failed to stop Reza in the mountains, but the strange shadow of Father Marius' was now his to follow. Marius had used his power in the battle with the Assassins, and now its echoes were discernable as footprints in the ethers. His imprint could be read in the lines of force. Kamose could now track Reza's party without confronting the Walladid. A part of Kamose was pleased the Assassins had failed. He did not trust the Old Man of the Mountain, and it still galled him to have such creatures as allies.

"You are pleased, Great One." Tawfiq said.

"Yes."

Sandor stroked his mustache. "You can track them."

"I can."

"What is your will?" Tawfiq asked.

Kamose raised an eyebrow. "What would you do, *Amir*?"

"Run them down and kill them."

The Egyptian looked to the Pole. "And you, Sandor?"

"They are now in the Kopet Mountains, and have a great lead upon us. I do not believe we can chase them down by following their path. I say let them weave their way through the mountains. Let them waste their strength. I say we head south, into the plains of Northern Persia, and parallel them. In the flatlands, we will make up the time we have lost. We may even get ahead of them when they choose to leave the mountains."

"And should they head north?"

"North of the Kopets there is nothing but the fringe of the Karakum Desert, and beyond that, the Great Waste. Even should they be so foolish as to enter it, we will make better time going through Persia and then cutting through the width of the Kopets than following their trail along their length."

It struck Kamose that Sandor's sense of geography stretched far beyond the plains of Poland. His logic was flawless, however, and he had to agree.

"Let us leave these mountains."

* * *

Coel eyed the brown mountains. Zuli assured him that they had left the Elburz far behind and were now deep in the Kopet range. Coel could not tell the difference. Each peak conquered offered the heartbreaking vista of more to come. Reza continued to commune with whatever lay within the box and lead the party ever eastward. They had lit no fires for a week and were near the end of their rations. Water and fodder for the horses grew increasingly scarce.

Coel eyed Orsini. The dwarf was ill. He was taking great pains to hide it, but his blunt face was pale and his features haggard. Coel had dug the arrow out, cauterized the wound and sewn it. Orsini had shown considerably better spirits with the arrow removed, but Coel believed the damage was done. The poison was still in the dwarf's body, and despite his inhuman constitution, it was slowly taking its toll. Cold food and cold mountain nights sleeping on the ground could not be helping matters.

Orsini insisted he was fine.

Coel pulled his horse to a halt.

Otto was a stone's throw away and staring at something intently.

"Snorri," Coel spoke softly out of the corner of his mouth. "What is wrong with your dog?"

Snorri scowled. "I don't know."

The hound held his head up into the wind. He sniffed intently at the rock wall before them. Coel slid from the saddle. His bow was strung. He had seen mountain goats in the distance for the past two days and been hoping for a pot shot. He nocked an arrow as he dropped to the ground.

"Otto!" Snorri freed his axe. "What is it, boy?"

Otto's head jerked but his eyes remained riveted on a clump of brown boulders.

Coel eyed the rocks. "Rabbit?"

"He's a hound. He'd be flushing it out."

Márta reined in beside them with her bow in her hand. "What is wrong with Otto?"

"He smells something."

Otto's lowered his muzzle. His haunches rose up high in the air. His whole body vibrated with excitement. His eyes never waved from the rocks. His tail started wagging so rapidly it made his whole body wriggle.

"Your dog's mind is damaged."

Snorri glared at Marius.

The rest of the party reined in. Otto leaped from side to side before a boulder wagging his tail and barking. Snorri hissed again. "Get it, Otto! Get it!"

Otto let out a bark of spastic joy.

Coel nearly dropped his bow as the rock rose up and spoke in perfect Latin.

"Stay your arrows. We wish no quarrel."

The rock threw back a brown cloak and was no longer a rock. Six other rocks underwent the same startling transformation. They stood straight as spears and looked at the party with lifted chins. Their brown cloaks were now a shimmering, silvery green. Beneath their cloaks they wore leather corselets embossed with golden scrolling and tooled with silver runes. Impossibly long, stiff-bladed thrusting swords hung by baldrics from their shoulders. They held bows in their hands that were neither long like Coel's nor compound like Márta's, but of curious flat construction and bound with gold, silver and brass wire. The speaker drew back his hood and braided blonde hair spilled out over his shoulders. Coel stared. Wide eyes as green as the sea met his own with a power that held Coel in place.

Coel knew the man before him was no man.

Coel was so stupefied he spoke in Gaelic. "*Siddhe!*"

"Elves?" Orsini shouldered forward. "Where?

The two parties stared at one another silently. The unhooded elf turned to one of his companions. He inclined his head slightly towards Coel and spoke Gaelic. "That one speaks a civilized language, and carries a serviceable bow."

The second elf's hood fell back and revealed a woman's face. Her eyes were the same green as her companion, and her golden braids glittered in the sun. Her eyes bored into Coel's. Coel yanked his gaze up between her sculpted eyebrows and raised his bow. The sea-green eyes twinkled and their intensity softened as she smiled. "I shall not try to charm you, man of Wales, you have my promise." Her head tilted thoughtfully. "Who are you?"

Reza's voice was a harsh grate compared to the woman's and in Latin. "You may direct your questions to me."

"I am Coel!" Coel blurted. "Son of Math!"

The woman stared intently at Coel. Something moved behind her eyes as she ran her gaze across the party. They stopped upon Zuli and became unreadable. Zuli glared. The elf woman turned back to Orsini. "Greetings, *Fomorian*, how are you called here?"

Orsini did not remove his hat. "Orsini, of Venice."

"I have heard of you."

"I am not surprised."

"I can smell your wound, and I can see its poison in your aura. I would not go east if I were you."

"You are not I."

She turned her glance upon Zuli. "Greetings, little one. Do you remember me?"

The little thief's face twisted with hate. "I remember you, Fiachna, and I remember your hospitality."

Marius spat upon the ground between them. He raised his Chi-Roh symbol up on its silver chain. "We should have no truck with these. They are the children of Lucifer."

"We are the Children of Danu." The woman eyed Father Marius with great distaste. "Though I would not expect you to know the difference."

"You are stealers of babes, and have sold your souls to Satan for immortality on earth."

She ran her eyes around Marius as if drawing his outline. "You are not one to be speaking of souls, Priest."

Marius blanched. He shook out his mace and chain from beneath his mantle. The elven woman's hand went to her sword. Several elves raised their bows.

"Coel! Son of Math!" An elf stood forward and interrupted. He looked much like the first two, save that his long hair was reddish gold and blew unbound in the wind. He carried a spear with a silver steel blade shaped like a long inverted heart. He gazed at Coel with guileless excitement. "Son of Megan?"

The other elves stared at him.

Coel felt a surge of emotion "I am, Coel! Second son to Math and Megan!"

"I am Fiachad!" The elf threw his heart bladed spear into the air jubilantly and caught it. "I know your mother!"

The elf-woman raised an eyebrow at Fiachad. The exuberant elf seemed to remember his place and tucked his spear under his arm as he stepped back in line. "My brother Fiachad is young," The woman said. "And never before has he left the Isle of Man. He must be forgiven."

Reza met her gaze impassively. "What do you wish?"

"Merely to pass."

"What are you doing here?"

"What are you doing here?" Countered the elf.

"Merely passing."

The two silently measured one another. The elf's eyes went to the saddlebag by Reza's right hand. Coel realized she was staring where Reza kept the box. She drew back slightly, and Coel saw fear in her eyes. She scrutinized Reza with immense concentration.

Once more her eyes darted around his form and drew a silhouette. Her sea-green gaze was deeply disturbed. "I have seen your signature in days to come. I have seen your signature in my dreams."

Reza nodded. "I am not surprised."

"You are Reza Walladid."

"I am."

She looked at his saddlebag again. "It is not my place to make this offer, but I feel I must. Give this thing to us. On the Isle of Man, there are those with the strength to destroy it. Be done with it, I beg of you."

"If you wish it?" Reza smiled. "Come and take it."

The first elf took a step forward. The woman stayed him with a hand. "I do not wish the thing, nor shall I contest you for it, but there are those who will." She looked at Orsini. "You have made a fool's bargain, Orsini of Venice."

"My destiny is mine own."

She shook her head. "You cannot go back."

Orsini was visibly startled. "That is none of your business."

"No. It is not." She suddenly looked at Coel. "Does your mother know the business you are about?"

"I . . ."

"Do you know what kind of business you are about, yourself, man of *Cymru*?" Sadness passed through her eyes as she used the ancient Celtic word for the men of Wales. She suddenly thrust out her finger and spoke in perfect Welsh Gaelic. *"Son of Math, for Megan's sake, who I know well, I tell you this. Death lays before you. Death lies behind you. Death follows your trail. You ride with death, and death is your destination. For the sake of your soul, turn back and go no further."*

Reza pointed an accusing finger at the elf. "What did you say to him?"

The elf answered him in Latin. "No secret of yours, nor nothing he did not already know. I give you my word upon it," She lifted her chin. "Will you let us pass?"

Reza lowered his hand. "Pass on, but do not think to follow me."

The elves filed by without another word. All kept their eyes on Reza until they had passed. Coel watched them go in an agony of unasked questions. Reza's voice spoke in harsh command. "We ride."

Coel stood where he was as the party moved past him. Reza's voice rose. "Coel!"

Coel ran after the elves.

"Coel!"

Even as he ran the elves drew their cloaks about them and seemed to shimmer and blend with the tumbled brown rocks of the landscape. Coel charged desperately down the path after them "Fiachad!"

Reza's voice sank to a baritone of anger. "Coel!"

"Fiachad!" Coel shouted out in Gaelic. "My mother! Tell me of my mother!"

Only the boulder-strewn valley stared back at him.

Coel hurled his voice to the sky. "I beg of you!"

In the distance the air shimmered. Coel could make out a brown shape among the rocks several long bowshots away. It was incredible that the elves had gone so far so fast. Fiachad's voice drifted back upon the wind in Gaelic. *"She lives, Coel! Her years are upon her! But she is well!"*

"Where? Tell me, where!"

Fiachad's voice dimmed. The shimmering shape in the rocks seemed insubstantial as smoke. *"She lives in Eire! In far Connemara!"*

Coel felt a great weight in his chest. Connemara was as far west as a man could go. It was the very edge of Ireland. It was the very edge of the world. "Tell her I live!" Coel felt tears spilling from his eyes. "Tell my mother I am alive!"

Only the sound of the wind blowing through the rocks came back

"Come on, Coel," Snorri rode up. "The Walladid is not pleased with you. Best we ride with the herd."

Orsini sat on his pony beside him. The dwarf looked intently at Coel. "What did the elves say to you?"

Coel wiped his eyes and bucked himself up. "They said death is all around us."

"That is true enough," Orsini snorted.

Snorri nervously made the sign against the evil eye. "Come on, Coel. The Faerie folk have always been fey. All Norsemen know this. They dream the future and speak in riddles. They are no friends to mortal men."

"Listen to him," Orsini counseled. "Elves have no honest emotions like men and dwarves, but are driven by their own peculiar passions."

"Fiachad seemed genuine enough."

"True, but he could not have been more than a century or two old," Orsini grimaced. "As for his sister, anything that has lived a thousand years no longer dreams like you or me."

"He told me my mother still lives," Coel felt his eyes grow hot again. "In far Connemara."

"Well, that's good news now, isn't it?" Snorri held out the reins to Coel's horse.

Coel took the Barb's reins. "Orsini?"

"What, Coel."

"What are elves doing halfway round the world from the Isle of Mann?"

"I can only guess."

"Guess, then."

"There were seven of them. Elves consider that a lucky number. They wore light corselets rather than byrnies of mail. They were lightly armed, and afoot rather than riding. They were expending great effort to remain concealed."

Snorri's chest puffed out proudly. "Otto found them! My dog

sniffs out elves! My dog sniffs out Assassins! My dog can sniff out a demon." He grinned down at Otto. "You are the best goddamn dog in the world, aren't you, boy?"

Otto wagged his tail in agreement.

Orsini nodded approvingly at Otto. "Elves live close to the cycles of the world. Much closer in some ways than men and dwarves. Animals sense this. I have never heard of a beast of the field that would harm an elf."

Coel kept to his question. "So what were elves doing in the North of Persia?"

Orsini turned his pony about and spoke over his shoulder. "I would say they were scouting."

CHAPTER TWENTY-EIGHT

Kamose continued to be pleased. Leaving the mountains had been an excellent strategy. They had galloped like the wind across the flatlands. His Inner Eye told him they were almost exactly parallel with Reza and his associates, though they were many miles and dozens of peaks deep within the Kopets. Kamose's party could now ride ahead and lay in ambush at a point of their choosing.

He looked at his encampment. Tawfiq had over a dozen armed Mamluks. Sandor had brought with him a half-dozen Rus from Cherson. The hand of the Blue-Robe sect reached far, and they had sent a sorcerer named Nuri to assist. Nuri had brought with him Daylami trackers. The Daylami were the mountain people of Northern Persia. They were savage fighters and those who had not been enslaved were the sworn enemies of the Assassins. The Daylami knew the Kopets well. Kamose kept their leader; an incredibly hairy man named Ciro by his side almost constantly. He turned to him now.

"Ciro."

Ciro was hirsute beyond description, and made more so by the wolf-fur vest and boots he wore. He looked up from under a single solid eyebrow as black as coal. "Yes, Great One?"

"How far are we?"

"We have paralleled a quarter of the Kopets."

Reza had no choice but to follow where his path led him. Kamose had learned the wisdom of not trying to follow the Persian's twisting path. Ciro and his Daylamis would decide the matter now. Kamose would use the Inner-Eye to watch Marius' shadow, and the Daylami would ensure that Reza and his associates bumbled directly into the jaws of the trap. Nuri was not a sorcerer of the first, second or even third rank, but he was much more skilled than Sandor's fool, Renatus, had been. Between the two of them, Kamose and Nuri would have the strength to overwhelm Reza and bind him. Tawfiq's Mamluks, combined with Sandor's Rus, would have the numbers to overwhelm Reza's few defenders. Reza's associates would be wearing little if any armor while they rode through the mountains. A nice small canyon would do. A shower of arrows would kill most of them in the first moments.

Ciro squinted at the mountains above. "Great One. Where are those you seek now?"

Kamose cut the Kopets with his hand. "They are close to the northern edge of the range."

"North?" Sandor had appeared soundlessly by their side.

"Yes."

Kamose looked out at the mountains. "What lies north of the Kopets from here, Ciro?"

"Little. Once it was the land of the Turkmenes. Much of it was the Karakum desert. Then the Great Waste poisoned everything," Ciro frowned at the mountains. "I have heard there is an arable corner of land between the Caspian and the Kopets. It is watered by the Attarak and Gorgan rivers, and fertile, but no one lives there."

"Why not?"

Ciro spat. "It lies between the Elburz and the Great Waste. Who would live on the path of the Assassin pilgrims and those things that come out of the waste? It has lain fallow for a hundred years, or so I am told."

Sandor stroked his mustache and stared at the mountains deep in thought.

Ciro scratched himself. "With horses, those you seek would likely take one of three paths. One was blocked by rockslides a year ago. Another is clear, but there is little water or forage. Camels could do it, but not horses. The third is wider, and there are many streams. It is a high path, but there are villages along it. I have kin in several of them."

"Are there many good places of ambush?" Kamose asked.

"Are there many grains of sand in the desert, Great One?"

Kamose smiled.

Ciro shrugged. "It is the Daylami way."

Kamose turned to Sandor. "In the morning we enter the mountains."

* * *

Snorri gazed towards Asgard for strength. "I hate these mountains."

Coel had to agree with his friend. He was sick of the endless vertical desert. "The peaks are getting lower. Reza is taking us north now."

"And what lies to the north?"

"Well, on Orsini's map, nothing but ice."

"Everything is nothing but ice on Orsini's map."

Coel stepped into the lion's den. "I think we should ask him."

"You don't mean Orsini or his map." Observed Snorri.

"No."

"You mean, Reza, and what it is we are doing."

"Aye."

Snorri hawked and spat. "You ask him."

"It would be better if we both did it, together."

"Strength in numbers?"

"Aye."

Snorri raised a scarred eyebrow. "And what if he tells us to mind our business, or worse?"

"I say we fling ourselves off that cliff when we come to it."

Snorri scowled unhappily. "It's those cursed elves, isn't it?"

"I will not lie to you, Snorri. They have set me to wondering."

"I told you not to listen to them!" Snorri clucked at his horse. "Well, then, by all means, let's go get ourselves turned into toads!"

The two of them rode up to Reza. The sorcerer smiled. "You wish to make a move, Yaroslav?"

"No," Snorri jerked his thumb at Coel. "This one has questions."

Coel shot Snorri a murderous look. Reza nodded knowingly. "It is the elves."

Coel sighed. It seemed everyone could read him like a book. "Yes."

"The rest of you, abide here a little while. I must speak with Coel and Snorri." The party pulled to halt. Reza looked at Coel frankly as they ambled on. "What exactly did they tell you?"

Coel saw no reason to lie. "They told me that death lay behind us. That death lies ahead of us. That we ride with death itself, and death is our destination," Coel summoned his courage. "I believe they meant the box you carry."

Reza was unperturbed. "And, so?"

"And so every tale my mother ever told me about those who ignored the warnings of the faerie folk ended badly. Perhaps it is not my place to ask, but I would like to know what it is we are about."

"Coel, everything the elves told you was the truth."

Coel and Snorri looked at one another.

"You have demonstrated your deductive reasoning before, Coel, think. The Assassins want you dead. The Church in Rome and quite probably the Orthodox Church in Constantinople want you dead, as well. Kamose of the Long-Eye, first of Blue Robes hounds our trail. Death indeed lies behind us."

"And before us?"

"Come now, who can know what lies before us? But enemies I can guarantee. There is very little mystery to that."

Coel eyed the sorcerer's saddlebag. "And what about riding with death?"

"Ah, now there they begin their riddles. I will speak plainly.

The box contains a talisman."

"A talisman?"

"I told you before I seek ancient mysteries. They involve the deepest esoterica of ancient sorcery. To unravel these mysteries, I must speak with one who is very powerful."

"The talisman guides us to this person, then?"

"Yes."

"Then why is it death that rides with us?"

"Because the one I wish to speak to is dead."

Coel paled. There was no higher sin in all of Christendom. There was no blacker art. Consorting with demons was considered a lesser crime. "You speak of necromancy!"

"I am. The talisman leads me to my subject's resting-place, where a summoning would be most effective, and it will help me speak with his shade if I am successful. It is typical elvish poetic wording, but we do, in a very real sense, ride with death, and towards it. However, I assure you, there is nothing to fear."

"Nothing to fear!" Coel was aghast. "It will start with rack and tongs and end with fire and the stake! You've condemned us all!"

Reza laughed. "No Christian Church knows of what I intend, nor any Muslim church, either. Kamose of the Long-Eye and the Blue-Robe sect are our true concern, and that is because they seek what I seek. They are our competitors. It is not Church Inquisitors or shades of the dead we must fear, but Assassin blades and Mamluk arrows."

Coel looked to Snorri, but the Rus was keeping his own counsel.

"I am a sorcerer of the First Rank, Coel, with all modesty, perhaps the most powerful of my generation, but, if I can unravel the mysteries I seek, the level shall have to be raised. I shall have power. Great power. My enemies shall be forced to bow to me. I will have the power to annul the contract the Assassins have taken to kill you, and you shall both be rich beyond your dreams. That I can promise," Reza stretched out his hand. "But I bid you, go ahead a little.

Discuss it between you. It is a weighty matter, and I want you firm in your decision. One way or the other."

"Come on, Coel," Snorri spurred his Arabian ahead. Coel and Otto followed. Coel could feel the eyes of the rest of the party boring into his back. He followed Snorri for half a mile before the Rus slowed his horse to a walk. "All right, so it's necromancy."

"And just how do you feel about that, then?"

"How by *Hel* do you think I feel?" Snorri shook his head. "They burn men for that!"

"So?"

"So, I've thought about it, and I want to go on."

"This is a bad business, Snorri. Do not lie, you would not have taken the job back in Moscow had you known of this."

"Oh, I'd have had my reservations, but I still might have taken it to save you and your goddamn leg, Coel, and Moscow is a world away. We're in the Kopet Mountains now. Farther afield than any Rus or Celt has ever been. If you and I turn back, what do you propose we do? Sneak across Persia past the Assassins? And Kamose and the Blue-Robe sect? I don't speak Persian or Arabic, Coel, and neither do you. Even with your dumb luck and my brain? It's still suicide."

Coel chewed his lip. "The sorcerer has put us in a pretty pinch."

"No, Coel. He's played us square. He's upheld his word every time, and stuck by the deal. Remember, when we first asked him about his business, he told us it was none of ours, and you and I both took his gold anyway. Now you've gone and kicked over the cook pot and complain because you don't like the smell."

"There's much he's not telling us."

"We're hired swords, Coel. Now, I like the way he calls us associates, but we're hired swords, pure and simple. We made a deal. I won't break my oath. The Angeli gave you a letter of credit for five hundred pieces of gold. You can pay off your debt to Reza and Orsini and ride, right now. I can't, and I'm not sure I would if I could. I want to see the world. I'm staying."

Snorri looked across at the peaks as the sun sank. According to Orsini's map they were very close to the northern edge of the Kopets. Their path dipped down into a tiny canyon and the peaks disappeared.

"I'll tell you another thing. I want to finish this chess game. I want to beat him."

"I thought you said Reza was finished in fourteen moves after you forked him."

"Don't change the subject!" Snorri visibly calmed himself. "Like I said, I want to finish this game, and I'll be honest, I want to be rich beyond my wildest dreams." Snorri drew his horse closer. "Listen, Coel. You're my best friend. I want us both to be rich, and we need to watch each others' backs."

"You know I won't abandon you, Snorri. So--"

"So it is settled." They rode around a bend in the canyon. "Listen, Coel. It's not that bad. People have spoken with spirits since spirits and people have--Odin's beard!"

"Jesus Christ!"

Snorri's horse reared. Coel's joined it. Otto snarled.

The great, canted amber eyes of the hobgoblins blinked in alarm. Their camels twisted their necks like snakes and groaned. A pair of hobgoblins blocked the path before them astride their humpbacked beasts. They wore heavy felt coats and bore lances. One hobgoblin threw down its lance and pulled a crossbow from behind his back. It shoved its boot into the cocking stirrup and grabbed the bowstring.

"Sic, Otto!" Snorri shouted. "Sic!"

Otto sprang. He sank his teeth into the hobgoblin's boot and hung flailing his body about furiously. The hobgoblin tumbled from his saddle pad. The other hobgoblin wheeled his camel about.

"I'll take this one!" Snorri leaped from his saddle with his axe in hand. "Don't let the other one escape! They must be scouts!"

Coel spurred his Barb and shot down the canyon. The camel raced ahead with its great stork-like legs swinging like boards. Its rolling gate was faster than Coel could have imagined. They burst out of the canyon onto a flat table of land. A rock face sloped a hundred feet upward a bowshot away.

Coel jinked his horse as the hobgoblin flung a handful of dark objects behind it. They fell to the rocky ground with the jingling of iron. Coel skirted them. They were caltrops, thistles of iron spikes that would always have one point up no matter how they fell. They were designed to split a horse's hoof. Coel spurred the Barb to make up lost distance. The hobgoblin bore down on the rock slope as if it intended to ride its camel straight up it.

Coel drew a javelin.

The hobgoblin leaped from its camel. It hit the ground hard and rolled up. The creature pulled a knife-axe from its belt and began clawing its way up the slope. Coel wheeled and hurled his javelin. It clattered into the rocks by the hobgoblin's heel. Coel hurled himself from the saddle and drew his sword as he bounded up the slope. The hobgoblin was tall, but its legs were short in comparison to its body. It leaned forward and used the butt of its weapon and its free hand to help it scrabble up the slope. Coel stretched his legs to take the rocks like a giant staircase. He gained quickly but the hobgoblin reached the top first. It whirled and swung its knife-axe down with both hands.

The Paladin blade rang and Coel arm ached with the force of the blow. The rocks shifted beneath his feet and he slid a dozen feet down the slope. The hobgoblin disappeared. Coel clawed his way to the top. The hobgoblin knelt a dozen feet away. It knelt before a large pile of wood. It furiously struck a flint against the great knife-blade of its weapon. Sparks jetted against a wad of char cloth.

Coel let out a shout and charged.

The hobgoblin rose and sliced at him. The two weapons clanged and the hobgoblin tried to hook Coel's blade away. Coel let his blade be pulled and came in with a knee to the belly. The hobgoblin grunted and rammed its face at Coel's hooking upward with its tusks. Coel's cheek parted down to the bone. Coel yanked his head back and rammed it forward again. His forehead smashed into the deep nictitating slits of the creature's nose.

The hobgoblin screeched and staggered back. It's great cat-like eyes squeezed shut in a rictus of pain. Coel took his blade in both hands and ran the hobgoblin through. It folded around the blade and dropped to its knees. Coel wrenched his sword free and the hobgoblin fell.

Coel staggered back and took great ragged breaths into his burning lungs. Blood spilled down his face.

"Coel!" Snorri's voice rang in the rocks below. "Coel!"

Coel ran to the pyramid of wood. He kicked away the kindling that was just starting to burn and stamped out the embers. He heard Snorri scrabbling up the slope. Coel walked over to the edge of the escarpment. The mountain he was on fell away to the foothills below. Past the foothills lay a great plain. Coel's eyes grew ever wider. Thousands of thin lines of smoke rose up into the reddening sky. As the sun set he began to see the twinkling orange lights of fires. A great portion of the plain was covered by something. Coel could make out movement. More and more fires winked into life as the sun fell. Coel's sword nearly fell from his hand.

It was an army.

The army covered the plain like a dark blanket as far as the eye could see. It was an army beyond imagining. Coel was stunned as he took in the scope of it. There had to be tens of thousands. Hundreds of thousands. It was a multitude beyond any army ever known.

It was a horde.

Coel looked back at the unlit signal fire and the dead scout.

It was a horde of hobgoblins.

CHAPTER TWENTY-NINE

Marius' voice was a whisper. "God have mercy on us all."

The seven stood on the escarpment under the glare of an immense full moon. They looked out upon the vast army camped on the plains below. Snorri shook his head in awe. "So many fires . . . "

It was like looking down into a starry sky. Reza stared with intense concentration and spoke to himself. "How could I have not seen it? How could the Long-Eye not have seen it? The Blue Robe sect, the Patriarch, the Pope in Rome, the Angeli, the greatest adepts in the known world, none have foreseen this. An army."

Coel could not believe what he was looking at. "A horde."

"An invasion," Orsini corrected.

"God's scourge," Marius turned on Reza. "God's scourge upon us for your pride, Walladid, and for mine. Is this where your devilry leads us?"

Reza ignored the priest and continued to argue with himself. "Why? Why would it lead us here? He could not be amongst the hobgoblins, how could he?"

Coel tried to comprehend what he saw. "Orsini, how can they feed so many?"

"Hobgoblins are carnivores, Coel. They eat whomever they kill in battle. Then they take every prisoner, every animal and all human non-combatants they find and eat them along the march. They are locusts upon the land."

Zuli's hand crept into Coel's. "They have hidden themselves between the Assassins and the Great Waste. The sorcery of their shamans has hidden them from the magicians and clerics of the East and West."

Snorri shook his head. "But Coel and I saw them on the steppes of Russia. Such an army could not have marched so far south so fast."

"No," Orsini's voice was deadly calm. "They could not, but, two hundred years ago, there were two hordes. One attacked through the Russias, and one came out of Asia and attacked south through the Anatolian Peninsula. I suspect there is, indeed, a second horde, and you and Coel have already encountered the forward elements of it in the Russias."

Coel's mind boggled at the idea of another army of similar size lurking in the north. "Sweet Jesus, we must--"

"The ring!" Reza's voice surged in triumph. "Their shamans have the ring! They would recognize its power, and keep it as a fetish, even if they could not work magics with it! They have his ring! There can be no other explanation!"

"What?"

"You, Coel!" Reza seized Coel by the shoulders. "You must go down amongst them and find the ring!"

"What?" Coel snapped his shoulders free. "Are you mad, then?"

Reza seized Coel again and shook him. "You must!"

"No!" Coel tore himself free. "We turn back! We warn the Empress of Trebizond and the Emperor of the Byzantines! We must warn the Shah of Persia! This is war!"

Reza's eyes burned bright. "That is exactly why you must do this thing for me."

Coel took a step back.

Snorri waved his axe across the plain. "Even the Roman Empire with all its legions could not field an army like that! You want Coel to go down there! To go poking about for a bauble?"

"Yes. There is no other choice. The ring is down there," Reza's voice was icy calm. "Coel must fetch it."

"Forget your ring. Forget speaking with the dead," Coel shook his head. "We must warn the world."

"Coel, listen to me! The talisman has led me here! The ring is the next step! If we do not find what I seek, the world may well be lost."

"No. We go south."

Reza's voice went dead. "Think well before you cross me, son of Math."

"Indeed, think well," Orsini stepped between them. "Look upon that host, Coel, and think. The hobgoblins now wield crossbows and ride camels. They sail in Chinese junks upon the Black Sea. They use Assassin poisons and have hidden the largest army the world has ever seen from the adepts and seers of both Europe and Asia. By your own adventures in the Russias, Coel, it seems a similar army lies awaiting just east of the Russias. Reza seeks a power beyond your imagining, and I give you my word, as a Dwarf, without it, this time, Europe may fall."

Reza mollified his tone. "My motivations may seem strange to you, Coel. I do not doubt it, but I also give you my word. I do not wish to live in a world ravaged by the hobgoblins. If I can attain what I seek, I swear to you, I shall smite them. As Saint Tomas Sander smote them before."

Snorri jerked his head at Zuli. "Why Coel? Why not her?"

Zuli glared.

Snorri folded his arms across his chest. "I bear you no malice, pet, but aren't you better at this sort of thing than Coel?"

"She cannot go amongst them undetected," Said Orsini. "It must be Coel. He is best suited."

"Best suited!" Snorri waved his arms. "She's a thief!"

"She is an elf."

Coel and Snorri stood thunderstruck. Orsini nodded. "At least, in part. You saw what happened on the junk, Coel. The hobgoblins smelled her through the cabin door. Hobgoblins have the noses of hounds, and elves have been their enemies since time out of mind. The scent of her down amongst their army would stir them like a nest of hornets. Their shaman would use sorcery to ferret her out. They would kill her and eat her and make black magics with her bones."

"What about Coel!" Snorri waved his arms in ever widening arcs. "What's to keep him out of the stewpot!"

Reza spoke calmly. "I have the power to let him pass unseen. As for his scent, that is a hobgoblin army. There will be thousands of humans chained to the food coffle. He will be just another human smell. We can dress him in the raiment of the hobgoblins you killed today to mask even that. If he is careful, he can wend his way through and find the ring."

"Coel," Márta spoke softly. "This must be done. You cannot turn back alone. The Long-Eye or the Assassins would kill you long before you ever reached anyone to tell of this."

Zuli squeezed Coel's hand. "I would go in your place, but I would fail and be torn to pieces. It must be you."

Coel struggled for something to say.

Snorri kicked the rocks at his feet. "Well, all right! But I don't like it!"

"Well, I am glad you object!"

Snorri shrugged. "I would do it, but you are a faster runner than I am."

Coel did not believe he could outrun a camel, much less a crossbow bolt. Everyone in the party seemed firmly committed to sending him to his death.

Reza beckoned Marius. "Heal his face. He cannot go down amongst them with an open wound."

"You are sending the poor savage to his doom."

"Heal his face anyway."

Marius walked up to Coel and raised a palm in benediction. His expression was strange and desolate. "Even the Philistines were men of woman born. You go down amongst those not of God's image. God help you." Coel jerked from the heat as Marius laid his hand upon him.

The ragged throb in his face was gone.

Reza faced him. "Will you do this? It is important to me that you do this of your own will. If not, I must make other arrangements."

Coel was not exactly sure if that was a threat. He looked

about at his companions. They all looked back at him in earnest concern. Coel looked down at the thousands of fires below. Swimming naked out to a Cathayan junk full of Chinese sorcerer's seemed like child's play in comparison.

"God . . . damn it . . ."

* * *

"Listen well, Coel."

Orsini filled Coel's ear with every facet of hobgoblin behavior imaginable.

"Their camp will be set up like a city. The tent of the Great Hobgoblin will be in the center, along with the tents of the shamen and other ranking beings. That is where you will find the ring. We call their armies hordes, but they are very well organized. Each tribal group will be encamped by its standard. They will have regular pickets and guards, but they will not be expecting any trouble. They will be as static and useless as any human on watch, save for their sense of smell. Of much more immediate concern is the lesser breed of goblin. They are the true camp guards. Packs of them will be roaming outside of the perimeter. Any human, animal, goblin or hobgoblin sacrifice that escapes the camp is considered fair game for them. If they find you, they will drag you down. If you put up a fight, the hobgoblins will come to see what they have found. Above all, think. Plan your route. Once inside the camp, stay close to other humans, animals, or latrines to mask your scent whenever you can. If you get in trouble, run. Do not go to ground or hide. They will sniff you out."

Reza raised a finger. "What you seek is a silver ring. It is large, and in the shape of an Egyptian scarab beetle. In its jaws, it holds a sphere of black star sapphire."

Coel felt the world crashing down around him. "How am I to find it?"

"Take this." Reza held out a piece of silver. Orsini had spent the last hour cold-working it with a hammer and an awl. It was a vaguely beetle-shaped lump with a chip of black gemstone in its mouth. "This is sympathetic to the ring you seek."

Coel took the silver token and nearly dropped it as it jerked and moved like it was alive in his hand. It suddenly stopped and vibrated in his fist. Coel opend his fingers and the token pointed unerringly toward the center of the hobgoblin camp. "I see."

"Good," Reza nodded. "Follow it to the ring."

Coel stripped and drew on the hobgoblin garb they had taken from the two scouts. Coel had run one hobgoblin through and Snorri had just about beheaded the other. Coel had to choose garments not stained with blood. The gray, woolen apron of one barely managed to cover his loins. He threw the cloak of the other across his shoulders.

Reza knotted his fingers into an almost inhuman configuration. "Now, I shall render you unseen. You will feel nothing, but listen to me. You will not truly be invisible. Light shall pass through you. In essence, someone looking straight at you will see what is behind you, and vice versa. The effect is not perfect. There will be some distortion, particularly when you move. The night will render this effect negligible. However, be careful, particularly when you move between someone and a source of light. The distortions will be magnified if something behind you is moving. More so if it is a source of light which moves, like burning flame."

Coel tried to comprehend what he was being told. "It will be like I am made of water, then?"

"Very good, Coel. You, your clothes, and what you carry will be like water."

"I think I understand."

"Good. Give your sword to Snorri."

Coel's stomach sank. "Your enchantment will not work upon it?"

"I fear not."

"I suppose the hobgoblins would find a sword floating in the air suspicious."

"Indeed, you are a clever man. Clever enough to succeed."

Snorri held out his great *sax* knife. "Take this, Coel. You took it out onto the Chinese junk and brought it back. It may not be magic, but perhaps friendship and luck can weave sorcery of its own."

Coel took the knife. "Thank you, Snorri."

"Just bring it back."

Coel mentally girded his loins and looked to Reza. "All right. Do it, then."

"Take this." Reza held out another token. A two-inch pane of glass cut into the shape of a man dropped into Coel's palm.

Snorri leaped back. "Odin All-Father!"

The whole party gaped in amazement.

"What?" Coel looked back and forth at his companions.

Reza nodded. "It is done."

Coel held up the token. There was nothing there. Not even his hand. He looked down at his feet and felt sudden vertigo when he felt his body but could not see any of it.

"Heed me," Reza warned. "If the token breaks, the enchantment is lost."

Coel's mind whirled. He struggled to keep his balance. "What if I just drop it?"

"It shall be like dropping a cloak, but, like a cloak, you can don it again. Guard it with your life, and, keep in mind, the enchantment will only last until dawn. Daylight will destroy it. Make haste."

Zuli crooked a finger. "I have found the path the hobgoblins took into the mountains. Follow me."

* * *

Coel clutched his magic tokens and wandered amongst the Hobgoblin horde. Wonder and horror filled his eyes. He had narrowly avoided the packs of goblins that roamed outside the camp. The hobgoblin pickets had been much easier. They leaned on their spears in infinite boredom, and Coel walked right past them. Inside the perimeter, he passed string after string of hobbled camels by the thousands of them. Coel gaped as he saw looming shapes that could only be elephants. Packs of great mastiffs lay about tethered to spikes set in the ground. He passed pens containing hundreds of miserable humans chained together and huddled for warmth. Vast herds of goats, sheep, pigs and cattle stood penned for the night. A sea of wagons carried timbers, ropes and chains of huge size that Coel knew were the disassembled pieces of siege engines. Thousands of oxen were corralled to pull them.

Coel swallowed as he entered the camp proper.

Never in his wildest dreams had he imagined an army so large, nor so disciplined. The hobgoblins bivouacked in great blocks of conical felt tents that stretched out to the horizon. High poles mounted the strange standards of each tribe. Some were flags, some were horsetails, and some were bizarre masks or carved totems. Others were the skulls of great beasts Coel could not recognize. There were hobgoblins beyond counting.

Cook fires burned everywhere.

Cattle and horse hides hung over fires as the meat simmered in its own blood. Sheep, pigs, birds, and small game turned on spits beyond counting. Human bodies turned over fires everywhere. The smell of cooking human flesh sent Coel's gorge rising up to his throat. Butchered corpses hung from hooks. In the lanes between the tribal blocks goblins shrieked and fought amongst themselves over the offal of the roasting beasts and humans. Coel stayed in the demarcated lanes between the tribal groups and wound his way towards the center. The silver token in his hand pointed him straight towards a citadel of larger tents and glowing bonfires.

A great mastiff sat up on its haunches and sniffed as Coel passed. The hobgoblin that held its tether raised its shovel jaw and the slits of its nose opened wide and snuffed the air. Coel moved by as quickly as he could. His sandals hung around his neck and he passed silently. The mastiff woofed and its nose followed him. The big dog rose. The hobgoblin let out the tether and pulled its knife-axe from the ring on its belt. It gave the dog its lead. Coel moved more quickly as the sentry slowly began to follow in his footsteps. A second hobgoblin left its own block and confronted the sentry from the other. They barked and hissed at one another for a moment, and then the two followed the mastiff as it sniffed at the ground that Coel had trod.

Sweat trickled down Coel's back.

A third hobgoblin hailed the first two. After a hurried consultation, it took the crossbow from its back and loaded it. Sweat broke out on Coel's forehead and he knew it was more fodder for the nose of the massive war dog trailing him. The mastiff pulled on the tether and dragged its keeper along.

Coel broke into a trot.

He ran straight for the pavilions in the center of camp. More hobgoblins joined the growing pack following him. Coel passed several large tents and wended his way amongst them. The mastiff unerringly led its masters along his path. They began jogging. Coel broke into a run. He found a break in the tent complex and charged across the open space. A smaller tent lay at its center. Great obese hobgoblins wearing leather aprons and bearing huge, leather bound clubs stood around it. Coel's pursuers broke into the open space. They skidded to a halt as the huge guardians rose up and confronted them in a line. They hailed the giants in their hissing language.

The guards began marching forward. Coel's pursuers began shouting and hissing more vehemently. Coel was pinned. He clutched his tokens in one hand and drew Snorri's sax knife. A huge hobgoblin guard came straight at him. The bloated guards let out a roar and broke into a lumbering run. Coel danced to one side and raised his knife to strike.

The guards charged straight past him. Coel's hunters shrieked as the huge creatures met their line and began to lay into them with their clubs. The mastiff took the better part of valor and ran off into the night. The hunters scattered in all directions.

The token vibrated in Coel's hand. It pointed straight at the unguarded tent.

Coel ran and ducked under the heavy felt. He found himself in a dark hallway of fabric. There was a tent within the tent. Light glowed dimly through the white canvas walls. The silver token vibrated in his hand as if it were alive. He listened intently to the howling and fighting outside. Slowly, he began to walk the perimeter of the tiny hallway between the inner and outer tent. The token turned in his hand to face the inner tent like a compass through all 360 degrees. Coel reached the entryway. The opening was roped shut in a series of very complicated knots. Coel listened and heard nothing within. He smelled a strange, musk-like scent he found vaguely disturbing. Coel walked to the back of the tent and the canvas parted in a long slit beneath Snorri's *sax*. Coel peered in.

The tent was well lit with lanterns in all four corners. Persian carpets and animal furs covered the floor. A round bed dominated the inner tent. Someone was sleeping upon it. Their back was turned, and some of the furs had fallen back to reveal a shoulder.

The shoulder was a deep olive green.

Coel crept inside. His bare feet were soundless on the carpet. He rose up and scanned about. The musk was much stronger in the room. It filled Coel's nose and made his loins itch. Chests lay about in the corners of the tent. A low table held a platter smeared with congealing blood and grease. Coel did not want to think about what the meal might have been. The chests were not large. Coel decided to creep by each one and hold his hand out over it. The token would tell him in which it lay. He would tuck the chest under his arm and go. Coel moved towards an ornately carved box of ebony.

The being on the bed sat up.

Coel's breath caught. Raiding instincts took over. He parted his lips and breathed shallowly through his mouth despite the hammering of his heart. He looked in awe at the creature on the bed.

Reza's chess piece had come to life.

She was bald except for the two-inch-wide mane of blue-black hair that formed a widow's peak at her forehead and ran down her back like a horse's mane. She had no eyebrows, but muscled ridges over her eyes rose in very human-like confusion. The great slanted eyes were yellow with slitted purple pupils. The pupils opened wide as she scanned about the room. Sensuous lips opened and her pointed chin thrust forward as she exposed her canine fangs. Her head tilted as she distended her jaw. Her nostrils flared as she breathed in. Coel had seen lynxes in the snow behave the same way.

She was scenting the air.

The musk scent grew more powerful. It made Coel's muscles tense against his will, and his eyes were drawn to the six breasts that jutted in pairs from her chest. The golden eyes bored holes in the air where Coel stood. She sniffed again and closed her mouth. She looked down and her eyes flared. Coel looked down.

His right foot stood on the lush, golden fur of some beast. No part of him was visible, but the fur crushed in the perfect outline of his foot. Coel dropped the crystal token and lunged with the sax knife.

The hobgoblin froze in shock as Coel materialized in mid-leap before her. The tip of Snorri's knife lifted her chin. Coel spoke very quietly. "Make no sound."

The great canted eyes looked Coel up and down and then bored into his own. "If I make a sound, you will die."

It was Coel's turn to be shocked. Her Latin was perfect except for a slight lisping around her fangs. "There are twenty guards outside. If I make any sort of sound that implies I am not alone they will cut the ropes holding up the tent. The tent will collapse and trap the both of us. We will be beaten unconscious with clubs. When it is discovered you are a human being things will go very badly for you."

"You speak Latin?"

"I speak three human languages. I am most fluent in Latin and Persian. Now, lower your knife, or I will call the guards."

"Why have you not already?"

"I wonder what you are doing here. Your presence implies powerful sorcery, yet you are no sorcerer. If you are a thief, you are far from the treasure wagons. If you are an Assassin, you have already passed the tent of the Great Hobgoblin, and you already had an opportunity to kill me." Stomach muscles like a Greek decathlete's clenched and the musk smell in the room grew thicker. "Also, I find your presence unexpectedly stimulating."

Coel gawked. "Who are you?"

"I am Gwall, First Consort of Matukash."

"Who is Matukash?"

"The Great Hobgoblin."

"You are the Hobgoblin Queen, then?"

The canted eyes narrowed in a very human fashion. "I am First Consort of Matukash, and a Prime Councilor. Your word, Queen, implies the human concept of royalty, or worth based upon one's forebears. My pedigree is impeccable. However, my right to breed, and rank of Consort to the Great Hobgoblin, was won in a series of single combats. I became a Prime Councilor through demonstration of mental ability."

Coel struggled to fathom this. His mind was strangely distracted from his task. "Why are you under guard, then, and why is your tent roped shut?"

"The moon is full." The creature leaned back from Coel's blade. "I am in heat. Any males in my presence would immediately seek to mate with me or fight amongst themselves for the right. No male can be trusted around me during the moon."

"What about your guards?"

"They are eunuchs. They prevent unplanned matings."

"Have you no say in the matter?"

Gwall flopped back on her elbows. She thrust out her triple bosom and her stomach muscles tensed again. The musk scent in the room could be cut with a knife. It filled Coel's mind like a fog. "I am in heat. Males cannot be trusted around me, and I cannot be trusted around males. In my condition, I would mate with a goblin if it managed to sneak into my tent and bare its fangs at me."

Coel's pulse hammered thickly in his temples. It took immense effort to change the subject away from mating. "What is your army doing here? Why are you invading us?"

"We travel the Great Path of Life. Your kind lay upon it. We are the superior species. You are in our way."

Coel struggled to order his thoughts as her scent sought to unravel them. "We defeated you before. We will defeat you again."

Her lips lifted away from her fangs. "You had cavalry. You had superior numbers. Superior armor and missile weapons. Superior sorcery. When Tuman Sunqur unleashed his sorcery upon us we were already reconsolidating to smash you. The survivors fled into the reaches of Northern Asia behind the Great Waste he created. The nomads hunted us. We were forced to eat the weakest among us in winter. Only the strongest survived, and we grew stronger for it. Over time we made slaves of the steppe people. We pillaged the Northern Chinese and learned new ways of battle. Those who were once left behind reinforced us as the Great Path of Life opened again. The mistakes of the past have been rectified. The powers of our shamen wax great. You will lose."

"Wait, what?" Coel shook his head to clear it. He knew he was missing things. "Who is Tuman Sunqur?"

"The Destroyer," She lifted her chin haughtily. "Your kind will betray one another for a fistful of metal that is too soft to make a decent dagger. Our agents already work amongst you. You are a fragmented people. You are riven with internal disorder. The Pope in Rome and the Patriarch in Constantinople are on the brink of declaring Crusade against one another. Every petty nation amongst you makes war upon its neighbor. The skills of your sorcerers and holy men have become weak and emasculated by the Churches. We will crush you."

"We will destroy your armies, north and south!" Coel spluttered.

Gwall reared up on the bed. "How do you know of the northern army?"

"I have seen it," Coel's tongue ran away with him as his lips skinned back from his teeth. "I have fought it."

"You are the Welshman!" The golden eyes bored into Coel's. "You are Coel son of Math!"

Her recognition registered only in a small and far removed corner of Coel's mind. Her scent filled all his senses. The musk of her sank into his groin and glowed like a ball of heat beneath his manhood. Coel dragged the back of his fist across his mouth and found that he was drooling. Her yellow eyes fell down his frame. The gray apron of wool he had taken from the hobgoblin scout barely covered enough of him for modesty. His flesh had lifted the hem away and freed itself. It felt like a winged piece of stone between his legs.

Gwall's eyes seemed to glow from within as she exposed her fangs. "You? Would mate with me? You are a human. Your nails are soft. You have no fighting teeth. You are unfit."

Coel shook with lust. He could no longer control his mind or his mouth. His flesh was slaved to the scent of her. "I am a man of Wales, six foot six, and seventeen stone if I am an ounce. I have killed more men than I can count, and more of your kind than I have fingers. Call forth your lover, Matukash, and I shall break his neck as I would snap the spine of a dog."

Gwall let out a shuddering hiss. Her stomach clenched so rapidly it shook her whole frame. The triple rows of her chest heaved with each contraction. She yanked away the sleeping fur covering her loins and rolled onto her hands and knees. Her musk filled the universe. Gwall lifted her hips and presented her hindquarters. Coel seized her ankle and flung her onto her back.

The thick, sharpened nails of her hands dug beneath his shoulders and tore bloody furrows down his back. Fangs sank into the flesh above his collarbones. The pain of it was like lighting bolts through Coel's body. He twisted his fingers into the horse-mane of her hair and he tore her teeth away from his flesh. The muscles within her clenched in rhythm to the contractions of her stomach like a bellowing vise. Coel met her rhythm and matched it. The heat between his legs expanded like a sun to fill his whole being. The sun exploded. Teeth sank into his shoulder again and her nails gripped his back. The body beneath him locked. Coel's vision went white and the bottom dropped out of the world.

Coel finally fell against her and shuddered. He lay there for long moments. Her tongue lapped at the bloody fang wounds in his shoulder. Clawed fingers combed through his hair. Coel slowly raised his head. His body locked in shock.

Márta stood only three feet away.

She wore nothing but a hobgoblin cloak over one shoulder belted at the waist like a toga. Her yataghan was drawn. She stepped forward and rammed its ivory pommel into the hobgoblin's temple. Gwall's body went limp and the heat that sheathed Coel relaxed and slipped away. Coel flinched at the loss and cringed under Márta's eyes.

"For God's sake, Coel!"

"Márta, I--"

"Cover yourself!"

Coel arose shakily and pulled the apron back down over his hips. Márta rapidly went from chest to chest and held her fist over them. She quickly turned back to the bed. She unceremoniously shoved Gwall to the floor with her foot and pulled the wicker frame to one side. The bed had been hiding a wooden box. Márta yanked it open. Coel collected his two magic tokens. The silver beetle oriented towards the box. Márta ran her hands through many strange objects of metal, wood and stone. Her hand came out holding up a silver ring in the shape of a beetle. The token in her hand leaped of its own will and clicked against the ring. She put them in a leather bag on her belt.

She held out her hand. She'd tied a leather thong to her wrist. "Take hold, so we do not get separated!"

Coel took an end of the thong and wrapped it around his wrist. Márta closed her hand around her crystal token and winked out of sight. Coel made a fist and he could no longer see himself. The thong yanked against his arm. "Come on!"

They slipped from under the tent. One of the eunuch guards turned and lifted his club. His golden eyes sought about in the moonlight and he took great sniffs of the air. The thong yanked again and Márta pulled Coel along at a fast walk. The guard chuffed and hissed, and two of his fellows joined him.

Márta and Coel cleared the open area surrounding Gwall's tent and began winding their way through the narrow alleys and the webs of tent ropes. Heads lifted wherever they went and they were forced to double back again and again. More and more armed guards seemed to be patrolling among the pavilion complex. More and more of the guards had dogs with them.

Coel clutched Snorri's knife. "What the hell, then?"

"It's you!" Márta's voice was an angry hiss. "They smell her, Coel! They smell her all over you!"

Márta led them at a run between a pair of massive tents. They came to an abrupt halt before a courtyard full of hobgoblins. A great fire burned in a pit at the center. Three hobgoblins in loincloths stood close enough to the fire to scorch themselves as they howled up at the moon in their inhuman tongue. Well over a hundred hobgoblins sat cross-legged in a circle around the fire. Each sat with a pair of knife-axes across its knees and watched the howling three around the fire with total concentration.

One of the three took up a human skull. He held it upside down and swept it at the fire. Liquid flew out and the fire hissed. Coel smelled burning blood. The orange flames of the bonfire turned a brilliant crimson. The hobgoblin took a second skull and poured it over his head. Blood streaked his green flesh. He stretched out his arms and stepped into the pit. The fire roared around him.

The blood on his body hissed and bubbled. The hobgoblin raised his arms to the moon above. He did not burn. He began to speak in a slow, rhythmic cadence, and the assembled hobgoblins hung on his every word.

One of the hobgoblins sitting closest to Márta and Coel turned from the circle and craned his head around. It sniffed the air. Around the circle heads began jerking up and looking away from the ritual. The hobgoblin in the fire stepped forth and hissed in great anger at the distraction. The courtyard filled with the sound of snuffing hobgoblins. The thong went limp in Coel's hand. A massive hobgoblin at the head of the circle rose. He was as tall as Coel but not fat like Gwall's eunuch guards. He raised his knife-axe and swept it in a circle. The hobgoblins all rose as a unit.

The tent rope behind the leader suddenly parted and a portion of the tent behind him collapsed. Márta shouted out in Latin. "Run!"

The hobgoblins let out a great roar and charged towards the tent. Guards began pouring in from all sides and Coel had to move aside as more came in from behind him. He weaved through the charging hobgoblins. Stealth was unnecessary in the bedlam. He threw elbows and shouldered a path for himself. Twice he was knocked down and nearly trampled. Coel found a clear space near the fire and crouched a moment as he looked for an avenue of escape.

Coel locked eyes with the hobgoblin leader.

It stood apart and stared at the space he occupied while others surged around him in all directions. Its head tilted curiously. Reza's warning rang in Coel's head. He was like a bottle of water. He would refract light.

He was standing directly between the hobgoblin and the bonfire.

Coel turned to bolt and bounced off the blood covered hobgoblin shaman. The hobgoblin leader let out a roar and charged. Coel dropped to a squat as the knife-axe scythed the air. He rose up and shoved the sax-knife into the creature's belly up to the hilt. The hobgoblin gasped and fell toward Coel. Coel rose up and shoulder tossed the spitted hobgoblin into the fire-worshipper. The two hobgoblins tumbled into the flames. Whatever blood magic had protected the shaman in the ritual was gone. Both hobgoblins screamed as they thrashed and burned. War horns sounded out all across the camp. Screams and moans erupted from the human pens. A drum began to beat in urgent cadence and was answered by a dozen more. Dogs began barking and howling. The trumpeting of elephants split the night. The full moon lay low in the sky. Dawn was not far away.

Coel ran for his life.

CHAPTER THIRTY

Coel limped exhaustedly through canyon land. His lungs burned and his feet bled from his wild run from the camp. The crystal token had turned black at dawn and he could see himself clearly. The sun had risen over the peaks. The party had moved, but the silver token had not lost its enchantment. Coel followed the twitching of the silver token and prayed Márta had made it back to Reza unscathed.

"Coel!"

Coel turned and saw Snorri. The rest of the party filed out of a narrow cleft in the cliff wall and crowded around him.

Snorri grabbed Coel and thrust a skin into his hand. "Here, sit down."

Coel sat on a rock and gulped water.

"Lad, I'd thought we lost you!" Orsini thumped him on the back happily. "Every day you teach me never to underestimate the Welsh."

Coel gasped and drank more.

Reza stepped forward. "Márta told me what happened."

Coel choked.

"Giving her the ring and creating a diversion so she could escape was extremely bold, and selfless. I shall see to it that you are suitably rewarded."

Coel sagged with inner relief and gave Márta a tentative smile.

Márta's lip lifted in disgust.

Snorri cocked his head at Coel. "What is that smell?"

"What?" Coel blushed bright red. "Nothing! What smell?"

Otto scampered forward and shoved his nose into Coel's crotch. His tail wagged furiously.

"Get your damn dog off of me!"

"Christ, Coel! It's all over you!"

People began sniffing the air curiously. Márta rolled her eyes in infinite scorn.

"I do not know what you are talking about!"

"No! Listen!" Snorri said. "Smell yourself! You smell like, like . . . "

"God's balls!" Orsini's jaw dropped in shock. "He's humped a hobgoblin!"

"What? Wait! No!"

"Márta?" It was the first time Coel had ever seen Reza startled.

"Forgive me, Master. When I found Coel he was having, relations, with a . . ." Márta folded her arms and looked away. "I found it too revolting to discuss."

Reza looked at Coel in utter amazement. "Coel?"

"I--"

"Oh . . . Coel!" Zuli ran her hands down her thighs as if someone had just spilled a chamber pot on her lap.

"You do not understand!" Coel waved his hands helplessly. "I had to!"

"I have to go wash!" Zuli ran back into the gorge.

"The Celts have always been a dirty people, but this is a sin against God and Nature." Father Marius turned his back.

"But--"

"Now, you see, this is why I do not sleep with human females," Orsini shook his head gravely. "You can never tell where their men have been."

"You do not understand!"

"Forgive me, Coel," The dwarf looked away uncomfortably. "But I do not wish to understand."

Coel turned to Snorri desperately.

The Rus would not meet his eyes. "Coel, I have broken bread with pagans. I have seen firsthand the perversities of the Byzantines, but this? This is," Snorri shook his head incredulously as he uttered the word. "Bestiality."

"She spoke Latin!"

"I mean, I had heard jokes about sheep-shagging Welshmen, but--"

"You go to hell, then!"

"Come now," Orsini waved a hand. "Let us forget Coel's, peculiarities, at least temporarily."

Coel glared.

Orsini diplomatically changed the subject. "We have more pressing concerns. Zuli was keeping watch on the ridge before we broke camp. At last glance, she said she saw no signs of pursuit by the hobgoblins. I find this very odd."

Márta deigned to look at Coel again. "During our escape, we interrupted a ritual of some kind. The horde's leaders were all assembled. I think Coel killed several important personages."

"Killed someone important!" Orsini grabbed Coel and shook him in exultation. Coel's bones rattled. "That is it!" Orsini enthused. "There can be no other explanation! You have killed the Great Hobgoblin! Of course there is no pursuit! The hobgoblins can do nothing until they have a duel among their tribal champions to determine who the new Great Hobgoblin will be! You have struck the first blow against the horde, Coel! And more immediately, you bought us time!"

Snorri looked at Coel thoughtfully. "So, Coel has killed the Great Hobgoblin?"

Orsini nodded smugly. "So it would appear."

"Does this mean Coel is the Great Hobgoblin?"

A moment of profound silence followed. Orsini's huge white teeth flashed in high amusement. "Well, yes, technically, I believe so, but were I he? I would not go back and try to press my claim to the title."

Coel was desperate to change the subject. "Reza, you have

what you sought?"

"Indeed, Coel. Despite your, inclinations, you and Márta have succeeded admirably."

"What do we do now?"

"We go east, and speedily."

* * *

Gwall sat upon a stool and watched the duel of champions. Two hobgoblin males wrestled collar and elbow and sought to rip one another's throats out with their tusks. War drums pounded in encouragement. The tournament robbed the horde of some of their better war leaders, but they needed an undisputed Great Hobgoblin immediately lest they lose the initiative over humanity. Gwall sat surrounded by a phalanx of her eunuch guards. She was still in heat, and her presence drove the combatants to even greater effort. That was as it should be. Gwall observed the bloody duel. Fourteen claimants from various tribes had died already. It had come down to this final combat. She considered the two contending males. One of them would be her next mate.

"Whom would you choose?"

Gwall cast her eyes upon the human sitting next to her. The man wore black robes that covered all of him except for his hands and feet. His reddened eyes stared out from a slit in his burnoose. Gwall answered the man in his native Persian. "My preference is irrelevant, however, had I one, I would choose Nijumet of the Ten Skulls."

"Ah, the brother of Matukash, your fallen master," The Assassin watched the fight. "His opponent is younger, larger and stronger. He will lose."

Gwall's pupils narrowed to slits like a cat. The Moon, the Welshman, the death of Matukash and the bloody combats already had her in a high state of agitation. She decided the Assassin should die for his impertinence. She watched Nijumet fight. His opponent was slowly gaining the upper hand through sheer strength. "Nijumet is clever. He will win."

"Ah," The Assassin clearly did not agree. "How much gold would you wager?"

Gwall found the concept of money alien. The idea of risking precious resources gambling was absolute proof that humans were inferior. However, the human concept of money had become an important weapon in the New War. "The Old Man of the Mountain was paid the weight of one hundred axe-heads in gold by the Great Hobgoblin to kill Coel ap Math."

The Assassin was silent.

"Why, then, was I mating with him last night in my tent?"

The question remained unanswered as the assembled hobgoblins roared. Nijumet's back was beginning to bend like a bow. The tusks of his opponent strained towards his throat. Nijumet suddenly dropped and sank his fighting nails into the flesh of his opponent's shoulders and heaved. The larger hobgoblin tumbled to the ground by the sudden change in leverage. Nijumet shoved his tusks into his stunned opponent's throat and ripped upwards. His opponent flailed in his death throes. The hobgoblins in attendance raised their weapons in salute as Nijumet stood. The representatives of the Ten Skulls Tribe were jubilant. Nijumet was Brood Brother to the fallen Matukash. The Ten Skulls Tribe had now raised a Great Hobgoblin twice in a row from the same brood. It was a great honor and a testament to the fitness of their bloodline.

Nijumet walked over surrounded by his warriors. His chest heaved, and his scalp was torn. His opponent's blood ran down his tusks. "I am Nijumet of the Ten-Skulls. My blood is fittest. I am the Great Hobgoblin."

The sight of the victorious, blood covered male before her set Gwall's loins to burning and itching. It took an intense effort not to bend over the stool she sat upon and offer him her hindquarters. "You are the Great Hobgoblin. Your bloodline is First in the Horde. Yours is the First Choice in Mating. Your totem leads us in war. The Council of Tribes, the Council of Females, and the Circle of the Shamen all recognize you."

Nijumet's self-control was admirable. He spoke calmly even as his eyes raked her body. "It is true? You mated with the human?"

Gwall exposed her fangs. She remembered the feel of his skin tearing under her nails and fangs. She thought about how his flesh and blood had tasted like food as they had mated. It had doubled the excitement, as had his unorthodox method of mounting her. No hobgoblin male would expose himself to the nails and fangs of a female during mating. The human had seemed to revel in it.

"You know the Law of the Moon."

Nijumet thrust his lower jaw forward to further expose his bloody tusks. His yellow eyes glowed with more than victory. It was clear he liked what he saw. "I know the Law of the Moon. I feel its pull. But, will there be issue from this mating with the human?"

Gwall considered the idea even as the sight of Nijumet's fighting teeth excited her. "The Line of our Blood is many times removed from the humans. I am inclined to say no."

"If there is issue, it will be destroyed."

"Of course."

"What else occurred?"

"The human was Coel ap Math. One of the humans encountered by the Northern Horde. Matukash ordained his death. He had an accomplice whom I did not see. Sorcery was used."

"The Shamen tell me they took a fetish from us."

"They stole the ring of Tuman Sunqur."

The Assassin sat upright. He did not understand hobgoblin speech, but he had heard the name.

Nijumet was startled by Gwall's indiscretion in front of the Assassin but ignored it. "What can they accomplish with the ring of The Destroyer?"

"Normally, I would say nothing. However, according to our spies, the two humans, Coel ap Math and Snorri Yaroslav, travel in the company of a sorcerer of great power, one who is a renegade, and practices magics the various human churches have forbidden. The consequences of this are uncertain, but I fear them."

"What is the will of the Council of Females?"

The fact that the Prime Females of each tribe were all in heat and willing to kill each other for the right to mate with whomever the new Great Hobgoblin might be had not helped cohesion, but they had agreed on some basic facts. "Any attempt by the humans to reclaim the power of Tuman Sunqur must be stopped. If the Assassins find out those we seek have the ring, they will become unreliable and seek their own agenda." She peered at the Assassin from the corner of her eye. He had heard the name of The Destroyer twice now and watched them intently. "The cooperation of the Assassins is a key to our plans. You are now the Great Hobgoblin. Speed is of the essence."

"We are in agreement," He gestured to a warrior who stood beside him. I will send my Right Hand, Nadrud, in pursuit of the humans."

Gwall knew Nadrud. When she had come of mating age, he had sired her first brood. He had been old then, and was much older now. He was nearly past breeding age. His left tusk was broken and the other yellowed with years. Over the broken tusk, his eye socket was an ancient wound puckered with scar tissue. The green of his flesh had weathered and lined to a dusky gray raddled by age-lines and scars. His massive shoulders stooped. Still, his good eye roved over her. He had won the right to breed seventy-two times, and he still wore the twin knife-axes of a Single Combat Champion on his belt. He was the Right Hand of Nijumet, and now the Right Hand of the Great Hobgoblin. It was clear he remembered her flesh. Gwall's lips pulled back from her canines as she remembered his.

"Nadrud," The Great Hobgoblin raised a bloody hand. "Take what warriors and beasts you need. Request the aid of the shamen. Find and kill the humans."

"I am the Right Hand of Nijumet," Nadrud gave Gwall a final look and lumbered off.

Nijumet looked at the Assassin and then at one of Gwall's massive guards. "This human has twice heard my First Consort speak the name of the Destroyer. He is no longer reliable."

The obese eunuch grunted. His club rose overhead and whipped down. The Assassin barely had time to flinch. His burnoose collapsed under the club as his skull shattered. Nijumet gestured west. "Send word to the Old Man of the Mountain that his emissary has died in an accident and that we wish him to send us another. The Waste taints this one's flesh. Let the Lesser Ones have his meat."

Warriors dragged the dead assassin away by his heels to be thrown to the goblins.

Nijumet's eyes traveled down Gwall's body. "Twice, deliberately, you spoke the name of the Destroyer before the Assassin."

"The Law of the Moon rules me. I wished you to win. He spoke disparagingly of you during the combat, and I wished him dead. However, it was poor judgment politically." Gwall tensed her stomach muscles. "Do you wish me to re-affirm my position as First Consort by combat?"

"The Law of the Moon rules us all," Nijumet watched the wall of her stomach clench in fascination. "I claim my right of Primary Mating. Immediately."

Gwall exposed her fangs. She had been hoping he would say that.

* * *

Coel rode his mount disconsolately. Márta would not speak to him. Zuli had gone back to sleeping with Snorri and took great pains to let Coel know it. Snorri made no effort to hide it, either. Reza was obsessed with his box and had little time for anyone save to give orders. Marius shunned him like a plague victim. Coel found himself too embarrassed to try and speak with Orsini. He took point during the day and the first watch at night. He ate by himself. By day, he thought about Márta. On watch in the rocks, alone, he thought about Zuli.

Late in the night, in his bedroll, his thoughts turned to Gwall.

He thought about her fangs sinking into his flesh while he buried himself in hers. Marius had refused to heal the injuries. The wounds in Coel's shoulder itched, and the torn flesh of his back stung when he drew on his armor. The smell of her filled his mind each night until he realized the hobgoblin apron he'd worn was stuffed into the bag he used as a pillow. He'd ripped the garment out and flung it away into the night.

Coel rode point and scanned the land ahead. He heard the clop of a pony's hooves on the rocks but did not turn his head.

"It has been hard on you," Orsini observed.

Coel ignored the dwarf.

"Well, would asking me a question divert your mind from your troubles?"

Coel gratefully accepted the opportunity. He considered the thousand questions tormenting him. "The elves called you *Fomorian*."

Orsini shifted uncomfortably in his saddle. "What of it?"

"Well, in Celtic legend, the *Fomorians* were a race of stunted giants. Greedy for gold, who would do anything for . . . "

The expression on Orsini's face killed the words on Coel's tongue.

Orsini rolled his eyes. "We are an ancient race, Coel. We have come through the doors between worlds to this place of yours before. We fought the cave bears and hunted the fur bearing elephants here in your world before we could forge iron. The race of man has many names for us. The elves like the Celtic tongue. It has seven vowels and is structured much like their own."

Otto came padding between their mounts sniffing at the ground. The dog went onward sniffing the path ahead. Coel and Orsini looked at each other. Coel dropped from his horse with his bow in his hand. Orsini shoved his foot into the cocking stirrup of his crossbow and pulled back the string. "It would not surprise me if that dog has found a dragon."

The rest of the party came forward. They all looked expectantly at Otto. The dog peered intently at the entrance of a small cave in the rocks. Orsini kept his crossbow leveled. "Too small for man or elf."

"Not too small for a goblin," Snorri hissed. "Get it, Otto! Sic!"

Otto barked and charged down the hole.

A shriek of terror came from the cave. Otto barked and snarled, and his hindquarters appeared in the cave mouth. The dog wagged his tail back and forth and dug his hind feet into the dirt as he heaved backward. Otto twisted and pulled at a small boot. There was a leg attached to it. A second leg kicked and flailed. The wails of despair increased as Otto dragged his prey into the light.

"Down, Otto!" Snorri dismounted. "Release!"

Otto released.

A boy sat cringing in the dirt. Thick blonde curls stuck out in tangles from his head. Dirt caked his white tunic and trousers. Huge blue eyes red from weeping stared up the party in terror. He could not have been more than ten years of age. He flinched away as Otto sniffed at him.

Coel stared at the boy. "He does not loo much like a Tartar."

"He's a Cuman," Snorri bent down on one knee. "They are called the Yellow People. They do not look much like Huns, but they are steppe nomads just the same."

Snorri asked a question in a strange language. He repeated it again more firmly and the boy snuffled and wiped at his tear-streaked face. "Luko."

"His name is Luko."

"He is adorable," Zuli came forward and held out a piece of bread. The boy looked at it for a moment and snatched it. Zuli looked up at Reza. "Can we keep him?"

Snorri spoke more steppe language. The boy began crying again and stuttered out his responses. Snorri frowned. "From what I can gather, his family was taken by the hobgoblins. They ate his father on the march. He says there was a great commotion several nights ago. His mother had cut at the ropes holding them with a sharp stone. He says they ran away during the trouble. I think the goblins got his mother outside the camp. He kept running."

Coel felt another load of guilt pile across his shoulders. "We cannot leave him here, then."

"That is exactly what we should do," Father Marius gazed down upon the boy steadily.

Shocked silence followed

"God damn you!" Snorri went white with rage. "If this is Christian charity, then by God I'll sacrifice an ox to Odin this very day! God damn you, Marius! God damn you to hell!"

"I'll be there soon enough, Rus. We all will." There was no anger in Father Marius as he spoke. His voice was so desolate it sent a chill down Coel's spine. "As for the boy, it would be better if you split his head now, rather than--"

"Marius!" Reza's voice was a snarl of rage. Marius flinched like he had been struck. The priest's lowered his head and walked his horse slowly on.

Coel repeated himself. "We cannot leave him here."

Reza nodded. "You are right. We bring him with us."

Zuli licked her fingers and wiped the dust from Luko's face. The boy smiled at her tremulously. She smiled back and took his hand. He followed her and she boosted him up onto her spare pony.

"Good boy!" Snorri rubbed Otto behind his ears. Otto wagged his tail happily. Snorri looked up at Coel and then at Luko with a grin. "Well, now we are eight again."

CHAPTER THIRTY-ONE

Nadrud sat his camel and honed his unbroken tusk with a well-scarred dowel of ironwood. He ran his single eye along the peaks of the Kopets calculatingly. The humans had several days lead on him. Their horses gave them a speed advantage, but his camels had the endurance to grind them down. He looked back upon his forces. He had a half dozen proven single combat champions and ten more hobgoblin crossbowmen. All were Ten-Skull tribe as he was. He did not doubt the blood of any of them

He also had the skills of the shaman, Retep.

Retep was reputed to be the most highly skilled shaman among the Elf-Skinners. Their reputation for producing shaman of great power was well known. Nadrud had asked for Retep by name. It was a testament to the importance of the mission that Retep was here. Several dozen goblins milled at the heels of the camels. A dozen more fanned out both ahead and behind the war party. The Lesser Ones were always useful to have about. They served equally well as scouts, trackers, camp guards, arrow fodder and emergency rations.

Nadrud looked down upon the Lesser One that shifted from foot to foot before him. It was a pack leader. It would not meet Nadrud's gaze as he spoke. "You have lost the scent?"

"Yes! No!" The Lesser One cringed. Lost humans! Lost dwarf! Lost elf! Not lost horses! We find dung! We track them!"

Nadrud ceased his sharpening. He had been informed there was dwarf among the humans. His blood moved with the ancient hatred at the news of an elf. The Lesser One looked upon Nadrud's single tusk in abject fear as he pondered. "An elf?"

"Blood is mixed! Blood is weak! But scent is elf!"

"Why have you returned?"

"Must choose! Three paths ahead! Must choose! No blood! No fresh dung! Path is rock and dust! Three paths! We track! We follow, but you must choose!"

Nadrud leaned back on his saddle pad. The Lesser Ones had found three paths and not enough of a trail to choose between them. This one had come back rather than plunge on blindly out of fear of retribution. Indeed, it had come back and reported even though it clearly feared for its life. Its bloodline was strong in brains. Nadrud decided to let it live. "Shaman."

Retep rode forward. Rather than knife-axe or crossbow, the shaman carried a curved knife and a set of bolas at his belt. "I serve the Right Hand of Nijumet."

"The humans have taken one of three paths. Elves and dwarves ride with them. Their path is not fresh enough for the Lesser Ones to choose. I must know their path."

Retep's lips smacked around his tusks in thought. "One of the humans is a sorcerer of great power. He will see me if I try to look upon him."

"Can you look upon him in such a way that you are not seen?"

Retep smacked his tusks again.

"Can you do this thing?"

"It will require blood."

Nadrud looked upon his warriors grimly. "Lesser, or Greater?"

"Lesser will suffice."

Nadrud gazed at the goblins among the camels. He pointed his sharpening stick at the smallest amongst them. "That one."

The demarcated goblin shrieked in terror. Retep smoothly pulled his bolas from his belt as the Lesser One bolted. When The Path of Life required sacrifice, even hobgoblin single combat champions were known to flee the Blood Rites. The stones whirred over Retep's head. The shaman released, and the bolas scythed through the air. The fleeing goblin wailed as the leather straps cinched around its ankles and it fell to the ground. Two hobgoblin warriors leaped from their camels and seized it.

Retep had his camel kneel, and he drew his curved knife as he dismounted. The two warriors held the goblin upside down by its ankles as it screamed. Retep took a wooden bowl and placed it below the goblin's head. He cut the lesser one's throat with a single slash. Blood poured down into the bowl. "Remove its head. Peel its skull, and bring me its eyes intact."

The warriors set about butchering the goblin. Retep took his knife and drew it across his palm. He made a fist and squeezed it over the bowl. His own blood fell to mix with that of the goblin. "Those we seek have walked this path?"

Nadrud nodded. "Yes."

"Fetch me dust of the path."

A warrior brought Retep a handful of brown dust. Retep sheathed his knife and took the dust in his clean hand. It sifted between his fingers as he blew upon it. Some of the dust rose up in his palm. Retep's clawed hand shook. The dust in his hand began to whirl. The funnel of dust grew and Retep upended his palm. It fell to the ground whirling and bulging. A dust devil half his height soon swirled before him.

"Shaman," A warrior stood forward. He held the goblin's skull in one hand and its eyes in the other. The lesser ones were already fighting over the meat of their sacrificed brother. Retep took the eyes and bathed them in the blood of the bowl.

He tossed the eyes into the whirlwind.

The wind and dust streaked red. The eyes swirled and bobbed about in the eye of the vortex. Retep extended his wounded hand, and the dust devil whirled off down the path. Retep raised the goblin's skull and peered into the bloody pits of its eye sockets.

Nadrud leaned forward. "Do you see, Shaman?"

Retep gazed deep into the skull. "I see."

* * *

Coel munched on roasted pigeon as they rode along the high cataract. Luko had already become a valuable asset. Zuli had woven him a sling out of leather, and the boy had proven himself adept. Snorri had given the lad his sax-knife. Luko wore it thrust through his sash like a sword. He looked ready to burst with pride. At dawn he had clambered up among the rocks and come down with a sack full of doves. He'd covered them with clay from the river and shoved them in the coals of the campfire. When the clay had dried, he had broken them open and the birds' feathers had come away with the clay. It was work to get the meat from the tiny bones, but Coel could not remember a juicier pigeon in all his life.

Snorri spat out a bone as they rode and raised his voice over the crashing water. "The boy has possibilities. Perhaps I should adopt him."

The Rus smiled at Coel's amazement.

Snorri shrugged. "Why not? We have to do something with him. I have relatives in the Orkneys. I could foster him there. Trouble is brewing, and I can think of no safer place."

"You'll have to get in line. He follows Zuli about like a lost gosling."

"Not that you or I would know about that."

Coel snorted. "You have me there."

"Perhaps I should make an honest woman of the wench. That would solve everything."

"Marry her?" Coel's jaw dropped. "Zuli?"

"We would make an interesting little family, would we not?"

Coel tried to imagine Snorri, Zuli, Luko, and Otto living in a sod house waxing cheeses in the treeless Orkneys.

"What about all your talk of travelling the world?"

"I think between the two of us we'll have all ready seen most of it."

"She's barren."

"We'll adopt Luko, as I said. Besides, she has only been riding the Spear of Odin for two months, so it's too early to tell if she would be barren with me, and I am more of a man than most." Snorri raised his scarred eyebrow. "But, if in seven months' time, she should drop a red-headed bean-pole, I promise you I'll be kind to it."

"Snorri."

"Yes?"

"You and I are friends."

"You are my very best friend in the world."

"We may speak plain, then?"

"I would have it no other way."

Coel struggled for the most diplomatic words that would not be insulting. "You know I am fond of Zuli."

"Yes, I do know, and I'll thank you to keep your fondness above your belt rather than below it from now on."

"No. That is not what I meant." Coel shook his head. "Snorri, I want no quarrel between us, but . . . "

"But what?"

"Zuli is a thief, an Assassin, and a whore."

Snorri's eyes narrowed. "She makes me happy."

"You really want to marry her?"

"I said perhaps I should. It is only a thought."

"Does she know these idle thoughts you've been thinking?"

"Not yet. Nor will she, unless you go farting off at the mouth."

An idiot's grin broke across Coel's face. "Well, then I guess I--Snorri!"

"By Odin!" Snorri reeled in his saddle. An arrow stuck out of his chest. The Rus roared in outrage. "Archers in the rocks!" The Rus yanked the arrow out and an iron scale of his vest came with it.

Coel leaped from the Barb with his bow and a sheaf of arrows in hand. An arrow struck his brigandine vest and another caromed off his steel skullcap and tore away his hat. After the poisoned arrows of the Assassins, the party had taken to wearing armor as they rode. The ambush was perfect. The path was narrow, and one side of it was a cliff that dropped away to the river below. The roar of the river falling down the mountainside had covered any telltale noises of the ambushers.

Arrows hissed and sparked off of the rocks. Coel loosed an

arrow and threw himself behind a boulder.

"It is the Long-Eye!" Reza dropped down behind his horse. Márta loosed arrows up into the rocks. Two shafts already stood up from the shield strapped to her arm. Snorri knelt by Coel's side clutching his throwing spears. Half a dozen arrows stuck in his shield.

"This is bad!"

Horses pounded down the path. Egyptian Mamluks rode shoulder to shoulder with their swords on high. The Mamluks were heavily armored and bore shields, but the range was closing to spitting distance. Coel rose and loosed a shaft into the lead Mamluk's face. Coel nocked another arrow as the Mamluk fell from the saddle. The man riding beside him pulled his long oval shield up to cover his head and torso. Coel lowered his aim and loosed. The Egyptian jerked in agony as his mail skirt burst and his leg was skewered. His shield lowered. The Mamluk took Coel's third arrow in the throat.

Coel heard fighting behind him and could only guess that Marius and Orsini were engaged.

The riderless horses reared. The riders behind piled into them and milled. Coel's own Barb stamped and reared behind him. Snorri hurled a spear at a Mamluk. "Coel! Stay between the horses! Ware the archers!"

Coel dropped back behind his stamping Barb and nocked an arrow. A riderless horse screamed as a Mamluk urged his mount forward and shoved it over the cliff. Snorri hurled his second spear. The Mamluk raised his shield and the spearhead scored the brass and skated off. Coel loosed his shaft under the shield's rim and sparks flew as the Mamluk's mail failed. The Egyptian collapsed over his saddle horn. Snorri's third spear bounced off another Mamluk's mail.

Large men on foot waving axes and longswords pushed between the Mamluk horses with their shields. A man with a forked blonde beard raised his axe and shouted in Russian. "Your head is mine, Snorri Yaroslav! Mine!"

"Take it!" Snorri waved his axe. "Take it if you can, you stoneless sausage!"

The man dropped his shield with a roar of rage and took his axe in both hands. Snorri dropped his axe. His hand went behind his shield and whipped forth to let a goblin dart fly. The dart sank into the man's shoulder.

"Bastard! I'll--"

Snorri threw again, and his second dart flew between the fork in the man's beard and pierced his throat. Forkbeard fell to the ground slobbering blood.

The Rus behind him pushed through. "Coward! You--"

Coel loosed an arrow into his screaming mouth. A Mamluk horseman pushed through and charged. Coel dropped his bow and drew his sword. He fell back to his Barb and yanked his shield from its pack straps. Snorri lashed out at the horseman and axe and sword met with a clash.

More Russians howled and pushing forward. Hill men in fur boots and vests leaped down the mountainside like goats and flung javelins. Arrows flew as Mamluks up in the rocks loosed.

There were too many.

Coel flung a desperate look over his shoulder. "Reza!"

"Coel!" Snorri hooked the rim of the Mamluk's shield with the edge of his axe and yanked it down. Coel lunged and thrust upward at the mounted man. The point of the Academy blade punched through mail links and slid deep between the Egyptian's ribs.

"Bastards!" Snorri's axe fell from his hand. An arrow skewered his forearm. He cast down his shield and took up his axe in his left hand.

"Coel!" Márta was still mounted and her bow was in her hand. Arrows pin cushioned her shield and others stuck in her armor. "Coel! Reza is beset! Kill the Long-Eye!" Márta dropped a hillman who flung a javelin from the rocks.

Coel looked about frantically. Zuli was suddenly at his side. "The Blue-Robe, Coel! Up on the hill! Márta hasn't the range! Kill the Blue-Robe!"

Coel sheathed his sword and picked up his bow. A stone

thudded into his back as he tried to pull an arrow from the quiver on his stamping horse. Zuli and Luko stood behind Snorri. Their slings whirled and released. A Russian blocked one lead bullet but the other cracked his temple. Zuli and Luko ducked back behind the horses as arrows sought them. Wounded horses wheeled and screamed. Coel could not see Kamose, but Márta could from horseback.

Coel leaped atop the rocks that had partially shielded him.

Kamose was a blue figure at the top of the ridge. His hands clutched his white turban in mental effort. The shot was long. An arrow hissed by. Coel ignored it as he laid his own arrow and drew. A screaming hill man bounded towards him down the rock face like a goat. His spearhead flashed.

A sling stone struck him, and a second later an arrow took him in the stomach.

An arrow struck Coel's chest, but his armor held. He took the bow to full draw. Another hill man came at him with his shield held at a slant and his hand cocked back. Márta's arrow skated off of his shield. Coel ignored his closing opponent and let out half a breath. He sighted over the gleaming point of the arrowhead atop his fist. Coel loosed. The hill man flung a river stone into Coel's face.

The world constricted down to darkness and purple pinpoints of light. Coel toppled from his perch. The air blasted form his lungs as fell flat onto to the stony path.

"Coel!" Hands seized Coel's arm and pulled him up. Someone drew his sword and put it in his hand. His shield was shoved onto his arm. Zuli's voice rose in strident urgency. "Coel! You must get up!"

Coel's right eye was blind and his left smeared with tears. He rose to find a Rus upon him. He managed to push his shield up as a glittering axe blade swung down at his head.

The axe blade split the rim of his shield and bit down deep into the wood. The Russian slammed his shoulder into Coel's shield and drove him backward towards the cliff. Coel went with the shove and fell upon his back and took the Rus with him. He kicked up with both feet and the Rus flew over him. Coel's shield ripped from his hand. The Rus fell to the cataracts below.

Coel rose unsteadily. All was confusion. Horses reared and stamped all around him. The air shuddered and thunder rolled. Lightning seemed to flash and crack out of the blue sky. A gleaming Mamluk suddenly towered over him on horseback. Teeth flashed in the dark face and his black eyes burned with hatred. "Now, red-haired whore's son! Now you die!"

The Mamluk's mace swung down and smashed the academy blade out of Coel's hand. The backhand return slammed against Coel's chest and sat him down again. Snorri leaped forward. His axed licked out against the Mamluk's brazen shield. The Mamluk swung back. Snorri raised his wounded right arm as he tried to manage his axe in his left hand. Snorri's forearm broke beneath the blow. The Rus fell to one knee. The Mamluk leaned from his saddle to strike Snorri down.

"Tawfiq!"

Reza Walladid strode out from among the horses. He held the box crooked in one elbow. His black eyes blazed. He raised his fist and the scarab ring gleamed upon his hand. "Tawfiq al Salim!"

The *Amir* froze in the saddle.

Reza opened his fist. "Die!"

Tawfiq screamed.

Black winged locusts erupted out of the Amir's mouth.

The Amir fell flailing from his horse. The thrum of wings drummed like thunder as the stream of insects coiled out from his throat like an unending serpent that twisted into the air. A Rus back-pedaled in horror. Reza pointed his finger. The flying river of locusts streamed into the Rus' face. The Rus' head disappeared in a heaving mass of ebony insects.

The locusts fountained on and on out of Tawfiq. Reza raised his hands, and the sun darkened as they formed a dense cloud over the party. Swirling storms of locusts engulfed Rus, Mamluk and hill man like tornadoes touching down.

Coel scooped up his sword. He staggered back against his horse and grasped the Barb's mane to steady himself as his head spun. He still couldn't see out of his right eye. It felt like someone had driven a nail through it. Snorri rose once more but fell as an arrow sank into his thigh.

"Snorri!" Coel moved to help him. He started as his rock throwing nemesis leaped from behind a boulder. The man grinned and flung another stone. Coel raised his sword instinctively but he was not the target.

The stone struck Reza in the skull.

Márta screamed and leaped from the saddle. "Master!"

The sorcerer sank to the ground.

The droning cloud of insects above broke apart on the mountain winds. Coel grasped his horse's reins and dizzily tried to pull himself up into the saddle. A horseman thundered down upon him. A black stallion's hooves rang sparks off the rocky path. The horseman wore a gleaming cuirass and carried a trapezoidal shield. His saber pin-wheeled around his wrist. Coel snarled in shock and anger as he recognized Sandor. Coel hopped with one foot caught in the stirrup. Sandor sliced down at him left-handed with a saber. Their blades belled. The stallion reared and lashed out its hooves. Air crushed out of Coel's lungs again as horseshoes met his armor and smashed him to the ground.

Coel's Barb reared above him. Hooves thudded into flesh as the horses fought. The Barb screamed as the stallion sank its teeth into her neck and savaged her. Sandor spurred his horse and the stallion bulled the Barb out of its way. Sandor's teeth flashed. Coel's sword wavered like a reed in the wind as he rose. Sandor spoke no insults. The smile on his lips spoke more than any words. The saber rose in his hand.

"Hey!" Snorri tottered on his good leg. His broken and skewered right arm hung limp at his side. His axe teetered across his shoulders. Snorri thrust out his jaw. "Try me, silk pants!"

Coel raised his sword.

Sandor laughed and spurred his horse at the Rus. Snorri hopped a step forward to meet the charging Pole. He swung his axe. The blow was with his weak hand and had but one firm leg behind it. Sparks flew as the blades grated. Sandor leaned out of the saddle and used his height and leverage to forced the axe down. He turned his wrist over and thrust. His curved blade slid along Snorri's axe like a serpent. Sandor's point slid inside Snorri's mail sleeve and sank deep into his armpit.

"Snorri!" Coel staggered forward. "Snorri!"

Snorri's mouth opened and closed. Sandor twisted his blade in Snorri's body and ripped it free. Snorri's axe fell from his hand. He stared up at the Pole incredulously. "You . . . bastard."

Sandor's laugh rang above the sound of battle. He raised his saber high for the finishing blow.

"Snorri!"

Armored scales flew as the curved blade cut Snorri down. The Rus toppled backward over the cliff and fell to the cataracts below.

"Snorri!"

Sandor wheeled his horse upon Coel.

"Kill you!" Coel lurched forward screaming. "I will kill you!"

Sandor aimed his saber at Coel with a smile

"Hold!"

Sandor turned his head. Marius strode out of the milling horses. The top third of his shield was gone. His helmet had been torn from his head, and blood streamed down his face. His mace and chain whirled. Sandor spurred at him. Marius raised his weapon high as Sandor closed. The brutal iron ball arced at the Pole's skull.

Sandor lay back in the saddle beneath the blow. The spikes passed a foot over his head. The tip of the Pole's saber licked under Marius' chin in passing. Flail and shield fell from the priest's grasp. Marius dropped to his knees. His hands went to his throat. Blood flooded over his mail mittens. His eyes locked with Coel's.

Marius smiled and fell on his face.

"Now, Celt," Sandor wheeled his mount. "Now, for you."

Coel looked at Sandor as if from the bottom of a well. He gripped his sword and tried to summon rage to cut the fog in his mind and across his vision. Sandor had killed Snorri. Anger seemed to push his vision up out of the well. He looked at Sandor clearly out of one eye under the blue sky. Coel's hands shook. He was half-blind and too weak to fight. His thoughts became very clear. He would drop and cut the grinning bastard's devil horse out from under him. If his own head was still on his shoulders after that, then he would kill Sandor where he fell.

Coel gestured Sandor in.

The Pole laughed and spurred his horse.

Sparks flew from Sandor's helmet. He raised his shield and a second sling stone smacked off of it. Zuli and Luko came forward reloading their slings. Orsini limped forward with his war hammer in both hands. "You, Sir! Come and let us disagree!"

Sandor's smile faded. His eyes looked past Coel to the path beyond and escape. The Pole spurred his horse. Coel tottered forward to cut him off, but the black stallion thundered past before he could get in front of it. Sandor swiped at him in passing and the shock of their blades meeting sat Coel down yet again. The Pole galloped on around the bend.

"Come, Coel! You must rise!" Orsini gripped Coel's arm and pulled him to his feet. Coel put a hand on the dwarf's shoulder to steady himself. He turned his throbbing head to look about with his open eye. Marius lay on his face in a spreading pool of blood. Between the horses Coel could see Márta cradling Reza's bloody head in her lap. Snorri's axe lay on the ground. Coel's heart opened like a wound for his friend. "Snorri."

"He is dead, Coel."

Coel pulled away from the dwarf and staggered to the cliff's edge. The rushing river fell almost vertically down the mountainside. Blades of rock churned the water to roaring white froth. There was no sign of the Rus anywhere or any of the other fallen men and horses anywhere.

"Fetch a rope. I shall climb down."

"He's dead." Orsini's voice was like gravel. "He had two arrows in him. His arm was broken. I saw the wound he took under his arm." The dwarf looked at the roaring water. "He was in armor."

"No," Coel shook his head and even that hurt. "Fetch a rope."

An anguished howl rose among the rocks. Down the path

Otto sat on his haunches at the cliff edge. His muzzle lowered and then rose up as he howled out in inconsolable loss.

Orsini knelt and rolled Marius over onto his back. His slit throat gaped beneath his chin. The smile upon the priest's face was beatific.

Coel's battle instincts took over. "Reza?"

Márta held the sorcerer's head in her lap. "He is unconscious, but alive."

Coel tried to look uphill among the rocks. His left eye would not stop tearing over. He could not open his right. His voice was a croak. "Orsini, what happened?"

"Your arrow struck the Long-Eye. A most amazing shot. Reza's will was then free. He unleashed his power." Orsini pointed upwards. Clumps of boulders were blackened and smoking. "He did something that struck down the archers, and some of the Mamluks and Rus facing Marius and I. Then he turned to aid you and Snorri." Coel gazed at the face of Tawfiq. The fallen Amir's jaw was locked open and distended in death. His pupils were pinpricks of frozen horror. Orsini nodded. "Reza unleashed the power of the ring. The remaining Russians fled. Then that hairy little fellow hit him with a stone."

Coel's hand went to his face and he nearly fell again. "Orsini?"

"Yes."

"Do I still have my eye, then?"

"Your face is too swollen to tell. We'll know tomorrow. Unless you want me to cut you now to find out."

The idea was more than Coel could bear. "How many of them are left?"

"Not many. Sandor, and our rock-hurling friend. Some Rus. I do not know whether Kamose lives. He must have had some men with him up on the ridge. If they were clever they would come and finish us now, but I wager they won't."

Coel looked out over the cliff again. Zuli's back was to them. Her shoulders shook as she looked down into the cataract. Luko clutched her thigh and wept openly. Otto howled like it was the end of the world.

"We have to move."

"Yes."

Coel went to his horse. The Barb shuddered and twitched. Her chest was lumped and swollen from the stallion's hooves. Blood ran down her neck from the black stallion's teeth. He pulled himself painfully into the saddle and nearly swooned. "Zuli, string the horses together. Luko, find my bow." He turned back. " Márta?"

Márta looked up from Reza.

"Can you get him on a horse?"

Márta nodded and rose.

Coel held his face. The pain in his eye was a spike through his skull. "Otto."

The dog howled on like someone was killing it with a knife.

Coel winced as he raised his voice. "Otto!"

The hound looked at Coel and then turned tormented brown eyes back to the water and rocks below. Coel's head hurt too much to yell. He clucked at his Barb, and the battered mare shambled forward over the bodies of the fallen.

Coel clutched his face. His left eye teared over with more than pain. Snorri was dead. His best friend was food for fish. He would have no proper funeral.

Only a mongrel dog remained behind to sing his praises.

CHAPTER THIRTY-TWO

Coel awoke from terrible dreams. His eye cracked open. He was cold. He ached down to his bones. He could not remember his dreams, but he knew the gist of them. Oleg was dead. Snorri was dead. Marisol was dead. His family was ruined. He was an exile. His love for Márta was a crumpled poem lying in dust across the Caspian Sea. Coel's hand went to his face and felt the crusted bandage wound around his head. He was a bowman with but one eye. He looked up miserably into the dawn.

Father Marius stood over him.

Coel screamed.

Marius' beatific death smile was gone. Flattened, bloodshot eyes burned out from bruised and sunken sockets. The fish-pallor of his face was so pale it was tinged with blue. The hands that hung at his sides were corded and purpled with lividity. His mace and chain dangled from its thong around his wrist. The studded iron ball dragged behind him in the dust. A bloodstained kerchief bandaged his throat. His chainmail sagged on his bones like sackcloth on a scarecrow. Blood crusted his mantle from his neck to his belt.

Marius' voice was a broken rattle. " . . . Coel."

Coel leaped screaming from his bedroll. The morning chill shivered his flesh and told him he was not dreaming. His sword flashed in his hand.

" . . . Coel."

Coel's voice rose to a shriek as the priest shambled toward him. "Orsini!"

"Coel . . . kill me."

"Orsini!"

"What in--God's codpiece!" Orsini stood with his crossbow in his hand. "Marius!"

Coel staggered back a step and kept his sword point between

him and the priest. "You are dead!"

Luko shrieked in terror.

Marius came another step forward. He leaned towards Coel's blade. "Coel . . . your sword . . . please . . . "

"Get the hell away from me!" Coel kept backing up. "How in hell did you get here?"

"I summoned him."

Coel jumped at the sound of Reza's voice behind him. The sorcerer had a bandage wound round his head. Blood stained it at his right temple. He leaned heavily on Márta. He held the box under his arm and the scarab ring gleamed on his right hand. "Marius, stay where you are."

Marius lurched to a halt.

"No! Marius is dead!" Coel kept his sword between them. "His throat was cut! His life bled out all over the stones! We all saw it!"

Reza regarded Coel steadily. His face was pale and dark circles bruised the flesh under his eyes. "It is not my will that the spirit of Father Marius shall pass on yet."

"You raised him? From the dead?"

"To a certain degree."

Coel was dumbfounded. "You have that much power?"

A strange smile crossed Reza's face. "I have."

"But, then," Coel's mind raced. "What about Snorri?"

"The Rus?" Reza shook his head dismissively. "What about him?"

Coel's knuckles whitened on his sword hilt.

"Coel!" Zuli knelt on her bedroll. Luko clutched her and wept fearfully. She turned Luko's face to look away. The thief jerked her head at Marius. "Think carefully about what you ask for."

Coel looked at Marius. The priest swayed on his feet like he was standing in a high wind. The flattened, bloodshot eyes burned upon Coel's Academy blade with a hunger beyond imagining. Zuli's voice was very calm. "Do you really wish Snorri to receive such a summons?"

Snorri would prefer to burn in hell and Coel knew it. He turned his good eye on Reza. "This is blasphemy, Walladid."

"So is seducing a nun, Coel, but I hired you anyway."

"Reza!" Orsini stepped between them. "This serves nothing!"

Coel stopped with Orsini's hand against his chest. He thrust his sword past the dwarf and pointed it at Reza. "By God, watch your tongue wizard or I shall cut it out and show it to you!"

" . . . kill him, Coel." Marius whispered.

"I am sick of your impudence, Celt! Márta!" Reza yanked his arm from Márta's shoulder. He swayed on his feet like a drunk. His knuckles were white as he clutched the box. Fresh blood trickled from beneath his bandage. His breath came in gasps. "If Coel takes another step, kill him!"

Márta gasped. She looked back and forth between Coel and Reza in horror. Her hand went to the hilt of her scimitar. She looked desperately at Orsini. Reza raised his hand and light flickered off of the scarab ring even as his hand trembled. His face twisted with rage. "Listen to me, savage! Snorri Yaroslav is dead! Oleg is dead! Marius is an extension of my will, and Márta is my slave. Orsini has his priorities and Zuli knows her place. Not even the dog is left to defend you. You are out of friends, Coel! Now, either learn to heel like the dog you are or I will--"

"I shall put your head on a spike and give it to the Blue Robes myself!" Coel shoved Orsini out of his way.

The dwarf stumbled backward but seized Coel's arm. "Coel!"

Márta's scimitar hissed from its sheath.

" . . . Kill him, Coel." Marius' voice was like the sound of spiders walking on a wooden wall. "Kill him . . ."

Márta stepped into Coel's path. Her hesitation was gone. She wore the same eyes she had on the Olga when they had fenced. The watered steel of her blade crawled with menace. Orsini's hand closed like a bear trap on Coel's arm. The dwarf dug in his heels and Coel could not move forward. Coel turned to smite the dwarf with the pommel of his sword.

"I'll kill you!" Reza tottered behind Márta. His head reeled on his shoulders. "I'll kill you all . . ."

Orsini seized Coel's sword arm even as he looked back. "For God's sake, Reza!"

Reza collapsed.

The box tumbled from his hands and lay on its side in the dust.

"Master!" Márta's eyes flicked to Reza in consternation, but she stayed facing Coel. She stood with her legs wide and her blade held in a low guard.

"Coel . . ." Orsini warned.

Coel snarled. "Aye."

Orsini released Coel's arms. Coel lowered his sword back and turned away. Márta sheathed her blade and knelt beside her master. Coel saw Zuli held the curved length of an Arab *jambiya* dagger low along her leg. She slid it under her bedroll and hugged Luko. Her eyes never left Coel.

Coel wondered whom it was she was willing to stab.

Orsini sat down heavily on a footstool-sized rock. "I'm tired."

Coel collapsed on his blankets and clutched his bandaged head. His pulse still pounded. His injured eye throbbed horribly. "I am sorry I laid hands upon you, Orsini."

"You have lost your best friend, and you may have lost your eye. Reza should not have baited you. It is understandable." The dwarf shook his head. "Though, you should not have been able to shove me like that. I must be getting old."

"You're sick, Orsini. The poison is still working within you."

Orsini said nothing. Coel focused his eye at Father Marius. The wind plucked at the tufts of his blood crusted blonde hair. The priest watched unblinkingly as Márta and Zuli pulled Reza on top of his bedroll. "He is just going to stand there, then?""

Orsini looked over at the priest with foreboding. "I suspect until Doomsday, or until Reza commands him otherwise."

"He has changed."

Orsini nodded. "Indeed, the priest was a handsome man, once."

"You know I mean Reza. He has changed ever since he put on that ring."

"No, I would not say that. I would say he has become more of what he already was."

"I do not like it."

"Neither do I. However, in his defense, he called down lightning to defend us, and the scarabs from the Mamluk, Tawfiq. Like you, he took a stone to the skull in the battle, and, more to the point, while you slept he summoned Marius. He is riding the razor's edge of his power, even with the help of the ring. He is coming close to his objective, yet he barely has the power to stand." Orsini shook his head at Coel. "The last thing he needed was impertinence from you. He needs rest. Perhaps this little misunderstanding is for the best if it forces him to sleep."

Coel looked at the box where it lay in the dust. He turned his good eye on Orsini. The dwarf looked back haggardly. "And while the wizard sleeps, you have questions."

"You seem no stranger to honor, Orsini. Yet this is black business, and I want to know why you are about it."

"I have my reasons."

"And just what are those, then?"

For a moment Coel thought Orsini would not answer. Or perhaps smite him. The dwarf finally sighed and stared wearily off into the mountains. "I want to go home."

"I thought your home was covered in ice."

"It is."

"Why, then?"

"Not all of us came through the doorways, Coel. Some stayed, to eke out whatever living they could."

"Your wife."

"You are intuitive, Coel, but not my wife, my betrothed." Orsini's anthracite eyes gazed across time and distance unimaginable to Coel. "My Finivar, her eyes as clear as crystal, her brow like a lioness. I could close my hands around her waist, and her hips?" The dwarf shaped an hourglass with his hands in the air. "No kohl-eyed Queen of Egypt could light a candle to her." Orsini's hands sank to his sides. "She didn't want to come to this world ruled by humans. I begged her, but she would not come. So, I left. I walked through the doors of worlds."

"If the ice claimed the north, why didn't your people just go south, then?"

"The Hill Dwarves were in our way."

"Hill dwarves?"

"Look well upon me, Coel. Am I like any dwarf you have ever seen?"

"Well . . . no."

"Of course not. You have seen the Hill Folk, they are the dwarves you are accustomed to. I am of the mountain breed. The Hill Folk? They can live anywhere, but we Mountain Folk, we love the high air and the mountain fastness. There were never many of us, and many of us died fighting the hobgoblins in our world, more died fighting the ice, more still gave themselves to the fight here in your world. I fear we are a vanishing breed." Orsini scowled. "The Hill Folk were already heading southward, making pacts with the those who lived there. The lowland dwellers are no friends ours. We never made slaves of them, but when they had something we wanted, we would raid them as often as we would trade for it, and we never let them forget who their betters were. If they sent their armies up into our mountains, we slaughtered them. But, to go south, our people would have to leave our mountains and go down amongst them, our wagons loaded with our families and herding our livestock. We knew they would take a mighty revenge upon us, either in extortion or battle. Some of us stayed in our mountains, the rest, we treated with the elves, and we went through the Doors."

"You came here."

"I came here to make my fortune, and quite a fortune it was." The dwarf's head sank back in his hands. "Now I have spent nearly all of that fortune trying to make my way back."

"Could not the elves help you?"

"Elves care little for coins," Orsini scowled. "And by myself, I have nothing they would take in payment."

"Reza can send you back, then?"

"He can, if he finds the power he seeks. He is one of the most skillful adepts this world has ever seen."

"But what would you do there?"

"Marry Finivar, if she still lives. Then carve a new life from the ice."

"But you said the dwarves fought the ice and failed."

"Yes, we fought it and failed. I will not fight it any longer. I will work with it. I have watched you humans. You are nothing if not adaptable."

"What would you do?"

"Live like the northernmost savages for a time, like the Lapps of Finland or the *Skraelings* of Greenland. Hunt seals, herd reindeer. Build boats and grapple the mighty whales. Make a new way for ourselves. In time, perhaps go to Vinland."

Coel's throat caught as he thought of his friend. "Snorri's land across the sea?"

"Yes, the Norsemen no longer fare as far as they once did, but rumors of the place are still told around the fire. If such a place exists here in your world? Then somewhere, across the ocean, it exists in mine."

Coel sagged. "I wish Snorri was here."

"I miss the Rus, too. He was as good a human as I have ever met. His heart was as big as a mountain."

"He said," Coel smiled and felt tears stinging his good eye. "He said he was thinking of adopting Luko and making an honest woman of Zuli."

"Yes, he ran the idea past me."

"Can you imagine the three of them in the Orkneys, then?"

"I can."

"You think she would have gone with him?"

Orsini glanced over at Zuli. She sat cross-legged on a blanket playing some kind of finger game with Luko. The boy laughed happily, his terror already forgotten. "I believe she would. The world has only become more dangerous for a woman like her, and even harder times are coming. The Orkneys are far, almost untouched by time and the troubles of the world. It would be a safe place for her, and she cared far more for Snorri than she would admit."

"She would not stay faithful."

"You're wrong," They watched Zuli play with the boy. "She would stay until Luko was well grown, and Snorri was old and gray. She would have stayed with him until the end of his days, and sung the songs of mourning over his grave."

"Just how old is she, then?"

"I do not know. She has not a line upon her face, but from things of which we have spoken, events and such, I would say at least a hundred years, if not more. Her elvishness does not show in her looks, but the blood runs strong within her."

Coel brought a hand to his throbbing head. "I do not like this business."

"If it makes you feel any better, neither do I. We do not have to like it. Some things simply must be done."

"There was a man on the Mamluk ship."

"Oh?"

"He spoke to me in Latin. He said I was on the wrong side."

Orsini considered this. "An Egyptian?"

"I do not know. He looked like Jesus. He had blue eyes." Coel took a deep breath. "The elves told me to turn back for the sake of my soul." He looked over at Father Marius. "They said death was our destination."

Orsini grunted unhappily. He winced as he shifted his weight.

"Orsini, you are sick. The elves told you to turn back."

"Bugger the elves!" Orsini visibly calmed himself. "Coel. If you wish to leave, go. Go now, while the Walladid sleeps. I forgive you your debt to me. Though know that the Walladid never will. However, listen to me, and listen well. We need you. Luko needs you. Márta and Zuli need you. Snorri and Oleg are dead. Reza is on the edge of collapse. I will not even speculate about Marius, and, you are right, Coel. I am ill. We are all in terrible danger. We need your sword. We need you. I beg of you, stay."

Coel grimaced.

Orsini twisted the knife. "Snorri would."

It was a low blow, but that did not change the fact that it was true. "Orsini?"

"Yes?"

"I do not believe Reza had told me the whole truth."

"And?"

"What is in the box?"

"Ask Reza, if you must," Orsini looked away. "But I do not think you will like the answer."

* * *

Nadrud peered over a rock and nearly took an arrow in his remaining eye for his trouble.

The Mamluks were excellent archers. They were a tribe of humans who caused the War Councils great concern. Nadrud was learning why. Luckily there were not many of them this day. The ones Nadrud hunted had decimated the Mamluk party. Nadrud had the Mamluks pinned down and outnumbered. The Mamluks also had a handful of Rus with them. Nadrud did not think much of the Rus as a tribe, but as individuals they were capable of great ferocity, and these were mercenaries bearing great axes and long swords.

Nadrud did not relish this battle. It was a distraction, but these humans were inextricably in his way.

"Shaman."

Retep moved closer. "I serve the Right Hand of Nijumet."

"Our prey is several days ahead of us. We cannot waste the sun going around these here, and none of these must escape to warn the West of our coming. I must slay these humans quickly. I need your power."

"I smell sorcerers amongst them. One is of great power, but wounds thin his blood. There is a lesser adept as well."

Nadrud was not pleased by this news, but his task remained. "I must slay these humans."

"Yes." Retep smacked his tusks in thought. "I will engage the human sorcerers to the best of my ability. Have your warriors ready themselves."

Nadrud hissed at his second in command. Athuc looked to him. Nadrud grasped the hafts of his knife-axes and raised his thumbs. Athuc drew his hand drum from the leather sack at his side and quickly thumped out the order to prepare for the charge.

Nadrud drew his weapons from the rings on his belt. He carried the double knife-axes of a Single Combat Champion. His left-hand weapon was curved like a scythe with the inside edge wickedly sharp for hooking and shearing. His right hand blade was a straight, double-edged dagger blade with a reinforced armor piercing point. He wore a knee length byrnie of chainmail from Persia and over it a blood red corselet made of seven layers of rhinoceros hide from India. The lacquered rhino hide was heavy and stiff, but Nadrud was pleased by the way arrows skated off its hard slick surface. "Shaman, are you prepared?"

"I am."

Nadrud gazed at his opponents' position. He could see the two-dozen goblins that had crept upon the humans through the rocks. The human sense of smell was almost worthless, and these humans had not the sense to bring dogs with them. The goblins crouched and hid almost right next to the humans as only the Lesser Ones could.

Nadrud pressed two fingers between his tusk roots and

blasted out a high-pitched whistle. The goblins shrieked and leapt from their rocky hides. Nadrud leaped out from cover with his warriors.

The goblins fell upon the Mamluks, seizing their bow shafts and hacking at them with hatchets and knives. Nadrud had made his will clear to the Lesser Ones. Ignore the hairy faces. Attack the archers. Those who survived would be allowed to breed. Meat, fear, and the right to breed were the only things that motivated the Lesser Ones. The Mamluk archers were caught flat-footed by the goblin attack, but they were well armored. They threw down their bows and drew their swords. The Rus leaped in hewing with their axes. However, the Lesser Ones had succeeded. The Mamluks were all engaged. There would be no arrow storm. Nadrud and his warriors charged the human position.

Two humans rose up from the rocks. Both wore blue robes and white turbans. One human was old, and his chest was bound with bandages. A younger Blue-robe stood at his side and supported him. The younger human brought a hand to his turban and closed his eyes. The older one watched the hobgoblins come on.

Nothing happened.

Nadrud's blood went cold as he bore in. Nothing would happen. Retep's power had been engaged by the younger of the two sorcerers. There would be no offense from Retep in time. Nadrud bellowed at the top of his lungs for the Lesser Ones to attack the Blue-robes, but he could not make himself heard above the shouts and war cries of the humans and the goblin shrieking.

Nadrud wished vainly for his crossbow. He pumped his arms and ran faster.

The older sorcerer looked directly at him. Nadrud's blood thinned with fear as the old human extended a single finger.

Another human appeared behind the sorcerers. He carried a curved sword. The young blue-robe screamed as the blade sliced across his spine. The old one stumbled as the one supporting him fell. A Rus turned to see what was happening and fell with his throat slit. The human then turned and cut down another Mamluk from behind. Another human in the garb of the local hill tribesmen ran a Rus through with a javelin.

Nadrud closed. An Armored Mamluk stood in his path, but a pair of goblins clutched his legs. The Mamluk raised his sword. Nadrud hooked it with one knife-axe and pulled the blade aside. The other knife-axe chopped down to pierce the mail on the side of the Mamluk's neck. Nadrud ripped his weapon free. A howling Rus swung an axe at him. Nadrud blocked the blow with the haft of his right weapon. He crouched and hooked the Rus behind the knee with his left and hamstrung the human. Lesser Ones fell upon the crippled Rus as he toppled.

Nadrud looked for another opponent. Nearly all the Mamluks were down. They could not fight hobgoblin warriors while the Lesser Ones slashed and grappled their legs. The Rus were all dead. They were strong fighters, but they were lightly armored and did not have the skill of the Mamluks. They were no match for hobgoblin single combat champions.

Athuc stood over the old sorcerer. The Blue Robe lay on his back spread-eagled. He strained as if he bore a great weight upon his chest. Nadrud peered down at the blue robe. "What did you do to him?"

Athuc popped his lips against his tusks happily. "I have not touched him. The Shaman holds him from afar."

Nadrud looked back. Retep had risen from cover. His head was bowed, and his hands were held out open at his sides as his will held the Blue Robe. Nadrud turned to look at the two surviving human warriors. The dominant one was tall with dark hair. The facial hair of his upper lip was carefully trimmed. He regarded Nadrud calmly. The shorter one was extremely hairy. He stood a little behind the tall one holding a sheaf of javelins. Nadrud could smell his fear. The two had retreated to the cleft in the canyon where the humans had hobbled their horses.

Nadrud cleared his throat and spoke around his tusks in human speech. "You speak Turkish?"

The human exposed his feeble teeth in what Nadrud knew was a smile rather than a challenge. "I do."

"You slew your comrades."

"Yes."

"Why?"

"So they would not slay you."

Nadrud considered this. "Why?"

The human sheathed his saber. He reached slowly into the neck of his tunic and pulled a medallion from under his clothing.

Athuc sucked his tusks. Nadrud peered closer with his one eye. The human held a medallion of hammered iron. It was of hobgoblin workmanship. It was lumpy like a flattened cluster of grapes. It had ten lobes. Each lobe was a crude carving of a hobgoblin skull.

"Shaman!"

Retep came forward. He nodded at a pair of warriors and they bound the human sorcerer and gagged him. Retep approached the two human warriors and extended his hand. The human took the medallion from his neck and gave it to the Shaman. Retep closed his hand around the medallion and closed his eyes. Seconds passed.

"It is a genuine token of the Ten-Skulls. It was fashioned by a Shaman of your tribe, Nadrud."

"How did it come into the human's possession?"

"By the will of Matukash. This human is one of those who have seen the wisdom of serving us. This token came from the hand of Matukash, and, through intermediaries, into the hand of this human."

Nadrud switched back to Turkish. "You serve Matukash?"

"I serve the Great Hobgoblin, Matukash, of the Ten-Skull tribe."

Nadrud was surprised by the sound of a human using hobgoblin formalities. "Matukash is dead."

The human did not blink. "Who is the Great Hobgoblin?"

"Nijumet, of the Ten-Skull tribe."

The human nodded. "I am not surprised. The blood of the Ten-skulls is strong."

Nadrud was irrationally pleased to hear a human say this.

Retep spoke in hobgoblin. "This human is clever. He is flattering you."

"Yes, but his words are truth." Nadrud went back to Turkish. "How did you serve Matukash, and how do you come to be here?"

"In the Russias, I arranged ambushes to prevent the discovery of the Northern Horde, as well as facilitated bribery and assassinations to pave the way for the invasion. When men discovered the Northern Horde, I arranged to have them killed. When the attempt failed, I followed them south to ensure their death."

Nadrud squinted his good eye. "Humans who had discovered the Northern Horde?"

"Yes, Snorri Yaroslav and Coel ap Math, and the party they joined."

"We seek them. You fought them with the Mamluks. What can you tell us?"

"They go east. Even now they must be descending from the Kopet Mountains. They are ahead of you."

"This we know."

The human stroked the facial hair above his lip and again exposed his teeth. "I have slain Snorri Yaroslav and the priest who wielded power." He gestured at the hill man. "He wounded Coel ap Math, and the sorcerer, Reza Walladid, as well. There is a dwarf, a swordswoman and a thief with them, as well as a boy I do not know."

"What of their horses?"

"They have the finest available, a gift from Hypatia the V, Empress of Trebizond."

"They go east?"

"Yes."

Retep spoke again in Hobgoblin. "The humans seek the Destroyer. It is the only explanation."

"Can they know where he is?"

"Something guides them."

"What guides them, Shaman?"

"I do not know."

Nadrud consulted his mental map. "The Kopets skirt the Karakum desert. Beyond that lays the Land that Fell Beneath the Hand of the Destroyer. They will skirt that land as long as possible. With good horses they can keep their distance from us."

Retep sucked his tusks. "What do you propose?"

"We must not let them find the Destroyer. That is our task. We cannot be sure of catching them by following in their footsteps."

"You mean to cut them off."

"Yes. We have camels. We will use them to our advantage."

"You mean to enter the Karakum."

"Yes."

"You mean to enter the Land that Fell Beneath the Hand of the Destroyer."

"If I must."

Retep sucked his tusks. "The desert is lean in meat and dry of blood. In the Destroyer's Land, there is nothing but poison and the death of our people."

"We can survive it for a time. We must catch the humans. We must slay them."

Retep was quiet for a time. "I serve the Right Hand of Nijumet. What is your will?"

"Slaughter all of the humans' horses save those of these two, and let the warriors eat their fill of meat and blood. Give the bodies of the slain humans to the Lesser Ones. Let them gorge themselves. Have all pack as much meat as they can carry."

"What of the humans?"

Nadrud fixed his eye on the human and spoke Turkish. "You shall go west. Take your horses. I shall give you a Lesser One to lead you to the Southern horde. Tell the Great Hobgoblin, Nijumet, that Snorri Yaroslav is dead. Tell him that the sorcerer, Reza Walladid, seeks the Destroyer, and I seek to stop him. Tell him to send reinforcements and mighty shamen east in case I should fail." He pointed his weapon at Kamose where he lay bound in the dust. "Take this one to the tents of the Shamen. They will have use for him."

Retep returned the Ten-Skull token to the human. He spoke in Hobgoblin to Nadrud. "I do not trust this one."

"Do you trust him to do what I have told him?"

"He will do that much. It is in his own interest."

"Then let him deliver my messages unto Nijumet. Then Nijumet, himself, will judge him." Nadrud switched to Turkish. "Do you understand?"

Sandor bowed slightly and smiled. "I serve the Right Hand of Nijumet."

CHAPTER THIRTY-THREE

Coel rolled up out of his blankets. Zuli made a sleepy noise but did not stir. The fire was out. The moon was bright. Márta was on watch up on a crag above camp. Coel slipped on his tunic. He stared over at Reza's bedroll. The wizard slept like a rock. He had been asleep for two days. He had woken briefly to tell Márta to keep the party heading east and to tell Marius to guard the camp each night. Reza and Coel had not spoken to each other. Coel looked up into the sky.

He had dreamed of Snorri and Oleg. He dreamed of the words of the Angeli and the warning of the elf, Fiachna. Then the dream had become horrible, too horrible to remember. He'd had the same dream and awoken sweating and shaking from it for the last three nights. He stared, red-eyed at the sorcerer where he slept. Reza's head rested upon his saddle. The box lay beneath it.

"Coel," Zuli's voice was very quiet. "Don't."

Coel belted his tunic and thrust his dagger through it. He walked over and looked down upon Reza. The sorcerer's face looked serene. Márta had mixed him a draught from powders in one of his bags. He had slept like the dead since.

Coel looked at Marius.

He stood a few feet away from the sleeping sorcerer. The priest had taken to wearing the hood of his mantle pulled low, and it was just as well. The hot weather was having no good effect on Marius' dead flesh. The priest sagged on his feet. His shoulders tilted at an angle that no one but a hunchback could sustain. He held his mace and chain in his hand, and the spiked ball swung slightly in the night wind.

"Marius."

The priest's head rose and his shoulders squared. Coel was thankful he did not have to look into Marius' eyes.

" . . . Yes."

"What is in the box?"

"In this rotting box of flesh?" Marius' voice was still a rattling, halting whisper, but it was stronger, as if he was relearning to use it. "Nothing, not even a ghost . . . naught but a shadow . . . twice removed from the man."

The hairs stood up on the back of Coel's neck. His hand went to his dagger as he stepped back. He swallowed his horror and steeled himself. "You know I speak of Reza's box."

"Yes . . . but I am forbidden to tell you."

"What is it that Reza truly seeks?"

"I am forbidden to tell you."

"Marius, is that you? I mean, truly, are you Father Marius Von Balke?"

The evening wind blew through the rocks. Coel nearly jumped when the shape before him spoke again. "Who is Marius Von Balke? A priest? He was ex-communicated for his sins . . . his order disbanded. A Crusader? He had believed that he who lived by the sword . . . died by the sword . . . so he killed women and children with an iron flail. A man? Marius Von Balke died under a saber before your eyes three days ago . . . what stands before you is . . . a cadaver . . . meat, putrefying off its bones. A soul?" The hood shook slowly.

Coel stared in horror. "What does that mean?"

"I am forbidden to tell you."

"What can I do?" Coel knew the answer even as he asked. "You said you wanted me to kill you."

Marius ceased his swaying. Coel could not see his eyes, but he could feel them boring into him from under the hood. "Yes . . . despite Reza's will . . . your sword . . . it could sever the bonds that hold me here."

Coel's skin crawled but he forced himself to take a step forward. "I have no love for you, Marius, or for your church, but by God I will not leave you like this. Tell me what I must do. Run you through? Through the heart? Behead you? Tell me what must be done, and I will do it."

Marius leaned forward. "No . . . I was wrong to ask it of you. It is . . . Reza's will that I go on; he requires my power . . . he will kill you if you release me. I am damned, Coel . . . and I can bear no more sins."

"You told Snorri it would be best if he split Luko's skull. What did you mean?"

"I am forbidden to tell you."

"Reza has the ring. What does he require your power for?"

"I am forbidden to tell you."

Coel looked down at Reza. "You protect him."

"Yes . . . it is his will."

The decision came to Coel with great clarity. "I am going to open the box."

Marius stood silent.

"Is it forbidden?"

"I am sure that it is . . . but it is Reza's word that binds me . . . and he has said nothing about the matter to me."

Coel knelt beside Reza. Snorri had told him he'd seen Reza go off with the box with a heavy iron key from a thong around his neck. Coel looked across the little camp. Orsini snored softly. Márta was still on watch. Coel drew his dagger as he reached for the neck of the sorcerer's tunic.

The chain of Marius' flail rattled as he took a step forward.

Coel tossed the blade onto a saddlebag some feet away. Marius made no move, but the intensity of his presence lessened with the dagger's threat removed. Coel lifted Reza's collar with a single finger and hooked the leather chord with the other. Reza slept on. His breathing was regular. Coel took a deep breath and closed his hand on the iron key and took the slack of the thong with the other. He smothered a grunt of exertion as his fists and forearms flexed. The chord broke in his hands.

The key was very old, wrought of black iron with three large teeth. He reached under the arch of the sorcerer's saddle and his hand closed upon the box. It was heavier than he had imagined. He drew it forth, and the scrape it made against the horse harness seemed loud enough to wake the world.

The iron straps that bound the box were ridiculously large for its size. They bound all six sides and culminated in a massive lock bolted to the front. The box itself was something other than wood. Coel could feel carvings on it but it was much to dark to read them. He went over to the embers of the fire and lit a torch in the coals. When it kindled he thrust it into the earth. Coel set the box on the ground before him and inserted the key. He turned the key and the iron straps clicked away from the lock.

Coel opened the box.

A large black hand in the shape of a fist lay within. It might have been ebony or ironwood, and even in the flickering firelight it was obviously carved with great cunning. The knuckles and tendons stood out in high relief. Coel thought it--

The hand flicked open.

Coel hurled the box away from him with a shout. The hand was already on his wrist and scuttling up his arm like a spider. Coel screamed and toppled backwards. The hand flickered up his chest unerringly as he fell. The fingers closed around Coel's throat.

The hand was huge, even though mummification had left almost no meat upon it. Thick finger bones sank into the flesh of Coel's neck and closed off his windpipe with sickening strength. Coel pulled at the fingers with all of his might. The grip was implacable as Orsini's. Coel rolled about kicking and flailing as he choked. The torch toppled. His foot struck the fire ring and embers flew up and coals crackled and popped.

A weight slammed onto Coel's chest. Zuli sat on him and her fingers clawed Coel's throat as she tried to gain purchase on the hand. She was screaming at the top of her lungs. "Orsini! Orsini!"

"Zuli!" Orsini's voice boomed. "What is wrong with him?"

"It's killing him!"

"What are you—God's balls!" Zuli's weight disappeared as Orsini flung her aside. Coel rolled and twisted. His blood pounded in his temples and his vision darkened. The dwarf's knee suddenly sank into Coel's chest and pinned him to the ground as if he was staked there. Orsini's thick fingers dug cruelly into Coel's throat. His flesh compressed as the dwarf dug under the fingers of the hand and gained purchase. Coel would have screamed if he'd had any air to do so.

Orsini tried to pry the fingers from around Coel's neck without ripping out his throat. The dwarf roared with effort. The effort failed. Coel's flailing weakened.

Zuli screamed in his ear. "Coel!"

Zuli pressed Coel's sword into his hand. His fingers closed around the hilt of the Academy blade. Even as he slowly died, the thrill went up his arm. Orsini pulled his hands away. Coel laid the blade across his throat and sawed it back and forth against the clutching horror.

The hand wriggled violently and twisted out from under the blade. It fell to the ground beside Coel's head. Coel lurched aside and shoved his sword's point feebly at it. The hand had already crawled out of range. Air flooded Coel's burning lungs as he pushed himself up to his hands and knees.

The hand scuttled towards the fire. Orsini and Zuli leaped out of its path. The box sat open, smoldering in the embers.

The hand crawled across the glowing coals and slithered inside.

Orsini lunged. He seized the box from the fire and squeezed it closed under his arm the way a wrestler would squeeze the head of his opponent. The dwarf shoved the iron straps into the lock and turned the key backwards. The mechanism clicked. Orsini tossed the box to the ground and stepped away clutching the key. The dwarf's eyes were wide and his shoulders shook with fear and revulsion.

"You have done some damn fool things, Coel! But this time you could have killed us all!"

Coel wheezed through his bruised windpipe. Even if he could have talked, he could think of nothing to refute the dwarf's words.

"The reckless courage of the Celts is legendary. It is what made them great, and it is what has nearly destroyed them as a race."

Coel lifted his head up. Reza Walladid stood over him. "Coel, it is time you and I talked."

* * *

Nadrud picked his inner teeth with a sliver of wood. There had been no hunger in the Southern Horde. Humans and livestock were plentiful, and would only grow more so as they marched into the crowded peninsula the humans called Europe. However, it had been some time since he had eaten horse. It was a delicacy, and one that hobgoblins rarely partook of. Horses could not stand their smell, and hobgoblins could not herd the rearing, powerful beasts like cows or goats. Horses could only be slaughtered when humans had fallen to hobgoblins in combat, and only then if the horses could be caught. The Mamluk's horses had been hobbled in place like a gift. Nadrud belched happily.

He and his warriors had gorged themselves. There was so much meat they did not know what to do with it all. There was no way they could pack it all with them, even on camels. The Lesser Ones lay about with their bellies distended. They had eaten the fallen humans and then gone on to eat themselves sick on horseflesh the hobgoblins could not force themselves to eat. It was probably the greatest day of their lives. The praise of their master, more meat than they could eat, and the promise of breeding rights when they returned to the horde was more fortune than they could comprehend. They belched and groaned and farted as they lolled by the fires, their pack squabbles utterly forgotten.

Nadrud rubbed his belly and looked about at his warriors. A few made a pretense of tending their weapons or mending armor. More picked their teeth or honed their tusks. The majority just held their bloated stomachs and drifted towards sleep. Nadrud allowed the lapse in discipline. Come the sun, they would ride. They would not stop until they were within the desert. The Daylami human, Ciro, had told them of secret water sources, but even they would fail once they were in the deep desert, and once in the Waste, only what they could carry would sustain them. On the meal they had eaten this night alone they would be able to march or fight for days. His warriors were champions, but Nadrud had few illusions. Soon enough, hunger and thirst would gnaw them all like rust chewed away even the finest steel. The trek across the Great Waste was a calculated gamble. It would be a death march. Many of his warriors would not survive it. Nadrud took up his knife-axe and began honing the nicks out of its scythe-like inner edge with a stone.

The humans had to be slain at all costs, and once in the waste, Nadrud had allies he could call upon.

CHAPTER THIRTY-FOUR

"Let me tell you something, Coel, something I suspect you already know."

Reza looked worn to the bone, but his eyes were clear. Coel sat on a saddle and regarded the sorcerer across the campfire and rubbed his throat. His voice was little more than a rasp. "What is that, then?"

"Everything the Church has told you is a lie."

Coel stared. His anger and distrust with the Church in Rome was deep and longstanding, but to hear the sorcerer say it aloud still startled him. He had to fight the urge to look behind him to see who might be listening to their blasphemies. "Why do you have a dead man's hand in your box?"

"It acts as a compass."

"To find what?"

"To find the rest of his body, as you already suspect."

"What do you mean everything the Church has told me is a lie? And whose body do you seek?"

"I seek the man you call Tomas Sander."

"Tomas Sander!" Coel shot to his feet. "Saint Tomas, himself?"

"Yes."

Coel's mind reeled and he wondered if this was a nightmare. "What, you want to speak with his shade, then?"

"No, I intend to raise him from the dead and take his power."

Coel nearly stumbled backward over his saddle. "You are insane!"

"I feel somewhat fatigued, but I assure you, I am not insane. Were I a lunatic, Orsini would not associate himself with me in a business venture."

Orsini nodded. "This is true."

"You are going to resurrect him?" Coel pointed at Father Marius. "Like that, then?"

"No. Father Marius has not been resurrected."

"Well, he looked god damned dead to me!"

"Yes, it is unfortunate that his body was killed. However, his spirit was still bound to it. What was required was the re-animation of his flesh, a related, but much different sort of sorcery."

"And just what is that supposed to mean?"

"I could explain it to you, but you and I have more important matters to discuss. What matters is that to achieve my goal, I need the powers of a man like Marius. I could not afford to let him die. So, I used the ring to re-animate his body. His powers remain intact."

Coel stared at the armored, rotting scarecrow that had once been Marius. "That is a hell of a thing to do to a man."

"There was no other alternative, and, had you seen Father Marius' behavior amongst the pagans in the Baltic on crusade, you might not feel so sorry for him. Snorri knew somewhat of these things, and you saw how he felt about it. Nevertheless, I give you my word, when my use for Father Marius has ended, I shall release him to face his maker."

Coel looked at the box where it sat at Reza's feet. "So, that is the hand of Tomas Sander, then."

"Yes."

"You and Marius . . . re-animated it? In the Angeli's tower in Trebizond?"

"Yes."

"And that is his ring you wear?"

"Yes."

"His hand led you to the ring in the hobgoblin camp."

"Yes."

"And now it leads you to his body."

"Yes."

"Saint Tomas is a Holy Martyr." Coel shook his head. "What is a Christian Saint doing with an Egyptian ring, much less one with the power of necromancy?"

"Because Tomas Sander is not a Christian Saint."

There was absolute silence around the campfire.

Coel blinked. " . . . What?"

"He was neither Christian nor Muslim, but a pagan, and a wizard of great power. His real name was Tuman Sunqur."

Coel just stared.

"The Church has lied to you, Coel. The Hobgoblin Hordes had, indeed, been driven from Europe, but they had consolidated in the plains of Kazakhstan, and they were far from beaten. Another wave of them was coming through the Doors between Worlds. The armies of man, elf, and dwarf were nearly spent. The Pope and the Patriarch both called upon any who could wield power to aid humanity in the final battle. Tuman Sunqur answered that call, and called upon power unlike that ever seen before in this world. The hobgoblins were annihilated, the Doors between Worlds closed, and the Great Waste was born in the aftermath. Sunqur himself was consumed by his sorcery. Or so it was thought."

"Saint Tomas is entombed in Rome. People make pilgrimages to his shrine. I know men who have seen it."

"I suspect people visit the bones of some poor priest who shall never have a marker of his own. The Holy League of Humanity could not have a pagan sorcerer for a savior, Coel, so history was re-written, and the legend of Saint Tomas was born. Who was to know it was not really a pious priest from Flanders who had been anointed by God in humanity's darkest hour? The assembled armies only saw a man in a monk's robe before they fell back. Today, only the Pope, the Patriarch, the Grand Master of Grand Triumphe and a few of the highest cardinals know the real truth. There are some, such as the Blue Robe sect, who also know. The elves and the dwarves know, and some others may suspect, but they know the wisdom of silence."

Coel was incredulous. "Orsini, is this true?"

"What Reza has told you is one of the things we dwarves are

foresworn from revealing in exchange for the tolerance of the two Churches. The elves must indeed know as well, of course, but no one communes with them but madmen and the Irish."

Coel looked back to Reza. "So, you intend to resurrect this Tuman Sunqur and steal his power, then?"

"I intend to have his knowledge, one way or another. I will not lie to you, Coel. I seek his power for my own reasons. However, as I told you before, I have no wish to live in a world ravaged by the hobgoblins. I will use that power to destroy them or turn them back if I am able. To acquire that power, I must have the aid of Father Marius. To reach Sunqur's resting place alive, I suspect we will need your sword arm as well."

Coel scowled into the fire.

"The question is, Coel, do you wish to remain with us?"

Orsini looked at Coel pointedly. Coel looked away from the dwarf. Zuli caught his eyes and held them. Her eyes slid to where Luko lay curled in his blankets and then back. Coel closed his eyes wearily. Facing the Empress Hypatia had been easier. He did not need the dwarf's accusing looks to tell him that Snorri would have stayed. He would stay for Zuli and Luko. He would stay to honor his contract with Reza. He would stay for Márta because . . .

Coel stared into the campfire and the glowing coals offered him no counsel.

Boots crunched in the darkness, and Márta walked into the circle of the firelight with her bow in her hand. She glanced about at the party assembled around the fire and then looked inquiringly at Reza. The sorcerer opened his hand casually. "Coel had questions, Márta. I have done my best to answer them."

"I will go back if you wish to speak further."

Reza smiled at Coel. "Do you have more questions?"

"Many," Coel rose and took up his bow. "But I will go take my watch."

Coel wished for the thousandth time that Snorri were here.

* * *

The mountains grew lower as they rode. Past the lower peaks, Coel could see the Karakum Desert shimmer off in the distance. Reza frequently consulted the hand, and Coel clucked his horse to a safe distance whenever the sorcerer opened the box. Coel rode up to Orsini. The dwarf sat slightly hunched in the saddle, and his face told Coel his wound was bothering him more than he could hide anymore. He also knew the dwarf did not wish to discuss it.

"So where are we?"

Orsini seemed pleased for the distraction. He scanned the mountains ahead and the desert to the north. "We are dropping elevation steadily. We descend out of the Kopets and will soon be in the mountains of the Afghans. South of them is the Hindu Kush, northeast the Tien Shan, and southeast the Himalayas. In between are vast deserts and plains, jungles and forests. Asia is huge, Coel, it could swallow the world you know half a dozen times and still not be filled.

"But, the Great Waste splits it, does it not?"

"Oh, yes. The Great Waste closed the Silk Road, decimated the Tatar peoples and swallowed the Aral Sea."

"So we ride towards it, then?"

"We are still south of most of it."

"Then where does Reza take us?"

"Where he is led." Orsini shrugged. "I do not believe he yet knows, though he has suspicions." The dwarf changed the subject. "Let's have a look at your eye."

Orsini reined in his pony and slid from the saddle. He winced as he landed. The rest of the party halted as Coel dismounted and took a knee. Orsini's hand's shook as he pulled at the knots of the bandage. Márta stepped forward. "Let me do--"

Zuli shoved herself in front of Márta and knelt before Coel. "I will do it."

Márta bit her lip and walked back to Reza. Orsini rose up heavily. "Perhaps I will walk a bit and stretch out the kinks."

Zuli began slowly unwinding the bandage around Coel's head. She wet her fingers from a water bag and pressed it against the cloth wherever blood had caked to loosen it. Coel peered at her with his good eye.

"Why do you hate Márta so?"

Zuli shrugged without taking her eyes from her work. "She is young, pretty, and innocent. You are in love with her. She is in love with you. That is more than enough reason."

Coel grew distinctly uncomfortable. "Well, you know I--"

"You are fond of me, Coel, but you are not in love with me. Do not bother denying it."

Coel didn't. He switched tactics. He looked at Zuli soulfully with his good eye. "You are saying you do not love me, then?"

Zuli's lips twisted into a smirk. "You have a certain loutish charm."

"Did you love Snorri?"

Zuli stopped fussing with his bandage. "You and I share a blanket, and I am fond of you. So I will tell you something. Love is not a word that comes easily to me. I have lain in the palaces of pashas while they sifted diamonds across my body like sand between their fingers, and I have been beaten and raped in the gutters of Cairo. I have had more lovers than you can possibly imagine and more of them are now dust than alive. I can count the people I have loved with one hand."

"Did you love Snorri, then?"

"I loved the first boy who took me. Though that was long ago. I loved Hypatia the IV, and because I loved her, watching her grow old killed me. She was never jealous of it, but I know it killed her, too." Her blue-green gaze misted with memory. "I left before it could become a bitterness between us, and because I knew I could not stand to watch her die."

"How old are you, then--Gah!"

Coel flinched as Zuli squeezed his swollen nose. "Even a Welshman should know that is a terrible question to ask a woman." She smiled slightly. "However, I will tell you something no one else knows."

"What is that?"

"I found my first gray hair twenty years ago." She shrugged. "I am still awaiting the second."

"How much elven blood have you, then?"

Zuli's face went hard. "One fourth, or so I am told."

"We have not spoken of it, but the elvish woman, Fiachna, you and she recognized each other."

"I told you before. I once made an attempt to find my family. I made my way across Europe. I went to Ireland, and from there I was granted an audience on the Elvish Isle of Man."

"What happened?"

Coel drew back. It was terrible to see a face so beautiful twisted with hate.

"I was a mongrel amongst them. They spurned me. They said my blood was too weak and my life too tainted. Oh, I met those who were my blood relations. Fiachna is the head of my clan. They treated me like a mutt whining at the kitchen door. They stopped short of throwing stones at me, but they made it very clear I was not welcome. I was lost after I left your islands in the west. Any human relations I had were dead, and I was a pariah amongst the thieves and street performers I knew in the east. It was not long before I fell in with of the Assassins."

Her eyes softened as she stared into the distance. "To answer your question, Coel. I loved Snorri, and yes, I would have married him. I would have gone to the Orkney Isles with him had he asked, and I would have stayed with him until he died. I loved him so much I was afraid of him, and that is why I fell into your blankets in the Caucasus."

"Oh."

Zuli covered his right eye with her palm as she pulled the last of the linen away. "Can you open the eye?"

"I think so."

"See if you can flutter your eyelashes against my palm."

Coel blinked his eyes. Zuli smiled. "Good." She cracked her fingers open slightly. Coel snarled and squeezed his eyes shut at the piercing light. She kept her hand shading his face. "Open your eyes."

Coel opened them a crack. Zuli held up a finger near the corner of his left eye. "Follow my finger."

Coel tracked her finger. His right eye ached as it followed. Her finger passed his nose and went to the right side of his face. "Can you see it?"

"Yes."

"How many of them do you see?"

"One."

"Is it blurry?"

"No."

"How does your eye feel?"

"It hurts."

"Good. Marius could have healed your eye had you been blinded, but I do not think you would have liked it."

Coel looked over to where the priest sat hunched in his saddle. His black mantle covered him. Each day his horse grew more hesitant to carry him.

Zuli licked her fingers and began wiping away the dried blood from Coel's face. "Orsini has told me of your exploits in Moscow and Smolensk, and I have seen firsthand your adventures since. I have two pieces of advice for you."

"Oh?"

"Yes, stop sitting down during swordfights, it is suicidal."

Coel stiffened.

"And second, you are a very handsome man. You must cease this stopping of stones and fists with your face."

Coel grinned. "Is that why you dove from the yardarm of the *Olga* to save me?"

Zuli lost her smile. "Orsini spoke the truth. Elves speak in riddles and dream the future. I am not an elf, but their blood runs in my veins. Sometimes I have dreams, Coel. Sometimes they come true, sometimes not. Sometimes I see things I cannot understand. Sometimes they nearly drive me mad."

"I cannot imagine."

Zuli rose. Her eyes stared into some terrible distance. "Remember your promise to me, Coel. Do not let me fall into the hands of the Assassins, nor those of the hobgoblins. It would be far better for me to die by your hand than to endure anything they have in store for me."

CHAPTER THIRTY-FIVE

The party approached the village fully armed and armored. Dogs barked in alarm and village men peered over walls of piled stone. Coel led, looking out for archers on the clay rooftops. The little party presented quite a sight, though precautions had been taken. Father Marius wore the cowl of his mantle low with one of Reza's woolen shawls pulled over his head even lower. He kept his rotting hands covered under the thick knots of the garment's fringe. Together, Márta and Zuli had poured nearly all of their perfume over the priest. Marius rode in an invisible cloud that reeked of jasmine and rose oil, but up close, the lingering stink of death was still unmistakable. Zuli had produced a black robe and veil for herself and sat her horse sidesaddle looking every inch a respectable Muslim woman. Márta wore her full armor, but her mail aventail was pinned to the front of her helmet so that the glittering chain formed a veil that showed only her eyes, and they were heavily kohled. Both Reza and Orsini wore low white turbans. Reza wore his best silks, while Orsini rode sheathed in his full plate armor.

Coel felt ridiculous with a turban on his head, but he kept his mind on business. He dismounted with his bow in hand and arrows sheafed as he fell into step beside Reza. "What is this place?"

"A village, like many others in these mountains, but this one is near the river Morghab, so it is larger than some and more accustomed to strangers. We are in the Paropamisus Mountains. The Morghab is the biggest river running through them. This village is part of the trade route through the range and the path of pilgrims from the east who go to Mecca. They will have camels for sale and will be pleased at the profit we give them."

They did not look pleased. Spearheads glinted dully over the rock wall and dark-eyed, bearded faces glared. Reza stopped a little distance before the wooden gate and raised his hand as he hailed them. There was a great deal of murmuring behind the wall.

"What are they doing?"

"Deciding whether to kill us outright or see what we want. Our garb, armor, and horses show that we are wealthy, and our lack of numbers make their sword arms itch. The strangeness of the two, together, fills them with uncertainty," Reza smiled. "Let me do the talking."

An older man came through the gate. He wore white homespun like the rest, but the wide belt of his tunic was worked with silver and his beard had been hennaed red. Men in sheepskins and festooned with swords and knives whose blades curved in every direction followed him. The men here wore woolen caps rather than turbans. They gazed long at Reza's silken robes, and they looked at Coel's red hair and the height of his bow with wariness. When Coel looked upon them they averted their gaze and made the sign against the evil eye.

Reza made a graceful motion with his hand and spoke in a language Coel did not understand. He spoke for some time, and the headman's gaze went from wariness to awe. Reza turned to Coel and spoke quietly in passable French.

"This is the village headman, Nasuh. I have told him that Marius is a great holy man from North Africa named Sahid. He is on a pilgrimage to spread the word of the Prophet amongst the idol worshippers of the Indias. You are a barbarian infidel of the West who was converted by him, and Orsini is a non-human who embraced Allah at his feet. Zuli is his sister. Márta was a gift from the Seljuk Sultan who bowed to him in Ankara. I was a gift from the Vizier of Baghdad so that he would have an interpreter as he went into lands unknown by the faithful. He has freed me for my devotion and piety. There are few greater deeds than freeing a fellow Muslim who is a slave. I have also told him that Marius has taken a vow of silence until he has reached his destination."

"That much manure may just break the backs of our horses."

"That is why we are acquiring camels."

Coel swallowed his misgivings. He bowed and touched his forehead and lips. "*Ah Salaam a-likam, Nasuh.*"

Nasuh beamed at Coel and returned the gesture. "*Wa a-likam Salaam!*"

Reza smiled. "That was well done."

526 | CHUCK ROGERS

"I learnt it in Spain."

Orsini slid from his horse and took Marius' reins as Nasuh ushered them through the gate. Crowds of children clustered about gawking. Men bowed before Marius as he rode in, and veiled women stood in doorways and whispered to one another. Goats watched the commotion uncomprehendingly. Chickens and dogs ran underfoot. Reza spoke with the headman as they walked and translated for Coel.

"Nasuh says they have camels for sale, though not many. He says that many strangers have been coming into the mountains. Mostly Persians, and they are paying good silver for camels and oxen, but not horses."

"Those would be the agents of the hobgoblins."

"Those are my thoughts as well. Nasuh also says he has told these strangers he would have more camels by the end of the month, but he considers it an honor for them to be in the hands of a great holy man on pilgrimage amongst the unbelievers."

"For a suitable price."

"Indeed. He has asked if we would stay the night, but I have told him that our master's vision tells him he cannot rest until he has reached the Indias."

Men took their mounts and led them to the corral. Children scampered about oohing and aahing at the fine horses. Luko watched the other children eagerly. He looked up at Zuli, and she inclined her veiled head. Luko ran shouting amongst a group of boys as they kicked a stuffed leather ball. Shouts and laughter rang out as Luko ran zigzagging through the other boys and usurped the ball.

Coel smiled proudly. "The boy is fast."

"These are village boys," Reza shrugged. "Luko is a Cuman from the steppes."

Márta spoke through her veil of chainmail as they watched him play. His blonde hair flew as he ran. "Perhaps this would be a good place for him. The Hobgoblin Horde has passed this place by. He would be safe here."

"No," Reza frowned. "We shall keep him with us."

Orsini cocked his head. "I think I must disagree with you, Walladid. Wherever it is our path leads us, I have the utmost faith that it shall be no place for a child."

Reza's face tensed but his voice stayed pleasant. "I think I must disagree with you, as well, Orsini. These are hill people. Luko is a child of the steppe. Once we left, they would make a slave of him and sell him. The boy is young, with blonde hair and blue eyes. Can you guess what kind of slave they would make of him? He would end up in the harem of some local satrap within a week."

Coel scowled. "I agree, but what if you tell them that he was a slave, freed by our great holy man, wouldn't they take him in for his holiness or luck or some such?"

Reza visibly smothered his irritation. "I could do that, and he would grow up, grow old and die in this mud pit tending goats."

"Better that than the hobgoblins or the Assassins."

"Both the hobgoblins and the Assassins are behind us!" Reza unclenched his teeth and took a weary breath. "Listen, Coel. I have thought for some time that I could use a new apprentice. Your friend, Snorri, was thinking of adopting the boy. I do not think he would want him dropped off here. The boy has shown himself a quick learner. Already we know he can cook, ride, and is an able shot with a sling. When we return to civilization, I was thinking of having him instructed in letters and mathematics. When he is older? The bow, the lance and the sword. With us, he has a future. Here, his future will be decided with the first basket of dung they have him carry. Would you choose this for him?"

"Well, I mean--"

Reza tossed his head. "Why do we not ask the boy, himself? Luko!"

The blonde head whipped up. Luko ran through his new playmates and skidded to a halt before Reza. "Yes, Sir?"

Coel had to admit the boy was learning Latin remarkably fast under Zuli's tutelage. Reza took a knee and looked Luko in the eye. "Luko, Coel would like to know if you want to stay here with your new friends."

Luko's blue eyes flew wide with alarm.

"Or would you like to go on with us?"

"Stay with you! Go with you!" He looked fearfully at Coel. "Please!"

Reza spoke again in French. "Now, you tell the boy he is staying here."

Luko stared up at Coel pleadingly.

Coel reached down and rumpled his hair. "You are with us, Luko. I just wanted to know what you wanted."

Luko looked back at the boys playing and then back at Coel uncertainly. Coel jerked his head. "Go play, but be ready to leave when we call you."

"You promise?"

"I promise."

Luko sped back into the game. Coel shook his head at Reza. "Remind me never to play chess with you."

Reza nodded. "Ah, and here are our new mounts."

Nasuh came forward, and behind several men led two strings of camels. Coel eyed the dozen or so humpbacked beasts warily. "I have never ridden such an animal."

"You are about to learn."

Coel had seen a few such beasts in Spain, and again when he had first encountered hobgoblins on the Russian steppes. This was his first good look at a camel up close. He was revolted. The animals stank. Their stilt-like legs and long necks made them look ridiculous even without the double humps. Their fluttering eyelashes and harelip faces made them positively unmanly as mounts. The animals looked like some terrible mistake or an even worse joke.

Coel folded his arms. "I do not like them."

"I suspect they will not like you, either. They rarely like anyone. Be careful. They spit upon those they dislike, and bite and kick those who handle them with an uncertain hand." Reza and Márta began appraising the line of camels and picking out specific animals.

"God's codpiece!" Orsini lurched back a step. A camel had

curled its serpentine neck over his shoulder, and a thick swath of green goo ran down the chest plate of his blue-steel armor. "Bastard! Get away from me!"

Márta giggled behind her armored veil. "That one is a cow."

"I do not care!"

Coel spoke with his newfound knowledge. "It is spitting, Orsini. I do not believe the beast likes you."

"On the contrary," Márta could not keep the mirth out of her voice. "She is not spitting. She is drooling. It is not unknown for camels to fall in love with their masters. This one has grown fond of Orsini."

The villagers laughed and clapped their hands on Orsini's armored shoulders. Orsini glared as he tried to wipe the camel froth away. It formed thick, viscous webs between his fingers and his armor. "The beast has befouled me!"

Nasuh smiled and spoke. Reza smiled as he translated. "Nasuh says you have a love match with that camel. He says such a thing is rare and that you are very lucky. He says that camel will carry you to the ends of the earth."

"Well, find me another!" Orsini flinched away as the camel's head craned towards him. Its huge brown eyes gazed dreamily at him through its smoky lashes.

"I have already purchased it for you. I suggest you make friends with it."

Orsini glared. "If the vermin soils any of my silks, I shall crush its skull!"

"You will thank me before this journey is over," Reza suggested.

"I thank the gods we are not purchasing elephants!" Orsini shoved the drooling beast's head away from him. "Be off!"

The camel rocked forward and bent its legs, kneeling first from the front and then the back. It rested on the ground and waited to be saddled. The villagers cheered the dwarf's apparent command of camels. A man pressed a long riding switch into Orsini's hand.

The villagers began saddling the camels. Men came out of

houses carrying saddlebags of brightly patterned carpeting. Others began filling hide water sacks at the well. Women were wrapping dried meat and filling sacks with parched grain.

Coel watched the proceedings. "What about the horses?"

"We leave them."

Coel's heart sank in his chest. "It grieves me to leave my Spaniard."

"Yes, they are fine horses, but they cannot last in the desert. Camels require neither shoeing nor fodder. They can travel forty miles a day carrying four hundred-pound loads. They can go days, indeed weeks without water and live on thorn and scrub. Your Barb would die in places where we may go."

"It seems like a lopsided trade."

"It is. Nasuh and his people cannot believe their good fortune. The legend of Sahid, the pious pilgrim, who traded horses for camels will live in these mountains for generations."

Orsini began overseeing the transfer of the party's goods onto the pack beasts. Other beasts were saddled for riding. Coel eyed the A-framed, four legged saddles. "They look like stools."

"And function as such in camp," Reza agreed. "You will find them quite convenient." Coel watched with interest as Reza took a riding switch and expertly stepped into the saddle of his chosen animal. He took the reins and flipped the switch lightly against its haunches. "Hut!"

The camel lurched up onto its feet with a great rolling motion. Reza called out. "Luko!"

The boy came running as the rest of the party eased themselves onto their beasts. Coel swung a leg between the two humps of his camel and took the long reins. The creature rose beneath him like a boat in a high sea. Coel checked to see that his bow and his javelin case were within easy reach and was satisfied. Despite being so far up in the air, it was a surprisingly comfortable perch.

"Orsini!" Reza's voice sparked with annoyance. "Come along!"

Orsini stood with his hand on the hilt of his shortsword. His camel gazed upon him with adoring doe-like eyes. Thick drool spilled down its lips and hung suspended in the air.

The dwarf was horrified.

"Orsini!" Snapped Reza. "Mount the beast and let us be off!"

"Yes, Orsini," Coel smiled. "Better you mounting the beast than the beast mounting you."

"You are not one to be talking of unnatural conjugations, Celt!"

Coel whipped his switch through the air and made a pretense of listening to the sound it made. It pleased him immensely to have finally one-upped the dwarf.

"And wipe that smirk off your face!"

Coel ignored him.

"By the Great Spirit's sweaty stones, I swear I will . . . "

The villagers took the reins of the camels and lead the party ceremoniously through the village. The villagers shouted and bowed and wished them well. Some of the women made u'uing noises as they approached the gate. Nasuh clasped his hands and spoke rapidly at Reza. The sorcerer turned and looked back at Marius with a frown.

Coel looked about. Everyone seemed very happy. He spoke low in French. "What is it?"

"They want Marius to bless the village."

Coel looked back at the huddled form under the shawl. Reza spoke in French. "Marius, give the villagers a blessing."

Marius did not move.

"Marius," Reza's voice stayed pleasant, but his eyes lit. "Give the villagers a blessing. I command it."

Marius sat up in the saddle. The villagers became very quiet. Many knelt. Marius raised his hands, and the shawl's fringe fell away. Coel flinched as he looked at the priest's mottled hands. The nails had fallen from several of the fingers. Marius hands went to cowl and he pushed back his shawl and hood.

"Marius!" Reza shouted.

The mid-morning sun fell on the face of Father Marius.

Villagers screamed.

Marius' straw blonde hair lay matted against his skull. The flesh of his face sagged on his bones and was purpled and blackened with dead blood where it was not white as chalk or gray as slate. Cracks in the skin exposed open wounds. Insects had been at him. Coel had seen men wearing such faces before. He had seen them on the fallen, littering week-old battlefields. Only Marius' flat bloodshot eyes were alive. They looked down upon the villagers with horrible intensity. Village men shouted in outrage as Marius began slowly drawing a cross in the air with his right fingers. They retreated in mortal terror as the German priest's voice rose in a horrid rasp.

"*In Nomine Patris, et Filius, et Spiritus Sanctus . . .*"

Women seized children and ran into their homes. Nasuh howled and made the sign against the evil eye. The village men shook their weapons in religious rage and retreated in mortal terror. Others seized up sticks and stones. Márta's bow was in her hand. Coel drew a javelin.

"*Amen.*" finished the priest.

"Damn you, Marius!" Reza's face was horrible to behold as he raised the ring. "You will pay for that! By the White Christ you worship, I shall show you what suffering really is! Now, cover yourself!"

Marius covered himself again. Nasuh stood transfixed in terror before the gate. Reza pulled a sack of coins from a saddlebag and tossed it at his feet. Nasuh stared at it as if Reza had thrown him a scorpion. Reza's face twisted, and his switch flicked across his camel's haunches. "Hut! Hut! Hut!"

The camel lumbered forward, and Nasuh leaped from Reza's path. Reza shouted back. "Márta! Coel! Guard the rear!"

Coel switched his camel as he saw Márta do and the beast turned beneath him. He slid his shield onto his arm. The rest of the party filed through the gate. Marius' camel made no effort to move forward and Zuli seized its reins. The village was turning into a mob. The shouting and screaming rose in volume. Coel raised his shield and a thrown stone thudded against it. "Zuli! Get Marius out of here!"

Zuli cringed as a clay brick hit her in the side. A javelin sank into Orsini's saddlebag. Coel's camel honked as a stick struck it.

"God damn it! Márta! Get them moving!" Coel leaped from his camel. He had no idea how to fight from atop it. He dropped his shield and the Academy blade sang forth. Coel whirled it about his body in the two-hand sword drill. His voice rose to a parade-ground roar.

"By God, I will behead every last one of you!"

The mob knew not his words, but his intentions were clear. A rock hit him in the chest of his armored jack. Coel pointed his sword towards the stone thrower. "Fine, then! You first, fuzzy!"

The man howled forward brandishing a huge knife. "*Allahu Ahkbar!*"

The villager raised his knife overhead. Coel crouched and ran him through with a stop-thrust. The man gasped in surprise and fell to his knees. Coel yanked his sword free, and the man fell on his face.

Village women screamed. Men roared in indignation. Four ran forward with fanatic fervor in their eyes. One stumbled as an arrow sank into his chest. A second shaft sprouted next to it as if by magic. The man fell, and another of Márta's arrows transfixed the next man through the belly. The third villager took a wild cut at Coel with his longknife. Coel used the reach of his own blade to intercept the blow and lop off the man's arm at the elbow. The Afghani sank to his knees screaming and clutching the stump.

The fourth man threw his club at Coel and fell back into the mob. The villagers shrieked insults and imprecations. Coel pinwheeled his bloody sword around in an arc overhead. "Come on!"

The u'uing of the women rose to a fever pitch. Men howled and shook knives and fists, but no more stones flew and no more of the mob came forward. Coel scooped up his shield and backed up towards his camel. Márta sat her mount with an arrow nocked.

Coel snarled. His camel was six feet at the shoulder and had no stirrups. "How the hell do I mount this thing?"

"Just climb!" Marat cried. "I'll cover you!"

Coel sheathed his sword and shoved his shield into the pack straps. The camel groaned and listed to one side as he leaped up and grabbed the saddle horns of brass. Coel grunted with the weight of his armor as he pulled himself up between its humps. He swung a leg over and reached for reins.

"Go!" Márta covered the crowd with her bow. "Use your switch as Reza did!"

Coel pulled his switch from his saddle strap and whacked the camel on its side. "Hut! Hut! Hut!" He nearly fell off as the camel lumbered forward in a great rollicking motion. Coel hung on for dear life as the beast charged down the path after the rest of the party. He could feel the blood of the fallen villagers staining his hands. He felt like throwing up. "Zuli! Are you--"

Coel's head whipped around. His blood froze.

The villagers had turned away from the gate and clustered back into the village square. The chorus of their screaming and u'uing rose and fell in an orgiastic frenzy. The sound had changed from fury and fear to bloodlust. Cutting through the sound of human hatred were the high, heart-stopping screams of horses being slaughtered.

Coel leaped from his camel.

"Coel!" Márta shouted above the din. "Do not!"

"Bastards!" Coel shook with fury. "Bloody red-handed bastards!" Coel's world turned red with rage. His sword sang from its sheath. The thrill of it ran up his arm and sat in the lowest part of his brain like a glowing halo of vengeance. He took the sword in both hands and broke into a run back towards the village.

"Coel!"

The war scream tore out of his throat in savage response to the howls of hate in the village and the mortal agony of the horses.

The scream cut short as a loop of rope fell over Coel's head from behind and suddenly cinched his arms against his sides. He ran out of rope and his feet flew out from under him as his momentum met the weight of Márta's camel. Coel struggled to his knees. Boots crunched behind him and Márta seized his shoulders. "Coel! For the love of--"

"I will kill them! I will kill them all!" He heaved Márta off as he vaulted to his feet. The party had left over a dozen mounts behind. The screams grew more horrible as the hobbled horses were hacked to death beneath the villager's knives.

"Control yourself!" Coel fell forward as his leg was yanked out from under him. Orsini's voice thundered. "There is nothing we can do!"

Coel heaved beneath the hands that held him. Tears spilled out of his eyes as he thrashed. He knew the sound of his own horse even among the cacophony of agony. He could hear his Barb being butchered. "I will kill them! I will--" Coel's muscles contracted against his bones like cables as he fought the ropes and hands that restrained him. He got a knee beneath him and heaved.

"Orsini! Hold him!"

Coel reared up with insane strength.

"Márta!" The dwarf shouted desperately. "Help me! He's--"

Coel's crazed scream echoed off the cliffs.

"I will kill you all! Do you hear me? I will come back and kill every last one of you! God as my witness, I will come back and kill you in your kitchens! I will kill you in front of your children and burn down your houses! I'll sow the earth with your blood and salt it! I will--"

The halo of hate in the bottom of Coel's skull shattered apart. His head snapped forward beneath a heavy blow. Pinpricks of purple light spattered across his vision and he reeled around drunkenly. He watched with detached interest as Márta pulled back her mailed fist.

Márta's armored hand flew at his jaw as slow as a dream.

It was the last thing Coel saw.

CHAPTER THIRTY-SIX

"How can anything live here?" Coel had seen first-hand the severities of the Russian steppes and the seared scrub of Spain. He had heard tales of the burning sands of the Sahara. The desert before him was the harshest place he had ever seen. Everything was burned brown by the sun. The rocks and soil were all umbers and burnt siennas. The very air, itself, seemed to boil over the land.

"This is the Karakum. Much lives here." Zuli's finger swept the arid vista. "There, you see the channel in the sand? During the rains, there is a river there. There is water here even now if you know where to look for it. It is a harsh place, but more life abounds than you can imagine."

Orsini's shoulders rounded with fatigue. "It looks dead to me."

"No," Coel pointed as a hawk wheeled across the sky. "Zuli is right. Where there are hawks, there is meat. Where there is meat, there is water."

Zuli smiled.

Orsini made a weary noise. His camel ambled forward without needing direction. Zuli watched him. "He's not well. He's not well at all."

"How are you?" They had lain together but not made love for the last two nights. Zuli's side was blackened and swollen where the villager's brick had hit her. Coel had bound it tightly with linen.

"I think the bastard broke my rib, perhaps two of them."

"You could--"

"I do not want Marius touching me."

"I understand."

"No, you do not. It is not him. It is just that what he has become resembles things I have seen before. I do not think I could stand it."

"Well what do you think possessed Marius to do that, then?" No one had spoken of the incident in the village. They had ridden almost non-stop for the last two days and gone almost due north. They'd had cold camps and stopped for only a few hours rest each night. They left the mountains behind them. It was hard to tell, but Coel thought they might well have covered a hundred miles.

"Well, despite his current circumstances, he is a Catholic priest. Reza told him to bless a village full of heathens," She shrugged. "He was bound to react badly."

"Do not play games."

Zuli was silent.

"What is his relationship to Reza?"

"I do not know," Zuli's nose wrinkled. "I first met Marius in Kiev, but I knew in that moment he would be trouble. He is Brethren of the Blade. They were an Order of Crusaders and Christian fanatics, as Snorri told you." Zuli watched the priest's back as he rode. "I have seduced Crusaders and Catholic priests. They have their failings like other men, but I can tell you, a man like Marius would never serve a Persian sorcerer. At least, not willingly."

"So Reza has some kind of hold on him, then. One that stretches back, back before he was killed."

"That is a reasonable assumption."

"You think he was trying to defy Reza, then?"

"Perhaps, within the limits of his condition, he was trying to rebel against Reza's will. You might do the same if you were in his state."

"I might," Coel's jaw set as anger sparked in his breast. "But I will not forgive him for my horse. Not now, nor ever." He shook his head. "And his little rebellion against Reza nearly killed us all."

"Perhaps that was his intent."

Coel's anger was startled out of him. "And what does that mean, then?"

Zuli peered off into the sands. "Perhaps he thought getting us killed would be a kindness."

"Now that is a hell of a thing to say."

"I am thinking of Luko," Zuli's eyes went to the boy. He rode beside Reza and sat his own camel like he was the king of the world.

"You mean what Marius said when we found him."

"Marius said it would be best if we split his skull right then."

"And Snorri nearly split his for saying it."

"Yes, but I do not think Marius said it to be cruel. As I said, I think it was meant as kindness."

"Snorri called that kind of Christianity salvation on the end of a sword."

"You are still angry over your horse. You are not listening to me."

"Bloody right I am angry about my horse! God damned heathen savages!"

"You are not one to speak of heathen savages," Zuli shook her head at him. "Killing them in their kitchens, Coel? In front of their children? You should have heard yourself. There is a reason why the Romans feared your kind and a reason why Caesar conquered them. You Celts are a mad, beautiful people. Pride and passion rule you. It makes you dangerous and foolish."

Coel's lips twisted with spite. "Did Hypatia whisper that in your ear while you were embracing, then?"

"You were absolutely the furthest thing from our minds."

Coel ground his teeth but could think of no rejoinder that would not seem infantile. Zuli lifted her chin. "Would you like some advice?"

"Have I a choice?"

"Talk to Márta."

Coel's anger was startled from him for the second time. Zuli switched her camel to catch up with Orsini.

* * *

Coel checked the stars and rose to take his watch. Zuli had crept into his blankets and not said a word to him. He had stroked her hair as she snuggled against him, and they had slept. He donned a tunic, breeches and pulled his armored jack over it. During the day, the sun had been so hot he could not stand to wear armor. Now he welcomed the weight of the jack and its warmth. He took his sword and bow and walked out into the dark. An outcropping of rocks screened the party from anyone watching from the south, and its elevation gave them a good view of the desert surrounding them. Márta's voice spoke out of the dark. "You are early."

"I know."

"Is everything all right?" Márta rose from her perch as Coel clambered up.

"We have not spoken much of late."

"I know."

"Are you all right?"

"No, I am not."

Coel was startled by the admission. "I am sorry."

"I did not like killing the villagers. I did not like it at all. I feel sick."

"Aye, I felt much the same, until they started slaughtering our horses, and now?" Frustration tightened Coel's chest. "It was senseless. All of it."

They stood together in silence and listened to the desert wind moan through rocks.

"Coel, I am scared."

"Scared? You?" Coel tried to force levity into his voice. "Márta of the Magyars fears neither man nor beast."

"Everything scares me. You scare me, Coel, with the things you say and do and the thoughts I think about you. Marius scares me. I am frightened for Orsini," Her gaze tracked out into the dark desert. "Reza scares me most."

"Do you fear him, or fear for him?"

"I have never seen Reza like this. He is at the limit of his strength. The potions he has me mix for him at night empower him, but even they extract their costs, and I hate that ring. He leans upon it like a crutch. The battle with the Mamluks, raising Marius, every use of power has its price. He cannot endure much more."

"And we go to resurrect a saint, or the most powerful sorcerer the world has ever seen. We raise him to steal his power."

Márta remained silent.

"Can he do it?"

"I fear he may be too weak."

"What happens if he fails?"

"Perhaps nothing."

Coel did not like the way she said perhaps. "Or perhaps what?"

"If he succeeds in the resurrection, then they will grapple, power to power, will against will. Either Reza will take Tuman Sunqur's power, or Reza himself will be taken."

"Taken?"

"Taken. Possessed. A living man, become a tool of the dead."

"So, the lich of the man who made the Great Waste, alive again, with one of the most powerful magicians of our day to serve him as Father Marius serves Reza."

"Do not say that!"

They were silent again. Coel stared up into the night sky. Even halfway around the world the stars were still the same. It was summer. His eyes tracked the familiar signposts. Draco's tail twisted as the dragon crawled between the Big and Little Bears towards Hercules.

"We are heading almost due north."

"Yes."

"We head straight for the Great Waste."

"If we continue on this course, we will be within the Waste before sundown tomorrow."

"Reza means to enter it, then?"

"I believe so. I believe the hand leads him there. I had thought he might know secret paths through the mountains that others did not. I thought perhaps he meant to enter it in a quick sojourn to Samarkand, or perhaps to find lost Tashkent."

"What do you believe now?"

"I believe we go to Bukhara."

The cities were little more than names from dim fables to Coel. Dimmer than Cathay or the Indias since the Great Waste had split the world. Sorrow stabbed at Coel as he thought of his friend. Such names would have lit fires in Snorri's heart. "Where is Bukhara?"

"Bukhara was a major way station upon the Silk Road. It was an oasis in the Karakum desert, watered by Zerevsan River and ruled by the Karakhitai. They were a steppe people. They were decimated when the Hobgoblin Hordes appeared in their midst. The Great Waste annihilated what was left of them."

"The Great Waste is poison. We will die."

"My master does not enter the Waste to die. He has a plan."

Once more Coel hated the word "master" on her lips. "I am worried about Luko."

"I am, too."

"I do not believe Reza wants him for an apprentice."

"It is odd, however, that is often how things happen."

"What does that mean?"

"It means my master is a very powerful adept. He was searching for warriors in Moscow, surrounded by scum serving their Frontier Commissions, yet he found you, Coel. The son of a chieftain, a Paladin candidate, and an archer and swordsman of unparalleled skill. And he found Snorri, a former officer of the Byzantine Emperor's Varangian Guard. He seeks Tuman Sunqur, and the great wizard's ring falls into his hand from the midst of a

Hobgoblin Horde. If my master seeks an apprentice, it does not surprise me at all that Luko appeared on his path in the midst of his most dangerous quest."

Márta looked up at the stars.

"I told you I helped Reza in his work when I was still too young for military training. He taught me many things. He taught me there are patterns in the world, Coel. Patterns in the world around us, and patterns in the world unseen. Adepts, priests, prophets, fortunetellers and fools, consciously or unconsciously, they can see these patterns, or pieces of them. Some see them through cards or crystals, others in dreams or trances. Reza says the patterns are the pathway to power. He would say the only difference between himself and a man like Marius is but a matter of interpretation and training."

Coel thought on his childhood. He thought of all the things his mother had tried to teach him as she took him over every inch of his father's land. Things he had turned his back on to please his father and become a Paladin. Things his Norman tutors had scarred his hands with switches for. Things for which the priests in the Paladin Academy had reached into his mind and punished him. They seemed far away and half-remembered.

"My mother spoke of such things. The veins of a leaf, the clouds in the sky, the alignment of the stars. Looking back? I think my mother wanted me to join her Circle. I think she wanted me to follow the Old Ways, but my father would not have it."

"Reza believes you are quite sensitive to these patterns. However much the Church tried to beat it out of you. You have power latent within you. He says you might well have made an adept had you studied. He believes it has much to do with your luck."

"Snorri said I was lucky. He said with my luck and his brains we would become kings."

"Snorri was a good man," Márta's voice caught. "He was a good friend to me."

Coel smiled at the memory of his friend. "He made fun of me all the time."

"Well, that is because you need it."

"Well, I am glad everyone is in agreement on that, then."

"I am sorry I hit you."

"Oh, well, I am often in need of hitting. That is something most everyone agrees upon as well."

Márta laughed. Coel's heart skipped a beat at the sound of it. Silence fell between them again. Márta slipped her bow into the case on her hip. "I should be getting back."

"Wait."

"What?"

"What do you know of Marius?"

"What do you mean?"

"I mean what do you know about him?"

"As much as you. I met him on the Dnieper when he healed my legs."

"You know something of sorcery."

"As I told you, I helped Reza when I was younger."

"What kind of hold could a Persian sorcerer have on a Christian priest, and a crusader?"

Márta shook her head rapidly. She turned to descend down the rocks. "I do not know."

"But you have your suspicions, have you not? I can tell by the tone of your voice, and I can tell you do not like them, either."

"I had begun to enjoy your company again, Coel," Márta's voice lowered. "I wish you had not ruined it."

"I am sorry, Márta. I miss your company, too." Coel swallowed. "I miss you."

There was no sound but the wind.

Coel fumbled for words. "I do not want us to go back to not speaking."

"Nor do I."

"If there are things you are forbidden to speak of, then, we do not have to speak of them."

"I have not been expressly forbidden to speak of Marius, but I know my master would not be pleased if I did, and I do not particularly want to speak of such things, either."

"I am sorry. It is just that . . ." Coel looked back at the camp. He knew Marius stood over Reza like an armored scarecrow in the dark. "Marius asked me to kill him."

"Reza told me."

"It is more than that. Orsini is sick, and he is getting worse. Going home is his only concern. Zuli grows fey and strange. Snorri and Oleg are dead," Loneliness caught in Coel's throat. "Reza said it himself. I have no friends left. There is no one I can talk to."

"You can talk to me."

"I know, but your loyalty is to Reza."

"And so long as you do not oppose him, we do not have a problem."

"No, it is, just-- "

"Coel, I will tell you this. Reza has told Marius to kill you if you try to open the box again. My orders are similar."

"No, that is not what I meant. I mean, we cannot talk. You and I. I mean . . . I mean I wish you had not . . . I wish I had not . . . "

Silence fell between them again. Coel cursed his tongue. Whenever he spoke to Márta, it either ran wild like a dog let off its leash or stood stubborn like a mule and refused to move.

Márta broke the silence. "I will tell you a secret."

"Oh?"

"One I have not spoken of. Not even to my master."

"What is that, then?"

"I have your poem."

Coel swallowed.

Márta's voice dropped to a whisper. "I went back and picked it up before we broke camp. I read it every night."

Coel closed the distance between them. Márta's head tilted back as he ran his fingers through the glory of her hair. He traced her face and felt the fullness of her lips beneath his thumb. Her lips parted beneath his as he kissed her. The stars broke loose and wheeled behind Coel's closed eyes. He felt like he might fall from the earth and spin upward into the heavens. His hands went to her hips.

Márta pulled away gasping. Coel's breath caught, and he swallowed with difficulty as he gasped himself.

Márta's hand went to her mouth. "I must go."

"I know," Coel's chest heaved. "Stay."

"Coel, I must not!"

"All right."

"You cannot tell Reza! You cannot tell anyone! You--"

Coel kissed her again. Márta's shoulders sagged even as her hips pressed against him. She pulled her face from his as if she were drowning. "Coel, I must go!"

She turned her face away as he tried to kiss her again. Coel moved his mouth to her bared throat. Márta moaned as his lips moved upon her. She bent her head down half-heartedly to keep him from her neck. He breathed in the scent of her hair and breathed out across her ear. Márta shuddered. Coel could feel her face smile against his hand as her head tilted back again. His mouth sought hers and their tongues met.

Márta shoved him away with both hands. She squared her shoulders and tried to bring her breathing under control. "I must go."

"I know," Coel grinned giddily in the dark. "Stay."

"I cannot."

"All right."

"You must promise me, Coel. Promise me you will not tell a soul."

"On my own soul, Márta, I swear it," Coel's lips tingled. "But you must swear something to me."

Márta drew back a step. "What?"

"I am going to write you another poem. If it pleases you, you must kiss me again when we switch watches tomorrow."

"Coel!"

"Swear it!"

"I will kiss you tomorrow," Márta darted forward and pressed her lips against his. "I swear it."

CHAPTER THIRTY-SEVEN

The party traveled across the Karakum. They set out just before dawn each morning and stopped to pitch lean-tos and nap upon carpets at mid-day when the desert sun burned its hottest. They would ride again in the late afternoon and not stop until after the sun fell. The wind never ceased. Dawn rose over their third day in the desert.

Coel ate dried dates and composed poetry from the back of his camel.

His eyes strayed to Márta beneath the brim of his hat. He watched her shoulders sway with the roll of her camel as she rode. The hot wind blew the folds of her burnoose and moved the red tassels of her camel's saddlebags. Reza's little caravan crossed the desert, but as Coel watched Márta he thought of the sea. His words took shape like waves in his mind.

"I wish you would kiss me like that."

"What!" Coel nearly fell off of his camel. "You were watching, then?"

Zuli smirked up at him. "Of course."

"What! Why?"

"Perhaps I am jealous."

"You told me to go to her!"

"I told you to go talk to her, Coel. Not suck forth her lungs."

"Well, hell. What did you expect? You--" Coel straightened. It occurred to him that Zuli might have set up both Márta and himself for a falling out with Reza.

Zuli's smirk grew insufferable. "First you flush, Coel, and now you turn pale. I swear, you Celts have such charming complexions."

"You would not . . . " Coel's stomach knotted.

"You had that far away look in your eyes as you were riding. Were you writing another poem for her?"

Coel could not believe he was so utterly transparent.

"Well?"

"Well what, then?"

"Let's have it."

"Have what?"

"The poem," Zuli rolled her eyes. "Let us hear it."

Coel blushed again. "It is not finished."

"I do not care."

"It does not rhyme."

"The best ones do not."

"I do not wish to."

"Recite it, or I will tell Reza you are molesting Márta."

Zuli's blue-green gaze was as steady as a gambler's. Her lips quirked infuriatingly.

"Very well," Coel let out a doomed sigh of resignation. "I dream of--"

"Say it like you mean it, with passion. Not like a drill to please your Latin tutor."

Coel cleared his throat and fixed his eyes on Márta. Her kisses came to his mind once more. Again he thought of the sea.

"I dream of crashing waves,

under nighted sky, two souls yield to an ancient tide,

swimming out beyond buoy or lighted caution,

immersed in Ovid's ocean,

delighting as currents of desire and experience entwine,

spirits courting, a dance on dappled waters,

stars above, reflect in the water about us, merging,

until vault of sky and depth of sea seem as one,

merging, as boundaries of flesh yield and merge,

swirling, surging, limbs entwined in the eddies,

swept helpless towards a maelstrom of wrenching sensation,

unable to stop, unwilling,

better to drown, to be thrown and broken,

than alter the thundering course,

to reel, borne aloft on towering crests, tumbling,

to lay exhausted in ebbs of indolent pleasure,

weightless, languid, in the lagoon of Eros' afterglow.

Márta . . . swim with me."

Coel took his eyes from Márta. He found Zuli gazing up at him unblinkingly. Coel's nervousness came back in a rush. "Well?"

"Now I am jealous."

A silly smile crossed Coel's face. "It is not bad, then?"

"It is beautiful." Her eyes bored into him. "Snorri said you were a man of destiny, and he was right. You are a warrior and a poet, Coel. A credit to the race of Celts." She shook her head slowly in admiration. "I swear you walk like a man out of myth. It is easy to see why she loves you."

Coel's heart and head swelled in equal proportions. He looked back at Márta and dared to dream. "You think she--"

"I suppose this means we shall no long be sharing a blanket."

Coel's head whipped about. "What?"

Zuli sighed wistfully. "Not even . . .? "

Zuli made an obscene gesture with her mouth and her hand.

Coel made a choking noise and looked about wildly to see if anyone watched. His ears burned beneath his hat. Zuli's laughter rang like a bell. "You will have to teach her that one, Coel. It does not occur to most women naturally."

The sound of laughter was alien under the vast horizon. Both Reza and Orsini looked back to see what was going on. Zuli stuck her tongue out at them and they turned back around. Coel pulled his hat lower.

"Have you had your fun, then?"

"I have not even begun. Why do you ask?"

Coel leaped for a change of subject. "Márta said we would soon be entering the Waste."

"We are all ready in it."

"What?" Coel snatched off his hat and looked about. "I see nothing!"

Zuli's own gaze ranged across the desert. "What did you expect? Lightning and fire? Boiling pits and a black gate with Charon collecting coins?"

"To be truthful, I do not know what I expected. But I do not see anything."

"Oh, you can see it. I know you can. Look closer."

Coel thought of Márta's words the night before and the things he had learned from his mother. He looked for the patterns of life. He grinned as they came to him. "No, this is not the desert. There are no tufts of withered grass. No weeds amongst the rocks. No hawks soar in the sky and no flies follow the camels anymore."

"What else?"

Coel looked at the ground more closely. "The desert beneath us was a tapestry of rock and sand and parched dirt." He watched as the red-brown ground puffed up in tiny clouds like flour beneath the camel's feet. "This is dust. What we cross now was once grassland."

"Very good. The Karakum was a patchwork once. Rivers from the Kopets and the Paropamasis watered parts of it and created plains and fertile hill land in its midst. There are even some lakes and marshes around its edges. However, all is poisoned now. The soil here died, and nothing has replenished it. All now is death and dust."

"Nothing lives here, then?"

"Nothing."

"I had always heard that horrors walked the Waste."

"Nothing can live in the Waste, Coel, but that is because there is nothing to live on. However, there are things born of the Waste and its effects. These things are usually born on the fringes. Some are carried in from elsewhere by watercourses or wander in lost during dust storms or deranged by the sun. Most sicken and die. A few live long enough to wander out again. Those that do have been changed. Some survive to breed. Over time, some creatures who have survived such changes or been born of such broods will actually re-enter the Waste, pulled back by the power of the place, and change more."

Coel thought of the thing they had met fishing in the Caspian.

"The whole Hobgoblin Horde died here, Coel. Who knows how many of their shades walk the Waste? And a place exposed to so much power, and so much death, who knows what other kinds of things it could attract?"

Coel had received Paladin training in Grande Triumph. He knew what other kinds of things would be attracted by the Waste.

Demons.

"Nothing lives in the Waste, Coel. But you can meet horror here. Do not doubt it."

"And what of the Assassins?"

"The Assassins worship the Waste. They traffic with demons and worship Tuman Sunqur as their patron saint." Zuli's voice went flat. "They consider the Great Waste a Holy Land. They seek its blessings."

Coel looked upon the dead land and dread crawled within him. "I do not feel any changes."

Zuli's eyes went to Orsini. The dwarf was coughing. He had begun coughing when they had entered the desert two days ago. Now his coughing was almost constant. He rode with a kerchief held to his lips. "Orsini has carried the poison of the Waste within him since the Kopets. Now he has carried it back to its home. He feels it."

"Will he die?"

"He is a dwarf. Short of beheading them, killing dwarves is very uncertain business. But he cannot withstand it much longer. Not like he is. Not here."

"What about us? We are but humans," He remembered Zuli's mixed blood. "Mostly."

"There is Marius for that," Zuli looked upon the cowled priest, and Coel did the same. The desert had been good for him. The hot wind and sun had dried out his flesh, and carried away much of his stink. Zuli sighed. "We will all begin feeling the effects tomorrow."

* * *

Nadrud coughed. He would have spat the vile taste from his mouth, but he could not afford to lose the moisture. His warriors sagged in their saddles. The camels' heads hung low on their long necks. The Waste was taking its toll. One of his warriors had sickened and died. Others were ill. They were nearly out of water. The sun of the Karakum beat down upon them in vertical brutality. The camels were close to failing.

Nadrud's voice cracked. "Shaman! Athuc!"

Retep and Athuc slowly plodded forward. Nadrud looked at the warrior who was his Right Hand. "Athuc, what of the warriors?"

Athuc straightened up in the saddle. "We are Ten-Skull. The Great Hobgoblin has said the humans must die."

Nadrud took weary pride in the answer. "Shaman?"

"We will die before we intercept the humans. We have gone too far to turn back."

"We walk the Great Path of Life, Shaman. These humans obstruct it. They must be slain."

Retep smacked his tusks in thought. "We cannot succeed without the camels to carry us. Give what water we have left to the beasts if you wish them to live."

"What of our warriors?"

"One of our warriors has died. Kill his camel. Let the warriors drink its blood and eat of its meat."

"The meat will sustain our stomachs, and the blood fill our veins for a day, but this place pulls the blood from our bodies. How are we to live days without water?"

Retep smacked his tusks in thought. "In some ways, the Lesser Ones are hardier than ourselves."

Nadrud looked down upon the goblins. They showed signs of hunger, heat, and thirst, but it had only sharpened their expressions. They were used to such hardships. Their flesh thinned across their bones, but they showed no sign of sickening and kept up with the camels. When Nadrud's first warrior had fallen, he had intended the flesh to be shared among his fellows. However, when the blood had bled forth blackened by the Waste, the polluted carcass had been thrown to the Lesser Ones. They had fallen upon the usually forbidden flesh of Hobgoblin with disturbing relish. They seemed to have suffered no ill effects from eating it. The Lesser Ones were indeed a hardy race. When meat was scarce, the Lesser Ones sustained themselves with roots, vermin, and insects. Crude as they were, their law was the same as that of their masters. The strong ate. The strong survived. The strong earned the right to breed. "Shaman. You suggest something."

"Yes. Slay two of the Lesser Ones each day, morning and evening, so that each warrior can begin and end each day with fresh meat and a bowl of blood to fill his veins. That will sustain us against sun and sand. As for the poison of the Waste, there is nothing to be done. The strong will survive. The weak will not. It has always been so."

Nadrud was pleased. The reputation of the Elf-Skinners for cleverness was well justified. "Slay the riderless camel. Let the warriors gorge and drink their fill of blood. Give what remains to the Lesser Ones." He looked at the goblin skull Retep carried beneath his arm. "You still watch the humans?"

"I do."

CHAPTER THIRTY-EIGHT

Coel dreamed of a man who looked like Jesus. Like Coel, the man crossed a desert, but the man's desert was nothing but sand, yellow as the seashore, with endless dunes and no ocean anywhere on the horizon. The man rode no camel. He walked. His bleeding feet sank deep into the sand with every step, and his limbs were weighted with heavy chains. In the dream, the man knew that Coel was alive. He had thought Coel was dead. The man who looked like Jesus continued his death march across the desert. The sun burned him. A whip laid open the flesh of his back. The man was happy.

He was glad Coel was alive.

Coel awoke confused. He was sick to his stomach and his joints ached. He rolled out of his blankets feeling like an arthritic old dog. His teeth and tongue felt disgusting, though he'd drunk no wine the night before. There was no twig to be found in the barren wilderness of the Waste, so he took a scrap of cloth from his saddlebag and scrubbed his teeth. He swigged water from a gourd and spat. He frowned as dust rose up in a puff around the water's impact. Sand would have thirstily sucked the moisture, but the dust just clogged and beaded around it. Coel jerked back as he looked at the scrap of linen in his hand.

It was bright with blood.

Coel spat again. Undiluted by water, his spittle was as red as the dust it fell upon. He reached into his mouth and felt his teeth. None were loose but they did not feel firm either. "Jesus . . . "

The others still slept beneath their lean-tos. Marius stood still in his silent watch over Reza. Coel took up his bow and sheafed a few arrows. He walked out across the dust to find Márta. The wind blew unceasingly and a dust devil twisted in the distance. The land they were on was flat save for a few clumps of rocks to break the monotony. Coel went to the closest. As he neared he heard a disturbing sound.

Márta was weeping.

Coel broke into a lope. "Márta!"

He came around the rocks and found Márta huddled clasping her knees. Her eyes were red with tears and her nose was bleeding. "Márta, are you all right?"

"No!"

"What is wrong?"

"Nothing!"

"Márta! Tell me!"

Márta held her comb in her hand. It was carved of tortoise shell and a thick clump of her hair jammed its teeth. Another clump lay in the dust at her feet. Coel knelt and put his hand to her hair. Márta flinched as he ran his hand through it. Thick strands fell away between his fingers. Márta would not meet his eyes. She wiped her nose against the back of her forearm. Blood smeared her arm from wrist to elbow.

"I was combing my hair! And it just came out! My head is throbbing, and my nose will not stop bleeding!" Márta scraped her arm across her face harder and more blood flowed across her lips. Her voice rose towards hysteria. "It just will not stop!"

Coel seized her shoulders and pulled her to her feet. "I am taking you out of here! I am taking you out of this place right now!"

"No! We must not!"

"No! We go! Now!"

The sorcerer's voice called out from camp. "Coel! Márta! Come!"

Márta would not look at Coel as she wiped her eyes and collected her weapons. They walked back to camp together. The rest of the party was up. Reza looked at the two of them as they approached. Coel spoke before the sorcerer could say anything. "The Waste is sickening us." He looked at the dwarf. Orsini sat hunched with his saddle for a stool. He coughed into his handkerchief. His coughing had gone from a dry hack to a gurgling rale. His lungs were filling. The desert morning was cool but sweat had broken across his brow. His camel gazed at him longingly but no longer made any attempt to lick him. "It is killing Orsini."

"You are right, Coel. We are beginning to feel its effects. We must take action against it." The sorcerer turned to the priest. "Marius."

Father Marius straightened up. His hood blew back in the morning wind. His face was horrible to behold. The desert had sucked the moisture from his rotting flesh and stretched it like faded parchment across his skull. His lips had shriveled so that his yellowed teeth bared in rictus. His bloodshot eyes were so far sunken they seemed to stare out of darkness. They were flattened and empty, yet still horribly alive.

His nose had fallen off.

" . . . Pour water."

Reza nodded. "Márta."

Márta reached into a pack and took the large wooden bowl the party mixed its morning gruel in. They watched as she filled the bowl from a goatskin bladder and stepped away. Marius lurched forward and stood over the bowl. "Embers . . . from the fire."

Márta pulled a riding glove over her bloody hand and scooped embers from the fire. She blew on them as she brought them to Marius. The priest pulled forth a tiny bible from the pouch on his belt. He cracked it open randomly and tore out a page. Coel could see the page was from the Gospel of Luke. It was the start of Chapter V. Coel had learned the scriptures by rote at the Academy in Paris.

Christ's cleansing of the leper seemed singularly appropriate.

Marius turned his palm up. Márta balked a brief moment before pouring the glowing embers into his hand. His shriveled flesh sizzled. Marius took the tiny page and placed it atop the embers and partially closed his hand. The parchment flared to light, and flames flickered between his fingers. He slowly closed his hand. Smoke curled from his fist as the flame smothered. His dead fingers worked and ground the charred paper. He turned his fist over and slowly opened his hand. Ashes drifted down into the bowl.

His hand hovered. He raised the other to close around the sword-bladed Chi-Roh pendant on his chest. Coel squinted as he watched Marius' mouth. The priest's lips and tongue were shriveled but Coel knew the scripture and could see the words form silently in Latin.

"Lord, if thou wilt, thou canst make me clean . . . "

Marius' burned hand trembled over the bowl.

The water made a thumping noise as something shifted deep within it. No bubbles came forth, but the water roiled. Coel watched the ashes littering its surface spin about. He squinted in surprise. For just an instant, they seemed to form some sort of meaningful pattern, but within an eye blink he had lost it. The water ceased its roiling and stilled as quickly as it had begun. It appeared to be nothing but a wooden bowl of water scattered with ash.

" . . . Drink."

The party stood and stared at the bowl.

Reza nodded at it. "Márta."

Márta looked at Marius and paled.

"I will go first." Coel knelt and picked up the wooden bowl. It was as wide as a washbasin and heavy with the water within it. Coel tilted it to his lips. He took a half sip and held it. The water tasted clean across his tongue save for the grittiness of the ashes. Coel closed his eyes and took three long swallows.

The hollow nausea in his stomach left him with the first swallow. The water filled him as if he had eaten a meal. Coel stood with the bowl in his hands, and the aching in his joints was forgotten. His teeth felt hard, slick, and clean again under his tongue. He nodded and held out the bowl of consecrated water to Márta. "Aye."

Márta took the bowl and drank. Her hands ceased shaking and she smiled as she lowered the bowl. Reza and Zuli drank next. Zuli held the bowl for Luko. The boy made a face at the dirty water but drank as Zuli prodded him. She took the bowl back and held it for Orsini. The dwarf waved her away. "I'll have none of that, thank you."

"Fool! You'll die if you don't!" Everyone was surprised by the passion in Zuli's voice.

"Then the quicker we stop--" Another coughing fit overtook the dwarf. His face contorted as he held the kerchief to his mouth.

He took a wheezing breath as it passed. "The quicker we stop standing around, the quicker we can be about our business, and the quicker we can be out of this accursed place!"

Coel found himself turning to Reza. "For God sakes, do something."

"It is within my power to destroy him, but as for making a dwarf do anything against his will, I know of no living adept with that kind of influence." Reza shrugged. "Failing that, I must agree with him. Saddle the camels. The quicker we are finished and away from this place, the better."

Coel watched the wizard turn away. The sorcerer's words rang hollow in Coel's ears. It occurred to Coel that Reza did not really care whether Orsini lived or died. With the hobgoblins behind them and the Assassins passed, Reza did not really need Orsini any more. One ailing dwarf no longer assured the mission's success. In fact, no longer needing his war-skills or wealth, Orsini was just one more mouth thirsting for water in the Waste. Coel watched a dust devil dance in the distance. A remark of Snorri's about Reza's chess game with the wizard came to mind.

The Persian had no qualms about sacrificing pawns.

* * *

The goblin screamed as two warriors hoisted it up by its heels. The scream cut short as the edge of a knife-axe sliced across its throat. The blood of its life poured forth into the breakfast bowls of the warriors. As the blood drained, others worked at removing the meager meat from the Lesser One's scrawny carcass. The rest of the Lesser Ones sniffed and whined at the camp's perimeter and waited for the bones and entrails of their sacrificed comrade.

Nadrud ignored the noise and stared at Retep intently. "Shaman. Do you see?"

"I see," Retep gazed deeply into the weathered goblin skull. "The humans are now well within the Waste."

Nadrud leaned forward. "Where?"

"They are south of us now."

"Which way do they go?"

"North," Retep's great yellow eyes regarded Nadrud respectfully. "The Right Hand of Nijumet is wise. We no longer follow the humans. We now lay in their path and await them."

Nadrud unrolled an ancient human map. The characters upon it were written in the language of the Persians. Nadrud could not read them, but he had memorized the major features that Gwall had recited to him. The map was over two hundred years old and depicted a Central Asia before the Great Waste had swallowed it. The map was heavy. The original human artisans had carved the map's features onto heavy leather with a steel stylus. Hobgoblin artisans amongst the Council of Females had re-inked and repainted the features for the field commanders.

Nadrud traced a line with a thickened fighting nail from south to north. "Due north takes the humans to the city of Bukhara," The city had fallen before the Horde during the first invasion. It had fallen a second time beneath the hand of The Destroyer. It was a fitting resting-place for The Destroyer's bones.

"Here," Retep pointed. "They must cross a river to reach it."

"The Amu Darya," The river cut the Waste from the foothills of the Afghans to the Aral Sea. "Yes. They must ford it."

"The river runs the breadth of the Waste." Retep's bloodshot eyes regarded the map. "It will be a place of great poison."

A warrior brought Nadrud a bowl. Nadrud slurped the blood of the Lesser One around his tusk. Four more warriors had died. All of them were sick now. The push to the river would probably kill more, but the fresh blood was strength. "The river is two day's journey. We must reach it before the humans."

CHAPTER THIRTY-NINE

Coel rode with stolen kisses tingling his lips. Every night as they switched watches he recited Márta poetry. Some his, some Welsh, some from the Greeks and Romans. Each night Márta made him earn her embrace. Each night she stayed longer in his arms. Coel's eyes sought her out. Márta rode point with Reza just a little behind her. The box was the sorcerer's constant companion. Zuli rode beside Orsini with Luko and offered the dwarf what support she could. Coel suspected there was little comfort she could offer other than kind words and a steady arm to make sure he did not fall out of his saddle. The rest of the party was holding its own. Marius' ministrations had cut short the sickness they had all felt. Coel thought more of Márta. He took off his hat and ran a hand through his hair. It was growing out nicely. It was still a far cry from what he considered a manly length, but at least he no longer looked like a thrall. He--

" . . . Coel."

Coel flinched as he found Marius riding next to him. He tried hard not to stare at the priest's face. He tried hard not to look away in horror as well. Coel found he was not comfortable at all conversing with the undead. "Marius?"

"We must speak."

Coel could not help looking ahead to where Reza rode. "I thought it was forbidden."

"It is. In some ways, but, I have found in using my power, I mean God's, power, to heal you all has . . . strengthened me."

Coel had not heard such strength in Marius voice since the day Sandor had slain him. "You are free of his control, then?"

"No. I cannot yet, defy, Reza's will, but I find I can move, obliquely, against it. I must obey, the letter, of Reza's word, but by obeying them to the letter, I can defy, the spirit, in which they were intended."

"What are you saying?" Coel steeled himself and stared into the priest's tormented eyes. "You want me to kill you, then?"

"More than anything," The shriveled lips pulled back, and Coel realized Marius was trying to smile. "But, as I have told you. Reza will kill you if you try to end my, suffering, and my orders are quite explicit about, killing you, if you try."

Coel glanced nervously towards the front of the caravan. "Marius, you are a man of God. What kind of hold could Reza have upon you? I mean, not now, but before, when we first met you on the Dnieper. How did you come to serve him?"

"It is forbidden."

"Well, what can you talk about, then?"

Marius' dead, sunken eyes gleamed. "Would you like to hear a story?"

Coel's flesh crawled. "More than anything.

"I will tell you of Albrecht."

"Who?"

Sir Albrecht von Orlamunde. The founder of my order, the Brethren of the Blade, centuries ago. He had just been knighted on Crusade in the Holy Land, in Antioch, when the hobgoblins fell upon Europe. It was he who had . . . the vision . . . he who first forged the Chi-Roh from the sword blades of martyred crusaders. Our Order fought the hobgoblins with the credo to never retreat. Many were knighted. Some became Paladins. When the hobgoblins were destroyed, Sir Albrecht had a new vision. He returned to declare war on all pagans in Europe. Our Order wished him canonized, but both Churches refused, despite his heroism in the east and the north. The Brethren followed the creed after his death . . . never retreat . . . no mercy for the pagans."

"What of you, Marius? How did you come amongst them?"

"I was a young priest, in Westphalia. So very pious. When the power came upon me? Miracles came forth from my hands. The Archbishop spoke of sending me to Rome, to serve the Pope, but a Knight of the Order came to my church. He said the Brethren had heard of my, ability. He told me there were crusades to be fought and crusaders who needed help. I was, inspired, by his words. I told him of my vow, to live by God's law. That he who lives by the sword, dies by the sword." Marius raised his hand. The mace and chain rattled by the thong on his wrist. "He gave me this, and asked me to serve God's will in the Baltic. I was inflamed with crusader zeal. I joined the Brethren of the Blade. I fought. I healed. I was knighted. My power . . . God's . . . power . . . flowed through me. It was said no knight would die save by being beheaded if I was with him. They said I could raise the dead . . . and I knew the Sin of Pride."

"Snorri said your order was disbanded."

"The Rus was correct. Rome was never, pleased, with us. We kept most treasure we took to arm and equip the Brethren, to hire, mercenaries, for we were never many. Our mercenaries were, Christians, but most were not men of God. Freebooters, pirates, landless rogues. They pillaged and burned in our wake, and we did not care. There was only, the creed. No mercy for pagans. Our reputation grew. Our wealth grew. We were, feared. The Orders Templar and of Saint John, they spoke against us. Our order was, disbanded, our members put under Papal Ban. Many were slaughtered. Our castle, our, temple in Saxony was besieged, burned. The Grandmaster was taken to Rome in chains and, burned, at the stake for heresy. The Brethren, scattered, to the east. We hid amongst the Greeks, who did not care what the Pope in Rome said, as long as we could pay in gold . . . "

"In the east, where Reza found you."

" . . . Yes."

"How did you come to be in Reza's service?"

"It is forbidden."

"Damn Reza's will! You said God has given you new strength! Try!"

"I cannot."

Coel thought of what Marius had told him. "Then talk around it, then, as much as you are able."

"Our Order . . . was founded by Grandmaster Orlamunde."

"Yes, you told me."

"It is he who had the vision. He who first forged the bladed Chi-Roh of our order. Forged, from the swords of fallen Paladins in Antioch."

Coel waited, but nothing more was forthcoming. "Yes. The holy symbol of your order, I know."

"Yes."

"The one around your neck, it is forged the same, then?"

"No, this one is but a symbol of silver."

Coel stared at Marius. The way he said *this one* gave Coel pause. The dead eyes yearned at Coel horribly as he pondered. "But the first one was."

"Yes."

"The first one. It was lost."

"Yes."

"When your temple was sacked."

"Yes."

Coel filled with sudden certainty. "And Reza has it!"

"No."

Coel sat back, stymied. "No?"

"No."

Coel's eyes narrowed. The symbol was the key to the dead priest's riddle. He was sure of it. "But Reza sought you out. He'd heard of your healing power."

Marius said nothing.

"He sought you out and told you he had it."

Marius said nothing.

"He offered you a bargain of some kind."

Marius was silent.

"You made a bargain with Reza for the symbol you thought he had."

"No."

"No?"

"I am a Brother of the Blade. Even, for that, I would make no bargains with a pagan sorcerer."

"But he showed it to you, offered it to you, asked you to identify it or some such."

Marius was silent.

"You saw it, you were exposed to it, you were . . . " Coel's eyes slowly widened. Marius would, indeed, have made no bargain. He was a Christian, a priest, and a knighted crusader. He was a fanatic.

He had been forced.

"It was a trap."

Marius was silent.

Coel suppressed a shudder as he looked at the Christian priest with his flesh rotting off his bones in the Great Waste. Coel thought of the conversation they'd had before and what Father Marius had said. He could barely bring himself to speak above a whisper.

"Reza has stolen your soul."

Marius was silent.

"He has your soul in his goddamned saddle bag!" Outrage boiled up out of Coel. "By God, I will kill him! I will kill him right now, and then I will do you if you wish it, I--"

Marius' arm whipped upward and his mace and chain whirled up with it.

"I will not kill him!" Coel jerked his hands away from his weapons. "I will not kill you! I will not kill anybody!"

Marius' arm froze in mid-strike and slowly lowered. "Coel . . . ."

"I know, you will kill me if I attack Reza and defend yourself if I try to slay you."

"Remember, Márta is, conflicted, now. I have seen the two of you, together, in the night, but, if you attack Reza, she will, defend him."

Coel's lips thinned with the taste of it. "I know."

"The non-human . . . "

"Orsini."

"Sick as he is, and fond of you, nonetheless, given a choice of going home, or backing you, against Reza . . . "

"I know."

"Only the elven whore is on your side, and she knows not to cross the sorcerer."

"I know. I cannot count on anyone," Sudden intuition struck. "Why are you telling me this, then? You are speaking around the point again, aren't you?"

"Márta has served a sorcerer, but she is a virgin, trained by nuns."

"Yes, I know."

"The boy, Luko, has been raised a pagan, but he is only a child."

"You are saying they are innocents."

Marius was silent.

"You are saying they must be saved."

Marius was silent.

"You are a priest and it is your duty to save them."

Marius spoke not a word.

Things became very clear. Coel kept his hands away from his weapons and chose his words with great care. "You are saying that at some point you are going to try and resist Reza's will, when he is weakened, or has over extended himself."

Marius was silent.

"You are asking for my help in this," Coel kept his eye on Marius' mace hand. "When the time comes."

Marius was silent.

Coel clucked his horse forward. "You may count on it."

* * *

Nadrud stared at the Amu Darya and saw his death.

The river was dead. Nadrud had pictured the poisoned river black with banks choked by slime. The Amu Darya ran a dirty grayish red. Nothing lived in this place, and nothing held the dust to ground when the wind blew. Nothing held the riverbanks to its sides. Dust and silt choked the watercourse as it ran sluggishly down from the mountains far to the south.

Nadrud sagged in the saddle. He was down to five warriors. Mighty Athuc was two days dead and food for the Lesser Ones. Even the Lesser Ones had begun to sicken and die. Only a dozen of them remained. The camels staggered beneath the weight of warriors to weary to walk. Nadrud could feel the poison coursing through his veins. It ached in his old bones and throbbed in his fevered skull with every pulse of his heart. He was too weak to span his crossbow, much less wield the double knife-axes of a Champion.

The Destroyer and his wrath had won.

"Nadrud."

Nadrud looked blearily at the shaman. "Shaman?"

"Look."

Retep raised a palsied hand and pointed up the river. Nadrud's one eye squinted across the high sun's reflected glare.

A boat moved upon the river. Oars dipped into the poisoned waters and carried the craft towards them against the slowly moving current.

Nadrud slid off of his camel and nearly sat down as his knees threatened to fail him. He had removed his armor in the heat. Now he was too weak to put it back on. Nadrud drew a single knife-axe from the ring on his belt and rested its haft across his shoulder. His voice was a cracked lisp around his single tusk. "They come from the north?"

"Yes," Retep swallowed with difficulty. "It is strange."

"Nothing lies to the north."

"Nothing but Waste."

"These must be Assassins."

"We agree."

Nadrud's remaining warriors slid from their camels and loaded their crossbows.

The boat approached. The half-dozen occupants all wore black robes and veiled burnooses. The sweet smell of the Assassins wafted from the boat. The Lesser Ones crowded about the legs of the camels and cringed instinctively at the smell.

A very large individual stood in the prow. Black robes covered him from head to foot. Nadrud noted with weary interest that even the hands and feet of the Assassin were covered. The filmy black cotton gauze of a veil uncharacteristically hid his eyes. There was something wrong about the way the human stood. The boat ground to a halt against the bank. The tall Assassin spoke. "I am given to understand you speak Turkish."

Nadrud responded. "Yes."

"You are Nadrud, the Right Hand of Nijumet."

"That is correct. Who are you?"

"When I was a man, I was Faud Meqta. Now I am One Blessed by the Waste." The one who was once Faud tilted his veiled head. "It has come to the attention of the Old Man of the Mountain that you, Nadrud, the Right Hand of Nijumet, walk the Waste. The Great Hobgoblin, Nijumet, did not see fit to tell us of your excursion into our most Holy Land. You have hurt the feelings of the Old Man. How are we to offer our friends our hospitality if they wander in unannounced?"

Nadrud considered the inane remarks. He spoke two human languages, and he was intellectually aware of the double speech of humans and the concept of sarcasm. However, it took him several moments to recognize it. He decided he did not like it. "I am the Right Hand of Nijumet. He stretches forth his hand as he chooses."

"Ah," The Assassin placed a shrouded hand upon the prow of his boat and draped himself languidly across it. "But the Waste is no place for but a handful of warriors to walk alone. I was given to understand you had many more. Do the Blessings of the Waste not agree with you then?"

Nadrud had been challenged in personal combat more times than he could count. If a hobgoblin considered another's blood unfit, he told him so. Ritual combat settled the accusation. Specific rules determined when, where, and how such challenges could be conducted. It would never occur to a hobgoblin to taunt another, much less the sick and weakened. One who was sick or weakened would live or die by the strength of their blood. Such was the Path of Life. The humans farted forth words in such profusion that it was often impossible to be sure of their intention. However, this one's intentions seemed clear. Insults were another human weakness. Nadrud's hand tightened around the haft of his knife-axe.

The Assassin should have had a sword in his hand.

Nadrud snuffed the air. He was weak and sick. The human was larger than he was. The poison that blackened the blood within Nadrud's own body undoubtedly strengthened the human somehow. The human did not stand correctly. His body language was wrong. Then there was his smell. All Assassins smelled, but this one barely smelled human at all.

Nadrud decided to sick the Lesser Ones upon him and then reap the Assassin's head while he was preoccupied.

Retep interrupted. "Nadrud."

"Shaman?"

Retep spoke in Hobgoblin. "We should see what the human wants before we kill it. We walk the Path of Life. You are the Right Hand of Nijumet. The Law of the Moon does not rule us this day. We must think of our mission. The humans are here for a reason. We are but six now, and weakened by the Waste. If we are to kill the sorcerer and his companions, the aid of six Assassins will be invaluable."

Nadrud controlled the flood of fighting blood that filled him and spoke in Turkish. "What do you want?"

"What do we want?" The human brought its veiled hands to its chest. "We want to help you. You have hurt the feelings of the

Old Man, but he is yet your friend, still he wishes to offer you the open hand of his hospitality. In this most Holy Place, I am that open hand."

Nadrud sought about his feverish mind for human niceties and failed. "Shaman, speak with the human."

Retep bowed slightly, and his Turkish flowed around his tusks. "Forgive us, Blessed One. We have ridden hard across the desert. We have lost many warriors. The Blessings of the Waste are for the chosen ones, such as yourself. The power of this Holy Place is too great for such as ourselves. That which destroyed us once slowly destroys us now. We accept the hospitality of the Old Man of the Mountain with gratitude."

"Ah," The Assassin pushed himself up from where he languished on the boat's prow. "Then, let us offer your warriors refreshment." The Assassin gestured, and the others in the boat began unloading wooden casks.

Nadrud stared. "What is in them?"

"Fresh water. The Old Man cares for your welfare, and well knows that many are not prepared for the Blessings of the Land. Upon occasion, there has been need to have, shall we say, guests, in this place. Priests upon our Mountain have treated the water. It is a simple matter of sorcery. Like attracts like. You and your warriors must drink as much water as you can stand. When you have relieved yourselves, drink again. The water is attuned to this Holy Place. It shall pull the Blessings of the Land forth from your flesh and flush them out."

The Assassins struggled with a large crate covered by a blanket. As they moved the crate, there were scrapings inside it and the unmistakably squealing of swine. "The Old Man has sends you fresh meat and blood as well, to strengthen you."

Nadrud inclined his head. "The Old Man of the Mountain is generous."

"Indeed, he is." The Assassins began broaching the kegs. Nadrud's warriors found themselves crowding forward at the smell of fresh water. "And once you and your warriors have refreshed yourselves, we shall speak of the fate of Reza Walladid and those who ride with him."

CHAPTER FORTY

Coel looked upon the Amu Darya River with great unease. "I do not like it."

Orsini coughed into his kerchief. "Neither do I."

"How deep is it?"

"I do not know."

"Can the camels swim it?"

"I believe the question may be more one of willingness rather than ability."

The camels groaned and honked unhappily along the bank. Coel's mount had literally shrunk beneath him as they had ridden the Waste. Márta had told him the beasts lived upon the fat and water already in their bodies and so they suffered the Waste less than most animals would. Still, the camels looked tired and bedraggled, and they were becoming ever more stubborn and harder to control.

"The water is poison, then?"

Reza spoke. "Highly. Much more so than the dust beneath our feet. I suspect the slime on the bottom is highly concentrated. That is why I had you wax your boots to waterproof them. Keep yourself out of the water. We must ford the river, but whatever you do, do not fall in it. If do you, do not let it get into your mouth, ears, or eyes. Marius' ministrations may not be enough to save you."

Coel watched the greasy, sluggish river run. "What about beasts?"

"Beasts?"

"I mean monsters."

Reza shook his head. "Nothing lives in that river, Coel. Not for long."

"What will swimming in that dishwater do to our camels, then?"

"Probably kill them, in time." The sorcerer shrugged. "We should be well away with new mounts by then."

The Persian seemed to care as little for the lives of his animals as he did for his companions. It was one more thing Coel found himself despising the sorcerer for. He had been waiting for Marius to make a move for two days. The priest sat his camel by day and stood his watch over Reza by night in total silence. "Well, let us cross it, then. Shall we rope ourselves together?"

"No. Should one of us go down in that, we do not want the rest to follow."

"Huh," Coel grunted and switched his camel. "Hut! Hut!" The beast groaned and twisted its head about. It did not budge. The rest of the camels groaned and lowed in solidarity.

Orsini sighed, and the effort ended in fresh coughing. "One must lead, then the rest will follow." He ran his hand across his camel's withers. "Come along, old girl. You and I, together."

The cow craned her head around and seemed to give the dwarf a last, despairing look of love.

"I am sick with shame, girl," Orsini ran his hand along the camel's jaw. "You do not deserve this, but I must ask it of you. Hut."

The beast reluctantly began to move forward at his words. She made a sorrowful lowing noise as her broad feet squelched into the shallows.

"I know, I know," Orsini murmured. "I do not like it, either."

The camel began splashing out across the Amu Darya, and Orsini's pack camel followed. Reza spoke out. "Father Marius, follow him."

Marius switched his camel, and it fell in line with Orsini. Reza watched as the camels waded. "Coel, go next."

Coel grimaced and urged his camel in. It was reluctant, but it followed the tail of the camel in front of it. Orsini's camel honked and splashed as its feet left the bottom. The camel sank halfway to its humps. It craned its neck upward and rose up in the water as its feet started paddling. Marius' camel followed behind. The camel suddenly sank in the water, and Coel yanked his knees up around his ears with an oath. The camel rose up again and swam. It swam remarkably well. The beast's broad feet propelled it along better than a horse, and it was far more buoyant. The pack camels swam alongside, blissfully unencumbered by riders and carrying only the swiftly dwindling stores of supplies.

Coel looked back. Zuli and Luko rode behind him and then Reza. Márta brought up the rear. Luko waved a javelin Coel had given him. "Coel!"

Coel grinned. The lad held the javelin like a lance. Orsini had given Luko his steel buckler and taken Snorri's shield in its stead. The boy carried the little shield with pride, and Snorri's sax-knife hung like a sword at his hip from a baldric the boy had made himself. He still wore the turban Márta had wound for him; and he'd thrown the green half-cloak Zuli had cut for him over one shoulder and pinned it at the hip.

Luko was the most war-like looking ten-year-old in the world, and he knew it.

"Do not fall off, lad!" Coel waved back. "You will sink with all that iron!"

"I won't fall off! I promise!"

Zuli beamed.

The river erupted.

What emerged was not human. The creature was naked, and its flesh was so white the glare of the desert sun off of its skin was blinding. Thick black veins twisted across its hunched, freakish musculature. The screaming face was a misshapen horror. Teeth grew forward out of its mouth and met like the beak of a parrot inches past its lips. Its eyes were pink pits in its face.

It held a huge push dagger in each hand. Water from the Amu Darya River beaded on the viscous black poison coating it.

The creature punched a ten-inch blade into Father Marius' side.

Marius jolted with the blow, and his cowl fell back. His mace and chain rose up and whirled around his head. The Assassin drove its second blade into the priest's side. The spiked iron ball blurred down and crushed in the top of the inhuman skull.

Coel pulled a javelin from his saddle case.

Another Assassin with white skin and its head wrapped in dripping black gauze rose up behind Marius. It rammed a short bladed stabbing spear into the priest's back. Marius rocked forward. As he sat up, his flail whipped around in a backhanded blow. The side of the Assassin's head smashed in.

An Assassin swam at Coel.

Its skin was the same reddish-gray as the water of the Amu Darya. Silvery scales clustered around the heavy muscles of its shoulders. It swam with gleaming double push daggers in its hands like paddles. It swam without raising its head out of the water. Its red eyes locked with Coel's as it swam. Coel flung his javelin. The blade skittered over the silver scales of the Assassin's back. Coel drew his sword and yanked his shield from its pack straps.

The Assassin rose up as it closed. It grinned at Coel with the shredding triangular teeth of a shark.

Coel lashed out with his foot. Teeth broke beneath his heel. A poisoned blade scraped and slid on the waxed leather of his boot. The second dagger punched into Coel's shield splitting leather and wood. Coel chopped his sword down. The Paladin blade shaved off a fungal looking ear and sheared into the Assassin's shoulder. The Assassin yanked desperately with its good arm to free its blade. Coel leaned over and rammed his sword pommel down between the Assassin's red eyes. The Assassin's head snapped back and Coel struck it again. The Assassin reeled. Coel reversed his sword in his hand and thrust his point down like a spike through the hollow of the Assassin's throat. The three and a half foot blade sank down to the Assassin's bowels. Coel ripped his blade free and the Assassin sank back into the water.

Reza shouted above the combat. "Forward! There are goblins behind us! Marius! Slay them all!"

Coel swatted his camel across the flank with the flat of his blade.

Hobgoblins came up out of covered pits on the far shore. Goblins ran amongst them. Coel raised his shield as the hobgoblins leveled crossbows. The weapons thrummed, and a bolt crunched into Coel's shield. Orsini and Marius pushed forward. Orsini kept his shield up. Marius jerked as bolt after bolt pierced him.

"Coel!"

Coel turned at the sound of Zuli's cry.

Her camel foundered with a stabbing spear in its side. Zuli whipped the flagging beast towards Coel desperately. A few feet away a misshapen Assassin tread water feebly as Márta mercilessly shot arrow after arrow into it.

Zuli thrust Luko towards Coel. "Take him!"

Coel reached back and hauled Luko onto his camel by his baldric. The boy screamed and flailed. "Zuli! Zuli!"

An Assassin breached like a dolphin. Its skin was as black and shiny as marble. Spurs of white bone thrust out from its elbows and wrists. The bones of its brows and cheeks formed an ivory mask around the darkness of its eyes. The fingers of its huge hand fused like a great flipper. The paddle-like hand curled around Zuli's arm and yanked the little thief out of the saddle.

Zuli disappeared beneath the surface.

"Zuli!" Coel struggled to turn his camel but it kept making for the shore. "Zuli!"

"Zuli!" Luko howled as he tried to break from Coel's grip.

"Coel! Do not!" Reza shouted at the top of his lungs. "Forward! Forward or we all die!"

"Márta!" Coel struggled to keep his shield up as a quarrel struck it. "Find Zuli!"

"I do not see her! I do not see her anywhere!"

"Find her!"

"Forward!" Reza's voice boomed. "Forward!"

"God . . . damn it . . ." Coel squeezed the boy between himself and his shield and swatted his camel forward. Orsini had reached the other shore. His pack camel lay on its side in the shallows with a pair of crossbow bolts in its neck. Orsini stood on the beach with his hammer in his hand and Snorri's shield covering his body. Marius slid off his camel and marched through the shallows. He stumbled slightly as another crossbow bolt struck him but trod on implacably. The hobgoblins dropped their crossbows and drew swords and knife-axes.

A lanky Hobgoblin as tall as Coel stood on the shore. It wore red armor and held a loaded crossbow. It raised its aim from Marius and pointed its weapon at Coel. Coel tried to cover Luko with his body and huddled behind his shield as he awaited the bolt's arrival.

Coel's camel let out a honking groan of agony as it was shot out from under him.

Coel shoved Luko aloft as the camel sagged sideways into the water.

The water of the Amu Darya rose up around Coel's waist. He cringed as the coolness of it ran up his legs and filled his boots. Coel struggled to get Luko onto his shoulders. "Luko! Hold my shield before us!" Luko's little hands grasped the shield. Coel waited for a poisoned dagger to sink into his back as the slime of the riverbed sucked at his boots with every step.

Marius and Orsini were beset. Coel could not afford to look behind him. He splashed into the shallows as the red-armored hobgoblin ran at him. Coel dumped Luko onto dry ground took back his shield "Stay behind me!"

The hobgoblin closed swinging a knife-axe in each hand. Coel's sword rang against the blade of one weapon. The second hooked down and bit into the top of Coel's shield. The hobgoblin yanked Coel's shield down and pulled him off balance and they wrestled blade to blade. The hobgoblin suddenly thrust his knife-axe forward. The iron socket of the axe-head punched Coel in the jaw.

Coel saw stars.

The hobgoblin swung the knife-axe down, and the second weapon sank into Coel's shield next to the first. It heaved back with both blades and ripped the shield from Coel's grip. Coel staggered back spitting blood and took his sword in both hands.

The hobgoblin came forward whirling its weapons. Coel slashed, and the twin knife blades hooked Coel's sword and pinned it.

The two of them slammed their bodies together to smother each other's attack. Coel and the hobgoblin went face to face as they jockeyed to overbear each other. A single, huge, cat-like yellow eye glared into Coel's. Coel spat in the remaining eye and nearly lost his nose as the hobgoblin hooked at his face with its single tusk. Coel yanked his head back, and the hobgoblin slammed him its shoulder and buffeted Coel backward into the shallows. Coel swung wildly to fend the hobgoblin off. The double weapons crossed and trapped Coel's sword again. Coel sagged to one knee in the shallows as the hobgoblin kicked him in the stomach.

The knife-axes rose to finish him.

Luko darted in and thrust the wide blade of his javelin into the hobgoblin's calf.

The hobgoblin roared and tottered to one side. Luko leaped away as the hobgoblin took a wild swing in retaliation. Coel rose up and swung his sword like he was splitting wood. The hobgoblin could barely stand, much less maintain its defense. It crossed its weapons in a desperate 'X.' Coel hacked down at the hobgoblin like he was chopping a tree. His first blow sent the hobgoblin down to one knee, and the second knocked the knife-axe from its left hand. His third and fourth blow beat down its guard, and the fifth split its skull. Coel heaved a ragged breath as he strode out of the shallows. "Luko! Stay behind me!"

The boy retrieved his javelin and ran behind Coel. Coel dared a look back as he slogged ashore. Zuli was nowhere to be seen. Márta's camel slowly floated downstream. Márta stood waist deep in the river and held the reins of Reza's camel. Her bow was gone and her scimitar drawn. Reza's hands were upon his turban and his face twisted with strain.

A hobgoblin struck at Marius on the shore. The priest's mace and chain was twisted about one knife-axe, while the other hacked into him again and again. Orsini traded exhausted blows with a sword and shield armed hobgoblin. A spear's throw back from the battle, a hobgoblin stood with its arms outstretched and its eyes clamped shut with effort. Coel knew the hobgoblin was battling Reza mind to mind. The hobgoblin shaman barked out a command in its language.

A half-dozen goblins swarmed through the thick of battle.

They streamed towards Márta and Reza as the pair struggled ashore.

A hobgoblin ran at Coel bearing sword and shield. Two goblins with longknives ran at its heels. The goblins spread out to either side. Coel dug the toe of his boot into the slime of the bank and flicked his foot. The closest goblin shrieked as poisone muck flew into its face. The other made to run around Coel. Coel could do nothing as the hobgoblin swung at him.

"Luko! Look out!"

Luko's javelin flew but the goblin danced aside. The creature got behind Coel but he could give it no attention. The hobgoblin buffeted at Coel with its shield, and Coel stepped back and thrust at its eyes. The hobgoblin raised its shield. Coel kicked it in the knee. The knee buckled, and Coel put his foot into the hobgoblin's shield and shoved as it fell. Coel skewered the hobgoblin through the middle as it landed in the muck. The first goblin howled and clawed at the poison mud in its eyes. Coel cut it down and turned.

Luko and the other goblin rolled locked in battle in the dust. They shrieked and screamed on the bank trying to stab one another. Luko rolled on top. Coel strode forward and booted the goblin in the temple. Its limbs went limp. Luko drove his knife into its chest with both hands. "I hate you! I hate you!"

Coel ran to help Márta.

"Coel!"

He skidded at the sound of Zuli's desperate scream.

Across the river a half dozen goblins danced and shrieked and brandished their knives in victory. The black skinned Assassin emerged naked from the water. Impossibly wide shoulders and tapered limbs made the Assassin look like a Greek athlete carved of dark marble. The ridges of white bone sticking out from its skin made it a thing of horror. The Assassin dragged Zuli behind him through the muck by her hair. Her cloak was gone and her clothes half torn from her.

Coel broke into a run.

"Coel!" Orsini's voice boomed. "Do not! Swim the river, and you die!"

Coel ignored the dwarf. The burning feeling running up his

578 | CHUCK ROGERS

legs and filling his boots told him the river was already having its effect. He knew he could never reach Zuli in time, much less emerge from the poisoned water ready to fight.

Coel ran for his bow.

His dead camel lay in the mud of the shallows. Coel yanked his bow from beneath its body and snarled in rage. The great bow was a dead piece of wood in his hand. The string had broken beneath his camel's fall, and his spares were packed away in the saddlebag beneath its body. He hurled the weapon away from him with a curse.

"Coel!" Márta shouted from shallows. "Kill the shaman!"

Márta was besieged by goblins. Her scimitar flashed and severed their spindly limbs. Reza still sat atop his camel clutching the box. He reeled in the saddle under the onslaught of the hobgoblin shaman.

Zuli screamed as she was dragged ashore. "Coel!"

A crossbow lay in the dust where a hobgoblin had dropped it. Coel ran to the hobgoblin he had killed and seized bolts from its quiver. There was no time to unstrap the claw on the hobgoblin's belt to help him draw the bow. Coel took a bolt in his hand and stuck another between his teeth as he fell to the ground. He put his feet on the inner side of the bow and grabbed the string with both hands. Coel strove to straighten his body with all of his might. The string bit into his hands, and his shoulders shook with strain. The string slowly moved back. Coel let out a shout and heaved backwards. The string clicked behind the trigger nut and the strain was gone. He slapped the quarrel into the guide and rolled up.

The ebon Assassin pulled Zuli down the shore towards some rocks while she kicked and screamed. From his vantage, Coel could see a boat hidden among the boulders. The Assassin had only to shove it into the water and the current would take them north.

Coel raised the crossbow. They were not his favorite weapon, but he was familiar with them from his Academy days. The range was not long. He laid his thumb across the top of the stock and lined his knuckle with the head of the bolt. His fingers slowly took up the slack on the trigger lever.

Zuli's dagger appeared in her hand. The wicked curve of the

jambiya flashed as she hamstrung the Assassin. The Assassin's back arched as he began to fall, and Coel fired. The bolt punched between the abomination's shoulder blades and slammed him to the ground.

Zuli swayed as she rose. Blood smeared her lips. Her shoulders heaved, and blood spilled out of her mouth. She fell to her hands and knees and vomited forth more. The blood was black. Coel's heart froze. Zuli had not been wounded. She was bleeding from within.

The river was killing her.

The goblins on the far shore surged towards the dying thief.

Coel dropped and thrust his feet into the bow of the crossbow again. He heaved backward. He cursed as the string pulled out of his bloody hands. He seized it again and yanked back with all of his might. The crossbow cocked, and Coel slid a bolt into the guide as he rose.

Zuli was beset.

The goblins danced around her. She slashed at them with her dagger. They darted around her, thrusting with their long knives. In the time it had taken Coel to load the crossbow they had wounded her twice. Bright blood splashed her thigh and smeared her skin under her rent tunic. The shrieks of the goblins rose as they smelled her weakness.

Coel snarled as he tried to take aim at the darting, leaping creatures.

Zuli screamed as one got behind her and rammed its knife into her back. She spun and slashed, and the spindly creature fell back clutching its face. A goblin dove into her legs and Zuli tottered. A goblin leaped upon her back. Coel's teeth clenched as his aim wavered from target to target. He could not shoot them all. He could not shoot any without shooting Zuli.

A knife sank into Zuli's side. Another goblin seized her thigh. Zuli slashed and hacked at the creatures that swarmed her. Zuli's tunic was torn from her, and she was clothed only in goblins and blood. Her eyes locked with Coel's across the river dividing them.

"Coel!"

The creature on Zuli's back yanked her head back by the hair and bit into her neck.

Zuli screamed.

The crossbow thrummed in Coel's hand.

The bolt hissed across the river and sank between Zuli's breasts up to the fletching. Zuli's eyes rolled back in her head as she fell beneath the goblin knives.

The crossbow fell from Coel's fingers. No rage came to him. There was nothing within him but a graveyard filled with everyone he had ever cared for. Coel turned his head. The sounds of battle still raged on the shore. Coel scooped up his sword and waded into the river.

Márta's grave was still empty.

It would not be filled this day.

Márta fought knee deep in the shallows. Dead goblins floated in the gray water turning it red. Two still lived and tried to aid the hobgoblin she fenced with. The water was waist deep to them, and it hampered their movement. Márta kept Reza's camel to her back as she fought. Her scimitar rang as she parried blows.

An Assassin crept towards her from the shallows with poisoned push daggers in each deformed hand. The veins and sinews crawling across its flesh and its exposed bones made it look like it had been turned inside out.

Coel drew his dagger and flung it.

It was a poor throw, but Coel did not care. All he needed was a distraction. The dagger's handle bounced off of the Assassin's back, and its head turned. The face that regarded Coel was little more than a jawed mass of raw meat. The Assassin let forth a gurgling scream and came splashing at Coel.

Coel raised his sword overhead with both hands. As the thing thrust at him he hacked off one of its hands. He circled to its wounded side and slashed down through its knee and sent it floundering into the river. As it turned Coel thrust the point of his sword through its eye socket and rammed its head beneath the water and pinned it to the riverbed. He twisted his sword violently within the deformed skull and yanked the blade free.

Coel waded in and cut down one of the goblins besetting Márta. She snarled as she parried the hobgoblin champion's whirling knife-axes. "Coel! Kill the shaman!"

Coel ignored her. He took a great two-handed swing at the hobgoblin. It had to cross its weapons to stop the overhead blow. In an eyeblink Márta opened its throat. The remaining goblin screeched as Coel skewered it. Márta looked up at Reza. "Master!"

Reza reeled in the saddle. He clutched the box and rammed the key in the lock. The iron straps clicked free. Reza hurled the box to the shore. He put one hand to his turban and stretched forth his fist as the box tumbled in the dust. The scarab ring gleamed at the hobgoblin shaman.

The black hand scuttled towards the shaman through the dust.

Coel went to aid Orsini. The dwarf had lost his shield, and a hobgoblin chopped at him with sword blows. Orsini could barely block them with the haft of his hammer. He faltered as he was driven back towards the river.

The hobgoblin backed up as Coel ran in. Coel thrust at its face and it raised its shield to block. Orsini bellowed with effort and swung his hammer down on the hobgoblin's foot like he was driving a tent spike. The hobgoblin howled as its foot splayed like clay beneath the blow. Coel half-beheaded it with a chopping stroke to the neck as it faltered.

Orsini fell to his knees wheezing. "Well, that was timely." Coughing wracked the exhausted dwarf. Coel looked to Marius.

Both of his opponent's knife-axes stood imbedded in his body. The priest held the hobgoblin up in the air at arm's length. The tips of the hobgoblin's boots barely brushed the ground. The chain of Marius' flail was wrapped around the hobgoblin's throat. Marius held the feebly flailing hobgoblin aloft and choked the life out of it. The hobgoblin's eyes rolled back in its head, and Marius dropped it to the ground. Daggers, crossbow bolts, and knife-axes pierced Father Marius' body like a pincushion.

Coel strode towards the last hobgoblin.

The shaman lay in the dust, thrashing with its hands at its

throat. The green skin of its face purpled as the hand of Tuman Sunqur choked it do death. Spittle drooled around the hobgoblin's tusks. Its legs kicked and its fighting nails tore at the hand. Coel shoved his sword through the hobgoblin's chest. The shaman jerked once as the steel slid into its heart. Coel pulled the blade free as the hobgoblin went limp.

There were no more opponents.

Coel fell to his knees. Blood ran down his chin and his cheek. He leaned on his sword and sobbed for breath. Burning and itching ran up and down his sodden legs, and his limbs would not stop shaking. Coel looked to the river. Reza's head hung like a drunk as Márta dragged him up onto the bank.

"Coel." Orsini raised a shaky hand. Coel looked to where the dwarf pointed. The hand crawled off into the dust. Coel was of a mind to let the thing go and be done with it, but he rose and limped in pursuit. The black hand scuttled across the Waste like a spider.

Coel caught up. He staggered beside it and realized he did not have the box nor anyway to force the horror back where it belonged. He was not going to pick the thing up with his hands. Coel matched its pace for an exhausted moment. Every movement was an effort. The bones of his hips ached arthritically. The skin of his legs and groin burned as if they were blistering. Anger kindled in Coel's breast.

Coel raised his sword and drove it down like a spike. The hand spasmed as it was pinned it like an insect. The fingers of the hand scrabbled and clawed frantically at the dust. Coel knelt and flipped his first two fingers at the hand as he took a ragged breath.

"That for you!"

Coel reeled and looked about at the emptiness of the Waste. He spat on the hand. "This is all your doing, then, is it? Is it?" Coel's voice rose toward hysteria. "Your bastard owner stretched you forth and did all this! Did he not? Did he not, then! Well, bugger him! And bugger you! Bastard! You're not going anywhere, then, are you! And neither is sodding Saint Tomas or Sunqur or whatever the one-handed sheep-shagging shite's name is! Oh, I will bloody well see to that! God as my witness I will! I will--"

"Coel!" Orsini leaned on his hammer and jerked his head at

the river. "The boy!"

Coel blinked.

He had forgotten about Luko.

The boy stood by the bank of the river. The goblin he had killed lay at his feet. Snorri's bloodstained knife hung in his hand. Orsini's buckler lay in the dust. Blood covered Luko's tunic. The boy stared across the river without moving. There were five goblins on the other shore. One lay in the dust rocking and holding its wounded face. Another sat and cradled its bloody shoulder. The other three squatted on their heels in a huddle.

They tore at Zuli's flesh with their knives and teeth.

Coel ran to the river and scooped Luko up in his arms. The boy's blue eyes stared wide as saucers, but they stared into Coel's without seeing anything. Coel carried him over to Márta and Orsini. The dwarf knelt with his head resting on the head of his hammer. Blood dripped from his beard. His camel slowly walked over to him. Its brown eyes watched the dwarf with immense sadness. Orsini's voice was little more than a whisper. "Coel. Gather up the camels that remain. The heat of the day comes. Set up a lean-to. We must rest for a few hours, but we cannot camp here. We must be well away from the river by nightfall. The Old Man of the Mountain knows we are within the Waste. He will send more Assassins."

Márta threw down her cloak and Reza fell out of her arms upon it. Coel laid the boy next to him. Luko's eyes were open but his body was limp. Márta handed Coel a water skin and he gulped at it. He lowered the skin with a gasp and looked at Reza. The sorcerer's skin was gray as ash. His eyes were closed, and his mouth hung open. "Does he live?"

Márta wiped at his face. "He lives." Her eyes grew bright with tears as she looked at Luko. "What is wrong with him?"

Orsini sighed. "The boy has seen too much. The hobgoblins killed his father. The goblins ate his mother. He watched Snorri die. He killed for the first time today, and then he watched the goblins eat Zuli. He has lost two sets of parents. It is too much. His mind has gone elsewhere."

Tears spilled out of Márta's eyes. "Will he . . ."

"Make him a sleeping draught, like those you have been mixing for the Walladid. One quarter the strength or less. Sleep is what he needs now. If his mind is still hiding when he wakens, well, the Walladid is a master of mesmerism. Perhaps he can lead the boy back from wherever he is."

Coel stood and went to the camels. He did not let his eyes stray across the river. He could restring his bow and shoot at the goblins, but they would only scatter into the rocks with the first shaft, and return to their feeding come nightfall. Coel splashed to his dead riding camel. He cut its pack straps with his dagger and dragged his saddlebags ashore. Seven of their sixteen camels still lived. The beasts stood about shaking and huddling in ones and twos. Two lay dead in the shallows. The others slowly floated downstream. Coel gathered as much equipment as he could and piled it. He pounded stakes with aching slowness and set up a lean-to to give shade against the growing heat of the sun.

His hands shook as he finished. He found a wineskin and drained nearly half of it. The wine steadied him. He looked over at Marius. The arsenal of knife-axes, push daggers, and crossbow quarrels he had pulled from his flesh lay piled at his feet. Coel looked over at Luko. Coel forced himself to look across the river at the feasting goblins. He slowly looked back at the sorcerer where he lay.

Coel made his decision.

He reached into one of his saddlebags and pulled forth a heavy piece of folded parchment. He walked back to the others with document in hand. Orsini had risen to his feet again. "Coel, help us carry Luko and Walladid to the shelter."

"I have something to say," Coel looked down upon Reza and his face twisted. "While his lordship here still sleeps."

Márta's head jerked up at his tone. Orsini shook his head in infinite weariness. "And what is that, Coel?"

Coel handed him the parchment. "This is a letter of credit for five hundred ducats of Venetian gold."

Orsini stared at it. "It is."

"That is the seal of Hypatia Angeli the V."

"Yes."

"Do you accept its worth?"

"It is as good as gold, Coel. Just what is this you are about?"

"Then my debt to you and Reza is paid. I am dissolving our association, as agreed to in our contract. I owe you my friendship, Orsini. Know that you always have that." Coel nearly spat as he looked down at Reza. "Him I owe nothing."

Márta gasped. "Coel!"

"Come sundown, I am leaving. I am taking Luko with me."

Orsini closed his eyes. "Coel, you will die."

"No, Orsini!" Coel stabbed his finger at the dwarf. "You will die! Look at you. You can barely stand, and look at him!" They all gazed upon Reza where he lay like a corpse. "You think he can raise the shade of Tuman Sunqur? Look around you! Look at this place! If Reza is to be believed, Tuman Sunqur created this place! And you think Reza can control him? Looking like that?"

Orsini said nothing.

Márta cradled Luko's head. "Coel, Luko needs Reza. He can heal the boy. He can--"

"Reza shall not touch him!"

"Coel," Márta's lip trembled. "Please."

"Come with me."

"You know I cannot."

Coel's heart broke apart in his chest. "Please."

Márta shook. "I cannot."

Coel turned away. He looked out across the Waste for long moments. It resembled his life. He could not save his family. He could not save Marisol. He could not save Oleg, or Snorri. He had fulfilled his promise to Zuli, and she had died by his hand. Orsini was dying. Coel's eyes grew hot. Márta would not leave her master. He could not save either of them. Coel wiped at his eyes angrily. He could save Luko.

Or he could die trying.

Coel turned. His eyes met Márta's. She wept bitterly.

"I am going to follow the river south. If I get out of the Waste, I will head back into Persia. I will take the boy to Cyprus. I will go to the Sisters of Limmasol. You said the nuns there are skilled healers. I will see to the boy's healing and see that he is educated in art and letters."

Márta wiped her eyes and said nothing.

"You told me that Reza will free you in four years. In four years, if I live, I will return to Cyprus. I will go to the convent in Limmasol. I will wait for you there through the summer."

Márta made a choking noise.

Coel took a pair of cloaks and took up Luko in his arms. He looked at Márta one last time. "Meet me there and I will marry you."

Coel went off to wait out the heat in the shadows of the two camels he had selected for his trek.

CHAPTER FORTY-ONE

"Son of Math!"

Coel jolted awake. His hand went to his sword.

The Academy blade was not by his side.

Reza stood over him. Coel had slept longer than he had intended. The sun was low in the sky, and it made a blood red glow around the wizard. Father Marius stood at his right hand. Márta stood at his left. Orsini stood beside her. The dwarf held the Academy blade. Reza held the box under one arm. The iron straps had been relocked. Reza looked horrible. His skin was ashen and dark circles bruised him beneath his eyes. The whites of his eyes were as red as an Assassin's. He held up the letter of credit from the Angeli.

"Is this true?"

Coel looked over at Luko. The boy still slept from the draught that Márta had given him. Coel rolled to his feet. The burning and itching of his skin and the ache in his joints was gone. He'd been healed in his sleep. He looked at Marius, but the tormented eyes told him nothing. Coel glanced at the red ball of the sun as it sank across the Waste. Coel met the sorcerer's gaze squarely. "I leave within the hour."

"You are not going anywhere."

Coel felt his anger rise. His eyes flicked to Father Marius. He knew if he threatened Reza in any way Marius would kill him. It occurred to Coel that such a thing might be exactly what Reza wanted. The rotting priest's mace and chain hung from his wrist. Coel reined in his temper and ignored the sorcerer. He turned his attention to Orsini. "That is my sword you have there."

"It is."

"May I have it back?"

Orsini sighed. "You may--"

"He may not." Reza interrupted.

Coel held out his hand to Orsini without taking his eyes off of the wizard. "My sword."

Coel kept the relief off of his face as Orsini slapped the hilt into his hand. The dwarf's voice was a weary beyond words. "Good luck, Coel. You are going to need it."

Coel's eyes flicked to Father Marius. The priest's flail was cocked. Coel slowly sheathed his sword with his left hand. The flail lowered slightly.

Reza glowered. "Orsini, I told the son of a slave he could not have his sword."

"Do you think I am deaf?"

Reza blinked.

The dwarf's eyes glittered. His great teeth were stained with dark blood as he smiled. "I held Coel's sword. He wished it back. If you think about it, the transaction is really none of your business."

Reza's ghostly pallor darkened.

Orsini's smile remained fixed on his face like it had been painted there. "You hold a letter of credit from Hypatia Angeli the V for five hundred pieces of gold. The Celt has honorably fulfilled his contract."

"He has fulfilled nothing!"

The smile died on Orsini's face. "It is you, Walladid, who told me to make the Celt an offer. It is I who hired him and it is I who stipulated the terms of his contract. I quote, *'In the second, his Commission of Debt to the Holy League shall be paid in full, and all obligations of duty to the Church shall be dissolved. These debts shall be assumed by myself and the Walladid, to whom he shall pay the remainder, from earned pay, spoils, or other negotiable methods of compensation. Once the debt is paid, he shall be considered a free contractor,'* and, further, in the fourth sub-clause, *'He shall be allowed to keep all surviving said weapons, armor, equipment, horses and livestock so issued to him when his duties are finished or terminated by mutual agreement.'* Now, it is I who paid the Pope five hundred pieces of gold, my gold mind you, to free Coel from his Commission of Debt. I acknowledge this debt as satisfied. I say our contract with him is terminated by mutual agreement. I say he was issued two camels. I say he may have them, and I say he is free to go. Now, is it truly your wish to try and dishonor our contract with him?"

"I say he is a dog. I say he has insulted me, hindered me, damaged my goods, and molested my property."

"Well, now, those are personal matters. I suggest you take them up with him." Orsini's bloodstained smile slid back onto his face. "However, you should know that I consider the Celt a friend of mine, and, were I you, I would think very carefully before I did anything rash."

Reza closed his eyes. When he opened them, he looked at Coel. His voice was very calm. "Go then, Coel, but go knowing this. Things walk this waste. Things you do not want to meet. Things only my power has kept at bay. Things worse than death shall befall you."

"I will take my chances."

"You will die, long before you can retrace your steps to the Kopet Mountains."

"I shall not retrace my steps. I shall follow the river south, to the mountains of the Afghanis. I shall keep going south until I find the Arabian Sea. From there, I will take ship to the Red Sea, and I will cross Egypt to reach the Mediterranean."

"You shall meet Assassins long before you reach the sea."

"I like killing Assassins."

"You cannot cross Egypt without meeting the Blue-Robes."

"Then I will bloody well give them your regards when I see them!"

"Enough!" The outburst cost the dwarf. He doubled over with a fresh fit of coughing.

"Yes, enough." The sorcerer's black eyes calculated Coel's mounting anger and the dwarf's weakness. The sorcerer smiled. "Go, then, Coel. Scurry away like the coward you are, and know that when next we meet, we meet as enemies."

"As you like," Coel spun on his heel. He took half a step and then turned back.

Coel took his last look at Márta.

Márta turned her face away. The desert wind blew her brown hair. Her eyes stared out into the Waste in utter desolation. The tears on her face cut Coel like knives. He sought for something to say, but he could only repeat himself. "Four years, Márta. In Limmasol. I will be there in the summer. If I live."

She did not turn to look at him. Coel's heart stuck in his throat. "I love you."

Márta did not turn. Coel turned to gather his gear.

"The boy stays."

Coel's hand went to his hilt. He heard the rattle of Marius' mace and chain. Coel shoved down his anger and shook his head in disgust as he turned. "If this is the extent of your spite, sorcerer, then it is a sad sick day for you."

The Persian wore his chess-face. "The boy is mine."

"I see no slave collar around his neck, Walladid." Coel spat the Walladid's own words back at him. "But, why don't we ask the boy himself, then? When he awakens, you may give him the choice between staying in the Waste with you and consorting with the dead, or going to Cyprus with me and riding horses and learning swordsmanship. I will abide by whatever the boy decides."

Reza's cheek twitched.

"Find yourself another apprentice, sorcerer. Snorri was going to adopt the boy. Were he alive he would never have let you take him into the Waste. I failed him in that."

"You fail everyone, Coel."

Coel went rigid.

"Walladid," Orsini struggled for breath. "This is foolishness. Let them go. It matters not."

"Well now, this is a personal matter between myself and the Celt. I will thank you to stay out of it." Reza turned his attention back to Coel. "Let us take account. You failed your father, your mother, your family, and your clan. You failed your Academy masters in Paris, and Oleg and Snorri both lay dead because you failed them in battle."

Coel's jaw muscles flexed.

"You failed Marisol, and now she burns in hell, a suicide, while maggots pick her bones in an unmarked grave."

"Walladid!" Orsini took a step forward and fell to his hands and knees in the dust.

"Master!" Márta pleaded. "I beg you!"

Coel seethed. Marius stood ready. Reza smiled on. Coel knew the sorcerer was engineering his death. "You are a bastard, Walladid, but you have a way with words, I grant you that."

"You are failing Márta now."

Coel felt like he'd been kicked in the stomach. His eyes flicked to Márta against his will. She looked back and forth between Coel and her master in anguish. Her hand was on her scimitar. Her eyes met Coel's pleadingly.

Reza's voice dripped spite. "You have failed everyone who was ever fool enough to care about you."

"Aye, there is truth enough in that."

"I am glad you admit it, and think of poor little Zuli. You promised to protect her, and yet she died, naked, beneath the goblin's knives. They dragged her carcass behind the rocks while you slept. They should be breaking her bones for marrow by now."

Coel clenched his fist to keep it from his sword.

"Allah only knows how many assassins had their way with her before she fell into your arms. Do you know how many times she offered herself to me, Coel? How she crawled on her belly and begged me to take her? There is nothing so vile I could have asked of her that she would not have done. Indeed, that she had not already done." Reza shrugged. "Of course, I do not swim in dirty water. Unlike you and your friend Snorri. You passed her back and forth between you like the whore she was."

"You . . ." Orsini whispered. "Shall not speak of ladies of my acquaintance in such a way." The dwarf struggled to rise. He failed and wretched dark blood into the dust of the Waste. Reza smirked at him, and then turned his smirk upon Coel.

Coel felt his composure fleeing him.

"Now, as for your friend Snorri?" The sorcerer grinned at the snarl that leaped unbidden onto Coel's face. "The boy is better off without such a fool for a father. Yaroslav fashioned himself a Viking, but he was just one more pretentious Rus peasant, born squalling in the snow to some Slavic sow who could not say no to sailors with coppers in their hands."

"By God I will . . . " Coel's teeth ground as he clung to the last shreds of will within him.

The flail of Father Marius rattled as he cocked his wrist.

"Snorri Yaroslav was a buffoon, and a drunk. He followed his pizzle to his death. To think he actually loved that diseased, half-breed whore you killed. Perhaps the ailments of Cupid that crawled between her legs like pestilence were what they had in common. I do not know, but I am sure in a few weeks you will be able to tell me."

Marius' undead eyes burned over the rim of his shield. His right hand drifted back for the blow.

Coel no longer cared.

Reza smiled on. "However, I can tell you this, Coel. Your friend Snorri died, like the swine he was, squealing like a stuck pig, and I am glad of it."

Coel grinned crazily. "I am sure you are."

"Would you like to know something else, Coel?" Reza's tone dropped low. "I could have saved him. I could have stopped Sandor's blade, but I did not. I simply could no longer stand the stench of him."

The rage within Coel did not break free. Instead it hardened into something clear and cold. "Do you know the last thing Snorri told me, Sorcerer?"

"Pray," Reza's smile was sickening. "Tell me."

"He said he was going to beat you in seventeen moves."

Reza's smile faded.

"He said barge captains had given him better games than

you."

Reza slowly straightened. His eyes closed and he turned his head away. "Very well then," He waved a hand carelessly in dismissal. "Marius. Kill Coel."

"Master!" Marta moaned. "No!"

Father Marius did not move.

Reza's eyebrows bunched with effort as he raised the scarab ring. "Marius! I command you! Kill Coel! Kill the son of Math!"

"Master! Please!"

Father Marius shook like a leaf in the wind, but he did not raise his weapon.

Reza stared in disbelief.

Coel bared his teeth like a wolf as he stepped forward. "You have overextended yourself, sorcerer. Snorri always said you would."

Reza took a startled step back. It was the first time Coel had ever seen fear in his eyes. Coel waggled his eyebrows at the wizard in savage exultation. The sorcerer's dark eyes blazed.

"Márta! Kill him!"

Coel stopped in his tracks. Márta's jaw dropped.

"Kill him!"

Márta drew her scimitar, but she stepped back from the both of them. "You cannot ask this!"

"I said kill him!"

"I beg of you!"

Reza's voice cracked like a whip. "Who is your master!"

Márta stepped back shaking and weeping.

"Kill him! It is my will!"

"No!"

Reza's voice thundered. "Obey me!"

Márta cast her scimitar into the dust. "I love him!"

594 | CHUCK ROGERS

Coel's heart burst from his chest. "Come with me, Márta! Come with me right now! We can--"

Reza whirled upon him. "Then I will!"

The sorcerer's right hand rose. The scarab ring glittered with far more than the light of the fading sun.

Coel's sword cleared its sheath.

White light erupted out of Reza's palm. The light was so bright the sorcerer disappeared behind it. Coel's sword rose. For a fraction of a second the blade silhouetted into a thin black line before him.

The Paladin blade rang like a church bell.

The sword shivered in Coel's hand as though he had swung it against a tombstone. The vibrating ache of it ran down his arm like an avalanche and roared through his body. Coel lifted from his feet as his muscles rippled beneath his skin like a wave. The shuddering convulsions threatened to shatter his joints and break his bones as he hung flash blind and suspended in the terrible light. The force rang within him like a thunderclap. His heart hammered as if it would rip loose within his ribs. His brain bounced back and forth within his skull. The white light snuffed out like a candle. Coel fell to the ground.

His unconscious body quivered and twitched in the poison dust.

CHAPTER FORTY-TWO

The wind blew cold across the Waste. Coel awoke shivering in the dark. He lay face down upon the ground, and his nose and throat burned with the dust he had been breathing. Coel coughed, and his body cringed with the pain of his battered lungs. Every square inch of him ached like lockjaw. He rolled over with a groan. The stars shone down hard and bright.

"So," Orsini's voice was little more than a whisper. "You are awake."

Coel held his ribs and coughed. A coughing fit shook Orsini in sympathy. The dwarf was a dark bulk sitting against a rock a few feet away. Coel spoke in a parched croak. "What happened?"

"Well," Orsini wiped at his lips. "You have managed to get us stranded again."

"Reza left you here, then?"

"He did, indeed, and he took all the camels and the supplies."

"What?" Coel tried to sit up and couldn't. "What has happened?"

"Well, you and the Walladid came to disagreement. I do not know what it is exactly that the sorcerer tried to do to you, but whatever it was, your sword seemed to take the brunt of it."

"My sword . . . "

"It seems intact. I put it back in its sheath. It is beside you."

Coel fingers fumbled and clasped the blade. "Ah."

"Well, anyway, you fell, and the Walladid nearly fell himself with the effort. He could not make Marius finish you off, and Márta refused. I think he was considering slitting your throat, but I managed to stand in his way. So he ordered Marius to string the camels. Refusing to kill you seemed to have taken most of the fight out of Marius as well. Though Reza told Marius to kill me if I tried to stop them or mount. I do not think Marius had it in him to refuse that, even if he wanted to, and, to be frank, if Marius and I traded blows this day, I think I would get the worst of it. I am sorry, Coel, but it was all I could do to just stand between you and Reza's knife."

"What about Márta?"

"She loves you, Coel, and she refused to kill you, but the Walladid still has immense emotional influence over her. He told her to take Luko and mount her camel. She was weeping, but she obeyed him."

"What of Luko?"

"He was still sleeping, last I saw him."

Coel stared up at the stars. "So, we have neither food nor water nor weapons, then."

"Well, you have your sword, and I have my hammer. Reza made off with the rest of our belongings. As for food and water, I am not sure."

"What do you mean you are not sure?"

"I think Márta cut some things loose for us when she and Marius gathered up the camels."

"Like what?"

"I do not know. I was too tired to investigate. When I was sure Reza had gone, I decided to take a nap. I awoke some hours ago. I have not had the will to do anything since."

"I know how you feel."

"I am glad somebody does."

Coel held his ribs. "That wizard needs killing."

"I agree. Let us swear vengeance against him."

"All right." Coel felt light-headed and punch-drunk. "Do you know the Greek poet, Archilochos?"

"I do."

"Good, then this for the Walladid." Coel tried to clear his throat.

"Let the wind and waves

drive him off course.

And let the longhaired Thracians seize him

naked and without a friend,

at Salmydessos

And let him eat slave's bread

and be beaten

Then let him freeze in the cold,

tangled in seaweed, flat

on his belly like a dog,

teeth chattering, at the sea's edge,

puking up brine

And let me watch it happen,

for the way he double-crossed me."

"And then let him be delivered into our hands." The dwarf let out a pleased sigh. "I liked the Hellenes. Now there was a race of humans who really knew how to bear a grudge."

Coel lay in the dust. "So, how shall we kill him?"

"I do not know. We have no camels. We could try to swim the river. The Assassins left their boat on the other shore. Perhaps there is food and water in it. We can push it into the river and let the current take us. Once we are out of the Waste, we can plan our revenge."

"I do not fancy swimming that river."

"Neither do I, and there are at least four goblins hiding in the rocks on the other side. They have eaten Zuli and are refreshed. They know we are here. I would not make it across that poisoned water; and if you did emerge on the other shore, I fear they would make meat of you."

"I do not fancy taking the river North."

"Indeed, only assassins are likely to be there."

"No, I mean I do not fancy fleeing. Reza must be stopped."

"I had thought you might say that."

"Have you no ideas, Orsini? You almost always have one."

"A number of things have occurred to me while I have sat here, but I do not like any of them."

"What do you mean?"

"For one, you are going to have to kill Reza."

"You do not wish to help, then?"

"More than anything. However, I fear I shall not be available."

"What do you mean?"

"I am dying, Coel. I cannot walk. The coughing has eased, but I have been vomiting blood since dusk. I feel the poison within me. There is no part of me it is not eating. I have stayed strong as long as I can, but now my bones are hollow within me. The battle is lost. I shall be dead before the dawn."

"No," Coel's eyes stung with more than the dust of the Waste. "No."

"I am sorry, Coel. I wish it were different, but there is simply nothing left of me."

Coel had seen war and plague. He had seen such unnatural calm upon its victims. The dwarf had accepted his death.

Orsini was finished.

"Kill Reza for me, Coel. Send him to hell, and I swear to you I shall make a detour from my own journey and meet him there for a reckoning."

Coel closed his eyes. "All right."

"I have had other, unhappier thoughts."

"Unhappier, then?"

"Yes. Reza baited you so that you would attack him and Marius would kill you."

"I had guessed that." Coel rolled his head painfully to look at the dwarf. "You let that go on a bit too long, I should think."

"I was in poor shape to stop it, and I will admit, once the wizard began insulting Zuli's memory, I rather hoped you would run him through."

"I wish I had."

"You would have most likely died in the attempt. You nearly did anyway."

"Ah," Coel's head rolled back to look at the sky. "So, what are these thoughts that trouble you so?"

"Insulting you was a clever ploy, but his stubbornness about keeping Luko was foolish."

"Yes."

"Reza is not a foolish man."

"No."

"Reza was once of the Blue-Robe sect. When they initiated him into the Inner Mysteries, he learned the truth of Tuman Sunqur. He then dedicated his life to resurrecting him and taking his power."

"Aye, and?"

"I know little of sorcery, but I know that the resurrection of the dead is either a miracle bestowed by the gods or the work of blackest magic."

"No god smiles upon the Walladid. If one did, he would not need Marius."

"I agree."

"So, what then?"

"I have heard the blackest magics require blood sacrifice. I believe the blood of virgins is preferred."

The image of Márta naked upon an altar leaped into Coel's mind. He saw her bleeding heart carved from her body by a knife held in Reza's hand. Sickening fear shivered his guts. "No!"

"I should have deduced this before, but my own ambitions blinded me. Márta is a virgin. The Walladid raised her from childhood. He kept her by his side in her youth and put her in a military convent when she came to womanhood so that she would not be spoiled. I think perhaps he acquired her from the beginning so that he would have the virgin blood he needed always at hand. Until this day, she has been as faithful as a dog to him. She will defend him to the death, and she has helped him in his magics before. When he goes to sacrifice her, she will not see the knife until it is too late."

Coel's skin crawled. "And Luko is a ten-year-old boy."

"Yes, Reza must have thought that Márta might be killed on the journey. There was no guarantee whom amongst us would survive to see Tuman Sunqur's tomb. With her military training alone, Márta is an extremely valuable asset. One he need not expend now that he has the boy."

"She would never let him kill Luko."

"Who knows what lies he will tell her? Or how he will make it happen. He may mesmerize her so that she never remembers Luko save in fragments of her dreams. Of course neither you nor Snorri would have let this happen. So, to my undying shame, I believe your deaths were written the night I hired you." Orsini hung his head "I beg you in this moment to forgive me."

"I forgive you, and I promise you," Coel grit his teeth and forced his muscles to obey. "I will kill him." He rolled over and gathered his knees beneath him. Coel looked out into the starlit gloom. He spied a dark lump out in the dust where the camels had been. "You say Márta left us supplies?"

The dwarf sagged against the rock.

"Orsini?"

The dwarf's chin fell upon his chest. His breath came in short shallow gasps.

Orsini was dying.

Coel tried to stand and failed. He crawled on his hands and knees through the dust. He felt like crying from the effort of it. He dragged his aching bones onward and found a pair of saddlebags.

Coel pulled at one and heard the slosh of water. He opened it up and pulled out a wineskin. Coel opened the stopper and squirted the water into his dust-poisoned mouth.

Well-being filled Coel's belly. His pain and weariness fell from him like a dirty cloak. Coel arose and stared at the skin. It was one of the two they had stored the remaining water Father Marius had consecrated. Coel examined the rest of the bag's contents. He found a full-sized water bag and a brick of dates wrapped in paper along with a bundle of dried meat strips. The other saddlebag held another full-sized water skin and a pouch of parched grain.

Coel took another long swallow of consecrated water and felt strength fill him to the top of his head. He looked over at the dark lump of the dying dwarf by the river.

Orsini's breaths were labored sips of air. They came slower and slower.

Coel strode back over. The giddy strength of the healing filled him. "Orsini."

" . . . What?"

"I have heard that long after the skimming feet of an elf have stumbled, a dwarf will march on."

"That is true enough."

"I have heard that long after a goblin's back has broken, a dwarf will dig."

Orsini did not look up. "I appreciate what you are trying to do, my friend. But go, now, and leave me in peace."

"I believe even the Venetians who named you would shudder at how a dwarf can nurse vengeance."

The dwarf sat silent.

"Orsini, what would you endure to see Reza dead?"

The dwarf raised his head with great effort and groaned. "Short of being buggered, Coel, I would endure just about anything, why do you ask?"

"Good."

Coel put his foot into Orsini's chest and pushed him over.

The dying dwarf wheezed as Coel took a knee on his chest and pinned him to the ground. Coel thrust the spout of the wineskin between Orsini's teeth and squeezed. The dwarf thrashed feebly and tried to spit the water out. Coel slapped his palm over Orsini's mouth and leaned on it.

"Swallow!"

The dwarf swatted at Coel with the strength of an infant.

"Swallow it, damn you!" Coel leaned back and punched Orsini in the belly. Orsini made a strangling noise as he swallowed. Coel shoved the spout into the back of the dwarf's throat and pinched off his nose. Orsini gagged as Coel forced a stream of the consecrated water directly down his gullet.

Orsini's hand seized Coel's shoulder with bone-crushing force and flung him away like a rag doll. Orsini was a menacing bulk in the dark as he rose. He reached out and took up his hammer.

"Damn you! Damn you to hell and die, Son of Math!" The dwarf strode forward. "Now, you get up! Get up or I shall pound you where you lay!"

The consecrated water put springs in Coel's legs and he leaped to his feet. His sword rang free. "You said you would endure anything!"

"Do not bandy words with me, toothpick! You know what I meant, God damn you!"

"No!" Coel thrust out his finger accusingly. "God damn you, Orsini! Márta or Luko must die so that the fiend who created this Waste shall live, and yet you would rather rot by the river than do anything about it!"

"I would rather rot here than have that priest's power upon me! You know that full well! It is a matter of religious principle!"

"Well, then, by God, let us talk about Marius a moment!"

"Bugger Marius! And bugger you!"

"No!" Coel roared. "Marius has been fighting Reza's will since the beginning! The sorcerer stole his soul, and still he fights! When I first offered to kill him he refused! He stayed on! He rots in his own flesh, and still he is trying to save Márta and Luko, and if you and I are to wreak vengeance upon the Walladid? Then by Christ you will endure a Christian healing and be bloody thankful for it!"

They faced each other for long moments beneath the stars. Orsini lowered his hammer. "What else was in the saddlebags?"

"Are you healed?"

"I am not well, but I will not die."

Coel held up the wineskin. "Will you drink more?"

"No, and it will go ill for you should you try forcing me."

"Good, because I am going to need it."

"What are you planning?"

"We have no camels. The Walladid is many hours ahead of us. He will not stop to camp. I do not think he will rest until he reaches Bukhara."

"That is a reasonable assumption."

"I am going to have to run him down. I do not expect you to keep up, but I expect you to follow me. Reza will need to rest before he attempts his abomination. Perhaps I can reach Bukhara and kill him before he begins."

"And if he kills you, you want me to finish him."

"You were already dead to him when he stranded us. He will be surprised to see me, but he will never expect you. He has our camels and weapons. Were I you, I would find my way to where he has hitched the camels and find your crossbow. Put a bolt through him on sight. That way you can avoid trading blows with either Marius or Márta."

"It is as sound a plan as any."

"I will leave you half the food and water." Coel looked out across the Waste. "When the hand tried to escape it crawled northeast. I think it would make a straight line towards its master."

"I agree."

Coel looked up at the stars. The Great Bear, Ursa Major, hung in the northwest. It pointed him to Polaris. Coel looked upon the North Star as he calculated the hour of night and the day of the month. He tracked his finger across the night sky. "There. The Crown of Cassiopeia. It would be due northeast. Beneath it we shall find Bukhara."

"Good," The dwarf's voice was stronger than it had been in weeks. "Good enough to steer by this night, but in this dust their trail may not last until the dawn. Listen well. Bukhara was once a great metropolis. Even in the Waste, you will find its signs. There will be the ruins of outposts, outlying towns and villages, milestones and the remnants of roads. All will lead to the fallen city."

Coel went to their meager supplies. Orsini walked beside him. "It would be best if you could wait for me and we do this together, but circumstances prevent it. However, it will take Reza and Marius many hours to prepare for what they must do. So, do not kill yourself to get there. Be smart. If you stagger in upon Reza half dead upon your feet, he will strike you down; and I will not be there to save you a second time."

"I understand." Coel unbuckled his war belt and sheathed his sword so he could carry it in his hands as he ran.

"Also, take heed. Marius may have resisted the Walladid once on your behalf, but he may not be able to do it again. You do not want to have to fight them both, much less Márta, as well. Take your own advice. First, find where they have tied up the camels. Find your bow, and then fill the Walladid with arrows from a distance. This is not a matter of honor. Nor even of revenge. This is a rescue, Coel. Do not let the Walladid see you if you can help it. Shoot him. Shoot him on sight. Shooting him the back would be best, and keep shooting him until he falls. Then shoot him some more just to be sure. Sorcerer's often have unnatural vitality."

"Aye." Coel wound his warbelt and thrust it into the saddlebag. He took half the food and gave the other half to Orsini and gave him the heavier of the two water bags. Coel held up the wineskin with the consecrated water. It had been less than full when he had found it. Now there were but a few swallows left. "You are sure?"

"I am sure, but a word of warning about that. Remember the rowers on the Dnieper River. Drink of that only when you must.

When the enchantment fails, so shall you."

Coel remembered the men who had fallen shuddering and twitching across their oars when Marius' power had left them. "Aye."

He took off his riding boots and put them in the saddlebag. The dust was soft and cool beneath his bare feet. He would run better without them, but when the dust burned by day he would need them or be lamed. Coel threw the bulging saddlebags across his shoulder. "I am off, then."

Orsini held up his right palm and spat upon it. "Luko and Márta shall live. The soul of Marius shall go free. Tuman Sunqur shall not rise. The Walladid does not leave the Waste alive."

Coel spat upon his own hand, and he and the dwarf shook upon it. "Luko and Márta shall live. The soul of Marius shall go free. Tuman Sunqur shall not rise. The Walladid does not leave the Waste alive."

"Then off with you," Orsini's great horse teeth gleamed in the dark. "I shall be along presently."

CHAPTER FORTY-THREE

Coel laid his sword across his shoulder and slowed to a walk.

The last star had fled the sky. The sun threw a golden crown over the horizon as it prepared to rise up out of the dust of the Waste. He had been running for hours. Coel took great ragged breaths as he walked. He stumbled slightly as he raised one foot and then the other and examined them. They had yet to crack or blister. The dead dust of the Waste was a blessing in that respect. It was like fine flour beneath his feet as he ran. A flour whose poison would rise like yeast within him once his feet did break open and the dust entered his flesh.

Coel aimed his right shoulder at the sun's corona and kept walking northeast as he tried to bring his breathing under control.

There had been a time when he could run up one side of Snowdon and down the other. He remembered running barefoot through fen and forest from dawn 'till dusk to bring down a stag, and slinging its meat across his shoulders to return late in the night. Seeing his thirtieth birthday in the Russia's eating thin gruel and sniveling in the cold had robbed him of his legs.

Coel glanced back. Somewhere behind him Orsini marched. Coel was reminded of the Tortoise and the Hare. He filled his lungs determinedly. If this was the best he could do, by noon the dwarf would have caught him and by nightfall the dwarf would be carrying him. Coel reached into the saddlebag for some food. He took out the dates Márta had wrapped for him.

Coel stopped walking as he took a handful from the package.

The wrapping was a page from the book he had given her. There was fresh ink upon it. Coel stuffed dates in his mouth and squinted as he held the paper up against the dawn's light.

-Beloved,

Coel's forgot his fatigue in an instant and started again.

-Beloved,

You must forgive me. I died when you and my Master came to blows. I gave thanks to God when I saw that you lived. I beg you, forgive me. I must go on. Reza is friendless in the Waste, and with each step walks as close to death as Orsini. Reza is my Master. I am his sworn bodyguard. But it is more than that. He is the only family I have ever had.

Whatever I do now is wrong. You once shared with me the words of your father, who said the last refuge of a warrior is honor. Coel, Reza is the only father I have ever known. However much I hate what he did to you, it would be utmost betrayal if I were to abandon him in this terrible place.

I know you loathe him and would see him dead, but know this. My Master never lies, nor does he ever break a bargain. He has told me that upon my twenty-fifth birthday I shall be freed, and I shall be free to choose my path.

Beloved, I choose you. I bid you, I beg you, think not of Reza or revenge. If you truly love me, then live. Go south as you said you would. Save Orsini. Then, in four years, if I am still your desire, sail for the Island of Cyprus. There, in the City of Limassol, I shall await you, my arms open to your every embrace, and all sweet longings shall be addressed. I must go, but my heart, my love, and my longing go with you.

I love you. I love you. I love you.

- Márta

Coel folded the paper and slipped it into his tunic over his heart. He took the full sized water skin from the bag and drank until his thirst was gone. He saw no reason to ration himself. He would either reach Bukhara in time or he would not. He would expend the food and water as he needed it. The consecrated water he would use when his legs failed him. Coel adjusted the saddlebags across his shoulder and took his sword back in his hands.

He would marry Márta. Luko would live. His legs would carry him. He would give them no choice in the matter. Once he had been the greatest runner in Gwynned. There had been no Spring Fair when he had not left his competition gasping in his wake. If his muscles did not remember, then he would forcibly remind them.

Reza would not leave the Waste alive.

Coel examined the ground. The softness of the dust was also his enemy. The tracks of the camels were already fading as the desert wind began to blow across them. In an hour there would be no sign.

Coel ran into the rising sun.

* * *

"Augh!"

Orsini awoke with a roar. Vileness covered his face. Orsini snatched up his hammer as he rolled away from his assailant. A bestial head loomed silhouetted by the high sun. The dwarf blinked at the blinding glare and retreated deeper into the boulders he had been using for shelter. Orsini brought up his hammer as he could retreat no further. The great yellow head of the creature snaked into his redoubt on its serpent-like neck. Its harelip split to reveal massive yellow teeth. Huge brown eyes mooned at him through eyelashes as thick and dark as a courtesan's.

"God's salty balls!"

Orsini's camel groaned at him plaintively. A foot-long strand of drool stretched precariously from her lips and dangled in the afternoon wind.

Orsini wiped froth from his face and shook his head in wonder.

The camel looked awful. Her twin humps sagged like a pair of deflated bladders on either side of the saddle. The skin hung loose upon her bones, and fur matted where it wasn't falling out. Her exposed skin scaled and flaked. Orsini dropped his hammer and took his mount's head in his hands. He tsked as he surveyed his animal. "Oh, my poor girl, how I've misjudged you. You are faithful to the last."

The camel grunted lovingly.

The beast was fully laden. Orsini shook his head. The camel was like a sinking ship. If she were to carry him anywhere he would have to lighten the load. Orsini began unburdening his camel. He threw away his paper, pen and ink, his razor, brush and basin, and his spare clothes. His crossbow and his quiver of bolts lay packed as he'd left them. He looked upon his weapons grimly and pulled his heavy spear from the pack straps. If he could not win with crossbow and hammer, then the deed could not be done. He unbuckled his warbelt and abandoned his sword. The dwarf continued sorting his belongings and stopped. Orsini's eyebrows bunched in anguish. There was no other choice. He knew where the really useless weight lay. Orsini pulled a set of saddlebags from the harness and grunted with effort. He opened one, and had to close his eyes as he upended it.

He flinched as his sacks of gold struck the dust of the Waste. The silver came easier. Orsini pulled his purse from his belt and tossed it upon the pile. He turned his back on what remained of his wealth and patted his camel. "Look at us, girl, like Jesuits sworn to poverty. Pilgrims, walking in the Shadow of Death. I fear all we have is each other, now."

The camel drooped its eyelashes at him.

His mount carried four water bags. Orsini greedily finished the water and food Coel had given him. He took a water bag from the camel's harness and uncorked it. "Here, old girl, I'll buy you a drink for your troubles."

The camel took the spout between its teeth and tilted its head. Drool dangled from her mouth but not a drop of the water. The great neck undulated as the camel swallowed. Orsini upended the water bag and squeezed until it was dry. "There you are, pet. Share and share alike. You and I, partners, to the end."

Orsini's camel gurgled at him in agreement.

Orsini lowered the skin and eyed his camel's reins. A piece of halter rope hung from them. He ran his thumb across the soft tuft of the severed rope thoughtfully. A blade that would shear silk had cut it.

Orsini smiled. "Márta."

He rummaged through the saddlebags again but found nothing. Only when his camel knelt for him to mount did he see the note tied with twine to one of the brass saddle horns.

> *-Orsini,*
>
> *If you read this, you live, and your faithful beast has found you. Your camel resisted leaving you from the moment I tied it to the coffle. I cut it free while my Master slept, and it wandered back west without urging.*
>
> *Orsini, I beg of you, drink of the consecrated water when Coel offers it, if you have not already. You must live, and if our friendship has any meaning, take Coel south. Beat him and bind him across the saddle if you must, but take him from this place.*
>
> *In four years I am free. I have chosen to marry Coel, if he will still have me. Plead my case, I implore you. You of all people know that I cannot leave Reza now. For what he has done to you and Coel I cannot forgive him. In four years, I will be free of him, forever.*

I love Coel, and I love you. It is my dearest dream to marry Coel in Cyprus in the Cathedral of Limmasol. In my dream I see you there, in your finest silks, shaming every dandy in Florence with your glory as you give away the bride.

My love, like sunlight through a diamond, for you my friend.

- Márta

"Ah, Márta. You deserve a fine, fine husband." The dwarf gazed across the Waste. "Though, I suspect the Celt shall have to suffice."

The sun was falling to the west, and the shadows thrown by the rocks grew long. Fatigue had overtaken him and he had overslept. He had been marching a day and a night. Coel and the camel must have passed one another in darkness. Somewhere ahead, the son of Math still ran, if he was not yet face down dead in the dust.

Orsini winced as he threw a leg over the saddle and settled himself. The poison within him was losing the battle, the might of Marius had seen to that, but the rearguard action it fought was stiff. When death was claiming him, he had felt light as a feather. Now, his body felt heavy as clay, and his joints seemed filled with hot sand. Living was always harder than dying, and though death was not so strong within him, it still hovered all around. Death was the dust of the Waste. Death was the sun in the sky. Death was a mace and chain waiting in the hands of poor dead Marius. Death was a million and one vile magics pouring forth from the fingers of a vengeful Walladid.

Orsini's eyes glittered.

What he owed that wizard would fill a sea of vengeance.

Orsini suddenly looked up from his ruminations. "I stand and impugn the Walladid, but it is I who have been remiss with my friends."

Orsini dismounted the camel and picked up his spear. He

took the small knife from his eating utensils and began working his spear's haft. A small pile of shavings quickly piled at his feet. He held up the spear and surveyed his work with a nod. He let out a shout and rammed the blade down into the dust so that it sank to its lugs. Orsini opened his hands westward in supplication at the falling sun.

"My friends, it is a poor marker I leave you, but it is the best that I can do. I bid you, take my sword to ward you on your journey and my gold to pay the ferryman if you must. Walk arm in arm, wander well together, and know this. If Valhalla, the Christian Heaven and the Elven Halls of Light keep their cold doors closed, then go you both to the place all good Dwarves go. There my kinsmen shall give you warm welcome. There shall they do you great honor. There shall you both be feasted for the friendship you have shown me. Wander well, until the day we meet once more."

Orsini remounted his camel. She rose up upon shaky legs and steadied herself beneath his weight. Orsini rubbed the beast's withers in sympathy. "Believe me, old girl, I know how you feel; but, I give you my word I shall be lighter before this is done."

They rode northeast.

Behind them Orsini's spear stood in mute testimony. Silver, gold, weapons and goods lay piled around it like offerings. The exposed white wood where Orsini had done his carving stood out like fresh paint in the black lacquered shaft. Only a dwarf would be able to read what was written there.

"Zuleikha and Snorri, lovers, and beloved friends."

CHAPTER FORTY-FOUR

Coel staggered to a halt. The road he stood upon was paved with smooth stones and wide enough to accommodate four wagons abreast with ease. He had not known what to expect, perhaps blackened ruins or walls fallen like Jericho.

Coel gazed upon glory.

He gazed upon lost Bukhara.

Great granite walls glowed pink in the setting sun. Above them, minarets rose, and gilded domes of gold caught fire in red light. Magnificent manors with domes and arched roofs almost glowed in sheaths of turquoise tile. Frescoes and Mosaics seemed to cover every square inch of the towers and buildings. Mighty Kiev was a rude collection of logs in comparison. Only as he came closer did Coel begin to see signs of the hobgoblin siege.

A deep moat surrounded the city. Coel peered down into it. It was not a moat, but a ditch. Two hundred years had left much of it filled with dust, but it was twenty feet across, and judging by the angles, the ditch had to be at least twenty feet deep. Sharpened stakes thrust up from the dust. The ditch was not part of the city's defense. It was an offensive weapon.

The hobgoblins had circumvallated Bukhara. The great ditch encircled the entire city to prevent counter attacks or escape. In the dust below Coel saw the bleached skull of an elephant. Coel forded the dry moat warily and followed the road to the great gate. The brass-sheathed timbers had been broken by battering rams. The squat towers on either side of it had been crumbled by catapult stones.

Coel walked under the broken arch and entered the lost city of Bukhara.

As he entered, he saw the signs of war. No withered bodies strew the streets. Hobgoblins took the living as cattle. They ate the fallen. Nothing went to waste. Some domes had been smashed by catapults. Other, stouter buildings were blackened by fire. Great stones lay about where the hobgoblins siege engines had flung them.

The doors of nearly every building had been forced as the human inhabitants had barricaded themselves against the horde when the great gate had been breached. Many streets were pocked with goblin holes. Coel could imagine the citizens of the great city, starved by siege, their gates falling, suddenly dealing with the horror of goblins erupting from their tunnels by the thousands within the walls.

The great city, itself, showed no signs of whatever had created the Waste. Only that nothing lived. No birds roosted in the eaves. No cats or dogs prowled the empty streets. The few trees that had not fallen stood like gray skeletons. Rows of marble planter boxes that had once held legions of flowers were empty save for sere twigs and dead soil. Not a single weed grew anywhere. It was as if the Lord of Hosts had smote Bukhara as he had smitten Egypt. Only here he had not taken the First Born, but had smitten life itself. There was no sound but the moan of the wind through the breached buildings and sifting of the dust.

Coel stopped before a tattered bag in the street before him. Thick pieces of gold lay spread before him where the bag had ruptured. In his mind, Coel could see its owner, herded from his house by the hobgoblin invaders, his sack of his riches torn from his grasp and discarded as wasteful weight. Hobgoblins did not fight for silver and gold. They made war for meat. Iron armor and weapons of steel were the spoils of battle they prized.

Coel rested a moment. He'd drunk the last of his water hours ago. He had last eaten a day ago. In the wineskin, perhaps two or three swallows remained of the water empowered by Father Marius. Coel had run and walked for two days and nights. Scant sips of the consecrated water had strengthened him. Coel felt light-headed and boneless. The holy water was no longer a source of healing. He was using it now as a source of strength. It was a strange, hollow sort of strength. Coel knew his body had failed him long ago. The strength he possessed now was borrowed. He wondered if he could pay the debt once that strength had departed him.

Coel raised the wineskin and took a deep swallow.

Strength filled him. His head cleared. Coel took a deep breath and took stock. The city was huge, but it would have a central square and a marketplace. From there, he would be able to locate the citadel. There would have to be a mausoleum someplace.

Coel walked down the main street. He walked until he came to the great square in the city center. Ancient stalls lay wrecked and broken wagons overturned. Coel turned about. Streets radiated out from the square like the spokes of a wheel.

The breeze blew, and Coel lifted his nose to it. The lack of sound was startling enough, but Bukhara was so lifeless it had no smell. Coel smelled something now. He smelled camel dung.

He followed his nose. There in the middle of the street lay a pattern of fallen droppings. Coel knelt and examined the scat. The excrement was thin and shriveled, but it was less than a day old. The camels had drunk little and eaten nothing since entering the Waste, but they still attempted to rid themselves of the poison dust they breathed and swallowed. Coel rose and walked down the street. A great building loomed ahead. The falling sun left the city streets in shadow, but the spire of the building ahead was still in sun. Its golden dome blazed in the dying light. Coel heard strange noises upon the evening breeze. He drew his dagger and left it lying point first down the street as a marker and broke into a jog.

It was actually a series of buildings. Their walls stood higher than that of the city. It had to be the citadel. The gates here had been smashed down. Here, the signs of fighting were thicker. Siege engines had crushed whole sections of the exterior walls. Tiles were torn in great strips where the grapples and the hooks of siege ladders had ripped into them. Coel heard the grunt of a camel.

He entered the courtyard. Six of the beasts stood hobbled and looking much the worse for wear. Coel spied his pack camel and moved to it. He grinned to himself. They had not unloaded all the camels. Two water bags hung from the saddle horns. Coel took one and drank until he was full. He took dried meat from another and wolfed it down almost without chewing. He took deep breaths between bites of food and drank more water.

Coel looked at his bow. It rested in its waxed canvas case. Coel took out the bow and strung it, and then examined his arrow bags. An idea came to him as he examined his selection of remaining arrows. He took twelve arrows and sheafed them. Coel pondered half a moment and then began unpacking his armor and donning it. When he was clad, he dusted off his battered black hat and put it on over his skullcap. He buckled his warbelt around his waist and girded his sword to him.

Coel laid a gleaming arrow across his bow and entered the citadel.

The vast halls were caverns of shadow, but the high windows and marble latticework allowed enough light for Coel to see the results of horrific carnage. The last stand in the city of Bukhara had been fought room by room within the citadel. Arrow shafts and broken weapons littered the floor. The clothes of the dead lay in torn piles where the corpses had been stripped and carried away as meat.

The noises were louder within the halls. Ghostly moans echoed, and hollow thumps seemed to emanate beneath Coel's feet. He moved to the foot of a great staircase and paused at an even odder sound.

Someone was clapping hands above.

A second later Coel heard the sound of a child's laughter. Márta laughed and the clapping resumed.

Coel took the stairs four at a time.

He ran down a gallery. Ensconced balconies overhung the great hall below. Even here all the doors had all been forced. At the end of the hall a door had a tapestry drawn across it. Lamplight peeped out from the folds.

Coel halted at the doorway. Márta's voice rose in song. She sang in a language Coel did not know, but it was in time to the clapping. Luko's voice butchered the words in rhythm with her as they clapped their hands together. Someone missed, and Luko burst out laughing once more.

Coel pulled the tapestry aside.

Márta and Luko sat on a divan playing a clapping game.

"Coel!" Luko jumped up from the divan and charged full tilt. "Coel! Coel! Coel!" The boy vaulted up into Coel's arms.

"Hello, Luko!"

"Coel!" Luko shook his head and nodded and smiled all at the same time. His Latin tumbled from him in an awkward torrent. "You are alive! Márta said you were alive! I believed her, but I was afraid! But you are alive!"

"Aye, lad. I am alive."

Luko flung his arms around Coel's neck. "I am glad!"

"I am glad, too."

Coel looked over the boy's shoulder. Márta stood in her silks. Her scimitar was in her hand. Once more, the lines within the watered Damascus steel crawled up and down the blade with a life of their own.

"You are not happy to see me, then?"

"No!" Tears welled up in Márta's eyes. "Why are you here? You know I cannot let you kill Reza! And I cannot prevent him from killing you! I begged you to forget vengeance! I told you I would meet you! I told you I would marry you! Why must you be so stupid?"

Luko craned his head around at the outburst. "Why is Márta mad?"

Coel grinned. "Because she loves me."

"I love you, too."

"I love you, Luko."

Luko hugged him again.

"Oh, Coel," Márta shook her head. "Why?"

Coel shrugged as he hiked Luko onto his hip. "I love you. I came for you. I came for the boy."

"God damn you for a liar!"

Luko started. Coel set him down. Márta pointed her blade at him accusingly.

"Look at you! You have donned your armor and carry your bow! You come sneaking in like an Assassin! Do not rest your vengeance on Luko or me! You are here for the sake of your stupid pride! You are here to murder my Master! Well, Coel, you had best draw that bow, for you will have to fight me first. Do you understand?"

"No," Coel shook his head. "I shall not fight you."

Fresh tears spilled down Márta's face even as her brows drew down in anger. "I told you I cannot run away with you! I will not abandon my Master! Why can't you understand? If your stupid pride says you must take Luko with you, then do it now, while my Master is busy. That is the one thing we agree upon. He should not be in this place."

Luko looked between them unhappily.

"Your loyalty is misplaced."

"For God's sake!" Márta threw up her hands. "You are a mule once you have made up your mind, and when you are not acting like a mule? You are a pig. You know I owe Reza everything. My life, my loyalty, everything! Why can't you understand that?"

"You owe the Walladid nothing."

Márta shook her head wearily. "And what is that supposed to mean?"

"I mean he has meant to murder you from the day he bought you."

Márta straightened in shock.

"He need not murder you now, for he has the boy. But if I take Luko, then that leaves you. To resurrect Tuman Sunqur, Reza will require the blood of a virgin."

Márta turned white.

"It is Orsini who deduced it. He lives, and he follows in my footsteps, and you are right, I am a liar. Orsini and I have sworn oaths of vengeance against Reza."

"No!"

"We are sworn to set the soul of Father Marius free. We are sworn to stop Tuman Sunqur's rise, and we are sworn to stop Reza from spilling the blood of you or the boy."

"No! It is a lie!" Márta shook her scimitar at him. "A foul lie, concocted by men so deluded by vengeance it has driven them insane! My Master would never do such a thing! Never!"

"I ran for days to get here, Márta. Only the consecrated water you left for us keeps me standing. During that time, I have done much thinking. I knew you would not believe me, and you know I will not fight you. There is only one answer. You must see for yourself. Night is falling. Tonight is the full moon, and midnight is the witching hour. I know that much. Reza will come, and when he does, he will give you some pretense to take the boy."

Márta looked as if she might be sick.

"Márta, you have assisted Reza in his work, you know more of magic than I. Orsini said resurrection is either a miracle bestowed by God or blackest magic. In which manner would you describe the ring Reza wears and the powers it has given him?"

Márta's lip trembled. The scimitar drooped in her hand.

"Orsini says the summoning of demons and dark spirits requires blood. The blood of virgins. Reza has done everything in his power to keep you a virgin since you were ten years old."

Márta's legs failed her and she sat down heavily upon the marble floor. Tears spilled from her eyes, but she did not sob. Her eyes stared past Coel into some terrible place where hearts were betrayed. She shook her head slowly from side to side. She spoke in a broken whisper. "No . . . it cannot be true . . . it cannot."

"I told you, Márta. I have run for days, and I have thought long. I am no sorcerer. It is possible Orsini and I are wrong. If that is true, then I swear to you, I shall forsake my vengeance. I shall intercept Orsini. I will make my way from the Waste and go to Cyprus. There I shall take a monk's robe, and know no other until you come. But if I am right, you must not stand in my way."

Márta looked up slowly. Her brown eyes were bleak with despair. Her voice was devoid of emotion. "If you are right, I will kill him, myself."

* * *

Father Marius' dead flesh shuddered on his bones. The will of Reza Walladid closed around him like a fist.

"Marius, why do you still seek to resist me? It shall avail you nothing. Just look upon yourself." Reza held a mirror up for the priest to look in. Marius tried to look away but he had not the power to resist Reza's command. He had performed healings and Truth-Tells, and had looked into men's minds to find their sins and make them do penance. Father Marius knew that the eyes were the windows into a man's soul.

Marius stared into the empty horror that was his own gaze.

Reza lowered the mirror. "Tell me, Father, what is there within your rotting flesh that still battles on? I must admit that I am intrigued. There is no soul inside you, for your soul is in my keeping. You have no mind, for your brain rots within your skull. The insects feasted upon it until the poison of the Waste eradicated them. Your heart is little more than a shriveled fist of flesh within your ribs. What is it? An imprint? An echo of your personality? It pains me, but I must admit that I do not know."

Reza reached into a leather bag. He pulled forth a gleaming Chi-Roh medallion. Swords formed the *chrismon's* six arms. A black stone sat in its center. The stone was a match of the one clamped in the jaws of the scarab ring Reza wore. "Here is your soul."

The German priest stared in hopeless longing at the shining christogram in Reza's hand.

"Listen to me, Marius, and listen very carefully. You have done your part well. The preparations have been made. All is in readiness, and the hour has nearly come. You are almost free, but I will brook no more resistance from you. You will do as I command, instantly, and without fail. You shall obey me in all things. Do you understand?"

Marius shuddered and fought in Reza's grip.

"If you do not, I shall leave you here, in one of the tombs. I shall seal you in stone deep beneath the citadel. You will remain as you are forever, here in the poisoned Waste where no one shall ever find you. Not even rats or insects shall strip your flesh or gnaw your bones. You will lie in darkness, a mewling, and insane thing, preserved until the end of the world. Tell me you understand."

Father Marius voice grated unbidden through his slit throat. "I . . . understand."

"Know that I take no pleasure in your suffering. It is a by-product of necessity. It serves me only in that it ensures you obey my will. However, there are those who enjoy seeing the suffering of others. There are those to whom the separation of your soul and your rotting body would be a source of endless amusement. Disobey me, and perhaps I will not entomb you here. Perhaps I will sell you and your soul to the Old Man of the Mountain. I am sure the Assassins could find many uses for a man in your situation, and devise unendurable torments to match them."

Marius would have wept were he still able; or moaned and howled his torment if Reza's will allowed it. All he could do was stand where he was and face the Walladid.

Reza held up the holy symbol that housed Marius' soul. The sorcerer's eyes were clear and he was no longer pale. He'd had a full day's rest and partaken deeply of the consecrated water. He had mixed fresh dosages of the drugs that gave him strength and clarity of mind. His hand slowly closed around the symbol so that only the hilts of the swords were visible between his fingers. The gem in the center was engulfed in his grasp. "You will obey."

Marius' last resistance shattered beneath the hammer of Reza's will. Reza turned his back upon the priest. "Now, follow me."

Marius followed his master up the stairs.

* * *

Orsini rode through the empty streets of Bukhara. His crossbow lay drawn and cocked upon his knee. The full moon rose above him and turned the empty city into a twilight of ghostly gray and black boulevards. Orsini admired the architecture and the magnificent stonework. He observed the classic signs of a hobgoblin siege.

The dwarf came to the central marketplace. His eyes picked out details invisible to any human in the darkness. The city was vast, but what he wanted was the palace or the citadel. The Karakhitai had mostly been pagan shamanists, Buddhists, and Manicheans. They had persecuted the Muslims. They would not try to make their temples and fortresses face westward towards Mecca. They would have no prohibitions about burying their dead within the city walls. The royal mausoleum would probably be below the citadel.

Orsini rode his camel in a circle around the market's perimeter. He stopped upon seeing a ghostly gleam in the road ahead. Orsini smiled at the moon's reflection on steel. Orsini touched his camel's haunch with his hand, and it knelt with a lowing groan. The dwarf slid from the saddle.

A double-edged, bronze hilted dagger lay in the middle of the road pointing up the road.

Orsini nodded to himself. "You are thinking, Celt." The dwarf took his camel's reins in one hand and began marching quickly up the boulevard. The domes of great buildings glinted in the moonlight ahead, and great dark walls defended them. It could only be the citadel. Orsini crept through the gates with his crossbow ready.

A string of camels knelt hobbled to one side in the vast courtyard.

Orsini approached them. He spied Coel's pack camel, and a pile of the Celt's belongings lay next to the beast. The dwarf quickly surveyed the situation. Coel had donned his armor and taken up his bow. Orsini looked into Coel's arrow bag, and his eyebrow rose as he noted the arrows that were missing. "Well done. You have not rushed in like a fool, and you've had a good idea, at that." Orsini took the loaded bolt from his crossbow and put it back in the case at his waist.

He followed the example Coel had set. He slid one of the silver-headed bolts he had forged on the Dnieper into the guide.

Orsini eyed the darkened spires of the palace.

"Very well, Coel. Let us see what you have accomplished."

CHAPTER FORTY-FIVE

"He comes! Hide yourself!"

Coel lurched awake. He had dozed against his will. His limbs felt like lead as he rose. He stumbled as Márta shoved him. "Behind the tapestry! Quickly!"

Coel pulled the heavy tapestry aside and fell into the alcove behind it. He shook his head to clear it. His bow and arrows were already in place. Reza would undoubtedly have Father Marius with him, and Coel had little hope for the arrows to have any effect on him. Coel put his hand on his sword. He opened his mouth slightly and began taking slow, shallow, silent breaths.

He recognized the dragging scrape of Marius' boots out in the hallway.

Coel peered through the narrow slit he had cut in the fabric. Luko lay curled upon the divan. It seemed he had fallen asleep as well. He'd been upset, but understood little of the argument. Márta reclined next to Luko and took up her book of Greek poetry. The footsteps grew closer. Coel reached down and took up the wineskin.

He took the last swallow of the consecrated water. Once more strength filled him and fatigue fell away.

Reza and Marius entered the room. Marius wore his mail hood and helmet and carried Snorri's shield. His mace and chain dangled from his wrist. His skin had turned grayish red to match the poisoned dust of the Waste. His pale blue eyes stared hideously out of his skull. Reza gestured about the room with his hand. "And how do you both fare?"

"I am bored," Márta closed her book and sighed. "I had hoped to find some books, but all I have found are old, un-illuminated scrolls in some strange steppe language. Perhaps you can make something of them."

Reza nodded at the book in her hand. "Well, there are always the Greeks."

"Yes, but I have read the Greeks."

Reza smiled. "I suspect you have memorized the Greeks."

Márta's chin dimpled.

Reza looked to Luko. "How is the boy?"

Márta did not miss a step. "He is tired. He has seen too much."

"Yes, we have all seen too much, but soon it shall be finished."

"Master?"

"Yes, Márta?"

"I have concerns."

"I am not surprised. What surprises me is how you have stayed silent about them for so long. It is not your usual manner. I was becoming concerned myself."

Márta blushed. It faded as she looked at the undead priest. "When it is accomplished, you will free Father Marius?"

"His current state is necessary, Márta. I could not let him die. Without him, all my work is for naught. However, as I have already told you, and sworn to him, when the act is accomplished, I shall free him." Reza cocked an eyebrow. "Do you doubt my word?"

"No, never. It is just . . ."

"It is a terrible thing, and you have a compassionate heart. I understand it pains you to see such suffering. It pleases me not to inflict it either, but it is born of necessity."

"I understand." Márta looked sidelong at her master. "Master?"

"Yes, Márta?"

"I wish to marry Coel."

"I know."

"This is not some infatuation like Sandor," Márta paused. "I love him."

"You could do better, Márta." The sorcerer's sudden smile

was disarming. "Then again, I suppose you could do worse."

Coel's eyes widened behind the tapestry.

Márta blinked in surprise.

Reza shrugged. "Well, he is tall and well-fashioned, bold and passionate. A warrior and a poet in the way of the Celts. It is easy to see why you love him. The two of you are well matched."

Márta shook her head in confusion. "Master, you tried to kill him."

Reza smiled ruefully. "Oh, I most assuredly did."

"But--"

"Márta, have I ever lied to you?"

"No. You have never lied to anyone."

"Then listen. Indeed, when I was insulting Coel, I wanted your beloved dead. However, as you well know, I was not myself at that moment. I was at the limit of my power. My strength, my endurance, my concentration, my self-control, all were at the point of breaking. I had just fought the hobgoblin shaman and it was a battle I nearly lost. Coel's rebellion at the time, and Orsini's afterward were more than I could tolerate. I felt betrayed, and my anger broke free.

As for Coel, Oleg's death hung heavy upon him, and he had lost his best friend in Snorri. When he was forced to give Zuleikha the final mercy, it was more than his heart could bear. When confronted by fear or loss, Coel is the kind of man who summons anger to sustain him. All of us have suffered on this journey, and after the battle, Coel and I became the focus for one another's rage. I will admit it. At that moment, when we confronted each other, Coel's death was my dearest desire, and you must admit Márta, your beloved had no qualms about cutting me down."

"I know," Márta looked down at her slippers. "Master, I have disobeyed you."

"Well, I never specifically forbade you to kiss him."

Márta blushed to the roots of her hair. "I have disobeyed you in other ways as well."

Reza sighed. "Well, I suppose I did not specifically give you instructions not to leave Coel and Orsini provisions, either."

Coel stiffened.

Márta's head snapped up. "You knew?"

"I deduced it a few hours ago, when I noticed we were a wineskin short of consecrated water." Reza frowned slightly. "Márta, there are things I must say to you. Things you are not going to like. Things perhaps you have already deduced yourself. You know that throughout our journey, Orsini refused all of Marius' ministrations. He also refused any of the tonics and philters such as I have been taking to strengthen myself. These were his spiritual principles, and we must respect them, but they had their cost. The battle with the Assassins finished him. His last act was to defend Coel against my anger. His defiance was one reason I did not balk at abandoning him, though I know you despise me for it."

Márta flinched.

"The other reason is that he would not have survived these last three days it took us to reach Bukhara. He will have already refused to partake of the consecrated water you left, and he will have died without it. I know he was your friend, but Orsini is surely dead."

"I know."

"As for Coel, I know you love him, but you must steel yourself. It is most likely that he is dead also. The Waste is wide and filled with horrors. He is alone and without a mount. A single saddlebag of rations is slim provisions in this place."

"But if he lives?"

"He is resourceful. There is that possibility."

"In four years, he said he would meet me in Limmasol, and he would marry me."

"Márta, you could do better."

"I have never met a finer man."

Coel's chest swelled.

"I do not speak of the man, I speak of the match, and its future. I ask you to think of this. His debt to the Church in Rome is paid, but his name is on their rolls of disfavor. He became romantically entangled with a nun, a handmaid of the Pope. She committed suicide. The Church will neither forgive nor forget that."

Coel's face tightened. Márta was right. Reza never lied, and the truth of his statements cut like knives.

Márta's face fell. "I know."

"He has nowhere to go, Márta. Even should he walk out of the Waste alive? He cannot go back to Wales. He has shamed the name of the Paladin Academy in Paris. He is a pariah in Spain."

"I know."

"What's more, the Old Man of the Mountain has taken gold. The Assassins shall not rest until Coel is dead. Every dark alley will hide a poisoned blade. Coel's name is also known to the Blue-Robes in Cairo, and it was Coel's own arrow that struck down the Long-Eye. They will want vengeance. Coel is a landless man, with few friends and very powerful enemies."

Coel closed his eyes. For the first time, he thought of the life he would be dragging Márta into.

"Remember, also, war is nearly upon us. The hobgoblins come. When I have the Sunqur's power, I will give them battle. However, it seems likely that Coel really did kill the Great Hobgoblin, and, not to be indelicate, Coel has given the Horde, how shall we say? Other, offenses, as well."

Coel cringed.

Márta looked back at her slippers.

"I fear the newly seated Great Hobgoblin knows Coel's name, and has marked it." Reza shook his head. "Márta I care about you. You were as a daughter to me in your youth, and you are like a sister to me now." Reza smiled again. "Though, more recently, you sometimes act more like my mother."

Márta's lip trembled.

Reza's smile fell. "Márta, you and I are like family. You are the only person whom I trust. So, I must tell you honestly. Even if Coel still lives, it very unlikely he shall survive the next four years."

Márta's voice was very small. "I know."

Coel had to look away. Until this moment, all he had thought of was having Márta. He had thought nothing of the future. He realized very clearly he did not have one. The life he could offer Márta was no life at all. It would be a lifetime of running, and a short one.

"And know this, and know that I say it not in spite, but I will not take Coel back into my service, nor extend my protection to him. There is too much bad blood between us. Nor, do I believe he would take it, even if I offered."

"All that you say is true." Márta raised her head and looked in her master's eyes. "But, if in four years, he lives, what if I still wish to meet him in Cyprus?"

Coel held his breath.

"In four years you are a free woman. You may do whatever you wish without asking my leave."

"You would not try and stop me?" A tiny smile crept onto Márta's face. "Or take vengeance upon him?"

"Márta, if in four years, you wish to leave my service and marry the Celt, then he shall be staggered by the size of your dowry."

Coel gaped.

Márta's smile broke across her face like the sun.

"Beyond that, he and I shall have nothing to do with one another." The corner of the sorcerer's mouth quirked slightly in thought. "Though, I suppose I shall have to be polite to him at your child's christening. That is, if I am invited."

"Master!" Márta leaped up and flung her arms around the sorcerer.

"For that matter, I do not believe that there is any rule that says in-laws must like one another." Reza shrugged in Márta's arms. "Indeed, I believe it is traditional that they do not."

Márta stepped back smiling and crying. "Master?"

"Yes, Márta?"

"What would you do if you were Coel?"

"Why do you ask?"

"I love him. I want him to live. Perhaps I can send word to him somehow. There must be a way."

"Indeed, there might, but I cannot take any such action now. All my powers must be reserved for what must transpire this night."

"I know."

"However, I believe Trebizond would be his safest haven. The Angeli bid us leave her city, but she meant myself and my party of associates. If Coel returned, alone, she might extend him her hospitality. He performed an invaluable service for her, and her consort, the *Strategos*, was very impressed with him. War is coming, and Trebizond is always short of soldiers. He could rise high in the Angeli's service; and the power of the Angeli women would be an invaluable shield against his enemies, at least until the hobgoblins reach the Anatolian Peninsula. But then, once they do that no one shall be safe."

"Yes, the Angeli," Márta nodded. "Coel should return to Trebizond."

Coel stared in wonder from his hiding place. The sorcerer had thought further into his future in a minute than he had in six weeks.

Reza stretched his arms and yawned. "Well, the hour comes swiftly when I must be about my task. I would take a light repast if you would prepare it for me."

"Certainly." Márta bent to shake Luko awake.

"Let the boy sleep," Reza waved a hand. "He is weary."

Márta shrugged. "He has slept for hours. He can help me cook."

"It is not as if we have game that needs dressing or water to spare for boiling. All I require is some moistened gruel and dried meat. Let Luko sleep. It is the kindest thing we can do for him at the moment."

Márta reached out for Luko's shoulder. "It is nothing, I--"

"Márta, I have much to do. Now, please, do as I ask. Go fetch some food."

"You are right, I am sorry," Márta stood. "Master?"

"Yes, what is it?"

"Was it always your intention to murder me this night?"

Reza did not blink. His eyes widened slightly as they stared into Márta's. His voice softened into an even tone. "Tell me, Márta. What has made you--"

"You always told me that one cannot mesmerize an unwilling subject." Márta's face went hard. "Now, I would like an answer. Did you buy me with the intention of sacrificing me to the abomination which lies below?"

Reza's face went flat. "Give me the boy."

Márta's scimitar blurred from its sheath. "No."

"Marius," Reza jerked his head. "Kill Márta."

Marius raised Snorri's shield before him. The iron ball whirled overhead.

Coel burst from behind the tapestry. Reza stared in shock. Coel ignored the sorcerer and charged straight for the priest. Father Marius had said the Academy blade could sever the bonds that held him to his dead body. Coel aimed a cut at his neck. "Márta! Defend Luko!"

Luko awoke with a cry.

"Marius!" Reza snarled. "Kill Coel and Márta!"

Coel's sword slammed down against Marius' shield.

Reza circled towards Márta. She held the point of her scimitar between them. Her eyebrows drew down into a vee of rage. Murder shone in her brown eyes as she thrust Luko behind her. "You shall not have him."

Reza drew forth the heavy *kindjal* dagger from his sash. "Oh, but I shall."

Márta whipped her scimitar on high.

Reza made no effort to defend himself.

Márta's blade blurred down in a skull-splitting stroke.

Blue light flared from the blade as it shattered like ice a foot from Reza's head. Márta staggered like an invisible ocean wave had struck her and she crumpled to the floor.

"Márta!" Luko pulled Snorri's *sax* knife from his belt.

"Márta!" Coel's heart stopped as she fell. Marius' flail came an inch from taking his head off as he tried to go to her. Coel dodged the blow and Marius slammed him back with the boss of his shield.

Reza's voice rose. "Luko!"

The boy stood over Márta as she slowly pushed her herself to her knees. Her hands and face were bloody from the slivers of her exploded blade.

"Márta!" Coel desperately hurled his shoulder back into Marius' shield to move him. The priest clouted Coel with the haft of his flail. Coel staggered back blinking at stars.

"Luko," Reza held the boy's gaze with his own. The wizard's voice was unnaturally calm. "Drop the knife."

Snorri's *sax* clattered to the tiles.

"Come to me."

Luko walked to the wizard like a puppet. Reza bent down and took Márta's hair in his fist. He lifted her chin to cut her throat.

"Márta!" Coel slashed desperately at the priest, but he could land no killing blow nor force him back.

Reza leaped away from Márta with a curse and pressed his hand to his side. His hand came away bloody. The sorcerer retreated holding his *kindjal* before him.

Márta rose to one knee. She held her *yataghan* dagger in her left hand. Blood dripped from her torn brow into her eyes. Her right hand hung useless at her side. She smiled at the Walladid and brandished the bloody dagger in her hand. "Come, Master. Let us cross blades."

"Luko!" Reza jerked his head at the boy. "Come! Follow me now!"

"No!" Márta lurched to her feet as the boy ran past her and fell again. She struggled to rise. "No!"

Reza strode from the room. Luko heeled behind him like a

dog.

Coel's blade belled in his hand as it met the iron ball of Marius' flail. The vibration shuddered his arms and nearly took the sword from his grip. Marius jerked as Márta rammed her dagger into his back. He whipped his shield about to strike her. Coel took the opening and thrust his sword two handed through Marius' middle.

The iron ball arced at Coel's head. He yanked his sword free and dropped low as the weighted chain flew past. Coel stabbed Marius again. "How do we kill him?"

Márta ducked and the iron ball smashed marble from the wall. "I do not know!"

Coel's blade threw sparks as it sliced across Marius' mail armor. The priest whirled upon him. Márta leaped in and thrust again. They circled Marius, stabbing and slashing. The priest was sheathed in heavy mail. Few blows drove home. Those that did had no effect. Márta's breath came in ragged gasps. "Do something!"

Coel leaned back as the studded iron ball sought him. Perhaps Orsini had the strength to behead a man wearing a mail hood; but even with an Academy forged blade Coel knew it was beyond his ability this night. If he failed Marius' return stroke would crush his skull like an egg.

Coel met Marius gaze.

The pale blue eyes gazed out from their sunken sockets and burned at Coel in horrible empty fever. Marius was dead. Reza had his soul. Coel's mind grasped at strands of things his mother had taught him in his youth. His mother had taught him all things were connected. The sun, the moon, the stars, all wheeled within a man's body even as they wheeled in the heavens above. There were paths and gates, places within the human body. The seat of the heart, the seat of the soul . . .

Coel swung his sword like an iron bar to try and batter Marius away from Márta. He held the priest's terrible gaze. Marius was dead. Reza had his soul. The eyes were the windows of the soul, but if Marius was dead and his soul was stolen, how could he see?

Coel retreated back as Marius advanced. Coel's mind clutched at the thought. His mother had said there was a place within him. A place she called the Window to the World. Reza had called it the Inner Eye. It was an eye that could be opened to see the worlds without and within. An eye that pierced the veils between life and death. It had to be the bridge for Marius' soul. Separated from his body, it had to be from there that he saw through the gates of his dead flesh and directed his dead body to enact Reza's will.

It was the Third Eye that was active within him. Coel knew its location. He snarled as Marius swung at him. "Between his eyes!"

"Do it!" Márta flung down her dagger and dove at Father Marius' legs.

Marius stumbled as Márta ploughed into his knees. His shield lowered as he tottered. He raised his flail to smite her.

Coel lunged.

His point punched between Marius' sunken eyes. Coel's blade sang through Marius' skull and rotting brain and only stopped when it hit the back of his helmet. Coel violently twisted his blade and ripped it free. Father Marius collapsed like a boned fish on top of Márta. Márta struggled beneath the weight of the armored corpse.

Coel hauled Marius off and raised the Acadmey blade. The priest did not move. The feverish light in his eyes was gone. The right eye had gone cross-eyed from Coel's blow. The left stared up at the ceiling without seeing. Coel knelt at Márta's side. "Are you all right?"

"We must save Luko." She leaned heavily on Coel as he raised her to her feet.

"Is Marius free?"

"He is free of that," Márta gestured at the body on the floor. "But I fear Reza still has his soul."

"What of Tuman Sunqur? Can Reza summon him without Marius?"

"I think Marius has already served his purpose."

"Where lies the mausoleum?"

"In the crypts below us."

Coel sheathed his sword and fetched his bow from the alcove. "Let us finish this, then."

* * *

Orsini held his torch high. He did not like what he saw.

He was well below the citadel. The winding passages were narrow and vile black moisture seeped the walls from the nearby poison of the Zerafshan River. Orsini stood before a massive portal of black marble. The heavy bronze door lay open. Stone seals above the door and on either side were cracked and fissured. Runes he could not read had been carved deep into nearly every square inch of the door. The symbols made no sense to him, but the dwarf knew what they stood for. Mighty magic had been used to seal the tomb. The cracked stone seals and the open door told him that Reza's magic had unlocked it. Light shone out of the tomb. Orsini stuck his torch in a sconce carved in the wall. He took his crossbow in both hands and entered.

Orsini gazed upon Tuman Sunqur.

The ancient sorcerer lay upon a massive basalt slab. A pentagram drawn in blue chalk surrounded the altar stone. A thick black candle burned at each of the pentagram's points. Runes and pictograms written in chalks of many colors filled the intersecting triangles of the pentagram. Reza's saddlebags lay in a corner. Strange vials, scrolls, carved boxes, and iron implements lay arranged in precise order on a blanket. Funerary lanterns lit in all four corners of the spacious chamber. Beneath them, open braziers smoldered with the scorched scent of vile, unnamable things. The entire chamber from ceiling to floor was seamless dark marble, as if a great cube had been sunk in the earth and then precisely hollowed out to form the chamber within. It was amazing work from a stonemason's view, and the dwarf puzzled over it for an awed moment. He dismissed the problem for later contemplation.

Orsini turned his eye back to Tuman Sunqur.

The body lay covered in a fresh shroud of filmy white gauze. Silver filings sprinkled upon the shroud drew the form of a great scarab. The glittering pattern covered Sunqur's body and matched the beetle on Reza's ring. The jaws of the scarab were drawn to close around the dead sorcerer's head. The shroud covering Tuman Sunqur's face was blackened with powder to match the dark gemstone clutched in the jaws of the ring. Orsini looked the Sunqur up and down. He could not make out any of his features beneath the shroud. By his length, Orsini judged Tuman to be a full head taller than Coel.

"Well, I see the guest of honor is here, but where are your well-wishers?" Orsini glanced about. The catacombs beneath the citadel were a rat's maze. No dwarf would have dug so haphazardly. Nevertheless, they were extensive, with many places to hide. It occurred to him that Reza might be laying in wait.

"No, Walladid," Orsini spoke aloud to encourage himself in the oppressive place. "You would never let anyone get so close to your prize."

Orsini glanced up at the marble above him. "Something has distracted you."

CHAPTER FORTY-SIX

Coel and Márta stood before the stairs. The darkness below led down into the depths of the catacombs. Coel kept an arrow nocked. "Do you know where the mausoleum is?"

"No, my master did not bid me follow him below," Márta sniffed at the air. Disturbing, burnt odors wafted up from the depths. "But it should not be hard to find."

"How is your hand?"

Márta held up the lantern she had taken from her room. The blood on her hand had dried. "I can hold a lamp, if not wield a sword or draw a bow." She held up the *yataghan* in her left. Reza's blood still stained the recurved blade. "This should suffice for my master."

"It is his magic that makes me nervous."

"Even now, he will seek to conserve it. His preparations have been made. He will strive to raise Tuman Sunqur at all costs."

"Then perhaps we can catch him while he is busy." Coel set a foot upon the steps and froze.

A thin wail of agony came from the galleries above them.

"Bastard!" Rage surged within Coel. Luko howled again in torment. "He has doubled back upon us!" Coel threw down his bow and drew his sword. Márta put a hand to his chest.

"It is a trap!"

"Aye!" Coel brushed her arm aside. "What of it?"

They charged up the stairs side by side. It sounded like Reza was skinning the boy alive. The lamps still lit the room where Márta and the boy had slept. Coel went through the door with his sword in both hands before him. He skidded to a halt on the tiles. Márta took a knife-fighter's crouch.

Luko stood off to one side by himself staring blankly. He slowly tilted his head back and let out a blood-curdling cry. His face showed no sign of effort. He resumed staring at nothing. Slowly, he tilted his head back and let out another heart-wrenching wail of agony.

"He is in no pain," Márta shook her head. "It is Reza's mesmerism. It is a trap."

Coel whirled.

Reza Walladid stood in the doorway. He had wrapped his sash around his lacerated ribs. He smiled amiably. "I see you defeated Father Marius."

Coel stared about the floor in shock.

Father Marius' body was gone.

Reza lifted his hand and beckoned behind him. "Do you think you can do it again?"

Feet scraped on the stone and a shape loomed behind Reza. The sorcerer stepped aside. Father Marius shambled into the room. His eyes were still askew from Coel's thrust. No light of life shone within them. Marius sagged and swayed like a marionette with twisted strings. Reza lifted his hand. The scarab ring gleamed in the lamplight. "Kill the man and the woman."

Marius raised his shield and shambled forward.

"Luko!" Reza curled his finger. "Come to me! Quickly!"

Luko bolted forward.

"Luko!" Márta lunged but the boy was already past. Marius barred their path. The sorcerer and the boy disappeared into the gallery.

Coel raised his sword. "I do not think spitting his skull a second time will work!"

Márta held the lamp up before her like a shield. "There is nothing of Marius left! It is a revenant! A Golem of flesh! The only way to stop it is to break Reza's magic or dismember it!"

Coel jumped back as the iron ball whirled at him. He lunged in return and thrust at the knee. The zombie lowered its shield to stop the blow and swung at him again.

Márta hurled her lamp. The glass shattered against the dead

man's mail. Burning oil splattered. Marius' dried and crusted mantle flared. Flames sheeted upward. Marius burned.

"Take his legs!" Márta dove in to hamstring Marius with her *yataghan*. Marius' arm whipped out from the fire that engulfed him.

The spiked iron ball met Márta's head mid-lunge with a sickening thud.

"Márta!" Coel charged screaming as she fell to the floor. Marius swung at him.

Their weapons met. The mace whipped around his sword and wrapped the blade with its chain. The zombie yanked Coel forward and rammed him with its shield. Coel grunted with the impact and flame singed him. Coel's head rocked as Marius uppercutted him with the rim of Snorri's shield. Coel staggered. The chain tightened on his blade. Coel's sword yanked from his hands.

The zombie shook out its weapon. Academy blade clattered to the floor. Coel faced the undead with empty hands.

The burning priest shambled towards him.

Coel seized up a chair and swung it at Marius. The mace and chain smashed a leg from the ancient furniture. Coel ignored the flames and rammed the chair forward. The flail swung again. The chain wrapped around the side of the chair and the ball smashed into Coel's armor. He gasped and dropped the chair. He staggered back and desperately seized a standing, wrought iron candelabrum. Coel brandished it like a quarterstaff as the dead priest came for him.

He was dead and he knew it.

"Coel!" Orsini's voice filled the chamber. "Do no battle! Retreat before it!"

Coel raised his makeshift weapon and backed up. The dwarf held his hammer in his hands. The zombie took no notice of the dwarf. It advanced on Coel. Orsini raised his hammer and charged up behind Marius.

The zombie's knees shattered beneath the dwarven hammer. Marius fell with broken legs beneath him. Orsini attacked relentlessly. He crushed the shoulder and elbow of the arm that held the mace and chain and then went on to shatter both hipbones. His hammer rose and fell like a man chopping wood as he worked his way up and down Marius' burning body. The corpse twitched as it tried to fulfill Reza's orders without any joints left to move its body.

Coel dropped the candelabra and ran to Márta. Blood pooled on the tiles beneath her. Blood covered his hands as he cradled her head. Her brown eyes stared up at the ceiling glassily. Her pupils were two different sizes. "No!"

Orsini knelt beside them. "She took the mace to the skull?"

"Aye," Coel's throat caught. "She did."

Orsini's blunt fingers gently probed Márta's head. He sucked a breath between his teeth. "I do not believe any bone has entered her brain, but her skull is fractured."

Coel looked into the empty stare of the woman he loved. "I could not save her," Despair filled him.   "I could not--"

Orsini's palm cracked across Coel's jaw. "Mourn her when she's dead!"

Coel sat back clutching his face.

"Fool!" Orsini glared bloody murder at him. "Márta lives! Luko still lives! You and I live! Márta and Luko may yet be saved, and should we fail them?   Then you and I remain sworn to vengeance! Remember that!" Orsini cocked back his massive hand. "Or must I remind you a second time!"

Coel held his swelling cheek.   He had seen many head wounds. Nearly all of them fatal. Those few that lived were often simpletons ever after. "You can save her? You can bind skulls?"

Orsini scowled. "I have earned my mastery in the Dwarven Guilds in wood, stone, and steel. I can raise a helmet from a single piece of iron or weld it from four so that you could not tell the difference. I cannot imagine bone being much different. It is merely a question of setting the skull without further damaging the brain beneath."

Hope surged in Coel. "You are that confident?"

"Not at all. Now, fetch your sword. Watch the door lest Reza return and do us further mischief."

Coel took up his sword and went to the door, but he could not take his eyes from Márta. Orsini picked up Snorri's sax and cut strips from Márta's silken sash. He slowly tied them round her head and began knotting and tightening. Coel snuck a glance out into the darkened hall. "I killed Marius to no avail. He came back a second time."

Orsini did not look up from his work. "No, Reza simply re-animated his flesh. There was nothing of Marius in it. That is how I destroyed it so easily. It was mindless. It knew only Reza's orders to kill the two of you. To the spark that animated it, I did not exist; so I was able to strike it with impunity," The dwarf folded his cloak and put it beneath Márta's head and then fetched a blanket from the divan to cover her. "There, that is the best we can do for her. Now, let us attend to Reza."

"We cannot leave her here!"

"Get a grip on yourself!" Orsini handed him Snorri's knife. "We cannot care for her and fight Reza. If we live, we come back for her. If we fail, she will never know," The dwarf slid his hammer into his belt and retrieved his crossbow. He took one of the hanging lanterns from its chain and checked its oil. "Let us be quick about this."

Coel thrust the knife in his belt. The two of them ran down the stairs. Coel's despair began to leave him as he left the room. Hatred crept in to replace it. "Death is too good for him."

"Steady down!" Orsini grabbed Coel's armored sleeve. "Stick to the plan! We shoot him on sight! No insults! No challenges! Do not look him in the eye, and do not let him get close enough to touch you. We must shoot him before he can utter a single syllable if we can."

"You are right," Coel forcibly reined in his hatred to keep it cold and calculating. "We kill him, and leave this cursed place."

"One more thing. If you must, kill the boy. It would be far better for him to die with one of our shafts in his chest than Reza's knife across his throat. I believe it is more than just his blood that is being sacrificed."

Coel found his bow and sheaf of arrows on the landing where he had left it. The two of them stood and looked down the dark stairway that led below. "Aye, then. So be it."

They descended into darkness and the stench of the burning herbs and unguents. The stair led to another hallway. Another set of stairs spiraled down to tunnels hewn from the dirt and rock. Coel had to crouch to keep his head from striking the low ceiling. He followed as the dwarf moved unerringly through the maze. Niches for the dead filled the walls. Some were dressed in rusted armor or faded gowns of costly material. Others lay as mere piles of bones. Strange noises issued down the narrow tunnels. A warm wind ruffled Coel's hair. "There should be no breeze in this place."

"No natural one."

Coel pointed at a red glimmer ahead. "There."

"Indeed. That is the tomb."

Coel followed the dwarf towards the glitter of light. The wind moaned up and down through the catacombs. They crept towards the entrance. Whispers upon the wind raised the hair on Coel's arms. He could feel the presence of others watching on the back of his neck. In this place, the veils between the seen and the unseen were growing very thin.

They came to the portal. The gleam had been the light of their lamp reflecting off of a bronze door. Orsini cradled his crossbow. "The door was open when I came down here."

"You were down here?"

"Yes, and Reza wasn't. So I came back up looking for you."

"You saw Tuman Sunqur, then?"

"All seven feet of him."

Coel looked at the twisting runes carved on the door. Staring at them made him feel nauseous. He could not read them, but their omen traveled his spine like a cold messenger. It was not a place he wanted to enter. "Is it barred?"

"No." Orsini gestured at the brackets on the door and the broken stone seals. "This door is meant to keep things in. Not out."

"What do we do?"

Orsini brought his crossbow to his shoulder. "Kick the door. Then step out of the way. Reza still imagines me dead. He will be surprised when I shoot him. Then, if I am not torn apart by demons or sundered by lightning, leap in and shoot behind me."

"All right."

The dwarf nodded. "Do it."

Coel put his boot into the bronze door with all of his strength. It flung open on oiled hinges. Coel spun out of the doorway. For a split second, he saw the sorcerer. Reza wore black silks and a black turban. Luko lay upon the altar next to a huge shrouded body. In his hand Reza held a heavy glittering dagger chipped from a single piece of obsidian. Orsini leaped into the entry. "Walladid!"

Coel stepped behind Orsini.

Reza's eyes flew wide at the sight of the dwarf. His mouth opened. The scarab ring rose. Orsini's crossbow thrummed. Reza staggered as the crossbow bolt sank into his stomach. Orsini lowered his weapon and shoved his foot in the cocking stirrup. "Now, Coel!"

Coel drew his bowstring to his ear and loosed. His arrow whistled through the air and sank into the wizard's chest. Coel drew another arrow.

Reza's eyes blazed. The ring pointed at Coel and the sorcerer's bloody lips began moving.

Coel raised his aim and let fly.

The broadhead arrow tore into Reza's throat.

The sorcerer staggered. His incantation choked around the iron barb in his neck; his words gurgled as they drowned in blood. Coel lowered his aim and sank his third arrow into Reza's chest. Reza's mouth opened wordlessly. Blood spilled over his lips. Orsini loosed his second shaft into Reza's guts and the sorcerer staggered vomiting blood upon the altar. Coel loosed his fourth arrow. Reza's eyes rolled. He folded over the altar and fell upon Luko and the body under the shroud.

Coel kept his arrow nocked and looked about. The whispers and moans had stopped. The warm wind ceased. The air grew dank and cold. The candles in the corners of the pentagram burned so steadily they might have been painted. The silence was total.

Luko let out a piteous cry.

"Careful," Orsini warned. "One must be wary with wizards."

He slid a silver-headed bolt into the guide. "I'll approach from the right. You go left."

Coel circled the altar. His every nerve was taut as he eyed Reza's back. Two of his three shafts had pierced the wizard front to back. Luko's arms and legs flailed feebly beneath the Persian. His cries grew louder. Coel glanced at Orsini and shrugged his shoulders in question. Orsini aimed his crossbow at Reza's head and nodded.

Coel eased off his bowstring. He seized the sorcerer by the shoulder and heaved him from the altar. Coel leaped back as if he had slapped a snake and redrew his bow.

Reza flopped limp to the dark marble floor. Coel dropped his bow as Luko launched himself into his arms and began wailing at the top of his lungs. Orsini kept his weapon trained on the sorcerer. Coel held the bloodstained boy and looked down. Reza gazed up at his eyebrows and did not blink. His mouth hung open. His body was riddled with shafts and he was covered in blood. His black turban hung askew. He did not appear to breathe.

"Is he dead, then?"

Orsini snapped the toe of his boot into the side of Reza's head. Reza's jaw wobbled and his head rolled. His eyes stared glassily. "As a doorknocker. He took six shafts. Two of yours have torn his heart."

"Should we not behead him or something?"

"That should not be necessary, but we might relieve him of the ring, just to be sure."

Coel looked at the body beneath the shroud. The scarab pattern was ruined where Reza's body had fallen across it. Reza's blood stained the pristine white gauze in great splotches. Coel set Luko down. The boy clung to his leg crying. Coel peeled the boy off and drew Snorri's sax-knife. "Luko, you are a warrior. Take your sword."

Luko's eyes widened at the sight of the weapon. He snuffled and took the knife.

"Are you all right?"

Luko nodded.

"Are you scared?"

Luko nodded.

"Aye, I am scared, too, but we must be brave for Márta. All of us, together. Can you be brave with Orsini and me? For Márta?"

Luko wiped his nose with the back of his hand. "I will be brave."

"Good. Go watch the door."

Luko went and took his station at the door with his knife in both hands. Coel grimaced at the massive body on the altar. "What about him, then?"

"What about him?"

"Should we burn him, or something?"

"My first instinct, which is the one I trust the most, is that touching anything within this place is a very bad idea. I think we should fashion a litter for Márta and hasten from here. We have saved the boy. Márta needs attending to. Reza is dead, and we have spoiled his magic. Let someone else deal with the mess. We can send word to the Blue Robes. They will know what needs doing, if anything." Orsini nodded to himself. "Indeed, that is exactly what we shall do. If we tell the Blue Robes that Reza is dead, Tuman still lays in his tomb, and give them the ring, they may not be so eager to kill us. We should also tell them of the hobgoblins. The power of the Blue Robes needs to be mobilized against the Horde as soon as possible."

Coel bent to pick up his bow. It sounded like an excellent plan to him. "See if there is any more of the consecrated water for Márta."

"I think Reza used it in his magics, however, he was using potions and philters to strengthen himself, perhaps--"

Luko screamed.

Coel started.

Orsini rose up through the air as if he had sprouted wings. He flew headlong across the tomb and struck the marble wall with frightful impact.

Tuman Sunqur stood upon the slab and loomed over Coel.

The sorcerer was seven feet tall. He shrugged back the hair from his face. It fell in cinnamon-colored ropes to his shoulders. His skin was darker than any Ethiopian's. The eyes that met Coel's were such a pale gray they seemed translucent. Tuman Sunqur smiled down at Coel with teeth whiter than Orsini's.

Coel raised his bow.

The sorcerer extended a finger.

Coel froze with his bow half drawn. The man's hands were immense, even for a man of his size. Coel's muscles locked beneath the pointing finger. All Coel could do was stand and stare. The man kept his finger pointed at Coel as he shrugged the stained and bloody shroud from his shoulder. He was naked save for a sky blue silk breechclout. His muscles stretched across his massive bones like ropes. The flesh that covered them was so emaciated it clung to every sinew and vein. He was like a giant who'd been sucked dry of every drop of blood in his body. The hand he extended was skeletal with nothing but parchment thin skin covering bones.

Coel had felt that hand upon him before. It was now re-attached to its rightful owner.

Coel fought to draw his bow but could not move. His body shook with strain.

Tuman shook back his hair again casually. The finger that held Coel in place never wavered. The sorcerer spoke in perfect Latin. "No, I am no Egyptian, but it does not surprise me that the Blue-Robes lie even amongst themselves to associate their sect with my power."

The sorcerer was reading his mind. Coel fought his arms to draw the bow, but his limbs felt like they did not belong to him. He tried to drag his gaze up between Tuman Sunqur's eyebrows and failed. Tuman's will held him like a vise.

"Go, now. Fetch me the boy."

Coel lowered his bow and started to turn. His joints popped as he forced himself to halt. His voice came out in a strangled grunt. "No!"

"No?" Tuman Sunqur stepped down lightly from the slab.

He stared down at Coel sympathetically. "Very well, then. The virgin upstairs. Either will suffice."

Coel's muscles writhed beneath his flesh like worms on hooks as they fought his will. The pale gray eyes stared deeply into Coel's. Coel could not look away. His vision doubled and skewed. The eyes of the sorcerer merged into a single eye that filled Coel's universe. The dark pupil of the eye opened like a window into a starless night. The darkness rushed toward Coel like a wave.

"Serve me."

Coal groaned. "No!"

The Sunqur's will pulled Coel in like a riptide. "Yes."

Coel plunged into a vast black well.

He could not feel his body. His mind floated in uttermost darkness. The voice of the sorcerer seemed to come from all around him, as if he had sunk into a sea of the Sunqur's will. The dark sea hardened around him like mortar. Coel felt suspended in stone.

"Serve me. Bring me the boy."

Coel could not answer. His mind shrank beneath the terrible force tightening all around it.

"Serve me. Make the blood pact with me. Bring me the boy. I shall strike down your enemies."

Coel resisted in agonized silence.

"Bring me the boy. I will save the woman."

Coel's will fissured and cracked.

"You will hold Márta in your arms again. I will make her whole. Even now, her damaged mind cries out for you to save her. Save her. Serve me."

Coel's mind flooded with unbidden images. The sorcerer drew forth his memories like a great hand sifting through a treasure chest. Coel saw Márta's tongue run across her lips as she ate honey by the Caspian Sea. He tasted the honey upon her lips as he relived their every stolen kiss under the stars in the Karakum. His every fantasy of their marriage night smoked across his mind's eye. He saw their children and grandchildren. Coel's daydreams of growing old with Márta played before him bathed in golden light.

The images changed abruptly.

Marisol lay naked in the bath, the water scarlet with the life-blood taken by her own hand. Oleg bled out his life, his veins blackened by Assassin poison. Snorri toppled into the cataracts sabered under his arm. Zuli fell with a crossbow bolt between her breasts, loosed by his own hand as goblins tore her flesh with their fangs.

Coel's mind squirmed at horrors he could not close his eyes too.

Tuman ripped forth a more recent memory and held it up before Coel's mind.

Coel saw Márta lying on the floor. Her eyes gazed sightlessly at the ceiling. A pool of blood spreading beneath her cracked skull onto the tiles.

"Not all you love must die, Coel."

Coel broke.

The crushing weight fell away from him. He felt a terrible sense of relief in giving up his will, as if he had a thousand mosquito bites all over his body and he had given in to the hundred hands that would scratch them. He would bind himself to Tuman Sunqur. He would cut into the flesh of his palm and mingle his blood with that of the sorcerer. He would make the Blood Pact and offer up Luko as his first act of fealty. The boy would die, but that thought was already lost in a distant place.

Márta would live.

In a far place he could not see Coel dropped his bow. With strange prescience, he knew Reza's stone dagger lay upon the black altar. His hand reached out for it. He could neither see nor feel the sacrificial knife, but his fingers obeyed and curled around the chipped hilt.

Coel sliced the glass sharp stone into his hand.

The darkness about him roiled with eagerness as his blood welled up from the wound. A hand half again the size of his own took the dagger from him.

Coel raised his hand to mingle his blood with--

The darkness shredded apart. Coel toppled as the candlelit tomb spun before his addled eyes. His wounded hand throbbed as it slapped the marble altar to catch his fall. It slipped and Coel fell to the floor. Tuman Sunqur stepped back. His emaciated face split into a snarl.

A crossbow bolt stood out of his chest.

"Coel, get out of there!" Orsini stood near the tomb's portal. He yanked back his bowstring and slid another silver headed bolt into the guide. He jerked his head at Luko behind him. "Run, boy! Run!"

Luko ran into the catacombs.

Coel seized his bow and the arrow from the floor and flung himself backwards. Tuman Sunqur extended a finger at Orsini. "Your kind I cannot dominate, dwarf. So it shall be a simple transaction between us. I will let you live."

"I shall not extend you the same courtesy." The crossbow thrummed. Tuman Sunqur jerked as the heavy bolt punched into his ribs.

Coel leaped to his feet. He nocked his silver arrow and took the great bow to full draw. Tuman's head whipped around to look at him, and the gray eyes sought his. Coel felt his will begin to leave his muscles. With his last effort, he forced his fingers to release. Tuman flinched as the silver sank into his chest. Coel felt his will expand as the spell broke.

Coel leaped over the altar as he drew another arrow from the sheaf on his belt. He ducked as Orsini loosed. Coel turned and drew. He released, and the arrow whistled across the tomb. The shaft barely penetrated an inch. Tuman Sunqur plucked it like a thorn. Coel realized he had loosed an iron broadhead. He had four silver arrows left.

Coel drew silver from his belt. The undead sorcerer ignored man and dwarf as he bent over Reza's body. Coel and Orsini both loosed. Tuman lurched as the two silver-headed shafts struck him in the side. He stood back up to his full height. He held the scarab ring. Tuman Sunqur grinned at them as it slid loosely onto his mummified finger and he made a fist to hold it in place.

"This is bad!" Orsini grabbed the lamp and shoved it into Coel's bloody hand. "Run!"

They bolted from the tomb. Coel kicked the bronze door shut. The bar that secured it was nowhere to be found. Orsini drew his hammer and shoved the iron bound haft down into the brackets. Coel followed Orsini down the dank tunnel.

Behind them the bronze door rang like a gong.

Coel ducked his head as they ran through the twisting maze. "Will it hold him?"

"What do you think?"

Metal rent with a scream behind them. The bronze door had not held. Coel's voice echoed down the tunnels. "Luko!"

Luko wailed somewhere ahead of them.

"Luko!"

The boy had not gotten far in the dark. He stood in a side-tunnel holding Snorri's knife in both hands. Orsini scooped him up and threw him over his shoulder without breaking stride. The dwarf bee-lined towards the rough-hewn stone steps that led up to the surface. They ran up the flight and Coel flung the iron bound wooden door shut behind them and shot the bolt.

"Jesus!" Coel panted. "What do we do?"

"How should I know?" Orsini put Luko down and took a moment to reload his crossbow. "Silver arrows but annoy him and iron does nothing at all. I do not think his body is totally resurrected, nor is his soul completely ensconced within it. I think that is why he has thrown no great sorceries upon us and why silver upsets him. However, I fear silver arrows alone will not be enough."

They ran on down the hall. Marble lions' heads marked the landing that led into the citadel. The door behind them burst off of its hinges. The figure of Tuman Sunqur arose in the dim outskirts of the lamplight. Orsini whirled. Coel held the lamp high. The dwarf took a half-second to adjust his aim and loosed. His bolt hissed for Tuman Sunqur's head.

The sorcerer jerked his head aside. The bolt broke against the wall behind him. Orsini threw down his crossbow. "That was my last!" He took the lamp from Coel. "Do something, Coel, and make it count!"

Coel wiped his bleeding hand on the hem of his tunic. He took his bow and drew the three remaining silver arrows in his belt. He thought of how he had dispatched Marius and of his mother's teachings. Coel drew his bow. He whispered to himself under his breath.

"The Seat of Life . . . " Coel dropped his aim and loosed. The silver arrow whistled through the hall and sank squarely between Tuman Sunqur's hipbones. The sorcerer's shoulders hunched, and his gaunt face twisted. Coel drew back his second arrow.

"The Gate of the Heart . . . " Coel's next arrow struck Sunqur in the sternum. The sorcerer staggered. Coel drew his third and last arrow. He raised his aim high.

"The Third Eye, the Window Between Worlds . . . "

Coel loosed. The arrow whistled down the hall straight and true towards the point between Tuman's eyebrows.

Tuman's mummified hand flashed before his face like a bird as he plucked the arrow from the air. The shaft of the silver arrow snapped between his fingers like a matchstick. Nearly a dozen shafts feathered his body. His melodious voice filled the hall. "You have some knowledge, Coel son of Math, but neither the tools nor the power to exploit it. Now, sacrifice the boy to me, lest I become angry with you."

Orsini snatched up Luko and ran up the stairs. Coel bounded up the staircase behind him. They reached the ground floor and Coel glanced back in the wildly flickering lamplight. There were no more doors to close and no more silver arrows.

Tuman Sunqur stalked up the stairs.

Coel seized the lantern from Orsini and flung it.

The glass shattered against the ancient sorcerer's chest. Fire spilled out across Tuman's chest and shoulders and slid down his torso and legs. The flicker of victory died in Coel's chest. The flame kept sliding down. The fire beaded and slid off of the Sunqur's dark flesh like oil from water. Orsini dropped Luko. He bared his great white teeth in rage as Tuman walked up the stairs and left the fire puddling behind him.

"By the Saint's sweaty stones! I have had enough of this!"

The dwarf strode to the banister. His great square hands seized one of the marble lion heads and his face bunched with effort. A great roar of effort tore from his throat. Marble cracked like the sound of a whip. Orsini staggered backward with his prize. He raised the two-foot sphere of carved marble over his head.

The dwarf hurled the massive lion head down the staircase like a catapult stone. "That for you!"

The stone struck the sorcerer's chest with a great hollow thump. Tuman Sunqur's arms flailed, and he staggered backward two steps. The sorcerer straightened. He squared his shoulders and tossed back his hair.

The Sunqur strode back up the stairs smiling.

"Bastard!" Orsini bent with his hands on his knees. His chest heaved. "Well, I am out of ideas."

The sorcerer approached the landing. The flaming oil backlit him in lurid reds and oranges. He looked like the end of the world.

Coel drew his sword.

Tuman Sunqur hesitated.

Coel held the point of the Academy blade high between his eyes and those of the sorcerer. For a moment there was no sound but the crackling of burning oil upon the stairs.

Coel jerked his head without taking his eyes of off his opponent. He spoke French so Luko would not understand. "Orsini, take Luko. Go upstairs where Márta lies. We left her dagger there. Take it. If he gets past me, cut their throats before he can lay hands upon them."

Orsini straightened and looked back and forth between Coel and Luko. "All right." He took Luko's hand and the two of them hurried across the great hall to the next staircase.

Tuman Sunqur watched them go. He turned his gaze upon Coel and the sword for long seconds. Sunqur backed down the stair and turned to the wall. His eyes never left Coel's over the point of the Academy blade. The sorcerer reached to the stonework over the banister. Stone cracked as he pulled free a five-foot length of fluted marble from the wall like picking a flower. The shaft was as thick as Coel's arm.

Tuman Sunqur ascended the stairs. "I have arrived at a decision."

Coel retreated.

"I have decided upon the boy."

Coel stopped retreating.

"First, I am going to shatter your limbs, son of Math. Then, whilst you writhe like a cripple, I shall let you watch as I take Márta's virginity. Then, I shall carve the boy's living heart from his chest and--"

Coel lunged.

Tuman Sunqur swung the length of marble down. Coel dove and yanked his blade away. The Sunqur had not swung at him. He had swung to shatter the sword. Coel rolled to his feet and lurched away as the white marble blurred at him. He leaped backwards to buy himself space. Tuman Sunqur closed the distance in a single stride.

The dark-skinned sorcerer became a phantom as they moved away from the light of the burning oil. Coel retreated helplessly. He had never faced an opponent who was larger, stronger, and faster than himself. He could not fence with a five-foot length of marble. He could exchange blows but once, and then either his sword or his body would be shattered.

Coel seized on an idea. If one exchange was all he would have, then so be it. Coel leaped forward and attacked with suicidal inspiration. He would use the Sunqur's own tactic against him.

He raised the Academy blade high and the Sunqur swung his marble rod to meet and shatter it. Coel whipped his blade back down and around in a lopping, underhand cut. Coel ignored the massive stone cudgel as it arced at him. He ignored the dark bulk of the sorcerer behind it. He aimed instead for the gleam of the silver scarab ring and the desiccated hand that wore it.

Tuman Sunqur's wrist severed beneath Coel's blade like a

hollow reed.

The marble shaft struck Coel's side with horrific impact and swept him across the hall like a broom. Coel rolled a half dozen paces lay stunned. Pain rippled through his side like saw teeth as he tried to breathe. Beneath his armor his ribs were broken.

"Coel!" Light suddenly shown down from the upper gallery. Coel squinted up wearily. Orsini held a lamp. "Get up!"

Blood dribbled over Coel's lips as he rolled over and pushed himself up with one hand.

Tuman Sunqur stood wavering on his feet. He looked down upon his severed hand where it lay on the floor. The great ring had slipped from his mummified finger and rolled across the hall. The mummified hand lay curled like a dead spider, twitching with the death nerve. The length of marble dragged on the ground in the grip of Tuman's remaining hand.

Orsini roared. "Get up, Coel! You have almost succeeded! He is neither dead nor alive! His soul is between worlds, and his body lies between life and death! Only a net of sorcery keeps him here! The ring and the hand were strands of it! You have severed them! Now, get up! Get up and finish him!"

Coel groaned. He used his sword as a crutch to push himself to his feet. He doubled over as his ribs shifted and stabbed within him. Coel grit his teeth and limped forward.

The undead sorcerer's eyes met his and had no power over him.

"Do us a favor, then, Sunqur," Coel raised the Academy blade. "Lift up your chin."

Tuman's gaze flicked around Coel's frame. Coel had seen the same sort of searching in the eyes of the elf-woman Fiachna when she had looked upon Orsini and seen the poison in him, and upon Marius and seen he had no soul. Tuman's eyes traced Coel's silhouette. Tuman was reading his aura. What he saw made him smile. Tuman's gray gaze locked with Coel's.

"You seem very tired."

Every ounce of strength drained from Coel's body. His sword felt as heavy as the world and slid from his hands. Coel's knees buckled and he fell on his face.

Orsini's voice shook the hall. "Get up!"

Coel lay on his belly while his muscles trembled and jerked. The power of the consecrated water was gone. Reza had struck him down with sorcery in the Waste. He had run for two days and nights. He had fought Marius twice. He had contested wills with Tuman Sunqur and been broken. His ribs lay cracked beneath him. All the strength that had sustained him had been borrowed. Nothing of it remained. Coel seemed to look down upon himself from the air above. He felt nothing. He gazed down upon his spent and broken body twitching prone upon the marble floor. Coel felt a strange, almost pleasurable detachment. He felt like--

"Coel!"

Coel snapped back. He was trapped once more in torn and exhausted flesh. The nausea of broken bones filled him. His head grew light. The room seemed to lighten and darken. Within the cracked cage of his ribs Coel's heart fluttered like a bird with a broken wing. His soul felt like a kite in a high wind. Only a slender thread held him to the tortured meat that clothed his bones.

He was finished. Orsini would go back into the room where Luko guarded Márta and take their lives. Then the dwarf would fall upon Tuman Sunqur with naught but a dagger and be torn limb from limb.

Tuman stepped towards the stairs.

Part of Coel wanted to die. Another part was frightened and wanted to live. A third stream of his consciousness did not care. Coel followed it. Images of his life floated across his vision. He saw himself back in Grande Triumphe. He saw the day of the dreaded Trial By Fire. For weeks the Paladin candidates had feared having to face torture or terrible sorcery.

What they had faced was merely more drill practice.

Disappointment had filled them. They had stepped barefoot into the snow of the fencing court in the thin, sleeveless tunics they slept in and been issued the double-weight practice swords they had long since graduated from. The sword drills had commenced. They were given the first and the simplest drill. They had repeated it endlessly. The cuts and guards flew rapidly as the Swordmaster called the cadence. The drill did not end. Its starting and ending movements flowed in an endless cycle. Steam rose from their sweating bodies. The practice blades cut the air until muscles burned and continued long after they felt like lead. The drill was an endless loop. The cadence continued without mercy. Candidates fell vomiting to the snow. Others pushed on, swinging arms they could barely feel.

For a few, Coel among them, something happened.

The act became effortless. The blunted and weighted practice swords whirled in their hands with uncanny speed and precision. No strength was required. The sword drill became an endless dance of perfection. It was ecstasy. It was--

The sudden call to halt had jarred them like a thunderclap.

They had stood, panting and steaming in the snow. Some laughed out of control. Others wept. For a few fleeting seconds, each of them had been in touch with something greater than themselves. There was a place beyond boundaries. There was a place that was a single step beyond where all limits had been reached. The priests said there was a place where a man who had surrendered all pride could gaze upon God. From such a place, the Mantle of Power descended upon Paladins.

His mother's teachings had been very different from the Church, but on some rarified level they became eerily and beautifully the same. Coel hung in a place beyond life and death. In that place, the disparate chains of his life began linking. His Academy blade was a lens for the power of the man behind it. A man was but a flawed lens through which the clear white light of all of life shined. A druid spent his life polishing that lens so that light would shine through it pure and harmonious. A Paladin cleansed himself to become a fit vessel of God's divine will.

These were the two great trainings of Coel's life. The two polar opposites that had torn him apart. In his present state, he had no will, no distraction, no thought. The two threads of Coel's fate twisted around the flickering light of his life in a spiraling double helix.

Coel felt light as a feather.

His hand stretched out and clasped the hilt of his sword.

Coel rose. Tuman Sunqur moved slow as a snail crawling across the tiled floor. He had not yet completed his second step towards the stair. Coel moved toward him without thought. The Paladin blade rose in his hand. The war scream rose from the pit of his belly and tore forth to shake the walls with its power.

There was a place of clear white light. There was a man named Coel ap Math. There was a sword forged in the Paladin Academy in Paris from the iron of fallen stars. For a split second, the veils between them lifted and the lenses through which each shined were without mortal blemish.

The sword in Coel's hands flared like the sun.

Tuman Sunqur turned like a man trapped in sand. The shaft of marble rose too slowly. Tuman's every feature stood out in high relief beneath the terrible light of the sword as it arced down upon him.

The Sunqur screamed as the sorcery that bound his undead body and departed soul shriveled and parted like a spider's web exposed to flame. The sword cleaved his body from collar to crotch. The shaft of marble fell to the floor like a toppled tree. Coel drew the blazing sword from the sorcerer's sundered torso and scythed it about in a terrible arc. Tuman's head flew from his body and fell to the floor in a whirl of cinnamon-colored braids. Tuman Sunqur's decapitated body collapsed to the tiles.

The light of the sword guttered out.

Coel swayed in the vague lamplight. He was only dimly aware of the pain and exhaustion in his body. He still felt the high wind that tore souls from the shallow anchorage of the world, but now he stood before that wind like a man facing the gale from the prow of a ship. He felt very peaceful. "Orsini."

The dwarf stood at the top of the gallery. His voice was tentative. "Coel?"

"Luko and Márta live?"

"Indeed," The dwarf paused. "Coel?"

"Fetch furniture. Whatever wood you can find. Build a

pyre."

"All right."

Orsini descended the stairs and began piling benches and tearing tapestries from the walls. Everything within the citadel had been protected from the elements and was bone dry with age. Coel watched with detachment. It was all he could do just to just stand and breathe.

Orsini disappeared. Coel did not know for how long. The dwarf came back with Father Marius' body over his shoulder. "You were right, Coel. He fought the Walladid as best he could. He deserves a pyre." The dwarf laid the dead priest upon the pile. He gathered up Tuman's corpse, head and hand and laid them atop as well. He opened the lamp's oil spout and tossed the lantern upon the pyre. Flames licked up around the corpses. Smoke rose up to the golden dome of the citadel.

Sparks danced and winked in the air over the fire. Coel watched their patterns. He knew they would tell him things were he not too tired to listen. At the moment, knowing that they spoke at all was enough.

Orsini gazed long and hard at Coel in the orange light. "Are you all right?"

"No. Why?"

"You are frightening me."

"I am sorry."

"I saw what happened. I have seen such things. Two hundred years ago. When the Paladins of Grande Triumphe rode forth against the Hobgoblin Horde. The light of their swords eclipsed the sun."

"I do not know if I could do such a thing again." Coel sighed. The sparks no longer spoke to him. His intellect and the distractions of his mortal flesh clawed their way into his lucidity. The cries of his overtaxed body rolled through him like an avalanche. Every crippled beat of his heart felt like the last.

"Coel?"

"Yes?"

"Are you going to die?"

"I do not know," Coel looked about blearily. "Where is the Sunqur's ring?"

Orsini held it up. "I fetched it. I fetched this as well." Orsini held up a Chi-Roh symbol with a black gemstone that matched the scarab ring.

"The soul of Father Marius."

"I believe so."

"Drop it upon the floor."

Orsini dropped the silver symbol to the tiles. Coel raised his sword. It was no longer like a thing alive in his hand. It was a heavy piece of steel he could barely lift. He raised it like a spike and stabbed it down into the black gem. The stone cracked with a spark and a hiss. The two of them stared in the firelight.

"Is he free?"

"I do not know."

Orsini raised the scarab. "And the ring?"

"Put it upon the banister."

Orsini went and set the ring upon the carved marble.

Coel tottered to the banister. He groaned with the effort of raising his sword. It crashed down mostly of its own weight. Sparks flashed as the blade sheared through the silver alloy and met the black stone. A great jolt ran up Coel's arms. Black powder spit as the gem shattered. The great, headless body burning on the pyre convulsed. The fire shifted and the flames rose higher. Coel staggered backward and sat down heavily upon the floor.

"By the Gods! Coel!"

Coel stared stupidly at his sword.

The blade had broken in half.

"Coel!"

Coel flopped back with the hilt in his hand and stared up at the glittering dome as the shadows of the funeral pyre danced across it like giants.

Orsini seized his shoulders. "Coel!"

"I am very tired."

"All right, my friend. Rest, then. I shall gather our weapons and goods. Luko and I shall take care of everything."

"My sword . . . the remains of the ring."

"Do not worry. Rest, now. Sleep the sleep of the just, and dream in the hall of heroes. When you awake, I shall have food and drink for you. Regain your strength. We have a very long journey ahead of us."

"Márta . . . "

"Márta rests, as you should. I shall lay you beside her. You shall share a blanket as you slumber."

"I love her."

"I know."

Coel felt Orsini hoist him up in his arms. He did not feel his fingers open. Coel did not feel his broken sword slip from his hand.

CHAPTER FORTY-SEVEN

Hilell Ibn Hammed of Jeddah sat on a patio overlooking the Arabian Sea and drank coffee from Yemen from a silver service. The docks of the Daybul waterfront bustled beneath him. It was late September, and he was well pleased with the summer's trading. The Italian who drank wine beside him was young, blonde, Christian and arrogant, but his partnership had been invaluable. The Italian's cousin was Portuguese, and his cousin's brother had married a Nestorian Christian woman in Karachi. A plan had been hatched and bargain struck. Hilell had never seen so much cinnamon and pepper as he now held in the holds of his ships. His three Dhows sat at dock below and smelled like the kitchens of the Sultan of Delhi. Hilell enjoyed the aroma on the afternoon breeze. He could not help but admire the Italians. It was said that Allah loved crazy men and fools. The Italians hurled themselves across the world, and luck went with them. It was quite late in the season, but against all odds they had beaten the rains and taken on the spices the Italian's cousin had promised.

Hilell smiled. His profit would be stupendous.

Signore Radovano Zannini peered over his silver goblet across the patio. "Well, Hilell, what is this? Surely these are no hirelings of yours?"

Hilell turned his gaze from the sea and blinked in surprise. The portico of the inn looked down upon the docks. A dwarf and a giant stood at the landing. Two of the proprietor's larger slaves stood before them with clubs and barred their way. Begging was acceptable on the docks, but not in the coffeehouses where the merchants took their ease and talked business. A serving slave scuttled over wringing his hands. "Forgive me, Captains, but those, individuals, they wish to speak of business with you," He looked fearfully behind him. "They are insistent."

Hilell frowned. Behind the giant and the dwarf a child held the reins of the scrawniest, most bedraggled and malnourished looking camel Hilell had ever seen. A woman lay bundled in a sling on the camel's side. Hilell stifled his irritation. He sailed for Jeddah. Jeddah was the port for pilgrims. If these people were upon *Hadj* heading for Mecca, he would be morally obligated to assist them, particularly after having made such a profit this day. Hilell arranged a neutral expression on his face. "Very well, let them come forward."

The burly slaves stood with their clubs ready and watched the ragged invaders enter the establishment with great distaste. Hilell sat up straighter as the beggars approached. The dwarf took the lead. Hilell took in the almost rectangular, anthracite eyes and massive, squared off hands and nearly choked on his coffee. The dwarf was not a human dwarf. He was a dwarven dwarf. The Imams in Mecca still debated whether or not non-humans were the spawn of Djinns and demons. Only Allah himself knew what such a one was doing in Daybul. The dwarf threw back his threadbare travel cloak to reveal weathered and faded silks of outlandish cut. He carried a *yataghan* dagger thrust through his warbelt. The dwarf doffed a battered silk hat with a broken plume and bent a knee as he spoke in Greek. Hilell shook his head. The dwarf switched to Latin.

"Greetings, good Captains."

The grim-faced giant took off his wide-brimmed black hat but did not bow. Hilell raised an eyebrow. The giant's eyes were green as jade, and his hair the color of blood. Hilell inclined his head slightly. "Greetings. Forgive my staring, but it is strange to find one of your race so far to the East."

"Indeed, good Captain. Fortune is a fickle mistress."

Hilell nodded at the wisdom of the statement. "I am told you wish to discuss business with me?"

The dwarf nodded. "You are Captain Hilell Ibn Hammed of Jeddah?"

"I am he."

"I am told you are bound homeward for Jeddah?"

"I sail to Jeddah, and then on to Aquaba."

"I would book passage with you."

"Ah," Hilell looked the dwarf up and down. He did not look like he could afford to book a bowl of gruel, much less passage to

Jeddah. "Forgive me, but I do not believe you are a pilgrim bound for Mecca, nor Jerusalem for that matter."

"No, I must admit I am not."

"Allah loves the merciful, so I may grant you a few coins, but I fear I cannot offer you my charity or credit."

"Nevertheless, I am forced to throw myself upon both."

Hilell found he could not smother his curiosity. "From whither do you come, if I may ask?"

The dwarf smiled. "Of late, I have traveled south, from the mountains of the Afghanis, just south of the Karakum."

Hilell stared. He had traveled far, and the places the dwarf spoke of were barely names to him. Names that lay unimaginable leagues away through some of the most hostile lands in the world. "And whither are you bound?"

"Cyprus."

"You seem to have traveled the breadth of the earth."

"A good bit of it, my Captain."

Radovano sipped his wine. "He is a liar."

Hilell was inclined to agree, but he was still appalled by the Italian's open rudeness. Radovano looked upon the dwarf's torn and faded finery with a sneer. "You are dressed like a clown. Tell me, do you do tricks?"

The dwarf's eyes glittered. He examined the Italian's cloak. His inhuman eyes fell upon the winged lion of Saint Mark that marked Radovano as a member of the Chivalric order of the *Cavalieri di San Marco* and the crest of his family heraldry that flanked it.

"I helped your grandfather turn back the Genoese freebooters from Crete, *Signore* Zannini. That was quite a trick, indeed."

Sir Radovano Zannini of Venice sprayed his wine across the table. "The Little Bear!"

Orsini bowed. "At your service, good Captain."

Hilell looked about in confusion. "You know him?"

"Why, he is Orsini!"

"Orsini of Venice?" Hilell had heard the name. Few merchants in the known world had not. He looked upon the dwarf with renewed respect.

Radovano rose from his seat and swept his hat from his head as he bowed low. "You must forgive my insult, *Signore*. One does not expect to meet the Little Bear in such a place."

"Indeed. I must apologize for my appearance. I am not the dashing figure of fashion I once was."

"Again, I apologize. Of course, you may book passage with us."

"Alas, good Captain Hilell is correct in his assumption. I cannot pay for it, at least not immediately."

"Your credit is good."

"I fear it is not. My fortunes are depleted. My business venture to the north was, shall we say, something less than successful. It will take me some time to repay you."

Radovano bowed low once more. "Then the honor of your company shall be your coin."

"It is you who do me honor." The dwarf bowed in return. "My business associates and I travel to Cyprus. The woman on the litter is from the Convent of Limmasol. She has taken grave injury, and the Sisters will take her in. From there, I must go on to Venice. I have urgent news for the Doge."

Radovano looked upon the giant and the boy. "These are your companions?"

"Yes, they are associates of mine."

Radovano turned to Hilell. "I, myself, shall bear the cost of the Little Bear's berth. The man and the boy seem likely enough to be able to work their passage."

"I will not hear of it," Hilell smiled. "I offer *Signore* Orsini of Venice and his associates the hospitality of my ship. The coin for their passage shall be the tales they can tell us. From the looks of it, the story should be an exciting one, and take many nights in the telling."

Orsini bowed low. "The Son of Hammed is too kind."

"Not at all."

Their eyes met. They understood one another. They were both warriors and merchants. Captain Hilell Ibn Hammed obviously considered having Orsini of Venice in his debt an excellent investment.

Signore Radovano nodded. "Very well, then, it shall be my honor to see to your every need, Orsini, and that of your companions, before we sail."

"When do we sail, if I may enquire?"

"We sail with tommorow's tide. I shall see to it that your injured companion has every comfort upon the voyage."

* * *

Coel opened the window to let in fresh air.

It was winter in Cyprus. For six days, they'd had leaden skies and cold gray rain that had turned the sea to chop. It was Sunday. The sun had broken out, and a warm wind that smelled of the desert blew up from Egypt. Sunlight streamed into the room and lit up the whitewashed walls. Coel looked upon Márta. Her hair had grown past her shoulders and spread in a silken brown fan over the pillows. Coel's heart skipped to look at it.

She slowly opened her eyes and smiled at him sleepily.

"Well, good morning, princess," Coel grinned. "And how are you this morning, then?"

Márta's eyebrows bunched with effort. Her mouth worked to force out words. "I . . . I . . . "

Coel waited.

Márta's face fell and she sagged back against the pillows in defeat. ". . . Iceland."

Coel smothered his disappointment. It was her one word. It

was the first word she had spoken when she had opened her eyes in Alexandria. It had been her only word ever since. It was a place she had never been. A place she had never shown the least amount of interest in. A place she had never spoken of. To Coel's knowledge, Snorri had never spoken of it in her presence. Now, it was the only thing she could say. Iceland was her request to open a window. Iceland was asking how many wounded crusaders were in the soldier's ward. Iceland was victory when she beat him at backgammon. Iceland was her smoky voice purring for a kiss when they stole moments together alone outside the convent walls. In the past months, Coel had learned every possible permutation and nuance in the pronunciation of the island of ice and fire.

Sister Blandine poured water from a pitcher. A leather cup covered the stump of her right arm. The Amazon Captain had returned to the convent after losing her forearm in the horse market of Trebizond. She had taken a nun's habit and taught the younger girls in training horsemanship. The Frenchwoman had assigned herself the position of chaperone. She turned a blind eye to their kisses, but she'd told Coel in all frankness that she would castrate him if he took his affections any further.

Márta had recovered more than Coel had dared hope. Orsini had sold Reza's implements and anything they could spare that they'd taken out of Bukhara. He'd paid any healer or shaman or witch they'd encountered to heal Márta as best they could. It had been little, and done in spurts here and there when they had not been fighting off hill bandits or suffering starvation in the endless march of mountain ranges and deserts that lay between the Karakum and Karachi.

It was a time Coel did not like thinking about.

There had been little the Sisters could do for Márta in Cyprus. They were a minor military order. Any nuns that showed extraordinary powers of healing were quickly called to Constantinople for service to the Emperor and the Patriarch. The Sisters of Limmasol trained Amazons, and they did what they could for wounded and crippled crusaders returning home from the Holy Land. They had done what they could for Márta. All they could offer now was shelter, comfort and safety. Márta still walked with a limp. Her right hand had little strength in it. She could not pull a bow or wield a sword. She could speak but a single word. Coel felt his heart smiling.

She was beautiful.

Márta looked out the window and frowned. The sun had risen to mid-morning. Sometimes Márta slept for entire days and nights, and Coel sat sleepless by her side sweating with the fear that she might never awaken. Blandine handed Márta a cup of water with the barest pink tinge of wine. "Would you like to go riding with me after luncheon?"

Márta nodded. "Iceland."

Blandine smiled and looked at Coel. "I will go see about horses." The Frenchwoman took her leave. She usually left the door slightly ajar. Coel raised an eyebrow as she closed it.

Márta raised a hopeful eyebrow at Coel. "Iceland?"

"No," Coel shook his head. "A ship did arrive from Venice this morning, but there was no new letter from Orsini."

Márta sighed. Her brow furrowed. "Iceland?"

"There are more rumors of hobgoblins in the east. Some say towns and villages east of Riazan, in the Russias, have been burned, but there have been no refugees. Some say these are lies being spread by the Patriarch to distract people from the growing enmity between himself and the Pope. Others say it is black magic of the Muslim steppe people and there must be a Crusade against them," Coel frowned in turn. "There is news from Holy Land."

Márta closed her eyes. No glad tidings came from the Holy Land.

"They say Tyre will fall any day now."

Márta gazed unhappily out the window. If the combined Mamluk and Syrian army took Tyre, the Crusader States would be cut in half. The Saracens would be on the coast of the Mediterranean less than a hundred miles from Cyprus. The fighting was terrible. No mercy was given on either side. The wards of the convent were filled with the wounded.

Coel suddenly smiled. "Next Sunday is Christmas."

Márta nodded.

"I thought it would be a fine day for you and I to be married."

Márta gaped in shock.

"I . . . I . . . "

Coel took a knee by the bed and took Márta's hand. "Marry me."

Márta looked about herself in panic. Coel squeezed her hand. "I am sick of this place, and so are you. It is safe enough for the moment, but there is nothing more they can do for you here. You can walk, and you can ride. Time is what will mend you best now, and now it is time for us to think of our life together."

Márta's big brown eyes grew shiny.

"Marry me, and I will take you anywhere you ask."

"I . . ." Márta stuttered. "Iceland!"

"Very well," Coel shrugged carelessly. "Iceland it shall be, then."

Márta scowled.

"Why not? Snorri always told me it was nice. He said his cousin Madia, the poet, lives there. He said she talks to glaciers and volcanoes, and they listen."

"Iceland?"

"Yes, well, Snorri said lots of things," Coel admitted. "But he also told me the Icelanders have no kings. He said they govern themselves by going to something they call the All-Thing. They all stand about in a mob and wave axes and shout at each other. I shall take you there. We shall live in a house of turf. I shall take you to the All-Thing. You can stand up and shout 'Iceland!' You will be very popular."

Márta raised a bemused eyebrow at him.

"But I know a better place I can take you. A place where there are no Assassins, no hobgoblins and no churchmen higher than a village priest. A place where no one shall ever find us."

Márta's eyes grew wide.

"I will take you to Spain. High in the Pyrenees Mountains, to the land of the Basques. The Pyrenees stretch from the Mediterranean to the Atlantic, with a thousand valleys in between. We shall go and make one our own."

Márta looked at Coel questioningly. "Iceland?"

"We shall raise sheep. That is what Basques do."

Márta looked at him disbelievingly.

"I am a Welshman, Márta," Coel waggled his eyebrows. "I know a great deal about sheep."

Márta's eyebrows rose in alarm.

Coel took both of Márta's hands in his. "I fought beside Basques when I battled the Moors. They are a beautiful people. Many are nomads. They say they are the descendants of Tubal, the grandson of Noah. Their legends say Tubal came to the Pyrenees before the Tower of Babel was raised. They have their own language they call *Euskera*. I have heard it spoken. It is like music. They say it was the language spoken by Adam and Eve, and they are last people on earth whose lips still speak it."

Coel looked deep into Márta's eyes. "Marry me. We will go there. We can leave today. We can forget about war and the Church. I still have some friends among the Basques. We can find a little valley all our own, high in the mountains and be forgotten by the world. We shall live together to the end of our days, and we will have children. Boys tall like me. Girls beautiful like you. They will grow up wild and free in the mountains, and speak the language of Eden."

Tears fell down Márta's cheeks. Coel's eyes grew hot. He smiled as they spilled over. "Just say Iceland, Márta. Say it and I will take you there."

Márta did not speak. She pointed at the little table by the bed and Coel fetched her inkpot and paper. She dipped her quill and wrote. Coel waited patiently while she wrote left-handed and then took the paper.

> *The hobgoblin hordes come. Soon it will be war. Soon the wounded here will be stacked like cordwood in the*

wards. The hobgoblins will eat
everyone in their path. I will not bear a
child just to see it spitted over a cook
fire. We cannot hide. We must fight.

Coel's heart twisted in agony. "You want me to go and fight, then?"

Márta shook her head violently. "Iceland!"

"I am sorry. I know you do not want me to go. It is just," Coel shook his head. "Do you know the two words I hate the most in the world?"

Márta gave him a lopsided smile. "Ice . . . land?"

"No." Coel laughed. "Those are my favorite. The words I hate most are 'I wish.' Wishes mean nothing. Only actions speak. It seems my whole life has been 'I wish.' Wishing about what I have done and what I have not. I am sick of wishing. I want to marry you. I want to have children with you. I want to grow old with you."

Márta quickly scrawled on a piece of paper.

You shall have it. I will marry you. I will run
away with you to Spain. But it cannot be now.
I do not lie to myself. The world will never be
safe for us. But I will not let the hobgoblins
have it. Not while I still breathe.

"Very well. I swore to you I would wait four years for your hand. I will hold that troth now."

Márta dipped her quill and wrote another note. Her hand shook slightly, and she blushed as she held the paper out.

Not all desires must be waited for . . .

Coel found himself startled and blushing as

well. "You mean . . . "

Márta nodded. Her voice dropped to a secretive whisper. "Iceland."

"You mean here?" Coel glanced about the nun's cell in sudden panic. "In the convent? Now?"

Márta nodded rapidly.

"But, what about Blandine? She will--"

Márta looked to the closed door and nodded decisively. "Iceland."

Blandine was in on it. Márta threw back the blankets and pulled Coel to her. On the terrible death march from Bukhara to Karachi Coel had fed Márta, cleaned her, changed her, and taken care of her every helpless physical need. It had only made him love her more. Now that body pressed up against his, utterly alive, and with a need that matched his own. Coel pressed himself against her. Márta wore only a linen nightshirt. Her lips hungrily met his. Her hips lifted in a heat he could feel to meet his. Coel felt the world start to break loose around him.

He suddenly pushed himself up and looked deep into Márta's eyes. "No. Not until we are married."

Márta nodded her head vigorously and pulled at him. "Iceland!"

Coel resisted. "I shall not take a whore for a wife. You shall just have to suffer."

Márta glared.

Coel bent down and kissed her throat. "However . . . " He began untying the laces that held her nightshirt one by one as he whispered in her ear. "Tell me, my love. Do you like the way I kiss you?"

Márta looked at him suspiciously but nodded.

"Would you like it if I kissed you someplace else?"

Márta's eyes flew wide in alarm. Coel began kissing his way down Márta's collarbones. He took his time doing it and visited places he had only dreamed about. Márta's stomach clenched as his lips and tongue brushed her belly in their southward passage. Her fingers combed through his hair. Her stomach relaxed. Márta let out a soft, helpless sigh.

"Iceland . . . "

* * *

The sun set as Coel strode down the hall. He grinned like an idiot at everyone he saw. Blandine had not returned, or if she had, she had not knocked upon the door. As he walked past the wards he heard the moans of wounded warriors writhing in pain and the cries of the unconscious reliving the horrors that had put them here. Some of the walking wounded took their ease in the unseasonable warmth out by the inner fountain or took light exercise in the galleries.

Coel nodded at a pair of Breton sergeants he had made the acquaintance of. The short one, Guys, held up his dulcimer and spoke in French. "Coel, my friend! Shall we play later? Christoff and I walked to town today and bought some wine."

Coel's heart filled at the idea. He was, indeed, in the mood to play his harp. It occurred to him that he and Guys should play outside of Márta's window. "That is a good idea. We should--"

Coel spun as a warrior blindsided him in the narrow gallery and shouldered him out of the way. Coel caught himself. His hand reached for the sword he no longer carried.

The warrior turned. He was big. He wore no badge or livery, but his breeches and tunic were of the latest cut in the east. Golden brown hair fell in lazy curls around his face, and his beard and mustache were unfashionably long. The man lifted his nose at Coel in distaste and kept walking down the hall. Coel smothered his anger and turned away. The Sisters had already warned him about fighting. The stranger muttered loud enough to be heard by all as he walked on.

"God damned Irish. Always getting underfoot."

Coel whirled.

"Snorri!"

The big man turned around. The golden brown locks belonged on a Saxon dandy and the long beard upon a woodcutter, but the scarred eyebrows that waggled at Coel could belong to only one man on earth. Snorri's smile widened so that it spread his drooping mustaches and his golden tooth gleamed.

"Did I fool you?"

Coel felt like the world might shatter apart. "It is you!"

"Yes!"

"You are alive!"

"Hah!"

Coel flung his arms around his friend and heaved him up off the ground. The Bretons looked on with vague suspicion.

Coel set his friend down. He clasped Snorri's shoulders and shook him. "How?"

"Well, now, it pains me to admit it, but that bastard Sandor got the better of me." Snorri stuck his hand in his armpit. "That wound there was nearly the death of me. I went over into the river, and I sank like a stone. Only there wasn't very far to sink. That river was a cataract falling nearly straight down the mountain. So I kept tumbling. Anyway, the next thing I knew, I was jammed up against a dead Mamluk horse that was wedged between some rocks. My head was above water, so I sat there for a few minutes and wondered if I was going to die. Well, I didn't. So, I decided to pull myself out. I nearly froze to death. That goddamn water was so cold I was hung like a goblin by the time I got ashore. Anyway, I warmed myself in the sun for a bit and waited to die, but I didn't. So, I jammed some moss under my arm and took stock. The goddamn horse was dead and of no use to anyone, and his saddlebags were still on him. So I crawled out onto the rocks. There was a hand axe, a flint and steel, and a good bit of gold. I made myself a fire out of driftwood and hacked off a haunch of the horse. I managed to burn some of the meat until it was edible and dried the saddle blanket in the meantime. So, I was full of meat, half-dead, and had a nice fire. I settled down to die, but I didn't. I awoke the next morning?" Snorri grinned. "There was Otto!"

"Otto!" Coel looked about. "Where is he?"

"Luko is playing with him. The boy told me you would be lurking about Márta's room. You've been lurking in there for four hours, I might add."

Coel's ears burned despite himself. "Snorri, how did you get here?"

"Well, once I had given up on going to Valhalla, I started to stumble my way down the mountain. I hated leaving the gold but I was in no shape to carry it. I was crawling by the time I reached the foot of the mountain. I swear at one point Otto dragged me, but I ran into some steppe people. The Southern Horde has left many refugees in its wake, and I know a little steppe speech," Snorri rolled his eyes. "I'm afraid I told them something of a lie. I told them I was a crusader who had come to fight the hobgoblins and been wounded and left for dead. They thought that was great. They were pagans, but a nicer bunch of pagans you've never met. They were Kipchaqs or some such. Anyway, they had some kind of mystic woman who managed a bit of healing on me. Fine woman. Got me up on all three legs again, if you know what I mean. I swear her braids fell to her ankles." Snorri sighed at the memory. "Anyway, I got better. Most of their men folk had been killed, so I spent a couple of days in the tents of the widows, you know, spreading comfort as I could."

Coel just stared.

"They had very liberal views about these things. Anyway, when I was well? My feet started to itch. So I told them I had to go. We had a big party. They officially adopted me into their tribe," Snorri shrugged modestly. "Snorri of the Long Shadowed Man-Lance is my Kipchaq name."

Coel just stared.

"Anyway, we danced the war dance, sang the war song, struck the war post, and swore eternal brotherhood. I told them about the Mamluk gold up in the cataract, and they gave me some food, a skin of fermented mare's milk and a spear. I had no idea which way you'd gone, so Otto and I started walking west."

"Where did you go?"

"Trebizond."

"You walked from the Kopets to Trebizond?"

"I did, and that is a god damned saga in itself. Anyway, I walked to Trebizond. I had an audience with the Angeli and gave her the news about that horde of hobgoblins hiding out behind the Caspian. She was suitably grateful," Snorri waggled his brows. "Ianthe was pleased to see me. So were Ghiday and Tabitha. So was Eulia. I gave them all your warmest regards," Snorri looked back up the hall towards Márta's chamber and shrugged. "Not that you would care. You were alone in there with Márta for four hours, and I'll bet my gold tooth you still haven't poked her, yet, have you?"

Coel stiffened in outrage.

Snorri shook his head in disgust. "God damned altar boy."

Coel took in Snorri's bizarre appearance. "What happened to you? You look like a cross between a harem boy and a goat."

Snorri's brows drew down. "The Assassins of Alamut are on my trail, and not even my best friend recognized me, thank you very much!"

Coel could not stop staring. "Snorri?"

"What?"

"Well?"

"Well, what?"

"You have hair."

"Of course I have hair! I have beautiful hair! Now where is my goddamn axe? Don't tell me you left it by that cataract!"

"I have it in my hut."

"He's living in a hut," Snorri rolled his eyes again. "Anyway, I took ship from Trebizond and sailed to Constantinople. I still have some friends there. Then a trade ship brought the news that Orsini of Venice had returned to Italy. So I set sail and met him there. Venice, amazing city. You should see it. Anyway, Orsini has become *Consiglieri* to the Doge. He told me where to find you and Márta. He told me what happened in Bukhara," Snorri looked sidelong at Coel. "Is it true?"

"Is what true?"

"Are you a Paladin?"

Coel looked away. "I barely remember what happened. Sometimes I dream about it, but waking or dreaming, it slips away from me when I try to think about it. Orsini says I almost died. For a week after he thought I would anyway. The sword is broken. We made our way south." Coel looked back at his friend even as the memories eluded him once again. Coel smiled. "Márta lives. That is all that matters."

"Orsini told me of Márta's injury. How long have you been here?"

"Since Autumn."

"He told me what happened to Zuli."

Coel's chest tightened. "Snorri, I couldn't save her."

"Orsini says you did save her. The hobgoblins did not take her for their Blood Rites, nor the Assassins for their revenge. You will always have my thanks for that."

Coel could think of nothing to say.

Snorri clapped him on the shoulder. "I am glad you are alive, Coel. You saved Márta, Luko, and Orsini. You stopped Reza and you stopped Tuman Sunqur. Your life is already legend worthy, and it is far from finished."

Coel looked down in embarrassment and changed the subject. "What shall you do now, then?"

"What will we do now is more the question."

"War is coming. We have to fight. That is what Márta says."

"Smart girl. You should marry her."

"I have asked."

Snorri looked away diplomatically. "So, she still hasn't forgiven you your hobgoblin, thing, yet?"

"We do not discuss it!"

"Oh, well, that is probably for the best. How is she?"

Coel thought of the hours they'd spent in her chamber together. He found himself smiling again. "She is better. Much better. She will go out of her mind when she sees you," Coel's smile faded slightly. "I asked her this very afternoon to come away with me, but she is intent on staying here. She intends to help with the wounded and train new Amazons as much as she is able. She says we must all do whatever we can in the days to come."

"She's right. Walking and sailing give a man time to think, and I have spent much time in thought the last few months. The hobgoblins come, and they are in league with the Assassins of Alamut. I think before the war starts, many important people will die by their hand. Kings, holy men, warlords, and heads of state. There will be chaos and dissension. That is when the hobgoblins will strike."

"So, what are we to do about it?"

"We warn the world, what else?"

"Snorri, no one will believe us."

"The Angeli and Sir Roger already do. They have sent envoys to the Patriarch, the Emperor of the Byzantines, the Kings of Georgia and Cilicia, and the Seljuk Sultan. Whether they can be convinced before it is too late remains to be seen. Orsini told me you have already sent word to the Blue Robes with the remains of the ring."

"Aye, but who will believe us here, in the West?"

"Hardly anyone, but I have thought about that, too. You and I should go to Paris. To Grande Triumphe. You must go before the Academy Masters. Tell them your tale. Show them your sword and tell them of all we have seen. The Crusaders and the Saracens must stop fighting in the Holy Land and turn their attention to the Hordes. We cannot afford to be fragmented. We need a new League of Humanity. The Paladin Academy is respected throughout the known world. If the Paladins lead, others will follow. We must convince them."

"Ships to Paris cost money, Snorri. I have none. I work around the convent for my keep."

"Work? What do you mean, work?"

"I dig ditches. Mend nets. Teach archery. The other day I fixed the well winch."

"Oh, for--Here!" Snorri pulled a pouch from his belt. "Orsini sent this money along with me. He says it is partial payment on your back wages, and, as I have already said, the Angeli was suitably grateful for the news I brought her."

Coel took the pouch. It was heavy. He knew without looking that it was filled with Venetian gold. "So, you would go to France with me, then?"

"Well?" Snorri drooped his wrist and fluttered his eyelashes like a dandy. "I have always wanted to see Paris."

Coel's face tightened. The idea of facing the Academy Masters whom he had failed at Grande Triumphe filled him with foreboding. But he knew Snorri was right, and Márta would agree with him once she was told. They were the two people he loved most in the world. His mother's words came back to him. Life was a circle. Omens were everywhere. Snorri's return was a sign. It was time for Coel, himself, to return.

"I suppose we must book a ship, then."

"I have already booked a ship. We have berths on a Venetian galley leaving for France by way of the Majorcas, with a Captain Zannini. I believe you know him. We sail at dawn."

Coel rolled his eyes. It seemed his destiny was once more firmly out of his hands. "Very well, dawn it is." Coel matched Snorri's grin. "But first, you must visit with Márta. She will be thrilled."

"Of course! We shall have ourselves a party! I shall tell her all about Iceland!" Snorri looked down the hall. His voice dropped low. "That Frenchman, the short one with the funny harp. He's a friend of yours?"

"Guys? Yes, he is a friend of mine. Why?"

Snorri grinned wide enough to show his gold tooth. "Well, my Frankish is rusty, but I could swear he said something about wine."

EPILOGUE

Gwall strode through the Citadel of Bukhara.

The winter wind shrieked through the open windows of the upper galleries. Gwall's face was veiled and muffled against more than cold. A hooded felt robe fell to the ankles of her boots. Mittens covered her hands and thick cloth treated with the blood of shamans covered her mouth and nose to keep her from breathing in the poison of the Waste. A thin layer of gauze kept it out of her eyes. She pulled the gauze away as she walked through the drafty hall. Her six eunuch guards formed a wall of flesh around her. The trip across the Great Waste had thinned them. They were all thinner, but none had succumbed to the poison of the place. Against all precedent, Nijumet had sent his First Consort into the Great Waste. He had asked the Council of Shamans to use their power to heal and preserve those whom he was sending into the Land of the Destroyer. The Council of Shamans had met. The Council of Females had met. The Council of Tribes had met. It was unorthodox, but it was deemed necessary. They all walked the Great Path of Life.

They would not be turned back from their journey a second time.

Gwall stopped in the great hall. Warriors stood guard at all entrances. Hundreds of the Lesser Ones fanned out throughout the city looking for sign. In the middle of the great hall, the four shamans stood around a great pile of ash. Gwall noted the presence of bones in the dead fire. A pierced skull peered up at her from empty eye-sockets.

Gwall gazed down at the skull. "Shaman."

Signeg, Shaman of the Big Knife tribe, answered. "First Consort of Nijumet, First of the Council of Females, in this place you speak for the Great Hobgoblin. What is your will?"

"The city is ancient. Our siege of it centuries past. This fire is recent. What does this represent?"

Signeg stooped and pulled the skull from the ashes. "This is the skull of the priest who served Reza Walladid."

Gwall turned to Sandor and spoke in Turkish. "You claimed you slew Father Marius."

The Pole nodded carelessly and tapped his fingers upon the saber on his hip. "I slit his throat."

Gwall's nostrils flared. There was no smell of fear or sweat. He gave off none of the body signals that humans revealed when they lied. She turned to Signeg and resumed Hobgoblin speech. "How is this possible?"

"Reza Walladid had the ring of the Destroyer."

"I see."

Signeg dropped the pierced skull and poked about through the ashes. He arose with a femur and another skull. The skull was larger than the first. The femur was longer than any Gwall had seen on a human. Signeg presented them to her.

"These are the bones of The Destroyer."

Gwall stepped back. "You are certain?"

"The very dust of this place resonates with his echoes."

"He was raised by the Walladid?"

"He was raised. Then he was slain. Then his body was burned." Signeg smacked his tusks at the enormity of the revelation. "I believe his resurrection was not total before he was slain."

"He is destroyed?"

"I do not know," The Shaman smacked his tusks again in thought. "Though I believe no known effort of human or hobgoblin sorcery can bring him back to this world. His ties to it have been severed."

"Who slew him?"

"We cannot be sure."

"How was he slain?"

"With a sword."

"Where is his ring?"

"We have found traces of it. We believe it has been destroyed, and its remnants taken from this place."

"First Consort!"

A shaman of the Long Walkers came up the stairs. Six single combat champions followed. The warriors bore a body. They came forward and laid it down before her. Gwall examined the arrow-riddled corpse. The poison of the Waste was a great preserver. No insects had been at the body and no decomposition had set in. The flesh was sunken only from dehydration. "We found this in the crypt of the Destroyer. There are many tools of sorcery in the crypt. Great magic was worked below."

Sandor spoke. "That is Reza Walladid."

The shaman confirmed it. "It is indeed the body of the sorcerer."

Gwall stared down at the body.

The Council of Females formed one of the Three Pillars of Hobgoblin society. The Shamans were the conduit of the Blood of Life, the link to the spirit world, and the opener of the Doors Between Worlds. They charted the Great Path of Life. The Council of Tribes represented each tribe at the Great Council, presided over by the Great Hobgoblin. Females cared little for tribal matters or the spirit world. They cared about the future of their next brood. It gave them a unique perspective. It was the Council of Females who had advised using the humans against one another rather than trying to overwhelm all as before. It was the Council of Females who had instigated the widespread use of spies and hiring the Assassins of Alamut. It was they who had instigated the learning of human languages and customs. Gwall had intensively studied the varying methods of warfare of the human tribes who stood in their path.

Gwall pulled two shafts from the body of Reza Walladid. She examined the first. It was nearly twice as long and half again as thick as the arrows of the steppe nomads. "Only the tribes of the far Western Isles wield bows so powerful," She turned to Sandor. "The Welshman's?"

"Yes. The Celt had a bow of massive proportions. I saw him bend it. This is one of his shafts. I recognize the fletching."

Gwall held up the other shaft. It was short and squat and thicker than her finger. Signeg smacked his tusks at the blue steel head. "Dwarven."

Ialbuk strode through the hall. Nadrud was dead. Nijumet had a new Right Hand. It was Gwall's duty to discern the truth of the situation and deal with any humans. In this she spoke for the Great Hobgoblin. In military matters, Ialbuk was in command. It was a new and strange division of duties. A small pack of the Lesser Ones swarmed about Ialbuk.

The Right Hand of the Great Hobgoblin stopped before her. "First Consort, the Lesser Ones have found sign. There were six camels kept in the courtyard. They were joined later by an seventh. In the galleries above, there is blood sign. Dried, but they believe it is human female. There is also fecal sign in the commodes. The Lesser Ones smell Dwarven, human male, female, and immature male. They say the camel sign leads them towards the south gate."

Gwall calculated. They had found Nadrud's Lesser Ones wandering the Waste. The poison of the place had begun to twist them, but their spoor had made finding Nadrud's bones easier. The elf woman was dead. The priest was dead. Snorri Yaroslav was dead. Reza Walladid was dead. The Destroyer was destroyed.

The Welshman, the dwarf, the swordswoman and the boy could still live.

Ialbuk glanced southward. "We pursue them?"

Gwall came to her decision. "No. If they live, they long ago reached the sea."

She turned to Signeg. "Shaman. Gather your Circle. Speak through the Blood and contact the Horde. Tell Nijumet that the Destroyer is no longer a threat. Tell him the Assassins must be contacted. Coel ap Math still lives, and they owe us his life. The Welshman is most likely in Europe. Tell Nijumet we must contract for the lives of the dwarf, Orsini of Venice, and the warrior female, Márta. They will try to warn the western tribes of humans. They must be killed."

"You are First Consort." Signeg turned and gathered the other shaman about him. They seized a shrieking Lesser One for sacrifice.

Gwall turned to Ialbuk. "Gather the warriors and the Lesser Ones that remain. We are finished here. We must return to the Horde. Blood Sacrifices must be made and the Gates re-opened. The axes must be sharpened. We must prepare to lift our feet. We take the next step upon the Great Path of Life."

Ialbuk looked down upon the body of Reza Walladid. "Burn this?"

"No," Gwall stared upon the sorcerer's corpse. "Bring it."

THE END

THE AUTHOR WOULD LIKE TO THANK:

- Marc Lee for his amazing cover art, and, his incredible patience with me during the process. I had never hired an artist before and it was really cool to watch him work up the cover. Can't wait to see what he does with the cover of Book 2.

- Ron Miles, fellow author, for both his technical assistance on the Kindle launch, literary advice, late night sessions and critiques, which leads us to his lovely wife . . .

- Kristine Miles, who made her opinions on the book known over Ron's shoulder as he and I texted, and re-read it again for the final push to Kindle file. ("Chuck, you nock an arrow, you don't knock it!") (How did that get overlooked?)

- Steve Burich for the author picture, my first green screen photo session, and for all of his encouragement of my writing, (including odd jobs in the technical writing world when I was starving), over the years.

- Terry Rudy, without whose Apple IT support this work might never have been published. (And who threatened "I am not buying you another beer until you launch this . . .") (He relented.)

- Alice O'Kieffe, who despite being TOO BUSY to read this before publication, ;), her ability to deliver glowing praise and savage criticism of my work when either are merited have sharpened up my writing skills over the past several years, and the "Alice's eye" in Chuck's brain was heavily involved in this draft.

- At this point I have to mention Brian Crebs, the last beta reader, who said he loved the book, and then said, "Where's the map? There's a bit of map on the cover, but no map inside. Where's the map? I'm a guy who likes history. I'm a guy who likes a map. Got map?" Which directly leads me to . . .

- Samuel Reyes, visual artist, graphic designer, DJ, and now? Cartographer.

- And, for William Castaneda "Billy C" Jr., Amigo Especial and London celly, who never read this work, expressed no interest in doing so, and yet was WTF appalled over breakfast when he found out he was not in the 'author would like to thank' section. So, Mr. C? For you? Wind beneath my wings, brother. Wind beneath my wings. ;P

- I would also very much like to thank those who took the time to read the manuscript in various stages and/or gave me critiques, advice, enthusiasm or encouragement, including: My father and fellow author, Patrick Rogers, who encouraged me to write so very long ago. My mother, Barbara Rogers, who married a writer, gave birth to one, and spent a lot of time as editor-in-chief of the Rogers household when she wasn't busy being Mayor. (Thanks Mom!) My fiercest critic, biggest supporter, and big brother, Roger Rogers, who, also, when I was trying to figure out some kind of squiggled map idea to give Samuel said "Give me that!" and knocked out what I needed, (and didn't need) in five minutes. My niece, Christy Rogers, who helped solve the "They are acting like they are in high-school" romantic dilemma. (It helps when your niece is a PhD in psychology, and a girl . . .) Best friend, and philosophical/literary/artistic sparring partner since high school, Walter Saleme. I believe he is the only human being who has literally read everything I have ever written professionally, and a great deal of the unprofessional. I know it is a heavy cross to bear. Thank you, brother. Your reward is in Heaven. Or . . . a beer.

Roth Rind, (No one else I want to produce, and DIRECT, (Get in there big man!) the series for HBO!) Steve Anderson, (Good night, Oscar Levant, wherever you are!), Linda Pendleton, (I have had the privilege of writing for her husband Don's series 'The Executioner' and the pleasure of trading emails for advice and about cover art, and the business/art of writing), Mark Caron, (More about you in Book 2!) Harry Kane, (My first agent!), Loren "Chuck, there was no Suez Canal back then!" good for a freak out and stop the presses, Rendler. Charles Eischen, (Liked it, but has informed me he is waiting for the Yoga instructor/Paperback writer/Silicon Valley Bukowksi book), (It's coming . . .), Biz Eischen, (Hated it, but her literary critiques are like straight razor sharp n' stuff), M. Cecilia Sternzon, (She read the book in foreign lands!), Nathan "So, obviously, you based Snorri on me" Meyer, fellow writer and brainstorming buddy, (Some of that brainstorming should just stay buried in the X-files of the NSA . . .) Fellow author Jack Murphy, (Thanks for the feedback, he read the book on flights from very interesting places, and thanks as well for awesome intel/stories on the Mack Bolan end), Cambria Smiley-Abrew, (She read the whole book on her phone!), Tamara Martin, (I am pretty sure she has never actually read anything I have ever given her to read, but her support has been unwavering) Jeanette Matthews, (Editing and Beer with Lida!), Maria Alva Roff, (If someone is going to save the planet it might as well start with an author/blogger in Iceland), and the many, many others who took some time to travel the Heroes Road with me. I know I forgot a bunch of people. Contact me angrily, and you are in the "author would like to thank" in Book 2.

- and Val, the Muse.

ABOUT THE AUTHOR

Chuck Rogers lives by his wits in the heart of the Silicon Valley

Made in the USA
San Bernardino, CA
17 September 2018